Other books by the author:

Fiction
Caveman Politics

Non-fiction
Legends of Winter Hill
Ice Time

City
in
Amber

Jay
Atkinson

LIVINGSTON PRESS
THE UNIVERSITY OF WEST ALABAMA

isbn 13: 978-1931982-96-2 trade paper
isbn 13: 978-1931982-95-5, lib. binding
Library of Congress Control Number 2007929951
Printed on acid-free paper.
Printed in the United States of America,
Publishers Graphics
Hardcover binding by: Heckman Bindery
Typesetting and page layout:Angela Brown
Proofreading: Margaret Walburn, Casey Smith
Cover design: Joe Taylor
Cover Layout: Jennifer Brown, Angela Brown

For my son, Liam:

the past, the present and the future

Cover Photos: In 1954 the Library received the records of the National
Child Labor Committee, including approximately 5,000 photographs
and 350 negatives by Lewis Hine. In giving the collection to the
Library, the NCLC stipulated that "There will be no restrictions of
any kind on your use of the Hine photographic material." Credit Line:
Library of Congress, Prints & Photographs Division, National Child
Labor Committee Collection, [LC-DIG-nclc-02208 (color digital file
from b&w original print) Call Number: LOT 7479, v. 4, no. 2275[P&P]

This is a work of fiction:
any resemblance
to persons living or dead is coincidental.

Livingston Press is part of The University of West Alabama,
and thereby has non-profit status.
Donations are tax-deductible:
brothers and sisters, we need 'em.

first edition
6 5 4 3 3 2 1

Acknowledgements

As a boy, I spent a great deal of time on my bicycle and on foot exploring the streets and alleyways of north Lawrence, already enthralled by its worn out grandeur and gritty style. If any and all 'real' fiction is about place, and I believe it is, I had the sense, even as a child, that I had found the place I wanted to write about. It would take some years before I was equal to the task I had set for myself, but I always knew in my heart that I was going to do it.

I could never have tackled such a project without the direct assistance of two individuals. Dr. Peter Ford, esteemed history professor at Merrimack College in North Andover, MA, a fine prose stylist and raconteur, was a vigorous and vocal supporter of this book and kicked me in the ass more than once in the early going. An expert on Charles Storrow and the Lawrence brothers, Pete offered numerous invaluable anecdotes and many lucid pages of his own writing on these men. His essays on Storrow, "'Father of the Whole Enterprise': Charles S. Storrow and the Making of Lawrence, Massachusetts, 1845-1860," (Massachusetts Historical Review 2-2000: 76-117); "An American in Paris: Charles S. Storrow and the 1830 Revolution," (Proceedings of the Massachusetts Historical Society, 104-1992, 21-41); and "Charles S. Storrow, Civil Engineer: A Case Study of European Training and Technological Transfer in the Antebellum Period," (Technology and Culture 34-1993: 271-99) are the definitive works on this era in American history.

The other early champion of my project was Ken Skulski, the overworked and underpaid director of what was then known as the Immigrant City Archives. Located on Essex Street in the former headquarters of the Essex Company, the archives, founded by the legendary Lawrence character, Eartha Dengler, was the repository of all things Lawrence, and Ken was—and still is—the city's most unabashed enthusiast. I spent many rainy and snowy afternoons listening to Ken talk about Lawrence's historical figures in a way that made them come alive in my imagination.

This project took several years and I am grateful to Joe Taylor at Livingston Press for his enthusiasm and willingness to bring my story into print. He's a great advocate of literary fiction and many writers share my feelings on Joe Taylor and his press, which is a labor of love for him and his associates at the University of West Alabama, just like our writing is for us. Peter McGuigan of Sanford Greenburger Associates in

New York negotiated the contract, and these two gentlemen concluded their business quickly, as gentlemen often do.

Dr. Patricia Jaysane and her staff at the Lawrence History Center dedicated many hours to sorting through and discussing archival records from Lawrence's time-honored institutions and corporations; old family histories; long out-of-print books on pieces of Lawrence arcana (Flow of Water in Pipes by Hiram F. Mills, comes foremost to mind); and hundreds of indelible photographs depicting various Lawrence scenes over the one hundred and sixty-odd years of the city's history. Many of these wonderful images, like the old black and whites of a crowded Essex Street in the 1930s and 1940s, helped me to develop my "illustration" of Lawrence and how it teemed with commerce and socializing across a large span of years.

The reference staff at the Lawrence Public Library helped me with many things, including the excavation of biographical information on various relatively obscure figures from the city's past. These generous folks also directed me through their vast microfilm collection of defunct daily and weekly newspapers that originated in Lawrence. (Additionally, I received valuable assistance from the reference staff at Nevins Memorial Library in Methuen, MA.) Pete Ford also introduced me to his colleague, Dr. Clarisse A. Poirier, and her doctoral dissertation, Pemberton Mills 1852-1938: A Case Study of the Industrial and Labor History of Lawrence, Massachusetts, published by Boston University in 1978, and the chapter "Aftermath of a Disaster: The Collapse of the Pemberton Mill," which appeared on pages 77-96 of a book entitled Labor in Massachusetts: Selected Essays (edited by Kenneth Fones-Wolf and Martin Kaufman, and published by the Institute for Massachusetts Studies, Westfield State College, Westfield, MA, 1990) were integral to my understanding of that historic mill fire and how it affected the city.

While I was poking around town, detectives in the Lawrence Police Department shared insights about the possible causes of the arson wave that struck Lawrence in the early 1990s, and, as always, I found members of the local law enforcement community to be hard working, informative and good-natured. Firefighters like the late Jeff Ness of the Lawrence Fire Department; chief Cliff Gallant, his brother Lieutenant Glenn Gallant, ex-Marine Steve Battles, Lieutenant Bill Giarrusso (or "Chief of the Italians" as he likes to be called; retired and loving it), and Deputy Chief

Bill Barry of the Methuen Fire Department; and old rugby pal Dan "Original Sully" Sullivan of the Manchester, NH Fire Department told me stories from the job and discussed the perils of fighting fires in the many old mill buildings that dot the local landscape.

Local historians Jonas Stundza (who was especially helpful, providing several photographs, as well as interesting material on the cultural meanings of amber), Philip Laudani, my old Pop Warner football teammate Dan Gagnon, former Methuen High teacher and track coach Mike Hughes, and legendary Methuen expert Ernest Mack were happy to share their encyclopedic knowledge of the Merrimack Valley with me. I am also grateful to the Boott Cotton Mills Museum at the Lowell National Historic Park in Lowell, MA, which is run by the U. S. Department of the Interior, as well as the Tsongas History Center located in the Boott Museum. There I was able to witness a mill floor in action and found the staff and re-enactors very knowledgeable and friendly.

As always, my friends offered ample encouragement and numerous local anecdotes, and I am grateful to Bob and Linda Sheehan, John "Surfer" Hearin, Salem NH police officer Mark Donahue and his wife Maureen, Dr. Karen Koffler, Dr. Marc Klein, Atty. Randy Reis, Norm Litwack, Bill and Kathy Fitzgerald, Jason and Stephanie Massa, Tim and Denise Croteau, Andrea Doherty, Atty. Mark Machera and family, Greg Cyr and family, Jay Buckler, Geoff Pitcher, Mary Beth Donovan and Tom Grassi, Martina Kalusova, Jim and Maryanne Connolly, Mass. State trooper Gene Kee (retired) and his wife Ellen, Atty. Joe Doyle and family, Mass. State trooper Mark Lemieux and family, U.S. Secret Service Agent Henry (retired) and his wife Diane, Revere MA Police lieutenant John Goodwin and family, Ken Greenwood and family, Father Paul O'Brien and Father Paul McManus of Saint Patrick's church in Lawrence, Father John Farren, Frank Posluzny and family, Somerville, MA police sergeant Joe McCain, Jr. and Maureen and Helen McCain and their family, and Bill DePardo Jr. and his extended family. Mostly, I eschew the company of other writers but you have to love these guys: Frank Baker, Paul Marion, Dave Daniel, Chuck Hogan, Keith Bowden, J. D. Scrimgeour, Perry Glasser, Halley Suitt, Joe "Dutch" Kurmaskie, Steve Whipple and Jay McHale. Adjectives and adverbs are mere child's play to all of you.

Growing up in our family was a lot of fun, and the candid sense of humor and bluntness that characterize our gang has always kept me from ruminating on the darker aspects of life. When I was writing this book, always foremost in my mind was the fact that my family connected me to this particular landscape and vice versa. Therefore, I'd like to thank John and Jackie Atkinson and family; Paul and Shirley Crane and all my beloved cousins and their families; Arthur and Natalie Wermers; Lawrence Berry and Peg Burr; Scott and Mary and Barbara Leonhart; John, Jodie, Matthew and Katelyn Berry; Patrick, Deanna, Owen and Reese Bower; Jill Atkinson; James Atkinson Jr., my late parents, Jim and Lois, and my wonderful 12 year old son, Liam, to whom I have dedicated this volume.

City in Amber

"History is a vast, inexplicable tale that seems to make no sense."

—Jack Kerouac

"The city lies in latitude 42 degrees, 42 minutes, 13 seconds, and in longitude 71 degrees, 10 minutes, 13 seconds, west from Greenwich; has a little more than seven square miles (4,577 acres) area, of which 2,216 acres are in the North District, taken from the town of Methuen; 2,097 acres, south of the Merrimack river, were taken from the town of Andover....The city is well situated in a broad and open plain. The central and more thickly-settled portions are upon the rolling swell of land on the north bank of the Merrimack river, where that majestic stream curves about the great mills. To the south the plain is a wide expanse, extending westward from the Shawsheen river, somewhat rolling and broken near the western limits. The highlands west of the city known as Tower Hill, as well as the rolling ridge, Prospect Hill, eastward, are sites of attractive residences, having an elevation of eighty to one hundred and fifty feet above the dam. The valley enclosed by these ridges is nearly two miles broad, extending to higher lands beyond the city limits."

—*Municipal History of Essex County in Massachusetts*
Benjamin F. Arrington, Editor; 1922

"That temporary causes have operated in Lawrence, as in other new places, to depress the public health, and to produce an unnatural increase in the number of deaths. Among these causes may be mentioned;—1. The transition from one place and from one mode of living to others;—2. The bringing together of persons and adventurers of different characters and habits, sometimes with broken fortunes or debilitated constitutions."

—*Sanitary Survey of Lawrence*, 1850

Principal Characters

Lawrence, Massachusetts

The Present Day

Walter Beaumont, retired banker
Philbin Bates, lawyer
Colin Isherwood I & II, newspaper publishers
Wilson X. Wilson, state senator
Father Tom Dailey, priest
Dr. Montgomery Tattersall, physician

Kuko Carrero, gang leader
Little Eddie, strong arm
Tito Jackson, street criminal

Joe Glass, handyman
Francesca Nesheim, his former girlfriend
Gabriel Glass, their toddler son
Pier Eriksen, Joe's elderly neighbor
Boris Johnson, landlord and fitness enthusiast
Charlie Kutter, radio station owner
Kap Kutter, his grown son
Billy Bruce, disc jockey

Thomas "Tug" McNamara, chief of police
Rick Maxwell, special agent, Bureau of Alcohol, Tobacco and
    Firearms
Rudy Pattavina, police detective
Paul Quebec Jr., city councilor
Ismail Citron, Holy Rosary altar boy
Hernan Diaz, his 4-year old half brother

1848

Abbott Lawrence, financier, principal of the Boston Associates
Gabriel Glass, laborer
Josiah Quebec, assistant chemist
Charles S. Storrow, chief engineer
Captain Charles Bigelow, principal field engineer
John Levy, barber
J. F. C. Hayes, newspaperman

Nathan Appleton, The Boston Associates
William Sturgis
Ignatius Sargent
Rev. John A. Lowell

1910

William Madison Wood, mill owner
Silent Dick Morgan, Wood's chauffeur
Frederick J. Ayer, Wood's father-in-law
Franklin Beaumont, overseer's second hand, Wood Mill
Ignatius J. Bates, lawyer
Colin Isherwood, newspaperman

1932

Franklin Beaumont, general overseer of the Ayer Mill
Gus Hearin, dye house foreman
Walter Beaumont, young Army veteran
Monty Tattersall, medical student
Judge Ignatius Bates, superior court justice
Phil Bates, high school student

1941

Paul Quebec, mayor
Charles M. Prescott, bank president
Chet Collins, jazz musician
Pier Eriksen, artist
Joseph G. Glass, short order cook

1

Lawrence, Massachusetts

The Present Day

Walter Beaumont felt the world slipping beneath his Oldsmobile as it zoomed down Tower Hill. Outdoors for the first time in a month, the retired banker was light-headed and queasy, his hands like two claws gripping the steering wheel. Even the contour of his neighborhood looked strange to him: the grand old houses with their medieval turrets and glassed-in widow's walks, the huge lawns whitened into dust from the September drought, and the iron fences and brick walls and bulkheads rushing by his windows. An old woman in a feathered hat spooked like a pheasant, flushed from an alcove when Beaumont inadvertently touched his horn. His face jerked downward in a sudden fierce apology, then he turned back to the careering pavement, the wheel twisting in his hands like a snake.

At the bottom of the hill, where the houses shrank and grew closer together, Broadway was crowded with men in nylon skullcaps and long parkas despite the mild weather, their syncopated music shrieking from huge radios. They stood arguing and pushing each other and calling out to the women in passing cars, obscured by steam rising from grates in the road. To Walter, it was like being visited by apparitions. These ghosts indicated there was another city, subterranean to Lawrence, that was heavy with steam and smelled of distant shores—dark, foreign and strange—to which they would return.

On the site of the Tip-Top Club, where the young Walter Beaumont had danced with his sweethearts, was a place called the Disco Very. It was aqua and pink with bars on the windows and a low concrete marquee. Down the length of Broadway, nondescript stores hawked items of used clothing and broken-down furniture lined the sidewalks. Everywhere there were signs misprinted in English: *Fine Cloths for Woman. Good Foo. Electric Waterheeter.* A lot of it Walter didn't recognize: *Jose's Otto Shop and Store 48 and Alexandre's X-press Likkors*, interspersed with several locksmiths and check cashing places.

Steering his car between the delivery vans and taxis, Beaumont aimed for the river. Hunched against the bright October sky were the Wood and Kunhardt and Pacific mills, expanses of brick that sagged in the middle and featured a thousand broken windows. Above the low buildings on Essex Street, Beaumont saw the six floors of the Ayer Mill rising up from the Merrimack. The mill tower was capped with a green copper roof and weather vane, pointing north in the wind, and the great disk of the Ayer Mill clock. In just a few minutes it would be ticking again, re-dedicated in his honor. But then his gaze drifted to the trash piled against the bulging fences and the storefronts with their metal shutters, and Walter despaired over what had become of his city. Lawrence was under siege.

He panicked at the next intersection when he attempted a left-hand turn and discovered Essex Street was now one-way. His mouth open in disbelief, Beaumont sat with his hands frozen on the wheel and sweat running in a deluge from his armpits and beneath his collar. Motorists whizzed past on both sides, cursing in Spanish and Portuguese and shaking their fists. Then a stout, hairy-chested man in fluorescent green shorts sprinted toward him, his legs churning as he ran among the moving vehicles.

"Go back," the man said.

With a screech from the undercarriage Beaumont rolled his car in an arc, back onto Broadway heading south. He tried another left at Lawton's Frankfurters but the traffic pulled him along, over the O'Leary Bridge and away from the Ayer Mill. On a girder someone had painted a blue crown and the words "Latin Kings Ruel." The Merrimack glittered beneath Walter's tires, and he heard the falls beside the Great Dam and a hum that sounded like ten million insects emanating from the power station.

A minute later Walter was in South Lawrence, trying to regain the river and approach from the backside of the Ayer Mill. Craning his neck in every direction, Beaumont stopped the car in front of a strange, V-shaped building at a fork in the road. Half the roof was missing, and where the front windows should have been were holes that looked like eye sockets. Although it was uninhabitable, several men and women in dingy clothes and even one fellow wearing a business suit hurried into the structure. Most came right out again, but enough stayed inside to mark the location as a busy spot.

A shirtless, dark-skinned man in loose-fitting yellow dungarees and a black leather hat loitered against the building. His head was down, the brim of the hat shading his eyes.

"Pardon me," said Walter, in a voice that sounded feeble to his ear. "I need some directions." The man didn't respond, and Walter removed a five-dollar bill from his wallet. "Sir, if you can assist me, I'll reimburse you for your time."

Immediately the man was at the passenger side door, smelling of bleach and old, ingrained perspiration. His skin was blotchy, stretched over a wiry frame, and he had a faded blue crown the size of a thimble tattooed on his abdomen. "You need a bag, *viejo*?" he asked.

Jay Atkinson

Beaumont realized the man was Spanish and thought about driving away. "I don't need anything except directions to the Ayer Mill," he said, holding the banknote like it was intended to ward off evil. "Show me how to get there and I'll give you five dollars."

"Five bucks won' feed the dog around here," the man said. He took the bill. Jerking open the door, he got in and slid over the upholstery. "But for *fifty* bucks I'll give you a tour of the whole city."

"I've lived in Lawrence my whole life," said Walter. He felt the sweat pooling against his shriveled belly. "I don't need you to show it to me."

"For a hunnert bucks, I'll give you the place back," the man said.

Beaumont slipped the car into gear, rolling away from the curb with the smelly man as his passenger. Perhaps if a police car came along, he'd flag it down. In the seat beside him, the man rifled through the glove compartment and filled the pockets of his dungarees with stale cigars and some foil packets of antacid. He discovered a pair of gloves under the seat and put them on, admiring the dexterity the thin leather provided him. Placing the five-dollar bill on the dashboard, the man snapped it up like a magician performing his favorite trick.

"Hey, hang a left," he said, jabbing Beaumont on the shoulder.

Walter felt himself spiraling farther away from the Ayer Mill, in a maze of tenements. He glanced around at the ruined hulks and the mangy, toothless people wandering among them. The chances of spotting a police car in this neighborhood appeared remote.

"Right here. That's Kuko," the intruder said, indicating a man wearing an abundance of gold jewelry and wraparound sunglasses. Kuko was standing beside a purple Mustang that had tinted windows and pipes sticking out of the hood. He looked like some sort of dangerous prince. "When you do bizness aroun' here, you gotta go through Kuko," said the smelly man.

Walter felt vestiges of his management posture rising up in him. "I have an appointment at the Ayer Mill. If you want to guide me along, fine," he said. "Otherwise, get out."

A truck that had been maintaining a safe distance ahead of them blocked the road. A man climbed down, set out some orange traffic cones and lowered a hose into the bowels of the city. Then a compressor started up with a roar and the hose on the sewer truck vibrated, a moment later settling into a loud, steady rhythm. Beaumont and his passenger gagged as the stench overwhelmed them.

Kuko spotted the marooned Oldsmobile and came sauntering over. He was dressed in black with an enormous ring on his left hand that spelled out *New* and one on his right that said *York*. "Bizness," he said, displaying his fists. Kuko scratched at the small blue crown tattooed on his neck. "What's happenin', Tito?"

"I got some guy here, *ese*."

Jangling his gold chains Kuko leaned in the window, removing his sunglasses to give Walter Beaumont the once-over. Beaumont felt the loose flesh quivering on his neck, and sat there sweating and powerless. His heart was booming in his chest, and he felt that his civil rights were being violated. But Kuko just smiled at him.

"Some old *jefe*," said Tito. "In the wrong fuckin' neighborhood."

"What do you think of my city?" asked Kuko. In his hand was a gold-plated tooth attached to a gold chain, which he spun in a circle like a propeller.

The retired banker held Kuko's gaze. "What happened to Lawrence is a real shame," he said.

"So, look what happen' to you," Kuko said, laughing at the man's earnestness.

Beaumont's passenger joined in Kuko's eruption of mirth. "Why don't you take all your money and fix it up?" Tito asked. "You're too fuckin' old to spend it on yourself."

When he had wiped tears of laughter from his eyes, Kuko put his sunglasses back on and straightened up. "Let 'im go," he said.

"C'mon, man," said Tito.

"A biznessman always recognize another biznessman, even if the biznessman don' recognize him," said Kuko. He walked away, his heels popping on the asphalt.

Fumbling into gear, Walter Beaumont directed his car past Kuko and the sewer truck and the purple Mustang. Two blocks later, he was outside the gates of the Ayer Mill.

"Here you are, *jefe*," Tito said.

Beaumont handed over another five-dollar bill. "Please get out," he said.

"You can find me at the triangle any day," said Tito. He slithered from the seat, found the sidewalk, and disappeared among the crumbling tenements.

Determined not to reveal this episode to anyone, Beaumont squeezed the Oldsmobile through the rusty iron gates to the base of the mill tower. He parked beside Reverend Cruikshank's old Pontiac, climbed out and maneuvered toward the doors.

As a lifelong bachelor, Walter Beaumont had reached the age where his most intimate relations were with his doctor and his attorney, and the future disposition of his wealth was of more concern to his minister than the state of his soul had ever been. All three men were present, waiting for him at the summit of the Ayer Mill. Sighting up the barrel of the tower, Beaumont saw his lawyer, Philbin Bates, leaning over the hole in the floor.

"Take the elevator, W. B.," said Bates, who was dressed in pinstripes. "We're not going anywhere."

Beaumont could hear the floor above him groan with the weight of two dozen celebrants. After a restoration campaign kicked off by Walter's fifteen thousand dollar ice-breaker, the giant clock, which had stood motionless and rusted and decrepit above the city of Lawrence for more than forty years, was going to be set in motion again. Walter was there to cut the ribbon, as his father had been in 1910 when the Ayer Mill opened for business and the faces of the clock were illuminated for the first time.

Jay Atkinson

The freight elevator deposited him on a platform one level beneath the clock. Clinging to an iron ladder, Walter's heart hammered in his chest and his head swam in the acrid stench of pigeon waste. It was a toxic material that had formed itself into great stalagmites inside the tower and gave off a vile gray dust. Experts speculated that more than a million pigeons had roosted there over the years, leaving several tons of waste that specialists charged one hundred thousand dollars to remove. As treasurer of the restoration committee, Walter Beaumont had signed every work order and authorized each and every payment. By the pound, pigeon shit ended up costing only a few dollars less than caviar.

Behind Walter on the ladder, a sturdy lad in the employ of the general contractor asked, "Are you all right, Mr. Beaumont?" when the pause in their climb had lasted several seconds.

"Just stopped to enjoy the view," said Walter, gesturing at the walls that surrounded them. Laughter came from above at his little joke. Portals on the final landing gave out to panoramas of the city, but from where the climbers stood on the ladder they had a vista of brick and nothing more.

Walter Beaumont was not well. He had lost weight, down to one hundred-fifteen pounds on his six-foot frame, and the simplest of tasks left him out of breath and defeated. It had taken a supreme effort to dress and drive himself to the clock dedication. Walter's cardiologist, boyhood chum Dr. Montgomery Tattersall, was present at the ceremony because of his concern for Walter's health. The physician waited at the zenith of the forty-by-forty-foot tower with a blood pressure cuff and stethoscope hidden beneath his jacket. He had warned his friend not to take part in the dedication, which they had learned about only days before, because of the difficult climb and the inevitable pigeon dust. Both conditions were sure to affect what Tattersall referred to as Walter's "chronic obstructive pulmonary disease."

"My emphysema is going to kill me, Monty. Not the pigeon shit," Beaumont had said, sitting in his undershirt in the doctor's Common Street office. "I'm going up there to see what the hell I was signing all those checks for. If the largest mill clock in the world isn't worth gasping over, I don't know what is."

It had seemed easy enough resting in Tattersall's office. But five steps into the climb the tower wobbled with each new breath, and Beaumont felt like iron bands were encircling his ribs. Exhaustive tests at Beth Israel Hospital had revealed a hardening of his lungs similar to a ninety-five-year-old man who smoked four packs of cigarettes a day. But Walter was only seventy-nine and, except for his brief Army service, had never used tobacco. Dr. Tattersall speculated that the fibers and resins in use at the Ayer Mill had done serious damage in Walter's youth and now, as the rest of his body was breaking down, the effects of that unregulated work environment were manifesting themselves.

"What these mill owners did was criminal," Attorney Bates had said when he heard the news. "You should seek redress."

"The mill's been closed for forty years. Anybody worth suing is already dead," Beaumont said.

Through the soles of his shoes, Walter felt the young man press upward to help him mount each successive rung on the ladder. When they were halfway up, the jowly face of Bernie L'Heureux appeared above them, framed by the hole in the floor. L'Heureux was the president of the Chamber of Commerce, an enormous man who wore a poplin jacket with stains under the arms and a polka dot bow tie. Undoubtedly, his intention was to take credit for another project his office had done nothing about, posing for photographers and giving his "pride and history and determination" speech. Each week L'Heureux sent out press releases on the city's bootstrap recovery, a laughable prospect with half of Lawrence boarded up and the other half on fire. He frowned at Walter Beaumont's slow progress and ducked away.

Finally Walter's head poked through the floor at the bell level, and he and the contractor's boy rested for a few moments. The two-ton bell had been cast in Denmark of brass so pure a master carillonneur could play Mozart on it. Walter remembered walking to work as an assistant foreman, listening to the different languages converging as they passed beneath the clock's shadow and through the gates of the mill. Snatches of Italian and Gaelic and Portuguese floated to him on the solemn tolling of the bell, as the yard filled with men and women prepared to work twelve hours with only a single tomato for lunch, or a twenty-cent pork pie.

The bell was so tall a grown man could stand inside it, and cold and smooth to the touch. Walter leaned against it, struggling for breath. Ten feet above him, where an assembly of community leaders and politicians surrounded the shiny brass workings of the clock, someone popped a bottle of champagne. "We've all worked so hard on this project," said the voice of Bernie L'Heureux. "It's a beacon—a sign that Lawrence is going to come alive again."

"I'd like to wait on that toast another minute," Attorney Bates said. "The project would never have gotten off the ground without Walter Beaumont."

Metal screens covering each gable afforded views of the Lawrence skyline and allowed in drafts of cool air. Beaumont steadied himself on the stairway that led to the clock, his breath coming in gasps, the boy waiting at his shoulder. "When you're ready, sir," he said. Nearby, a raft of pigeons formed a ululating chorus, swiveling their heads around as they defecated on the brickwork.

"I better get going," said Walter. "I don't want those pigeons to start refilling the tower."

He went up the stairs too fast. At the top, with Dr. Tattersall and Philbin Bates and L'Heureux crowding around, Beaumont wanted more room to breathe but his lungs were empty and he couldn't talk. Looming nearby, he saw all the color drain out of Tattersall's face. Walter blacked out for a second and woke to find himself sitting beside the clock's inner workings. Tattersall had the blood pressure cuff tightened on his arm and was listening to his lungs through a stethoscope.

Jay Atkinson

"You're having an episode," the doctor said.

"Nonsense," Beaumont said. "I'm fine."

When his head began to clear, he recognized most of the occupants of the drafty clock keeper's room. Scattered about nibbling on hors d'oeuvres and clutching champagne were local politicians, merchants who had donated money, and other sycophants and hangers-on. Lawrence's optimistic, deluded mayor, Elizabeth Temple O'Brien, was talking with Bernie L'Heureux, master of hyperbole and the gratuitous handshake.

Colin Isherwood II and Colin III, father and son publishers of the *Lawrence Tribune-Standard*, loitered in a corner aloof from the proceedings. In profile, they looked like twin Yankee cameos. If it was indeed true that the Cabots spoke only to the Lodges and the Lodges spoke only to God, then God required an appointment to speak with the Isherwoods. Dressed in crisp blue blazers and chino pants, the Isherwoods wore the patrician leers of men who spent their summers on Governor's Island and had prepped at Choate. Their thin faces, identical except for the father's graying temples, scanned the room like surveying instruments, keeping watch for a family mercury that rose as high as their own.

Once the Isherwoods had put ten cents of their own money into the clock restoration, the *Tribune-Standard* pimped for it as shamelessly as the hookers on Essex Street. The hours of the week and the clock faces and hands were symbolically sold. A column in the newspaper kept a running tally of the donations, and for over a month the Isherwoods published inspirational stories on the front page. Beaumont knew they had charged the restoration committee a significant sum to run features like the one about a retired jack-of-the-clock who gave five thousand dollars. But Walter kept silent because the *Tribune-Standard* campaign had enabled the committee to close an estimated two hundred fifty thousand-dollar shortfall with no single donation totaling more than ten thousand dollars. Claiming in a final editorial that "memories are the strongest human motivating force," the Isherwoods pocketed over nineteen thousand dollars.

That was how things worked in business. If someone was willing to help out but wished to make a profit, you emphasized the help and ignored the profit. Colin II and III played the game very well. Where Bernie L'Heureux's proprietorship was active to the point of comedy, the Isherwoods plied their interests with a nearly motionless resolve. Never so much as twitching an eyebrow, they pressured events down whatever chute they had devised with the unspoken and uncogitated will of peristalsis.

Some of the masons and carpenters hovered around a table filled with crackers and cheese, and a wobbly three-foot gelatin mold in the shape of the clock tower. Elderly state senator Wilson X. Wilson was there, wearing a hounds tooth hat and his Fireman's Appreciation badge. Beside him was the clock maker, Basil Morrisette, who looked like a man who reviewed films for public television. Dressed in wool and carrying tins of brass polish, Morrisette smiled at Senator Wilson's loose-dentured blathering and gazed across the room at his latest work of art.

The clock itself looked like a Model T chassis with some sort of Rube Goldberg device resting on it. An intricate system of gears, stainless steel pinions, and rubber and metal belts appeared ready to circumvolve. Suspended on the brick walls of the tower and connected by thick metal rods to the clock works were four glass faces. They measured twenty-two-and-a-half feet across, only six inches smaller than the Great Clock of Westminster, which housed London's Big Ben. Morrisette had created them by installing six thousand pounds of double-frosted quarter-inch glass, illuminated from within by spotlights that filled the tower with their brilliance.

A young man in an expensive trench coat stood nearby, poised to give a speech. Walter also noticed Kitty Axelrod, a widow and rival philanthropist who had married an Italian race car driver. With both of them staring in his direction, Walter became embarrassed at his infirmity. He struggled to his feet, pushing his doctor and lawyer away. "I've kept everyone waiting long enough," he said.

Bernie L'Heureux repeated his toast, while a photographer from the *Lawrence Tribune-Standard* jockeyed with his lenses. The fat man levitated on a cushion of air, turning his bulk to remain in the viewfinder. The photographer fired off several pictures of the shiny clock workings with Isherwoods II and III in the background, their lips glued together like those of funeral home corpses.

L'Heureux turned away, edging himself into the range of WKUT's microphone. A young woman in a tartan skirt was interviewing Philbin Bates about the perpetual easement he had secured *pro bono* from the mill's only lessor, a firm that made prosthetic eyeballs. During the early stages of the project, Walter had attended a meeting in the firm's office and been unnerved by a glass jar filled with their product. Bates was nattering on about rights of way and some thorny liability issue but Walter couldn't stop staring at the glass eyes. Under the roof of the Ayer Mill, he could sense the eyes of dead mill workers floating there, implicating him.

Once tall and straight and operating under the entitlements of the Ayer Company, Walter Beaumont had served as shop foreman at the age of twenty-one. The blue eyes of the Irish, the dark Italian browns, the olives of the Greeks had watched him give orders with the same impassivity as the eyes in the jar. Beaumont was a man born to medium position, of medium temperament, with the volatile ingredient of higher expectations. In 1932 productivity was up, his father was holding wages steady, and the mill owners had plans for their ambitious young foreman. Now the owners and the plans and the mill and his father were all dead.

The young man in the trench coat drew everyone together around the clock. The paper badge on his lapel was inscribed MY NAME IS: *Jay Bower.* Years ago Walter had known a Bower, a pudgy English baker named Ray. Working out of a cellar, this man Bower baked at night and then drove around in a horse-drawn wagon delivering his goods. He carried a huge ring of keys and would let himself into speakeasies around the city, where his pork pies were sold for a quarter with the bathtub gin. Perhaps the young man was a relation.

Reverend Wilbur Cruikshank, and then Father Tom, the young priest from Holy Rosary Church, gave their blessings. Trying to look pious, Bernie L'Heureux opened his mouth like he wanted to add another prayer but no sound came out.

"Ladies and gentlemen, today is a great day for Lawrence," Jay Bower said. "I want to thank the readers and staff and publishers of the Lawrence *Tribune-Standard*, the law offices of Philbin Bates, the Chamber of Commerce under the direction of Bernard P. L'Heureux, master clock maker Basil Morrisette, Mike Devaney Steeplejacks of Lowell, National Eye Prosthetics of Lawrence, New England Technical Abatement Specialists of Boston, the estate of Harvey Axelrod, city historian Philip Laudani, Immigrant City Archives director Eartha Dengler, State Senator Wilson X. Wilson, City of Lawrence Mayor Elizabeth Temple O'Brien, WKUT Radio, one-time jack-of-the-clock Joseph Plonowski, the hundreds of retired mill workers and citizens of Greater Lawrence who gave to the project, and last, but not least, the man who envisioned the Ayer Mill Clock ticking again and had the courage to step up to the plate for what some called Beaumont's folly—a nice round of applause for Lawrence Savings & Trust president Walter Beaumont."

"Retired," said Walter, to a surge of laughter and applause that filled the cap of the tower. When it died down, he got to his feet and said, "To me, the clock will always be a memorial to my father and mother, and to everyone who came here to work and make their lives better. I think it probably means something different to everyone here, and that's a good thing."

Beaumont was handed a pair of shears to cut a red, white and blue ribbon suspended over the clock. His narrow wrist fell out of his sleeve, and he remembered a pair of gold cuff links in the shape of the clock his father had once owned, wondering what had become of them.

"There we are," said Beaumont, as the ribbon fell away. "Time again."

Twisting a shiny brass key into the workings of the device, Basil Morrisette started the clock. Gears turned, metal bands began spinning and the entire contraption hummed with activity. In a minute, the connecting rods turned the hands on each of the four clock faces, and a cry of surprise went up from the assembly. Jay Bower shook Walter's hand, saying something that couldn't be heard in the din. The young man's performance had been masterful, summarizing the thousands of hours and hundreds of thousands of dollars that had gone into the project, satisfying just about everyone present. A real talent, Walter declared.

"Was Ray your grandfather?" he asked, resting his hand in the boy's.

"That's right," said Jay, smiling with all his teeth. "I didn't think anyone here remembered him."

"I remember him. Hardworking fellow. What kind of work is it that you do, Jay?"

"I was hired as a consultant by Mr. Isherwood. My job is to get to know everyone, and bring them all together, sort of as a team." He was about thirty years old, with an athletic build and thick brown hair. The young man leaned forward. "But I'm a writer, really. I'm writing a book about Lawrence."

"Oh. Congratulations. I hope to read it one day," said Beaumont.

"I hope so, too," Bower said, and WKUT interrupted him for an interview. Beaumont sank back into the metal folding chair, and Basil Morrisette came over to shake his hand.

"The clock looks marvelous," Beaumont said. "How accurate will it keep time?"

"To less than a minute each month," said Morrisette, who had salvaged most of the metal parts and reconditioned them himself. He and his wife and son had removed the clock's four sets of hands, and its two-thousand-pound physical movement. Using the original gearing as a pattern, the Morrisettes made exact copies of the clock's brass gears and replaced steel pinions that were pitted and worn. Over the course of fourteen months, the clock restoration took the Morrisette family three thousand hours to complete.

The two men turned and looked at the clock; it continued spinning and clicking like a miniature symphony. The E. Howard Clock Company in Waltham, Massachusetts had built the Ayer Mill Clock in 1909. "There's no other like it in the world," Morrisette said, pulling up a chair. He continued watching the movement with his hands resting in his lap.

The rest of the crowd stayed at a respectful distance, sipping their champagne. More than any of the others, the retired banker and the clock maker had believed in the project from start to finish. At the end of every working day, Morrisette had called Walter Beaumont to report his slow but steady progress. A bond had formed between the two men, who had traded stores of vast information on the exigencies of clock repair and fund-raising, and now were seeing, with the start of the clock, the finish of their professional relationship.

"What the hell is time, anyway?" Beaumont wanted to know. He turned his watery eyes to the clock maker.

The other man chuckled. "You might put that question to one of these preachers, or maybe a physicist or philosopher," he said. With a needle-like tool, Morrisette made an adjustment on one of the slower moving gears. "What I do know is, the duration of a second is defined as 9,192,631,770 cycles of the hyper-fine resonance frequency of the ground state of the cesium-133 atom."

Walter felt the tiny whirring of those atoms sending him earthward. Twenty years earlier he had been middle-aged, and forty years before that he was young. The true duration of that time had escaped him somehow. Across an arc he had been delivered to where he was at this moment, sitting beside a clock that overlooked the city of his birth, a peaceful ordinary life, and soon upon him, the moment of his death. Starting the

Jay Atkinson

clock up again where he had first gone to work and his father had put in more than fifty years, seemed a way to at least circle his unanswered questions.

Charging across the room, Bernie L'Heureux dragged a young priest by the arm and leaned toward Beaumont and Morrisette with the garlicky smell of his breath flying in their faces. "Father Tom says he might be interested in getting Holy Rosary's clock in shape," he said. "By my count, there's four unused tower clocks in the city. The Chamber supports any and all efforts to get them running again."

Basil Morrisette rose to make the priest's acquaintance. He lived from project to project, and was therefore interested in anyone who was interested in clocks. Beaumont remained in his chair; the energy that would have to be summoned to fix one more clock, let alone four, was beyond him. Already Morrisette was talking the poetry of reconditioning. He walked away with the priest, leading him toward the translucent orb of the nearest clock face.

Several people disappeared through the hole in the floor, back to their offices or to other appointments. Kitty Axelrod, followed by her husband, the slick-haired Alberto, went down the ladder first. She dropped a pair of high heels to the landing, and descended in her fur coat and cocktail dress. Mayor O'Brien departed in similar fashion, and then most of the others crowded down the ladder like ship passengers into the lifeboats. Soon only Beaumont, Monty Tattersall, Morrisette and two construction workers remained. Getting Walter to his car presented a dilemma. Shaky on his feet, he stood near the hole unable to squat into the proper position.

While the others scratched their heads, Basil Morrisette looked up to the ceiling and found the solution. With help from the two construction workers, he unstrung a boatswain's chair left behind by the steeplejacks and rigged it over one of the crossbeams overhead. Covering the dirty seat with a tablecloth, Morrisette and Tattersall fixed it beneath Walter Beaumont's rear end and suspended him over the opening in the floor.

"*Voila,*" said Dr. Tattersall. "Yankee ingenuity."

Walter clung to the ropes, his ankles extending beyond the cuffs of his pants and his feet dangling down. "More like Yankee infirmity," he said.

"I'm not interested in seeing you fall six stories, and then explaining to the authorities why I allowed it," said Dr. Tattersall. "I would like to keep practicing medicine for at least a few more weeks, and make it an even half-century."

The last to descend before this problem had arisen was Reverend Cruikshank. He was hailed through the opening and agreed to wait on the landing. The construction workers and Morrisette began paying out the rope, and Walter had a giddy feeling as he swung in the air. Excitement rather than exertion robbed him of his breath; his heart throbbed at a weak, rapid pace. Dropping down the tower, Beaumont pumped his knees like a child on a swing, and the rope twisted above him and the seat became unstable.

"Easy now, Walter," said Tattersall.

"He's coming to me," Cruikshank boomed in his preaching voice. "I almost have him. Only a few more yards."

Bald-headed, in his plain black suit and shiny shoes, the minister waited at the level of the freight elevator. Walter Beaumont dangled just above him. He felt Cruikshank grasp at his ankles and miss.

"Leave him be until he gets to you," Dr. Tattersall said.

"Sorry," said Cruikshank.

"Are you okay, Walter?" asked Tattersall.

The retired banker inched lower, until his feet were touching the floor and Cruikshank had hugged him to the fabric of his coat. Beaumont's nose filled with the scent of Cruikshank's aftershave, and the coolness of the minister's cheek brushed against his own. It felt like they were dancing.

"Right as the mail," Cruikshank said.

*

Joe Glass came down the stairs with his garbage and threw the bag to the curb. It gave off a lemon and mint smell, and elsewhere in the pile there was the rich dirt smell of coffee grounds, roasted garlic from the Marianno's on the first floor, and the odor of soiled diapers and brine. The temperature, which had been warm of late, was dropping and mists were rising from the pavement. From where he stood, the black bags in front of the tenements looked like pilgrims in sackcloth. They were huddled together in clumps, sodden from the rain that had fallen all night. Over the houses, Joe heard the grinding of a truck that was coming for the bags and the shouts of men working.

Next door someone threw four bags of garbage from an upper window and a well-dressed elderly gentleman drove by in an Oldsmobile. Then it was quiet again. Across the street, Mrs. Eriksen rapped on the window from inside her apartment and waved a thin, pale hand.

Pier Eriksen was eighty-two years old and lived in a narrow Victorian house that was balanced on its lot like a wedge of cake. The interior of Mrs. Eriksen's home was decorated with sepia wallpaper featuring trees hung with Spanish moss and a white-columned plantation that repeated itself every six feet or so. In the corner of her living room was a terrarium that glowed with a strange purple light. The lower level of the terrarium was filled with loam and held several varieties of fern, one row festooned with tiny white flowers, and the largest of the plants arranged like an Indian headdress in a circle of pointed leaves. On a glass shelf above were pink orchids and orange tiger lilies, mingled with tendrils and something resembling pea pods.

Mrs. Eriksen was often visible in the bay window of her house, wearing a rubber horticulturist's smock and canvas gloves, cultivating her miniature garden with a pair of shears. Her pendulous face wore a look of gentle but inexorable concentration, like a monk intent on translating some ancient hieroglyphic. None of the plants were marked with identification tags, and her plant foods and vitamins came in shaker cans and triangular vellum envelopes with foreign labels. Mrs. Eriksen

Jay Atkinson

worked in the eerie purple glow of the heat lamps, a cup of tea at her elbow.

When Joe got to the door, Mrs. Eriksen opened it before he could knock. She smiled at him with long yellow teeth. "I was hoping you could take out my residuals," the old woman said.

Occasionally Joe Glass ran errands or fixed a drainpipe for Mrs. Eriksen, but lately she had been calling him over just to chat. Her trash was bundled in two pastry boxes tied with string and a tall paper bag. Together they looked like a delivery order from an exclusive shop. Mrs. Eriksen wore a long wool skirt, fisherman's sweater and battered old tennis shoes. She was tall, with clear blue eyes and an impressive mound of white hair.

"What are you doing up so early, Joe?" she asked.

Joe Glass knew that Mrs. Eriksen rose at four AM and read from the King James Bible, Torah, and other more obscure texts and publications. The old woman also practiced for an hour each afternoon on the harp in her front room. During the summer, Joe enjoyed the music floating up to him on the warm fragrant air.

"I'm on my way to see Gabriel," he said.

Mrs. Eriksen smiled. "That child of yours is a treasure," she said. "Do you see him often?"

"As much as I can."

"A child is like a flower that needs cultivating," Mrs. Eriksen said. "You'll bring Gabriel by today, won't you? I have something for him."

"Francesca likes him to stay inside when it gets cold," Joe said. "She's afraid he'll get sick."

Mrs. Eriksen shook her head. "Children need the outdoors. It makes them healthy," she said. "It says in the Bible, 'Who by worrying can add a single hour to his life?'"

"Maybe I'll just bundle him up and stop over," said Joe.

"You do that," said Mrs. Eriksen.

Joe Glass had longish hair and wore a black leather jacket over a T-shirt that read *Guilty*. His hands were hairy like an ape's, and there was a scar beneath his lower lip that looked like a slot to put coins in. Nothing registered in his sleepy brown eyes except the desire to be agreeable.

"Have a cup of tea with me," said Mrs. Eriksen.

The teapot sat on a cozy upon the windowsill. Mrs. Eriksen placed a cup in Joe's hand that felt as light as an eggshell. Into it went a stream of hot greenish liquid that smoked upwards and gave off a sweet odor. Strangely, it didn't heat the edges of the cup.

Joe Glass sipped the tea, and a moment or two later found himself sitting in a chair although he didn't recall walking to get there. He felt like yodeling, and there was a ball of excitement turning in his chest. Mrs. Eriksen was smiling at him. "On a raw morning like this, nothing warms you like a good cup of tea," she said.

Reaching into the pocket of her skirt, Mrs. Eriksen took a pinch of something else and added it to the tea. "Now try it," she said. Joe Glass tipped the cup to his mouth. The smell of a root cellar filled his nasal passages, and the silvery taste of the brew spread downward through his torso. Now he was by the door, Mrs. Eriksen patting his arm. "Bring that boy here to me," she said. "I have something for him."

The old woman closed the door with a shaking of glass and disappeared toward the back of the house. Out on the street, Joe Glass couldn't resist opening up Mrs. Eriksen's neatly wrapped trash and peeking inside. One of the boxes contained the end of a turnip, along with some apple peels inside a tin can that had been stripped of its label. In the other box were stale croissants, toilet paper rolls, a plastic statue with the head broken off, and thick wads of dust from under sofas and chairs. The inside of the paper bag was waxed, filled halfway to the top with wet plant clippings and the waterlogged residue of Mrs. Eriksen's tea. Beneath the damp mixture was a rectangular packet of some sort. Digging in the humus with his fingers, Joe Glass shook it free of the plant clippings and pulled out an envelope filled with small pasteboard cards. They were a sheaf of yellowed photographs and Joe leaned against an oak tree to examine them.

The top one depicted a much younger Pier Eriksen dancing naked in a room filled with old furniture and a chandelier overhead that threw diamonds of light across her frame. She was approximately thirty years old, with blonde hair that flew over her shoulder, a hand raised across her eyes at the moment the shutter clicked. Bouncing upright on one long muscular leg, Mrs. Eriksen's ample breasts stood straight out and the Vandyke of her pubic hair looked like it had been drawn in with pencil. Except for her mischievous smile it appeared that she had been surprised by the photographer; an inexplicable moment in the life of a young woman.

In the next photograph Mrs. Eriksen was again naked, seated in a wing back chair. Perched on the arm of the chair was a fully clothed older man wearing a stiff collar and homburg hat. His clothing was expensive and distinguished. He was smiling at the camera, and Mrs. Eriksen was gazing at him. The man was also the photographer. He held a metal cricket in his left hand and there were flash burns on his lapel.

Four other photographs completed the set. In two of them, Mrs. Eriksen was naked above the waist and appeared alone in the room, posing with her harp. She wore an elegant brocaded skirt and toe shoes. One photograph depicted the room itself, empty, with the curving bay window and chandelier. The final photograph was the most curious. In it the man was bare-chested, and Mrs. Eriksen was attired in his jacket and stiff-collared shirt. Staring down at himself, the man appeared to be exclaiming aloud while the hat went flying in the air and Mrs. Eriksen glanced at him with a disapproving look. The lower half of the photo was missing.

He replaced the photographs in the envelope and slipped it into his pocket. Pinching some of the tea leaves beneath his lower lip like snuff, Joe molded the rest into a little ball he stored in another pocket. He repacked Mrs. Eriksen's trash and left it beside the oak tree. Far down the block, the garbage truck was approaching, snorting and grinding like a tank.

One day a few months after Gabriel was born, Joe Glass had wheeled the infant past the house and Mrs. Eriksen came onto the porch and addressed him for the first time.

"So. A son," she called out.

It was a brilliant October afternoon and the oak trees were arrayed in great cloaks of red and gold, shimmering with color when the wind blew. Gabriel was wrapped in a cotton blanket with a fuzzy cap on his head. Mrs. Eriksen asked his name and when Joe Glass told her what it was, she said, "The archangel and one true messenger of God."

The circumstances of Gabriel's arrival had been difficult; Joe Glass was not married, and he had not planned on becoming a father. Mrs. Eriksen's blessing had been unexpected, but welcome—the thought of his son as a gift from God was not something he had considered. From that day onward, he often stopped to say hello to Mrs. Eriksen and would do errands and odd jobs for her whenever he was asked. She seemed like a beautiful old soul.

People danced around the house naked; he probably did it two or three times a week. Why shouldn't Mrs. Eriksen? She had a right to her privacy and her past. Still, Joe Glass wondered about the man in the photograph, and about Mrs. Eriksen's homemade tea; it had done strange things to him.

Joe Glass floated toward Broadway. Every object in the neighborhood was cut out by strange blue light. The curbstone was fluted like pie crust, and each bag of trash was a historical marker. The garbage truck came down the street with two Puerto Rican attendants and they looked like dignitaries on a barge. Joe Glass saluted them, and they stared back like he was crazy.

At the corner, Joe turned onto South Broadway and there were some men from the gas company working under the road. Standing over the manhole was a Massachusetts State Trooper in his greatcoat, pinched motorman's cap, and glossy boots. With hands in his pockets, Joe closed his fingers on the naked eighty-two year old woman, afraid he was breaking the law.

"Morning," said the trooper.

"Cold one," said Joe. The clock above the Ayer Mill indicated it was 7:09 and he hurried along.

Francesca lived in a yellow brick building on Bailey Street. Punching in the security code, Joe pushed through the buzzing door and ran down the hall. "Frannie," he said, rapping on number six. When Francesca didn't answer, Joe let himself in with the key.

The apartment was filled with Francesca's scent, but she wasn't there. Water dripped from the faucet and a smoldering waffle was stuck in the toaster. In the bedroom, the covers were thrown off the bed and lay tangled on the floor. Gabriel's crib was empty; it looked like it had been robbed.

An overweight woman with red hair came to the doorway. "The baby's at my place," she said. "Fran figured you were gonna be late."

Joe's panic subsided, and he went next door to retrieve his son. Gabriel was standing in the middle of the filthy kitchen with a smile on his face. "Ha," he said. The little boy cocked his head, like Joe had been hiding just out of sight all morning. Dark-haired Gabriel was dressed in a one-piece corduroy suit with a patch on the breast that said "Fly Boy." He stretched his arms upward and Joe lifted him in the air, tossing him toward the ceiling.

"Hey, little man," Joe said. "Wanna go somewhere?"

The neighbor sat at her kitchen table eyeing Joe Glass. "Fran was gonna pay me if you didn't show up," she said, reaching for the boy.

"Too bad," said Joe. He snatched his son away from the woman, stopping across the hall to get Gabriel's snowsuit and his diaper kit.

He scribbled a note on the waffle box. *Picked up Gabe at 7:11. Don't pay the old bat a cent. Love, Joe.* Gabriel waited beside the table, his head encased in the hood of his snowsuit like a piece of china. His eyes dominated the top half of his face, huge and brown like Joe Glass was standing there looking at himself. The boy had his father's eyes, but his mother's perfect lips and fine black hair. While Joe was writing the note, an ambulance and two fire trucks passed in the street and Gabriel began swinging his hips to the sirens.

"The music of the city," Joe said.

Joe Glass went out to the street, carrying his son like a lawn ornament. Gabriel was seventeen months old and could walk, but not very steadily. At the corner of South Broadway, the state trooper and the men from the gas company were still at work, and the garbage truck came past and the men all waved to each other. Joe felt left out, and shifted Gabriel off his shoulder and spoke into the boy's round, happy face.

"Give your old man a kiss, even if he doesn't have a job," he said, and Gabriel rolled his eyes upward and opened his mouth.

Joe could see the pink flap of the baby's throat, and into the tunnel leading down to what he had eaten for breakfast. It smelled of milk. Joe blew a stream of air into Gabriel's mouth, and the boy squealed with laughter and pounded his father on the side of the head.

Joe Glass stopped at Marianno's Pizza to see if his landlord needed him to make some deliveries. Inside, John Marianno and another man were installing new ceiling tiles and smoking cigarettes. "Whatever you do, you pay a certain price, and the price I'm paying is death," said Marianno, coughing up a little cloud.

"What's wrong with you?" asked the other man.

"High blood pressure. Angina. You name it."

Joe Glass cleared his throat, and the two men looked down at him from the scaffolding. "Yeah?" asked the proprietor, his arms coated in dust from the job.

"I'll have a large, with pepperoni and asbestos," said Joe. "To go."

Marianno climbed down to pinch Gabriel on the cheek, and the boy started to cry. "Take it easy," said Joe, turning away.

"Crying is good for him," Marianno said. "It clears the lungs."

The pizza shop owner took a sponge and began wiping the counter

Jay Atkinson

with it. "I'm not gonna need you today. Too cold and wet. Soup weather."

John Marianno was seventy-five years old and healthy as a teenager. "In two wars I didn't see one dead Senator, believe me," he often said.

With Gabriel slung over his shoulder, Joe Glass remembered the nude photographs in his pocket and thought about showing them to Marianno. The tough old Italian had been in the neighborhood almost as long as Mrs. Eriksen had. Perhaps he knew the man in the homburg hat. "I took Mrs. Eriksen's garbage out for her this morning," Joe said.

"I bet that was a thrill," Marianno said, throwing a tarp over the counter.

"Was she ever married?" Joe asked.

"I dunno. No kids. She used to travel a lot and she had some famous boyfriends, movie actors and writers and big company men," said Marianno, as he wrung out the sponge. "I never planked her. I wanted to back then. Not no more. If I'm gonna plank anybody it's gonna be an eighteen-year-old cheerleader, not some old communist."

Marianno climbed back up on the scaffolding, and Joe Glass tucked Gabriel under his arm and went out. The trash bags had all been picked up and Bailey Street was deserted, like a boulevard in a fine old city. Oak trees towered over the street, scratching at the sky with their empty branches. At eight-thirty in the morning, it was gloomy enough for some people to have their lights on, but Mrs. Eriksen's house was unlit and she didn't appear in the any of the windows. Joe Glass crossed the street, and lugged Gabriel upstairs to his third floor apartment. Except for his bed and a kitchen table and a few boxes, it was unfurnished. In the midst of the empty living room, a red light was blinking on his answering machine.

Francesca's voice filled his apartment, while Gabriel toddled off to the kitchen. "Joe: I'm at the rink. We had a fire. They called an ambulance for me, and it's—"

The machine cut off, and then Gabriel walked by carrying a large kitchen knife. "Gimme that," Joe said, coming up behind the toddler. He removed the knife from his son's fingers. "You'll hurt yourself."

Gabriel had an expression on his face like a soldier who had been disarmed. He turned away, and continued walking down the hall. Joe Glass tossed the knife into the sink and swept the boy into the air and thundered back downstairs. Outside he hesitated, looking up and down at the bare trees and wide empty street. The rink was over a mile away and Gabriel weighed twenty-two pounds: they wouldn't make it on foot.

Crossing Bailey Street, Joe leaped onto Mrs. Eriksen's porch and rapped the brass knocker against the door. It swung open, and the old woman appeared in the foyer with her hands pressed together. "You brought the young man," she said, smiling at her visitors.

Joe Glass was unsure of why he had come to Mrs. Eriksen's. "Something bad happened to Francesca," he said. "I need to get to the rink right away."

"I have a car," said Mrs. Eriksen.

A grassy driveway ran alongside the house, leading to another building with a gabled roof and barn doors. Joe threw them open, and the snout of the car seemed to protrude outside of the garage. It was an old green touring car, its leather upholstery hung with netting and an oak steering wheel like the wheel of a ship. Joe turned the key, and the engine coughed and then started with a roar. Bucking first, and then easing into gear, the car rolled out of the garage and down the driveway, just missing the house. Joe left it running out front, and returned for Gabriel.

"The child can stay with me," Mrs. Eriksen said.

The touring car hummed at the curb like a giant insect. "I have to take him," Joe said, opening the rear door. "Ugh. There's no car seat."

Mrs. Eriksen poked holes in the netting that covered the back seat and threaded the baby into it. "There," she said. "He'll be fine."

Joe climbed behind the wheel again. The car was very powerful; it jumped forward as Mrs. Eriksen shrank in the distance, and Joe turned onto South Broadway and flew past Marianno's Pizza and the appliance store. The state trooper stood scratching his head as they went by.

South Broadway ran out of town, climbed a steep rise and arched over the railroad tracks. The ice rink was down in a hollow beside the tracks: F O S T A R E   A. Firemen were running back and forth, throwing great sheets of water onto the blackened metal. Smoke poured out through a hole in the roof and an "R" and an "N" were lying on the ground, toppled over like ancient tablets in the dust. Joe drove the touring car onto a siding and pulled on the emergency brake, then ran up to a fire lieutenant in his rubber macintosh and long-brimmed metal hat. The man's face was streaked with mud, and heat radiated from his clothing.

"I think my girlfriend's in there," Joe said. Through the open door he could see a wall of flame raging across the ice. It swept upward to the roof, and then a shower of water in little droplets fell onto the surface of the rink.

"We got them all out," the lieutenant said. "Two of the people went to the hospital."

Gabriel was struggling in the mesh of the back seat like a lobster caught in a trap. Streams of water from the fire hoses deflected off the rink and fell against the side windows of the car, causing the baby to cry out. Joe Glass got behind the wheel again, his jacket dripping with water from the hoses.

"Mama's not here," he said. Turning the car around, Joe pressed on the accelerator and shot over the gravel past another fire truck that had just arrived.

In the jumpy rearview mirror, Gabriel looked bewildered and a little frightened. Joe snapped on the radio, and Harry James and his orchestra's "Mr. Five by Five" played from the single round speaker on the dash. There was a lot of saxophone and piano and it filled the dank interior of the old car. Gabriel's head was free of the netting, and he rolled it from

Jay Atkinson

side to side and hunched his tiny shoulders to the music.

"You're a dancing fool," Joe said.

They were back on South Broadway, and then over the singing bridge above the river and down two blocks to the hospital. Joe left the car in front of the emergency room, ripped Gabriel from the netting, and went inside. A man he recognized as the ice rink manager was lying on a gurney coughing into an oxygen mask, and two nurses were standing over him. One of them was writing something on a clipboard and the other, who was young and pretty, was applying lipstick.

"Where's Francesca Nesheim?" Joe asked. The face of the baby hung next to his like a miniature duplicate. "From the ice rink."

"She's in there," said the nurse with the clipboard, pointing to a closed door.

Joe hoisted Gabriel to his shoulder. Swinging the door open, they entered and found Francesca sitting on an examination table with her head in her hands. "Are you all right?" Joe asked.

"I fell down and banged my leg against a pipe," she said. Lifting the edge of her jonny, Francesca displayed a lump the size of an apple on her shin. "The doctor said it's not broken, but I won't be able to skate for a month and when I can, I won't have a rink to skate in."

"In a month, you'll be able to skate outside," Joe said.

Francesca sneered. "Professional skaters do not skate on ponds."

Gabriel said "Aah!" and reached for his mother. Francesca took the baby in her arms, and kissed him on top of the head. "Hi Mister. How did you get here so fast?"

"We borrowed a car from my neighbor, Mrs. Eriksen."

"Does it have a car seat?" Francesca asked.

Joe fixed his eyes on the floor. "No. But he was all right."

"I told you, he never goes anywhere without a car seat," Francesca said, clutching Gabriel like she never meant to let Joe touch him again. "This is my baby we're talking about."

In his pocket, Joe Glass had nude photographs of a distinguished old woman and he hadn't said a word to anyone about them. Some things it was better not to know. People walked around with all sorts of secrets and it occurred to Joe that the world operated the way it did because of a delicate system of withholding information.

If he knew things about other people, then of course, other people knew things about him. It made Joe shudder to think that other secrets about him were circulating around town, vague things about his past that he could only guess at. Since Joe was the sort who would never ask Mrs. Eriksen about her nude photographs, he expected no one would ever say anything to him about his own weird little habits.

The hospital gave Francesca a pair of crutches and with Gabriel in the other arm, Joe helped her to the car. She fixed the child in the netting as securely as she could, and then sat beside him.

"Home, Joseph," said Francesca from the back seat.

"Right away, ma'am," Joe said, glancing in the mirror. He started the car, and it rolled along the hospital driveway. "I'll have you there in a jiffy."

Whatever they had given Francesca for the pain started to take effect and she gazed around the interior of the car, playing along with the idea of having a manservant. "My son and I would like to be driven along the river," she said, her nose in the air. "It's much prettier going that way, and we can stop and pick up something for lunch."

Joe nodded, and turned onto a road that was bowered with oak trees. Gradually the trees gave way to a view of the Merrimack River, and then a stone aqueduct that ran overhead to the gas company. The horizon had tilted upward, absorbing the afternoon sun, and long shadows cast by the mills were stretched along the river. In the distance, the clock tower on the Ayer Mill pointed at the low gray sky.

Another few weeks and the Merrimack would be frozen, covered with a skin that was ten inches thick and hard as concrete. Skaters would carve the ice in both directions, etching long silver trails from one end of the mills to the other. Furious hockey games were played in the shadow of the clock tower, and the teams used old bent harrows and metal flywheels and other refuse to make their goals. Girls dressed in long coats stepped upriver, with the curious one-legged stride of the novice figure skater. Some of the skaters were drug dealers, young men in expensive hockey skates, using the canals to make their drops, taking sharp unexpected corners, their legs whirring. They'd cut across nine city blocks in less than two minutes, and no one could ever catch them.

"It's so dreary here when winter's coming. Don't you think?" Francesca asked, giving the baby her thumb to play with.

Joe kept his eyes on the road. "I wouldn't know about that, ma'am," he said.

They stopped at Marianno's to buy pizza. Francesca stayed in the car with Gabriel, and Joe went in. The scaffolding had been dismantled and John Marianno was alone behind the counter. "Nice car," he said, glancing out the window. "Where'd you get it?"

"It belongs to Mrs. Eriksen," said Joe.

"I bet she used to get planked in the back seat by Warren G. Harding," said Marianno. "She dated Henry Ford when he used to ride a horse."

Joe went out to check on Francesca. Gabriel had been freed of the netting, and was standing in the well of the seat with his hands resting on the upholstery. He couldn't really talk, just sounds that imitated some of the words people used, but in back of the old touring car he said, "Kitty," and then the boy's eyes shone and he said, "My doggy."

"Wow," said Joe. "He talked."

Francesca had her injured leg stretched across the seat. "He sure did," she said.

Father and mother giggled, and Joe leaned over and kissed Francesca and their heads stayed together looking at Gabriel. "What does it mean, 'kitty' and 'my doggy'?" asked Joe.

"Maybe he's going to be a veterinarian," Francesca said.

The baby was playing with a piece of string and gave no indication he was going to reveal the names of other domestic animals. Inside the restaurant, Marianno was gesturing to Joe Glass. "I'll be right back,"

Joe said to Francesca. He ran inside. "My kid just talked! He said three words."

Marianno slid the steaming pie into a box and taped the corners. "Have your pizza. It's getting cold," he said, shoving the box along the counter.

"What do I owe you?" asked Joe, reaching for his wallet.

"Nothing," said the ex-infantryman. "Cops all the time want things for free, but a kid speaks his first words in front of my place, that's on the house." He reached into the cooler, handing Joe a bottle of beer that was dripping wet. "Good luck, kid," he said. "Once the first words are out, they never shut up."

Joe Glass put the beer in his pocket and ran to the car and drove it around the corner to Francesca's building. He carried Gabriel and the pizza with the bottle of beer flapping against his thigh, and Francesca limped along on the crutch. Balancing like a flamingo, she put the baby on the kitchen table and changed his diaper while Joe prepared a bottle of milk. When the baby was clean, Joe went into the living room with the bottle and Gabriel was let down from the table and followed him in there. From the couch, he could hear the sound of Francesca getting out silverware and plates.

"Do you need any help?" he called out, his voice ringing off the walls. Joe reached into his coat pocket and took out the bottle of beer. A short distance away, Gabriel raised the bottle of milk to his mouth just as his father brought the beer up, and they looked at each other and laughed.

Francesca came to the entranceway with tears in her eyes. Beyond her, the open pizza box was sending steam into the air. She walked toward Joe and the baby trying not to limp and then she collapsed onto the sofa, wiping her eyes.

"What good is a skater with one leg?" she asked.

Tense and quivering, she curled up beside Joe and then Gabriel came walking over the sofa cushions and toppled into her lap. Joe Glass put his arms around the two of them and crushed himself under their weight, stroking Francesca's silky hair, with his other hand cupping Gabriel's hard round stomach.

"Don't worry," Joe said, although he was plenty worried. Both he and Francesca worked sporadically, and the money from the local ice shows would be gone for a while. "I'll get some drywall work, or house painting or something. Maybe I'll just rob a bank."

After a while, Gabriel was asleep. Lying there composed with his hands by his sides he looked like a little elf. "Nap time," Francesca said.

After a few minutes, her limbs grew heavy and she was asleep, too. Joe reached into the pocket of his leather jacket and removed the wad of tea leaves salvaged from Mrs. Eriksen's garbage. He reached down and pressed the mixture on Francesca's injury like a poultice. She was in a deep pharmaceutical sleep, and Joe eased himself up and covered her and the baby with a blanket.

The pizza was room temperature, and he ate a slice and washed it down with the rest of his beer. Afterward, he stretched out on the floor beside the couch. Only four o'clock and it was dark outside. Lying on his back, Joe Glass stared out the window at the lights of an airplane sliding across the sky and wondered who was up there. He imagined he was flying a plane, looking down on the city, the houses arranged in rows radiating outward from the huge dark mills. The air roared at the windows of the plane and it was cold in the cockpit, suspended above the horizon. Here and there in the city were fires, some reflecting against the wide silver path of the river, others burning upward in showers of light. Fire trucks converged on them from the empty city streets, their turret lights revolving against the trees and darkened buildings. Every night the city was on fire, and circling in the frigid cockpit of his plane, Joe Glass pinned himself to the stars and watched.

He dozed for a while, and then woke to the soft humming of Francesca's refrigerator. She and Gabriel were still sleeping at opposite ends of the couch. With the stealth of a burglar, Joe rose to his feet, gliding into the kitchen. He took a slice of pizza from the box, then searched in his pockets for a ten-dollar bill and left it on the table.

Out in the street, people were coming home from work, banging storm doors and turning on lights that sent luminous yellow cones spiraling from their porches. A boy passed with the *Tribune-Standard*, and Joe bought one of his extras. On the front page was a photograph of the Frost Arena amidst columns of thick black smoke. In the foreground was Mrs. Eriksen's car, and Joe standing there talking to the lieutenant. The headline was *Fire on Ice. Arson Suspected in Rink Blaze.*

Joe Glass rushed down the sidewalk. The oak trees were arranged like monoliths alongside the road and he flew from one to the next. Joe turned onto South Broadway, which was glittering with neon above the tiny bars and liquor stores—at once reversing his course because he had forgotten Mrs. Eriksen's car. There it was, looking like a prop in a gangster movie, still parked in front of Francesca's. He slipped behind the wheel and drove off, the headlights throwing themselves against the pavement when he pulled a knob on the dashboard.

Joe imagined what it would have been like to wear a homburg hat and cavort with Mrs. Eriksen. Her white hair transformed itself to its original yellow, and her breasts inflated and the camera captured their movements as they went naked around the room. Soon Pier Eriksen was half-dressed in his clothes, and as the camera flashed she reached down and grabbed his penis. Squeezing it like a titan, Mrs. Eriksen hung on while Joe Glass straightened and the hat bounced from his head into the air. She had him, and wasn't about to let go.

He took a circuitous route back to Bailey Street. Switching off the headlights, Joe glided between parked cars and down the grassy driveway, easing into the tight fit of the garage.

At the front door, Mrs. Eriksen clicked on a light when he mounted the stairs. "Is everyone all right?" she said.

"They're fine," Joe said.

Coming inside he bumped into Mrs. Eriksen. Her arm was thin and hard, and he could feel the burl of her elbow beneath the skin. Mrs.

Jay Atkinson

Eriksen's face hung from her skull like pudding and the breasts that stood out in the photographs appeared only as odd lumps in her sweater. Still, he could make out a cast to Mrs. Eriksen's torso that appealed to him in much younger women.

Joe was sitting in a chair, perspiring. The old woman gave him a knowing glance, and he was certain she was going to cross the room and dig the stolen photographs from inside his leather jacket. Joe was outraged they had come into his possession. He didn't *want* to have a picture in his mind of Mrs. Eriksen's naked body, even a much younger and sensuous Mrs. Eriksen. Now it was too late.

"There's something you need to understand," said Mrs. Eriksen, looking at Joe.

Joe felt his heart tighten into a fist. He started in his chair, then swept his hair back from his face and let his gaze drift over the wallpaper. "All right," he said.

"I've been all over the world, and this is my home," said Mrs. Eriksen. "But it's changed. All the people are gone." She put a hand to her neck, staring out through the curving black expanse of the front window. "You don't know what it's like to have something like that taken away from you."

Mrs. Eriksen turned toward Joe's chair. "The city is burning," she said, looking at him. "And my past is burning with it."

In Mrs. Eriksen's blue eyes, Joe glimpsed for a moment the lost beauty of her youth. Sitting with her knees together and her long white hands slotted between them, the old woman's head trembled at the top of her neck. Up and down went her chest in a slow, shallow rhythm. She appeared to be waiting for each successive breath, measuring them as they leaked out of her.

"If you want to leave Gabriel here on occasion, you're welcome to," she said.

"It's Frannie. She wouldn't like it."

Mrs. Eriksen rose from her chair and approached the terrarium. She separated leaves, adjusted some of the stems and arranged the fronds on the upper level so they overhung the glass. "I never had any of my own. So there are no grandchildren to keep me company and none of the children of the neighborhood will come here. To them I'm just a crazy old lady who lives alone." Wind rattled the glass of the front windows, shaking the weights that were hidden inside the frames. "At one time, children loved me. 'Pier, Pier,' they called when I walked down Essex Street. But I had no time for them. I was busy with sophisticated things and the intrigues we adults make so much of." The old woman paused, a sprig of something between her fingers. "I have something for Gabriel," she said. "Let me get it for you."

While Mrs. Eriksen was out of the room, Joe rose to inspect the terrarium. The tiger lilies and orchids were saturated by purple light radiating from a tube across the inner edge. The air that emanated from the terrarium was humid, scented with flowers and a thicker underlying smell that was like earth and flesh combined. Joe looked closer, into the orange trumpet of one of the lilies. He saw a stream of tiny insects marching up the stem, and then down into the pistil of the flower. In a choreographed movement, the insects were extracting tiny measures from a single drop of liquid. Widening his field of vision, Joe realized they were carrying the liquid great distances across the terrarium to the orchids.

"Some labors go unappreciated," said Mrs. Eriksen, startling him.

The old woman was two inches taller than Joe Glass. Standing beside him, she reached into the pocket of her sweater and took out a box with a spring-loaded clasp holding it together. The box was no wider than her palm, and the velvet surface of it had been worn by constant handling.

Joe Glass touched the edge of the box with his finger and it popped open. Pinned to the satin lining was a pair of cuff links in the shape of the Ayer Mill clock. The cuff links were made of gold with a pearl inlay and twelve diamond chips ran around each tiny clock face. Inscribed on the edge of the cuff links was "1910."

"I can't take these," said Joe, shaking his head.

Mrs. Eriksen closed the box and pressed it into his hand. "For Gabriel," she said. Mrs. Eriksen escorted Joe toward the door and he put the jewelry box in his pocket, his fingers brushing against the old photographs. A wave of cold air swept in from the porch.

"Time flies," Joe said.

"It's always on the wing," said Mrs. Eriksen.

2

"The New City"
Lawrence, Massachusetts

September 18, 1848

An unusual sight greeted Abbott Lawrence when he stepped off the train in North Andover. Hard by the tracks, on the dirt apron extending from a warehouse that was situated there, a fat man in breeches rolled out a large wooden cask bound with iron hoops. Overturning the cask with a shove, the man chased after various-sized cement balls that ran in all directions. Several workmen unloading bricks from the train noticed the fat man and called out to him.

"Playing games again, eh Josiah?"

"Gather up your balls, and put them in thy breeches. Yonder comes my wife!"

Laughter followed, and then one young man with broad shoulders and thick black hair raised a hand to his fellows. "Oh, leave him be. Some men are born of a political nature and would rather fawn and supplicate than work," said the youth, lifting a hod of bricks to his shoulder. "Isn't that right, Josiah?"

The fat man placed his hands on his hips and, maintaining a cordial tone, told the youth: "Aye, Gabe'rill. There's the work of the limbs, all which is honest and good, but contrasted to the labor of the cerebellum it amounts to mere jerking and twitching." He lifted one of the cement balls, weighing it in his hand. "My position in the company requires a vast effort of the imagination—one you cannot see but that is quite real and taxes me, nonetheless. While thy arms and legs may take thee over the Great Dam fifteen or twenty times in a day, my thoughts carry me to the cement factories in Troy, New York, and onward to the ancient city of Troy in the same instant."

"Well said," whispered Abbott Lawrence to himself. He stood in the dust wearing a plain black cloak and narrow-heeled boots, waiting for the Essex Company strongbox to be unloaded from the train. Since he often traveled without clerk or secretary, the millionaire founder of the bustling settlement was not immediately recognized and no one spoke to him.

The workmen again laughed at Josiah standing among his cement balls, and one fellow said, "While you're off in New York, I'll carry myself over to shantytown and see about thy wife's knickers."

Abbott Lawrence came out of the shadow cast by the passenger coach and set down his portmanteau. He was clean-shaven, of average stature, with a high smooth forehead and well-set, regular teeth. This man, who had come within a single vote of the Vice Presidency of the United States, listened to the bantering workmen as attentively as he would have heard a congressional debate.

"Excuse 'em, sir," said the foreman, a man named Coolidge, who that moment had passed out of the Essex Company warehouse. He tipped his cap to Abbott Lawrence. "I'll see to those boys."

"Don't trouble yourself, Mr. Coolidge," Lawrence said.

But Coolidge, his face white, avoided a team of horses being led past and approached the first of many flatcars piled with brick. "Get on with it, you lallygags," he said. "And keep your tongues still. That gentleman there is Mr. Lawrence 'imself. The president of this-here Essex Company."

The men on board the train fell silent and went back to work. Abbott Lawrence often declared that he was the son of a simple Groton farmer and felt superior to no one—although he was a prominent Whig, an advisor to President Zachary Taylor, and a millionaire with wide-ranging mercantile interests. This enterprise beside the Merrimack River had originated with Abbott Lawrence and his brother Amos gathering several partners to form the Essex Company, and by Abbott's purchase of one thousand company shares at one hundred dollars apiece. Now, three years later, a city was being raised from a plot of empty woodland and thousands of men were employed in the endeavor.

As Mr. Lawrence made his way toward the Essex Company warehouse, intent on delivering bills of lading to his clerk and other perfunctory business, the railroad porters and teamsters and hod carriers shunted themselves to either side, avoiding his path and his gaze. But the crude humor of the masons had no effect on him, for Abbott Lawrence had labored among the lower strata since becoming an apprentice to his older brother's dry goods business at sixteen. He had long understood that the lives of working men were primitive and arduous. In a sense, their limited experience and education forced them to live below ground, deprived of food, water, and light. Lawrence felt only Christian charity toward these men, and pitied their inhospitable condition; the only foibles he would not suffer from the working class were drunkenness and the Lord's name taken in vain.

Laid out in the dust near the warehouse entrance were several large granite slabs, eight feet tall and a foot thick, numbered in red paint. Bits of mica and hornblende embedded in the granite caught the light; for an instant, the slabs reminded Mr. Lawrence of the family mausoleum in Mount Auburn Cemetery. But these headers and stretchers had been quarried from the company lot in nearby Pelham, New Hampshire, and by the sequence of numbers Lawrence knew they were designated for the crest of the Great Dam. Anchored to the hard blue gneiss of the riverbed, bound together with iron clamps and smeared with Rosendale cement, the tablets would crown a feat of civil engineering that was unparalleled in the New World.

A notebook containing a sketch of each stone and its measurements hung from the warehouse door by a length of string. Turning the pages of the notebook, Abbott Lawrence studied the sketches for a few moments, until one of the concrete balls rolled near him.

Bracing his sore kidney with one hand, Mr. Lawrence stooped to retrieve the ball; it was the size of a cannon shot and weighed ten-pound. With a smile playing over his lips, Lawrence carried the ball to the fat man, who had garnered most of his collection with the assistance of a wooden rake. Beside the overturned cask was a second, larger barrel, tarred black inside and filled halfway with water.

"Here is your specimen, my good fellow," said Abbott Lawrence, handing the ball over. "Let me ask, who are you?"

"Josiah Quebec, sir," the fat man said. "Assistant chemist."

"And what is your activity today?" asked Lawrence.

"The same activity it has been every day for nearly two year, sir: testing a sample from each lot of hydraulic cement. In the evenings, I form these balls by lamplight"—Quebec placed one atop the overturned cask, and split it in two with a stonemason's ax— "and twelve hours later I examine them for hardness and density and, since it's a dam we're building, sir, impermeability to saturation." With this, the portly chemist began dropping cement balls into the water cask.

Stacked beneath an awning on the side of the warehouse were several dozen casks stamped with the name of the cement maker in large black letters. "And has John W. Lawton & Company proven to be an able supplier?" asked Mr. Lawrence.

"Aye, sir." Quebec lowered his arm into the cask and began arranging the balls more economically. "When we began, one cask in fifty was of inferior quality and Captain Bigelow sent word to New York that he was again considering his original selection, Canvas White Company. For over a year now, it's less than one cask per hundred that's been lumpy or otherwise unfit for your Boston Associates."

In 1845 Abbott Lawrence and his brother Amos, proprietors of A. & A. Lawrence, had created a holding company, the Boston Associates, from among the merchant leaders of other prominent families, raising over one million dollars in capital by selling shares for a hundred dollars apiece. Boston Associates, in turn, had created the Essex Company, which purchased seven square miles of land on either side of the Merrimack River, above and below Bodwell's Falls, from North Andover farmer Daniel Saunders. For the sum of $30,000, the Essex Company also secured water rights, and chose an engineer named Charles S. Storrow to design and build a Great Dam across the Merrimack, as well as an industrial city that would make perpetual use of the ensuing waterpower. Mr. Storrow had hired Captain Charles Bigelow, a graduate of West Point, to supervise the construction of the largest mill dam in the world and its adjoining power canal.

"How have you found the judgment of Mssrs. Storrow and Bigelow?" Mr. Lawrence asked the chemist.

Quebec smiled with large wet teeth. "They don't always agree, sir. But each man believes in a free exchange of ideas, and they have always found a consensus," he said, wagging his head. "Mr. Storrow sees to that."

"If you continue to do your job so thoroughly, your employment with the Essex Company will never be gainsaid," Lawrence said to Josiah Quebec.

"God bless you, sir," said the chemist. His bulk sank toward the ground, wobbling as he attempted a bow. "Tomorrow's dedication will be a great event for you and your Essex Company."

"It will be a great day for all free Americans," Lawrence said, stooping to retrieve his portmanteau. "Building the dam was God's will, and employing the men of this valley is an attached and perpetual covenant, as the lawyers say, running with the land."

Abbott Lawrence watched as the strongbox was loaded through the rear hatch of the omnibus. The driver fixed a pistol in his belt and bridled the horses, and they stamped against the clay road just as the long-haired youth raced up. "I'm going where you are, and if it doesn't trouble you, sir, we can help each other get there," he said to Mr. Lawrence. The youth used a lever to unfurl a set of jointed steps, and then stuck his head inside the passenger cabin to make sure it was tidy. "A coach fit for a king or a sheik," he said.

"All it will contain, I'm afraid, is a God-fearing Christian," said Lawrence. He placed into the boy's hand a packet of small white cards printed with his brother Amos's favorite Biblical verse: *What shall it profit a man, if he gains the whole world and loses his own soul?* "When we get to the New City, please distribute these to the men who can read," Lawrence said, climbing inside the omnibus.

The youth clambered up, joining the omnibus driver on his bench above the cabin. Then the horses pulled away, and the youth glanced down at the cards and asked the driver to read the maxim printed there. "Some's only got their souls to keep," the youth said.

"Rich men are great believers," said the driver. "'Cause they believe it's God what made them that way."

The cart path led through a stand of oaks and then dropped toward the river beyond. Rolling through a patchwork of cultivated farms and forest, Abbott Lawrence gazed out the omnibus window, noticing how the September drought had begun turning the leaves a premature yellow. It was Indian summer in the valley, rife with the scent of apples and mown hay. Lawrence flapped his arms and beat his hands against his chest, inhaling great drafts of the cool morning air. Hidden in the glen, woodpeckers drilled for food, and the sound of their work brought the variegated landscape to him in all its dimensions.

Lawrence opened his portmanteau and, for a few moments, busied himself with some papers. But soon he was studying the pleated hay fields, and clusters of hardwood and firs passing outside his window. Also appearing on the side of the road were stacks of brick and an occasional broken nail keg or cask of cement. Overloaded wagons, Lawrence supposed. Several bricks were missing from each pile, and here and there fistfuls of nails littered the ground. As the omnibus passed through the last verdant stretch of farmland and approached the shanties huddled beside the Merrimack, Abbott Lawrence observed their foundations of pilfered brick, imagining that these shabby lean-tos were also hung with fugitive nails and papered inside with bills of lading.

At the foot of the Andover Bridge, the cart path flowed into the Loundonderry Turnpike and began to fill up with men on foot and horseback. Ox carts laden with granite slabs, coarse-gowned workmen carrying their hods, and other signs of the great labor that had consumed the energy of five thousand men sprang up on all sides. Across the river two imposing factories rose from a man-made island, six stories each and constructed of brick, their chimneys throwing black smoke into the sky. Between them was the giant cellar hole of a third mill.

Leaning out the window, Abbott Lawrence said, "Can it really be true? I've seen the plans and diagrams, and read all score of letters, but can my eyes be deceiving me?"

"There's your New City, sir," shouted the driver over the noise of the coach. "The dam and canal and factories all at work, and growing by the day."

"It's a magnificent sight," Lawrence said.

The gabble of hammers, chink of metal on stone, and the odor of tar and burning faggots wafted out from the New City. Hanging from the cabin window, Lawrence had to be shooed inside by the driver, but not before praising God and asking the youth to expound on the projected completion of the Upper and Lower Pacific Mills, and the Atlantic Mill that would separate the two.

"There's a lot of sweat and toil being put into them, and not half as many words as Josiah Quebec speaks in a day," the lad said.

As the omnibus made its halting way across the bridge, Lawrence looked through the northward window, staring with fascination at the dam that continued to rise above the Merrimack. During his absence, the Great Dam had grown to a height of forty feet; its bulk was thirteen feet thick at the crest, with a face of hammered granite slabs dressed in hydraulic cement. Atop its length, teams of workers were drilling holes and inserting iron rods to hold the flashboards. Another of Charles Storrow's innovations, they would allow the Essex Company to raise the millpond an additional three feet and, in the case of a flood, break away without causing damage to the permanent structure below.

The Great Dam, which had been built upon the parallel bluestone ridges of Bodwell's Falls, arched upstream at an oblique angle to the river. The huge bonded mass of the dam was trapezoidal in profile, arranged so the river's flow would always fall within the middle third.

"Wonder of God," Lawrence said to himself. "Charles has prevailed."

Upstream, earth-filled cofferdams extended two-thirds of the way across the Merrimack. Steam pumps were operating between the cofferdams and the still-rising monolith, and their din sounded like locomotives. The pumps were used to dry the last vestiges of the riverbed, while earth-filled rollers flattened the clay puddle that sloped out from the base of the dam. These huge wooden rollers were dragged up the apron by teams of horses, turned in painstaking arcs, and then separated from the horses on the way back down by men wielding iron-tipped pikes. Everywhere laborers scrambled, hallooing to one another above the noise of the steam pumps and journeying in a great pilgrim column across the cofferdams, which were each as wide as a country road.

Near the center of the bridge, progress halted when a cart loaded with timbers collided with an old high-seated wagon that advertised patent medicines for sale. Huge planks crashed to the deck of the bridge, and a great many bottles were shattered on board the wagon. Immediately a number of voices cried out, men on horseback and boys who had been racing along the bridge's edge, juggling their handloads among the small hackneys and other conveyances. They laughed at the patent manufacturer, a man named Bessell, who gathered his mangled goods while doing his best to ignore the taunts and imprecations.

Bessell was a wizened old fellow with a pointed beard and tufts of white hair sticking out from beneath his skullcap. Nearly half his colored bottles, the jagged necks hanging from the wagon by little curlicues of wire, lay shattered on the bridge. Their contents formed a sticky mass that continued to spread beneath the horses' hooves. Sliding this way and that, the little white-haired man tried to siphon up the liquid through a hollow cane tamped over by his thumb.

"Make room there, man, in the name of the Essex Company," said the driver of the timber cart. "There's work to be done, and no time for the likes of you. Get out of my way."

"In the name of Hiram Bessell, you may yoke thyself to thy cart and go braying over the countryside," the old man said. He retrieved a tin pot from among the appliances hanging on his wagon, and attempted to fill it with can-fuls of medicine.

"Halloo!" cried the long-haired youth, jumping down from the omnibus. "What's this—a few broken bottles holding up the completion of the Great Dam?" He assisted the patent manufacturer in retrieving his cartons and cases, kicking aside fragments of the broken glass.

The driver of the timber cart swore at the patent manufacturer, calling him an alien. But the youth smiled, hefting one of the errant timbers and tossing it into the superannuated cart with a flick of his wrist. "There are no aliens here," said the good-natured youth. "Just good, hard-working fellows trying to make a living." He winked at the patent manufacturer. "Isn't that right, Mr. Bessell?"

"There are some good fellows and some hard-working fellows and some fellows trying to earn a living here in the New City, and I suppose there are a few who are all three, although I have yet to make their acquaintance," said Bessell in his high-pitched voice. "Before I could complete my philosophy on the subject, some constables from the Essex Company requested that I collect my wares and depart."

Jay Atkinson

A few men who had gathered around laughed at this. "And were they good, hard-working fellows?" asked the cart driver, smiling and winking at his audience.

"They were not good, at least to me, and the work they did, in my humble opinion, was not worth doing," Bessell said. "But since I had no opportunity to examine their souls, I cannot offer any theories on their usefulness."

The youth laughed at this remark, lifting the patent manufacturer into his johnnyseat with the strength of one hand. He gestured toward the shanties on the south side of the river. "If you're not welcome on Essex Street, you should try our fair 'Dublin.' There's a whole lot of doers who reside there and not a few talkers, but none so's can talk like you."

"I was making my way there, when this man's horse threatened to stamp its hoof through my skull," said Bessell. He reached for the tin pot that the youth raised to him, and stowed it beneath his seat. "But I'd rather be a physician with a horse's hoof through my brain than a steward of this-here Essex Company."

"How's that?" asked the youth. The other workmen drew in closer, intent on this declaration. Nearby, horses tossed their heads and the stench of fresh manure went up from the bridge deck.

In all the commotion, Abbott Lawrence had stepped down from the omnibus and was leaning against the rail. He watched as the patent manufacturer yanked down on the lapels of his frock coat, raising his voice to include more prospective customers in his oration. "Because a city, even such a modern one, is merely a gathering of men"—Bessell pointed toward the north bank, where the massive brick structures of the Pacific Mills rose up from the island— "and men tend toward the organic and not the mechanical. To plan and raise a city is one thing, while trying to regulate the comings and goings of its inhabitants is another. Entering the streets of the New City, I did not realize that I would be a ball rolling along its runways, but rather, I believed I was a man going about my business."

The cart driver shook his head at this and, slapping the reins against his horse's withers, spat in the roadway. His retort to the peddler was lost in the clatter of hooves, and the men behind them sent up a cry to continue the procession.

"Are you coming, Gabe'rill?" asked the omnibus driver, unfurling his leather reins.

"No," said the youth, looking over the bridge rail. "I see Captain Bigelow, and that he needs me." With a discreet nod, he referred to the omnibus' paying customer. "But I should not start off if I were you, as your passenger is not occupying his cabin."

The omnibus driver had not noticed Abbott Lawrence standing on the bridge. "Now there, Mr. Lawrence," he said. "Mr. Storrow will be waiting, sir."

"And a great deal of commerce is waiting behind thee," said Lawrence, glancing back at the stalled carts and wagons, "while I stand here like a fool."

"In you go then," said the long-haired youth, yanking open the cabin door.

Before Lawrence could respond, the youth uttered a happy cry and then leaped over the bridge railing. Mr. Lawrence, dumbfounded for a moment, rushed forward and was relieved to see the young man descending one of the ropes fastened there. Far below, the waters of the Merrimack ran swift and black and dangerous, moving away from the bridge in long, foamy ripples.

Anchored among the pilings was a flat-bottomed scow, and a crew of dredgers were enjoying a respite from their work. They chewed loaves of bread with their faces turned up, watching the young man drop hand over hand into their midst.

Lawrence could not mistake the black-bearded figure in his military coat holding to the nether end of the rope. It was Captain Charles H. Bigelow, the Essex Company's principal field engineer, in charge of the construction of the Great Dam, the power canal, and the Lawrence Machine Shop. With his free hand, Captain Bigelow reached up for the descending youth and collected him into the scow. The captain wore an iron brace on his left leg, the result of an accident upon the river that had nearly claimed his life.

Abbott Lawrence retired to the omnibus. As it moved forward, he slid open the tiny panel that led to the driver. "You there, my man," he said.

"Yes, sir."

"Who was that remarkable youth?" Lawrence asked.

"Glass is his name, sir. Gabe'rill Glass."

"And what is his occupation?"

The driver jerked on his reins, lowering the omnibus from the bridge onto the muddy surface of the Loundonderry Turnpike. "General laborer in the employ of Carpenter & Gilmore, sir. Assistant to Captain Bigelow," the man said. "He's the one what saved the captain's life when the cofferdam overturned."

Abbott Lawrence had learned of this unhappy event through a letter from Charles Storrow. On October 12, 1847, fifteen men, including Captain Bigelow, were swept downstream when one of the cofferdams collapsed into the river. Bigelow, his foreman Coolidge, and several laborers in the employ of Gilmore & Carpenter were working aboard a large scow tied to the dam. Suddenly, the earthen bulwark dissolved and the crew were thrown from a height of twenty-five feet into the roiling water. Three men leaped out and clung to the remnant of the dam and were saved. One man dived from the stern of the scow and rode the current to the south bank, where he was pulled out by a frantic group of teamsters. Two of the men were killed; two others were crippled. Captain Bigelow suffered a broken leg, three broken ribs, a fractured jaw and other injuries; he was floating toward the precipice of the Great Dam when he was dragged ashore by a laborer who had been aboard the scow. Until this moment, the hero's name had been unknown to Abbott Lawrence.

"It is God's own mystery how a fellow could save another man's life

Jay Atkinson

and go on like nothing extraordinary had occurred," said Mr. Lawrence, his face thrust through the omnibus window.

The driver urged his horses beyond a slough of mud that occupied the Turnpike. "Gabe'rill's a practical lad, sir. It's a great thing he's done, aye. But yesterday's work won't feed a body today, is how he sees it."

Abbott Lawrence had intended to review a number of deeds and their covenants on his way to the New City. Recently Charles Storrow had sold several land parcels from among the prime lots on Essex Street, the price doubling to $1.25 per square foot after the initial offering of '47. But with the cost of raw materials going up, and the Atlantic Mill far from returning a dividend, the Essex Company found itself $400,000 in debt. For several months this situation had worried the correspondence of Mssrs. Lawrence and Storrow. In addition to marking the completion of the Great Dam, Abbott Lawrence had hastened his return from Washington to discuss with his colleagues the possible deregulation of land sales in the New City.

One way to amortize their debt was to ease the prohibitive covenants attached to Essex Company property, clauses that prevented the manufacture and distribution of spirituous liquor. This would speed land sales to tavern keepers and breweries and patent medicine manufacturers, increasing cash flow and thereby satisfying Boston Associates shareholders in the short term. Such a course, however, was not being seriously considered. The Boston Associates had agreed to Charles Storrow's recommendation that the Great Dam be constructed of granite and cement beton—instead of the wooden cofferdams used for power elsewhere in the United States. And they had approved the plan for several gigantic brick mills, the excavation of the one-mile canal and its walls of undressed granite and impermeable clay floor, because the shareholders of the Boston Associates believed in permanence and sobriety. As they had imagined it, the New City was meant to outlast the age.

Mr. Lawrence realized that Charles Storrow's question about the removal of moral covenants, in a letter dated July 21st, was a rhetorical one. For he knew that Charles upheld the same standards of temperance and faith in God that he and his brother Amos had dedicated their lives to. Still, Abbott Lawrence detected a note of worry in the neat slanted lines of Storrow's hand. And although fresh from political disappointments in Washington, the financier had come to the New City to see what man and God hath wrought, while allaying any doubts that Mr. Storrow had permitted to creep into his mind.

3

The Present Day

Christmas came to Lawrence and it was a drab affair. From one of the few stores remaining on Essex Street, "Jingle Bells" played from a speaker in a tinny beat. A scrawny Santa walked up and down, giving out lollipops wrapped in cellophane stiffened by the cold.

"Happy hour at the King of Clubs," said Kris Kringle. "Cocktails half price. Live band."

Rain had washed newspapers and other scraps into the gutter, and they were glossy in the old-fashioned streetlights. Joe Glass hurried along, his hands deep in the pockets of his leather jacket, head tucked against the wind. This wasn't the downtown of his childhood, decorated for the holidays and bustling with shoppers: McCartney's, Kap's, McQuade's, their windows filled with glowing plastic elves; the roof of Sutherland's frosted like a cake and stocked with reindeer; Woolworth's draped in silver bunting. All gaiety and sense of occasion had been washed out of Lawrence. It was a city with a terrified heart.

Wind howled among the chimneys, rattling the heavy sheets of glass in the stores and throwing grit that had eaten away at the limestone cornices until they looked like bones. Joe Glass turned the corner at Amesbury Street and looked up at the tangled electrical wires, the gargoyles looming on the roof. The cement trim was pockmarked with holes and turning gray with industrial pollution, like the gates of some cold-weather hell.

At the end of the alley was the canal, a frozen band appearing between the brick and cinder block buildings. A group of boys in youth hockey jerseys darted over the ice, swooping and turning with one mind like a flock of birds. Joe Glass watched them carve away from him, and then he ducked into the entrance of the King of Clubs.

A set of Christmas lights above the bar threw off garish colors and patterned the cigarette smoke with weird floating strands of red and yellow and green. Someone had vomited somewhere, and the high

Jay Atkinson

thin stench pierced the haze. Joe went to the bar, and called over to the bartender. "Seen Boris?" he asked.

The door to the men's toilet swung open and Boris Johnson was outlined there against the tiles. He was barrel-chested and hairy, wearing only shorts and running shoes although it was below freezing outside. Boris Johnson was a fifty-year-old fitness maniac and ne'er-do-well mayoral candidate, a man inclined to run all day through the most dangerous parts of the city, and up and down the hills of Bellevue cemetery. There he stole flowers and American flags that he later presented to shut-ins and prostitutes. Johnson owned several pieces of run-down property and Joe Glass sometimes worked for him as a maintenance man.

"Got anything for me?" he asked as Johnson walked by.

The other man stopped. "No," said Boris. "Got anything for me?" He began windmilling his arms, and executed several deep-knee bends.

"I just thought you might have some work for me," Joe said. "It's Christmas."

Boris took Joe's beer, which had arrived on the bar, and drank from it. "Merry Christmas," he said.

Joe Glass produced a dollar for the beer and followed the strongman out of the dark, vomit-smelling bar into the alley. Boris Johnson threw himself down and began doing push-ups on the frozen cobblestones, the muscles bunching across his hairy back each time he dropped his chin to the ground.

"Tell you what," said Johnson. "Go to Broadway and talk to one of the girls, and I'll run around the Common and meet you. That's worth twenty bucks."

"I'm not your pimp," Joe said.

"Either you're mine or I'm yours," said Boris, and he ran off toward Campagnone Common.

Joe Glass stuck his hands in his pockets and trudged up the alley. Winter light glared off the buildings ahead; at three o'clock, the sun was already sinking into the river behind him. Pedestrians were scarce, and he found himself alone at the intersection of Amesbury and Essex Street. In the space ahead, a trio of mangy squirrels flattened themselves and darted across the intersection, gray blurs dodging the traffic. Then the wind died down and Joe could hear their claws scraping the pavement.

The holiday was two days away and Joe Glass didn't have any money. He wasn't driving the Zamboni machine on weekends any more since the rink had burned down. John Marianno had his son home from college to deliver pizzas for him, and Boris Johnson was trying to wear the city out in court instead of fixing all his code violations.

Joe stopped into Gale's Jewelry to find out if the cuff links Mrs. Eriksen had given him were worth anything. He couldn't face the idea of giving Gabriel some homemade gift wrapped in the funny papers for Christmas. A bell rang over the door when he went in.

"Yes, what is it?" asked the elderly proprietor, like he feared a robbery.

"I have something I want you to look at."

The jeweler shook his head. He was a small man, sitting on a stool with his legs tucked under him. Bald, with tufts of gray hair sticking out his ears, the jeweler wore extra thick glasses that made him look like a rhesus monkey. "This isn't a pawnshop," he said.

"Just tell me if these cuff links are worth anything," Joe said, producing them. "They're not gonna tell me the truth at any pawnshop."

The gold caught the jeweler's eye, and he picked up one of the cuff links and brought it closer. While he turned it back and forth under a retractable light, humming to himself, he reached under the counter and took out a ledger of some sort. Beckoning for the other cuff link, Mr. Gale placed them on a rubber mat and opened the ledger with one of several ribbons laid between the pages. For a moment he was lost in study, his pupils widening and narrowing in their sea of blue.

"I'll give you three hundred dollars," Mr. Gale said. The ledger went back beneath the counter, and the jeweler took off his glasses and fixed his blue eyes on Joe Glass.

"I thought you said this wasn't a pawnshop."

"I'm not interested in buying these for re-sale. I'd like to keep them."

Mr. Gale was wearing a short-sleeved shirt with a woolen vest over it. He held his glasses in one hand and continued to look into Joe's eyes. "This is a custom item," he said, "so collectors aren't going to be interested in them. But the gold is in good shape, the inlay and chips are intact. It's a nice pair of cuff links."

"Why buy if you're not gonna sell them?"

Mr. Gale retrieved one of the cuff links, and turned it so the edge was facing his customer. "See here? 1910. The year the clock was dedicated." He raised a hand in the air and pointed behind him, toward the Ayer Mill.

"So what?"

"I was born in 1910," said the jeweler. "My father was from Italy, and he worked at the Ayer Mill as a weaver. Our name was Gallitelli then."

Joe shook the cuff links like dice, then opened his hand and gazed at them. "What are they really worth?" he asked.

"What someone will pay for them—same as anything else," Mr. Gale said, donning his glasses again. "You couldn't pawn them for more than fifty bucks. Take an ad in the paper, you might find somebody willing to pay more than what I am. I'm offering three hundred." The jeweler's lower lip rose to crease the upper one, and he looked down between his eyelashes at the cuff links. "It's a fair price."

"It is," Joe said, wagging his head. "I'll take it."

The jeweler went into the back room, returning with two hundred-dollar bills and two fifties. Then he took out a slip and wrote up the transaction. "How'd you come by the cuff links?" he asked, pausing over his pen.

"They're not stolen, if that's what you mean."

"I didn't mean that," Mr. Gale said. He handed over the bills. "There. It's a deal."

Joe folded the bills and put them in the pocket of his jacket. Acting on

Jay Atkinson

a hunch, he took out one of the photographs he had salvaged from the trash and folded it over to hide the naked Mrs. Eriksen. What remained was a grainy picture of a man wearing a suit and homburg hat. "Ever seen this guy before?" he asked the jeweler.

Mr. Gale squinted at the photograph. "It looks like old man Beaumont. Franklin Beaumont, I think his name was. He was the overseer of the Ayer Mill for many, many years," said the jeweler. "Is he a relative of yours?"

"Not me."

"My father worked for Beaumont," Mr. Gale said. "He was there for the dedication of the clock on October 4th, 1910. When my father got home, I'd been born."

Joe replaced the photograph in his pocket and moved toward the door. In the dimness of the shop, Mr. Gale raised his hand. "One more thing," he said. "I won't sell these back. I'm keeping them."

"Like you said, this isn't a pawnshop," said Joe. He went out.

As soon as he was outside, Joe reached into his pocket, folded one of the hundred dollar bills and shoved it in his boot and down beneath his stockinged foot. The rest of the money he divided between the front pockets of his jeans. Essex Street had fallen into darkness, wide and bare through six sets of lights, the wind blowing from the north again. Possibilities for Gabriel and a happy Christmas sprung up all around him. At that moment Boris Johnson sprinted across the intersection just ahead, bare-chested and pumping his arms.

"Go get 'em, Boris," Joe called after him.

Joe Glass passed through the alley and entered Campagnone Common. The statue of a World War I infantryman marched toward Essex Street, the brim of the doughboy helmet shading his handsome metal face.

All the trees on the Common were bare, and the paved paths were swept clean and looked like runways at an airport. Halfway across, a granite monument shaped like an upright book dedicated the park to the three Campagnone brothers, killed in separate engagements during World War II. Joe remembered Mrs. Campagnone, who used to march in the parades when he was a kid. Her porch on Jackson Street had three American flags hanging from it all summer and it was the only house the kids wouldn't play in front of. She was dead now, buried up at Bellevue with her sons.

Joe Glass went through the YMCA parking lot; inside the glass doors he could see Boris Johnson arguing with the desk clerk, a huge fir wreath in each hand. Deciding on a couple of drinks before he caught the bus, Joe pulled up his collar and headed for Murphy's Tavern. He was thinking bicycle and snowsuit and toboggan, an army of green plastic soldiers and a Christmas tree with lights. Maybe a train set and savings bond. The look on Gabriel's face when he saw all the stuff.

Murphy's was only a couple of notches above the King of Clubs but it was warm inside, molecules of turkey soup floating in the air. Joe Glass stood in the entrance, stamping his feet and looking for an empty bar stool. They had a kitchen and bakery, serving homemade bread and boiled dinners and a cake with pudding inside that felt like a brick in your stomach. When Joe had any money, he used to take Francesca there.

Billy Murphy was an old classmate from Lawrence High. At the sight of his friend, Murphy removed a stool from behind the bar and set it out so Joe could sit down. "Happy Hanukkah," Billy said, his eyes disappearing in pockets of flesh when he smiled. He was close to three hundred pounds, big all over, with forearms the size of two championship salmon. "Come to pay your tab?"

"Yeah, as a matter of fact," said Joe, opening the beer Murphy pulled up for him. "What is it?"

Billy pawed among the slips. "Let's try under 'Deadbeat,'" he said. His bottom lip fell open, exposing a row of crooked teeth. "Ah, here it is. Seventeen beers, four strawberry margaritas and one order of Nachos Grande. Sixty-three bucks."

Murphy watched Joe dig for the money. "Been busy?"

"Been broke," Joe said. He took out a hundred-dollar bill and laid it on the bar. As soon as he did it, he wished he hadn't. C-notes were pretty rare on Broadway.

"Mr. High Fuckin' Roller," said Murphy. "When'd your ship come in?"

With a quick glance, Joe measured the men looking his way. "Nah. Just been doing a little work," he said.

"Like robbing old ladies?" asked Murphy. He rang up Joe's tab.

Joe put away his change and wished Murphy would shut up. Already people were coming in and out, and he had lost track of who had seen the money. The thing now was to sit tight, have a few beers and let time pass. Two new customers came to the bar and Joe turned his back on Murphy and scanned the room. Bending over the pool table was a girl in leather pants and a tight purple sweater, her ass turned up like a valentine. She made the shot and pumped the stick between her legs. "Ten bucks," she said to her opponent, a guy wearing a flannel shirt.

"Double or nothing," the guy said.

"Gimme the ten bucks," said the girl.

The mousy guy went into his pocket, and then sidled toward the exit while the girl racked up the table again. Billy Murphy noticed Joe watching her and came back down to that end of the bar. "That's Brenda Steffanelli," he said. "From Steffanelli's Towing."

Joe peeled the label from his beer bottle. "I'm not interested," he said.

"Like hell you're not," Murphy said.

"What makes you so fuckin' smart?"

Murphy's eyes again sank into the doughy pockets in his face. "I can tell when people want something and when they're only looking it over," he said. "Most of the time they're reaching for their wallets before they even think they've decided."

Ordering a bourbon, Joe Glass watched the girl in the purple sweater light a cigarette and then swat the smoke with her free hand. She did a little dance, sucking on the cigarette and then trying to get away from the raggedy exhaust. After a moment, she gave up and the smoke swirled around and rose like ghosts, evaporating through the ceiling.

"Why smoke if you don't like the smell?" Joe asked, laughing at her.

"Because it makes me feel good," said the girl.

Joe took his beer from the bar. "I don't want to breathe that shit," he said. "I got a kid."

At least twenty people were smoking inside Murphy's, so it was a philosophical discussion. "Big deal: I got three kids," the girl said. She stood with the cue stick pressed against her hip, looking him over. "If you want a pat on the back, you're gonna have to do it yourself."

Brenda Steffanelli had oval hips and a thin waist with small upturned breasts rounding beneath the purple sweater. Her pale, smallish face was surrounded by dark hair gelled into a mane, and the shiny ringlets tapered to a point in back. The heavy eye shadow and lipstick meant she was from Methuen.

A postman in uniform began reciting an X-rated version of "The Night before Christmas." His friends cheered and the waitress stopped her rounds and stood in the doorway, smiling at the drunken mailman with a platter of ribs balanced on her shoulder. Joe ordered another beer, and a vodka-cranberry for Brenda. With the waitress gone into the kitchen, Murphy brought the drinks over himself.

The big man had a light, delicate stride that didn't seem to lead him anywhere. Carrying the two drinks, he went up and down like a drum major. "Watch out, Brenda. He's got a social disease," Murphy said, indicating Joe with his chin. "Cheap-itis."

"Here, Billy," Joe said, paying with a fifty dollar bill. "Now fuck off."

Across the room, the postman sang: "And Mom with her dildo and I with the clap, we both settled down for a long winter's nap."

"Ah, Christmas in Lawrence. It's like an old movie," Billy Murphy said, mincing back to the bar.

Brenda broke the rack, and they played high-low for ten bucks a game. She was a hustler, falling behind when it looked too obvious but winning three out of every four. Joe felt his pocket growing lighter as the balls rolled and clacked together on the bright green felt and more beers were delivered. He was rusty; to be a good pool player you had to practice in bars. The drinks cost money, and he usually didn't have any.

"I give up," Joe said. He clattered his pool stick onto the table.

Brenda counted the sixty dollars she had won and stuffed it in her pocket.

"I should've kept the fucking cuff links," said Joe.

"Huh?"

Joe shook his head. "Forget it."

Swinging her hips in a little circle, Brenda Steffanelli held him there. "Let me buy you a couple drinks. After all, it's your money."

The drunken postman had been carried out, leaving an empty booth near the windows. Ordering a longneck and shots of bourbon, Joe ran his eyes over Brenda's compact body when she turned her head. The Steffanellis had the municipal towing contract in Methuen and half of it in Lawrence. When Joe had owned a car, an old bomber with "Colt 45" spray-painted on the hood, it had been towed from a hydrant that was buried in snow. Steffanelli charged him a hundred bucks for the tow and thirty dollars a day for a week of storage. Joe thought the car had been stolen and when he figured things out, the bill was more than the car was worth but he had to pay it. State law.

Brenda had married one of the iron-jawed Steffanellis. There were four brothers, Steve, John, Mike and Rocco, all with police records that somehow never prevented them from acquiring city contracts. The Mrs. Steffanellis were as notorious as their husbands: with bright lipstick and gluey hair, pulled out of the nightclubs long enough to get hitched at St. Lucy's and then herded back inside. Brenda was Mike's wife, the second youngest and wildest of the brothers. Mike was an asshole, she said.

"I can't argue with that," said Joe, shooting the solid little tumbler of bourbon.

"You don't say much, do you?" Brenda said.

Joe Glass shrugged; he felt like a drunken mess. The room glowed, suffused with smoke and trembling with every heartbeat. There was a great roar of voices and rattling bottles, an odor of spilled liquor, and dozens of bodies crammed between the tables. Joe inched his hand across the vinyl seat and touched Brenda's warm sinewy back where her sweater rode up. The sweater was fuzzy, and Joe played with the lower edge of it, his fingers searching upward for more skin. Brenda arched herself over the table and looked away like she hadn't noticed Joe's wandering hand. She thrust her breasts forward, a little smile playing across her lips.

Joe watched through the windows as a tow truck with Christmas lights strung over the roll bar pulled up. It was a huge, steaming beast, painted black, with *Steffanelli Towing* written in script along the fuselage and *Mike* on the driver's side door.

"Oh-oh," said Brenda, grabbing for her cigarettes.

Mike Steffanelli charged into the bar, bringing a gust of arctic air. "Brenda, get in the fuckin' truck," he said.

He was a tall, pointy-jawed fellow, with large chapped hands and wavy hair that was turning gray. For a few moments, he had the attention of everyone in the bar. Mike Steffanelli wore a greasy canvas coat, thermal shirt, outmoded designer jeans and workboots. Around his neck was a gold chain with a miniature tow truck dangling from it, and he wore a gold pinkie ring studded with diamonds on his left hand.

"I have the Toyota," Brenda said, but she was already heading for the door.

Steffanelli scowled as his wife ducked behind him. "I'll tow the fuckin' thing," he said. "Get in the truck." He glanced over at Joe Glass, who still had his arm stretched across the booth. "You want some, Romeo? Come on outside, if you do."

"Nice pants," said Joe. He was encouraged by laughter that rang out from the bar. "About ten years ago."

"Let's go," said Steffanelli, thumbing the door again. "Outside."

Joe got up from the booth. Solid in his leather jacket and boots, he was still a head shorter than Mike Steffanelli. "Give 'im one for me," someone called out. Joe thrust his arms in the air, and followed Steffanelli outside. The laughter inside Murphy's died as the door closed behind them.

"Fuckin' wiseguy," said Steffanelli.

Brenda was perched high in the truck cab, smoking a cigarette and staring through the windshield. Joe scraped his boots on the pavement but she didn't look over. Even through a bourbon haze, fighting one guy with three brothers seemed like a bad idea. Joe decided to throw a couple punches and then take a dive and let Steffanelli feel good about himself. This seemed like a great strategy, until the tow truck driver took off his coat and displayed a physique straight out of the National Football League. Beneath the filthy thermal shirt, his chest was carved into two angled planes and the muscles behind his shoulders bowed up to his ears.

Joe Glass frowned at him. "You guys charge too much," he said.

"What?"

"You're a bunch of fuckin' crooks," said Joe. His heart thumped and he felt the bag of his stomach, inflated with beer, flopping against his spine.

Stefanelli came forward and hammered him with an overhand right. It glanced off Joe's left forearm onto his cheek. The truck driver's next punch landed on Joe's forehead. As he went down, he noticed the tow truck was in a handicapped space. "No parking," he said.

"Fuck you," said Steffanelli, from a dreamy distance.

The tow truck departed. Rising up, Joe floated for a ways down the sidewalk and then turned into an alley. Stumbling from wall to wall, he corrected himself and staggered toward Essex Street. Once or twice he fell and took his time getting up. His head felt like a cannonball on his shoulders.

He stepped off a curbstone and it was like falling twenty feet. The ground rushed at him, but he landed and didn't get up. From a doorway some shadows crowded around and Joe levitated for a moment, inches off the pavement. Then he dropped back into the darkness.

*

Father Tom Dailey awoke in the early hours of December 24th, washed and dressed himself, and then descended to the garage beneath the rectory. Housed there was a black late model Chrysler, and he started the engine and opened the electric garage door and drove the car out. Common Street was deserted, and the lights of Essex Street shone against the dim gray horizon. Not even the newspaper trucks were out.

On Essex Street, one building after another was closed tight, the windows all dark like row houses in the Depression. The street was arranged for one-way traffic, as wide across as a superhighway, and Father Tom cruised down the center lane. He noticed a huddled form on the sidewalk and stopped the car.

A man was lying there, dressed in a black leather jacket. Father Tom kneeled and touched him on the shoulder and the man sat up. "Are you hurt?" asked Father Tom.

The man smelled of liquor and had dirty hair and a scar beneath his lower lip. "I'm not feeling too good," he said. Father Tom gripped the man's jacket and hauled him to his feet. The chains attached to the leather jacket made a little music on the way up.

"What happened?" Father Tom asked.

The man looked up and down the empty street. "Shit: is it Christmas?" he asked.

"The day before," said the priest.

A light that wasn't really light had come up, and they could see the doorways and alleyways surrounding them although it was still dark. Father Tom's car remained in the middle of Essex Street with the door flung open.

"I got suckered," said the man. He had an enormous welt on his forehead. "I gotta get my kid a present."

Across the river, the Ayer Mill clock glowed against the paling sky. It was quarter to six. "Can I help you?" the priest asked, gesturing toward his car.

The man sat down on the curb and pulled off his left boot. His hand came up with a crumpled bill in it. "I'm all right," the man said.

"I hope you can turn the other cheek," the priest said.

"Sure, Father," the man said. He surveyed the desolate stretch of asphalt, then swiveled back to the priest. His left eye was swollen shut. "Around here, you gotta turn about fifty cheeks."

Father Tom felt useless among his new, independent flock. "Well, good luck," he said.

The young man blew on his fingers and regarded Father Tom before stamping his feet against the pavement. "Same to you, Father. Merry Christmas."

Climbing behind the wheel, Father Tom nodded as the man closed the door on him and hurried down an alley. Church bells struck the hour and doubled sheets of newspaper flapped like small dingy angels in his wake. Father Tom began praying the rosary as he steered the car down the wide, empty boulevard. His devotions went up into the heavy sky with a sense of certainty, but it didn't feel like activism. The town was already painted red from top to bottom, and his little scrapings didn't do much to take the color off.

Iron shutters were down on all the storefronts, and at the end of Common Street Holy Rosary Church was reduced to a Gothic shadow. At six AM Tivoli Bakery was doing a good business, with people lined up eight deep at the counter. Father Tom parked the Chrysler in their lot and went inside.

The aroma of baking bread was dense and warm, filling the space from floor to ceiling. Long yellow loaves were piled from one end of the bakery to the other, which was visible through the open doorway. Italian women dressed in shapeless wool coats placed orders for bread and *biscotti* and other delicacies while fresh young girls scurried around behind the counter. When Father Tom loosened his topcoat and his collar became visible, the proprietor rushed out of the back, his white shirt and pants singed at the edges.

"Father, for you: anything," Tivoli said.

The baker was a middle-aged man with his few strands of hair greased back over his skull, a square dark face hanging from it. His look of piety told Father Tom that he never attended Mass.

"I just want some rolls for dinner, and a bag of cookies for Monsignor Borinquen," said the priest. Under his topcoat, he hiked up his cassock and removed a worn leather purse from his trousers. "I'll pay for them."

The baker grunted and Father Tom realized that he didn't like the man. In the warmth of the counter space, elderly women who the priest had heard in the confessional stood in their orthopedic shoes, watching his every move. Slowly the last old Italians of the parish had come to Father Tom, confessing their minor lapses of faith—what Monsignor Borinquen liked to call "bingo sins"—as they took his measure. Father Tom was an Irish kid from Chicago who could speak Spanish, Portuguese, and a little Italian. The Cardinal Archbishop called him *Señor* Dailey, and said he would either be a gigantic hit in Lawrence (because he was young and good-looking and had a sense of humor), or he'd be ignored (because he wasn't Italian or Puerto Rican). Mostly Father Tom Dailey felt anonymous; no one called him by name except his boss.

The baker put two dozen snowflake rolls and a box of Christmas cookies inside a tall white bag. "We're struggling, Father," he said. "Please pray for us."

Father Tom strained to remember a particular verse from Matthew, and then something from John came into his head. "Who by worrying can add a single hour to his life?" he asked, and gathered the soft fragrant bag under his arm. Dropping the exact amount on the counter, he held the gaze of the baker and then went out the door into the morning light.

A woman carrying a child in her arms slipped from among the other women queuing up for bread, and followed the priest outside. The bell above the door jingled and Father Tom turned back. Hulking in their winter coats, the old women stood like football linemen inside the bakery, their kerchiefs battened on like helmets. For a moment, the baker spoke to one of them with an impatient look on his face and then returned to his ovens. The young girls behind the counter, in polo shirts and too much make-up, continued lifting the yellow loaves in the air, sheathing them like swords in the long paper bags.

Francesca Nesheim caught up to Father Tom on the parking lot. "Father, can I speak to you?" she asked.

Her gaze was fixed on the ground, but the child on her hip, red-cheeked with dark hair, was gazing at Father Tom with sorrowful eyes. The young vicar smiled at the little boy, cupping his hand for a blessing, and the child continued to stare with a grave look on his face.

"I'd be happy to speak with you," Father Tom said. He placed one hand on the body of his car like he was showing it to a prospective buyer.

"Would you prefer to come to the rectory? We can talk over some hot chocolate."

Attractive, with angled cheekbones and sleek black hair, the woman was dressed in a leather duster and black tights, her feet laced into tiny black boots. Her eyes swung up and met those of the young priest, and Father Tom felt himself looking into them beyond propriety. He held the bag and felt the warm rolls crushed against his chest. Several of the Italian women in the bakery had swung around and were watching him through the glass.

The young woman looked down the empty stripe of Common Street to the church. "Maybe I should meet you at the rectory," she said.

"Jump in," said Father Tom, his heart sinking in the gulf between them. "I'll drive you."

"Don't worry, Father. We're dressed for walking," the woman said. She hiked the child to her shoulder, heading off toward the church.

Father Tom glanced at the lighted bakery window and noticed five or six women looking at him. He waved and got behind the wheel of the Chrysler. The priest turned the key, but the engine was already running. It made a loud grinding sound that drew attention from all quarters and he cursed inside the thick glass of the windshield, stifling himself at the last instant.

Father Tom said a prayer of contrition. Easing into the street, he turned and passed without noticing beneath a red traffic light, coming alongside mother and child. In a moment the car rolled by them, its engine ticking beneath the hood. Father Tom glanced at the woman. Her long legs flashing out at the sidewalk, she kept her eyes looking ahead, toward the bright gold cross on top of Holy Rosary.

He parked the car in the garage and hurried into the rectory to start a pot of cocoa. Father Tom was dismayed to see Monsignor Borinquen at the kitchen table dressed in his mothy old bathrobe, drinking a cup of tea and reading the *Boston Herald*. Mrs. Castiglione, their combination secretary and maid, had the weekend off. As a result, Monsignor Borinquen had bypassed his early meal of tea and doughnuts in his office and was making do by himself.

"Welcome, traveler," he said, raising his cup. A brown and white cat named Jonah lay beside him on the floor. "Care to join me?"

Unable to hide his feelings of invaded territory, Father Tom said, "I'm expecting a parishioner any minute. For counseling."

"If it's Rocky Bonnano and his 'marital difficulty' again, I won't even change clothes," the Monsignor said. "I've heard all about Mrs. Bonnano's frigidity and soggy pasta a hundred times."

"It's a young woman," Father Tom said.

"Oh," said Borinquen, maintaining his good cheer. "In that case, I'll retire."

The older priest cleared away his cup and saucer and folded up the newspaper. A thick arm fell from the sleeve of his bathrobe, and the faint blue letters USMC were visible.

"After Korea, the priesthood was a cinch," he had once told Father

Jay Atkinson

Tom. "There's nothing like mortal terror to help you choose a career path."

Monsignor Borinquen rinsed his dishes in the sink, humming the tune to "South Pacific." He was the size of a fullback, but with varicose veins and a heart that speeded up and slowed down of its own accord. Shuffling in bathrobe and house slippers, Borinquen looked like an otherwise vigorous man institutionalized for some passing disorder. But in the two months they had lived together, Father Tom had sensed that his superior was not at all healthy, despite his regular afternoon rides on the stationary bicycle in the parlor.

During a recent confession, Father Tom spoke of doubts about his vocation and an urgent desire for pizza and beer. The Monsignor replied that without doubts there would be no faith and that pizza without beer was the real sin—and assigned the rosary for penance.

Footfalls came up the back stairs and then a young woman appeared with the silhouette of a child. Monsignor Borinquen could see them through the two-way mirror in the door, where visitors were confronted with their own reflections. A memorandum suggesting this device had come from the Archdiocese in response to several recent attacks against priests. Monsignor Borinquen had resisted the idea until a kit arrived *Special Delivery*, accompanied by a note from the Cardinal Archbishop.

"Pretty girl," Borinquen said, the words falling like two stones upon the table.

Something close to disapproval registered in his eyes, their color picked up by the gray stripes in his bathrobe. There was a moment of indecision where Borinquen worked the tendons in his throat, and then decided not to speak. He sucked in his lower lip, taking the newspaper with him down the hall, followed by the cat. Father Tom waited for the heavy oak door of the bathroom to close before admitting his visitors.

"Thanks for coming," Father Tom said, ushering the woman toward Monsignor Borinquen's chair. "The cocoa is almost ready. And you are...?"

"Francesca Nesheim. And this is my son, Gabriel."

The young priest untied the boy's hood. "Nice to meet you, Gabriel Nesheim," he said, shaking the toddler's hand.

"Gabriel Glass," Francesca said. "Glass is his father's name."

The priest blushed. "I suppose a lot of women keep their own names these days," he said.

"Especially if they're not married," said Francesca. Her oval eyes were fixed on the priest, unnerving him. She loosened her coat and the hard edges of it scraped along the floor. "I appreciate your time, Father. It must be your day off."

According to Monsignor Borinquen, the only day a priest had off was when he prostrated himself and took his final vows. Afterwards there was a celebration with cake and ice cream, just like a birthday, but from then on you worked for the Home Office and were expected to produce results.

"I'm always happy to meet with a parishioner," Father Tom said.

"I don't go to church very much," Francesca said. The boy had climbed down from his mother's arms and was standing beside the chair, one hand on a low wooden strut. Gabriel stared at the priest through intelligent brown eyes.

"Has the boy been christened?" asked Father Tom.

"I'm afraid he hasn't," Francesca said. "I never knew how to get it done."

"Is that what you wanted to see me about?"

The shiny black ponytail brushed her shoulders. "I have another problem," Francesca said.

"You can speak freely," Father Tom said, glancing down the hall. He heard the toilet flush, but the bathroom door remained closed.

The child left his mother's side and began exploring the kitchen, goose-stepping in his squeaky rubber boots. He made one loop around the table and then headed for Jonah's litter box. Francesca lunged across the room, lifting Gabriel in the air before he could grasp a pellet and put it in his mouth.

"No offense, but you seem pretty young," she said, holding the boy in front of her. He didn't struggle to free himself, but hung from his mother's grip, smiling at Father Tom.

"I'm thirty-three. I was ordained four years ago."

Francesca directed a look straight into his eyes. "Is this your first job?" she asked. "Holy Rosary, I mean."

"This is my second parish assignment," said Father Tom, his curiosity about the woman increasing. "You could speak to another priest instead, if that would make you more comfortable," he said. The faint sound of the shower running came from down the hall. "Monsignor Borinquen is more experienced than I am."

"No, thank you. You're probably gonna be more help than someone older."

"I hope so," said Father Tom.

The young woman returned to the table, encircling Gabriel with her arms to keep him there. "I'm pregnant again, and I'm not sure who the father is," Francesca said. She frowned at Father Tom. "There's three possibilities."

The young priest tried not to picture Francesca Nesheim in the midst of three separate passions. "Have you been to a doctor?" Father Tom asked.

"I took a home test," said Francesca. "I passed, or failed, depending on how you look at it."

"How do *you* look at it?"

Francesca stared out the window. "Like I'm in a lot of trouble," she said.

Jonah sauntered into the kitchen, his tail in the air like a flag. "Kitty," Gabriel said, pointing. Francesca let the child down to pet the cooperative Jonah, whose fur was damp from being in the bathroom when it filled up with steam. The cat stretched itself and then wandered over the linoleum, with Gabriel toddling along behind.

Jay Atkinson

The priest had a keen sense of the impracticality of his role in situations like this. Praying the rosary would not divulge the name of the unborn child's father, nor was there a sacrament that bestowed happiness or improved reasoning. The Archdiocese sent its vicars to Holy Rosary armed only with the New Testament, when they should have dispatched clairvoyants with money to give away, auxiliary police to arrest the drug dealers and muggers, and at least one politician with his or her pockets sewn shut. A church in downtown Lawrence was like a shop in the middle of the desert that sold bathing suits.

"Christ is not ashamed of you, or afraid of what people will think," said Father Tom. In his heart, he felt like he was talking about Someone he didn't really know. "Because you asked Him for help, He will provide it."

"I never asked Him for anything, and I'm not sure if that's a plus or a minus," Francesca said.

"He wants you to seek Him out. That's the sole reason for His ministry on earth."

Francesca crossed the room to prevent Gabriel from pulling on Jonah's tail. "From now on, I promise I'll be a steady customer," she said. "This problem isn't going away any time soon."

"Can you identify the father and get support from him, when the time comes?"

"It might be Joe—Gabriel's father. He's out of work, but does everything he can to make things easier for us," Francesca said. She stood against the wooden cabinets that surrounded the sink and raised the child to her shoulder, who seemed happy at the mention of his dad. "The other two, I have no idea. One is married already, and offered to leave his wife and kids to marry me. But that was before I got pregnant. The other guy is good for nothing. Your typical charming bum."

Father Tom was silent. He gazed at a spot on the wall where a crucifix had once hung, but had been removed for a painting job that never occurred. The ghost of the cross was still there.

"If I was a man, everyone would congratulate me for being so popular," said Francesca. "But if a woman sleeps with three people, I guess she's in a different category."

"You should think about how you are conducting your life and how it affects your children," Father Tom said. "You have certain responsibilities you must live up to and that often means practicing self-denial."

"That's easy for someone who's celibate," Francesca said. "I never made that promise."

"Everyone has desires," Father Tom said to Francesca.

Dressed in black trousers, his clerical collar and a gray-on-black Argyle sweater, Monsignor Borinquen exited the bathroom and swung his head toward the kitchen. Francesca happened to be looking that way and an introduction became necessary. Clacking in his leather soles, the Monsignor strode down the tessellated floor of the hallway to take her hand.

"Welcome to Holy Rosary," he said, stooping to make the sign of the cross with his thumb on Gabriel's forehead. "Christ have mercy on you."

The Monsignor smelled of lime aftershave. He looked on Francesca and then twitched his heavy eyebrows at Gabriel, who was stunned into silence. "Has your son been baptized?" Borinquen asked. The child spun on the linoleum and flung out his arms and Francesca gathered him in.

"No, Monsignor," she said.

"Bring him to the altar on January thirteenth. I'll put you on the list," said Borinquen. "No use waiting any longer. We all need God's blessing."

Francesca gazed at the floor, her hair coming undone from the ponytail and spilling over her shoulder. "Yes, Monsignor," she said.

Embarrassed that their meeting seemed more like a flirtation than a counseling session, Father Tom stood up and spoke to Francesca. "There's a class for parents and godparents on the night of the fifth. It's compulsory, so I'll expect you there," said the priest. To his own ear, he sounded stuffy and dogmatic. "We meet at six-thirty in the back of the church."

"Okay," said Francesca, without looking at him.

"Then it's settled," Borinquen said, again making the sign of the cross on Gabriel's forehead. "We'll be inducting another one of Christ's little troopers on the thirteenth of January."

Jonah was at the door, mewling to go out. "We should go," said Francesca, when the Monsignor opened the door for his cat. She clutched Gabriel to her chest and fussed with his hood. "Thank you both."

"No trouble," said Father Tom, his heart aching. "Please come again."

"I'll see you on January fifth," Francesca said.

"Have a blessed Christmas," said Monsignor Borinquen, closing the door. When he turned, Father Tom was against the counter, frowning at him.

"Was all that bossing around necessary?" asked the young priest.

"These young women have to be told," said Borinquen. "If we don't stand up as moral examples, they take their example from what they see. And what they see is not acceptable to Christ or His church."

"I think we must be aware of the human element in decision-making," Father Tom said, more tentatively than he wished to. "We make mistakes, too. I think the lay population find that comforting."

"The human element is weakness," Borinquen said. "It's not the job of a priest to be weak. Many other people are fulfilling that role. The most important job of the priest is to set a moral example."

Father Tom nodded. "I'll pray for understanding on that issue, Monsignor," he said.

"Good." The older man swung his head around, scanning the room. "Did you get the cookies?" he asked.

*

When Joe Glass arrived home, his left eye swollen into a ring on the side of his head, there was a message on his answering machine. It was from Harrah's Funeral Home, asking him if he wanted to work that morning. "The day before Christmas, I can't get anybody else," said Larry Harrah, son of old man Harrah. "I'm paying a hundred bucks. I have a topcoat you can wear, just show up with a decent pair of shoes. The service is at nine, here in the funeral home. Call me."

It was seven-thirty; a weak light was falling through the trees outside. First, Joe called Larry Harrah to say he would come in. "How long is your hair?" the funeral director wanted to know.

Looking at his reflection in the aluminum oven hood, his damaged eye blowing up large and black, Joe shook his head and the dirty strands of his hair brushed his cheek. "It's not bad," he said.

Larry covered the phone and gave muffled instructions to someone before coming back on the line. "Put it in a ponytail and tuck it under your collar—the collar of a clean shirt," he said. "Hurry up. I'm short-handed."

"I need half an hour to get myself organized."

"You've got fifteen minutes. I'll send somebody over," Larry said and hung up.

Francesca wasn't home or she wasn't answering. Joe let the phone ring while he stripped off his clothes. They stank of cigarettes and beer, his pants crusted with mud and a huge rash on his leather jacket from where he had fallen against the pavement. He threw the telephone back on the receiver.

In his closet, he had a pair of black twill pants and a white shirt with blue stitching on the seams that was a little worn but clean. He took a three-minute shower. Under the bureau he found a pair of socks and his dress boots. He slicked his hair back, and tucked it underneath his collar just as a horn blew in the street. There was a limousine in front of the house; he hoped the neighbors were watching.

Butch Dallon was behind the wheel of the limo. "What are you wearing that leather coat for? This ain't a Hell's Angel funeral we're running this morning," he said. Dallon was a bulky sixty-year-old man in a pin-striped suit, two fingers missing on his right hand from an accident in the Oxford paper mill. Joe leaped in beside him and the big Lincoln roared off.

"Larry says he's got a topcoat for me," Joe said.

Pointing two waxy-looking fingers, Dallon grunted with disgust. "He ain't got a coat that's gonna cover that eye," he said. "This is a funeral. Have some fucking respect."

Larry Harrah met them outside the garage next to the funeral home. He was wringing his hands, every few seconds pulling back the edge of a glove to check his watch. Behind him the garage stood empty. He rented all his cars from a bigger outfit across town.

"Jesus Christ," he said when Joe had hauled himself out of the limo. "Did you think it was Rocky Marciano's funeral or something? You look like shit."

Dallon lit a cigarette. "I told him," he said.

"I'll drive the flower car," said Joe. "They'll never even see me."

"You're fucking right, they won't," Harrah said. His eyes went up to the gloomy sky. "These people have to die on Christmas, right? They can't wait."

Larry Harrah was thirty-five years old, with brilliant black hair and the rich brown skin of the Lebanese. "Put on a coat and hat; they're in the garage," said Harrah. "And sunglasses to cover that eye."

"I don't have any sunglasses," said Joe.

"Butch, give him yours."

The smirking Dallon, a wattle hanging from his neck like a turkey, clutched at the sides of his head. "Let him get his own fucking glasses," he said. "My daughter gave me these."

"He's got the black eye," Harrah said. "Give him the fucking glasses."

Dallon continued grumbling, but turned over the sunglasses. They were worth about nine dollars and made everything glow with an unnatural amber tint. Just then the first car pulled into the parking lot. Harrah gestured for Joe to get the coat and hat out of the garage, and then rushed to open the car door for a large woman with a spray of plastic holly attached to her hat. Before the car had even stopped rolling, Harrah's face had transformed itself into a grave, obsequious mask. His heels pressed together, a green holiday scarf setting off his herringbone topcoat and striped gray-on-black trousers, Harrah turned every fiber of his being to the horsy woman who now stood beside the car, exhaling plumes of steam through her nose and looking bewildered.

Butch Dallon waited beside the limousine like a beefeater, unable of being roused, his face sunken around his dentures. Donning the heavy coat and visored hat, Joe Glass watched through one of the grimy windows as the rest of the mourners arrived, many of them looking put out by the occasion, on what was supposed to be the happiest day of the year.

Harrah was everywhere at once, making it appear that more help was at hand than actually existed. Butch Dallon continued his mannequin act until he was alone in the parking lot. Then he lit a cigarette and leaned against the gleaming hulk of the limousine. Inside the garage with the weight of the topcoat on his back, Joe Glass watched the mourners file beneath the awnings of the funeral home. He exited a side door, came around to the plain black station wagon that Harrah used as his flower car, and got inside. The keys hung from the ignition, and inexplicably, there was a woman's bra and panties on the front seat. Doused with perfume, the underwear bore certain markings that indicated it had been worn. Joe sniffed both pieces and hid them in the glove compartment.

When the engine was warm, Joe drove around front and parked behind the hearse. A few minutes later, Dallon brought the Lincoln out and motioned for Joe to make room for it. Joe steered the flower car in reverse for thirty or forty feet and got out with the motor still running. Then he and Dallon drove the mourners' vehicles out from the parking lot and placed them behind the station wagon, attaching magnetic funeral flags. It was going to be a small procession: only nine cars in all.

Butch Dallon stamped up the stairs to the funeral home and entered through the heavy black doors. After several minutes, it grew warm

Jay Atkinson

inside the flower car and Joe began yawning and then fell asleep. Only the coffin bumping against the hearse woke him up. A dozen well-dressed people milled about on the sidewalk, indicting him with their glances. The pallbearers and Butch Dallon and Harrah formed a brigade descending the stairs of the funeral home and began passing outside the floral arrangements and poinsettias. Joe Glass scrambled from the station wagon to assist them. Trying to hide his battered eye, his hair still wet and freezing in the cold air, Joe helped stow the flowers in the back of the wagon. A few of the cardboard pots were leaky, spilling water on his hands. In the frigid temperature the carnations and orchids withered, hundreds of dollars worth of stiff brown stalks.

After helping the last relative into the cars, Harrah came around to check the latch on the hearse. "No fuck-ups so far," he said to Joe and Butch, still wearing his death mask. "Keep it that way, and everybody goes home with a few skins in his pocket."

The cortege pulled onto Union Street, heading for the cemetery. As they passed the Common, Joe spotted Francesca striding along with Gabriel on her shoulder. She hadn't even glanced at the cars when Gabriel spotted his father and cried out. On Francesca went, her long legs devouring the sidewalk. Behind the flower car was the first set of mourners and Joe didn't dare toot his horn. The hearse and then the rest of the cars moved along the quiet frozen street, through a red light, and Joe watched as his young son receded in the mirrors attached to both sides of the station wagon.

They crossed Broadway and several cars tried to cut through the procession, zagging in front of the hearse and between the limousine and flower car. Joe saw the face of a truck driver swerve close, and then STOP AND SAVE unfurled as the truck went careering past. He jumped on the brake and in his mirror Joe watched the middle-aged couple behind him, their faces streaked with tears, as they exploded with curses at the truck driver and an instant later returned to blankness and silence.

Nine cars twisted around a small rotary, and then up toward the reservoir and cemetery. The hills of Bellevue were studded with granite tablets and spires and vaults, half-buried in the snow. Tattered American flags flapped in the wind that spilled over the huge bulwark of the reservoir. First the limousine and then the hearse turned beneath an iron arch, still climbing, up one small hill covered with graves and then beyond it to a valley large enough to make the rest of the world disappear. The little procession had entered the country of the dead.

Waiting on an icy plain was a grave surrounded by green plastic mats and covered over by a black tent. The hearse turned off the main thoroughfare and headed down a single-lane road, the snow brushing the hubcaps. Coming alongside the tent, the mourners waited inside their cars while the pallbearers struggled with the coffin and baskets of flowers were ferried out to the grave.

The minister was a young woman and she took her place at one end of the narrow ditch. She smiled at the pallbearers as they lowered the coffin onto straps that stretched across the grave, then took a bible from her coat. She found it impossible to turn the pages with her gloves on and stuck them in her pockets.

Joe Glass retreated to the bumper of the station wagon. A group of about twenty people huddled beneath the tent, which bowed in the wind. Unnoticed by the mourners, Larry Harrah held one of the support poles in his gloved hand. With a slight nod, he directed Butch Dallon to ground the pole across from him. The minister began praying aloud and her words were thinned by the cold and whipped away on the wind. Joe couldn't hear a word she was saying, only the flap of someone's coattails like a bird taking wing. He scanned the faces of the mourners. At the rear of the assembly was a hatless man wearing a powder blue leisure suit. The man wore an old pair of zippered dress boots and a cheap wristwatch.

When the minister reached the twenty-third Psalm, the man in the leisure suit recited it along with her. His hands were red in the cold and his eyes were deep in their sockets, his close-cropped hair riffling in the wind. The minister ended her prayers, offering condolences to the family before hustling back to her car. Larry Harrah intercepted her and slipped an envelope into her hand while shaking it, and then returned to the grave site and made an announcement about a gathering at such-and-such an address. It was Christmas Eve and everyone wanted to go home. They retreated to their vehicles.

All except the man in the leisure suit. While the others dissolved into the snowbound reaches of the cemetery, he walked closer to the coffin and stood beside it playing with his wristwatch. Since this man had arrived in his own car, Larry Harrah wasn't obliged to wait for him. In fact, the family of the deceased was ready to leave. Over by the limousine, Harrah whispered to Dallon to wait until the man finished paying his respects before breaking down the tent. Afterwards they would rendezvous at the funeral home.

Butch and Joe waited for the man to say his good-byes. He squatted on his heels like he was reading something on the coffin and then stood up, sobbing to himself. The buttons were stretched on his shirt, revealing sections of his hairy red chest.

"For the love of Mike, it's freezing out here," Dallon said under his breath.

Standing now, the man glanced around and realized he was the only mourner still in attendance. He fumbled with his wristwatch, placing it on the burnished surface of the coffin. Joe Glass watched him stride away from the grave, his legs bunched with muscle beneath the fabric of his pants, over to his dented Pontiac, which then wouldn't start. The man got out, threw open the hood with a squeal of metal, and adjusted the carburetor with a screwdriver he took from his pocket. On the second try, the engine caught with a whine and he drove off toward the shadowy horizons of Bellevue.

Down the slope, a front-end loader crawled toward them. "Let's get out of here," Dallon said, shivering.

The tent came down easily. Dallon unscrewed the poles and then

Jay Atkinson

stored them and the roll of canvas in the hearse. He moved aside the sheets of artificial grass, revealing mounds of frozen dirt underneath. The flowers, which were stiff in the wind and altogether dead, they chucked into the grave. "Nobody wants 'em," Butch said.

Dallon took the wristwatch and he and Joe lowered the coffin into the shallow cement vault by loosening the canvas straps. Too much slack jumped in at the end and they could hear the body thump inside the coffin.

"Who is it?" Joe asked.

Dallon was examining the wristwatch. "Who's who?"

Joe pointed into the hole. "Down there," he said.

"I don't know. Some guy," said Dallon. "A mechanic, I think he was."

There was a bitter wind, throwing cascades of snow over the grave. At the bottom of the shallow hole, the casket looked forlorn. Inside it, Joe guessed there was a guy with chapped hands and a blue leisure suit and zippered boots. It seemed criminal that they were about to leave him up here. Mechanics contained all their friends in seven cars and died on the installment plan, but they were just like everyone else. So quickly into the ground, cried over and forgotten.

Dallon tossed the wristwatch into the grave and it clattered over the lid of the coffin and landed in the narrow space beside it. "Crappy piece of shit."

They folded up the artificial grass and put the mats into the station wagon. "See ya back at the ranch," said Dallon. He jerked his thumb toward the grave. "That's gotta be the easiest two hundred bucks I ever earned."

Butch Dallon wheeled the hearse through the intersection, gunning it toward the cemetery entrance. He met the front-end loader coming up, and Joe watched as the hearse squeezed alongside and the window came down and Dallon handed a bottle of liquor to the operator. The man laughed and then rolled up his window, inching his way toward the open grave. Inside the Plexiglas cab, he looked like a pig wearing a quilted cap.

Joe Glass arrived at Harrah's just as Dallon pulled up in the hearse. The limousine was nowhere in sight and the funeral home was dark. They drove around back, but the garage was locked.

"Fucking Larry," said Dallon. "He took off."

"When are we gonna get paid?" Joe asked.

Butch Dallon rapped two yellow fingers against the hearse. "Not today, it looks like. Larry probably wants the three cents in interest."

Joe handed over the borrowed sunglasses, hat, topcoat, and the keys to the station wagon, then stood shivering in his threadbare shirt.

"What are you gonna do for Christmas?" Dallon asked him.

"See my kid, I hope."

"I'm gonna do the same I do every year," Dallon said to a question that hadn't been asked. "Sit around and hope somebody dies."

4

Lawrence, Massachusetts

September 18, 1848

A quarter mile beyond Andover Bridge, Charles S. Storrow stood in the doorway of the Coburn House. The director, treasurer, agent, and chief engineer of the Essex Company was thirty-nine years old, with a cropped beard, broad fleshy nose and a heavy forehead above melancholy black eyes. The omnibus stopped in front of the hotel and the driver unfurled the steps and opened the door. Clutching his portmanteau, Abbott Lawrence emerged from the cabin, hailing his friend and protege.

"Halloo, Charles of the New City," he said, with blustery good cheer. "Or, is it Constantine and his Constantinople I see before me?"

The younger man responded to his patron with demure nods. Mixing the attires of the businessman, pioneer, and man of letters, Charles Storrow was dressed in hobnailed boots, a double-breasted field coat draped over woolen trousers, and a top hat made of velvet.

"How is the health of Katherine and the children?" Mr. Storrow asked, as the two men gripped each other by the wrists. "Are they well?"

"God's blessing they are thriving, and I trust Lydia and your brood fall equally under the shadow of His Providence," said Abbott Lawrence, staring into the younger man's mirthless eyes. "Nothing gives a man such reams of joy as his family."

Storrow's characteristic reserve seemed to have deepened into gloom. "But, dear Abbott, the purest, most unalloyed sort of happiness comes from a man's work."

"Perhaps you are right, Charles. If so I choose abundance, then, over purity."

His gaze falling on the boots of his companion, Mr. Storrow said, "For my part, give me anything besides this wretchedness."

Abbott Lawrence thrust the other man to arm's length. "Why so black a mood? Tomorrow your Great Dam will have gone from paper to prospect in just three years, and thousands of men will cheer you. And

Jay Atkinson

so they should, Charles. You have won here in the New City and won handsomely."

"I have a tooth which pains me," said Storrow.

Lawrence gripped the wooden handle of his portmanteau. "Then we must decamp for the surgeon's," he said. "For nothing will do for a diseased tooth but pulling it out."

"First you must rest. It's a long journey from Washington to our outpost."

Mr. Lawrence shook his head, laughing at Storrow's earnestness. "For the past three days I've grown stronger in the bosom of my family. Let's see about that tooth, and a swift tour of all you've accomplished since my last visit," he said. "There will be time to go over accounts, and to rest, when we finish the day's more pressing business."

The smell of a brewery hung in the air and the streets were thick with elastic, fetid mud. Despite his heartiness, Abbott was taken aback by the clamor, the stench, and the wriggling vitality of the work camp. For it hardly could be called a city, where half the structures were unfinished, horses ran at a gallop through the streets, and everywhere were piled goods for construction: abandoned timber and barrels, loose shingles, bricks, and mounds of shale and stone rubble.

"Our frenetic industry can shock a visitor," said Storrow.

Abbott Lawrence started at the noise of an explosion; masons were blasting the last few ledges above the dam. "I entertain no doubts upon that subject," he said.

The wooden sidewalk in front of the hotel came to an end. Spread in front of Mr. Lawrence, and barring his way to the door he wished to enter, was a stinking sea of mud. "If our engineers can dam a river, our investors should not hesitate to bridge a mere swamp," he said, laughing at his own timidity

The Coburn House was three stories high and made of brick, with a mansard roof and gabled windows that added another story. Extending from the building and running for some distance along Common Street was an attached structure, comprising a stable on the ground floor and a gallery above. Three liverymen dressed in ulsters were standing at an outdoor bar, which was nothing more than a porthole on the side of the building. They laughed at the sight of Abbott Lawrence tiptoeing along, attempting in vain to preserve his boots. One of the men downed a yard of ale and cried out, heaving his tankard through the porthole.

"Is it the smell of so much manure that bothers you?" he asked, while his companions roared. The liveryman unbuttoned his trousers and sent a stream of urine onto Common Street. "Here, then. Here's some rosewater."

In the midst of their laughter, Mr. Lawrence's face grew tight and his small, smooth hands reddened into fists. "These men are brigands," he said. "Their employment with the Essex Company should be brought to its conclusion."

Storrow pre-empted his companion by thrusting an arm across the older man's chest. "They do not work for us, Abbott, but for one of the many livery companies delivering goods to the New City," he said. "Their conduct and their illegal beer are just two of the urges we are not free to control. Between our plots of land and company egresses lies an abundance of free space, and free men walk on it."

The strongbox, containing a month's wages for employees of the Essex Company as well as the quarterly payment for dam builders Gilmore & Carpenter, was carried from the omnibus by the driver and another man and loaded onto a wooden dolly. Two constables appeared, dismissing the driver and his man, and they wheeled the dolly into the Coburn House while Abbott Lawrence and Charles Storrow followed behind.

"How long will you be staying in the New City?" Storrow asked his employer.

"Today and tomorrow: the span of time that will empty my heart of family joy and command me to fill it again. Besides, Tuesday-week I must be in Washington to assist Old Zach in his preparation for the presidency."

Storrow shook his head. "All that for Mr. Taylor, after you have been so put upon? Why, Abbott, to give Millard Fillmore the seat of Vice President was passing it to the second-best man."

"To lose by a single vote was God's will," said Lawrence. "It reminds me that I am a man of commerce, who can do his good works by employing the men of this valley." He paused a moment at the entrance, scuffing his boots upon the doormat. "Why, Amos says it's all for the better. *Place* cannot impart *grace*, in my brother's estimation."

The interior walls of the Coburn House were covered with horsehair plaster and smelled of fresh paint. The dowdy little proprietor, T. J. Coburn, who wore a wig and suffered from coughing fits, popped through the door of his apartment. "Will you's be staying long, milord?" he asked, bowing to one knee.

"Up, fellow," said Mr. Lawrence, with a chortle. "The king has been banished these seventy-five year and his court along with him. I am an American."

"Sorry, milord," said the innkeeper. "I meant no offense."

"And there was none taken," Lawrence said. "Here in the New City it is my wish that men will not be wounded by words, and may labor together toward a plentiful future."

"If that be God's will," said Storrow.

"That is correct, Charles. For it was through God's will alone that an ocean was parted, and a tribe of outcasts was delivered into a land flowing with milk and honey. Doubts there were, and doubts there shall be, but men of faith will persevere."

T. J. Coburn listened to this sermon with his eyes turned up and a hand placed over his heart. "Amen, milord," he said. "I couldn't have said it better me-self."

The innkeeper led his visitors down a flight of stairs into the cellar. The constables pushed the strongbox along to a hole in the floor, and then down the ladder into a makeshift vault while the two burghers and T. J. Coburn lingered above. Storrow and Lawrence regarded each other

Jay Atkinson

over this chasm while the innkeeper crouched at its foot, his hand raised in benediction. A moment later, Coburn descended into the vault, carrying a taper lit from one of the torches along the wall.

Abbott Lawrence smiled at his chief engineer. "All your hard work is coming to fruition, Charles," he said. "A mill dam like no other in the world; a canal with more horsepower over a mile's length than the canals of Lowell deliver in three; a city containing enough labor to occupy ten thousand men; clean living quarters, churches, schools, and commons; and tomorrow's capstone, which is God's signifier. Yet surrounded with all these blessings, you seem mournful."

"The diseased tooth colors my sensations," said Mr. Storrow. "It is a mortal reminder."

"To be happy on this earth, that is as much God's reminder as any other."

The tread of the constables sounded on the ladder, followed by a halo of light and the innkeeper, raising his candle like a talisman. When they were all reunited on the planks, one of the constables swung the trap shut and fixed it with an iron padlock. He dragged a chair over the trap door and then the constable, a large, sturdy man with two pistols in his belt, sat upon it. The other constable, likewise armed, positioned himself at the end of the corridor.

"Will you be joining us for supper, milords?" Coburn asked.

"Mr. Lawrence and I will be dining at a temperance saloon," said Mr. Storrow, twitching his whiskers. "We do not approve of spirituous liquors."

"Nor do I, milord."

Arms folded, the principals of the Essex Company glowered at the innkeeper.

"We approve even less of duplicity," Lawrence said.

"There are no spirituous liquors on these premises, milord," said Coburn, bowing again.

"Up, man," said Lawrence. "Ask God for His forgiveness, for it is spirituous liquors that your stable man is dispensing along with his Hobson's choice. This is a violation of the covenant inked above your signature on the deed to this establishment. Best you remedy the situation, or see that deed revoked."

Trembling from head to foot, Coburn stopped himself in the midst of another bow. Clicking his heels together, he said, "I shall see to it, milord. And your quarters along the second story gallery shall be prepared to your liking."

"See to the abolishment of the liquor," said Lawrence. "A monk has his cell, and an Indian has but the stars for his roof. Neither takes libation, and both are said to be content. Only in like circumstances shall I be satisfied in your house."

"Is there nothing I can fetch for you, milord?"

"I ask only for a basin of clean water and a pair of dumbbells for my exercise," Lawrence said.

"I will get them immediately, milord," said the innkeeper, bowing once more.

Something about the man's impertinence irritated Lawrence. "And take off that confounded wig," he said. "It is an emblem of conceit and a badge of foolish pride."

"Yes, milord." Coburn snatched the wig from his head, which was shaped like an egg and contained only a few hairs. "I am a vain man, milord."

"All is vanity," said Lawrence.

The musty smell of powder hung in the air. "I will study on that, milord," the innkeeper said.

Lawrence and his engineer retired to the sidewalk out front. "In my prayers I must ask God for strength in these matters of supervision," Lawrence said. "For He says, 'Judge not, lest ye be judged,' and reminds us of our place."

"Our settlement will be cursed if we do not grow up a sober, temperate, industrious, and order-loving people," said Storrow.

Hands on hips, Abbott Lawrence regarded the hurly-burly of carts and men passing along Broadway. "Let's see about that tooth," he said. "For every New City must include a surgeon. Only then will you regain your good cheer."

"We have iron workers, fullers, sawyers, stone masons, carpenters, mill workers, a lawyer, a newspaperman, a minister, and recently, I noted in my journal the arrival of our first undertaker," said Mr. Storrow. "But no surgeon."

"Is there not a barber?"

"There is a colored man named Levy. His establishment is farther along Broadway."

"My father, God rest his soul, took especial pains to show kindness to the darker race. If there is no surgeon, a colored barber will do just as well. Let us go in search of his pole," said Mr. Lawrence. The two men stamped over the sidewalk into the muddy thoroughfare. "Remember, Charles, we must educate and elevate foreign emigrants or they will ruin our establishment. The health and wealth of a country is founded upon its labor."

"My tooth can wait," said Storrow. "First you must see the dam and the just-completed gatehouse for the canal."

"The barber's pole symbolizes blood and bandages, does it not? The application of which will help you shake off this gloom." Lawrence winked at his engineer. "Will your dam not keep for an hour?"

"It is my belief it will keep a fair bit longer," said Mr. Storrow.

"Let us make haste, then, for I have been traveling all day and will be wanting my supper," said Lawrence. He gestured for Storrow to open his mouth. "Let me see the tooth."

"It will offend you," said his companion.

Mr. Lawrence repeated his gesture. "Not nearly so much as it is offending you," he said.

Storrow removed his hat and tilted his head toward the sun. The tooth gave off an unpleasant odor. It was riven nearly in two, fixed in the

Jay Atkinson

engineer's lower jaw by puffy white flesh.

"Ugh," said Lawrence. "That certainly must come out."

Among the cooper shops, tanneries, and forges that had sprung up along Broadway was a narrow brick building divided into shops on the ground floor. To one side was a glass blower, and through the entranceway on the right was a card that read *John Levy, Barber*. Below that, in smaller script, was written *foul teeth extracted*. A newspaper occupied the floor above the barbershop and the thump of its printing press could be heard through the ceiling.

"Relief is at hand," said Lawrence, pulling open the door.

The barbershop was redolent of wintergreen oil and camphor. The two visitors were greeted inside by a strapping, mahogany-colored man whose pate was encircled by a ring of woolly white hair. John Levy was in his sixtieth year, a supple-limbed fellow dressed in a barber's gown, a pair of canvas leggings and yellow horsehide slippers. In the center of the room was a straight-backed chair and folded open there was a copy of the *Weekly Tribune*, which offered four pages of advertisements and a smattering of local news. Circled in pencil was a drawing of the Moorish barber and his chair.

John Levy flashed his large white teeth. "Which gentleman is it?" he asked in the musical tone of the West Indies.

"It is this fellow," said Abbott Lawrence, steering his engineer into the chair. "Mr. Storrow has developed an abscess which poisons his disposition and casts gloom over his accomplishments. We call upon you to resolve it, my good man."

"At the moment my tooth does not trouble me," said Storrow. "Merely arriving in this establishment has affected a remedy."

"Nonsense, Charles," Lawrence said. "The good Lord says we must exert ourselves to eradicate sin, and this foul tooth is sinning against your health and good temperament. It must come out."

Several vials and jars, and a few small iron tools that had been dipped in iodine lay on a nearby bench. The barber stood beside this arsenal, waiting to come forward. Turning his hat in his hands, Storrow cast his gaze in that direction and shook his head. "No," he said. "Perhaps tomorrow."

"You must do it, Charles," said Lawrence.

A sigh escaped from the engineer. Resigning himself, Mr. Storrow sat down, gripping the arms of the chair with his head thrust back. "On with it, then," he said.

"No need to worry yourself, sir," Levy said.

The barber removed a bottle from the pocket of his gown and pulled the stopper. Shaking into his hand several splinters of wood contained there, he lit a candle that was jerry-built to a flat piece of metal. Levy raised the candle to his patient, throwing V's of shadow beneath Storrow's brow. "Open, sir," said Levy.

Storrow pried apart his teeth. "I see it," said the barber.

With nimbleness belying his ample frame, John Levy took four splinters of wood and pierced the flesh surrounding the diseased molar.

They stuck out from the corners of the tooth, brushing the roof of Storrow's mouth. Immediately a cool sensation spread throughout the man's jawbone, eliminating all traces of pain. For the first time in many days the gloom lifted from him, and he was inclined to order a supply of splinters from the barber and forgo the surgery.

"Aarrghh-a-woo," Mr. Storrow said.

"I know, sir. It doesn't hurt anymore," the Negro said. "That's just the balm working upon your humor." Dipping his fingertips into one of the vials, Levy again reached into the open mouth and spun the twigs that penetrated Storrow's gums. A new feeling, of numbness this time, prevailed upon the injury. The barber removed his twigs and, raising the candle in one hand, reached into Storrow's mouth with a small clamp fastened to a polished iron rod, fitting it over the tooth.

"Uurrg-wharr-horr," said Storrow.

"Is he all right?" asked Mr. Lawrence.

"In a moment he will be, sir," the barber said. He braced his knee on Storrow's chest and flexed his wrist upward. There was a liquid popping sound. The engineer felt the roots of the tooth give way and his mouth filled up with blood.

"There," said Levy. "It is out."

Hanging from his clamp was Storrow's tooth, the twinned yellow root more than half an inch long and its head crumbled by the pressure of the extraction. The barber laid aside the tooth and his candle, raising a pail to the engineer's chin. "Here, sir," he said. A stream of blood gushed into the pail.

"Staunch the flow, man," said Lawrence. "That is a dangerous amount of bloodletting."

Levy did not reply. He dunked a wad of batting into yet another jar and applied it with force to the canker. "Hold it steady, sir," he said to Mr. Lawrence, pressing the financier into service.

"Most extraordinary," said Lawrence.

Running a thread through the eye of a needle and tying it off, the barber asked Mr. Lawrence to step aside and then removed the batting from Storrow's mouth and sewed the wound shut. Again he instructed Storrow to use the pail and handed him a bottle with the legend *Bessell Patent Medicine* printed on its label.

"Drink this," the barber said.

"Isth thith spirituouth liquoth?" asked Storrow.

But Levy was adamant. "I am prescribing a medicine, and since medicines by their very nature contain potents and spirits, you shall either violate your ban or suffer the pains that are soon scheduled to return." The barber looked at his patient. "It is not much of a choice, sir."

"His reasoning is irrefutable, Charles," said Lawrence.

"How muth shath I dranth?" Mr. Storrow asked.

"The contents of the vial," said the Negro.

Storrow's jaw began to throb again, and he held it in his hand and groaned.

Jay Atkinson

"Take the spirit," said Mr. Lawrence. "It appears to be the weaker of two evils."

Storrow drank from the bottle and then lolled in the chair, groaning.

"You speak very well for a colored man," said Abbott Lawrence. "Were you not once a slave? And have you been a barber all your life?"

"When I landed in this country, I first became a waiter at Harvard College, was employed as a steamboat operator by Captain Jake Vanderbilt, and for two-year was hand nurse to Governor John Jay, who signed the treaty with England in '94. The art of barbering I learned at sea."

"Harvard College must be where you learned to speak so eloquently," said Lawrence. "Mr. Storrow here is a graduate of Harvard. First in his class in '29."

"I remember seeing him there. I also knew your father, sir," the barber said to Abbott Lawrence. "I was present when the cornerstone was laid for the Bunker Hill monument, and Mssr. Samuel Lawrence and I spoke on that occasion."

Samuel Lawrence, the Groton farmer who had sired Amos and Abbott and five other children, was a Revolutionary War hero. On June 17, 1775, he and his band of irregulars joined Captain Farrell's militia for the onslaught upon Breed's Hill. During the battle, Sam Lawrence was wounded in the arm with British grapeshot and another musket ball parted his hair and rent his beaverskin hat in two. He lived another fifty years, and was in attendance that day when the battle was memorialized with a granite obelisk.

"Oh, charming fellow," said Lawrence. "You once spoke with my father?"

The barber wagged his head. "I had some few words with him," he said.

"And what did he tell you?"

"It was but a brief conversation, but the gist of his speech was that the battle had shown him God's light. Which in turn illuminated the way to Susanna Parker, who would become his wife and bear his children."

"Father told me that Captain Farrell had enjoyed such a revelation himself upon being shot through the body and grievously wounded," Lawrence said. "In fact, his men thought he were dead until Farrell cried out, 'It ain't true; don't let my poor wife hear of this; I shall live to see my country free.' And so they both did, those two good men."

"A free country is certainly worth the price of a musket ball," said John Levy. Then he smiled with dazzling teeth, and excused himself to empty the pail of blood.

Abbott Lawrence dropped onto a bench and began stroking his chin with his gaze fixed upon the floor. Old Sam Lawrence had been dead some twenty years, passed into memory and vanished from sight. His legacy was a fee simple of bounteous land and equal good sense, and to date those gifts had been more than adequate to remember him by. Now the recollections of this dusky barber had conjured Samuel Lawrence from the nether world once more, younger than his son had known him, in his beaver hat and armed with a musket.

Charles Storrow nipped at the patent medicine; the pain departed and he felt a certain giddiness. Feeling the gap between his teeth, he asked, "Arth thee all righth, Abbotth?"

"Yes, Charles," Mr. Lawrence said. "I was just reflecting on how people from a distant time were people same as we are, and how a colored man might deliver a whole city. For through your barber's reasoning our plans for a society guided by God and temperance are proven right. We shall not cancel our covenants."

Storrow gained his feet, swaying with the empty bottle in one hand and the other gripping his chair. "Agreeth," he said. "Ith Goth's will."

When Levy returned, Mr. Storrow paid for the extraction and another bottle of medicine with a silver dollar.

"Let us dine then, Charles, and look over our covenants," said Lawrence. "And then we can view your dam, like two pilgrims visiting the pyramids at El Gizeh."

"Yeth," said Mr. Storrow, staggering toward the exit. "I am famisthed."

After crimping the dollar with his powerful teeth, John Levy flung open the door to his shop. "Nothing but lemonade and oysters for you, sir," he said to Storrow. "The oysters will slide down your throat without the necessity of chewing them, and the lemon extract will tighten your wound. And no lying down for several hours. Let Newton's law act upon your blood, or you will find it running again."

"Where can we find oysters in the New City?" asked Lawrence. "A mess of these sea creatures and a hank of broiled cod is a meal I have not once enjoyed in Washington."

"The Temperance Oyster and Victualing Saloon at the foot of Essex Street will fill that bill," said Levy. He retrieved his newspaper and handed it to Abbott Lawrence. "You will find a notice here. I suggest taking a hackney coach, seeing as Mr. Storrow has lost so much blood."

"Sage advice," said Lawrence. "Would you care to join us?"

"No thank you, sir. I eat only beefsteak and drink my own small beer, which makes me sanguine."

"Is there not a moral covenant on this building?" asked Mr. Lawrence.

"There is one to the left and right, but none attached to this structure," Levy said. "It is deeded to its original owner, Mr. Erasmus Johnson, who, believing that an occasional small dram of spirits will bring good health, allows his tenants free reign."

"Such thinking can be dangerous," said Lawrence.

"Every man should think for himself," Levy said. "In my humble opinion, sir, a company should provide ample work and a clean space to do it in, and leave God to the rest."

The financier wrinkled his brow. "God bless us all," he said. "Come, Charles. Let us depart."

The two men left the barber's shop and tramped to the corner of Broadway and Essex Street in silence. Abbott Lawrence was reflecting

Jay Atkinson

on the boldness of the Negro and his remarks. It was true that A & A Lawrence ascribed to a brand of corporate paternalism: first in their endeavors at Lowell, then in Manchester with the Amoskeag Company, and now here in the valley. After all, men who were absorbed by the present moment, laboring in pits of grime and clouds of dust, could not be expected to navigate by God's light. In preparing their New City on the Merrimack, the Lawrence brothers and Charles Storrow had also roughed out a moral plan for its inhabitants. But despite their efforts to the contrary, Abbott imagined that all sorts of Bessells and Levys and Coburns were lurking in the shadows.

Charles Storrow was thinking about his father. Whereas Abbott and Amos Lawrence were descendant from an American war hero, his own *paterfamilias,* Captain Thomas Wentworth Storrow, was commander of His Majesty's First Regiment of Foot during the rebellion, and later a prisoner of war. After being emancipated, it was Captain Storrow's good fortune to meet and marry Sarah Phipps Brown, the daughter of a prosperous Boston merchant. Thomas Storrow settled into his father-in-law's employ, although he never lost his powdered wig, his Tory sympathies, or the stiffness in his back garnered from the Sudbury gaol.

His son Charles was born in Montreal during a sojourn in that city, and thereafter the Storrows sailed for France, where the children began their matriculation and learned the language. Later, Charles continued his education at Round Hill School in Northampton, Massachusetts, and then at Harvard College under the tutelage of Laommi Baldwin, the famous engineer. Baldwin encouraged the young Storrow to return to Paris and enroll as an *élève étranger* at the École Nationale des Ponts et Chaussées. With financial support from the Lawrence brothers, Charles spent two years in Europe, studying French-style mathematics, as well as the Roman aqueducts and quays that had been built along the Seine. Assisted by an additional five hundred dollars from his patron Amos Lawrence, young Storrow journeyed to Manchester, England to behold for himself the industrial revolution.

"One may study anywhere and everywhere," Professeur Baldwin wrote to him. "But public works are to be seen only in a few places."

With this Great Dam upon the river, the power canal, mill buildings, and his plan for a New City, Charles Storrow had combined the best of Old World engineering with typical American brashness and wherewithal. But for all his journeying, he never traveled beyond the regions of his childhood. Limping along Essex Street with his jaw pounding and no passenger coaches in sight, what rang out in Storrow's memory were the taunts of his Round Hill schoolmates, calling him Tory and traitor and mimicking the precision of his French.

Essex Street ran northwest for two thousand feet parallel to the canal, then made a twenty degree bend to the south and ran due west for an additional two thousand feet to Jackson Street. It was broad and flat, graded at considerable expense over quartzite ledges and bogs and, in its lower half, marshy sloughs that branched off the Spicket River as it joined the canal. Arranged on both sides of the street were several empty lots marked with wooden stakes and piles of fieldstone. Storrow envisioned Essex Street as a prominent thoroughfare, and had seen that Boston's most successful haberdashers, furriers, milliners, and tack shops were invited to open branches there.

Stopping in front of a building with painted windows, Abbott Lawrence unslung the newspaper that Levy had given them and donned his spectacles. The magnified type of an advertisement jumped at him:

TEMPERANCE OYSTER & VICTUALING SALOON
Meals furnished from 6 AM to 10 PM. Pies, cakes & hot coffee. The best New York oysters constantly on hand & served up to the taste of the customer. Prices in all cases moderate. Please call & see.

The name in the advertisement corresponded with that etched in the window glass, and the scent of broiling fish wafted through the doorway. Inside, several men crowded around a trough where the proprietor, dressed in a rubber apron, tended to his oysters with a short-handled rake. Nearby, another man was turning fillets on a brazier, his figure illuminated by the coals.

"This looks capital," said Mr. Lawrence, patting his stomach. "What do you say, Charles?"

Storrow had taken advantage of this respite to hail a wagon that had been passing on Jackson Street. Avoiding several piles of manure that lay in the roadway, he unhooked a bucket hanging from the tailgate and saluted the driver, an employee of the Essex Company. With a shaking hand, Storrow raised the dipper to his lips and swallowed some water, then doused his face and neck. "I have very little appetite at present," the engineer said.

"Come, Charles," said Lawrence, thrusting the newspaper back into his pocket.

The financier assisted his employee through the door. A group of respectable-looking men attired in frock coats ringed the oyster trough. Most of the clientele in the saloon were agents and fiduciaries; the traveling delegates of companies who did business in the New City, or wished to establish an office there.

Abbott Lawrence helped his engineer into one of the leather-lined chairs. Emitting another groan, Mr. Storrow reached into his pocket and withdrew the patent medicine.

"Careful, Charles," said Lawrence. "Too much cure is worse than none at all."

"The tonic is the only thing which soothes my discomfort," Storrow said. Uncorking the bottle, he took a long draught.

Two men wearing dusty field coats and top hats approached the table. "Good afternoon, Mr. Lawrence," said the larger chap, who had scraggly chin whiskers and a bulbous nose. He removed his hat and bowed, indicating the portly, red-faced man beside him. "Allow me to present

Jay Atkinson

myself, and my associate. I am Mr. Carpenter and this is Mr. Gilmore, of Gilmore & Carpenter, General Contractors to the Essex Company for the purpose of building the Great Dam and its canal."

"I am charmed, gentlemen," Lawrence said. "You are, of course, both acquainted with my chief engineer, Charles Storrow."

"We've never had the pleasure, sir," said Gilmore, pushing himself forward. He was a squat fellow who wore his hat indoors and sported a pair of side whiskers. "This is a happy coincidence, for it was our intention to address you both tomorrow at the capstone ceremony."

"A great day, indeed, where the planning of Mr. Storrow will be crowned by the fruits of your industry," Lawrence said. "But I am afraid my companion is feeling rather ill at present."

"We apologize, then, for disturbing you," said Carpenter, glancing at his partner.

"Not at all, my dear sirs," Lawrence said, placing his hand on the elbow of Mr. Carpenter. "Accompany me to the buffet, while allowing Mr. Storrow to conserve his strength. We have many topics to discuss and deliberate."

"Indeed," said the hat-wearing Mr. Gilmore. "Why we have waited three extra days for this month's payment, that is the sole topic I should like to discuss."

Frowning at him, Abbott Lawrence said, "Money is one subject I never broach in a public house, except to guarantee that full payment plus any interest will soon be yours. But we are tiring Mr. Storrow, as I mentioned."

"We hope your spirits improve, sir," said Mr. Carpenter, as he was being led away.

His stomach rumbling, Abbott Lawrence drew near to the fish trough, assisted by the impolitic wheedling of Mssrs. Carpenter and Gilmore. Employing the width of their shoulders, they positioned Mr. Lawrence front and center, where he had a commanding view of the halibuts, cods, blue-skinned mackerels, and row upon row of oysters, laying edgewise on a blanket of ice.

"Give way, sir," said Gilmore, using his elbow to drive off an oxen trader.

The merchant resisted, shoving his paunch back at Mr. Gilmore. "My, you are a pushy fellow," he said. "Deserving of a wallop, I should think."

"Please, my dear sir," said Carpenter. "Allow Mr. Abbott Lawrence to select his dinner."

At the mention of the financier's name, a murmur arose that spread to the nearby tables. The proprietor smiled, doffing his cap. "Mr. Lawrence: we boast the finest of smelts, clams, mussels, and hake, in addition to all that you see here, fresh from the briny deep of the North Atlantic. At your service."

Lawrence bent over the trough, examining the be-shelled and scaly creatures heaped upon the ice, as well as a brace of dead lobsters. Curious at the sight of an actual millionaire, and what a millionaire might choose to eat, the other customers pressed in around him.

"Get back, you rude fellows," said Mr. Carpenter. "This man is a patron to you all, yet you jostle him as if he were a mere fishmonger."

The proprietor reddened at this. "Mongering fish is as honest a labor as piling stones upon one another, or digging trenches in the ground," he said.

"I am fine, gentlemen," said the financier, putting up his hands. "And let me also remind you that every man who labors does so for God's patronage and not for mine." His eyes met those of the proprietor, and he pointed to the lank body of a cod nestled among the ice. "If you please, sir; a fillet of cod, broiled sans the head, and two dozen boiled oysters will suit Mr. Storrow and me."

The largest, fleshiest oysters were piled in a kettle and doused with seawater, which was then placed on the brazier. Other items were thrust aside and the force of a bellows was applied to the coals, which burned twice as brightly.

"Gentlemen, I must attend to Mr. Storrow," said the financier to Mssrs. Gilmore and Carpenter. "I trust ye shall have a hearty luncheon, and after a fair night's sleep, we'll greet each other again."

Casting a glance toward Lawrence's table, which contained only two diners but would accommodate twice that number, Mr. Carpenter smoothed his chin whiskers and said, "My associate and I had hoped to discuss some further business with you, as tomorrow the Great Dam will be completed."

"And in less than a month, our carpenters and masons will be forced to quit the New City," said Mr. Gilmore.

Lawrence fixed his gaze on the two contractors. "I never conduct business while dining."

"Of course, sir. My associate and I meant no harm in the suggestion," said Carpenter, bowing to Mr. Lawrence while Gilmore continued to block his passage. "If I may choose a seafaring analogy, we mean only that ships' captains are a lonely breed, and sometimes their sole opportunity to discuss the laws of navigation come at a tavern keeper's table."

"Felicitously expressed, my good fellow," said Lawrence. "But now that your work here is almost completed, the channel for our Essex Company lies straight ahead and quite narrow. We must tend to our New City—if you will pardon my shift to *terra firma*—like a farmer tends his fields; growing up businesses to fill our squares, providing nourishment to the workmen and their families, and most important of all, remaining vigilant against the sloth and drunkenness that would choke our enterprise like weeds."

Mr. Gilmore obstructed the aisle, touching his finger to Abbott Lawrence's coat button. "Allow me to communicate one significant piece of information," he said. "Our provision men, who range far and wide to secure all manner of goods, have visited a site upon this same river in the village of Amesbury. An inlet and high falls are located there, which house only a farmer's crude waterwheel. It is but half a day's journey—perhaps we could visit this site together with the intention of establishing another New City."

"Have you the capital for such a venture?" asked Lawrence, the mirth around his eyes hardening into displeasure. "Have you conducted surveys on this land, or calculated the length of a millpond and its possible effect on our endeavors here at Bodwell's Falls?"

Gilmore shook his head. "We barely manage to meet our payroll, and have speculated in Amesbury only so far that a new project might employ our men for another definite term," he said.

"Any dispossessed hirelings of Gilmore & Carpenter will find employment in Essex Company building projects, and in the mills of our New City," said Lawrence.

Gilmore stabbed at the financier's coat button. "We must hatch a plot that includes the future, sir."

"As should every company, and every man, as far as they are able to," said Lawrence, removing Mr. Gilmore's finger. "But we would be doing the Essex Company a disservice if we were to scramble along the banks of the Merrimack before making firm our establishment here at Bodwell's Falls." The financier reached up and tugged on his lapels. "So I wish you good day, sirs."

The two contractors stood in the aisle, turning to watch Lawrence move off between the tables. A coal dealer seated nearby raised his mug of ginger beer and snickered. Glaring at him and the other eavesdroppers who surrounded them, Mr. Gilmore kicked a stray oyster shell along the floor and then, without another word, he and his associate quit the premises.

Charles Storrow greeted the arrival of his patron with a flamboyant gesture. "If I were a prince of Araby, I would order my harem girls to bring you vessels of sherbet. Instead, I offer you a packet of tea and the stench of old clam shells. Such is our modern predicament."

Lawrence was aghast; he drew up his chair to the wounded engineer and looked at him. Storrow's pupils were enlarged and the flesh of his face, where it was visible above the whiskers, hung slack upon its framework of bone.

"Give me the tonic," said the financier. "For the effects seem to have passed on from your abscessed tooth to the pits of your brain."

The empty bottle clattered onto the floor. "I am now the reservoir of its contents," said Storrow. "And so my tooth is gone and forgotten; it twinges only upon the application of the lemonade." With his finger, he referred to a pulpy glass upon the table.

Lawrence glanced around the saloon, then directed his gaze back to the engineer. "Are your legs steady beneath you?" he asked. "Perhaps it would be best if we retired to my hotel."

Storrow squeezed himself above the knees. "At present, I cannot control my limbs," he said with detachment. "But the pain has fled, replaced by a mysterious sense of truth which inhabits me."

Deciding it was better to remain seated, Mr. Lawrence leaned closer. "What is this truth?" he asked.

"That we are all going to die, and that our dams and canals and even our children die with us."

Just then, the proprietor approached the table. He laid two platters in front of Abbott Lawrence: the steaming oysters on one of them, and the other with the broiled cod, its mouth parted, the cloudy eye aimed at the ceiling. Sensing a private conference, the saloon keeper backed away but Lawrence reached out and seized him by the wrist.

"I ordered this fish cooked and served without the head," said the millionaire.

Mumbling his regrets, the saloon keeper attempted to clear both platters from the table.

"What are you doing, man?" asked Lawrence, still holding him. "Leave the oysters while you rectify the error, or my companion and I might die of starvation."

The proprietor slid the tray of shellfish back onto the table. "My apologies, sir," he said. "I feel it is my own head what's been cut off."

"Blast you," said Lawrence, releasing the man's wrist. When the saloon keeper hurried away, he said, "Idiots and bumpkins will never operate a city."

"When you realize the truth, Abbott, fishmongers and contractors and every sum we've calculated on every scrap of paper all lose their significance," Storrow said, prying open an oyster shell. "The fiery-headed worm consumes them all."

"Blast your truth. It is merely the voice of that patent medicine which animates you," said Lawrence, dashing his oysters with black pepper. "Here. You must eat something," he said, shelling two of the mollusks and placing their plump, viscous bodies on the tea saucer.

Storrow looked upon the oysters with a cockeyed gaze. "How such a creature should travel from the deeps of Nantucket Sound to fuel my muscles is the riddle of the Sphinx," he said. "What silty currents, what arm of man has delivered them to me? The Fates are no more strange. Transactions of celestial mathematics, the march of Roman legions, barges missed and trains that didn't run on time, all have conspired to deposit me in this chair, lolling like an oyster."

"You are melancholy, Charles."

Shaking his head, Storrow said, "I have traveled to the edge of unlimited joy and found myself a stranger there. I would tear down our Great Dam stone by stone and let streams of this joy pour out, if only I had the mechanism."

The saloon keeper returned with his headless cod and then stood by Lawrence's chair, waiting for remuneration. "Less than a dollar has stopped this fellow from thinking," said the proprietor. "Money will do that; a little for some, a little bit more for the rest. For my part, fill a basket with silver and I will murder you an ocean of fish."

"Spare me your philosophy, sir," said Lawrence. He retrieved a banknote from his pocket and flung it on the table.

"That's very generous of you, sir," said the saloon keeper. "A cod's ransom."

Lawrence shooed the fishmonger away and reached for another oyster. He cracked open the shell and held it by the loose, scrawny neck.

"Some men are not worth listening to," said the financier, intent on his meal.

"If these oysters could speak, they might agree," Storrow said.

Lawrence chewed and swallowed his morsel. "Bah," he said.

For several minutes, no one looked in Abbott Lawrence's direction. Then a new patron entered the saloon: a man in knee-length breeches and a tarpaulin shirt, his arms streaked with printer's ink. Upon his head was a small, round hat with a turned-up brim, and he wore a pair of workman's boots and red tartan stockings. Several diners called out to this Mr. Hayes, inquiring on both his health and the latest news. The sound of coppers fell against a dozen tabletops; the pennies exchanged for newspapers that Hayes carried in a satchel beneath his arm.

Conferring for a moment with the proprietor, Hayes turned his gaze on Abbott Lawrence. The newspaperman had a thin mouth spread over by jet black mustaches and a pair of eyebrows drawn sharply on his pallid skull. Laying aside his papers for the moment, and drawing forth a tablet and pencil, Mr. Hayes approached the table of honor.

"Mr. Lawrence, I presume?" he asked, touching the brim of his hat with the pencil.

"You are nothing if not presumptuous, sir," said Lawrence. Eager to continue his dinner, the financier did not so much as glance upward.

"I wish to ask you a few questions, sir," Hayes said.

"Indeed. Who are you?"

"I am J. F. C. Hayes, sole owner, publisher, editor, reporter, and advertising salesman for the *Weekly Tribune*," said the man, with a distinct Scottish burr. "And might I add that the recipe for a successful newspaper calls for a dash of presumption. Not to mention ample doses of luck and more than a pinch of boldness."

"I have little understanding of newspapers," Lawrence said.

Hayes indicated the paper that extended from Lawrence's coat pocket. "As you have fed on the early edition, so others will feast on the scraps you'll provide for the later ones. Why should you cram yourself into the narrow columns of the Boston papers when I have a full broadsheet you may lounge across?"

Lawrence glanced about him at the traders and masonry agents and waiters who, if they were not leaning to process his conversation, were engrossed in the pages of the *Weekly Tribune*. "I will grant you a brief interview," he said. "It may encourage our efforts to publicize all that God has accomplished here in the New City."

Hayes seated himself. "I understand that Mr. Storrow has today undergone surgery, and lost a great deal of blood. Do you care to comment on that, Mr. Storrow?"

"That item has no redeeming social value," said Lawrence. "Mr. Storrow and I refuse comment."

"You need not comment, as the bucket I detected behind my establishment spoke volumes."

Hayes reached into his pocket for a handkerchief; thrusting the cloth forward, he uncovered a human tooth. It emitted a rotten odor, and bore the imprint of an extraction. Without saying a word, Charles Storrow parted his lips to reveal the corresponding gap along his jawbone.

"Remove that foul object from these premises," said Lawrence.

Hayes folded up the handkerchief and replaced it in his pocket. "A man retains something in his body and demands respect for it as part of himself, but no sooner does it leave him, that he curses its foulness. I suppose the same could be said for the body politic: even the most revered candidates are later expunged. Thus a man short of votes is reduced to a dung heap."

"Do not tempt my patience, Mr. Hayes," said Lawrence. "Or tomorrow you might find yourself with a new landlord and a foreshortened lease."

The newspaperman began writing again. Throughout the tavern, the only sound was the scratching of his pencil. "What puzzles me, is why this sort of resolve had no effect on your efforts to secure the Vice Presidency," he said. "In any event, is it not accurate that you are several days in arrears for the final payment to your dam contractors? And are you so strapped for cash, as my sources have informed me, that a twin venture proposed for Amesbury Village is beyond the reach of your Boston Associates?"

"You are a disagreeable fellow," said Lawrence. "If you do not quit the premises, I shall summon our constables and have you thrown out on your ear."

Stooping for a moment, Hayes retrieved the newspaper from beneath the table and smoothed its pages. "Since at least two good men have read what is printed here, you should have no qualm if I seek another penny for my efforts," he said, adding the paper to his satchel. "I wish good day to you, sirs, and an equally good night, as it must be difficult sleeping with so many dubious affairs weighing upon your conscience."

Mr. Hayes strode away toward the rear of the saloon, pausing at three or four tables to sell his newspapers. One gentleman offered him a grilled lobster tail, which he speared with the point of his pencil. Hoisting the tidbit into the air, Hayes said something under his breath, and he and the other man glanced at Abbott Lawrence, stifling their laughter. Then, tipping his hat to the proprietor, J. F. C. Hayes crashed his teeth into the lobster and disappeared through the exit.

"The editor of such a periodical would wear his soiled drawers for a hat if it would cause a sensation," said Abbott Lawrence.

"I believe Mr. Hayes would prefer our soiled drawers to his own," Storrow said.

After downing three more oysters, Lawrence felt a twist in his guts. He inquired about the privy, following a waiter's direction toward the rear of the saloon. Entering the hallway, he passed through a storeroom filled with a number of crates and soggy casks. A rank sea odor permeated this space, and extending from one of the crates, Lawrence could see a pair of claws grasping at the sawdust. He pushed on the outer door, barging it open to take several great draughts of what he hoped would be clean air. But the stench of the outhouse gagged him.

"Blast," said Lawrence.

Jay Atkinson

A single, muddy plank led from the saloon to a cylindrical vault. The vault had been built on a foundation of bricks, and was topped by a shack made from weathered boards and strips of tin. Several burnt matchsticks littered the entrance. Visitors to the privy lit matches to drive off the foul smell, but in such an open space the sulfur drifted away and the technique did not accomplish very much. The stench was pervasive.

The financier crossed the trembling plank, which gave him a queasy, weightless feeling. Inside the shack were two makeshift booths, suspended over the pit below. It was plain to Abbott Lawrence that not every exigency had been anticipated when the drainage system for the New City was installed. The floor of the privy lay inches deep in mud and the smell was overpowering. Covering his nose and mouth with his handkerchief, Lawrence fumbled with the door to one of the cabinets.

"Hallo, comrade. This one is occupied," said a voice. "But feel free to enter the other confessional and unburden your sins, if you be a Papist."

Lawrence glanced down and saw the tip of the man's boots. He maintained his anonymity and opened the other door. The abundance of night soil contained in the vault, stuccoed over with clamshells and the hinged backs of lobsters, rose to the level of the seat.

Lowering his trousers, Lawrence squatted over the fixture and awaited the disbursement of his guts. He had been suffering lately from dyspepsia, and, during periods of sleep, vivid nightmares; a condition for which his surgeon had prescribed "cannibal salad," a diet of raw beef and field onions. And although he still followed a regimen of strenuous exercise and meditation on the bounty that God had provided him, Lawrence feared he was creeping toward the invalid condition that had long ago afflicted his brother. Amos's mind was free to roam among the spreadsheets and tables of the Boston Associates and he maintained correspondence with a great number of friends, but suffered bouts of weakness that kept him bedridden. Nor could he enjoy connubial relations with his wife, Nancy. It was a condition that Abbott Lawrence feared more than death, or bankruptcy.

The gasp of a man's sphincter in the adjoining cabinet was followed by some satisfied groaning. Prompted by this success, Lawrence released his own manure and then noticed that the cabinet was devoid of wiping-paper. After a moment, he rapped on the other cabinet and stuck his hand beneath the wall that separated them.

"Can't help you, guv'nor," came a familiar voice. "All I have is me newspapers, and heaving one under the divider will cost you a penny." The laughter of J. F. C. Hayes echoed in the vault. "I might as well hand you a portion of mutton steak from tomorrow's dinner, or a pot of ink with which you could paint shut your hole. Why, if it was Abbott Lawrence sitting here he could pass you a stack of bank notes and you could cleanse your buttocks with the United States Treasury, as he does."

Refraining from comment, Lawrence searched in the pockets of his dropped trousers but found no copper coins there. Hearing another gasp from the neighboring cabinet, he rolled a silver dollar beneath the wall and heard it traveling over the planks toward the newspaperman.

"What's this? A sovereign, bestowed on a commoner like myself?" Again the newspaperman laughed, shoving an issue of the *Weekly Tribune* at Lawrence's feet. "Your generosity has purchased relief for us both," said Hayes. "Armed with this flimsy product of my industry and abetted by the wellspring of your own imagination, you may hereby entertain the cockles of your mind before wiping the cockles of your arse."

In the midst of a furious silence, Lawrence rent the newspaper in half and then ripped it again into quarters. His plan for a quick exit was foiled by another spasm of his intestines, and since the newspaperman was similarly affected, he maintained his crude monologue.

"Through the partition I cannot surmise which aspect of commerce brings you to the New City, or where it is you call home, but I would guess it has a more pleasant odor than this chamber we find ourselves in," said Hayes. " 'Tis rotting money you smell, and it's my intention as correspondent for the *Weekly Tribune* to spread that humus beneath the sun's light, for that is the only way to aerate the truth."

There was the rustle of paper and fabric, as the newspaperman attended to some secret business. Lawrence shuffled his feet as a signal for the monologue to continue.

"Every foundation in this camp is as rotten as the one we are sitting on; purchased with the same money Abbott Lawrence and his Whig cronies attempted to buy the Vice Presidency with," Hayes said, between the strange noises he was making. "Their reasoning is that the congressman must have his payment today, but a poor carpenter can always wait until tomorrow. If Mr. Lawrence were sharing this privy with us, the great man could stay all day and transact his affairs here, as he long ago decided that certain varieties of shite have no odor."

Lawrence grunted at this.

"You find yourself in agreement, sir," said Hayes. "Or perhaps these facts wedge against your digestion and make you uncomfortable. They do me." Another internal gasp came from his cabinet, accompanied by the rustling newspaper. "I would publish this sort of vileness to the world, if there were enough pennies in the camp to buy my papers. But the truth is very dear; my old mam taught me that. Just the ink and my press and the cost of newsprint threaten to evict me from my premises. But if next week brings about the final issue of my humble little toilet-paper, believe me, sir, it will contain the truth about this blasted Essex Company."

Lawrence tore off a page of the newspaper, emblazoned with the headline "Great Dam To Be Completed Soon," and used it to tidy himself. Fastening his trousers, the millionaire burst out of the cabinet, covering his face with a handkerchief while making for the outer door.

"Like I say, I do not know your political inclinations, sir," said Hayes, still ensconced within the booth. "But if you see a clean-shaved man

Jay Atkinson

riding on the boulevard, pull your carriage to one side and hold your nostrils together. This is Mr. Lawrence and his preferred way of doing business has a musky odor to it."

Again crossing the plank, Lawrence choked on the fresh air and entered the tavern with a long, muddy strand of newspaper attached to his boot. It dragged across the floor behind him, exciting snickers and whispered comments from the patrons scattered among the tables. Approaching his companion, Lawrence noticed the muddy paper and scraped his heel against the parquet in an effort to remove it.

"Are you finished, Charles?" asked the financier, tossing a handful of coins onto the tabletop.

"I have eaten but one oyster, and feel it paddling across an ocean of misgiving," said Storrow. He glanced up, and Lawrence noticed the dark rings beneath his eyes.

"Don't talk nonsense," said the millionaire. He picked up Storrow's top hat, brushed some lint from the crown and handed it over. "Come, Charles. There is a lot of work to be done."

A murmur arose from the tables and around the fishmonger's trough as Lawrence and Storrow departed the saloon. A surveyor wearing a pince-nez jabbed his dining companion with the point of his elbow, and both men collapsed into fits of merriment. Another fellow rose from his chair to make the sound of a cuckoo. The noise was repeated here and there until a mad chorus filled the room, and even Charles Storrow took up the cry. His face white with anger, Lawrence pressed against his colleague, steering him toward the exit. They passed through the swinging doors and trod on the boards outside, followed by shrieks of laughter.

His jaw fixed, eyes sweeping the thoroughfare from left to right, Lawrence entered the muddy cart path with a determined air while his engineer ambled along, hands in his pockets. Ahead a short distance was an Essex Company wagon, its horse munching a bag of oats tied on a pole.

"Hurry, Charles," said the financier, striding in that direction. "We must not dawdle now. Cities have fallen in the blink of an eye, and none so tenuous as this one."

The wagon was stationed outside a shed at the corner of Jackson and Essex Streets. Hanging from cords was a sign that said "Essex Company Headquarters." The shed was scheduled to be demolished at the end of the year, to make way for a compound housing the company offices, archives, drafting rooms and library.

"You there," said Lawrence, as the wagon driver exited the building.

The man doffed his cap. "Hallo, sir," he said.

"I have an errand which must be completed immediately."

The wagon driver nodded. "Yes, sir."

Using the wagon seat as a desk, the financier produced the nib of a pencil and an old lading slip and scribbled a note there. "Have you the seal, Charles?" he asked, knowing that the engineer often carried this brass instrument in his pocket.

"I do," said Mr. Storrow. "But no lump of wax to make the stamp."

Abbott Lawrence signed the note. Taking the seal from his companion, he rummaged through his pockets for a suitable material with which to create an imprint. Meanwhile, the driver mounted his horse and waited there, the reins tight in his fist. "If you please, sir, I can run inside and ask one of the clerks for a bit of wax," the man said.

"No time for that," said Lawrence.

Storrow had taken a seat in the horseless wagon and pantomimed the act of driving the car forward. "Give me your missive, Abbott, and I shall race to the goal like Helios, driving his sun across the horizon."

"Put an end to these absurdities, Charles," said the financier. He directed his attention back to the horseman. "Hold just a moment," he said. Reaching beneath the wagon, Lawrence grasped a lump of manure and, fitting paper and manure into the handpress, made an imprint. Then he handed the stinking paper to the horseman.

"Go on," Lawrence said. "Take this to the depot at full speed and give it over to Mr. Coolidge. Acquire a receipt and fetch it back to me at the gatehouse. Do you understand?"

"As well as I can, sir," said the horseman. He folded the paper, storing it in his tunic. Then, with a glance at his employers, the messenger dug his heels into the horse's belly and headed off toward the Andover Bridge.

Lawrence led Mr. Storrow back onto the cart path and around the block to Canal Street before making a reply. "That was a confidential despatch to Mr. Coolidge, and something that must be acted upon immediately—if we do not want to see our teamsters, masons, and carpenters fleeing the New City like ants doused with vinegar," he said. "It needs to be taken seriously, and as you well know, the *imprimatur* of seriousness is our company seal."

In a trench alongside the road, a boy of about seven or eight years of age ran toward them carrying a satchel of newspapers. One hand clutching his cap, he sped with all possible fury, his knees rising toward his chin. The men stood and watched him pass along the ditch and up the shallow embankment, his feet ringing across an iron footbridge, the satchel flying behind him. On the far side of the canal, the newsboy disappeared between a mechanic's shed and an adjacent stable.

"See? Already our enemies improve their network, in order to mount a campaign of infamy against us," Lawrence said. "They conspire to send all God-fearing businessmen to the poorhouse."

Both men turned at this instant and saw the boy materialize on the far bank, a quarter mile away. He scrambled down the apron, heaved his satchel of newspapers across the face of the canal, and plunged into the water. A moment later, his head appeared like a bobbin on the oily surface and he swam its width, yanked himself out, and grabbed the newspapers and ran off. "How could this poor creature tear down our dam, foul our yarning machines, and demolish our covenants?" asked Mr. Storrow. "And if a mere stripling is able to disrupt our undertaking, what can Mr. Coolidge possibly do to prevent it?"

Lawrence resumed his course toward the head gates of the canal. "My trip to the privy was an enlightening one, Charles," he said. "Entombed in the next booth was this Hayes fellow, who, unable to recognize me, mused aloud on the subject of printing detestable rumors about the Essex Company in that wretched newspaper of his."

"What sort of rumors?" asked Storrow.

"Rumors of usury, of miserliness, of underhanded practices, and of bankruptcy." The financier stamped his heel against a paving stone, and the sound rang out in the evening air. "This bastard son of a mean Scottish bitch intends to spoil our efforts by publishing all manner of lies and conjecture. Well, if the marvels of French engineering can turn water into money, Charles, as you have done, then the bare fist of an old Groton farmer can turn horseshit into printer's ink and vice versa, God blast him."

Storrow emitted a whistle of surprise. They continued walking along the canal, until the engineer asked, "What else did Hayes reveal, and what instructions are printed in your despatch to Mr. Coolidge?"

"I am a hard man, but a fair one. And though I am guided most by God's hand, just as the puppeteer guides his marionettes, there is enough play at the end of my string for the whirlings I must execute to maintain my grip on the American stage. Think, Charles. We have done nothing here in the New City but provide opportunity to a host of men who would be our employees. So, what have I now set out to do? Provide this Mr. Hayes with the same fortuitous circumstance."

A man carrying a hod of bricks passed by, and Lawrence waited before continuing. "Hayes confessed to me that the sales of his newspaper were insufficient to meet his rent and the cost of his supplies. Within two weeks—two editions where he would publish enough slander to ruin us, no doubt—he would be back on the Loundonderry Turnpike with his carpet-sided trunk, following the emigration of honest laborers to their next enterprise. From atop that foul dung heap where we kept our hatch, an idea occurred to me that we needed this J. F. C. Hayes, in the same manner one needs the devil he knows as an antidote to the one he does not. So I have instructed and deemed Mr. Coolidge to visit the offices of the *Weekly Tribune* with utmost speed to offer Mr. Hayes a proposal."

"What sort of proposal?"

"That Hayes gather up his one-armed press and pots of ink and quit his crammed attic, while an entire floor of our newest structure on Essex Street is placed at his disposal," said Lawrence. He made a sound in his throat, craned his neck, and spat into the canal. "For these accommodations, we will levy but half the rent he now suffers. Included is a lease of two years, with an option for eight more, if both parties are satisfied with the arrangement at the end of twenty-four month."

It was Storrow's turn to be flabbergasted. "Even the upper floors of those buildings are prime space and should attract treble what Johnson gets for his hovel alongside the Turnpike," said the engineer. "Why, if a colored barber can afford to occupy the ground floor just think what a pittance the attic must render."

"Your calculations are no doubt accurate, Charles, as always," said

Lawrence. "But I am no fool as a negotiator. This agreement contains a codicil, *quid pro quo*, as it were, exchanging an attractive rent and a discount on supplies for our perusal of Mr. Hayes' typesetting each week. For that purpose, I have designated our faithful Mr. Coolidge. Henceforth, the Essex Company, in effect, will become publishers of the *Weekly Tribune*."

"Do you really put such stock in what might be printed in a penny newspaper?"

"While you have been nestled in the maw of rustic pursuits, I have felt the sharp teeth of the press in New York, and in Washington. A printed word, even in agate type barely visible to the eye, can end a man's career—even his life—and the livelihood of his family after him. Remember, Charles: it's the little things, the details. There are dozens of men who once walked the street of Georgetown in plumed hats and brocaded jackets who now sleep out of doors, either in brothel sheds or much narrower apartments in the national cemetery."

During the conversation, Lawrence and his engineer approached the Lower Pacific Mill, which lay across the canal on a man-made island. The path at their feet, beaten into dust, climbed a small mountain formed by leftover and pulverized bricks. They gained the crest and surveyed the monolith before them. The Lower Pacific was six stories high, broad and dark against the glow of sunset, and in full operation. Smoke puffed from its chimneys, and the rattle of yarning machines shook the windowpanes with an infernal racket.

Pointing his finger along the sluiceway, Storrow indicated how the force of the canal was drawn through breaches in the foundation and then sucked through the turbines. The water, brown and roiling, was released back into the river on the far side, streaked with ribbons of foam. "Our canal is an engine that will never wear out," said Storrow.

Beyond the mountain of bricks was another footbridge leading onto the mill island. Stripped of all foliage and just under a mile long, the elliptical mass of land was home to the Lower Pacific; the unfinished bulk of the Upper Pacific; and the gigantic cellar hole where the Atlantic Mill would be constructed. According to Storrow's plan, the island would contain at least nine and perhaps twelve of the largest, most productive textile plants in the world. The Essex Company controlled all the water for powering these factories, leasing it per running foot; they owned the land beneath the structures; and they would, for a price, build a milling or manufacturing facility, from schematic drawings to shingled dormers.

At this moment, the only structure on Storrow's mind was a company privy. "All that tea and lemonade has created a hydraulic crisis," he said to Lawrence, hurrying through the shadow of the Lower Pacific. "And the sound of the canal is doing little to alleviate it."

Ahead in the rubble was a narrow building, topped with a placard that said "Essex Company Employees Only." Based on the *pissoirs* Storrow had seen in France, the outhouse was fitted with pipes that ran beneath the vault and deposited the effluence in the river. Although freeholders and lessors were barred from this activity, Mr. Storrow had deigned it a right of ownership; providing comfort to the builders of this great empire, and saving money on gangs of sewer men, who would have gathered the night soil in carts and sold it as fertilizer.

Inside the privy were three stalls. Choosing the middle one, Storrow unfastened his trousers and stood over the pit. His gaze strayed to the wall as he sent forth a steaming arch of urine. Pinned there was the most recent *Weekly Tribune,* and scrawled in red ink above the masthead, "Next issue: shallow-pocketed Abbott Lawrence visits his New City." The engineer was so startled by the advertisement that his stream petered out, sopping his trousers.

Storrow dashed into the other stalls and saw identical posters in each one. "Holy goblins of God," he said. Tearing down the sheets, the engineer gathered the newsprint into a spiky ball and dropped it into the pit.

Mr. Lawrence waited for him up island, gazing at the spray that hid the dam. A great stream of water poured over its unprotected half, appearing now and then in the mist like a band of jelly. Hurrying toward his employer, Storrow cried out, and Lawrence turned to the younger man with a contemplative look on his face.

"You are right, Abbott," said the engineer. "Something must be done about this Mr. Hayes and his ridiculous newspaper."

As the gravel vibrated around his feet, Mr. Storrow reported what he had seen inside the privy. Once again, the financier made a deep rumbling sound and expectorated into the canal. "My brother says to look after our clerks well, if we aim to keep them honest," said Lawrence. "Our first goal, therefore, is to make Mr. Hayes one of our clerks."

The two men hurried toward the gatehouse and their appointment with Captain Bigelow. Just ahead, the river and canal were divided by the tip of the island, and off to their left, the dam rose to its middle height of forty feet. With its substantial wing walls, also of dressed granite, the Great Dam formed a curve that ran 1,629 feet in length. On the north side, a covered walkway suspended over the channel housed a series of head gates, designed to measure and regulate the canal's force. Greenish water ran through the gates and emerged on the other side of the weir, scribbled with foam.

Ascending the granite stairs, Storrow held the door open and then followed Abbott Lawrence into the building. Inside, sturdy wooden levers attached to the penstocks could be manipulated by the gatekeeper. Captain Bigelow stood upon the planks in his braided military coat, a cigarillo clenched in his teeth, one hand resting on a lever while his eyes examined a gold watch. The bristles of his beard fanned out from his jaws, and the sweet damp odor of the cigarillo saturated the room.

"Captain Bigelow," said Lawrence, over the noise of the water. "I do not approve of smoking."

Bigelow turned his mournful gaze on the two visitors. With an unconscious movement, he closed the watch and deposited it in his coat while, at the same moment, releasing the lever. There was the sound of falling weight, and the rack and pinion system closed the breach.

Bigelow extended his hands and took those of Lawrence and Storrow in an iron grip, as the smoke from his cigarillo formed a wreath around his head. "My apologies, sir," said the Captain. "I came here to smoke unobserved, so as not to encourage the men to imitate me. This hemp tobacco is a medicinal cure, and I curse it even as it brings me relief."

"What troubles you?" Lawrence asked.

The large, fleshy man before him heaved a sigh. "What does not? The spines of my lower back radiate pain from morning til night, my head throbs with distemper, and there is a constant gnawing sensation at each point where my bones were broken." He dropped his cigarillo through a space between the floorboards and watched it disappear on the current.

"And your cigarettes cure you of these ills?" asked Lawrence.

"Nothing cures me; they divert my attention. All day long I bite my teeth together, cursing this horror, and then in the evening I smoke. My mind drifts out and I think of other things: sailing upon the Hudson, my campaigns in Ohio, and the laughter of my beloved children. Then the *cannabis sativa* allows me to sleep, and I dream the most curious, vivid dreams. Last night I dreamed of a great fire, and how I walked inside it like a salamander and was not consumed. Men were dying on all sides, reaching out for me, and I dared not look at them. Out through a fire-ringed exit, I crossed the river, scaling its waves as if they were dunes of sand."

Captain Charles H. Bigelow, the Essex Company's most experienced field engineer and a man of vast, practical knowledge, reported these fantasies as if they were weights and measures, the exact specifications of a project he had mounted in his free time. "The hulk raged in fire behind me. To my right was the Great Dam, and far ahead was the southern bank, where yet another blaze awaited. I was over the deepest part of the river, where our sounding ropes have dropped to seventy-six feet and still swung free of the bottom. Trudging through ankle-deep water, I looked down and saw my reflection, dappled by the flames. I had grown thinner, beardless, my clothes were strange: a thin-lapeled jacket, white shirt collar, the strand of a necktie. It was not this face you now see before you, and yet it represented the self I had known. My hands were long and yellow, grasping at the air, and I was overcome by tears."

Lawrence directed his gaze at Mr. Storrow. "Did not our Essex Company provide Captain Bigelow with a physician upon the occasion of his accident?"

"It was, in fact, Dr. Charles Ellis of Harvard College who prescribed the *cannabis*. He sends me a packet every month," Bigelow said. "Dr. Ellis believes my injuries would have caused death in ninety-nine of a hundred men, and I am serving my penance for having such a strong constitution. Apparently, God has plans for me."

"Indeed He does," Lawrence said. "But is there no other way to bring relief?"

The sound of running water seeped between the floorboards. "According to the good surgeon, there is nothing more he can prescribe for my condition besides the narcotic poppy flower, which I thus far refuse to take," said Captain Bigelow.

The party withdrew to a small office in the rear of the gatehouse. From the windows, they could see the crown of the dam and two men hanging a drape of red, white, and blue bunting. Scaffolding had been erected just below that point and was also draped in bunting. Upon the coffer dam the last of the workers departed, shovels and picks angled over their shoulders like muskets. Already the thread of supper fires mingled above the river, forming a great Arabian plume that rose toward heaven.

Several blueprints were spread on the drafting table. Using his pencil, Captain Bigelow explained how the contractors' men would operate a block and tackle to raise the final slab to the top of the dam. There, one sturdy lad would press the granite header into its slot while Abbott Lawrence and Charles Storrow cut a ceremonial ribbon.

"Who would be this deserving fellow?" asked Lawrence.

Hunched above the drafting table, Bigelow fixed his employer with glowering eyes and said, "Gabe'rill Glass; the man who saved my life."

"An appropriate choice, Captain," said the financier. "I have twice today seen this chap and he is a hard-working employee, no doubt."

Bigelow laid aside his pencil. "He has the courage of us three, and more," he said. "Mr. Glass was himself injured when the coffer dam overturned. And while I hobble across the deck of my scow, or scribble on these parchments, he produces more labor and conducts himself with more energy and zeal than any other man on the works."

"Have you met this lad, Charles?" Lawrence asked Storrow. "He is a force of nature."

"I do not know him. Spending so much of my time in Boston, I would not have recognized Mssrs. Carpenter and Gilmore before today."

"You should know these men who built your dam, Charles," said Lawrence.

Shaking his head, Storrow said, "Our dam. Since my jaw aches, and the dusky barber has advised me to remain on my feet, perhaps this evening I will accompany our constables as they collect the ground rents. We must perform this unhappy task before the mass of laborers quit the region."

Captain Bigelow started from the table. "If you do not mind my opinion, sir, Dublin after sunset is no place for a gentleman like yourself," he said. "It is a wild settlement, full of rough talk and even rougher men."

"Nonsense, Captain. I have walked the streets of Paris in the midst of a revolt, dodging musket balls in order to witness the birth of men's freedom. General Lafayette himself, who was no stranger to revolutions, commended my patriotic spirit upon the occasion. And these men of the New City are honest, God-loving Americans. We have nothing to fear from them."

Bigelow removed his tobacco from an inner pocket and opened a drawer that contained a device for rolling his cigarillos. "I agree they are Americans, but they are also men who sometimes act before they think and who argue with their fists. I have seen their like in the Army."

"Do not fear for me, Captain. I am especially lucid this evening and will be in the company of no less than five of our constables."

Pinching some tobacco into a narrow cone of paper, Bigelow inserted the tip of the cone between the rubber rollers and with the action of his thumbs made another cigarette. "As you wish, Mr. Storrow. I ask you only to remember that the constables are collecting money from men who have performed great labors and not yet been paid for them."

His hands pressed behind his back, Abbott Lawrence cleared his throat and walked over the hardwood floor to the windows. After the echo of his heels died away, he said, "The payroll was delayed by my order, and arrived with me today. I wish to collect the chits from these men myself, and hand them each a silver dollar beyond their wages, as symbols of gratitude from the Boston Associates."

Bigelow again fixed his black eyes upon his employer. "A piece of silver tomorrow will not provide their children with food this evening," he said.

In order to change the subject, Storrow leaned over and unfurled the blueprints for a structure to be called the Pemberton Mill. This factory, designed by Captain Bigelow, would occupy a parcel on the lower third of the island. "Can you inform us of the progress on this site, Captain?" asked Mr. Storrow.

While Storrow held his sore jaw and Lawrence stared down through his spectacles, Captain Bigelow detailed the excavation and scaffolding for the Pemberton. He had drawn up the plans and ordered most of the materials; viewing the endeavor as a worthy addition to his portfolio as a civil engineer, which to date had consisted of earthworks, roads, sea walls, and coffer dams. Bigelow's enthusiasm for the project superseded his physical discomfort, as he moved about the drafting table, with his meaty hands describing the oak pillars and pediments and conjuring bulwarks in the air.

The clatter of hooves on gravel, and the neighing of a post horse interrupted the financier and his employees. Outside, a granite promontory afforded a view of the weir, the millpond, and the curving bulk of the dam, amidst watery clouds of mist. Abbott Lawrence and the engineers exited the rear of the gatehouse, ducking to fit through a small door, and gathered on the pier to await their visitor.

It was Mr. Coolidge. Dripping with sweat, he stood on a tiny peninsula separated from the gatehouse by a lagoon of deep black water. Coming into view behind him, the horse nibbled on some clover at the edge of the lot.

"Well, Coolidge. What is it?" asked Lawrence, over the noise of the weir.

"I have spoken to J. F. C. Hayes, sir, and he has a response to your offer," said the foreman. He twitched his large black mustache. "I thought I should relay it myself, sir."

Lawrence was vexed. "Don't shout at me as if I were the cook's assistant," he said. "Come through the gatehouse."

"Yes, sir," said Coolidge, catching up his horse and disappearing around the corner.

At dusk, the hatch of mites skating above the millpond was like dots of violet. Hoping to alleviate the pain returning to his jaw, Storrow asked Bigelow to roll an extra cigarette and together they stared out at the lagoon, puffing on the hemp. Lawrence watched their smoke dissipate on eddies of wind. "Are you sure this *Nicotiana tabacum* will not be deleterious to you, Charles?" he asked.

"In Paris, I suffered from headaches due to excessive reading and my professors there suggested *cannabis*," said the engineer. "It has been many years since I have partaken of the weed, but I once found the effects quite beneficial."

Mr. Coolidge passed through the gatehouse, joining them on the pier. He was Bigelow's principal assistant, in charge of the depot, all six company warehouses, and the transportation of goods between various work sites in the New City. With his cap removed, he inclined his head toward Charles Storrow and Captain Bigelow, who stood at the edge of the promontory smoking their cigarillos.

Then the foreman directed his attention to Abbott Lawrence. "I received your instructions, Mr. Lawrence, read them thoroughly, and addressed the matter therein with my full attention," he said.

He produced the document in question, which still contained a faded brown imprint of the company seal. The paper stank in his hand. "What do you wish done with the original order?" asked Coolidge.

"Destroy it," Lawrence said, grimacing at the sight. "In what manner has Hayes responded to our offer?"

"Mr. Hayes is a difficult fellow to transact business with," said Coolidge. Wetting his fingers, he smoothed the edges of his sideburns. "The whole time I was speaking to him, he sat crouching over his drawers of type, choosing letters with a tweezer and arranging them in a shallow box. He insisted that he was hard at work on his new edition, and if I and the Essex Company wished to deliver a proposal then we would be forced to make our case with only half his attention."

"A confounding individual," said Lawrence.

"Indeed, sir. He kept a jug of beer at his elbow and interrupted me more than once on the spelling of various words. But what dearth he suffered in education, Mr. Hayes made up with energy. In the space of ten minutes his box was full. The story of the year, he called it."

Hands clenched behind him, Lawrence chopped his teeth together and began measuring the pier, three paces up, three back. "This fallow ignoramus. Exploiter of another's industry," he said, his posture straight as a surveying rod. "A single Scottish bumpkin would undo the work of five thousand God-fearing, Christian men, armed with only his bad diction and a drawer filled with misspelled words. Confound him and his blasted newspaper."

In the three years Coolidge had been acquainted with Mr. Lawrence, he had never heard him raise his voice in anger. The foreman's gaze ran to Bigelow and Storrow, who occupied the farthest tip of the pier, smoking their cigarettes as evening settled over the millpond. Lungs working in unison, the engineers stood counter-passant to one another and released fragrant plumes into the air, their faces blank as slate.

Again, Coolidge groomed his mustache and the furry tips of his sideburns. "In the end, Mr. Lawrence, this Hayes chap said your offer was, in his words, 'pregnant with possibilities.' But he insisted he was too busy with his journal to respond in person, and that I might be trusted to deliver an answer on his behalf."

"What is it?" asked Lawrence.

Gazing at his employer's boots, Coolidge said, "I told Hayes that his suggestions were too preposterous to bear repeating. That men of your stature, Mr. Lawrence, do not suffer fools."

"Did you not see the company seal on the order I sent you? This is no trifling event. What is Hayes' counteroffer?"

Coolidge raised his eyes. His tongue darted out to flirt with his mustache again, and he began hemming in his throat. "I—there's some discrepancies between—I cannot in good conscience—"

"Out with it, man," Lawrence said.

"Mr. Hayes addressed three issues in his proposal. One, that his firm be given the upper floors of the building under construction at the intersection of Essex and Methuen Streets, at a rent of twenty dollars per month and a lease of seven years, with an option for ten additional years at the same rate."

Lawrence gestured for his foreman to continue.

"Secondly, Mr. Hayes requires that his current measure of paper stock, Indian inks, and soft lead type be purchased by the Essex Company on his behalf from Mitchell & Pipkin, Stationers, of Rowes Wharf, Boston, Massachusetts, and delivered to him monthly for the first three years of the lease term, at which point the option to double the order will be his, with a term of four additional years, the cost of the increase shared in half by the *Weekly Tribune.*"

Coolidge saw that Mr. Lawrence wanted him to go on. He cleared his throat and said, "Lastly, Mr. Hayes agrees to report, compose, edit, and peddle the *Weekly Tribune,* providing all copy a day in advance to myself or other designee of the Essex Company, in exchange for all income generated by advertising and the sales of the paper each week." Coolidge lowered his eyes, as if he were speaking to an insect between Abbott Lawrence's feet. "In addition to these profits, Mr. Hayes will require a monthly salary from the Essex Company in the amount of one hundred and fifty dollars."

"One hundred and fifty dollars in salary each month, plus whatever profits generated by the newspaper, minus twenty dollars in rent?" asked Lawrence. "That is larcenous."

"It is a ridiculous proposal, and I apologize for bringing it to your attention. I only wished to be thorough in discharging my duties in this matter."

Lawrence turned away, and for several moments contemplated the expanse of the millpond. Just then a great bass tore apart the surface, gobbling from the hatch before disappearing back into the water. The financier glanced across at his fellow shareholders in the Essex Company, but was met only with mortal disinterest in the eyes of Captain Bigelow. The old soldier clenched his cigarillo between stubby yellow teeth and said nothing. Beside him, Mr. Storrow wore a stupefied expression and his cheek bulged at the place of his missing tooth. After the splash echoed away, the only sound that could be heard was the water combing through the weir and in the distance, the cry of a locomotive.

Uneasy at such a silence, Coolidge said, "I entertained thoughts of calling our constables, and impounding this man's printing press. What he suggested is nothing short of extortion and blackmail. My hesitation was precipitated only by the succinct nature of your order, Mr. Lawrence. If you had not instructed me to make an agreement with Hayes, I would have had him arrested on the cusp of his lewd proposition." He nodded in agreement with himself. "At the very instant, sir."

Lawrence's right shoulder drooped toward the pier, and he staggered for a moment. Putting out his hand, the financier caught himself and sat down on the berm, his legs dangling toward the water. "How does Mr. Hayes wish us to signal our assent to his offer?" he asked.

"Forgive me, sir, but how could we agree to such threats?" asked the foreman.

"If I wish be queried on my decisions I will invite such inquiry," Lawrence said. The financier allowed his rejoinder to find its mark and then, enunciating each word, he asked: "How will we signal our assent to Mr. Hayes' proposition?"

All color and expression drained from Coolidge's face. "Mr. Hayes plans to spend this evening at a Freemason's gathering in Methuen," he said. "And since no one but members of this secret society may be admitted, he instructs me that your acquiescence to his offer be signaled on the morrow by a tartan band worn around your hat. Since you will be on the scaffolding and he will remain with the crowd below, the colors of his clan will advertise to him and no one else that the Essex Company and the *Weekly Tribune* have come to an accord."

Lawrence spat into the millpond. "I have no tartan band," he said.

"Here it is, sir," said Coolidge, fetching a ribbon of cloth from his pocket. It was red with intermittent black bars running vertically, and three horizontal blue lines. "I took the band from Mr. Hayes only to be thorough."

Lawrence received the band and hid it in his pocket. "I wish you to draw up some papers, Mr. Coolidge. List the basics of our agreement and the codicils proposed by Mr. Hayes, and leave room for our signatures and a space to be witnessed and countersigned by yourself and Mr. Storrow."

"When shall I accomplish this, Mr. Lawrence?"

"Do it now. Bring the documents to my room in Coburn House when they are completed, and in the meantime, do not speak of these matters to anyone."

Once again the foreman inclined his head. "I will see to it immediately, Mr. Lawrence."

Coolidge withdrew to the little office, and through the gatehouse window they could see his pate hovering over the table while he copied out the contract. Pressing upward on the granite pier, Lawrence was steadied by the arm of Captain Bigelow, who had stepped forward at the first sign of an effort.

"Are you all right, sir?" asked Bigelow.

"It has been a long year for me, my family, and our company, and today has proven to be quite strenuous. I wish to retire, take a cup of tea, and say my prayers," Lawrence said. He freed himself from Bigelow's grasp, straightened the folds of his cloak and cravat, and beckoned across the pier. "Charles, if I can prevail upon you, walk me out to the Turnpike and we will put a cap on the day's business."

Storrow assisted the financier through the office, where Coolidge did not dare look up from his writing, and then out the gatehouse, down the steps and onto the gravel apron. Tied to a post, Coolidge's horse bared its teeth and neighed, shuddering through large black nostrils.

There was a sputtering noise from the horse's rear end, and Lawrence and Storrow backed away as manure thundered to the ground.

"The stench," said Storrow.

"When the war ended in '15, I made passage to England on a stench-filled cattle ship and returned with a hold full of dry goods that we sold for a handsome profit," Lawrence said. "A long, backward trace of our accounts would conclude that the settlement here on the Merrimack rests on that profit—just as all men stand upon invisible foundations, on the deep root of things they cannot see or understand."

As the two men flanked Coolidge's horse, a squad of six constables and a lieutenant turned into the gatehouse lot, their boots crunching over the gravel. The constables were dressed in coarse woolen shirts, armless tunics crossed by rawhide belts, and stovepipe dungarees. The officer at the head of the column had a pistol in his belt, and the rest carried lengths of black oak fashioned into pikes. Additionally, each man had a ration bag slung over his shoulder.

"Here come our mercenaries," Storrow said.

While they yet remained at a distance, the officer halted the column and began drilling his charges. The constables sounded the roll, presented arms, and then were ordered to a nearby embankment where they ate dried cabbage and strips of corned beef from their ration bags.

"Tell me your dream, Charles," said Lawrence.

The engineer furrowed his brow. "Which dream are you speaking of?" he asked.

"The one you mentioned earlier. Your dream of the New City."

Storrow turned away, gazing across the precipice of the dam. The water approached the open half of the structure in an unbroken mass, changing from black to silver as it poured over the crest. "That was merely the trifle of a fatigued mind," the engineer said.

Lawrence's voice was tinged with paternal forbearance. "Is it always the same dream, or a series of episodes?" he asked.

"Always the same," said Storrow. He kept his back turned, facing the river. "I am sitting in our offices in Boston, alone at my high desk. It is

Jay Atkinson

late, snow is falling past the windows, accumulating on the lamp posts and hitching rails of Beacon Hill. Everywhere the streets are deserted."

As the sun disappeared, the hatch had turned black and now the surface of the Merrimack was teeming with specks. They thronged over the millpond, and the sound of their wings beat a million-fold on the air. "Before me on the desk are my plans for the New City, from the earliest sketch to the finished blueprints for the Great Dam and several of our mills, each embossed with the company seal. I am deep in some calculation, my drafting pencils and rules scattered about. But as much as I endeavor, the sum will not arrive; there is a number that refuses the space I have prepared for it, and without this figure, all my plans are for naught."

The phalanx of constables rose in the dust and their lieutenant, a man named Treachey, got them moving along the road again. Storrow paused in his monologue, and when the column neared the gatehouse, Lieutenant Treachey recognized his superiors. "Good evening, Mr. Lawrence. Mr. Storrow, sir," the officer said. "We're to report to Captain Bigelow. Tonight we'll be collecting the ground rents."

Lieutenant Treachey wore a hard, round hat, like a pith helmet, and the other men were bareheaded. His brow was heavy and dark, and above a well-attended regimental mustache, his shaven cheeks were blue-black with stubble. Since he found himself in private employ, and Mssrs. Lawrence and Storrow were not military men, the lieutenant was caught between removing his helmet out of respect and leaving it on to salute. As night winds began to sweep over the dam, swirling the dust of the Loundonderry Turnpike, Treachey and his squad stood grim-faced and silent.

Just then, Captain Bigelow thrust open the door to the gatehouse. "Treachey," he said.

"Here, sir."

"Bring your men inside the gatehouse. There are orders to be dispatched."

"Yes, sir," said the lieutenant.

Treachey threw out his chest and started the column with a short marching order that sounded like "*Ho.*" The constables passed Lawrence and Storrow in route step, disappearing through the gatehouse door. Lieutenant Treachey came last, removing his helmet on the way, the hair plastered down over his forehead and showing the imprint of his headgear. The lieutenant glanced at his employers, a note of condescension in his voice. "Sorry to interrupt you, gentlemen," Treachey said. "Please carry on." His boots were heavy on the stairs, and the door flapped shut after him.

"Impertinent fellow," said Lawrence.

"Chalk it up to military bearing, Abbott. As Captain Bigelow noted, our constables spend their hours among intemperate men and their profane talk."

A caisson pulled by two sturdy horses arrived at the Andover Bridge. On the driver's bench sat three additional constables, and the deck of the flat-bottomed wagon was emblazoned with the Essex Company seal. Lashed to the deck were two slotted casks, for the money and chits that would be collected, and a mechanism consisting of two black rubber siphons, a hydraulic tank that would allow the siphoned water to build up in pressure, and extending from there, a canvas hose with a brass nozzle and two brass handholds.

"In addition to collecting rents, do our constables expect to be putting out fires this evening?" asked Lawrence, studying the wagon from a distance.

Storrow gazed across river at Dublin shantytown, and the wires of smoke that now formed a laughing death's-head above the encampment. "I believe they aim to extinguish the spark that blazes in men," he said.

"It is the ghost of that diseased tooth which troubles you," the millionaire said. A row of granite tablets ringed the lot, and he drew himself up to one of them and inspected it before seating himself. "Please, Charles, finish your dream," said Lawrence.

Coolidge's mount neighed once more and when the call traveled downwind, the two bay horses answered, twisting their heads and stamping their hooves against the paving stones. One of the constables stood up, yanking the reins and cursing at the beasts, and their whinnying resounded over the water. "I have suffered this vision three times, identical and clear, the night that I return from the New City to my family in Boston," Storrow said. He watched as the driver removed feed bags from the back of the caisson and fixed them to the horses' heads.

"Maybe it is a presage to our impacts here in the valley," Lawrence said.

Charles Storrow gazed into the mists above the dam. His flabby lip dropped open, and a line of spittle fell onto the ground. "In the dream I am figuring a sum, an ephemeral number that, when plugged into various calculations, fastens together all my science here in the New City—the engineering of a world that I would see made whole after ten years' effort."

"That we would all see whole," said Lawrence. Squatting on the granite tablet, he fussed with the ends of his trousers and drew up his sagging hose.

"Of course, there is no such number. My drawings and calculations have always been piecemeal, and in the spirit of Professeur Baldwin, my great mentor, I finish each segment of our enterprise before passing on to the next. But that is the conceit of the dream."

"Perhaps it is a symbol to tie the fragments together in your mind," Lawrence said.

"But the elusive figure cannot be grasped. My theorems and computations form a scaffolding that rises before me, as tall as Ararat. The pieces of paper on the desk are filled with scribbles; yet as passes to the realm I wish to enter they are useless. I hold one in my hand and the numbers are transformed into hieroglyphics, into gibberish. Several times I am on the brink of discovery, weaving through this labyrinth, and then it all falls away, collapsing into vaporous pits. The Great Dam and canal, the mill buildings, and every cobblestone in the New City are released from their bonds and sent spinning into the ether."

Here Storrow faltered. "I cannot . . ." The engineer stared into the dust at his feet. He removed his top hat, pressing it against his hip. "Abbott, this is scandalous."

Lawrence's voice was a whisper: "Go on."

The engineer approached Coolidge's mount. With his fingers, Storrow brushed the horse's cheek, looking into its wise, unblinking eye. "In the dream, snow falling against the window rouses me from my chair. I circle the desk, and peer through the smoky glass at the storm. The blizzard is strange, without wind or cold. There is a figure coming toward me, through the drifts: a woman, her shoulders bare, her gown wrapping and unwrapping about her slender legs."

"Your wife?" asked the financier.

Storrow shook his head, gazing at the pebbled ground. "It is a foreign woman, and recall that I have had the dream at home, my dear Lydia sleeping beside me, and three times I have awoken in the midst of this fever."

"It is a mental invention, Charles. Such a phantom cannot harm you."

The afflicted man raised his eyes, huge and black, fixed there in the loose flesh of his face. "I am not shivering in fear, but in lust," said Storrow. "The woman is pleasing in her shape, her tresses long and yellow. She beckons me. Somehow I pass through the window into the street and take up her hand. The flakes from above are motes of ash, ghostly white, and piling against our shins as we walk."

"Preposterous," said Lawrence. He retreated behind Coolidge's mount, peeking at Storrow over the swag of the horse's back.

Storrow expressed his disagreement with a brief, mirthless smile. "God save me from it, but I can hardly wait for a repetition of this vision. It thrills me in ways you can never know."

"That's the end of it, then," Lawrence said, his face puckered like he had tasted something foul. "You and this mysterious woman strolling among ashes."

"There is one more portion of the dream," said Storrow. Again he stared into the well of the horse's eye, soothed by its neutrality. "The blizzard subsides and the streets of Boston magically transform themselves into this thoroughfare before us. Hand in hand, we approach the bridge. Although I am afraid to cast my gaze upon it, the Great Dam is erect, its bulwark smooth and perfect. But the river has disappeared. Where once the Merrimack swept downward from Lowell to form this millpond, there lies a dry and rocky bed with only a trickle of water meandering down the center.

"The woman laughs but her expression does not change; the sound comes from an empty chamber in my head. I look more intently and see the dam is stained and misshapen, pocked full of holes. It breathes in and out with the action of my lungs, tattered at the edges, no more substantial than an old piece of muslin. Across the way, our New City lies in ruin. A vast number of buildings are merely holes in the ground, scorched black. Some of the farther mills are standing, but windowless and empty. Others are arrested in mid-construction, the raw materials lying in heaps, frosted with cobwebs and dust. Scores of shovels and picks and mason's trowels litter the island, as if their handlers have fled or been incinerated."

His hand gliding over the horse's back, the engineer staggered toward the granite tablets bordering the lot. Storrow's legs collapsed, and his hat tumbled to the ground as he sat upon one of the stones. "Take your best ideas, your best moments, your passion, youth, and idealism, and pitch them all into a cocked hat." Storrow kicked at the top hat with his foot, and it rolled away. "Take off your pince-nez, gather up your skirts, and gambol about the church-house. Take your beloved children, and drown them in the sea."

"Banish these anxieties from your mind, Charles. You have achieved wonderful things here."

Storrow gripped the ball of his skull. For several moments the engineer sat with his face concealed, and the only sound was that of water rushing through the apertures in the dam. From high above, a hawk spiraled down to the river, and then flew into the piles of smoke above Dublin.

When Storrow spoke, his voice was muffled. "We are all damned," he said.

Leaning over for the top hat, the millionaire knocked dirt from the brim and came forward. At the sound of his mentor's approach, Storrow lowered his hands. The engineer's visage was deathly pale; an aureole of dark, twisted hair stood up on his head. The flesh of his lower jaw was distended, and he reached to cradle the morbid tissue that hung there. "In my waking hours, I know that the dream is a cipher; that the sum I am calculating is mythical; that the woman who accompanies me is not a woman but a wraith, sprung from some gloomy recess of my spirit," Storrow said. "There is no monstrous pivot in the universe upon which all our ambitions teeter. I know this, Abbott, but that does not stop my heart from smashing against my ribs when the dream reaches its climax."

Lawrence lowered himself onto the tablet beside his protege. "What is it, Charles?"

"I dare not speak of it," he said.

"You have kept this secret for too long. It rots your soul the way standing water rots the inside of a cask. Speaking about it perhaps will cure you."

From across the gravel, Coolidge's mount watched the engineer through deep black eyes. As Storrow continued his account, the horse spread its teeth and laughed, black nostrils shuddering. "My escort and I abandon the bridge, heading for the south bank. The ground is scaly and arid, and our journey is a harsh one. Yonder, where this evening lies nothing but verdant hills and pastures, the land has been scoured by some infernal process, raked into great furrows. One of these descends into the earth. The trickle of water appears, and it is the subterranean canal, which heretofore existed only in my notebooks. Along the passage we travel, this female Vergil and I, her skirts gliding over the stony ground. The motion of her buttocks is arousing; my tool lengthens, it strains against my breeches—"

The financier raised his hands. "Let me remind you, Charles, that we are both married men."

"But we are also human, subject to the temptations and fluctuations that besiege our kind," said Storrow. "As a man, you should comprehend my despair at these visions, commingled with my excitement."

Abbott Lawrence considered this for a moment. "Go on," he said.

"The woman and I ascend a narrow pitch of stairs. The walls take shape around us, and I realize we are inside the rectangular vault of a building, a milling facility of some kind. Passing upward, each floor contains several rows of dormant machinery, some as large as an omnibus, and sheathed in billowing veils that match the garments of my escort.

"There is a tower. A spiral staircase leads to the top, and as I climb, I can feel my limbs becoming decrepit; my hands grow warty and my breath shortens. Up the final steps I rise, pulled there by my companion. Her grip is strong, her skin fragrant and inviting. I grow old, yet the woman remains young, and together we gaze out the capped tower at our New City: a feckless Adam and his comely Eve, afloat above the industrial garden. The woman's breasts are full of sweet milk; they swing against me. Her nether region is warm, soft, and wet; our kisses deep. Summoning me, the woman climbs out onto the ledge. I follow, hard as monument stone. My tensility meets her resistance; we couple.

"Spreading in every direction, the New City lives again. The stacks bellow, locomotives cry, the streets are filled with racing millwrights, jobbers, peddlers, and an inordinate amount of clergy, in their pleated vestments and wearing advertisement-boards for various products. High above them, my partner and I engage: our copulation is tender, and exotic pleasures fill the interior of my being. The woman twists, she grapples. All the wires of my body sing with a mysterious static power . . ."

Storrow glanced away, the pouch of sickened flesh hanging from his jaw, which had turned a yellowish color and rocked against his neck like a wattle. "The more deeply I abhor this behavior in myself, the greater the relishing of it; the more I endeavor to stop myself, the more frenzied I continue on," he said.

On the adjoining tablet, Lawrence sat with his mouth gaping. "A fantastic tale," he said.

"There is yet a frightening denouement," said the engineer. "The woman and I are lying spent on the ledge. Shame overcomes me, for in sight of the New City I have shattered my vows and desecrated my family. The woman, once so soft, so temperate and obliging, is transformed into a harlot. Her flank shrivels, the tresses of her hair weaken into string. I look into her face, which ages ten, twenty, thirty years with each beat of our hearts. 'Stay with me,' she whispers. But I am choked by horror; and with a thrust of my arm, I cast her from the ledge. Her fall is elongated and silent, as the tower continues to grow." With his knees drawn up, Storrow pressed his thumbs into his eyes and began sobbing. "Everywhere the landscape is smoldering, and all the figures who once traveled there are dead."

Suddenly the door to the gatehouse was thrust open and Captain Bigelow stumped down the stairs, followed by Lieutenant Treachey and his constables. Mr. Coolidge emerged last, a parcel of papers squared with black ribbon under his arm.

"Compose yourself, Charles," Lawrence said.

Captain Bigelow approached the two men, and Abbott Lawrence rose to meet him. "I trust that all is made ready," said the financier.

"Aye, sir," Bigelow said.

They watched as Treachey checked his squad with a brief order, saluted Captain Bigelow, and then restarted the marchers with a downward motion of his arm. While Bigelow held the reins, Mr. Coolidge secured his papers in one of the saddlebags, caught his heel in the stirrup and lifted himself onto the horse.

"Any further instructions, Mr. Lawrence?" Coolidge asked, as Bigelow lobbed him the reins.

"Just get on with it."

Coolidge wheeled the horse around. "Then I ride for the company offices," he said.

Kicking his mount, Mr. Coolidge leaned against the horse's neck and went galloping down the drive. Immediately Charles Storrow felt a void where the horse had been. Gazing into the horse's eye had comforted him somehow, and now the empty place in the park loomed within his spirit.

"I trust you will watch over Mr. Storrow this evening," Lawrence said to Captain Bigelow.

The captain shook his head. "My wounds prevent me from touring the camp. But rest assured, I have given Lieutenant Treachey specific instructions to remain at Mr. Storrow's side, armed with his pistol," said Bigelow, leaning on his good leg. "Just this week, I moved my quarters into the gatekeeper's shack in order to restrict my movements. Hobbling from skiff to scow, drawing on my papers, lately I have become more contemplative, which grates against my active nature."

Placing his hand on the other man's shoulder, Lawrence said, "This evening I shall write to Katherine, beseeching her to pray for your recovery."

"As nightly I pray for my dearest cousin, and all your brood," said Bigelow. He disengaged himself from Lawrence's grip. "Now, if you will pardon me, I must retire."

"Go, my good man," said Lawrence. "Even as you rest, we will continue your work."

The captain bade his employers good evening, hailed Lieutenant Treachey once more and limped over to the gatehouse steps, disappearing inside. Abbott Lawrence beckoned to Mr. Storrow, and arm in arm they followed the marching constables toward the road. Both men were near

Jay Atkinson

exhaustion. Lawrence stumbled in the gravel like he was navigating among boulders, and next to him, Charles Storrow felt Newton's force pulling his cheek downward, until he imagined a giant underlip bumped against his knees and went dragging on the ground. Aiming for the surveyor's stakes that marked the lot, they leaned together like boys in a three-legged race.

A short distance ahead, two constables spread a tarpaulin beneath the wagon, crawled on it and greased the axle, while the horses remained cowled by their feed bags. As they approached, the financier dropped his voice and said to Storrow, "I apologize for curtailing our talk, Charles, but the trials of these last few weeks compel me toward slumber. One thing bears repeating: venture out this evening with all possible wariness, to learn, as a man of science must, by direct experience, but forbearing from any actions that would place you in danger, and conceding to the authority of Lieutenant Treachey."

"I will," said the engineer.

One of the constables stacked blankets onto the tailgate of the wagon, providing an upholstered seat for Mr. Storrow. Uttering an apology, Lieutenant Treachey grabbed the engineer by the belt and collar and hoisted him up. "There you go, sir," he said. "Safe as old Midas on his throne."

"You have your orders from Captain Bigelow, and no doubt your methods, Treachey," said Lawrence. "But take every precaution in safeguarding Mr. Storrow, at the certain peril of your employment here in the New City."

"I'd cleave a lad's skull before I'd let somebody tamper with the hair on Mr. Storrow's head," said Treachey.

"You are to collect ground rents and make an accounting of our chits, but lay hands on no one."

His chin jutting out, Lieutenant Treachey threw his shoulders back and remained silent. In the ranks the other constables were motionless, their heels pressed together, staring ahead at the Turnpike. Suddenly a droning sound filled the air. Driven by the wind, a swarm of honeybees flew onto the bridge, well-separated from one another and interspersed with river spray. The hum increased as the bees got closer but no one dared complain, except the horses. Blinded by their feed bags, the two bays tossed their heads, stamping on the gravel and shuddering beneath their harness.

"*Yeah*-up," the driver said, tightening his reins. "Hold on there, *yeah-up*."

The honeybees were confused and wet, buzzing against the men without using their stingers. But as they massed in the twilight and their droning grew more intense, terrifying the horses, the constables eyed each other, gripping their pikes.

"May we proceed, sir?" Treachey asked Mr. Lawrence.

The millionaire encountered a trio of honeybees, and began waving his arms. "Go on, then," he said, bumping against the caisson. "Godspeed to you all."

Clapping Mr. Storrow on the arm, Abbott Lawrence whispered farewell into his protege's ear, and then turned and made for the Coburn House. Treachey detached one of his men and the constable followed behind the millionaire, his pike clicking on the gravel. Just then the honeybees rose above the bridge, concentrated into a single black cloud and flew south, toward Dublin.

"Constable Flanagan, make sure Mr. Storrow is made fast," said Treachey, removing his helmet to scratch at his head.

"Right, sir," Flanagan said. He was a tall, red-headed fellow with long arms and the words *Gilmore* and *Carpenter* printed on the cuffs of his dungarees. Leaning over the caisson, Flanagan inspected the engineer's top hat and whiskers and then called out to the driver: " 'E's all fit and comfortable, 'iggins."

Clutching the reins, Higgins nudged the fellow beside him and the man jumped down and removed the feed bags, tossing them onto the deck of the caisson. In an instant he was back up on the johnnyseat, and Higgins signaled they were ready.

Lieutenant Treachey waved his hand, and the constables passed on either side of the caisson and reassembled in front of the horses, their pikes aimed at the low violet sky.

"For the Essex Company: *ho*," said Treachey, leading the way, and with all six marchers in step, the column set out. Behind them, Higgins clapped the reins together and the two bay horses jerked the caisson forward and began clopping over the wooden bridge.

His feet dangling from the wagon, Charles Storrow gazed at the New City and recalled the innumerable happy hours he had devoted to its construction. But soon he was interrupted by thoughts of his dark-haired wife, Lydia, and their parcel of seven children. Lydia had suffered in childbirth the preceding year and afterward complained of dryness and pain during lovemaking, which had become rare as they reached middle life. Then Storrow recalled the passion of his dream, and how three times he had awakened, his breeches wet and viscous, and cursed its insubstantiality. Again his wife appeared among these memories, prim-faced and severe, and he found the intrusion unpleasant.

Far off, Storrow saw his mentor reduced to a speck on the Turnpike and regretted not telling Abbott of his dream's final segment. In it, his decrepitude leads onward, pulverizing him into dust, yet he remains invested in the particles, conscious of the past and all his vanities. A young man appears in the tower, rising over the balustrade with his shock of black hair and ruddy complexion. Clutching a broom, the youth climbs onto the ledge and whisks the dust away, the bristles of his instrument scattering Storrow's consciousness into the void.

As the engineer mused on these visions, addled by Bessel's cure and his inhalations of cannabis, the wagon became a fiery chariot and mounted into the sky. Ahead, lifted on ether, the constables ascended invisible steps and were transformed into angels. They acquired large, feathered wings, their hair grew long and white and they floated upward, shouting hallelujahs to the Lord.

Jay Atkinson

5

Lawrence, Massachusetts

The Present Day

Walter Beaumont stood in the window of his second floor bedroom looking over the city. There was a glow from downtown near the Pacific Mills, a gush of light he mistook for a holiday celebration until he saw the fire trucks cutting across town and realized what it was. Reaching behind him, Walter fiddled with the amount of oxygen coming through the mask. His breath flowed more evenly now, after the heart-straining walk up two flights from his study. For several minutes he was forced to sit on the bed, arms and legs jittering, his oxygen blasting at six liters. It frightened him to feel nothing as he sucked on the gas coming through the line, his limbs ratcheting around outside his control. When he could reduce the oxygen to three liters and sit with his hands on his knees, surveying the tin ceiling and ocher walls and solid, tongue-in-groove floor, the illusion returned that he might get better.

It was cold in the upper rooms of the house. He put his cardigan back on over his pajamas and switched on the electric blanket, unfurling several loops of tether from the oxygen tank to allow himself more freedom. Every few nights his bedtime ritual became more elaborate, the machinations of oxygen and pill-taking more demanding—a larger and larger investment that produced an ever diminishing return. Elise had suggested hiring a part-time nurse, but the thought of a stranger arranging his meals and tucking him into bed at night sickened him. In his mind he felt no more than thirty-nine years old, and could not believe his body was shutting down. But taking more than three steps made his head swirl with stars, and the floor warp and breathe like a diaphragm between the here-and-now and some lower world. Everything around him was becoming immaterial by degrees, and he sensed himself fading toward even less defined quarters.

It was eleven-thirty, Christmas Eve. Walter remembered driving up Tower Hill in his father's Pierce Arrow, every house glowing with decorations except the Shiebel's across the street. For a week around the holidays the Sheibel family would have a menorah in the window, lit with candles, and then nothing but darkness. When Walter was a young man, his father would invite the Sheibels to an open house on December twenty-fifth. Each year, they would decline. But there was great affection between Franklin Beaumont and Egonne Sheibel, and the next day the Beaumonts would douse their tree and put away the nativity scene, and they would have the Sheibels over for brunch. Walter would sit in a chair with the *Saturday Evening Post*, listening to his father and the man from next door exchange stories as the champagne flowed into the afternoon. Walter resented making the house dark for these people, who didn't believe.

Now all the houses were dark, including his own. He wanted the scent of evergreen in the foyer, carols sung from the driveway, Santa's sleigh and reindeer running over the roof. He remembered fireworks shooting up from the back yard, those he and his father launched in 1937, '38, '39, and '46. In the old days, Walter would turn the calendar with delight at more money in the bank, more parties, more young women to meet and woo, and the strength of his family, which was galvanized under the pressure of years like steel was galvanized. The passing of time had made him richer and more influential, but with one proviso: it had made him older until his age grew beyond function and dignity. Now the thought of another year and what it might bring terrified him.

Walter Beaumont crawled into bed, trailing the plastic cord. Light through the window made a pattern of branches throughout the room. On the bare walls, skeletal trees loomed, waving all around him. As cars passed in the street, rectangles of light filled with the shadow of more branches and then slid across the ceiling, stopping at a certain point before they disappeared. Breathing into the oxygen mask, the covers pulled up to his chin, Walter felt abandoned in the middle of the woods.

But it was cozy under the electric blanket. He reached into his pajamas and squeezed his penis. His fantasies, when he could manage any, featured his companion of recent years, a lovely young woman named Elise Dominaux. He and Elise spent little time together now; his illness had deepened the gulf of years that separated them. But Elise always brought fresh air to this musty old house, carrying flowers, throwing open windows. It was only in the last six months that her love had evolved into caretaking.

Outside, branches tossed in the wind, striping him with their shadows. For a moment, an image of Elise filled his thoughts. Scented with flowers, she came toward him. But his penis lolled in his hand like an earthworm and he dropped it.

Walter tried saying the Lord's Prayer, forgetting the lines after "Give us this day our daily bread." He was suspended over the gap in his recollection for several moments, and then drifted on to other matters. For more than thirty years, he had served as a board member of the United Church of Christ on Common Street. When his father died, Walter visited the Reverend Wilbur Cruikshank's office and gave him a check for six thousand dollars. As Vice President of Lawrence Savings & Trust and Franklin Beaumont's executor, Walter was in a position to help the church while cementing his reputation as a community leader.

"In the bible it says 'Who, by worrying, ever added a single hour to his life?' " said Cruikshank, pocketing the check. "But I have to admit, I was getting an ulcer over the weekly collection."

The gift became the keystone in the young minister's drive to build a Sunday school behind the church. Later, under Walter's supervision, the church invested in South African diamond mines and rolled the profit into municipal bonds. Twice, the church built additions, until their lot couldn't hold another brick. In 1960, Beaumont helped his minister negotiate an employment contract based on investment dividends, one that put overruns straight into Cruikshank's heretofore-meager salary. The annual twelve-percent earned through this arrangement sent the minister's three children to Ivy League schools, and financed an experimental kidney operation for his wife, Julia.

When Walter became ill himself and was yet to the point where he could be cavalier about it, he asked Reverend Cruikshank to visit him at home. In recent years, the church's portfolio had been depleted by a sluggish market, as well as Walter's retirement from the bank. Cruikshank, now a widower with all his children grown and gone, was scraping around for money to de-lead the chapel, hire a new Sunday school teacher, and buy a dozen computers. Over brandy, Walter presented him with a check for thirty-two thousand dollars.

"This is very generous of you, Walter," Cruikshank said.

"There's more to come," said Beaumont, serving the drinks. "It's all in my will. I just hope you'll remember me when I'm gone."

Reverend Cruikshank folded up the check and put it in his suit pocket. He was a dapper man, thin and bald with a face like a sea horse and damp brown eyes. Cruikshank's own health was vigorous for a man of sixty-nine, although his wife's death from kidney disease had reduced his episcopal optimism. "The congregation will not forget your largess, and the Lord will be reminded of your commitment to His work by the volume of my prayers," he said. Pausing with the snifter halfway to his lips, he added, "But that's a long time in the future. First, you must get well."

But there was an addendum to Cruikshank's addendum. "God willing," he said. Reverend Cruikshank placed his glass on a coaster, his wet eyes roaming over Beaumont's face. "Because it is by God's will that the lame walk and the blind see. The sick get well by His disposition alone."

This pronouncement had irritated Walter Beaumont. Every few months, he went to see his lawyer, Philbin Bates, and tinkered with his will. At his next appointment, Walter reduced the bestowal to United Church of Christ from seventy-five thousand dollars to less than half that figure, limiting its use to capital improvements. He also instructed Attorney Bates to parcel out the money only upon receipt of work orders. If the sick recovered only by the will of God, then goddamn it, he said, the rest of the Cruikshanks could pay for their own goddamn kidney operations.

Beaumont had no children, and only a few distant relations he hardly ever heard from. Most of them were successful and lived in the southwest or around Atlanta somewhere. He couldn't understand why anyone born in Massachusetts would move away. Walter's father once pointed out that the entire United States was a subsidiary of the Massachusetts Bay Company, a bunch of English capitalists who could see raw materials and cheap labor all the way from their chilly offices across the Atlantic. The Industrial Revolution had taken seed here like nowhere else, and reached its fullest flower in planned communities like Lawrence. To be the founder of a new settlement, company or family was Walter Beaumont's highest ambition; one that he had never reached.

Because of his status as a wealthy old bachelor, there was a great deal of jockeying among community groups to get a share of his estate. Walter had instructed Attorney Bates, who would act as his executor, to set up a Beaumont scholarship at Lawrence High School with an annuity of one hundred thousand dollars. Each year someone majoring in finance or textile engineering would get one thousand dollars, providing he or she attended a state college. He reasoned if a student could afford Harvard or Brown or some other classy school, they didn't need his money. His lawyer, a graduate of Pennsylvania, concurred.

The heaviest lobbying for Walter Beaumont's money came from Manchester College, a small but prestigious Catholic school in nearby Ballardvale. For some time, Walter had served as a financial advisor to the school president, Father O'Connell. Walter himself had not attended college; at least, he never earned a degree. Over the years, Lawrence Savings & Trust paid for his enrollment at dozens of two- and three-week seminars on the latest services and innovations in the banking industry. Framed in his study were the accompanying certificates from Brandeis and MIT and the Wharton School of Business. But Walter Beaumont, like many working men, retained for his entire life a hankering after academic honors and recognition.

For many years now, the president of Manchester had been a wily and indefatigable Jesuit named Eamonn Carr O'Connell. During his illness, Walter Beaumont received two telephone calls from Father O'Connell, who he had not seen or heard from in several months. The first call came the day after Reverend Cruikshank's visit. Although the Jesuit never mentioned Beaumont's substantial donation to the United Church of Christ, every intonation and pause coming through the receiver indicated he had been informed of it, no doubt through some ecumenical grapevine. Past conversations between the retired banker and Father O'Connell had more than once included the subject of Walter Beaumont's estate and his intentions regarding the college, but none of these talks had been very detailed or specific.

"I hear you're in a real fight and wanted to pass along my concern," O'Connell said, in his flat Ohio baritone. "The Episcopals are close to Christ, and I add my prayers to theirs in petition for your comfort. Your

Jay Atkinson

generosity of time and spirit is in all our hearts here at Manchester."

O'Connell omitted other sorts of generosity, and not because Beaumont was tight with his money (he had always been an easy touch for five hundred or a thousand dollars). Nevertheless, an inquisitiveness lurking in Father O'Connell's manner implied the retired banker could have given more. The priest was on an expedition, chipping with his little hammer, taking measurements. The size of the check delivered to Cruikshank meant a very rich vein was lurking below the surface of Walter Beaumont.

Huffing into the telephone, Beaumont said he had enjoyed his long association with Manchester College. "I pray for an even longer one," O'Connell said. "But I'll let you get some rest."

In his onrushing anxiety Walter had forgotten about the conversation with O'Connell, until this evening when the Jesuit had reached him before he climbed the stairs to bed. The time for subtlety had passed, and after speaking of the Christmas lights that adorned the campus, Father O'Connell came to the point while the invalid panted against the balustrade.

"I've been giving thought to our long association, Wally," he said. "You've been a true friend of Manchester, and this June I've decided to bestow upon you an honorary doctorate. It needs only to pass a vote of the Board of Governors after the first of the year. Congratulations, old friend."

Walter could feel the Reaper bearing in, throwing gusts of his foul breath. The banker knew he would be dead when spring came to the campus, and the Manchester College orchestra struck up "Pomp and Circumstance." Still, he felt his chest lighten at the thought of the doctorate. Academic recognition would fill one of the gaps he had always imagined in his life.

"I'm very grateful, Father O'Connell," said Beaumont.

"Call me Eamonn," the priest said, which was an absolute first. "And Wally, I'm pleased to make this offer to you. Very pleased, indeed. The only problem we might have is with Kitty Axelrod."

Kitty Axelrod had a hand in all the major charities on the north shore: United Way, American Cancer Society, Manchester College, and every other organization large enough to have a marketing director. With a portfolio equal to anyone in Lawrence, the tire heiress could afford it. And like the other members of the Board, she was a Manchester college graduate and a Catholic, two clubs Walter Beaumont was never be able to join.

"Kitty has a problem?" asked Beaumont. His heart rate was climbing although he remained motionless at the bottom of the stairs.

O'Connell made a sound indicating the situation was difficult, but manageable. "Well, to be honest, I haven't even broached the subject of your doctorate yet, but in our past conversations Kitty has questioned your commitment to the college by asking about your donations to our capital campaigns." The priest let that sink in for a moment. "And we both know, you haven't really made any of those."

Struggling for breath, Walter Beaumont felt the room make one quick revolution around him. "I've donated countless hours of advice," he said. The college improvements Walter was responsible for crowded his brain—the sports arena, the employee pension plan, the dormitories, the biochemistry and engineering laboratories, and several extended mortgages two points below prime—but he couldn't summon the air to give them voice and settled for saying, "I rest on that."

"Please don't upset yourself," said O'Connell in his pastoral tone. "Your name is on a lot of plaques around here. You'll be remembered." His enunciation hardened a little. "But there's strong sentiment among the Board that to reach the ether, so to speak, to get your name on a building—or a doctorate—the recipient has to go higher than time and expertise. Only money can make them sing, I'm afraid. You see, Wally, it's a measuring stick they all know how to use, and it helps make everyone equal. The Board is straight down the line on that one. And as Thomas Hardy wrote, 'What the potent say so oft, can it fail to be somewhat true?'"

Walter Beaumont flashed on Kitty Axelrod, and the grand old Axelrod home topping Prospect Hill. Kitty could throw a hundred long ones at O'Connell and still go off to Monaco and have her teeth bonded. At one time, Walter Beaumont might have held his own with her, but not anymore.

"How much money are we talking about?" he asked.

"We're not really talking about specific sums of money," O'Connell said. "We're talking about commitment. An amount that is significant to Walter Beaumont is a sign to other community leaders that Manchester College is a priority. *Res ipsa loquiter*, the thing speaks for itself. In that way, your assistance has an effect that goes far beyond the total of your contribution."

In his head, Walter bumped the number O'Connell was driving toward from one-hundred-thousand to two-hundred-thousand dollars. It worked against his business judgment, but with his other bequeathals unattached to any contingency such as an honorary degree, the sum was available to him. The idea was to make the deal now, since his power to negotiate was failing and the money would be left behind in any case.

"I can speak to Philbin Bates right after the holiday," Walter said, seeing no reason to be coy. "Something like a quarter million dollars might be do-able. I'd have to shift a few things around."

Bells began chiming on campus and the sound of them came through the telephone. "That would really be a blessing no one could have anticipated," said O'Connell, although his tone indicated otherwise. "This is true Christian magnanimity you're talking about."

"I'm happy to put my efforts where they will do the most good," Beaumont said, gazing into the darkness at the head of the stairs.

"Let's talk in January," said Father O'Connell. The bells continued pealing. "I must go prepare for Midnight Mass, but I'm very encouraged by this. May you know the peace of our Savior, Jesus Christ."

In the strange blue darkness of his bedroom, Walter Beaumont

Jay Atkinson

considered the thirty-seven-thousand in cash transferred to the United Church of Christ and his promissory notes for an additional two-hundred-fifty-thousand for Manchester College, wondering if indeed God would bless him for it. Beaumont knew his financial maneuvering was no substitute for a pure spirit and genuine good fellowship, but the money was what he had to give. He would part with it gladly, as it had never been his intention to hoard wealth, and only luck coupled with his hard-earned technical skill had imparted such sums as he had in the bank. In his heart, he had wanted his children and grandchildren to have the money. But that was impossible now, as it had always been.

On the bedside table, the numerals of his radio alarm clock turned to twelve. Christmas had arrived. In the distance he heard the bells from Holy Rosary and a few other churches in South Lawrence, and perhaps even Methuen and Andover. He thought he felt what clock maker Basil Morrisette called the hyper-fine resonance frequency of an elapsed second whirring more slowly inside him. All his atoms were winding down like clocks.

Walter raised his hands toward the ceiling. He imagined the quilt on the bed weighed down with his money and he scooped up the cash and threw it into the air like confetti. He continued scattering the ephemera of his life until the arc of his hands became smaller and he descended toward sleep, and what perhaps lingered beyond.

*

The cab reached the zenith of Tower Hill and then rolled to a stop. Inside, Elise Dominaux removed a compact from her bag and flipped it open. The compact was lit with tiny bulbs that illuminated the dank interior of the car. Turning the mirror, Elise hunched forward and her image floated into position. After a quick glance, she clicked the mirror shut.

"All right," she said.

The driver was a clean-looking young man dressed in a pea coat with short dark hair and serious eyes. Inside and out, his cab was immaculate. A statue of Jesus was glued to the dashboard and rosary beads dangled from the mirror. "Six dollars, please," he said.

"This is where my boyfriend lives," Elise said. "He's a pretty old guy but he's not weird or anything: he's just lonely. He used to be a big mucky-muck at the bank."

"I'm sure he'll appreciate your visit," said the cab driver.

Elise handed the man ten dollars, telling him to keep the change. "It's not healthy for anyone to be alone," she said.

The driver wished her a Happy New Year and zoomed off down the hill. Pulling the ends of her short fur jacket together, Elise scurried to the curb, looking up and down the street. Rising above her, one shutter banging in the wind, was a massive house with arched double doors. There was a wrought iron fence surrounding the property, black and fierce in the darkness, a row of barbed spears aimed at the low January sky. The grounds, which were covered with snow, rolled in a great bulk to the curb and downward at sculpted angles to the fences on either side. The front yard was clear of trees, giving it a regal sweep, but behind the house a line of trees swayed in the wind, their interlaced branches clattering like sheaves.

Elise had known Walter Beaumont for three years, and dated him for the year in the middle. They had met one February afternoon at the drugstore across from Breen's Funeral Home. Walter was healthy then, a tall, distinguished-looking man in a tweed overcoat and cashmere scarf, rummaging among the racks for a sympathy card. Elise walked past and he glanced over his shoulder, catching her scent. At the end of the aisle, she paused beside a display of chocolate hearts in gaudy red boxes. He had an aristocratic face and thick gray hair. Elise smiled at him.

"My friends are dying," said the man. "And I'm having trouble choosing a card. I've sent every one of them at least once."

Elise was beyond her youth, with gold-blonde hair and willowy legs. "You might try a blank one, and just write in it how you feel," she said.

"That won't do," he said, with a short confidential laugh. "Because I'm just glad it wasn't me."

Elise found him strangely attractive—strange because she had never been attracted to older men before. Together they went for a stroll down Essex Street. Many of the shops were closed down or marked with yellow police tape, but Walter Beaumont talked about the city's downtown when it had been one of the great retail strips in New England. Stopping in front of the elongated metal wings that formed the entrance to Sutherland's department store, Walter rubbed soap off the window with his elbow and peered inside.

"When I was Vice President of the bank, Sutherland's once grossed half a million dollars in a single week," he said. "Christmas, 1954. It was amazing really."

Mr. Beaumont was a witty man who remembered things that had occurred many years before Elise was born, and still lived in the present. They walked to the Cedar Chest Restaurant and Walter sauntered in and handed their coats to the denture-wearing proprietress. Then he gave twenty dollars to one of the boys who worked in the kitchen, sending him down the street for a bouquet of flowers.

"One night after the war I ate here with Senator Wilson X. Wilson and a young man by the name of Jack Kennedy," said Walter, inhaling the aroma of chicken pies and pot roast. "Back then, Lawrence was the place to be."

Nearby in one of the cedar booths sat Charlie Kutter, an announcer who had called the World Series every year since 1945. Kutter was seated with a younger man, who was obviously his son. Retired now, Charlie Kutter gave speeches, making thousands of dollars to tell stories about the day he met Babe Ruth and how Ted Williams shot the eye out of a caribou on a hunting trip they once took together. Kutter was a native of Lawrence and owned the city's only radio station, WKUT, but Beaumont had not seen him for many years.

Hailing a waitress, Kutter turned around and caught Walter's eye. "Hello, my friend," he said, in a reverberating tone that was familiar to baseball fans everywhere. Heads turned up and down the aisle. "Nice to see you. You look well."

Walter returned the compliment, and then Kutter introduced his son. "Starting today, Kap's the general manager of WKUT, Radio Nine Hundred. We're all hoping it's in his genes," said Kutter, assuming that everyone present was interested in his doings. "It's about time he quit fishing and playing golf. So I put him to work."

Staring at Elise, then shifting his gaze to the old man beside her, Kap Kutter nodded his head like Walter Beaumont had said something, although he had not spoken a word. The young Kutter was dressed in a rumpled but expensive suit, with a fleshy face that had once been handsome and a brush of hair turned prematurely gray. At his elbow was a water glass and another filled with scotch, same as his father.

The senior Kutter was smiling in a way that invited attention to his son. Kap Kutter folded his arms across his chest, gazing over the silverware to the mismatched couple in the other booth.

"What are your plans?" Walter asked.

"To be the best AM station in the country," Kap said.

Walter smiled. "That's a mighty tall order," he said.

Charlie Kutter shook out a napkin and draped it over his lap. "That's why I hired him," he said, turning back to his scotch.

"In business, it's always prudent to have a contingency plan should anything go wrong," said Walter. "But there's no contingency for hiring a son. I wish you both all the luck in the world."

The bouquet of flowers arrived at the table. Instructing the delivery boy to fetch a vase, Walter snapped one of the roses off and pinned it to his overcoat with a spray of baby's breath. Then he refolded the overcoat beside him so the flower and tiny white bells that surrounded it were exposed, like a badge of heraldry.

"That Kap Kutter, or whoever he is," said Elise, "is very rude."

Walter had his hand in the air. "Manners first, and then money: that's a gentleman," he said. A waiter saw his signal, and crossed the dining room. "Money itself is horseshit." Elise tittered at the idea, and Walter added, "When my father first told me that, the city was filled with money and horses."

A very old man in a stiff-brimmed hat and a jacket with thin lapels walked by their table, and Walter leaned across and whispered to Elise. "There's Wilson X. Wilson right there," he said. "He's been our state senator for fifty years—from FDR to George Bush."

"Maybe he'll join us," said Elise, craning to see Wilson totter down the aisle.

"The funny thing about old friendships is that you get embarrassed about them after a while," Walter said, grasping Elise's warm young hand. For a moment, his eyes lost their focus and he stared into the clatter of the dining room.

Walter had always referred to that February afternoon as the day Elise seduced him. But in actuality it had been the other way around; he had lured her into his life with the promises of history. Elise Dominaux was thirty-seven years old and had moved to Lawrence from northern Maine, where the once-booming lumber industry had given way to whining environmentalists and the age of the computer. Her past was unremarkable: divorced parents, high school failures, and a list of going-nowhere jobs. But Walter Beaumont was a man who had eaten chicken pie with presidents. He knew just what to say to famous people, and to waiters and busboys. After months of talking on the telephone and meeting for lunch, Walter invited Elise to dine with him at home. He lived in the family manse on Tower Hill, he said, and from there they could look down on the entire city.

For a time, Elise was often seen at the Beaumont house. Tonight the front walk had been cleared and swept, and later dried with some kind of hot air torch that left the flagstones as crisp as they were in summer. Elise paused at the gate, and then started up toward the bulk that rose in front of her. A voluntary stay in the hospital right after Christmas, and then recovery at home for a few days had prevented Elise from visiting Walter any sooner. She felt bad about it, but since she had planned to show off what he had given her for Christmas, she was determined to look her best. Clicking up the walk in high heels, wearing a dress that fit her like a second skin, Elise felt certain that she did.

Running along the promenade of the house, broken only by the arch of the doors, were four large sections of stained glass. Together the leaded windows formed a mural depicting the Lawrence skyline, and the Ayer Mill clock tower and Merrimack River. It was the sort of architectural detail that had fallen out of fashion; a light behind the glass made the river run blue and painted the sky with streaks of gray. Glowing in the darkness, the mural was a sign of old money and influence.

The brass knocker let out a boom. Inside the house, Elise sensed movement coming from behind the miniature city. A voice called out, "Yes. I'm coming," and then the door swung inward to reveal a tall, elderly man wearing a red turtleneck jersey, green cardigan sweater and a pair of tan slacks.

Walter Beaumont was narrow-shouldered, with a head of stiff gray hair and pop eyes that shook in their sockets. Much darker hair sprouted from his ears and nose, and his skin was a grayish color with dark spots covering his hands and the flesh of his neck. He wore a cannula looped over his ears, and the whisper of oxygen that ran through the plastic tube made it seem like the space behind him was filled with murmuring. In his right hand was a portable oxygen tank that he pushed along the carpet like a golf caddy.

"Hello, my dear," he said, gasping from the effort. "This is a surprise."

Elise kissed him on the cheek. "I had to show you what you bought me." She opened her fur coat and began shrugging it from her shoulders.

"Hold on," said Beaumont. "Let's have some champagne. I've got a bottle somewhere."

He rolled the oxygen tank toward his study. Elise went ahead, switching on the electric sconces along the way. Her fur discarded,

Elise smiled as Walter followed the steady up and down motion of her buttocks.

"They're beautiful," she said. "You're gonna love them."

The study was lined in walnut and had a fireplace, which was kept unlit because of the danger posed by Walter's oxygen. It smelled like the empty bowl of a pipe. Two high-backed chairs faced a cherry wood desk that was empty except for the blotter and a photograph of Walter's father, framed in gold. Franklin Beaumont had white hair and fatty, pinkish skin. Behind rimless spectacles he stared outward with a chilly expression.

"So," said Walter. "How are you?" Collapsing into one of the chairs, he waved his hand toward the wall where a refrigerator was concealed. Elise took out the bottle of champagne, and then fetched two long-stemmed glasses from a cabinet behind the desk.

Walter insisted on opening the champagne himself, although it taxed him. The two chairs were facing each other, and despite the fact that his shaking hands were in close proximity to Elise and her velvet dress, gleaming like sealskin in the lamplight, the old man seemed not to be talking to her but to the photograph of his father.

"Let me propose a toast," he said. The champagne fizzed like tooth powder in the glass. Elise was already drinking, and she stopped when Walter frowned and placed his own glass on a coaster and refilled hers. Taking up his drink again, in a quavering voice Walter said, "To the hope of new friends and the memory of old ones. To youth and beauty and all good things."

"Hear, hear," said Elise. They clinked glasses, and she drank the entire contents in one draught while Walter barely touched his. "Now I have one to make," Elise said, laughing. She refilled her glass, and hovered above Walter's before realizing there was no room for any more champagne in it. Elise raised her chin, and golden wisps of hair touched her shoulders and curled upward. "I want to propose a toast to the best Christmas gift ever."

The oxygen streamed into Walter's nose and he wet his lips in anticipation. With a flourish, Elise rolled down the top of her dress and exposed a pair of rigid breasts that bulged outward and were mapped with tiny blue veins. At the end of each breast was an engorged nipple—like the stems used to inflate car tires. "Aren't they the greatest pair of tits you ever saw?" she asked.

"They're wonderful," said Walter, shaking his head at what he had wrought. "You are very welcome, my dear. Merry Christmas."

"Merry Christmas, my ass," said Elise. "Feel 'em."

Walter's face was gray against the leather of the chair. "You'll catch a chill," he said.

"Go ahead."

Walter's spotted hands twice left his knees, each time stopping a little short. Above the new breasts, Elise's eyes were closed and her lips were curled back over her teeth in a little smile. Walter stared at the breasts like they were something in a museum. Finally he touched them, his fingertips scraping the tight warm flesh.

Elise's eyes remained shut. "Oh, go on," she said. "Give 'em a real squeeze."

The breasts standing like they had been carved from alabaster, and with the cold eyes of his father upon him, the old man reached a third time and took hold. The breasts thudded in his hands like a pair of beating hearts. He curled his fingers beneath them, and their weight fell into his palms. Pulling the cannula over his head, he tossed the plastic loop to the floor and bent upon Elise. He could smell her perfume and the aroma of feminine sweat behind it. Walter buried his nose between the swelling blivets. Moaning to himself about all he had once possessed and then lost, he began weeping.

"Don't cry, Walter," said Elise. Her ears strained to pick up a word that sounded like Pier. "I'll come over whenever you want, and you can feel them as much as you like."

Walter's gaze darted around the room, and Elise realized that he was looking for the cannula. She picked it off the carpet for him, lowering it over his head like a war decoration. The old man tried to catch his breath so he could speak.

"Can't...won't," he said. "Nothing helps."

It took several minutes for Walter to regain control. He was turned sideways in the chair, chest heaving, and his arms thin through the cardigan sweater. His eyes remained wet, fixed on the portrait of his father. Behind the gaze of Franklin Beaumont there had once been an expansive and calculating mind. Walter stared at the wrinkles on his father's brow, and remembered how it had furrowed during conversations in this very room. Advice sessions that went on until Walter was fifty years old.

"He did..." Walter said, still unable to process enough air for talking. His lips formed words but all that came out were inaudible sounds, like a dog whistle.

"He did what?" asked Elise, patting the old man's shoulder. "What did your father do?" She was overcome with curiosity, but saw that Walter's desperation was leading him toward an attack of some kind. "Please. You're getting too upset."

By the time the mill shut down, Walter was Vice President of Lawrence Savings & Trust; and at his father's urging, he had purchased municipal bonds for a planned suburban community in Levittown, New York that turned out to be a stroke of financial genius. Walter's share of that transaction, coupled with his stock from the bank, eventually had given him a net worth of eight-hundred-ninety-thousand dollars plus real estate and capital investments. The last time he had checked, his estate was growing by $1,276.92 a week. He had worked hard, but his father had provided him with the proper framework. Every business decision Franklin Beaumont ever made was clock accurate.

When Walter relaxed again, drawing his breath in a steady rhythm, Elise leaned forward to massage his groin. Her naked breasts fell to the old man's knees, and her eyes were steady on his. For six months during the previous year Walter and Elise had been lovers. After lunch or dinner at one of the city restaurants, usually Bachop's with its opulent decor and elderly tuxedoed waiters, the couple would return to Elise's apartment in a rehabilitated mill beside the river.

Lovemaking between them was orderly, their clothes removed facing away from each other and then folded, the bed turned down like children were going to sleep there. Walter needed no assistance, and his stamina was remarkable for a man of seventy-seven, but he never kissed Elise during the act or told her that he loved her. Looming there in the dark, he pressed his case like an old farmer plowing the land. He even looked like a workman without his clothes, long and spare with hardly any fat but long wrinkles across his chest and a heavy smooth hardness to his knees, the balls of his shoulders, and his narrow skull. His joints clicked, snapping like mousetraps when he moved, and if the moon was down and there was no light, Elise had the awful sensation that she was being ridden upon by a skeleton, the fleshless jaw grinning at her in the darkness.

All that came to an end after the emphysema got worse, and for Elise, gratefully so. She wasn't one to let an age difference trouble her, but any fool could see there was no future with a seventy-nine year old man. They had been together maybe a dozen times, in her apartment, at Wentworth-by-the-Sea, even one time behind the clock faces of the Ayer Mill. Never once had they made love inside Beaumont's mansion on Tower Hill. Asked why that was, he said, "Home to bed is where married people go."

Elise could see that he was almost asleep. Through the fabric of his pants his genitals felt like two marbles and half a wet cigar. Releasing them, Elise looked about the room for a pillow or an afghan. Unable to navigate the stairs, Walter had a bed arranged here on the main floor of the house. He was very stubborn about his independence, and had refused to employ a visiting nurse or to allow Elise to prepare meals for him or have them sent over. If they dined together, they dined out.

Light snores came from Walter's mouth. Elise pulled the velvet rim of her dress over her breasts, which she still wasn't quite used to, and tugged them into place. Walter's hands twitched on his knees, like he was feeling for something. She thought about a farewell kiss, but decided it might wake him. Tiptoeing from the study, Elise picked up her fur in the entranceway and went out the front door, the mural shimmering in her wake.

6

Lawrence, Massachusetts

September 18, 1848

Long after Captain Bigelow had been poled ashore in the skiff, his dredging crew was busy hauling up chunks of mud from the river. Their oversize buckets, which were fifty pounds empty and dropped into the current on ropes, featured an elongated lip on one edge that sliced muck off the bottom, allowing the Essex Company to deepen the Merrimack foot by painful foot. Captain Bigelow and Mr. Storrow had calculated that such an enlarged channel pouring into the sluiceways could be invoiced to the mills at a higher rate. And so crews were assigned to this unending labor, interrupted only by the encroachment of swiftly passing nights.

There were five buckets aboard the scow, each of them handled by a team of three dredgers. The foreman, Old Pete Driscoll, sat raised above the stern in the coxswain's seat, exhorting the teams through a megaphone. The scow was fifty feet long and half as wide, and each evening, when the bed of this ship was filled with debris, its gunwales stood mere inches above the river.

While the men hauled and spat and swore and upended their buckets, Driscoll cast his gaze over the day's work, which had risen at his feet like a yeasty black loaf. He estimated that the scow contained more than three tons of mud—any more and it would founder. "Last bucket, lads," he said. "One more pull, and we're all home for supper."

Laughing as he coiled his rope and then swung the bucket above his head, Gabriel Glass winked at his mates and said, "I never seen you choking a bucket line, Pete, but your end of the load seems to rise every time a skirt passes over the Andover Bridge."

The long-haired youth whirled his bucket like a lasso and then flung it into the river, as the dredgers erupted in laughter. "I pull up my load of ore every night at half-eight," said a redheaded fellow, nudging the man next to him. "Your wife catches it in her bonnet."

"She has a hatful of ginger-haired children," said another.

Jay Atkinson

The offended man laughed along with the others. "Feed those and mine as well," he said.

"You've got a mule's habit for work, Master Glass," said Old Pete, using his megaphone to speak over the commotion. "But mark me, that wagging tongue will finish you one day."

Gabriel and his two mates felt their bucket sinking fast. Hauling the line against the current, they aimed with a surveyor's precision for the chasm they had dug that day. The other four teams dropped their lines in the same proximity. Eyeing the men closest to him, Glass smiled as the five buckets pierced the muck beneath them.

"First up?" asked the long-haired youth.

One bucket over, a stout fellow spat into the river. This crew was a trio of brothers, all the same size and stature who appeared to have dredged their way out of the earth. The Murphys were balding, their backs and chests were covered with thick black hair, and they had the constitution of moles.

The Murphy brothers, all straining at the rope, displayed their stubby teeth to one another. "First up, a dollar," said the ugliest of them.

"A dollar from each man on board," his brother said. "That's...ahh..." He attempted to count on his fingers while maintaining a grip on the rope. "That's surely more than ten dollars, I reckon."

Old Pete spat into the Merrimack. "The Essex Company does not approve of wagering," he said.

"No wagers, then," said Gabriel. "We'll make it a race."

All five crews steadied their buckets, looking at Driscoll through slit eyes. The only sound was the lapping of waves against the gunwale.

"Yes, a contest," the Swede called out. His name was Jorgensen, and although new to dredging, he was a man of extraordinary strength who could bend an iron rod with his hands. "I, the Swede, will win," he said to Gabriel Glass. "I will rip out your tongue and feed it to the eels."

"Then turn your muscles into feathers, Jorgy, and try to catch me," said the youth, to the merriment of his crew. "After I put my empty bucket over your head, I'll disappear like Caesar's ghost."

High in the catbird seat, Old Pete sat chin in hand, twisting the lower half of his face. "A contest it is, then. The winning crew can ascend the ropes while the rest haul us in."

There were groans, sprinkled with a few cheers. The first and heaviest of the Essex company scows had been built without a capstan, which would have allowed the dredgers to wind the boat ashore, and every evening they damned the carpenters for this oversight. For when the stars began to glisten above the Pacific Mills, Old Pete clipping his hasp and harness onto the fixed line meant the crew would have to pull until they reached the gatehouse.

"I, the Swede, will win, and haul this scow with my teeth," said Jorgensen.

The ginger-haired man broke wind. "I say you'll pull us home with your arse," he said. "In ten minutes, Gabe'll be having his supper and yours, too."

"On my mark, then," said Old Pete, raising a hammer he used to bang out the dented buckets. "Ready, ready, lads. Now pull!"

Exhaling through his nostrils, Gabriel Glass created a rhythm that sent six fists alternating onto the rope. The other crews worked in silence. Most of the men were tired, and although the buckets were invisible beneath the waves, Gabriel and his crew were the only ones piling up coils at a steady rate. Across the bow, Jorgensen watched these loops accumulate, grabbing the line in huge swags and bashing his elbows against his teammates.

Two of the crews gave up. They sat down on the pile of muck and each man yanked at the line in turn. The Murphy brothers were far behind; only half the length of Gabriel's rope lay about their feet.

"Curse this mud, this scow, and this bunghole of a New City," said the first brother, clawing at the rope. He lost his grip and fell down, slicing his forehead on a cleat. "I pull buckets out of this river until I'm exhausted; eat, drink, fart, and work some more; and at night have nothing to show for it but calluses and blisters."

"Don't quit now, boys." said Old Pete. "Do it for the pride of the Essex Company."

The ugliest Murphy glanced up from where he was lying. "I do it for the *pay* of the Essex Company," he said. "And the pay is late."

Jorgenson continued yanking at the line. The muscles of his chest wobbled beneath the blouse he wore, sailcloth trimmed with blue piping that was the envy of the other dredgers. "I, the Swede, will empty the river," he said. "Alps made of mud from here to Amesbury will I, the Swede, make."

As the hands of his team plunged one on top of the other, Gabriel Glass felt the bucket swimming upward to him. "Here she comes," he said. "Steady now."

Old Pete raised his hammer. "For the Essex Company!"

Glass and his team yanked their load, now close to 150 pounds, out of the Merrimack. They made an aperture in the river that quickly disappeared, and foam trailed the bucket as they heaved it against the pile of mud. The other four lines were still in the water.

Jorgenson let go of the rope. "You win," he said. "The better man say I, the Swede." Reaching behind his head, he shucked the blouse from his torso and threw it into the mud at Gabriel's feet.

The Swede, etched with various muscles, hopped over the bowsprit and grasped the other team's bucket in his hands. Turning it upside down, he emptied the mud onto the pile with a loud suction noise. Then Jorgenson crammed the bucket onto his head, with the handle drooping beneath his chin. "I, the Swede, see Caesar's ghost," he said. "Oo-ooo."

The dredgers laughed at these antics, while Old Pete banged on a stanchion with his hammer. "You won't be so merry if Cap'n Bigelow is waiting on the pier," Driscoll said. "Let's heave to, boys."

A heavy tarpaulin, which acted as sort of a windbreak, hung down from the Andover Bridge and was lashed to the scow. As the men worked to free themselves from the pilings and Old Pete attached his hawser

Jay Atkinson

onto the fixed line, the tarp came free and made a loud snapping sound against the water. The Swede removed the bucket from his head, tossing it over the pile of mud. Retrieving his prized blouse, he slogged through the debris littering the scow and presented the item to Gabriel.

"I, the Swede, make you a gift," Jorgensen said.

"Keep your garments, Jorgy," said the long-haired youth. "It is a queer part of my constitution to work hard in order to avoid working."

But the Swede gestured again for him to take it. Glass removed his filthy undershirt; the blouse hung down to his knees and the hand-sewn sleeves covered his hands. "It sure is a fine shirt," he said.

"My wife is the greatest seamstress in all of Stockholm, and I miss her and my children—who are the most beautiful sons and daughters in the world—more than a fish misses the water," said Jorgensen. He rested against the gunwale, all his muscles sagging. "I came to this New City to make my fortune and have found nothing but stacks of mud."

The youth was admiring his new blouse: sailcloth trimmed with blue piping that was the envy of the other dredgers. "Don't fret, Jorgy," he said. "All of us will return home someday, wherever home is."

"When I told them I was a sailor, they took away my bo's'n's pipe and made me empty out the sea," said Jorgensen, slumped over the gunwale like a colossus. "Such a man will never set foot in the Old Port again."

The dredgers began untying the half hitches that secured their mooring. Bowing in the wind, two lines streamed down from the bridge, attached to cleats that decorated the gunwale. "Anyone galumphing up those ropes better do it now," said Old Pete.

One of Gabriel's mates who had a sore shoulder pronounced himself unfit for this task, joining the other dredgers on the fixed line. Gabriel Glass and his remaining crew member, Ephet Asadoorian, sat hunched on the stern. The Armenian had blunt, swarthy features and tufts of hair protruding from his ears and nose. He was ten years older than the youth who sat beside him, and although he was tattered and dirty and stooped with weariness, his forearms resembled chunks of granite. "Up you go, Gabe," he said, smiling at the lad. "You and your fancy new shirt."

"Why not come along? Hasten up those ropes, and there'll be roasted bass for supper."

Asadoorian gazed at his feet. "Too tired," he said.

"Thirty minutes sweating over the fixed line, I'd hardly call a rest," said Glass.

Old Pete ordered the mooring lines to be unwound from the fore and aft bollards, and the boat swung with the current, ripples flowing from the stern in a great V. "Now or never, boys," he said.

Glass slapped Asadoorian's knee. "Come on," he said. "For the pride of the Essex Company."

"For the *pay* of the Essex Company," said the Armenian. He stood and grasped the nearest rope.

While the crew of dredgers huzzahed, Gabriel Glass ran across the stern, leaped up, and stabbed at the other line. Fifty feet above the scow loomed the Andover Bridge. Hugging the rope between his knees, the youth ascended hand over hand, chewing his way like an inchworm.

Asadoorian was not faring so well. A little more than a third of the rope lay beneath him but he was motionless, gripping the line with both hands, his head askew like a sailor who had broken his neck in the rigging.

Gabriel Glass dangled just a few feet below the bridge deck. "On you come, Ephet," he said. "Soon we'll have our feet in a pail of hot water, and our mouths full of river bass."

The other man sighted up the line. His hands trembled and slowly his body uncoiled, drooping toward the river. "No," he said.

The youth watched as the Armenian let go of the rope and fell with a whistling sound through the air. Just then the dredgers, fighting against the current, began to pull on the hawser, angling toward shore. They were loosened from the pilings and, just as the scow threatened to slip away, Asadoorian plummeted into its cargo of ooze, knifing to his armpits.

The dredgers laughed, and the shock of their laughter reached the Pacific Mills and echoed back to them. As the scow ran free of its moorings and the fixed line sawed back and forth over the mud, Asadoorian grabbed at it, wrenched himself free of the quagmire, and joined the other men hauling the barge toward shore. "Home and supper, boys," said Old Pete, while laughter exploded in the air.

Gabriel Glass felt the space yawning beneath his feet and hurried up the last stretch of rope, hauling himself onto the bridge. For a few moments he rested there, listening to Old Pete's cadence while his arms burned and the muscles of his back twisted with spasms. Wreathed in shadow, the Great Dam loomed beside him, spilling water at one end.

"I will eat a whale for...pick my teeth with his bones," said Jorgensen from below, his voice separating on the wind.

Gabriel picked himself up, straightened the folds of his new blouse, and glanced about him. His rib cage was tender, on the spot where he had smashed against a rock while saving Captain Bigelow. Far off, he saw men approaching from the New City. They marched along in step and then turned into the gatehouse lot—a squad of constables. Not wishing to be seen on foot, covered in muck and wearing another man's shirt, Gabriel plunged his hands into his trouser pockets and hurried toward Dublin.

Ahead, the horizon closed to a single red line demarcating the land and sky. Gabriel could sense the weight of all that water behind the dam, its mass turned against the bulwark and running for the canal. Although he had contributed his labor to other projects—the grading of Essex Street, building the coffer dams and five months spent dredging the river—this was his finest achievement. Among the three hundred headers and stretchers that comprised the Great Dam, Gabriel reckoned that he had handled at least one third; using oxen to stand the tablets upright, fitting them with canvas harnesses, and cranking the windlass as the strength of one man lifted into the air what four men couldn't budge. The previous morning, while another laborer wound the stem of this device, Glass helped raise slabs marked 274, 275, 283 and 286 into their notches, his arms spread over the granite, the whorl of his ear pressed against each stone as it ascended.

As Gabriel's feet rang over the bridge, he imagined that the dam housed some portion of his energy and that one hundred years in the future, the joy he had felt would remain there, caught between the stones. Back in April, while working with a crew of sawyers, the youth had discovered chunks of amber inside a tree cut down to make way for Essex Street. Upon closer examination Glass found an entombed dragonfly, its wings, spindly legs, and antennae preserved in the yellowish-brown resin. Using his hatchet, Glass freed the amber and retained the dragonfly as a keepsake. For months he had carried it in his pocket.

At noon that very day, while taking their luncheon on board the scow, Captain Bigelow had informed Gabriel that he had been chosen to guide the final stretcher atop the dam. This distinction was not based on a whim, or a form of apology for vexing the youth during the collapse of the coffer dam. Nay, Bigelow's choice was popular among the men; from the consulting engineers to the mute who spent his day scouring out masonry buckets for a half-penny apiece. No other fellow had expended his sweat on so many projects, and done it all so cheerfully; nobody else had applied such vigor to the largest mill dam in the world, the grading of the most efficient power canal in human history, and the dredging of a moving river as had Gabriel Glass—offering ideas that saved his fellow employees many hours of hard labor and the Essex Company a commensurate number of dollars, while shrugging it all off as mere commonplace wisdom.

That morning when the burghers in their top hats and frock coats would mount the platform—never once setting eyes on the Great Dam before the moment that they stood upon it—at least one deserving fellow would be among them, wearing Gilmore & Carpenter dungarees and a ribbon of appreciation from the Essex Company, which Captain Bigelow then presented to Gabriel Glass. The moment Gabriel received the ribbon and badge into his hand, Jorgensen's cries lured the other dredgers away, to watch the Swede wrestle with a giant fish he had hooked on a dropline. Reaching into the side pocket of his trousers, Gabriel Glass produced the nugget of amber containing the dragonfly.

"Here, Captain," said the youth. "A man of science like yourself could fathom such an object better than I."

Stooping over his game leg, Captain Bigelow had grasped the amber between thumb and forefinger and raised his hand to the sun. *"Odonata Anisoptera,"* he said. "Called the devil's darning needle, and distinguished from the damselfly by the horizontal position of the wings while at rest." In the sunlight, bands of gray and green flashed across the dragonfly's body, and its net-veined wings sprang to life, until it appeared the insect would fly from Bigelow's grasp.

"It's an apt memento from our New City," said the Captain. Beyond the river, the Upper Pacific Mill threw smoke from its stacks and a number of shiny conveyances could be seen rolling along Essex Street. "For our prospects here will never be as bright as they are at this moment. Encase us all in amber, and this is the way we would always be."

A tumult upon the stern drew their attention. With the line taut in his hands, and the string zagging back and forth, Jorgensen had bent in the pose of an archer, his right arm drawn up behind his head and his left hand extended. Utilizing all his strength he raised the fish to the surface, its mouth gaping. The Swede seized the carp in an iron grip, maiming its eye, and lifted the huge coppery fish into the air.

"What a monster that one is," Old Pete said.

The body was three feet in length, covered in dull gray scales. Jorgensen tossed the fish, which weighed close to a hundred pounds, onto the pile of muck aboard the scow and immediately the carp began losing its scales by the fistful. The sides of the great fish heaved, the loosened eye hung by a sinew, and its tail flapped and pounded against the mud.

"There's your trophy, boys," said one of the Murphy brothers.

Jorgensen stood high on the stern, his feet spread apart, arms akimbo. "I, the Swede, will catch a boatload of such trophies and feed the whole of your shantytown each and every night."

"You can eat that carp, Jorgy, if you fancy it," said Asadoorian. He nudged the man beside him, and was shoved back in return. "A beast which feeds on the shite running from our privies."

Bigelow's final comment to Gabriel Glass had been lost amid laughter from the dredgers, but he had smiled at the youth, tucking the dragonfly into the pocket of his waistcoat.

*

As Gabriel descended from the bridge onto the Loundonderry Turnpike, streaks of red fumed along the horizon, bloodying the river and promising fair weather for the morrow's ceremony. Immediately a cart path branched off from the Turnpike, and Gabriel jumped down from the abutment and followed it toward the cluster of shanties that lay a mile ahead. Part of an old harvest road that had once circumnavigated Daniel Saunder's farm, the path to Dublin bore the impression of two wagon tracks and dropped into a field of briars.

Gabriel tucked his trouser cuffs into his boots and pulled up the collar of Jorgensen's blouse to guard against ticks, which were rife among the briars. Once a mule had been borrowed from the Essex Company to drag a granite slab into camp for use as a hearthstone. Progress through the briars was so slow that when the mule arrived in Dublin, quivering and shuddering through its nostrils, its hide was embedded with so many wood ticks it took a half dozen boys the entire night to remove them. They touched the insects with brands pulled from the fire, causing the mule to yelp in a strange human voice and the agitated ticks to back out of their furrows.

Beyond the thicket, the road sloped into a marshy area that served as an elephant's graveyard for the company. Rusted turbines, fragments of stone, shattered railroad ties, and brick rubble formed various piles across an open field. Everything useful had been scoured from the area—including the wooden crates that later became the shanties of Dublin—and what remained were iron routers too huge and heavy to move, eerie-looking cairns of stone, and rotten flashboards covered in algae, surrounded by footprints that had filled up with water. There were hidden springs beneath all the refuse; none of this was arable land.

The residents of Dublin, their boots gooey with mire each time they passed to their shanties, often noted that Daniel Saunders had realized $150,000 from the Essex Company for a parcel of land that brought in fourteen dollars a year—the sum collected from beekeepers who kept their hives there—and still the old gent could be heard fretting over the lost honey rights. In spite of the old man's penuriousness, the teamsters and masons and dam builders admired Saunders. He remained a fixture in the valley, driving in each Saturday to the Essex Company headquarters on Jackson Street. At the stroke of noon, he presented himself to the clerks in order to receive his weekly payment.

The wagon tracks softened into mud and Gabriel Glass picked his way along, until the mire became so pervasive that trekkers were forced to wade knee-deep through the duff. Behind the stump of an oak tree, Gabriel fished among the roots for something he had deposited there. It was a pair of flat, oval disks woven from river reeds and mule skin. Bound with twine to his boots, they became crude snow-shoes that allowed him to travel over the muck without sopping his trousers.

The long-haired youth kept a pair of these devices hidden at each end of the boggy trail. They served him so well that other laborers had begun clamoring for them, but Gabriel was preoccupied with his new fishing enterprise and concealed the snow-shoes in order to prevent them from being stolen.

Although he generated a number of such ideas on his own, Gabriel Glass's happiest moments were spent collaborating with Captain Bigelow. Referring to his soiled boots one morning, Gabriel had expressed a desire to go skating over the trail, in order to avoid spending the day with wet feet. His superior listened with interest, and disappeared when the masonry crew began hauling stones to the foot of the dam. Returning at noontime armed with a picture-book, the Captain showed Gabriel an engraving of Esquimaus wearing strange webs attached to their mukluks. These allowed the arctic tribes to tread over great banks of snow without breaking through the crust, Bigelow explained.

Possessed of this notion, Gabriel attempted to make a pair of snow-shoes on his own, but was unable to round the tips or bind the outer edge, and the mats disintegrated when he tried to walk in them. He turned to Captain Bigelow and they spent half a Sunday studying the picture-book while the Captain made some drawings. Together the inventors decided that they would substitute mule hide for what appeared to be bearskin on the uppers of the shoe. While Gabriel roamed the lot outside the gatehouse in search of a springy bow with which to form a last, Captain Bigelow discovered that he could produce a natural adhesive from the boiled hooves of the mule. And so the beast who had died from an abundance of tick bites served Dublin once more, its skin glued to reeds and bound to Gabriel's feet, enabling the youth to avoid what had been the mule's downfall.

City in Amber

The encyclopedia fascinated Gabriel, and the Captain invited him to borrow this book so he could leaf through the illustrations. From that day on, an unspoken bond grew between Gabriel Glass and Charles Bigelow. Gabriel's mother had died in childbirth in Andover and his father was a drunkard, who within a year had turned the child over to a storekeeper named Glass and fled the region. It was a household of nine children and meager rations of love. By the age of ten, Gabriel Glass, as he became known, was working for local farmers and shop owners, laboring in exchange for food and a bundle of hay to lie down on. He found that the life of an itinerant suited him and he learned to survive through a combination of grit, a pleasant nature, and compassion for his fellow man.

When he was fourteen, Gabriel apprenticed himself to a stonemason for two years; and at sixteen, he worked for a year as a blacksmith in North Andover. There he met Daniel Saunders while shoeing one of his horses and, broad in the shoulders now and sturdy on his feet, he joined the employ of the old man for two dollars a week, a place at the Saunders' table, and lodging in the granary. Soon after, the Essex Company surveyors arrived to measure the lower lands beside the river, and Daniel Saunders began traveling to Boston on the train. Rumors circulated about a Great Dam that was to be built, along with a power canal and mills, and the labor force swelled as men arrived by foot and on horseback. On such a project, local folk might learn one of the mechanized trades, while living in sparkling new dormitories and eating company bread, as did their cousins in Lowell.

For weeks, the farmhands buzzed with speculation. Then red stakes were driven into the ground, and a deal was consummated between Daniel Saunders and the nascent Essex Company. It was true: the men would build a mighty dam thirty feet high, with wing walls a mile wide; they would cut a canal along the Merrimack that would drop a mere six inches along its length and yet generate 10,000 horsepower. Modern factories would appear on the banks of the river, and these mills would clothe half the world and employ the same families for generations.

Gabriel Glass couldn't sleep that night. In the morning, the principal field engineer for the New City was due at the North Andover station. People said that he was a military man, and that he would bring with him the clerks and secretaries who would enroll the first workers for the dam. Although many claimed they would join him, only Gabriel arose at three AM and was standing by the tracks when the train arrived, hooting in the dimness. The first man to disembark was wearing an army field jacket with gold epaulets. His eyes were clear as the river, and his black beard ran in a thatch from ear to ear.

"Good morning, sir," said the sole member of his welcoming party. "I want a job."

Captain Bigelow shook the youth's hand and found a huge leathery mitt. "What sort of work do you do, son?" asked the Captain.

"Any kind at all," Gabriel said. "But I'd like to build a dam."

Bigelow glanced around at the empty lot, as two men carried a wooden table off the back of the train and set it in the dust, accompanied by two chairs. "You are hired," said Captain Bigelow. He nodded toward the company scribes, who were sharpening their quills. "Tell them your name should be entered first in the ledger, and that you will report to me. And what is that name?"

"Gabriel Glass."

Bigelow mused on the youth's name, and what it might signify. "Tell them to write, 'Gabriel Glass. First man to appear, first man hired, under the auspices of the Essex Company, 17 May, 1845.' And then hasten to the baggage car and help me unload my instruments. There's work to be done, if we are to build a New City and see it grow."

*

At the end of the bog, Gabriel removed his snowshoes and hid them inside a tangle of ferns. The ache between his ribs had grown into genuine discomfort, and the spot burned when he knelt to lace up his boots. Soon he heard the sound of twigs breaking underfoot— another laborer was coming along the trail. Scratched by briars and muddy to the knees, the man emerged from the underbrush and began stamping his feet and combing his fingers through his beard. He was six and a half feet tall, with a thick torso and legs like two bridge pilings.

"William," said Gabriel. "You are a sight."

The giant smiled in recognition, his beard parting to reveal a set of yellowed teeth. Then his throat convulsed, and something like a cough mixed with growling emerged from his mouth.

As a young boy, William Bower had enjoyed the gift of speech, until the day his mother discovered a growth on his tongue and an Andover surgeon was hired to cut it out. Although the operation was botched and there were torrents of blood, the patient managed to survive. Now his thoughts began as words in his brain, but when the mute compressed air in his mouth and attempted to launch them, they disintegrated into the wild sounds he was known for. Children taunted him and visitors to the New City laughed, calling him an idiot, and under the pressure of these insults William went around with his jaw clenched tight and his enormous hands balled into fists. But the sight of Gabriel Glass caused happiness to overtake him, boiling into an expression that only a few intimates could fathom.

"Shall we go on to Dublin?" Gabriel asked, clasping the hands of his friend.

William made another bawling sound, and the youth nodded in agreement. "Nothing short of a river bass and brown bread will stop the rumbling in my guts," said Gabriel.

Strapped to the soles of William's boots were shattered river reeds, which hung down like muddy webs when he lifted his feet. It was the fourth pair of snow-shoes that Gabriel Glass had fashioned for William, but his customer's size and weight had so skewed the engineering of these devices that the young inventor once tried weaving barrel staves together and still the giant crushed them. Mute William growled his apology.

"It's my lack of skill that makes them a failure," Gabriel said. "Before we try again, I shall consult with Captain Bigelow."

Standing so close, the youth noticed a tick burrowing into William's neck, and first pointed to his own neck before reaching for it. "An uninvited guest," said Gabriel, the shell of the insect crackling as he twisted it out. "Let's hurry back to camp," he said, squinting in the gloom. "We must examine you by the fires."

Ahead was a field of boulders, which over the ages had pushed up from beneath the earth's crust. They were huge and moss-covered, some of them cracked in half by tree roots, so cleanly it appeared they had been struck by a stonemason's ax. Running over more navigable ground, the cart path turned west through meadows of goldenrod until it disappeared into another forest. Men in wagons and driving mule teams were forced to detour in that direction, but those on foot could follow a more direct route into shantytown. The trail between the boulders was narrow and hard, winding among rock canyons that were cool to the touch and around smaller stones and jumbled tree roots in a series of switchbacks. The logic of this pass had been printed into the earth over centuries, first by fox and bear, and parties of Algonquian heading north to make war; then explorers and conquerors, white men toting bibles and white men armed, settlers, hunters, sawyers and their blades; the farmer dragging his mattock and behind him the farmer's wife, then their children, and grandchildren, and great-grandchildren; and those who came by train to see the sights; and Sunday fishermen, beekeepers, burghers, and speculators; and the five thousand men who built the Great Dam and the New City that would follow it.

There was one cleft in the rock where Mute William was forced to turn sideways, raise himself on tiptoe, and draw in the billow of his stomach as he attempted to squeeze through. A short distance off, Gabriel Glass waited in the clearing, one hand massaging his sore ribs. "No bread and beer for you," he said, grinning at his friend. "Just a filet of bass—and not too much of that."

William struggled for a moment, chafing against the rocks, then his rib cage flexed inward and he popped free, shaking out his beard and jangling his arms. He made another gargling noise in response to Gabriel's jest, patting his stomach to indicate his readiness for the evening meal. Smoke from the fires of Dublin filled the air, which was just out of sight now and redolent of broiling fish, venison, and other sundries. Extending for a quarter mile beyond the rocks was a cluster of elms, each a yard in diameter and rising more than five stories before expanding in a crown of branches.

High above, the elms were turning yellow, streaked here and there with a brilliant red. Gabriel Glass and his companion lingered in the grove, the smooth trunks like monoliths all around them. A breeze wafted in from the river, and for a moment they listened to the murmur of the leaves. Then they heard the sound of a flute coming from shantytown, and doubled their pace.

Before they emerged from the wood, they circled a pit that had been

Jay Atkinson

dug among the trees. Each morning, residents of Dublin hiked out here carrying buckets and deposited their waste into the communal sump. Chunks of builder's lime and sweet ferns by the bushel had been sprinkled into the night soil to help control its reek, but the odor was unmistakable. A strange humming noise rose from the pit and, as the two men approached, they saw it was teeming with honeybees. The swill was black with them, crawling and buzzing.

"Ugh," said Gabriel. "Thom Maddox's bees have been making a foul nectar."

The oldest shanties had been built side by side on the edge of the clearing. These were of flimsy construction, hammered together from broken railroad ties, crates, scraps of driftwood and pine boughs. In hot weather, the crooked pine boughs exuded sap that gave off a pleasant odor but stuck to everything in the shanty, and the old railroad ties sweated tar and other resins that fouled the air, making the inhabitants sick. As more and more workers arrived in the New City and Dublin grew, these dwellings were abandoned, left behind by men too fatigued at the end of their labors to demolish them.

Only one of these shacks was still in use. Its occupant was known as Cob, a small, pointy-faced chap who went about dressed in a woolen shawl. As far as anyone knew, Cob had never worked a day in the New City, but subsisted on the generosity of his neighbors during times of plenty, and in winter on the dried corn from which he drew his nickname. The ground outside his window became littered with dozens of corncobs. The children of Dublin shied away from this hovel, and rumors grew that the old man who lived inside was a cannibal, and the discarded cobs were the gnawed-at bones of his inquisitors.

But really he was a gentle fellow. Sometimes Gabriel Glass brought an eel or horned pout that had been caught in his fish traps, and Cob would boil it in river water sprinkled with handfuls of maize, making a poor soup. He liked to sing while he prepared his dinner, an old song about a winged chariot and kingdoms of gold, and when the soup was ready he sat with his legs folded beneath him and a toothless grin upon his face. Before he commenced eating, he would ask his visitor to pronounce a blessing and when Gabriel intoned the Pater Noster, the old hermit would often shed a tear.

The old shanties were pitched along a grade, and as Gabriel and William Bower passed by, turning their feet sideways to skid down the little slope, Cob thrust his head from the window. Recognizing the two travelers, he asked, "Anything for Cob?"

Gabriel waved the man back inside. "Later, the head and tail of a bass, but nothing at the moment," he said. The hermit retreated into his cabin with a grunt.

Standing on level ground, the youth and his companion surveyed the four hundred shanties that dotted the glen, in various sizes and methods of construction. A town built of necessity rather than an engineer's plan, it was a place meant only to nourish the bodies of its inhabitants and not their minds or souls. Many of the roofs were fashioned from tin, which shined in the firelight; others were shingled and bits of mica glistened in the flames, and some were blackened by tar paper. In the middle was a common, formed by a brook that ran from higher ground across the meadow where Dublin stood, divided by a grassy ravine. The brook dropped some two hundred yards through this park and into the Merrimack River. After circling the field of boulders, the old cart path returned over the course of a mile, then followed the brook into Dublin and veered toward the northern boundary of Saunders' farm.

It was a masculine encampment. Men in greasy dungarees and overalls tended their supper fires, grilling flanks of venison and hare, and turning open-mouthed fish on rotisseries made of pine branches. What few women lived in camp were hanging out clumps of wash carried up from the river, and a number of children gamboled along the cart path, firing stones at a terrified mole they had driven into the brook. Unaccustomed to being wet, the mole darted back and forth, seeking refuge beneath the overhanging sod as the children made sport of him.

Parked on the cart path in the midst of this commotion was a varnished patent-medicine wagon, and occupying the johnnyseat was Hiram Bessell, surrounded by his wares. The bespectacled old man had lain out some parchment leaves and was scribbling on them with the nib of a pencil.

"Hallo, Mr. Bessell," said Gabriel. "I see you have found our Dublin, after all."

Looking up, the peddler hailed the youth as he waded across the brook. "I used the divining rod of my own good sense," Bessell said.

Mute William gestured that he would return after conducting some other business, and then set off across the glen. Along the way, he passed Thom Maddox, standing among the soft gray bulbs of his hives wearing an apron and gauzy headdress. Maddox was pulling fistfuls of honey from the hives and stuffing it into glass jars. From over the rooftops the sound of a flute grew stronger, accompanied by someone scratching a washboard and another musician beating upon a kettle.

"Are you preparing an oration?" Gabriel asked the peddler.

"Upon conclusion of yonder symphony, I will deliver a message of good health to the camp—bolstering the advice with sales of my elixir," said Hiram Bessell. His whitened beard and the tufts of hair sticking out from his skullcap gave his head a triangular appearance. "If any settlement ever cried out for my prescriptions, it's this one."

Standing before the wagon, the youth gazed at the hanging bottles, which tinkled in the breeze. "What pains will your tonic resolve?" asked Gabriel, massaging the tender place between his ribs.

"Bessell's Special Patent Cure is an all-purpose remedy, palliative, and antidote; effective against ills of the heart, brain, kidneys, liver, intestine, and gall; aches of the muscle and sinew; vague and general discomforts; and alleviating and mitigating infestations of screwworm, tapeworm, hookworm, ringworm; persistent ringing in the ears, and the mad whirling dizziness. Bessell's Cure also gives certain and verifiable relief to unpleasant dreams, impure thoughts, irregular digestion, and previously unnamed and undetected diseases of the mind; as well as toothaches, rashes, itches, boils, carbuncles, and parasites of every sort."

Raising himself in the johnnyseat, Bessell gripped a dusty lapel in one hand and a bottle of his panacea in the other. "For the past twenty-nine years, I have concocted Bessell's Special Patent Cure from a secret mixture of herbs practiced by Siamese mystics, and never once has my elixir failed to produce the desired result: balanced humor, supple limbs, and a pleasant and agreeable disposition."

His eyes widened and mouth agape, the youth asked, "How much is it?"

"A precise sum arrived at through exacting processes, whereupon I calculate to the far decimal point the value of each multifarious ingredient, allowing only that knife's-edge margin with which to fuel my peregrinations from village to town." His customer stood dumbfounded by this, and Hiram Bessell said, "One dollar."

Gabriel thrust his hands into empty pockets. "That's a dear price for a working man," he said.

"As any diseased person will tell you, no fee is too extravagant when it comes to good health," said Bessell, as he lowered himself back onto the johnnyseat. Making sure the cap was snug, the old man returned the bottle to its place on the rack. "Do you have an ailment, sir?"

"Some months ago, I injured myself when a coffer dam failed," Gabriel said, pressing a hand against his damaged ribs. "The ghost of that event pains me at times."

"The circulation of Bessell's Special Patent Cure will resolve all such phantoms," said the old man. "Last autumn, I was in Lincoln and met a man named Henry who lived beside a pond. The iron had sprung from my cart wheel, and he was kind enough to build a large fire and help me smelt it back into place. When I asked him why he dwelt in the woods, a mile from any neighbor, he answered, 'What do we want to live near to? Not to many men, surely.' Noticing that he suffered from wheezing, at the conclusion of our labor I offered him a bottle of my tonic, which would calm the agitation in his lungs. Just as a small gray bird flew overhead, he refused, saying that only when my elixir was as plentiful as the water in his pond would he feel the need to swallow it."

Gabriel had never in his life drunk anything besides water, cow's milk, and occasional draughts of cider. "The men of Gilmore & Carpenter do not receive their salaries until tomorrow," he said.

"So let us bend time, and make it serve us," said the old man.

"I don't understand your meaning."

Bessell rummaged beneath the johnnyseat. "For you, sir, who rushed to my assistance upon the Andover Bridge, I will provide a heretofore unprecedented opportunity," he said. The wizened old fellow retrieved his cane and then brought up a battered tin pot, using the cane to extend the vessel toward Gabriel. Inside was a puddle of thick, dark liquid, flecked with grit and tiny splinters of wood. "For the greatly reduced sum of one-half dollar, I shall impart to you this entire batch of my cure. In a further display of my gratitude, I invite you to sample it at no cost or risk to yourself whatsoever. And I will be happy to extend one day's credit—if you will make your mark inside my ledger, and bind over an item of at least two-fold collateral."

Again Bessell thrust the pot toward the youth. "Go ahead, sir," said the old man.

Peering into the vessel, Gabriel tipped it up and swallowed some of the potion. It was bitter, with an aftertaste of licorice that filled his sinuses, and he gagged as the elixir burned a trail toward his stomach.

"A man soon learns that any true cure is a harsh one," Bessell said.

Even as the youth began choking and coughing, he felt a warmth spreading through him that included the sore place in his ribs. "It has a remarkable effect," Gabriel said. He tried another draught.

"One half-dollar," said Bessell, using his cane to hook the vessel and draw it away.

"I have a picture-book worth twenty dollars, which I can sit with you until tomorrow when we are paid," said Gabriel, making his X in Bessell's ledger with the pencil he was handed. He took the pot of cure back from the old man. "Just allow me time to visit my fish traps, and I shall hasten a return."

The peddler listened to the haphazard music drifting over the shanties. "Go on, then," he said. "I believe this entertainment will continue at some length. There is a great deal of conviviality here tonight."

The impending dedication of the Great Dam had saturated Dublin with an air of merriment, but as Gabriel waved at the old patent manufacturer and hurried off, he also detected a grimness in the camp, born of late wages and the uncertainty that crept in when such a grand labor was finished. Every morning the shantytown teemed with rumors—of another dam being built in Amesbury, the Essex Company deciding on a new mill, or that construction of the south canal was about to begin—and each evening brought the death of those rumors.

There were a thousand men living in and around Dublin, according to the ground-rent schedule, and more than six hundred would be out of work now that the dam had been completed. The first hireling Gabriel Glass encountered on the way to his shanty was a concrete mixer named Bresnahan. Like many in camp, the Irishman kept his family in Andover while he labored on the Great Dam, visiting his wife and four children on Sundays. Coming along the path with a pair of dead muskrats, the gray-haired Bresnahan stopped and removed a cut of tobacco from his pocket.

"Hear the news?" he asked, clipping the quid with his teeth. "The Essex Company won't start digging the south canal for three years, now. Why, a man could die from privation in three days."

A dog came trotting up the path behind him, and Bresnahan lifted the muskrats by their tails and slung them over his shoulder. Heads hanging toward the ground, the muskrats gave off a foul odor and the dog raised itself and stood against the Irishman's back, sniffing at their heavy wet coats. "It were no use getting our hopes up," said Bresnahan, spitting tobacco juice into the weeds. "I suppose a fellow can mix concrete up in

Manchester as well as he can in the New City."

"A good man should be able to find work here," said Gabriel.

Shrugging off the dog, Bresnahan hoisted the muskrats to the other shoulder and spat into the bushes again. His gaze was mournful and dark. "Aye, lad, he should. But even a vast territory's too small once enough men begin to fill it."

Gabriel Glass saluted the Irishman, and proceeded on. Certainly, there were undertakings in the New City that would employ a large number of men: the construction of rowhouses, framing the Atlantic Mill, and grading the many new roads that branched out toward Methuen. Some of the laborers would jump on flatbeds in the morning and ride to Manchester, New Hampshire, where the Amoskeag Company was lengthening its power canal, and others would hike the old Indian trail back to Lowell, in order to apply for the fire and police departments that were opening up. But even taken in aggregate, these projects were not large enough to absorb the men who had built the Great Dam. Just a few days earlier, Captain Bigelow had appointed Gabriel to the dredging crew, guaranteeing him another three month's work. No such luck for Bresnahan.

Gabriel's shanty stood on the edge of the clearing, shaded by a box elder and near the spot on the Merrimack where he kept his fish traps and trotlines. Inside the canvas flap that served as a door, Gabriel opened up the chest that old Mrs. Saunders gave him when he left the farm. In it he placed the ribbon of appreciation from the Essex Company and Jorgy's blouse, donning a woolen tunic and knitted cap in its stead. He left the pot of cure on the table, covered by a piece of cheesecloth. Then slinging the frying-pan by its strap, the youth pocketed his flint and a handful of shavings and headed for the river.

Pods of milkweed grew up along the trail and Gabriel pinched them in his fingers, releasing their downy spores. The path dropped into a marshy hollow filled with skunk cabbage and the youth passed among these ill-smelling plants, holding his nose together. A stench rose from the spathe of each cabbage, creating a natural obstacle between the shanties and Gabriel's secret little fish camp upon the Merrimack.

Half a mile wide, the river curved around a steep promontory that was thick with pine trees, forked to allow the sliver of Rapeseed Island, and then ran straight and heavy for the dam. Loosestrife grew in purple clumps along the bank, and the moist air was filled with whistles and chirrups. Bent under its own weight, a willow tree spread above the current, forming a deep eddy that was perfect for fishing. Here Gabriel baited his traps each morning and dangled his trotlines. But tonight the youth was puzzled by what he encountered. Of the four trotlines only one remained fastened to its branch; two of his fish traps, modeled after an Algonquian drawing that Captain Bigelow had shown him, lay on the sandy beach. Half the wooden slats were missing, the bait removed; nothing was inside.

After taking off his boots, Gabriel waded into the cold black water, following the single trotline with the pressure of his hand. He felt a heavy weight on the line and began yanking it up. Thinking there was a turtle snagged on the hooks, the youth was surprised to find a large book dangling from them. The binding had been broken and the leaves were a sodden mess. It was the illustrated text he had borrowed from Captain Bigelow, which his mentor had purchased during a trip to Boston. Paying for it would mean the loss of half a month's wages.

That morning at five o'clock when Gabriel had departed for work, the encyclopedia was wrapped in a blanket inside his shanty. Now the youth felt the book come apart in his hands; sections of it escaped his fingers and thudded to the ground until only the warped covers were left. He dropped to his knees on the muddy bank and, groping in the darkness, tried to reassemble the pages. Gabriel had no enemies; no one bore a grudge against him. Except for a few women and their bedraggled children, visitors to the camp were rare during the daylight hours. Who could have done such a thing?

From an upper pocket, the youth took his flint and shavings and upended the frying-pan. Piling the tinder there, he struck the flint. The shavings caught, illuminating the river bank for a few moments. Sections of the book had swollen to grotesque size and were lying in clumps. The ink had washed off some of the pages and as his little pile of shavings blazed, Gabriel understood that what had been undone could never be fastened back together. He saw a picture of an ignorant-looking bird with webbed feet—Captain Bigelow had called it *Raphus cucullatus*, the dodo—then the light shrank to a dot and the rail of smoke from his little fire turned black and drifted away. In the darkness, Gabriel shuffled the manuscript into a bundle and carried it off, smashing his knee against one of the fish traps as he passed. He kicked the shattered trap into the river.

Gabriel was soaked to the waist and his dungarees rasped against each other as he went back through the skunk cabbage. Scrambling up the embankment, he thanked Providence that yesterday's catch, two good-size bass and a yellow perch, had spent the day swimming in the reservoir he and William had dug astride the brook. The fronds parted and two men coming along with fishing poles spoke to him, but Gabriel kept on, speeding toward his shanty. Inside, he lit the lantern and hung it swaying from a cross beam. He examined the thickened pages of the encyclopedia and determined that no part of the book was salvageable.

The youth took up the tin pot of Bessell's cure, as frustration entered his bloodstream like a poison. Without any sensible thoughts, Gabriel drank off half the elixir, swirling the liquid as he stared into the pot, the splinters of wood in a tide around the rim. From the encampment, he heard shouting and other noise. Taking down the lantern and gripping the cure in his free hand, Gabriel passed through the doorway into the evening air. A great many torches lit the cart path, and the youth soon extinguished his lantern and followed the procession of fire.

There was tumult upon the green—intersecting haloes of light, a great hubbub of voices, and piercing it all, the high-pitched wailing of William Bower. The mute stood knee-deep in the brook, his hands held

Jay Atkinson

out. Floating past were the upturned bellies of half a dozen large fish: his and Gabriel's enterprise had been destroyed.

In the midst of the common, men were dumping buckets of swill into the creek, turning it black in the torchlight. The foul waterway passed through the center of Dublin and the men cheered it, many of them carrying staves and hoisting flasks of Bessell's Patent Cure. In the commotion a pair of stonemasons knocked against each other and a fight ensued, but it was broken up and the two tradesmen shook hands and laughed. A short distance away, Bower was in full cry, his large, shaggy head thrown back, arms thrust out to either side. As men passed, drinking from their bottles, they tore at themselves and mocked his wailing, then roared at one another.

Wading into the creek, Gabriel took the mute by the hand and led him out. "Drink this," said the youth, offering the pot of cure. "It will numb you."

Standing above the throng on his wagon, Hiram Bessell delivered his oration; or at least, his mouth moved amidst the din and sheets of parchment flashed in the torchlight. Leading the mute, who drank from the battered pot, Gabriel made his way toward the peddler.

There was a stench rising from the brook. Atop the ravine, more of those who were quitting Dublin in the morning were dumping their buckets into the creek. Warned of this activity, the other settlers emerged from the shanties and began taking umbrage with it. Their shouting and shoving increased. Those leaving Dublin formed a higher percentage than the rest and although they did not all participate in spoiling the creek, neither did they speak against it.

Once on the green the polluters spied Bessell's wagon, its varnish shining in the firelight, and descended upon it for sport, for relief from their ailments, and for the old man's commentary that some remembered from the Andover Bridge. A number of coins speckled the johnnyseat and Hiram Bessell was prodding some of the revelers with his cane and shouting out something that could not be heard. Hands reached out for bottles of the elixir and when they began disappearing out of proportion to the coins that rained down, the old man used his cane as a saber, cutting swaths in the air. The laborers were threatening to overturn his wagon when Gabriel Glass and William Bower arrived.

"Are you in danger, Mr. Bessell?" asked the youth.

A teamster drinking from a flask jostled Gabriel's arm. "As long as he offers his goods at a cut-rate, your professor will find a wealth of friends here," the man said. There was a jagged scar on his cheek where a raccoon had bitten him. "Otherwise, his wagon and its contents belong to the village."

"The price is, and remains, one dollar," said Bessell.

The patent-medicine wagon began to twitch, shaken back and forth by the action of many hands. Fearing it would be overturned, Gabriel and William combined their strength to push back the crowd. Soon after, Bresnahan the concrete mixer joined them. Together with his dog, the gray-haired Irishman helped clear a space in front of the wagon.

"Let Mr. Bessell speak," Gabriel said.

"He needn't speak—he need only peddle his wares," someone in the crowd said.

"Aye, at a price we can afford," said another.

Bessell gathered up his parchments and stood with one foot upon the johnnyseat. "Let me remind you that this great Commonwealth was founded on the principle of free enterprise, and it is that principle that I am exercising," he said.

"We've had our fill of such enterprising," said the man with the raccoon bite on his face. He raised his fist. "Let's see a morsel or two for the public welfare," he said.

"Hooray! Hooray for the men who built the dam!"

At that instant Old Pete's crew reached the green, coming straight to where the mob had gathered. "Tomorrow you'll have your hoorays," said Ephet Asadoorian. "Let this fellow do his business."

The Armenian drew up and next to him was the tall, strapping Jorgensen, his muscles standing out in the torchlight. At this show of strength, the moat around Hiram Bessell widened enough to allow the Murphy brothers to patrol there, armed with hammers and quirts. A man with a coat thrust over his head reached for one of the bottles and the ugliest Murphy smashed his hand with a sap, breaking the man's knuckles.

"Christ, brother. What have you done?" he said. "I shan't be fit for work tomorrow."

"Don't test me," said the dredger.

Hiram Bessell seized the moment. "For all who have discomfort and who suffer, whose anxiety of mind prevents them from sleeping, for any man who swings a hammer by day or carries the hod and whose muscles jump involuntarily at night, I offer you my cure, steady draughts of which will sooth any ailment, alleviate your anxious mind, and quiet the muscles that refuse to do your bidding," he said. "Through a long apprenticeship to the writings of Thales and Hippocrates, with painstaking science I have fashioned my spring tonic after the drink that Hercules received from the hand of Hippolyta, restoring him to life."

Bessell raised one of the coins that had fallen on the johnnyseat, holding it in the circle formed by his thumb and forefinger. "For a dram of this remarkable potion I ask only one dollar. It represents both the lowest common denominator in our monetary system and, as you see here, the world, the globe, the *yin* intercepting the *yan* of good health." The coin sparkled in the light from the torches, and the old man grinned and put it in his pocket.

Kept back by Gabriel Glass and his friends, the mob questioned itself. "Will it take this burr out of my shoulder?" asked one fellow. "I can't lift my arm above my head."

"My knees throb from morning till night. What about my knees?"

There was a myriad of aches and pains among the despoilers, but Mute William and the giant Swede and Asadoorian and the rest of the dredgers prevented them from stripping the peddler of his wares. Wild-

Jay Atkinson

haired and swarthy in the torchlight, young Gabriel stood before the wagon, swigging from his pail of cure. Everyone present knew he had saved Captain Bigelow's life. What they respected about the lad was that he never asked for anything in return—as if any member of the burgher class would have done the same for him. Among the crowd that had gathered, those who loved him intervened when Gabriel began to say something and a few of the rabble-rousers shouted him down.

"Let the lad speak," said one fellow.

The man with the raccoon bite objected and Bresnahan went eye-to-eye with him. "You've said your piece. A man what's twice you are should have at least half your say."

"Give him some air. Let the boy talk!"

A group of men began swinging their torches to clear a space in front of Bessell's wagon. The brands swooped through the air, embers crackling, drops of liquid fire scattering across the ground. Here and there tiny blazes caught, and the laborers stamped them out with their boots.

"Go on, Gabe'rill," said Asadoorian.

But young Glass was not suited to public speaking. He stood in the firelight, staring at the faces that surrounded him while a knot ascended his throat. Mute William handed him the battered pail of cure and the youth swallowed the dregs and then handed back the empty vessel.

"The cure is good," Gabriel said. "It made me feel better."

"Then it will make all of us feel better," said the raccoon man, his eyes black in the glare of the torches. "Let's have it."

"Mixing the cure is the old man's work, same as yours is mixing cement"—Gabriel indicated the raccoon man, then Thom Maddox the beekeeper, and another and another—"or making honey, or carrying the hod, or dredging. Taking a man's work and leaving him nothing ain't right."

A murmur of assent swept over the crowd. "Aye. The blasted truth it ain't right," said the raccoon man. "Then why is the Essex Company doing it to us?"

At that moment, the squad of constables and their wagon emerged from the forest. Bracketed by torchlight, the procession angled down the slope, the two bays stamping at the turf and the light gleaming from the brass buckles of the marchers. Riding on the caisson was Charles Storrow, the clerk of the works, who had never before set foot in Dublin.

"Here's your man," said one of the drovers. The crowd was hushed as the glassy-eyed Storrow rocked and bumped his way toward them. "You can ask 'im yourself, if'n he cares for the truth."

Seeing this assemblage on the green and with scant clues to its meaning, Lieutenant Treachey ordered his squad to quicken their pace; the laborers of Dublin, hoisting axes and tree limbs and bathed in torchlight, appeared to be armed against their masters. Ordering the caisson to the fore, which would require any man foolish enough to stand down the two horses, Treachey formed his men into a blockade around Mr. Storrow and unholstered his pistol.

In a loud voice he called out, "Essex Company detachment for the necessity of collecting ground rents and chits. Make way there."

Spurred on by the raccoon man and several other grumblers, the crowd turned and began massing along the creek. The torchbearers closed on one another, their globes of light reaching to the treeline and illuminating the lower branches. As these forces came together, Bessell's wagon was left behind and several men took a bottle from his rack as they passed. Incensed at this, the old man struck at them with his cane. When a stinging blow landed on the neck of a teamster, he and his companions rallied against the side of the wagon and began rocking it to and fro. Bessell was ejected, flying through the air like a squirrel, only to land in the creek. Next the wagon toppled over, with a great crash of glass and crunch of varnished wood.

Bessell's sway-backed horse fell to one side, struggled to regain its footing, and then broke free of the harness and trotted off. The men laughed, and hands reached for the many unbroken bottles of cure that lay on the ground. Emerging from the shadows, Cob the Hermit darted out and began pillaging the wreck. He grabbed Bessell's cane, some of his mixing utensils, and even the old man's skullcap, stowing them beneath his shawl as he scurried into the darkness.

Faced with a mob carrying torches, wielding staves and scythes, and drinking from flasks of patent cure, Lieutenant Treachey leveled his pistol and took dead aim at the raccoon man. "Halt, in the name of the Essex Company. We're here to collect the ground rents," he said. "Agreed to by all the residents of this settlement, and signed into the covenants on the land."

The men slowed their advance upon recognizing Treachey's pistol, but milled about in the torchlight, their faces grimed with sweat and ash. "How can I settle my rent when I haven't been paid?" asked one of the millwrights.

"Give us our wages," said another fellow. "We didn't go hunting for you with pistols when *our* money was late."

More of the laborers joined in the protest but their sentiments were lost in the general confusion. At the back of the crowd, a man with two large pleats of hay strapped to his back leaned close to a torch and caught on fire. Unable to shed his burden, he stamped his feet and ran wildly about, braying like an animal. "Shoot him!" said a voice, as several teamsters put their hands out and tried to corner the man. Around the side of the caisson, he dodged them willy-nilly, a trail of sparks fizzing along the ground.

But Lieutenant Treachey had been trained at West Point. "Mr. Flanagan," he said.

"Aye, sir."

"Knock the man down and put out the fire."

"Aye, sir." Grasping his pike sideways, Flanagan exited the ranks on the quick-step, herding the man toward the creek. While the teamsters pursued, the man turned to elude them, still screaming, his arms flagellating among whorls of fire. The constable veered across the glen and accelerated, cutting the man off. With a short upward stroke, he found bone in the midst of all those flames, knocking the settler off the embankment into the creek. The teamsters dived in after him, splashing the man with handfuls of water.

He staggered out of the creek, still afire, still screaming. His agony stirred and terrified the assembly, and there was an odor of charred flesh. Acting on impulse, two of the constables jumped down from the caisson and ran their siphon hoses into the creek. A third man began turning the hand pump and within seconds, water spewed from the canvas hose. By raising the nozzle, the constables directed the stream onto the injured man. But the arc of water, flecked with excrement, incited the crowd and a melee ensued.

The raccoon man, wielding a rake, and a band of drovers carrying torches and staves attacked the caisson. A constable was knocked down before the hose was trained on the raccoon man, smashing him back against his confederates. Drenched in human waste, the raccoon man let out a string of curses.

Lieutenant Treachey and his squad, disciplined but outnumbered, fell back in a ring, their pikes forming a barrier around the caisson. Men were fighting everywhere. The bay horses reared and snorted, hooves pawing the air, and Higgins and his assistant tightened their grip on the reins. With the wheels chocked—something Bart Higgins had done at the first sign of trouble—the heavy rig kept the two beasts in the traces, bucking and stamping though they were.

Charles Storrow was curled on the ground in a fetal position, staring into the bowl of his hat. Kaleidoscopic images were projected there, as the whinnying horses and exclamations of men penetrated his consciousness. Treachey stood over the engineer with his pistol, a constable on either side. Not everyone in the settlement was fighting; most watched from the rim of the meadow, torches in hand, shouting out names, raising their voices in prayer, or cursing the Essex Company. When one of their number was knocked over with the hose, they sent a blizzard of stones against the caisson.

A constable was struck by a stone and fell to the ground. Raising his pistol, Treachey discharged two shots over the head of the rock thrower and the activity ceased. After half a minute, the hoses running into the creek sucked air and the constables found themselves without their main defense. Although most of the settlers had lost the will to fight, a trio rushed in with branches and rakes, striking blows of vengeance. There were also laborers trying to quell the violence, chief among them Gabriel Glass, Ephet Asadoorian, and several members of the dredging crew, moving to disarm their neighbors with strong hands and words of consolation.

As this was occurring, a group of skirmishers made a foray inside the ring of constables. While Lieutenant Treachey was busy giving an order, a settler trampled upon Mr. Storrow and cursed at him. Treachey whirled about, his pistol raised; with the din in his ears and scuffling all around, he fired a shot. The train of the bullet missed several men who were in close proximity, traveling the length of the meadow before it struck Jorgensen in the temple.

The giant Swede had been standing beyond the fray, with his outspread arms convincing a newly-arrived group of teamsters to remain neutral. The shot echoed away, and dozens of peacekeepers and constables and instigators froze in tableau, studying the fallen man. They had all seen death before.

Halfway between Treachey and his victim, Gabriel Glass felt the bullet cutting through the air and understood the result before it had even unfolded. He raised his arms and in a great voice cried, "Enough," striding up the little slope toward the caisson. No one was fighting. Pulled upright by Flanagan and another constable, Charles Storrow stood beside the horses, staring down into his hat. A few feet away, Lieutenant Treachey gripped the stock of his pistol. He was furious—at himself, at his failure to carry out Bigelow's order, and at the troublemakers who the bullet had missed.

But Treachey knew this was no time for a plea of *mea culpa*. Still under the mandate to safeguard Mr. Storrow, it was imperative that the constables withdraw without further incident. He eyed the youth who was closing on his position.

"Is this how your workers are rewarded?" asked Gabriel, his arm flung back toward Jorgensen.

Treachey spoke to Mr. Flanagan. "Take care of this fellow," he said.

When Gabriel was within a dozen paces of Lieutenant Treachey and Mr. Storrow, Flanagan stepped into his path. The youth's gaze never wavered, passing through the constable to its target. Setting himself, Flanagan reared back and swung his pike at the other man's head. Gabriel ducked and shot forward, charging the constable off his feet. Before matters got out of hand, Treachey struck the youth behind the ear with his pistol and the meadow went black.

*

Gabriel woke to a circle of faces, which spun faster and then settled over him for a moment, a single torch blazing in the center and motes of ash rising from it. All at once, Jorgensen's death returned to him and the youth sprang up and delivered a terrific blow to the first man who stood in his way. Mr. Storrow's nose exploded with blood and he went down in a heap.

It was all Lieutenant Treachey could do to prevent his squad from killing the boy. They jabbed and stroked at Gabriel Glass with their pikes, until his face was battered into mush and his ribs broken. Treachey fired his pistol into the air, stuck it in his belt and began yanking men aside.

"Maintain your discipline," he said. "You are Essex Company constables—not a mob."

Mr. Storrow and Gabriel Glass were helped to their feet—the engineer by two constables and the youth on the hands of his fellow laborers—and stared at each other across the dividing line. Each man's head was encased in a thickening flab and rivulets of blood spattered their boots. On the lower end of the common, revelers had seized Hiram Bessell's wagon and piled it onto the bonfire. The flames from this pyre encompassed a hundred torches, and a column of embers rose into the night sky.

Lieutenant Treachey's helmet had been knocked off during the scuffle. The dark crown of his hair, encircled by gray, made a serrated edge across his forehead. "Who is this fellow?" Treachey asked, pointing at the battered youth.

Ephet Asadoorian spit on the ground. "I don't know."

But Treachey had already made the hard decisions. "At risk of a company fine, you will identify this man. The incident must go in my report to Captain Bigelow."

Asadoorian stared back at the constables. "Never seen him before," he said.

Treachey looked across at the other employees of the Essex Company, their faces drawn in straight lines and fists clenched. "All right," he said, reaching to the ground for his helmet. He placed it on his head and adjusted the crown. "Since this fellow shall remain nameless, it is my recommendation that each man registered in camp be docked three dollars pay." He glared at the Armenian. "So let me test your memory one more time."

Once again Asadoorian spit into the chasm separating the men.

"Hoist Mr. Storrow onto the wagon and turn it around," Treachey said to the driver. Then he addressed the workers: "The company shall deduct the ground rents from tomorrow's pay—less another three dollars. I'll fill out the chits myself."

Treachey ordered four of his constables to throw Jorgensen's body onto the pyre. The Swede had stiffened like iron and the pallbearers struggled down the little hill, his great blond head riding between them. With a muttered cadence, they swung his weight in an arc and dropped it onto the bonfire. The corpse sailed through the wall of flame, making a temporary breach, and some of the men cried out in despair. Jorgensen's body crushed the superstructure of Bessell's wagon and the constables leaped back to avoid the sparks that charged out, beating at their trousers like fireflies were attacking them.

Higgins and his assistant maneuvered the caisson uphill, and while Mr. Storrow was fixed to the tailgate with a strap and the constables re-formed their ranks, flames ate at the giant Swede and his body dissolved into the coals. The dejected laborers, who that evening had intended to celebrate their accomplishments, trudged back toward the shanties. Gabriel Glass was alone on the meadow. His head reeled from the concussion of several blows, and once, twice, three times the entire settlement swooped about him. The youth tried to speak but no sound came out, and he raised a hand toward the departing constables.

"Lieutenant Treachey, sir," said Flanagan. "Here this fellow wants to say something."

Treachey halted the caisson and returned to the spot where Gabriel stood. "Out with it," said the constable. "I have a lot of work to do before this night is over."

The youth stated his name and Treachey's mouth dropped open. "The one what saved Captain Bigelow?"

Gabriel nodded his head.

"Listen to me, son," said Treachey. "Leave Dublin now, and forever avoid the New City, and I'll put 'Missing: anonymous,' in the report. That way, you won't ever have a mark against your name and nobody'll lose any pay."

The youth started to say something but Treachey cut him off. "No need to mention the dam dedication," he said. "There's no chance of that now."

On the lower half of the common, William Bower and Ephet Asadoorian and the rest of Old Pete's dredging crew stood near the bonfire, looking into the flames. Treachey clapped Gabriel on the arm. "It's a rotten business," he said. He left the youth standing in the meadow and followed after the caisson, which was disappearing between the trees.

Gabriel ran up the opposite slope and into the forest until he couldn't run anymore—until he felt a strange, satiated feeling in his legs. Then he dropped into some fronds, gasping for breath. Over a mile away, lying against the Great Dam, was the last granite header. That afternoon the other dredgers had teased Gabriel about it, asking if he could handle this great beast all alone, as the principals of the Essex Company looked on with their feeble arms and silk hats.

His back bowing as he hauled up his pail, Gabriel remained silent, the tiny wavelets lapping against the barge. Just as he had when the coffer dam overturned, stroking for the injured Captain Bigelow whose greatcoat ballooned with water and than sank, dragging the man downward into the pools, Gabriel kicked after the stream of bubbles, which came in a smaller and smaller trail as light evaporated and the water grew deeper. He felt the sting of his own wounds until he entered the thermocline, where the intense cold numbed him.

Twenty-four feet deep by the sounding ropes there was little visibility and the current, powerful at the surface, had subsided. Waving his arms for ballast, Gabriel reversed positions by executing a slow somersault. As he settled downward, his boots sank in the ooze of the riverbed and his head began to ache. Groping about, his lungs bursting from the pressure, his hand touched something solid but it was an outcropping of ledge—too substantial for the dredgers to move, so they had dug around it. Here in a shallow depression he had found Charles Bigelow, crumpled against the rock. Gabriel bore into the other man's armpit with his head, flung his right arm over the Captain's back, and grabbed Bigelow's left wrist with his left hand. The youth popped his head free and, bracing his feet against the rock, launched himself downstream, the Captain soaring beside him like Daedalus.

Light returned to the deep and Gabriel could make out the details of Bigelow's face: the matted clumps of beard, a broken nose, the eyes vacant and staring. Their heads broke the surface as one—next, a confusion of shouts and water noise—then the current changed and they began dropping again, skewed by the Captain's weight. Not knowing where his strength came from, and without any sensation besides the implosion of his lungs, Gabriel dragged the Captain's bulk upward and, flapping his legs like a merman, raised him to the surface.

That time he felt the probe of a gaff, and then he and Captain Bigelow were hooked by their clothing and pulled ashore. When they reached the embankment all the men congratulated him, but the youth just lay there exhausted, his sides heaving like a great fish.

7

The Present Day

The day after New Year's, general manager Kap Kutter sold the station's entire catalogue of holiday music. Morning disc jockey Billy Bruce watched in dismay as a van pulled up, and two long-haired young men in World War I trench coats entered the station and began pulling armloads of tape cartridges from the shelves. Bing Crosby's "White Christmas"; Peggy Lee's "Rockin' around the Christmas Tree"; "Blue Christmas" by Elvis Presley; *William Shatner and Leonard Nimoy Sing Rudolph the Red-Nosed Space Alien*; "God Rest ye Merry Gentlemen" by Sammy Davis, Jr.; as well as the most requested Christmas song in the twenty-eight years Billy Bruce had hosted *The Morning Show*, Leonard Bernstein's "Christmas Cantata," all clattered into the van.

The sight of these tapes being carried out by doughboys who reeked of marijuana was too much for Billy Bruce. He put on a Duke Ellington number and raced down the hall to register a complaint with his boss, the man WKUT employees referred to as Boy Blunder.

"Kap, what the—" he said, bursting into Kutter's office. Kap put his hand up, sitting with the telephone in his fist, and Father Tom Dailey looking uncomfortable in the chair opposite him.

"That's right, Dad. It's a black line rising up the chart," said Kutter. "Good management, that's how."

The priest smiled at Billy Bruce, and the deejay sank into the chair beside him It dawned on Billy why the holiday music was being sold. After suffering eighteen consecutive losses on its monthly balance sheet, WKUT would show a positive bump—allowing Kap a little more time to run the station into the ground. Behind the desk were photographs of Charlie Kutter and the teen-age Kap kneeling beside a deer with a huge rack of antlers, and holding up wild turkeys and grouse with their wings hanging open. In a short time WKUT would be just as dead, mounted like a trophy on some discount broker's wall.

Kap hung up the telephone and launched right back into his

conversation with the priest. "So Father, I can go as low as twenty-five bucks per spot. I'd like to see you spruce up the church, but if I said yes to everyone that came in asking for a handout, we'd be in the poorhouse."

"I've started driving a cab to help out with parish expenses. At the price you quoted, I might be able to purchase half a dozen commercials," Father Tom said. "Would that do us any good?"

Kap Kutter's face, boiled by excessive drinking, lost its salesman's arch. But before he could shoot the priest down, Billy Bruce mentioned *Hot Line* as a potential solution. "I need a guest for Thursday's show," the disc jockey said. "How does that sound, Father?"

"Will it cost us anything?"

"Not a cent, Father," said Kutter. He cleared his throat. "I'm sorry to hurry you out, but I've got a big meeting today and I've got to get ready for it."

Father Tom stood up. He was dressed in a black shirt and his Roman collar, with blue jeans and boots and a canvas jacket, on account of all the snow. "Is there anything I have to do?" he asked.

"Just come in at noon on Thursday, and we'll chat about the church and anything else you want to talk about," said Billy Bruce. "We'll take telephone calls and have a cup of coffee together. It's fun."

Kap waved his hand toward the door. "Billy will handle everything," he said.

"Monsignor Borinquen says that years ago hundreds of people came to Mass on Christmas Eve, and Holy Communion would last three-quarters of an hour. This year the furnace wasn't working right, and we only had about thirty parishioners there. The church is in very bad repair."

"Right," said Kutter.

Billy Bruce showed the priest to the door. "See you Thursday, Father," he said.

"Thursday at noon. Thank you," said the priest, and he went out.

Turning to the window, Kap watched Father Tom walk past the barbed wire surrounding the station. "The Catholics have all the money in the world," he said. "They've been mining it out of here since Irish Mickey ate his first potato." Kutter shook his head. "You tie a basket to the end of a stick, go up and down the aisle, and everybody pays through the nose. What a racket."

Jerry Schindler entered the office. Dressed in a snakeskin suit and with lifts in his shoes, he crossed the rug and removed a cigarette from Kutter's pack. WKUT's director of sales was a dainty man, no more than five feet, three inches in stocking feet, with razor cut hair and modish tinted spectacles. Winking at Billy Bruce, he took a light from the boss's ember, and then he and Kutter puffed on their cigarettes.

"Selling our own catalogue," Schindler said. "What a couple of geniuses."

It was time for Billy Bruce to return to the studio. "What are we gonna do for music *next* Christmas?" he asked his boss.

"I just want to show a spike this month. Keep the old man happy," said Kutter. "We play that shitty music for two weeks, and then it sits for fifty."

Billy Bruce hightailed it down the hall and into the glass booth. He flipped on the microphone. "Good morning, friends. That was the inimitable Duke Ellington and his orchestra featuring Gene Kruppa on drums. Bringing you into this new year by helping you remember old times, here on WKUT Radio Nine Hundred."

He pushed in a cartridge with the station jingle, and searched through a tangle of papers for the weather report but couldn't find it. Leaning backwards until the cord on his headphones was stretched to the limit, Billy peered through the window for a look at the sky. "Back with you this chilly morning, friends, as I am every weekday morning from five-thirty until ten o'clock. Weather predictions today say partly cloudy skies with light snow, followed by little boys on sleds and temperatures in the mid- to high-twenties. Coming up next, my friends, George Gershwin's 'Rhapsody in Blue.' "

Billy Bruce turned off the microphone, sighing into his WKUT coffee mug; the station was going to the dogs. Noting that a chill had crept into the studio, he grabbed his coffee and went out to check the back door. It was open, blowing gusts of frigid air into the building, and the two long-haired zombies had finished with the holiday section and were loading another row of tapes into their van.

"What are you doing?" asked Billy Bruce. He stood in the hallway, the men passing by him with armloads of Cab Calloway and Louis Armstrong, the Andrews Sisters, and *Les Brown and his band of Renown*. "Those tapes are part of our everyday catalogue."

"The man said the first three rows of file A, so we're taking the first three rows of file A," said one of the trench coats.

Billy Bruce spilled some coffee onto his pants. "What the hell am I gonna play?"

The maw of the van was filled to the roof with WKUT's library, including some Benny Goodman and Charlie Parker and all the Trini Lopez ever pressed onto wax. Billy Bruce twisted around to listen for Gershwin, but from the hallway behind him came the sound of dead air.

In the general manager's office, Jerry Schindler and Kap Kutter were discussing the station's receptionist, Elise Dominaux. "You can't just call her up and ask her," said Schindler.

"Bullshit," Kutter said, picking up the telephone. He dialed zero for the front desk. "When someone takes three days off, I think I have a right to know what I'm paying for." In a sugary voice, he said, "Elise, I'd like to speak with you a moment." Kutter replaced the telephone in its cradle. "The little minx is on her way."

Schindler wagged his head in admiration.

A moment or two later, the pretty blonde came through the doorway. Elise Dominaux was dressed in a black turtleneck, green mohair skirt, and matching blazer that was fastened above the midriff with a colorful silk scarf. She had been with the station for a year, and never wore the same outfit twice.

"I've been worried about you, Elise," Kap said, grasping her thin white wrists. "Did everything go all right?"

"Did what go all right?" she asked.

"Whatever procedure you needed to have done. You looked fine when you left, and finer even when you came back, but I wanted to make sure." Kap waved at a chair. "Please, have a seat. Cigarette?"

"No, thanks."

"You're right," Kutter said. He stubbed out his cigarette. "It's bad for the lungs," he said, rolling his hands with an expansive gesture.

Schindler made a short hiccuping sound while his eyes darted over Elise's mohair blazer. "Do they bother your chest, er, the cigarettes, I mean?" asked Kutter.

"I don't like the smoke," Elise said. "Otherwise, I'm fine."

Kap flicked his gaze toward the door, and Schindler rose and left the office. "We have a nice benefits package here," Kutter said. "It covers just about everything, even cosmetic surgery. Did you need extensive coverage?"

"What do you mean?" asked Dominaux.

Her boss came closer, and Elise found herself sitting inside the odor of Kap's soiled thousand-dollar suit. "If you had some cosmetic surgery, I'd just like to see it, that's all," Kutter said. "To make sure it turned out all right."

Elise met Kutter's eyes. "Can I go?"

"Sure," said Kutter. "I'm glad you're feeling all right."

The receptionist clicked down the hallway and Schindler eased back into the office. "Well?"

"A brand new pair of tits," said Kutter. "She's got them hidden under that hairy jacket. At least a thirty-six double D."

Schindler's eyes popped out of his doll's head. "She *showed* them to you?"

"In all their glory. And believe me, they were glorious."

The sales manager lit another cigarette. On the speaker in the hall, Billy Bruce was signing off with "Happy Trails." Schindler danced around the office, clutching his cigarette like a wand. "I gotta see 'em," he said.

"Not a chance in hell," said Kutter, picking up the telephone again.

*

Behind the locked door of his office, Billy Bruce removed his three-hundred-dollar toupee and put on a WKUT fishing hat. The rug was the only vanity he permitted himself; it was his natural brown flecked with gray and swept up in a 1960s curl. His wife Belinda had given him the toupee as a present on their twenty-fifth wedding anniversary. On the card she had written: "Turbans for Valentino/Antlers on a Moose/Sugar in my coffee/And hair for Billy Bruce."

His name was Bruno Finklestein, a *mensch* from Oyster Bay, Long Island. After enlisting in the Army, he spent two years broadcasting for the National Intelligence Service and then another year making documentary films at the Army Pictorial Center in New York City.

Discharged in 1952, he met Charlie Kutter when they applied for the same overnight position at WINS in New York. Kutter got the air shift, and Bruno Finklestein changed his name to Billy Bruce and went to work in the mailroom. A friendship ensued, and over the years the two men kept in touch. When Kutter made it big in television and purchased WKUT, he brought in Fink, at that time doing overnights at WELS in Nashville, to anchor his morning show.

"Where the hell is Lawrence, Mass?" asked Billy Bruce.

"In the asshole of the world," Kutter had said. "I'm gonna put you on, so I never have to go there."

The walls of Billy Bruce's office were papered with autographed photos and letters of thanks from an assortment of former WKUT disk jockeys. Because of his guidance, a dozen young stars had broken into radio and were now featured in Atlanta, New York, San Francisco, Houston, and other important markets around the country. During private moments with his wife, Billy Bruce talked about Bruno Finklestein like he was someone else, using the affectionate but disappointed tone reserved for failed uncles. If Bruno Finklestein was a baseball player, Billy often remarked, he would have been "a good field/no hit" kind of guy, who lacked the indefinable something that would have put him over the top. But he played his heart out, and he knew talent when he saw it.

Billy Bruce searched through the old scripts and tape cartridges piled on his desk for Charlie Kutter's telephone number. Before locking himself in his office, Billy had tiptoed by the general manager's office to find Kap Kutter cleaning his shotgun with a bottle of Wild Turkey sitting open on the floor. Against the wall, a video monitor was playing the tape of Kap's recent fishing trip to British Columbia. Dressed in waders, Kap Kutter had hauled in a beautiful leaping salmon and gestured to the woman on shore, who wasn't his wife.

Billy Bruce found the Kutters' number on the back of an old dry cleaning slip. Charlie Kutter picked up on the second ring, loaded to the gills. "Fink! Why aren't you on the air, you fucking gonad? What am I paying you for, if you're not swapping Old Yankee Snot, or whatever that show is." There was a college football game playing in the background. In weird stereo effect, Charlie Kutter's drunken ramble mingled with his call of the football game coming from the television. "You know what I'm watching right now?" he asked. "The 1967 Rose Bowl, that's what. Listen to me: I was fucking A-1. And that O.J. Simpson. He could play a little football, couldn't he?"

"I want to talk to you about WKUT," Billy Bruce said. "Kap sold half the music."

"What? You sold the what? What the fuck are you gonads doing up there?" There was a loud bang, and Billy Bruce was afraid Charlie Kutter had fallen over dead. But in a second he was back on the line. "Whoo-ee! I just went for a fucking loop. First down! First down on the play!" Another voice chimed in, a woman this time, pleading with Charlie to turn off the television. It was his wife, Katherine.

"Third quarter. Two minutes left," Kutter shouted at her. "I'm not going anywhere."

Billy Bruce could hear USC driving for a touchdown. Leaning away from the receiver, Kutter mimicked his own voice, "The thirty. The twenty. The ten. Touchdown Trojans!" The telephone banged down against something while a hundred thousand football fans roared in unison. From twenty years in the past, the USC fight song faded out and commercials came on for products that were no longer being sold.

Katherine picked up the line. "Who is this?" she asked.

"Bruno Finklestein. Is Charlie all right?"

"He passed out on the floor," Katherine said. There was a muffled pause. "I don't know what I'm gonna do, Fink. He won't go to a clinic, even though I've asked him a hundred times."

"Has he been doing a lot of drinking?"

There was a sigh at the other end of the line. "You know, the same," said the 1949 University of Wyoming Homecoming Queen.

Billy Bruce pictured Katherine Kutter, a faded beauty wearing a silk pantsuit and sandals with her toenails painted red. "Charlie was playing tons of golf, and doing a little fishing once in a while. Then somebody in New York called him about writing his memoirs, and that bloody Touchdown Club in Lantana invited him to give a speech." A tightness came into her voice. "They were feeding him Cutty Sark all night. I knew the horse was out of the barn when he started playing those old football tapes of his, and the '65, '66, and '67 World Series—he's got a million of them. Now there's a piece of paper in his typewriter doesn't have fifty words on it. He can't write a book about the good old days. The good old days are killing him."

"You've gotta get Charlie into a hospital, and then—" said Billy Bruce, just as someone knocked at his door. "Hold on a moment, Katherine."

It was the jock who came on after *The Morning Show,* a chubby redhead named Sheryl Sherbrooke. "Rhapsody in Blue" was again wafting through the hallways of the station.

"This isn't supposed to be on," said Billy Bruce. "I just played it."

Her hands full of tape cartridges, Sheryl Sherbrooke was in tears. "Half the stuff the log says to play isn't in the library. What am I gonna do? Where are all my friggin' songs?"

Billy Bruce grabbed some of the cartridges, looking through the titles. "Screw the log. From now till the top of the hour play all the B sides, the obscure stuff, anything you want. Call it...call it 'Sherbrooke's Grab Bag of Forgotten Hits.' No novelty songs or trick stuff, just the good ones. When Barry comes in for the news tell him to stretch it. I'll be there, and we'll write a log for the afternoon from what we've got." The young dee jay looked encouraged. "And from now on, get here an hour early and put your show together. Let's go, kid. You're on."

Billy Bruce locked himself back in the office. "I'm sorry, Katherine. Just a little snafu I had to fix," he said into the telephone.

"How are things at the station?" she asked.

Something in her voice told Billy she didn't want to know. "We're driving a horse and buggy in a rocket ship world, but we're surviving," he said.

Charlie Kutter groaned from the living room floor. "I have to go, Fink. Thanks for all your help," Katherine said. "And please look after Kap for me."

"He's a fine boy," Billy Bruce said, and hung up.

Pulling his WKUT fishing hat over his ears, Billy went down the hall to the library and started scribbling a new list of songs for the afternoon. Most of the jazz collection was gone, the rhumba and salsa, and a good chunk of the classical music they used on the overnights. A ball of fury rose in Billy Bruce's chest. The strength of programming that stayed away from Top Forty and other pop music was an endless variety, and WKUT prided itself on owning seventy-five years of the best American songs. Now by Billy Bruce's calculation more than a third of their catalogue was gone, sold off to nitwits who probably thought Jell Roll Morton was a dessert.

Billy Bruce stormed down the hall toward the broadcast booth. The flip side of "Boogie Woogie Bugle Boy from Company B" came on, and Billy Bruce gave Sheryl Sherbrooke an OK sign and wagged his head. Beyond the studio, a flickering motion caught his eye. *Whish. Whish.* Something fine and silver flashed across the lobby opening; a tiny dot of color drifted by an instant later.

The disc jockey went to investigate. Kap Kutter stood at the end of the corridor dressed in fishing waders, a fly rod bent and twitching in his hand. From behind a row of potted plants, he drank whiskey straight from the bottle and fished an imaginary stream while Elise Dominaux frowned at him from the reception desk.

Four times the fly traveled up and back the length of the room. With a perfect flick of his wrist, Kutter dropped the hunk of colored thread on the tip of Billy Bruce's shoe. Its tiny hook glistened against the leather.

Kutter smiled. "Ace," he said.

*

Somebody had put a bumper sticker on the back of Joe Glass's leather jacket that read SAVE THE PLANET—KILL YOURSELF, and he couldn't get it off without pulling up the finish. With Gabriel beside him in the high chair, playing with a few cubes of shredded wheat, Joe tried soaking the sticker in water but only the outer paper would come off, not the gluey backing underneath.

"Shit," he said. A smile crept over Gabriel's face.

Joe Glass tried to control the muscles of his face while he shook a finger in warning. Opposite him, the boy knew he was about to do something fantastic and watched for his opening with a sly smile. For several seconds, father and son regarded each other. "Don't do it," Joe said. Raising the gate on the high chair, he lowered Gabriel to the floor. "Go play with your toys."

Gabriel circled the table. In a white T-shirt that snapped between his legs, he looked like a bandy-legged little wrestler. "Shit!" he said, raising his fists toward the ceiling.

Jay Atkinson

"Your mother's not gonna like that," said Joe. He carried his leather jacket to the sink, and tried spreading a dab of shaving cream on the sticker and scraping it off with a razor blade. This succeeded in removing the shaving cream but nothing else.

Someone knocked at the door. "Come in," said Joe.

Francesca entered wearing tights and a thick gray FROST ARENA sweatshirt. Gabriel dropped his little hockey stick and she swept the giggling child into her arms and flexed him toward the ceiling. The boy squealed with laughter when Francesca lowered him nose to nose and then threw him upward again.

"Hello, bear," she said. "Mummy missed you."

Sitting on the floor, Joe Glass swept the hockey stick in an arc that controlled a little orange ball. In front of him, Francesca's skater's rump showed through her tights. They hadn't slept together in months and Joe suspected she was dating someone else. He was no angel; Brenda Steffanelli was the closest he'd gotten lately, but he wasn't staying home nights.

"How's the ice?" he asked.

"Good enough for you," Francesca said, smiling at him. She put Gabriel down, and the child kicked the orange ball into the corner and went chasing after it. "What time's your game?"

"Ten o'clock. I was thinking I'd drop by your place afterward."

"Soon as I put the baby down, I'm going to bed," said Francesca, shaking her head.

She sat down on the floor next to Joe, and they watched Gabriel chase the ball around the room with his hockey stick. "I hope he doesn't want to play hockey when he gets older," Francesca said.

"He's got the right amount of teeth," Joe said. "Four."

Gabriel took a swing at the ball and missed, landing on the seat of his pants. "Just like his dad," Francesca said, nudging Joe in the ribs. They held hands.

"How's your love life?" Joe asked.

"I wish I could meet a millionaire."

Joe laughed. "Rich guys are dull," he said. "Poor guys like me are a lot more fun."

"Poor guys are a lot more accessible," said Francesca. She swept her hair to one shoulder and Joe nibbled at her salty neck. Gabriel dropped the hockey stick and streaked toward them, leaping at the tiny space between their hips. Mother and father threw up a latticework of forearms and the baby landed in the net they had made, laughing and burbling.

Joe Glass and Francesca Nesheim had met during a free skate at the rink two and a half years earlier. In that hour, which started at midnight, no one was on the ice except the two of them. Francesca was tracing figures in the center circle, forward on one edge in a perfect oval and then backwards on the other. Around the perimeter of the rink, Joe was doing long sprints up one set of boards, his skates throwing little chips of ice over his shoulder. Down the back stretch he glided, kicking his edges together, jangling out his arms, and Francesca batted her eyelashes and smiled at him. She was finesse and he was strength, and their workout led to hot chocolate and a long conversation at De-lite Do-nuts, which was open all night.

"Let's go, bear," said Francesca. She zipped him into his snowsuit on the kitchen table.

"I'll see you in the funny papers," Joe said.

Francesca threw the baby bag over her shoulder, and hoisted Gabriel to one hip. "Yeah. I'll see ya," she said, waving the boy's hand for him. "Say bye-bye."

Gabriel's eyes were round and wet and sad. "Bye," he said.

After they left, Joe drank three more beers.

On the radio, WKUT was playing some Elvis Presley songs he had never heard before, scratchy blues accompanied by just a guitar and piano, sometimes with what sounded like old black men singing in the background. After Elvis came more music Joe Glass didn't know, big band stuff with a lot of great drums, and an old Eddie Cantor record, and the High Hat All-Stars featuring Miles Davis and pianist Al Walcott recorded at Boston's High Hat Club in 1955. The disc jockey followed that with Ray Charles, then Woody Guthrie singing "This Land is Your Land" and something called the "Workingman's Blues." Joe Glass marveled at this new program they called "Hidden American Treasures."

Tapping his beer can against the kitchen table, Joe passed the time until nine o'clock. He pulled on the cord running down from the light bulb, and it made a teeth catching sound and the room went dark. Then shouldering his hockey stick and canvas equipment bag, he thundered down the stairs to the street. Snow was piled up to his shins and more was falling. A city truck with a huge yellow plow roared down Bailey Street, sending a wave of snow against his knees. Two men laughed inside the cab, laborers making time and a half for a night's work. And it was pretty easy: one watched for hydrants while the other plowed. Joe Glass computed their paychecks with the exactitude of an accountant as they turned the corner onto South Broadway.

Striding toward him through the drifts was Pier Eriksen, her overcoat buttoned to the neck. Joe went into the roadway to meet her, his stick held over his shoulder like a lance.

"You look like a knight errant," said Mrs. Eriksen. Her white hair showed beneath a Russian fur hat, and she smiled with long wet teeth. "Out to slay dragons and rescue all the maidens."

Joe laughed, and they stood together exhaling steam that rose in plumes above their heads. "The dragon's kicking my ass," he said. The snowflakes angled down at them, flying through the cones of light from the streetlamps.

"How's Gabriel?" asked the old woman, her cheeks glowing. "Growing up, is he?"

"He was playing hockey all day."

Pier Eriksen balled her fists on her hips, surveying the street. "When I was growing up in Norway, we would build great bonfires on the ice and skate for hours," she said. "It was marvelous exercise."

Jay Atkinson

An old station wagon rumbled toward them with one headlight out. "Here comes my ride," said Joe. He heaved his bag through the rear window of the station wagon and skidded his stick in after it. Then Joe came around to the passenger seat, waving to Mrs. Eriksen as they drove off.

*

Father Tom wheeled his cab through the slush on Essex Street. With several taxicabs out covering Lawrence's six square miles, he had had only a few fares all afternoon but enjoyed being away from the rectory. During his shift, Father Tom had ferried several women from the Stadium projects to the welfare office and back. The women, who spoke little or no English, would hand over fistfuls of change to come up with the two-dollar fare. They crowded into the back seat with their children, rode to the Bay State Building and home again, clutching their voucher envelopes and boxes of condensed milk. To Father Tom, it was emblematic of Lawrence's decay: all these idle young people, staring at the blighted landscape.

At the corner of Essex Street and Broadway, two black women wearing miniskirts loitered in the roadway. They waved at passing drivers, cocking their hips and whistling at anyone who glanced in their direction. For a moment, Father Tom thought the women were in distress until he realized they were prostitutes. Saying a quick prayer, he pulled into a nearby taxi stand and began watching the two women in his rearview mirror.

A bare-chested man wearing shorts and a stocking cap hailed the prostitutes and sprinted toward them between lanes of traffic. The women ran in different directions; the more successful of the two hurdled a snowbank in her high heels, making off through a vacant lot. The other woman hesitated for a moment and then changed direction, running for the taxi stand. But her shoe lodged in a sewer grate, which sent her tumbling into the gutter. From across Broadway, the half-naked man bore down on her, his legs churning.

"Tomorrow," the man said. He high-stepped through puddles and lunged at the woman, but she snaked over a snowbank. Landing belly-first on the sidewalk, she scrambled to her feet: a rail-thin black woman with scabby legs and garish make-up.

The man stepped backwards like he was measuring a high jump attempt. "I love you," he said.

Taking several bouncy steps, the man heaved himself into the air and flopped over the muddy embankment. He landed on a huge cushion of snow, staggered up, fell back into the snowbank and then regained his footing. The black woman emitted a shriek and then dashed into the roadway, her eyes searching the empty storefronts and alleys for an escape route. Quickly backing up his cab, Father Tom fishtailed into her path and thrust open the rear door.

"Get in," he said.

The prostitute dived into the backseat. Before Father Tom could speed away, the bare-chested man threw himself at the cab, adhering there like a spider. "Don't leave me," he said. He was flecked with mud from head to foot, and his torso was covered with dirty black hair.

"Get movin', " said the prostitute.

The spinning wheels of the cab found a purchase, and lurched forward. The bare-chested man fell in the roadway, but was back on his feet in an instant. "Come back," he said.

Father Tom watched the man diminish in the mirror. The buildings on Essex Street loomed overhead, traffic thickened, and the woman stared at her pursuer through the window.

"I hope somebody kill that motherfucker," she said.

While working as a cab driver Father Tom wore a plain black turtleneck and denim jacket, and made allowances for the range of humanity that ended up in the back seat. "I can take you to Bread and Roses," he said to the prostitute. "They'll feed you, and you can get warm in there."

"I ain't goin' to no shelter. Drop me down the Methuen line. You pointin' that way."

A call came over the radio, and the dispatcher announced that there was a fare waiting outside Dr. Tattersall's office on Common Street. Father Tom acknowledged the call and signed off. In front of a sign that said "Welcome to Methuen. Established 1726," he let the prostitute out of the cab.

"What's your name?" he asked.

"I go by Tomorrow, because Tomorrow never comes," she said, slamming the door.

Father Tom cut across town, past George's Syrian Bakery and the old jail to Campagnone Common, drifted now with snow. Standing at the corner of Common Street and Jackson was an elderly man wearing a baggy gray suit and raincoat and a tweed hat. He waited there in a little cleared space, his gloved hand clutching a portable oxygen tank. Father Tom eased over to the curb and rolled down his window. "Are you waiting for a cab, sir?" he asked.

"I certainly am," the man said. He coughed at the effort, covering his face. "Thank you. That wind is getting a little cold."

Father Tom set the brake, and sprang from the driver's seat. He took the man's arm, and unspooling some of the plastic cord, lifted the oxygen tank over a snowbank and helped the man into the cab. "There you go," said Father Tom.

"Ugh," said the man, easing back with some difficulty. "Thank you very much."

When both fare and driver were situated, Father Tom asked, "Where to?" His passenger's breath came in long raggedy gasps, and the man held up one yellowish finger indicating he needed a moment to compose himself. "No hurry," said Father Tom. He did not start the meter running.

The man was wearing a green and black striped necktie, and a starched white shirt that was loose at the neck. His shoulders were hunched like a vulture's wings, and with each breath the gentleman's face seemed to lose more of its color. Watching him in the mirror, Father Tom became

Jay Atkinson

alarmed.

"Are you all right, sir?" he asked, turning around to look at his passenger.

An accordion sound came from the man's throat, and he sputtered to get the words out. "I feel pretty good, believe it or not," he said. "I've been invited to a Chamber of Commerce meeting. This is my first day out of the house in a while."

"We'll set a flat rate of ten dollars, and I'll take a drive around town while you catch your breath," said Father Tom. "How does that sound?"

The man made a dismissive gesture. "I can afford to pay," he said.

At the foot of Common Street, the taxicab made a right-hand turn in front of the Pacific Mills building. It rose up six stories, flowing for several blocks in both directions. The windows were in neat rows, trimmed in articulated brickwork and sandstone that created a fan-like effect above each one. The lowest floor housed a dye-cutting operation, which was marked by a small metal sign, and the rest of the building was vacant, sealed off like the pyramids of Egypt.

Bent to the taxicab window, the elderly man peered at the mill, his view segmented by each dark broad window as they passed. Then the cab stopped at a traffic light on the corner. "The wool that came out of that building clothed half the world," the man said.

"I didn't know that," said Father Tom. He extended his hand into the backseat. "My name's Tom Dailey. I'm from Chicago."

The man offered his skeletal hand. "Walter Beaumont," he said. "It's my pleasure."

The light changed, and the bluish saints and gargoyles of Holy Rosary Church passed overhead. Father Tom squeezed the cab between a delivery truck and some pedestrians and turned onto Canal Street, running parallel with the snow-covered trough of the canal. At intervals, suspension bridges led over the Merrimack River toward the Ayer Mill.

"I've lived in Lawrence my entire life," said Beaumont. "My father worked in the Ayer mill. I was there eleven years myself."

They crossed over some old trolley tracks, then the road turned to cobblestones beneath them, rattling the windows of the cab. "Where did everyone go?" asked the driver.

"The hardiest ones pulled up their bootstraps, and followed the work down to Georgia and the Carolinas. The others just scattered around. Some got work in the little shops here and there. Or they tried house painting, or got themselves on the fire department."

"What did you do?"

The old man pulled a scarf from his pocket and tied it around his neck, tucking the ends under his raincoat. "By then I was at the bank," he said, adjusting his breathing tube. "My father helped me get a position."

"The forces that were at work in these old mill towns were irresistible," the driver said.

"They were all too greedy, those mill owners and managers. Once the seeds were sown"—Beaumont glanced out the window— "no one could change the outcome of something like that."

City in Amber   143

Walter asked his driver to make a quick detour. Stopping in front of Lawrence Savings & Trust on Essex Street, the retired banker adjusted his lapels and smoothed the hair behind his ears. Then he disconnected himself from the oxygen tank. The driver, following these activities in the mirror, twisted around with a look of concern on his face.

"Are you going to be all right?"

"Fine," Walter said. "I'll only be a minute."

The taxi door opened, and Beaumont went over the cracked panes of the sidewalk. Reaching the door, he tugged on the handle but it wouldn't budge. Then he noticed the whitewashed windows and a sign that read: "This branch is closed except for the automatic teller. Please visit our branch in Methuen." Huffing for breath, Walter leaned on the glass and stared at the bank's rotunda, illuminated here and there by skylights in the ceiling. The zinc counter was intact but across from it, where bankers had met with their clients inside polished walnut carrels, there was nothing but blank space. A single coffee cup had been abandoned on the counter like an artifact at Pompeii, and dust mice huddled against the Ionic columns flanking the lobby.

For many years, silver-haired Evelyn Peachtree had sat at a reception desk that was now absent, greeting customers with an arched eyebrow and her terse, unwavering signifier: "Yes?" With that one syllable Mrs. Peachtree expressed annoyance at being disturbed from what she considered to be her engraved duty at the bank: answering correspondence, typing memoranda and whatnot, at the same time maintaining a note of politeness that indicated she valued each and every customer. Beaumont feared it was the tolling of a note that would never be heard in Lawrence again.

Suddenly the cab driver materialized. "Why don't you come back to the car, sir?" he asked.

But Walter was fishing for the plastic banking card he had received in the mail. "I'm all right," he said, going through his pockets. "I'll be with you in a minute. Thank you."

Walter plugged the card into a slot beside the door, buzzing it open. The tiny glassed-in vestibule smelled of body odor and urine; someone had spent several nights there bedded on a piece of cardboard. Beaumont remembered coming to the bank one afternoon in 1942, and his encounter with a panhandler who had swooped in to get warm. For a few seconds on that dim gray afternoon, Walter was alone with a man who smelled of slept-in clothing and grain alcohol. They stood on the gleaming marble floor staring at each other. A moment later, Mrs. Peachtree had arrived in the lobby, wearing an astrakhan coat with her eyeglasses suspended on a chain around her neck.

Raising her spectacles to the bridge of her nose, she took one look at the hobo and said, "Shoo." The man vacated the premises, and Walter sent an office boy after him with a ten-dollar bill.

The retired banker inserted the card in the teller machine, and punched in his code. He got the numbers wrong somehow and the machine digested his card. Immediately Walter was out of breath,

Jay Atkinson

trapped inside the urine-smelling cubicle. He rapped on the glass, and once again the driver came to his aid. Grateful for the help, Beaumont was led back to the taxi and hooked up to his oxygen tank. "I used to work there," he said, gasping.

"They don't make 'em like that anymore," the driver said.

His passenger took a last look as they pulled out from the curb. "Once it was new," Walter said.

Because Essex Street was one-way, the driver circled around the block and dropped Walter Beaumont off beneath the marquee at the Chamber of Commerce. Again toting the oxygen tank, he assisted his passenger over the soiled red carpet to the door of the building.

"Wonderful," said Beaumont, handing the driver forty dollars. They shook hands. "If you'd like to come back in an hour, I'll need a ride home."

Through the window of the cab, a burst of static announced another call from the dispatcher. "You can count on me, sir," the driver said.

Walter Beaumont entered the Chamber and made the first landing. In front of him were two steep flights of stairs. He heard the taxicab rumble off, and stood gripping the handle of his oxygen tank—he had forgotten the building had no elevator. Just then the door to the inner office was thrust open, enveloping him in the aroma of brewing coffee.

"Mr. Beaumont," said Jay Bower. "I'm pleased you could make it."

Walter Beaumont had never been so glad to see anyone in his life. He recalled the boy's grandfather, a pork pie baker with an English accent, meticulous and polite. The boy looked nothing like him; he was a lean, straight youth with a firm jaw and dark brown hair. But he had the same air about him, a man who exuded patience and usefulness.

The old man put out his arm and Bower stabilized him. "I need a little help," Walter said. "The stairs."

"Let's just move our meeting to the first floor," said the youth. "Wait here, Mr. Beaumont, and I'll see to it."

Jay Bower went bounding upstairs before the retired banker could object. He heard chairs scraping overhead amidst the rumble of conversation. Bernie L'Heureux stuck his head out of the conference room in doubting Thomas fashion, and then retreated and in a great artificial voice made an announcement about the change of plans. Braced against the doorjamb, Walter Beaumont concealed the oxygen tank behind the drape of his raincoat and girded himself for the onslaught of well wishers and apologists who would be descending toward him. But it wasn't the boy's fault; he was trying to help.

The assembly rushed out of the upper room. They swirled downward in a torrent of overcoats, grays and browns and blacks, their heels clicking on the stair treads. There were more than two dozen business executives, local politicians, and the police and fire chiefs in their dress blue uniforms. Doused with aftershave and perfume, animated by the change in scenery, their murmurs grew to a crescendo beneath the tin ceiling of the entranceway, like a crowd rushing out of the theater after a performance. Walter Beaumont shrank against the wall, terrified.

But they all passed within an eyelash and into the lower offices of the Chamber without addressing him, without even seeing him there.

Jay Bower came last, with a tray of Danish and other pastry in his arms. "Let me put this stuff down, and I'll be right back," he said, backing through the doorway. Then Walter was alone in the hallway, staring at the muddy tiles. Before he could exit to the street and hail another taxi, the young man had returned for him.

"Let's go in," Bower said.

Helped to a chair, Walter Beaumont struggled to remove his raincoat and scarf, and adjusted the plastic hose that fed oxygen into his lungs. Joined by his lawyer Philbin Bates, they sat with the rest of the dignitaries, facing an easel. Around them were desks and typewriters and adding machines, and the Chamber of Commerce secretaries who continued working in an unobtrusive fashion, flowing like spirits over the carpeted spaces of the office and modulating their voices to a pitch below earshot. In front of the assembly, the easel was divided into two parts: a washable slate with colored markers, and a map of the city that was fixed here and there with shiny stars made of paper. Beside the easel was a desk that supported a percolating coffee urn and the tray of pastry.

Bernie L'Heureux stood before the gathering with his fingers woven together in self-congratulation, beaming at the Mayor and city councilor Paul Quebec and a few others. Then L'Heureux explained that such meetings, on the first Thursday of every month, would be aimed at "cleaning out the riffraff" in Lawrence. At this initial session, Fire Chief Driscoll and a trim, hard-looking man with gray hair, Thomas "Tug" McNamara, the new Chief of Police, were the Chamber's honored guests. They had been asked to speak about the growing problem of arson. Chief Driscoll stood up first, wielding a marker that he used to pinpoint recent fires on the map.

"Seventeen residential and commercial buildings have burned down in the past nine months, with one fatality, a nine-year-old girl," said the Chief. "Our investigators have determined that at least thirteen of these fires were set, many of them by using the same kind of accelerant." He began marking these sites on the map. "So far it's cost the city four million dollars in—"

"Please, Chief, don't write on the map," said L'Heureux. "That's the only one we have."

Uncomfortable in his dress blue uniform, 48-year-old William Driscoll was a former private who had come up through the ranks of the Lawrence Fire Department. Before making Chief, Driscoll would not have been caught dead inside the Chamber of Commerce.

"Sorry," he said. "I thought that was what the marker was for." He looked back at the map and frowned. "Every time we have a big fire, we call in the neighboring departments and it's costing us all a lot of money. It's so bad, I see my fellow chiefs at mutual aid meetings and they run in the other direction."

Police Chief McNamara rose to his feet. He was a former Marine with two tours of combat duty in Vietnam, and fourteen years experience as

Jay Atkinson

Deputy Police Chief in Boston. Walter Beaumont had read about Chief McNamara in the newspaper but had never met him.

"Chief Driscoll is right, and it's only going to get worse," said McNamara, facing the semi-circle of chairs. "Arson will drive law-abiding homeowners out of the city, which means the tax base will continue to shrink, which means less money for public safety all around. Is this systematic arson? Is it drug dealers trying to intimidate, or absentee landlords trying to collect insurance? I don't know. And I don't have the resources to find out, either." He gestured to a man in a blue suit. "Come up here, Rick. Ladies and gentlemen, this is Special Agent Richard Maxwell, from the Bureau of Alcohol, Tobacco and Firearms."

A forty-year-old black man rose from his chair. He was six feet tall and lean, wearing shiny black shoes and a blue necktie. Agent Maxwell stood between the two chiefs, spoke to each of them, and then addressed the audience, his hands clasped behind his back. "You're probably wondering why the ATF investigates arson. Probably because most arsonists are drunk, smoking a cigarette and carrying an unlicensed, unregistered handgun," said Maxwell. There was some nervous laughter. "The truth is, usually we end up finding some connection to our other law enforcement mandates when we get to the bottom of things." He cast his gaze over the folding chairs. "And be assured, we will get to the bottom of things."

State Senator Wilson X. Wilson put his spotted hand in the air. Pinned to a lapel was his Fireman's Appreciation badge, and he balanced a prune Danish and a cup of coffee on his knee.

"Yes, sir," said Maxwell.

"How much is this gonna cost us?" asked Wilson. He glanced at those seated nearest him. "You federal boys never come cheap, and the till is just about empty."

Agent Maxwell leaned forward to catch what was scribbled on the elderly man's name tag. "That's a good question, Senator Wilson," he said. "We've got a certain amount of money for these projects, and Chief McNamara called early enough to catch that account full. You can thank him."

A look of profound dissatisfaction came over the elderly politician's face. Fixing the agent with rheumy eyes, Wilson creaked to his feet, the Danish in one hand and his coffee cup in the other. A roomful of people had just been told that their highest-ranking elected official had had nothing to do with a major service being provided to the city. Walter Beaumont smiled to himself at the federal agent's gaffe. It was like accusing Wilson X. Wilson of urinating in the city water supply.

"Over more than fifty years of public life I have dedicated myself to the city of Lawrence, young man. When I was first elected alderman in 1936, you might be interested to know, it was my motion that divided the job of Fire and Police Chief into two positions. Ten years later, at the conclusion of World War II, where because of my heart murmur I served as air raid warden for the great city of Lawrence, I voted to add six police officers to the department, and personally"—the senator raised his voice at this point— "*personally,* Agent Maxmore, hosted dances at the Arlington Club to raise the money."

Wilson X. Wilson drew a deep breath, no doubt intending to continue this spontaneous filibuster. Springing to his feet, Bernie L'Heureux made a time-out motion with his hands but the state senator ignored him.

"And furthermore," said Wilson, pointing at the ATF agent, "in 1970 I went to the mat for this city, and got my close personal friend Governor John A. Volpe to appropriate three hundred thousand dollars in order to give the police officers of Lawrence the raise they deserved. For many years, I have stood shoulder to shoulder beside a long line of Police Chiefs, sir, including the new one, Chief, uh, Macintyre. Now, normally I like to promote from within. There's no reason why a Lawrence boy, born and bred, shouldn't be good enough to wear the Chief's badge. But I did as requested when Mayor O'Brien called me at home for advice during the selection process. I checked around. Why? Because Mayor O'Brien is a constitoo-ent of mine, and I've never let a constitoo-ent down in more than fifty years of public service, believe you me, Agent Maxmint."

At the mention of the word "constitoo-ent," Beaumont recalled one of the many colorful episodes that Wilson X. Wilson had participated in. During a Knights of Columbus installation dinner years earlier, dressed in the beaded hat and gown of the Knights Templar, Wilson had learned that a voter from South Lawrence was being held at the state mental institution. Heeding the call, the elderly politician departed the banquet. Upon entering the gates of Danvers State Hospital, Senator Wilson leaped from his car and strode into the lobby with an imperious air, his gown flapping. He went straight past the reception desk into one of the wards, looking like some sort of wacky Shakespearean character.

An intern had stopped Wilson in the hallway, asking to see his identification. "I'm Senator Wilson X. Wilson, and I'm here to visit one of my constitoo-ents," came the reply.

"And I'm the Queen of England," the intern said.

Through a series of administrative errors, Wilson X. Wilson was then interrogated, sedated, and held overnight for observation. A picture of the State Senator appeared the next evening in the *Tribune-Standard,* sans the floppy hat, beaming on the steps of the hospital with his liberated "constitoo-ent" and the headline dated March 31, 1963: HE CAME, HE STAYED, HE WAS RELEASED. Also on the front page, Walter Beaumont remembered, was a story about the pandemonium at Kennedy International Airport when an English pop group called The Beatles arrived. The Beatles had long since broken up, one of them had even been shot dead by a madman, but Wilson X. Wilson still held onto his seat in the State House.

"Ladies and gentlemen, today I stand before you in complete accord with Chief Macintosh and Agent Michelson here," said Wilson, gesturing like a Roman orator. "With my full support and the support of the governor of the Commonwealth of Massachusetts and all the legislators of both houses, we will find the perpetrators of these crimes and after a fair trial, punish them to the extent of the law. I give you my word as a Lawrencian, as a Democrat, and as a man." The elderly senator bowed to the assembly. "Thank you very much."

Let it not be said that Wilson X. Wilson had forgotten how to mount a campaign horse. His face glowed with confidence, and the elderly politician nodded at the ATF agent and Police and Fire Chiefs like he had never interrupted them. One row distant, Mayor Elizabeth Temple O'Brien sat motionless with her hand pressed over her mouth, bug-eyed at the speech. The other elected officials present, Methuen town manager George Gomes and Lawrence city councilor Paul Quebec, a chubby young man, who, in deference to his late father, a former mayor, was known as Junior, were also taken aback. Wilson X Wilson's soliloquy had left them solid as statues; old pols never died, they just babbled on and on about nothing.

The momentum of the gathering had stalled. Jay Bower stood up, and directed another question at Agent Maxwell. "What will you do, and how can we help?" he asked.

"Well, sir, there's pretty tight security associated with what we're implementing, but I can share some of our ideas with you," Maxwell said. "ATF will send a number of agents in, targeting the problem areas. Having it all lead to one perpetrator, or a small group of perpetrators, would be the ideal scenario. Statistically, that's not going to happen. What we might have, which is more common in cities like Lawrence with large sections of vacant housing stock, drug trafficking, and densely-settled neighborhoods, is a mindless and random threshing out. Sort of a protracted Devil's Night."

"But nothing can be done about something like that," said Mayor O'Brien.

Chief McNamara smiled at the floor, then cut his eyes over to Agent Maxwell. "Don't worry, Mayor, a lot of things can be done," he said. "I want to start with higher uniformed visibility in certain neighborhoods." McNamara placed his hand over sections of the map. "There's no doubt the problems can be harnessed with the right sort of coordination between agencies. But we're talking about containment."

"You're right, Chief, in saying we're not going to war against these people," said Agent Maxwell. "We can't drag the neighborhoods, pulling people out of closets."

"I wish we could," said Bob Biddeford, who owned Biddeford Hardware, the last real store on Essex Street. "Show these punks who's in charge."

"All you have to do is violate one person's rights, and the whole thing comes down on top of you," Agent Maxwell said. "In Detroit, for example. People were being roughed up and arrested and they hadn't done anything. The political fallout starts, and you have to step back and watch the city burn to the ground."

Telephones began ringing throughout the Chamber offices. There was a call for Chief Driscoll about a three-alarm fire on Park Street, and Agent Maxwell occupied another line talking to someone in Washington.

The room buzzed with opinions.

"It's the goddamn Puerto Ricans," Bob Biddeford was saying to Junior Quebec. "They burn down the dumps they live in because they know the government will find them new places. It's like monkeys shitting in the monkey house."

The City Councilor glanced around the room, making sure the assembly was like-minded before speaking. "They'll fill out every kind of paperwork known to man when it comes to getting a handout, but they won't register to vote," he said. "If it wasn't for all the elderly in my district, I'd have to finish law school and get a job."

"When my people came here from England, they came to work," Wilson X. Wilson said. The whole row was joining in the conversation. "They were the first ones through the doors of the mill. These darkie types don't want to work. We should ship 'em all back."

"Back to where? Puerto Rico is a United States territory," said Junior Quebec. "They sign up for welfare here and in New York, and you watch, on the second Tuesday of the month, Essex Street is bumper to bumper with New York license plates. The Puerto Ricans are killing this city."

"The girl who died in that fire was a Puerto Rican," Biddeford said. "They'll kill their own, they don't care." The hardware store owner looked like he was going to spit on the carpet. "They're robbing me blind, all of 'em."

In the row behind him, Walter Beaumont and Philbin Bates sat in silence. Nine-year-old Luisa Gomez was the dead girl. There was a photograph of her that appeared in the *Tribune-Standard,* pretty and black-haired with delicate features. Lying on a ruined, waterlogged sofa clutching a stuffed elephant, Luisa Gomez appeared to be sleeping. Asphyxiation caused by smoke inhalation, the article said. She didn't look like someone who had refused to vote, or was lazy, or had made an unlawful flight to resist prosecution. Luisa Gomez was a murdered child, nothing more, nothing less.

"Are you ready to leave?" Philbin Bates asked his old friend, Walter Beaumont. "I don't want to hear another word."

Beaumont shook his head. "Out of breath," he said. "You go ahead."

The lawyer excused himself, and put on his hat and coat and left the meeting. Phil Bates had been approached by Luisa Gomez's family to represent them against the landlord of their apartment building, Boris Johnson, for neglect of the property, and against the city for not enforcing the building code. The house where the fire had occurred was a deplorable mess: exposed wiring, trash piled up in the hallways, ancient fixtures and not a single smoke detector or fire alarm on the premises. Luisa's mother, Angelica Martinez, had made repeated calls to Boris Johnson about these problems and even tried visiting City Hall to see the code inspectors, but nothing had been done. Unfortunately, the grieving mother had never put any of her complaints in writing, so it was unlikely that she or Attorney Bates would ever see a penny in damages.

To make matters worse, Boris Johnson ran up during the blaze and

Jay Atkinson

helped firefighters chop a hole through the back door to look for his tenants. Television crews interviewed Johnson dressed in his shorts and sneakers and a kamikaze headband. Against the backdrop of the fire, the landlord described the smoke and confusion inside 21 Park Street. To the television audience, he sounded like the reincarnation of Sergeant York.

"I'm sorry, ladies and gentlemen, but we're going to have to cut things short," said Agent Maxwell, hanging up the telephone. "There's been a fire across town in the Arlington District and we've made an arrest. Chief McNamara and Chief Driscoll and I have to get down there."

"Now, that's results," said Bob Biddeford.

Junior Quebec wagged his head. "This Maxwell seems like a whiz, for a black guy," he said.

Agent Maxwell and the two Chiefs departed the Chamber of Commerce. Through the front windows, all watched as they jumped into a late model sedan with the ATF agent at the wheel. Driving away from the curb, Maxwell reached out and stuck a revolving light on the car roof.

"There goes a couple of ass kickers," said Biddeford, rapping on the plate glass. "These monkeys will have trouble burning anything down from in jail."

Only Walter Beaumont was still seated, and Jay Bower, who had stretched a telephone cord over two desks was talking to someone in a low voice. Beaumont waited for Bower to hang up, and then asked the young man if he would make a telephone call to Central Taxi. "Sure thing," the youth said.

He gripped the edge of his chair. Nobody had spoken to him beside Bower and Phil Bates in the hour he had been at the Chamber of Commerce. At one point in his career, if such a crisis had affected the city, the Mayor and everybody else would have queued up for his advice. But a retired and infirm bank president, Beaumont decided, was of no more consequence than a retired janitor. Now he could start screaming, and no one would listen.

Eamonn Carr O'Connell entered the Chamber dressed in a plain black suit and his priest's collar. Late for the meeting and apologetic, he received an update from L'Heureux. The news, although distressing, had little effect on the priest's demeanor: he was solid as a rock.

From across the room, Jay Bower gave Beaumont an okay sign; his taxi was on the way. The old man donned his raincoat, and rolling the oxygen tank ahead of him, tottered for the exit. No one seemed to notice, but at the last moment Father O'Connell intercepted him. "Walter, it's a pleasant surprise to see *you* here," said the priest. He gripped Walter's bony hand, the eyes solemn beneath the white puffs of his eyebrows. "I've been meaning to call you about that matter we discussed. The honorary degree."

"I've instructed Phil Bates to make all the arrangements," Beaumont said.

"God bless you. Your contributions to the community will never be forgotten."

Walter Beaumont glanced at the men and women chatting before the windows, oblivious to his departure. "Right," he said.

The blast of a horn came from outside. With his raincoat draped over his shoulders, Walter Beaumont moved past the white-haired priest into the foyer, and then down the stairs to street level. His driver stood beside the taxi, clearing the pavement with a brush. There was a tapping at the window behind him, and Walter arched his neck and looked back. Perhaps the mayor or someone was saying farewell. But it was George Gomes and Biddeford and the specter-like figure of Wilson X. Wilson, gazing at something over his head. Together they pointed at a column of black smoke rising above Essex Street.

At the same moment, Boris Johnson burst from a nearby alley, wearing shorts and a headband emblazoned with the rising sun. He skittered between patches of ice, heading for the fire. Beaumont watched as Johnson's route took him alongside City Hall, and then up and over an embankment where the green metal doughboy marched down from Campagnone Common. The sound of footfalls could be heard, crunching over the hardened snow.

Walter felt himself marooned in the airless reaches of outer space. His tank continued its steady hiss, but he couldn't taste the oxygen. Dried lips parted over his teeth and the shriveled apple in his throat went up and down, but no sound came out.

"Here, let me help you," Father Tom said. He lifted the oxygen tank into the car and, with an arm across his passenger's shoulder, fitted Beaumont against the seat cushions. "There you go, Mr. Beaumont," the driver said.

Father Tom got behind the wheel. Three crows flew the length of Essex Street, arching upwards at the Pacific Mill building and darting like shadows into the rotunda. Then the door to the Chamber opened and Wilson X. Wilson emerged, tapping his cane along the sidewalk. In a moment, George Gomes and many of the others followed him out, dispersing to their cars. Only Bernie L'Heureux and Junior Quebec lingered in the window, hovering like barrage balloons above the street as they gorged on pastry and continued their meaningless pantomime.

Dusk was falling over the city. Weak light shone from some apartments, and the last empty commuter bus rattled toward the city limits. High above the Ayer Mill, the clock hands moved into place at five o'clock. Several peals came from the great Dutch bell, throbbing over the landscape like pulses from the city's heart. The last one echoed away.

"Bellevue Cemetery," said Walter.

His driver put the taxi in gear, and churned out of the gutter. Walter Beaumont looked out at the abandoned downtown for the last time. Nobody stirred on Essex Street. The metal wings of the Sutherlands Building were folded shut against the coming night, some trick of the wind that had pushed them against the facade. A short ways ahead was a traffic light that quickly went red.

Jay Atkinson

The light changed. Soon the driver had found the rotary at the foot of Bellevue Cemetery, climbing Gill Avenue to a bluff that overlooked the city.

"Stop here," Walter said.

Packed with dented and dingy snow, the cemetery loomed across the road. Walter Beaumont opened the door of the taxicab and struggled to his feet, dragging the oxygen tank with him.

From the vantage point of the hill, he could see steam from the gasworks rising over Lawrence. Hundred-foot smokestacks crowded the night sky and several fires burned in distant corners of the city. Straight ahead, the dial of the Ayer mill clock shone like an old coin.

On the nearest empty building was an advertisement for the *Tribune-Standard*. The billboard depicted a giant newspaper headline that read: THE TIME IS NOW. Silhouetted against the billboard, Walter Beaumont clung to the guardrail and swayed there for a moment.

"The old town," he said. "The grand old town."

8

Lawrence, Massachusetts

September 19, 1848

The outer world beckoned to him, impinging on his consciousness, and Abbott Lawrence emerged from a dreamless pool of sleep and sat upright in bed, gasping for air. It was a moment before the financier realized he was not in Washington or home in Boston, but occupying a rented room in the New City on the Merrimack. Lawrence rose in darkness and, after using the chamber pot, rummaged through his portmanteau for the striped trousers he would wear to the dam dedication. The windows leading onto the gallery were covered with hoarfrost, and his breath came in ghostlike vapors.

Taking up the poker, he stirred the fire and rolled another log onto the coals. A packet of papers impressed with the Essex Company seal was stuck halfway under the door. Slipping the documents into his pocket, Lawrence unhooked the latch, swung the door open and glanced into the corridor. The upper passage of the Coburn House was silent and empty. At his feet were a pair of Indian clubs and a samovar of tea, and Lawrence stooped to heft the weight of the dumbbells and then knocked them together. Off somewhere down the hall, he heard the complaint of a mattress and vague nocturnal bleating from another guest. With one of the Indian clubs under each arm, the millionaire retreated into his room with the vessel of tea and fastened the latch again.

Lawrence placed the papers on the desk, among the scattered correspondence of the previous evening. No doubt this latest delivery was the handiwork of Mr. Coolidge, working through the night on the agreement with J. F. C Hayes and his newspaper. Eager to peruse these lines and, if satisfied, to ink his signature, Lawrence turned the valve on the gaslight. Suddenly every item in the stark little room was thrown into relief. Frost on the nearby window had congealed into a spiral pattern and the millionaire scratched at it, the gray shavings curling over his thumbnail. He poured himself a cup of tea and then remembered to take his exercise, since so many obligations would weigh upon him in the next hours that he'd scarcely have time to dress himself.

Donning a short muslin jacket, Lawrence picked up the dumbbells again and unlocked the outer door. He went beneath the lintel and for a moment, scanned the second floor gallery that overlooked the street. At this hour the horizon was dark and he heard only the purling of water through the sluice gates. The previous evening, Lawrence had discovered a letter from his brother Amos, written some months before, that had ended up among the papers that awaited his return to Boston. In the letter Amos offered condolences for his brother's political disappointment this past June, but expressed satisfaction over their ventures in the New City: "If my vote would make you vice president I would not give it, as I think it lowering your good name to accept public office of any sort, by employing such means as are now needful to get votes. Your characteristic ardor and energy of will, in my opinion, are better suited to improving our firm and the lives of those who work for it." Following these lines was the postscript: "I hope 'Old Zack' will be president."

His feet cold on the planks, Lawrence stood the Indian clubs by the door and crossed the gallery to the handrail. Using a mouthful of tea, Lawrence cleared the foulness of a night's sleep from his mouth and spat into the mud below. He took several deep breaths of the chilly air, ruminating on the day that lie ahead and what it would bring. His brother's philosophy was the right one: How could a man profit by gaining the offices and entitlements of this world, if it meant sacrificing the next? Lawrence thanked the Lord for His bounty, as he would a dozen times before breakfast, and prayed that his colleague Charles Storrow would see God's glory in all they had accomplished together.

He could sense dawn coming in the warm air emanating from the river. Taking up the clubs again, Lawrence smelled the feculent odor of the Turnpike mingling with wood smoke—from fires arranged here and there to mark the night deliveries. The roadway had jelled in the colder temperatures overnight and now, as a single horseman trotted by, Lawrence could detect the earth beginning to loosen and the stench that accompanied it. At the foot of the Andover Bridge, the horseman reared, coaxing his mount onto its hind-legs, and glanced back down the Turnpike. Lawrence swung the dumbbells overhead at that moment, and the rider waved his farewell before dashing over the bridge.

Lawrence gripped the clubs by the neck and made large, slow circles with them, feeling the muscles bunch at his shoulders and the sinews stretch along his back. His youth on the farm had granted him a solid frame, and in his half-hour of exercise each morning the old Groton man reveled in the play of his strength. If there were no gymnasium at hand and no dumbbells, Lawrence took vigorous walks in the early morning darkness, alongside the brownstones of New York and Georgetown or over the cobbled streets of the Back Bay. But here in the New City, he didn't feel secure; every nook and cranny seemed the lair of a cutpurse or thief. It was a wild settlement.

When he felt rivulets of perspiration and his torso glowed beneath the muslin jacket, Lawrence waved the clubs in a tight figure eight, clenching his guts, the musculature of his back rippling in every direction. Beneath him, a man in a coarse woolen gown staggered out from the sheds and began fumbling with his trouser buttons. Lawrence struck one of the clubs against the railing and the stable man looked up at the gallery and muttered an oath. Confounded by the sight of Lawrence and his dumbbells, the stable man broke wind and then retreated into his sleeping quarters beneath the gallery. A moment later, a horse began whinnying and the man re-emerged wearing an old hat made of sheepskin. The boards groaned beneath his weight as he headed for the privy.

By the time Lawrence was halfway through his regimen, a thin border of gray lined the horizon and the first carts were rattling along the Turnpike. Far off, a train whistled into North Andover station, hauling its load of cement from New York and oak timbers that had been carted down from the Maritimes. Atop the papers on Lawrence's desk was a bill for a shipment of timbers that amounted to $650.18, and past invoices for brick totaling $1844.13. In addition to these debts was the payroll, calculated at $19, 294.92 for the labor of some 3,500 men over the past month. Total gross expenditures at the New City for the month of August 1848 were $26,494.72. Inside the strongbox beneath the Coburn House was $23,000 in treasury notes, $1,000 in silver coin, and $1,314.88 in promissory notes from vendors who had undershipped or supplied beyond their quota of damaged goods.

Vexed by the Essex Company's shortfall, Lawrence abbreviated his exercise and retreated into the room. He locked the gallery door, prodded the fire once more, and then hung the muslin jacket over the chair.

As light began to fill the room, Lawrence sat at the desk and plunged back into his calculations, before heeding the call to prayer. Kneeling beside the desk, he implored the Lord's Providence to guide his decision-making that day and in the future. He beseeched his God—the God of Abraham, of Isaac, and of Jacob—for the health of his five sons and two daughters, his wife, Katherine, and for each of his board members, investors, principals, field engineers and clerks. For the laborers he prayed en masse. Staring into the well of his life, he asked the Lord to drain away his vanity and to fill his remaining years with love for his fellow man, service to country, and the patronage of God's will on earth.

In his last, most intimate murmuring, Lawrence petitioned for the safe conduct of Amos' soul, which, he feared, would soon be called from this world. Beloved sibling, keen-minded advisor and a man of humility, charity, and Godliness, Amos had been the steady beacon of his brother's life, a life in service to others. The contemplation of this loss gripped Lawrence by the throat and he leaned against the wall and sobbed.

Stronger light was coming in the window and the birch log had warmed the room considerably; again the pile of papers beckoned from the desk. Within minutes, Lawrence had tabulated his books again, found the same sum wanting that he had discovered the evening before, and then a new terror struck him. Unless he signaled his assent to J. F. C. Hayes' demands, there would be no way to prevent the newspaperman from circulating his rumors while collecting new ones from the mob. Digging through his pockets, Lawrence found the tartan band that Coolidge had delivered to him and taking up his hat, fit the device over the crown. Still, it wasn't enough. Raised on scaffolding, it would be impossible for Lawrence to detect the Scotsman among the thousands who would gather for the dam dedication. While the millionaire fretted over this, a knock came at the door.

"Who is it?"

"Lieutenant Treachey, sir. I must speak with you."

Lawrence squeezed the nib of his pen until the ink ran over his fingers. "I do not wish to be disturbed," he said, wiping his hand with a chamois. "Make your report to Captain Bigelow."

A familiar voice boomed over the threshold. "I am also here, Mr. Lawrence," Bigelow said.

Barefooted, in striped trousers and the upper half of his dressing gown, the millionaire crossed the room and drew open the door. Lawrence's visitors were struck by his appearance and he was equally startled by theirs: both men pale from lack of sleep, dressed in muddy boots and holding their hats. Captain Bigelow looked more stricken than he had the evening before. The stench of his smoking clung to him and he grimaced every few moments, his free hand slotted inside his waistcoat where it pressed against his injuries. In the beam of the gaslight, Lawrence saw that his engineer had not slept for several nights.

Lieutenant Treachey was also in a state of agitation. The pistol in his belt had been discharged and reeked of gunpowder. His hair, uncovered by the helmet clenched in his fist, was stiff with perspiration and stood up on his head like wires. A large welt had risen over his cheekbone and blood ran in a stream from a notch that was cut there. His mustaches were also flecked with blood and looked like the pelt of an animal that had been slaughtered.

"What is the trouble?" asked Lawrence.

"Of the sort which must be discussed indoors," said Captain Bigelow. His gaze was steady and there was no panic in his voice, but Lawrence understood that something grave possessed the engineer.

"Come in, gentlemen," Lawrence said.

The room was small and contained only one chair. In the space between the bed and the desk, the three men stood facing each other. "Where is Mr. Storrow?" asked Lawrence.

"At the gatehouse," Bigelow said. "He was injured last night, but will recover."

"God blast these indiscretions," said Lawrence.

Lieutenant Treachey attempted to clear his throat. His jawbone quivered and he said, "Beg your pardon, sir. As the residents of shantytown hadn't been paid, they objected to us collecting the ground rents. A laborer in the charge of Gilmore and Carpenter even assaulted Mr. Storrow. The situation became so volatile I was forced to use my pistol." Treachey shifted his gaze to Captain Bigelow, who kept his eyes on Abbott Lawrence and nodded, and then the constable looked back again. "I shot and killed a man, sir."

"Lord hopes it was the man that attacked Mr. Storrow," said Lawrence.

Treachey studied the floor. "It was a bystander. A Swede he was, sir. They cremated him."

Lawrence staggered back against the desk and, reaching with his hands, found the chair and collapsed into it. "Holy God," said the financier. Head bowed, he began massaging his forehead. "A man shot dead, on company land? Were there any witnesses?"

"More than three hundred, sir. I regret my actions, and have offered to turn myself in to the sheriff but Captain Bigelow will not allow it."

There were several moments of silence, while the gravity of what had occurred in shantytown took hold of the little room. Finally the millionaire stretched his arms toward the ceiling and groaned aloud. "What say you, Captain Bigelow?" asked Lawrence, in the hiss of the gaslight.

The engineer spread one of his large hands and placed it on Treachey's shoulder. "I have spent the night interviewing the constables in our detachment, and even journeyed to the settlement to conduct interrogatories with men who were present, and have determined that it was an accident," said Captain Bigelow. "A tragedy, certainly; avoidable, perhaps; but in the midst of what I would characterize as a riot, Mr. Storrow was in peril and Lieutenant Treachey, given the means at his disposal, took reasonable action to prevent grievous injury to a superior."

"What is Mr. Storrow's condition?" the financier asked.

"He received many cuts and bruises, a slight concussion of the brain, and there is blood in his urine," said Bigelow. "But the barber has been called, a West Indian gentleman who insists that the wounds are superficial and that no danger to Mr. Storrow's mental or physical functioning exists."

While Captain Bigelow recited a full description of the events in Dublin, Lawrence's brain swam with a thousand horrible thoughts. One of the most troubling was the identity of the man who had assaulted Mr. Storrow. It was clear to Abbott Lawrence that the youth who had saved Captain Bigelow's life was a favored son of the New City. Just as plain, however, was the Essex Company regulation that *any quarrelsome, disorderly, incompetent, or unfaithful person shall be dismissed from the employ of the contractors.*

"It is most regrettable, Captain Bigelow, if all what I hear of the lad's exertion on your behalf is true," Lawrence said, "but there is no question that Gabriel Glass should be banished from the New City and prevented from collecting his pay."

Bigelow stood pale and gaunt, one hand inside his coat pressing against his damaged organs. "I was at the gates of death and Gabriel Glass snatched me away." The engineer gritted his teeth, and the cords in his neck stood out. "I will forever be obliged for that. But the rest of his conduct is beyond my influence."

Squaring himself to the desk, Lawrence signed the contract with J. F. C. Hayes and then rolled it up, scribbled instructions to Mr. Coolidge regarding the deduction of ground rents from the payroll, and wrote a hasty note to Mr. Storrow. He reached up to extinguish the gaslight and then delivered the contract into Bigelow's hand, retaining the two personal notes. "Seek out Mr. Hayes at the earliest possible opportunity and transfer to him this instrument, with the added consideration of a hundred-dollar note," Lawrence said. "Mr. Coolidge will provide the note."

As there was nothing left to discuss and Mr. Lawrence was about to make his toilet, the engineer bowed from the waist, Treachey saluted, and both men turned for the exit. Lieutenant Treachey marched through the open door into the corridor and, as Bigelow followed him out, Lawrence caught his engineer by the sleeve. "Just a moment, Captain," he said.

Bigelow closed the door and stood there holding the latch, while the financier threw his portmanteau onto the mattress and began assembling his wardrobe: cravat, satin vest, a shirt made of cotton broadcloth; then his swallow-tailed coat, English riding boots and doeskin gloves. The financier yanked the lower half of his dressing gown from within his trousers and pulled the garment over his head. His upper torso was white and hairy and blotched with salt rheum.

"Sometimes we must do things that run against the tenor of our principles, yet our principles are salvaged in the name of the common good," Lawrence said.

"Which deeds do you refer to?" asked Bigelow. "For I stand ready to execute them."

Sitting on the bed, Lawrence tugged on a pair of woolen stockings, squeezed into the shiny leather boots, and buttoned his shirt to the neck. "Brave, good fellow," he said. "I know your injuries trouble you, and that the banishment of the lad who came to your aid causes you pain as well. But now you must come to the aid of our settlement and stockholders."

A nod signaled that Captain Bigelow would assist the Essex Company. Lawrence glanced at him again, their eyes met, and he continued: "The matter of J. F. C. Hayes' cooperation must be decided. You are hereby charged with accomplishing this—whatsoever it requires. Is that clear?"

"Perfectly, sir."

There was a small pier-glass hanging on the wall and Lawrence moved within its range, fitting the cravat around his neck and looping its tether to the center button of his trousers. Gazing at his visage in the glass, he stuck his arms through the holes of the waistcoat and fastened its many tiny hooks and then, adjusting his cravat, stepped into the swallow-tailed coat that Bigelow held open for him. "Once you have detained Mr. Hayes and secured his assent to our proposal, turn your attention to Mr. Storrow," Lawrence said. "In less than three hours, he must be ready to mount the platform."

"Mr. Storrow is in no condition to attend a public ceremony," said Bigelow.

"He must attend or there will be speculation about his whereabouts and condition, which are mysteries the Essex Company need do without," Lawrence said. "Our investors must be assured that our financial and social condition is a sound one."

"Agreed. How may I assist Mr. Storrow?"

"Get some porridge into him," said Lawrence. "And we must take pains to disguise Mr. Storrow's bruises, in order to console the populace."

Captain Bigelow stuck a thumb inside his beard and scratched his chin. "There is an undertaker residing in Timothy Osgood's boardinghouse. I will send for him and his flesh paint."

The millionaire turned from the pier-glass and looked into the face of Captain Bigelow. "One more thing: we must avoid all taint of scandal relating to the incident in shantytown," he said. "This Treachey must be discharged from our service."

"Lieutenant Treachey has a wife and five sons," said Bigelow, his voice low and reasonable. "He has been in my employ for twelve years, three here in the New City and nine as second-in-command of my garrison in Ohio. I cannot, in good conscience, dismiss him."

His heels clacking over the floorboards, Lawrence paced up and down the little room. "Is this fellow more important than the future of our New City?" he asked, frowning.

"Neither Lieutenant Treachey's career, nor mine, is of greater significance than our work here," said Bigelow, his face stiff like iron. "Therefore I would tender my own resignation if forced to carry out such a task. It is repugnant to me, and I'm afraid its effect would hinder the performance of my other duties."

Gathering his papers, Lawrence stored them in the portmanteau and hid the case beneath the bedstead. Again he studied his field engineer. "Perhaps I spoke too hastily, and there is yet room for compromise," said the financier. "Our company can ill afford to lose one good man, let alone two."

"The Amoskeag detachment has been lacking an officer since James Connolly broke his leg," Bigelow said. "Send Treachey to Manchester and, with God's blessing, he will make an able substitute."

The millionaire thrust out his slender hand and Captain Bigelow enveloped it in his, brawny and hirsute, with double-jointed knuckles. "I agree to your proposal," said Lawrence, surprised by the coldness of Bigelow's flesh. "We must render unto Caesar those things which are Caesar's."

Bigelow dropped the millionaire's hand and unlatched the door and then followed Lawrence into the corridor. Lieutenant Treachey waited at the top of the stairs and without a word passing among them, the three men descended into the cellar. It was not yet six o'clock in the morning, and that space was dark and reeked of urine and spent kerosene. At the head of the passage, the chair that had been occupied by a constable the night before was empty. Groping in the darkness, Lieutenant Treachey found a lantern beneath the stairs, soaked the wick in kerosene and struck his flint.

The introduction of light alerted the constable slumbering in the farther chair, and he woke with a start. "What's this? Who is it?"

"Your employer," said Lawrence. With the captain and lieutenant tramping alongside, he strode toward the bewildered constable. "How long have you been thus occupied?"

"Not long, sir," the man said. "My shift began at five o'clock."

"On your feet, Mr. Donleavey," said Bigelow.

The constable jumped up from the chair and hurried into his tunic. Drawing closer, Lawrence noticed that the trap door beneath which the payroll had been secured, although fastened shut, was unlocked. "Stand aside," he said to the constable. "What sort of treachery are we subjected to? Where is the other guard, and where is the padlock to this door?"

"I came on alone, and the door was just as it is, sir," said Donleavey.

Another figure thundered down the stairs: a man in a nightshirt and wig, carrying a torch. "You can all go to the devil," said T. J. Coburn, fumbling along the passageway. "There has been noise to wake the dead beneath this house."

Coburn halted when he recognized Mr. Lawrence, snatching the wig from his head. "Beg your pardon, milord," the innkeeper said. "I didn't realize you were transacting business at such an hour."

Lawrence ignored him. "Captain Bigelow, secure this room," said the financier, indicating the constable who had been asleep. Bigelow extended his hand for the man's revolver and he complied.

"And Lieutenant Treachey, I'll ask you to bring up the strongbox this instant."

Taking the lantern in his fist, Treachey lifted the trap door and climbed down into the vault. A moment later, he ascended the ladder with the strongbox balanced on his shoulder. With a shrug, he flung the box onto the decking and stood aside. From inside the vault came the glow of the lantern, throwing shapes that danced over the walls.

Coburn's torch was flickering, and Lawrence motioned for Lieutenant Treachey to retrieve the lantern while he slipped the hasp on the strongbox. A halo of light rose from the vault as Lawrence threw open the lid. The treasury notes, arranged in rows and bound with strips of paper, had been disturbed.

"Cock that revolver, Captain Bigelow," said Lawrence, flinging a hand back toward his colleague. "There are thieves among us."

Bigelow pulled back the hammer on the confiscated pistol and motioned Donleavey to stand alongside the innkeeper, whose mouth hung open in disbelief. Kneeling beside the strongbox, Lawrence soon determined that the larger portion of the payroll remained intact. Only two of the smallest bundles, each containing one hundred dollars, had been tampered with and neither was empty. Tucked in the space between the piles of treasury notes and several paper tubes filled with coins was a blank tally sheet. The paymaster in Boston had included it for recording the disbursements. Lawrence pulled out the sheet and unfolded it within range of the lantern.

Using a pencil that had been left inside, someone had made an X on the top line of the spreadsheet; beneath it was an identical mark, countersigned with a much smaller x. Abbott Lawrence wet the index finger on his right hand and calculated how much money was missing from the two bundles. "Sixty dollars from one, and forty-five from the other," he said, waving the loose notes at Captain Bigelow. "A month's wages for a skilled laborer and an unskilled one, respectively."

Also discovered in the strongbox was a sheet of glossy paper. It had been ripped from an oversize book, the print arranged in dense columns and illustrated with Greek temples, steam engines, and various reptiles and birds. Because of water damage the ink ran in swirling patterns, and several of the illustrations were distorted into monstrous shapes. A single clear image was visible: that of *Odonata Anisoptera*, the dragonfly. Wrapped inside the soggy page was twenty dollars in scrip.

Captain Bigelow signaled for Treachey to relieve him, and with a grim face the lieutenant drew his own revolver and pointed it at Donleavey and the innkeeper. Pressing hard against his ribs, Bigelow stooped to examine the Xs on the company ledger, as well as the torn-out page. Then he thumbed through the ruffle of treasury notes. Making a noise in his throat, the engineer straightened up. "You can lower your pistol, Lieutenant Treachey," he said.

"Do you recognize the marks?" asked Lawrence.

"There are scores of illiterate men on these works, and I have seen many such Xs," said Captain Bigelow. "Nonetheless, I can induct a great deal from their presence, and from that of the twenty dollars."

"Odd that a thief would return a portion of the money," said Lawrence.

Just then, another intruder descended the stairs from the main floor of the house. It was the stable man, dressed in his woolen gown and battered sheepskin hat. He padded over the floor, surprised to find such a gathering at this early hour. "God's bones," he said. "What have we here?"

"An Essex Company matter, and your curses add nothing to it," Lawrence said.

"Beg your pardon, sir. I came in search of Mr. Coburn. There's a horse what's been stolen."

The innkeeper's bald head shone in the light. "An abundance of ill will is being heaped upon me," he said. "Which horse is it?"

"There is a glimmer of fortune in the choice," said the stable man. "It was not an animal belonging to this house, but rather, the piebald mare sent over by Mr. Saunders to be shod. I went to the privy this morning and noticed the stall was empty." With a nod of his head, he indicated the financier. "In fact, I saw you taking the air, Mr. Lawrence, though I didn't know it was you."

"Why didn't this thief alert you through his rumblings?" asked the millionaire.

" 'Cause he was a good horseman, sir. There's no other answer to it."

Captain Bigelow turned to Donleavey against the wall. "Who were the two men on duty when you arrived?" he asked.

"It was Bill Higgins and Jeremiah Getchell, sir," said the constable.

"Then I would swear that Mr. Coburn and Mr. Donleavey here are innocent of any wrongdoing," Bigelow said. "Nor was the money removed by the other two constables in our employ."

With the innkeeper going ahead, Lawrence and Bigelow ascended to the main floor of Coburn House. The front parlor had been stripped of its furniture and transformed into a standing room, in anticipation of the hordes that would be attracted to the dam dedication. His torch throwing shadows along the passageway, T. J. Coburn tied open the door to this room and, nodding to the two burghers, allowed Mr. Lawrence and his field engineer to pass inside. Gaslights burned on each of the four walls, illuminating the threadbare carpet and dented tin ceiling.

Lieutenant Treachey and Donleavey came into the parlor, lugging the strongbox. The stable man entered a moment later, and closed the door behind them. The stench of manure filled the room. "Have you summoned the watch?" asked Lawrence.

"I sent my boy," said the stable man. "There's not a horse unencumbered this mornin', and Joseph'd get there much faster than these old legs."

"Do you have a chaise or flatbed available?" Bigelow asked.

When the stable man said that he had a cart and two geldings, Bigelow suggested they withdraw to the stalls and wait for the guard to arrive. While the innkeeper lit another taper, the two constables picked up the strongbox and went out, trailed by the dung-encrusted stable man.

"Give me fresh air," said Lawrence. "For I am about to gag on that man's foulness."

Holding his hat by the crown, Captain Bigelow pointed the way. "A man comes not to recognize his own smell, no matter what constitutes the man and what sort of odor he emits."

Down in the stable, the cart and geldings were soon made ready and Donleavey sat on top of the strongbox with a revolver in his hand. The innkeeper used a candle to ignite the storm lantern hanging overhead, and made way as Mr. Lawrence passed alongside the cart. The horses were uneasy at all this traffic, snorting and bumping against the traces.

Lawrence walked out to the Turnpike and studied the light rising in the east, while Captain Bigelow chewed a splinter of hickory he had broken from the woodpile. "Where is that damned watch?" asked the financier. "Must I wait all morning just to move the blasted payroll?"

As if on cue, a boy of eight dressed in overalls and a knitted shirt came running over the Andover Bridge. Behind him were four constables double-timing on foot and someone riding Coolidge's mount. Boy and horseman arrived at the same moment, both Joseph and the mare out of breath and heaving. Young Joseph passed by Lawrence without looking at him and went to stand beside the stable man.

The financier thought he recognized the boy. "Were you the one delivering newspapers yesterday?" he asked. Joseph nodded, and Lawrence glanced at the stable man. "Is he your kin?"

The man draped his hand over the lad's neck. "Yes, sir. A good boy he is, sir."

"See he minds himself or I'll give him a good hiding, is what I'll do," said Lawrence. "We must all live within the covenants, even the mere striplings."

To the boy's utter confusion, his father slapped him in the head and then leaned back and kicked him in the hindquarters, propelling him toward the hotel kitchen: "You heard Mr. Lawrence. Get on your way and mind yourself." When the lad had flown into the dimness of the stable, landed in a pile of fresh manure, and then ran off, the stable man turned back to Mr. Lawrence and said, "I'd just as soon throttle my young'uns as look at 'em and I've got nine now, all of 'em boys."

"A man that has nine children ought to run a tighter ship than the one we are now adrift on," said the millionaire.

High atop the lathered horse was Mr. Coolidge, and he waved the constables past him into the stable and dismounted before Mr. Lawrence. "Sir, I trust you received the contract I drew up," said Coolidge, executing a bow.

"I did," Lawrence said. He reached into his pocket for the notes he had written. "Here are my instructions to you, and a message for Mr. Storrow. I'll ask you to ride ahead to the gatehouse and set to reckoning the ground rents. I will meet you there shortly."

Coolidge stowed the papers inside his field coat, saluted Mr. Lawrence, and leading himself back around the horse by the reins, hopped into the saddle. Inside the stable Donleavey and three other men loaded the strongbox onto the cart and rolled onto the paving stones just as Coolidge galloped away. Whipped into a canter, the geldings set off after him, the cart bumping along behind.

"I have a single matter to dispose of, and then I will go see about Mr. Storrow," Lawrence said to his engineer. "But I pray you, Captain Bigelow, be so kind as to identify the thief."

Bigelow spat his chewed up splinter into the roadway. "I believe 'thief' is a relative term in this instance," the engineer said. "My reasoning is that Gabriel Glass has deducted his allotment from the payroll, which he believes he deserves."

"That is a tenuous proposition," said the financier. "What is this man's prevailing wage?"

"Sixty dollars a month."

Lawrence exhaled. "How do you explain the additional forty-five dollars he has taken?"

"He has also deducted the wages of Jorgensen, the man who was slain."

The millionaire spat on the ground. "That is an injustice and he should be arrested."

Bigelow stepped onto the wooden sidewalk. "One could argue that Mr. Jorgensen's death was the true injustice here," said the engineer. "Knowing Mr. Glass as I do—and seeing the telltale mark of that smaller x—my sense is that he will forward this deduction to the man's widow."

Gripped by Captain Bigelow's logic, the financier spat once more. "I suppose he intends to mail her the stolen horse as well," he said.

"Since Gabriel was long employed by Daniel Saunders, I wager that he combined his need for transportation with the horse's return and left it off when he passed through Andover this morning," Bigelow said.

"What of the wrinkled page and the twenty dollars that was left behind?"

"All in character," said Bigelow. "The money represents payment for a book I had loaned him, which apparently was spoiled."

"A blasted and confounding situation," Lawrence said.

"I think all parties would agree to that," Bigelow said. Adjusting the brim of his hat, he reared up and stamped his leg, so that the iron brace rattled inside his trousers. "Now if you will excuse me, I'll make way on my errand."

When the sound of the engineer's boots had echoed over the sidewalk, Lawrence witnessed Lieutenant Treachey and one of the other constables saying farewell on the Turnpike. They gripped each other by the elbows while the lieutenant made a remark that was below earshot. Then the other man set off down Essex Street, as Treachey detoured between two buildings and veered onto the canal path.

The storefronts along the Turnpike were thronged with shadows, although the deep russet glow of a lantern came from Levy's barbershop. Lawrence headed in that direction but was compelled to wait a moment for a wagon to pass. It was loaded with apple crates and the driver, noticing the millionaire's finery, raised his hat as he came along. Just then the wheels dropped into a rut and the axle struck the ground, and a half dozen Baldwin apples rolled off the back. Their shiny red and green hides pocked the mud and Lawrence stooped for one as he crossed the thoroughfare. The upper half of the fruit was perfect and smooth, but clinging to the underside was a humus so foul Lawrence wavered in making the apple his breakfast. Reaching for his handkerchief he tried wiping off the mud but the smell clung to the apple regardless. He flung it away.

The millionaire stamped his boots against the sidewalk, cursing their lost finish, and approached John Levy's door. Mounted there was a hand lettered sign that read HAIRCUTS 10 CENTS. Just as Lawrence raised his fist to knock, the door swung open.

"Good morning, sir," said Levy.

"Let us hope we can salvage it," Lawrence said.

Clothed in a wool jacket and his leggings crusted with mud, the Negro gestured Mr. Lawrence inside, amid the lingering scent of wintergreen. "I've just come from visiting Mr. Storrow," said Levy. He placed a leather satchel on the bench, whereupon he began emptying its contents: two small glass vials, an empty thread-spool and needle, cotton dressing, and nine sticks of whalebone.

"How did you find him?" Lawrence asked.

"Beset by several injuries, none of them grievous," said Levy, as he cleaned his barbering instruments with a rag. "He has a cracked jawbone, internal ruptures and a dislocated knee. I strapped his knee with whalebone and muslin, applied a poultice to his broken jaw, and prescribed goldenseal and oil of calendula for the rupture. If there are no further complications, he will recover within a fortnight."

Availing himself of the barber's chair, Lawrence rubbed his forehead with both hands while the Negro shoveled fresh coal beneath the grate. Levy shed his coat and unwrapped the puttees, donning the yellow horsehide slippers he always wore indoors. Unhooking his smock from the wall, he pulled the garment over his head and cinched it about his waist with a hidden strap. From a basin on the sideboard, the Negro splashed water on his face and patted his scalp with it.

In his smock and slippers, Levy resembled the beadle in a country church. "How can I be of service to you, Mr. Lawrence?"

Lawrence rose from the straight-backed chair and met the Negro's gaze. "Mainly I desired your account of Mr. Storrow's condition," the millionaire said. "And relying on your circumspection in these matters, I also wished to discuss an ailment that plagues me." He studied the pattern of cracks in the wall, and his voice faltered. "It is quite persistent, otherwise I would not trouble you."

Levy drew closer. "How does it present itself?"

"It begins in the midsection," said Lawrence, placing a hand on his solar plexus. "There is a burning sensation there, and it does considerable harm to my digestion."

"Have you been aware of it long?"

"Some months. A physician in Boston suggested cannibal salad but I fear this affliction extends beyond the corporeal."

Levy gestured toward the chair and drew up a stool when the millionaire had seated himself. "If the ailment consisted entirely of the sensations you describe, I would hazard that you have a parasite, and that aided by rest and the application of herbs, the power of this toady could be mitigated."

"In my travels, I have encountered tropical fevers and all manner of listlessness and dengue. And although this grippe radiates from the bowel, it achieves the putrefaction of my entire self," said Lawrence. "Each time I am assaulted, my soul shrinks up so small it might dance a hornpipe in a mosquito's watch fob." Again the financier massaged his temples and then drew his fingers downward, leaving a faint red impress along his cheekbones. "Not always do I feel this way, but to increasing effect. Moreover, when I am restored to humor, I am left with the same apprehension: where is this darkness taking me, and how swiftly must I travel there?"

The Negro parted his lips and then sealed them again without uttering any sound. Rising from his stool, he went to the cupboard and returned with two small packets and a flask of Bessell's Special Patent Cure. "These are black cohosh and horsetail," he said, referring to the envelopes. "A dram of each in a goblet of water, taken every morning for two weeks, will initiate the purge I spoke of." His gaze swung up to encompass the man who sat before him. "It has been my experience that the phantoms that beguile most men are rooted in a fragile and precarious nature, mine own included. Address and bolster that nature, and you will perish the phantoms."

Lawrence received the thin paper envelopes from the Negro's hand and deposited them in his pocket. "What of the bottle?" he asked.

Levy turned the bottle to examine the label. "It is a spirit and therefore cures nothing," he said. "But given the sort of day you are faced with, Mr. Lawrence, you may choose to dismiss these apprehensions and so temporarily galvanize your mind." Both men regarded the bottle for a moment. "Knowing your thoughts on the taking of spirits, I leave that decision to you."

The millionaire hunched forward, elbows canted on his knees, and dropped his voice to a whisper. "Have you ever taken refuge there, Mr. Levy?" he asked.

"Small beer keeps me on the middle course. But I have known men who brace themselves with a drink and they are good, fine men."

One hand pressed against his stomach, Lawrence regarded the bottle of cure for a long moment. "A man is what he does," he said. "Therefore his actions must remain consistent with the character he has formed, otherwise he becomes like a house built on sand instead of stone, ready to fall over at the slightest tremor." The millionaire got to his feet. "Your counsel is much appreciated, but I shan't need the cure," he said, shaking Levy's hand. "How shall I compensate you for the herbs?"

Laying his free hand on their entwined fingers, the Negro said, "I knew your father, sir. To be of assistance to his son is a more than fair compensation."

9

The Present Day

The limousine turned at the corner of Jackson and Park Streets, making its way between the cars on either side. Kap Kutter, Jerry Schindler, and the two nineteen-year-old beer company girls bumped up and down as they crossed the fire hoses splayed across the roadway, and then were thrust backwards as the car plunged through massive puddles of water. Glowing against the night sky, the three-alarm house fire had spread to a neighboring tenement. Fire fighters outlined in bloody auras scurried back and forth, and the smell of ash and burned rubber infiltrated the limousine.

Outside on the sidewalk, a terrified Hispanic woman stared at the leaping flames and pulled her children together like a brood of chicks. Occasionally the whelp of a siren could be heard over the music playing inside the limousine: Hendrix singing "Purple Haze."

Pressing the intercom, Kap hailed the driver, a long-haired man with a scar beneath his lower lip. "Get closer," he said.

"I won't be able to turn around, and we'll be stuck there," Joe Glass said.

Kutter winked at the redhead. "I've got a case of Lucky Lager, two quarts of vodka, a carton of cigarettes and a cellular phone," he said. "I'll stay all night."

Cops directing traffic opened the barricade to let another ambulance in, and the limousine followed the big orange and white van straight to the fire. A man wearing a windbreaker with ATF printed on the back waved them to the curb. Kap Kutter lowered the window and stuck his head out. "What's the problem?" he asked.

"Where are you people trying to go?" the ATF agent asked.

Pointing toward the only spot among the fire apparatus large enough to accommodate the limousine, "I'm from the radio station, and we're gonna report on the fire," Kutter said.

The agent shook his head. "I just sent your reporter back fifty yards

Jay Atkinson

and that's where I'm sending you. There's no reason—"

Kutter raised his window, cutting the agent off. "Twenty bucks says you wedge us in right there," he said to Joe Glass.

"Right where?" asked Joe.

Kutter removed a twenty-dollar bill from his wallet and pointed toward a narrow space between two fire trucks. "Right goddamn there," he said.

The ATF agent was talking on a portable radio; he finished his call, and then ignored the limousine. Kap Kutter opened the sunroof, and he and Schindler and the two girls stood for a closer look at the fire and the city's effort to fight it. Nearby, a squad of firemen waved one of the hoses back and forth, keeping water running down the last intact wall of the structure. Neighbors stood guard on their front porches, armed with garden hoses and fire extinguishers, but most of the locals used the fire as a social occasion and loitered at the barricades, drinking from paper bags and calling out to their friends in Spanish.

Out of the shadows came a firefighter with an ax, his face streaked with dirt, and two uniformed policemen with a civilian between them, his hands manacled behind his back. The arson suspect walked along staring at the confusion like he was looking for someone in particular.

"Hey, fire bug," said Kap Kutter. "They should make you go looking for survivors."

Wearing a tattered Philadelphia 76ers sweatshirt, the curly-haired suspect waited between the two cops for several other police officers to arrive. Chief McNamara and a tall black man in a blue suit walked up and the Chief removed the handcuffs.

The man in the blue suit shook hands with the suspect. "Sorry for the fuck up, José."

"It's fucked up, all right," said the curly-haired man, who was wet and shivering.

The two cops glanced at each other, and then waited for Chief McNamara to say something. His arms folded on his chest, McNamara maintained a stony silence. Another plainclothesman came up and handed the suspect an ATF windbreaker. Jose turned with the Chief and the others to look at the fire, which had eaten away most of the façade and was capering through the eaves of the tenement.

"Got anything for us?" asked the black man.

José shook his head. "I was looking around and heard a pop, then this guy ran by me. I didn't get much of a look at him." He glanced at the two uniforms. "I was chasing him when they grabbed me."

"Did you guys just arrest one of your own agents?" asked Kutter.

Agent Rick turned to the man in the windbreaker. "What are these people doing here?" he asked.

"Somebody let them through the barricade."

"Get them out," said Agent Rick.

The agent nodded. "Yes, sir," he said.

The man in the blue suit walked over to the limo. "Rick Maxwell. Alcohol, Tobacco and Firearms," he said. "You can't stay here."

"Kap Kutter," the other man said. "Alcohol, tobacco and redheads." He squeezed the miniskirted girl. "Actually, I own WKUT. We came to see what was going on, and got stuck in the wrong spot."

"Don't worry, we'll get you out," Maxwell said. "But I'd like to visit your office and explain what ATF is trying to do. Maybe we can work together."

"This is my sales manager, Jerry Schindler, and our guests this evening are two promotional representatives from Lucky Lager"—he pointed first at the redhead and then the blonde— "Tawny and Amber."

A lot of things were happening behind Rick Maxwell's eyes. "I'll be talking to you soon, Mr. Kutter."

Maxwell walked away and the two cops remained, glaring at the limousine. Kap Kutter waved to them with his drink, and then he and Schindler and the girls ducked back inside.

"What a bunch of Einsteins," said Kutter.

While Chief McNamara directed traffic, the two fire trucks were disconnected from their hydrants and the limousine backed up, turned in a squealing arc, and moved away from the scene. Kutter and his entourage passed through the police barricade and down the tight confines of Park Street. At the next intersection, a man in swim trunks and a kamikaze headband sprinted past the limo.

"I bet that's him," Kutter said.

"Who?" asked Schindler.

"The fire bug," Kutter said. He called the driver on the intercom. "Did you see that guy running down Union Street?"

"Yeah," Joe Glass said.

"Catch up to him."

The limousine roared into overdrive. "Hold on," Joe said. "There he is."

The man wearing the headband romped through a series of puddles and turned onto Jackson Street, where they lost sight of him for a moment. Drinking vodka from the bottle, Kap tracked the man and shouted instructions into the intercom. "Cut him off and I'll give you fifty bucks."

The limo screeched around the corner, a roostertail of sparks flying from the undercarriage. "You're ahead of him," said Kutter, watching for a glimpse of the man.

The great black car skidded through the next intersection and formed a blockade across the roadway. Kap Kutter leaped out with the vodka bottle in his hand. "In the name of WKUT Radio, identify yourself," he said.

Boris Johnson came within a dozen yards of the limousine. Ice crusted on his chin, forming icicles in his hair and on his eyebrows, and his naked torso was streaked with soot. "I take the Fifth Amendment," he said. With that, he turned and ran off.

Kap Kutter jumped back inside and the limo raced up the hill to where Jackson Street met Berkeley. "I'll try the cemetery," Joe said. "That's probably where he's headed."

"The cemetery?" asked Kutter.

"That's where he brings his 'girls.' "

They went bumping through Methuen Square, past the little shops and the darkened firehouse, throwing sparks from the bumper.

"What are you going to do?" Tawny asked.

Kutter flexed his puffy arm, letting the girls squeeze it through the fabric of his suit. "Well, baby, I've been to the Rose Bowl, the Cotton Bowl and the Super Bowl," he said. "Had good seats, too." The girls laughed.

Climbing Gill Avenue, the limousine inched along with a steep view of the city: the gloomy mill buildings obscured by smoke and a tangle of power lines and steam pipes and tenements. The only other car in sight was a taxi parked at the apex of the hill. As they passed, the occupants of the limousine looked inside at the cab driver and his passenger, an old man with a plastic tube in his nose. The headlights of the limousine flashed in a quick strobe, the old man started up in horror, and then his head dropped again and darkness fell over the interior of the cab.

"Everybody's dying to get in," said Schindler.

In a wooded portion of Bellevue, two figures in dark clothing skulked among the graves. The small one carried a shovel, and the other was stiff-legged with a bulky object slung over his shoulder. Breaking from the trees, the two grave robbers stood upon one of the narrow roads. For a moment, they were in silhouette against the rising moon. Then the smaller figure pointed to something that lay beyond, and the two of them disappeared behind a mausoleum.

Kap Kutter called to the driver. "I saw two people back there. They were carrying something," he said. "Stop here."

Kutter climbed out of the limo and staggered through the cemetery gates. He had ventured only a few feet when he lost his balance and landed on his rear end. Sliding for a good distance, he didn't stop until he became wedged against a snowbank.

"Jesus Goldstein," he said.

Kutter tried to retrace the path of his descent but the road was shellacked with ice. He called out to the limousine; all he heard was laughter and electric guitars, and then his cry rebounded back to him. His feet plunging into the snow beyond his knees, he set off through the drifts. Picking his way among the headstones, he aimed for Gill Avenue about a hundred feet beyond the limo. He reeled from stone to stone, gripping them for balance, his fingers numb against the frozen rock. Beyond him was another roadway, which stretched over two small hills and then disappeared into a grove of trees. Just ahead the sound of footfalls scraped over the road; there was Boris Johnson running for the treeline. He was still bare-chested, but wearing a stocking hat.

"Hey, you," said Kutter. He tripped once more, landing hard on his belly. All around him snow flew upward in a soft fluttering wave. "Come back here."

Johnson was more than fifty yards away. Up and over the hoops in the roadway he went, and in a second he was gone into the woods. Kap

Kutter scuttled like a crab toward the limousine and then reared up, waving his arms, his entire body frosted with snow.

"Over here," he called to the limo driver. "I see the bastard."

The limousine turned into the cemetery, found the paved road and came forward. Before the car stopped, Kutter yanked open the rear door and tumbled in, gasping for breath. "He's here. There's two other people with him."

Bellevue cemetery was divided into rectangles, each one more than an acre in size. Some of the graves were in rows, but the majority of the plots were staked out over hills and in forests beyond the reach of any perpetual care agreement. The limousine was halfway along the access road when two dark-clad figures, without the bundle this time but still carrying the shovel, appeared a few blocks over. Kutter shouted instructions, but the only way to intercept the grave robbers was through the next intersection. By the time the limousine navigated the corner, the two figures were gone.

"This place is creepy," said Amber.

Jerry Schindler sat with his face blanched white and his hands pressed between his knees, looking seasick. The other girl was asleep in the corner, her miniskirt hiked up to reveal the tattoo of a butterfly on her hip.

"Some weird shit is going on," said Kutter, invigorated from his crawl through the snow.

Jerry Schindler opened the door and vomited. It rained in a torrent from his mouth, flooding the interior of the limousine with an acrid stench.

"Yeeooow, that smells *disgusting*," said Amber.

Kap Kutter got out of the car. In this section of the cemetery where no one ever visited, the snow was unbroken, lying in vast plains across an arctic wasteland. Fresh prints came out of the woods a short distance away and then angled back into the trees. Reaching for the vodka, Kutter went to the edge of the roadway and listened for the sound of crunching snow. He thought he heard several thuds from far-off, but wasn't sure. Then he took a swig from the vodka bottle, replaced the top and stuck it in his coat pocket. Turning up his collar, Kutter followed the footprints toward the treeline.

"Wait 'til Dad hears about this," he said.

In less than a minute, the woods of Bellevue had swallowed him up. Abandoned gravestones stood in dense thickets of undergrowth. Some monuments were broken at the base, lying on top of one another and connected by skeletal vines. Skirting one such area, Kutter paused for a moment beside an oak tree. Beneath the earth, he could hear a stream rushing through the catacombs. It ran on, gathering bones until their momentum smashed open the coffins, ripping up tombs in a single wide channel. A river of the dead, sweeping down the pitch into the sewers.

On the path ahead, which showed itself only as a trough in the snow, Boris Johnson appeared. He was bent over and panting like a run-out deer, his tongue lolling from his mouth. Kap Kutter's feet made noise in

Jay Atkinson

the snow as he came closer. He reached into his pocket for something to defend himself with, but found only the vodka bottle. Struggling for breath, Johnson didn't look up.

"Take it easy, fella," Kutter said.

Johnson turned sideways, his hands still on his knees. "I saw them two people," he said, icicles dissolving from his hair. "They were burying something."

"Like what?"

"I don't know."

Behind a granite obelisk, there were footprints and several places that had been disturbed with a shovel. Yards of undisturbed snow lay between Kutter and Johnson, and this trampled area.

Kutter took a drink from the vodka bottle, and then reached for his cigarettes. "Did you set that fire on Park Street?"

Johnson shook his head.

"So why did you run away?" asked Kutter.

"Because you were chasing me," the other man said.

Kap Kutter struck a match. He drew the warm smoke into his lungs, then capped the vodka and threw it to the hairy man across from him.

"It was a guy and a girl carrying something," Johnson said. He drank from the bottle; a large amount disappeared like water and he tossed the bottle back.

Together Johnson and Kutter advanced on the trampled area. The moon cast its tint over the surrounding snow, which except for the broken places was tightened into a smooth skin and marked by an infinite number of pores. The footprints came in a line from the undergrowth and then widened over a space of perhaps fifty square feet. Here and there, the prints accumulated beside gouges in the snow; apparently the trespassers had been searching for the right spot to unburden themselves.

"I bet they were grave robbers," said Kap Kutter. "Trying to steal jewelry or something."

"I know the grave robbers," Johnson said.

His gaze moving over the footprints, Boris Johnson came to a spot that appeared to have been dug up with a shovel and then covered with snow again. An effort had been made to disguise this activity by tamping it over, but markings from the back of the shovel were crosshatched on the site. Johnson removed a metal shiv from one of the graves. Wrapping the flag around his wrist, he used the shiv as a probe and began exploring the snow mound.

"Here it is," he said.

Kap Kutter was rigid, watching in silence from a few feet away. Dropping to his knees, Johnson carved at the mound with his hands, sculpting an image in the snow. After a minute, the shape of a person became distinct. Removing a piece of snow that had been hardened by the shovel, Johnson unveiled the face of a dead boy, eleven or twelve years old. The boy was wearing a short-sleeved jersey and blue jeans. His chin was pushed down, resting on his chest, and his frozen hands were laced together. The inside of the makeshift grave was lined with a blanket, not yet saturated with moisture.

"Jesus Goldstein," said Kutter. The cigarette dropped from his mouth.

Boris Johnson rose up. Icicles had formed again in his hair and the redness had evaporated from his skin, leaving him pale and shivering. The dead boy was half-revealed, the blanket fanned out around his head. It was yellow, decorated with tiny animals. Johnson stared over at Kutter for several seconds, then ran off through the trees.

Kap Kutter remained, staring at the boy's face. He groped for another cigarette, moving his gaze to the tree trunks and vines that surrounded him. High above, clouds streamed in, concealing the moon. Soon it was snowing; the first few flakes gathered on the corpse's eyelashes. Then the snow began covering the boy. Kap Kutter lingered by the grave a moment longer, expelling smoke from his cigarette. Finally he started backing up, and retraced his steps into the undergrowth.

*

In the course of three weeks, Father Tom and Monsignor Borinquen had lapsed into a prolonged, indifferent silence. Emerging from his bedroom one morning, Father Tom had seen his superior coming out of the shower wrapped in a towel. Normally they would each bathe and take care of personal grooming on separate floors of the rectory, and never so much as glimpse the other outside of his street clothes or vestments. But there was a frozen pipe in the second floor bathroom and no money to hire a plumber to repair it. In the name of further economy, the heat was shut off in all the unused rooms and the housekeeper, Mrs. Castiglione, had been let go.

The sight of the older man in a state of undress had shocked Father Tom, then moved him to pity. Monsignor Borinquen's stomach was rippled with varicose veins, bulging like a balloon with too much air in it. His command posture had also disappeared; the ex-Marine limped on flat feet. And the muscles of his chest were puny—unable to carry the great weight below.

The Monsignor fixed his gaze on Father Tom with a momentary candor. On each arm, Borinquen's tattoos looked like comic illustrations and the sparse hair on top of his head, mussed by the towel, was in disarray. He farted a single bass note. Then the Monsignor walked past his subordinate and into his quarters, closing the door behind him.

Holy Rosary and its vicars were in bad shape. Attendance at most masses had dwindled to fifteen or twenty parishioners, and throughout the gloomy reaches of the church the sound of dripping water could be heard. Father Tom was taking extra shifts driving the cab, which helped make ends meet and kept him out six nights a week. But the Monsignor had warned him several times about falling off his pastoral duties: visiting the elderly and sick, hearing confessions, and officiating wedding and funeral masses. For the latter services the parish charged a fee; less than what they would realize in a collection, but much-needed under the circumstances.

Jay Atkinson

One Saturday afternoon, while pulling a double shift in the cab, Father Tom had confused his schedule and was on the road when he was supposed to be saying a wedding mass. Monsignor Borinquen was in his room, suffering from the flu. There was a loud knocking at the door that persisted until the Monsignor roused himself and descended the stairs. Blinking in the light, he was startled by the father of the bride, who pointed to the wedding party assembled in the driveway.

Monsignor Borinquen hurried into his vestments, and the organist struck her first notes an hour later than scheduled. When Father Tom arrived at the rectory that evening and was informed of his error, Monsignor Borinquen related what the bride's father had said: "'I have four daughters and there's going to be more weddings, baptisms, the whole nine yards, but I'll be taking my business somewhere else from now on.'"

"He's right," said Borinquen. "Holy Rosary is like a restaurant: if a competitor is selling nine hundred chicken dinners a week and we're selling two hundred, we're just not cost-effective."

An irritated Father Tom had said: "Maybe the quality of our chicken isn't what it should be."

That night, Monsignor Borinquen set one place at the dinner table and cooked himself a steak that was the color of a bruise. It was the first time the two priests had not eaten a meal together in the eight months Father Tom had been at Holy Rosary. The older man made his displeasure clear in other ways, as well. All the early morning masses and all the funerals were put on Father Tom's schedule. Monsignor Borinquen signed himself up for counseling and confessions, and began referring to any woman who called the rectory looking for Father Tom as the younger man's "sweetheart."

Monsignor Borinquen stopped in the church one morning while Father Tom was conducting a funeral mass. The deceased was a fifty-one-year-old laborer named Bud Reilly, and from among the mourners his son got up to offer the eulogy wearing jeans and a denim jacket. All were startled when the young man recited a short verse in honor of his father: "Through mud, shit and blood, here comes Bud." Beyond the congregation, Father Tom noticed his boss, dressed in a plain cassock, with a stripe of anger descending from his hairline. In a moment, the Monsignor's entire face was crimson.

After the body was wheeled out of the church, and the pallbearers struggled with the coffin down the steep granite steps, Monsignor Borinquen caught the young priest by the elbow. "This is God's house," he said. "Not a barroom."

The coffin disappeared inside the hearse, and then one of the pallbearers slipped on a patch of ice. He cursed out loud and several people laughed. Another pallbearer yanked the man to his feet again.

"It's your responsibility to set the tone for what will and will not be permitted," Borinquen continued. The two priests were alone beside the parish automobile. "I'm sorry, but I've asked the Cardinal Archbishop to talk to you about your commitment to serve. Until then, Father

Daignault is going to come over from Lowell and help out."

"I'm working my tail off to keep this church going."

"I'm suspending you, Tom."

"Do you want to take over right now?" asked Father Tom. "You're welcome to drive up to the cemetery and do the prayers. Because I've had a bellyful."

"That's a good suggestion," the Monsignor said. He took the car keys, his gaze locked on Father Tom. "You can do some praying of your own."

Two days later, the Cardinal Archbishop arrived in his Town Car and placed Father Tom on an "internal retreat" where he was barred from performing any sacraments. The young priest's impression, upon meeting his superior again, was that he seemed like a politician.

The silver-haired Cardinal Archbishop exuded an air of cheerfulness that had more to do with public relations than warmth. Here was a man who played golf with United States senators and carried a cellular telephone beneath his vestments. In recent months the Cardinal Archbishop had spent twenty-five-thousand dollars for a promotional videotape, which had done more to advance his own career than meet its goal of encouraging men to join the priesthood.

The video images—the Cardinal Archbishop surrounded by children, and in a field of wildflowers—reminded Father Tom of the evangelists he had seen on television. At the finish, music swelled and the Cardinal Archbishop's face occupied the screen. In an actor's voice, he said, "Just as Jesus called the shepherds to tend His flock, I am calling you as the sheep of Christ to give service to His will. Call the 900-number that appears below. Operators are standing by to tell you how you can become part of the great flock of our Lord Jesus Christ. God willing, we will join as brothers and sisters to make the Archdiocese of Boston a strong link in the chain of Christian service. Thank you."

While the chauffeur kept his car idling, the Cardinal Archbishop had met with Father Tom in the Holy Rosary library. The ruby ring on his left hand was marked with the symbol of the Holy See. It was well known throughout the archdiocese that the Cardinal Archbishop had his heart set on Rome: he was campaigning to become the first American to wear the Pope's miter.

"Doubt is part of every vocation, Thomas," said the Cardinal Archbishop in the same actor's voice he had used on the videotape. "We recall that the Lord Jesus Christ himself suffered a night filled with doubt at Gethsemane. The way to quell it is not in good works, although I understand you are a man of action, but through meditation. If you pray, the Lord will give you the strength to follow your path, as He has given me the strength to follow mine."

Father Tom spoke up. "The problems in this parish are so far from the diocesan teachings that I feel like I'm from Mars," he said. "One man uttered a profanity straight from the altar and the congregation, such as it was, laughed."

The Cardinal Archbishop swung his blue-eyed gaze to the volumes lining the wall. *The Life of Saint Bonaventure. Francis of Assisi: Strong in Faith. The Teachings of Thomas Aquinas.* "Yes, Monsignor Borinquen informed me of that regrettable incident," said the Cardinal Archbishop. "Remember that Aquinas was carried off by his own brothers and imprisoned for two years in an attempt to obstruct his calling. Your superior here at Holy Rosary is a good man; you would do well to follow his example. He is like Aquinas waiting for the light. But unfortunately, our funding is at a low level and in many cases, we're retrenching in the suburbs, praying for our return to these neighborhoods. Each priest is being called upon to do more work, sacrificing much of the personal counseling and companionship that now must be considered a luxury."

The Cardinal Archbishop placed his hands on Father Tom's shoulders. His breath smelled of peppermint. "You have three weeks," he said. "To petition Jesus Christ to remain part of His new church. Think of Aquinas shut up in the keep, held by his own brothers, waiting for his deliverance to God's work. Think about it, pray about it, and I know you'll do a great deal about it."

There was a muffled ringing sound, and the Cardinal Archbishop reached under the folds of his cloak to remove a cellular telephone. "Excuse me," he said.

Father Tom retreated to the kitchen where the Monsignor sat brooding over a cup of tea. Silence reigned for a few moments. Then Jonah the cat tore across the room like demons were chasing him and the Cardinal Archbishop entered from the hallway.

"That was Father O'Connell from Manchester College," the Cardinal Archbishop said. "He had some exciting news about a donation that will keep our educational mission alive here in the valley. Father O'Connell's industry is an example for all those who must join in our efforts to remain viable." He put his arm around Monsignor Borinquen. "Come, Joseph. Walk me to my car."

Father Tom watched through the window as the Cardinal Archbishop placed his hands on the Monsignor's shoulders and spoke for a moment. Beside the Cardinal Archbishop's silver head, which was topped with a red satin skullcap, Borinquen looked wan and tired. Then the rear door of the Town Car clicked shut and the Cardinal Archbishop was spirited away, the cellular telephone again at his ear.

The Monsignor stamped up the stairs. "His Excellency told me that you're in his plans," he had said to Father Tom. "But there is only one man calling the signals. And on this squad, it's me."

*

Kap Kutter blew his nose into a fluttering handkerchief and inhaled two blasts of nasal spray. On his desk was a copy of the *Tribune-Standard* with the headline: BODY OF CHILD FOUND IN SHALLOW GRAVE. Although snow had fallen all night, obscuring his footprints and those of Boris Johnson, and the body had lain up at Bellevue for two more days before it was discovered, Kutter was worried about his appointment with Rick Maxwell.

The day after the fire, Maxwell had telephoned to suggest a meeting, and Kutter, his nerves frazzled by what he'd seen and not reported, put the ATF agent off until the end of the week. In the meantime, a man walking his dog had found the body of an eleven-year-old Hispanic boy in Bellevue. The newspaper said the cause of death was asphyxiation by toxic fumes. Further investigation had revealed kerosene on the boy's clothing, and second degree burns on his arms and legs.

According to Agent Maxwell, the boy's death was connected to the arson that had been plaguing the city. On the phone, Maxwell told Kutter that he wanted the media to be informed of developments in the case, as well as to report any tips that appeared in the course of news gatherings. The ATF had solved a string of gun store robberies in Houston by utilizing local radio, a strategy that might prove effective in Lawrence. Maxwell would explain how it all worked, in person.

For moral support, Kutter had ordered his sales manager to attend the meeting, but Schindler was late. Gazing out the window, Kutter saw a black sedan come through the gate and then Agent Maxwell stepped from the car. He was dressed in a plain blue suit and sunglasses.

A moment later, Jerry Schindler's car arrived in the parking lot and Kutter rapped on the window, beckoning the sales manager. Then the telephone rang; it was Elise Dominaux announcing the ATF agent's arrival.

"Send him up," Kap said.

There was a knock and Rick Maxwell came through the door, followed by Jerry Schindler. Kutter stood up, his nose inflamed, his face patchy and sagging. "Welcome to WKUT," he said, grasping the agent's hand. "This is my sales manager, Jerry Schindler. What can we do for you?"

Although the same age as Kap Kutter, the trim, well-built Maxwell looked ten years younger. His hair was worn short, and his face was unlined and square at the jaw. Compared to the draped European suits of the other two men, the ATF agent was poorly dressed, but he was tall and lean and his clothes were well-tailored.

"I'm sure you heard about the kid," Maxwell said. He glanced above the desk at a huge marlin nailed to the wall. "They found him up at Bellevue. Suffocation."

Kap Kutter reached for the *Tribune-Standard*. He pointed to the headline, and then shook his head and handed the paper to Jerry Schindler. "Yeah, I saw it," Kutter said. "What a shame."

"Two state police detectives and one of my guys are up at the cemetery right now, sifting for evidence," said Maxwell. "If they find a gas can, or a rag, or even a footprint under the snow, I might have my murder suspect *and* my arsonist."

With a shaky hand, Kap reached for his cigarette and then resisted the urge to fling it away. Two of his cigarette butts were under the snow at Bellevue, lying there like indictments. Kutter wanted to confess, but knew that if he mentioned the limousine ride through the cemetery there would be hundreds of questions to answer. It would take all day: an effort of civic responsibility that he dreaded.

"I've been listening to your station," Maxwell said. "Billy Bruce seems

Jay Atkinson

to have his finger on what goes on around here. He could be very helpful."

"I'll call him in here right now," said Kap, picking up the telephone.

Maxwell shook his head. "Not yet. I want to frame my discussion with you, first. Maybe with your help"—he gestured toward the *Tribune-Standard* on the desk— "and the newspaper's, we can flush out the arsonists."

"Screw the newspaper," said Kutter. "Jerry, tell him my idea."

The little sales manager teetered in his elevator shoes. "I'm a promotions guy," he said, smiling with his capped teeth. "So the other night at the fire, I says to Kap, why don't we do some kind of contest? Identify the arsonist and win a free trip. Something like that."

"Keep talking," said Maxwell.

Kutter broke in. "Jerry's original idea wouldn't work— 'Guess where the arsonist is gonna strike.' I mean, come on, every nitwit in the city would burn his house down. But I could offer a reward for information on who's lighting the fires. Billy Bruce will be our point man. Because you're right, people in Lawrence feel like they know Billy. Somebody just might call and spill his guts."

"My office can't sanction something like that," Maxwell said. "A hotline is more what I had in mind. We'd have Billy Bruce do the greeting. Then if you could make some public service announcements, it would all tie in."

"WKUT has always been a good neighbor," Kap said. "From the day my father founded the station, we've worked harder to improve the community than to make money. That's the solemn truth."

"Time is of the essence," Maxwell said. "I want to get the hotline up and running right away."

"Let me call Bruce in," Kutter said. He pressed the studio line and the disc jockey answered. "My office. Now," said Kutter, and he hung up. "When I say 'jump,' people around here set records."

"Cup of coffee?" Jerry Schindler asked Maxwell.

"I'd love one," said Maxwell.

Schindler rose from his chair and went out. Behind the desk, Kap Kutter extinguished his cigarette and then lit another, blowing smoke toward the ceiling.

"Did you see anything strange that night?" asked Maxwell, as soon as they were alone. "Anyone running from the scene, or cars with their lights off, or anything like that?"

Kutter wrestled with his conscience. "I probably would have," he said, "but if you remember, I was occupied with Miss Lucky Lager. Our clients are top priority."

"After improving the community," Maxwell said.

"Of course. After that."

Jerry came back without coffee, and Kutter glared at him. "Elise is gonna make some and bring it up," the sales manager said.

A knock at the door revealed Billy Bruce. "Whatever I can do to help," he said, after Maxwell informed him of the situation. "We'll set up a line right away, and I'll have all the jocks mention the number twice an hour. And you can be my guest on *Hot Line* tomorrow. How's that?"

"Spectacular," said Agent Maxwell. For the first time, he smiled. "I'd like to have Chief McNamara with me, if that's all right."

Elise Dominaux entered carrying a tray with three cups of coffee.

"Here's our waitress," said Kutter. "And a pretty one at that."

Elise tossed her golden hair. "Sorry, Billy, I didn't realize you were up here or I would have brought another one," she said.

"That's all right," said Billy Bruce. "Six gallons a day is my limit."

Kutter clapped the disc jockey on the shoulder. "What a personality. Always on," he said.

The taut pink fabric of Elise's sweater charmed every man in the room. Only Kap Kutter felt privileged enough to stare, and she caught him at it.

"My eyes are up here," said Elise, raising a finger to her nose as Kutter turned red.

Agent Maxwell laughed.

"That's a beautiful sweater you're wearing," said Kutter. "Is it cashmere?"

"Angora," said the receptionist. "You should recognize it by now. Every time I wear it, I'm picking your eyeballs out of the fuzz."

Kutter smiled at the ATF agent. "Everybody at WKUT jokes around a lot," he said. "Run along, now. Answer all those important phone calls."

When Elise left the office, the scent of her perfume lingering in the empty space, Kutter turned from the doorway and said, "They put those tits right out there on display, and get pissed off when you look at 'em. That's a broad for ya."

Maxwell nodded to Billy Bruce. "When do we get started?" he asked.

"Come downstairs and we'll make a tape," the disc jockey said.

Billy Bruce showed Maxwell the way to the production studio. It was equipped with an ancient reel-to-reel tape machine, two cassette decks and a control board that looked like an old high school science project. The disc jockey popped a cassette tape into one of the decks, and adjusted two foam-covered microphones. Handing the ATF agent a pad of paper, Billy Bruce put on a set of headphones and said, "Jot down the public service announcement, and we'll lay that track down first."

Maxwell finished writing and handed the pad back to Billy Bruce. The dee jay read through the copy once, then cleared his throat and switched on the microphone. "Hello, friends. This is your old pal, Billy Bruce, of WKUT Radio 900," he said. "As all citizens are aware, Lawrence has been suffering from fires that have cost dearly in human life, not to mention displaced families and devastated real estate. With me is Rick Maxwell from the United States Bureau of Alcohol, Tobacco and Firearms. He's working with local authorities to put a stop to the fires. How can we help, Agent Maxwell?"

Billy Bruce turned off his microphone, stopping the tape deck. He gave the pad of paper back to Maxwell. "We call this a doughnut. I lay down my part, your piece goes in the middle, and then I drop the instructions and telephone number on the end."

The agent chuckled. "You make it look easy," he said.

"It doesn't take a genius to talk on the radio," said Bruce, listening to the tape through his headphones.

When Maxwell finally got through his script, the deejay marked the pauses with a wax pencil, and then took a razor blade and sliced out the blank spots. Using thin strips of tape, Billy Bruce spliced the ends together and tightened the space between the three sentences. A chipmunk sound came from the tape player as he ran it back and forth, listening over his headphones. Then Billy Bruce played the announcement out loud, with the two voices blended together.

"Sounds good," said Maxwell.

"When everything was live, I was in here one time doing my show and had to pee so bad I went in a milk bottle and it sounded like Niagara Falls," Billy Bruce said. "The news guy came in and almost lost his dentures, he was laughing so hard." Billy Bruce cleared his throat once more and threw a switch. "Thank you, Agent Maxwell. To help WKUT Radio 900, the city of Lawrence and the Bureau of Alcohol, Tobacco and Firearms put an end to this menace, call"—he read the hotline number from a piece of paper that Maxwell held above the control board— "anytime, twenty-four hours a day. As I always say, friends, together we can build a greater Lawrence."

Billy Bruce ran the timer; the announcement came in at thirty seconds. He made several copies and then recorded a message for the police answering machine. During this activity, Elise Dominaux stopped to inform Billy she was going to lunch, and the ATF agent introduced himself.

"I thought you were coming to shut us down," said the receptionist. "If it wasn't for Billy, they would have pulled our license a month after Kap took over."

The woman's perfume flared up as she leaned over to kiss Billy Bruce.

"If my wife walked in right now, I'd be washing dishes for a year," said the deejay.

Billy Bruce had stacks of production work to take care of, and he shooed Rick Maxwell and Elise into the hall. The two young people stood looking at each other on the dingy carpet.

"Can I buy you lunch?" Maxwell asked.

"I'd love to, but I have to visit someone in the hospital."

"I'll drive you over, and then take you to lunch," Rick Maxwell said. "How's that sound?"

Maxwell opened the door to the parking lot. Elise Dominaux brushed against him as she walked by, scented with perfume. In the outdoor chill, she pulled on her jacket and buttoned it to the throat.

Up in his office, Kap Kutter beckoned Schindler to the window. "Check it out," said Kutter. They watched Maxwell and the receptionist climb into the black sedan and drive out through the gate.

"Even the federal government can't resist a great pair of tits," said

Kutter.

He opened a desk drawer and took a nip from a flask with *KK* engraved on it, then offered it to Schindler. "We have to get Billy up here and find out what he knows," said Kutter. "Maxwell has complete faith in him, and we should exploit that."

"I thought you were gonna tell him we were in the cemetery the other night."

Kutter took another drink from the flask. "I almost cut your throat to keep *you* from telling him," he said, wincing at the liquor. "Half the city is on fire and the cops don't have a clue. Why should I tell 'em anything?"

"What was going on up there?" asked Schindler.

"I know what I know," Kutter said. Standing up, he reached in his pocket and hustled his balls. "Keep your mouth shut, and you're dealing from a position of strength."

*

Lawrence General Hospital was dimly-lit, with cracked linoleum floors, high ceilings, and the overwhelming smell of urine smothered by antiseptic. Elise Dominaux tiptoed along the dark corridor, peering into each of the rooms. Beside her, Rick Maxwell walked over the squeaky linoleum, his gaze fixed on nothing in particular. Stifled sobs and an occasional plaintive cry floated out from the patients sprawled upon the beds. The rooms were unnumbered, their wooden doors propped open. Nametags were inserted into brass holders fastened to the wall, and Elise examined them one by one.

Elise stopped in one of the doorways. "He's in here," she said, disappearing into the room. Rick Maxwell looked at the cadaverous figure under the sheets. He was an old man with pencil-thin legs, hooked up to an electronic bellows that forced air through a tube into his lungs. On the bedside table, a radio played an old jazz number.

"I'll wait for you," said Maxwell.

Elise unhinged the door from its rubber stopper, letting it swing shut behind her. Twisting sideways, she felt the weight of Walter Beaumont's generosity tumbling beneath her sweater. Then Elise pulled up a chair and took hold of Beaumont's hand. "Walter, it's me," she said. "Elise."

From someplace where his mind was wandering, Walter Beaumont narrowed his focus. "Pier," he said. "You've come."

The room was filled with a horrible stench. Elise took a vial from her purse and sprayed a brief shower of perfume over the bed.

Beaumont's lips curled into a nearly toothless smile. "Father," he said.

The door opened, and an old nurse with a chest like a bulkhead came stomping into the room. "You'll have to leave, Miss," she said, fanning at the perfume. "Your father needs his rest." Above the bed, she gave Elise Dominaux a forlorn look.

"Walter's a friend," said Elise, retreating from the bedside. The music ended, and after brief mumbled comments from the WKUT jock, a requiem began to play. Walter's hand fell over the edge of the coverlet and hung limp.

"I'm sorry, Miss. I thought he said 'father.' "

The nurse escorted Elise to the door, and she took one last glance at her benefactor. Walter Beaumont was curled up facing the wall, his hands drawing the sheet toward him.

Elise looked back. "Goodbye, Walter," she said.

In the corridor, Elise slumped against the wall. Maxwell came out of the lounge, spotted her, and ducked back inside, emerging a second later with his overcoat. "Are you all right?" he asked.

"It was a shock seeing him like that," Elise said.

A minister dressed in black with a stiff white collar passed by and entered Walter Beaumont's room. Just a few seconds later, the elevator revealed a white-haired priest in an expensive overcoat and another dignitary wearing a red skullcap with a huge ruby ring on his left hand. These two men also went into the sickroom.

Elise rode the elevator in silence. "I'm sorry," she said, when they arrived in the lobby. "I'll have to take a rain check on lunch."

"Let me give you a ride back to the station."

"Thank you, but I'll take a cab." A taxi pulled up out front and Elise broke away. "Call me sometime," she said. Elise Dominaux ran to the cab in tears. "WKUT, please."

The driver was the man who had taken her to Walter's house right after Christmas. He was about to speak when someone else rapped on the window glass. It was the minister, huddling in his threadbare coat. "Can I share this cab?" he asked. "I need a ride downtown."

The driver glanced at Elise and she opened her door. "Of course. Please come in."

The minister was a bald man with a narrow face and filmy brown eyes. He sagged into the rear seat of the cab, blowing on chapped hands and with tears streaming from his eyes because of the cold.

"Where to?" the driver asked.

"United Church of Christ on Park Street," the minister said. He smiled at Elise, and thanked her for holding the cab. "I need to get back and make some phone calls. God bless us! Running a church these days seems to have more to do with lawyers and accountants than anything else."

Steering past a delivery van, the cab driver looked into the mirror. "Amen," he said.

Reverend Cruikshank introduced himself to Elise and she gripped his hand; it was cold even through her doeskin gloves. "I was so happy to see you visiting my friend, Walter Beaumont," she said. "And those two other ministers as well."

"That was Father O'Connell from Manchester College, and the Cardinal Archbishop of Massachusetts," said Cruikshank. "A couple of heavy hitters, you might say."

"It's good to see so many people concerned," Elise said.

Reverend Cruikshank's eyes bugged out and he pursed his lips, drawing his face to a point like a sea horse. "There's a lot of concern when someone like Walter Beaumont is dying," he said.

"Did Walter speak to you?" asked Elise.

"No, Miss. I only stayed long enough to pay my respects," said Cruikshank, running a hand over his bald head. "The others were there to administer what they call 'extreme unction.' The Catholics are very big on rites and ceremonies, you know." Reverend Cruikshank gazed at the boarded up tenements along Jackson Street. "We Episcopals can't really compete with that sort of thing."

*

Walter Beaumont was attending a party on the main floor of the Ayer Mill. All the machinery was gone, and the rafters were filled with thousands of balloons. Torches were mounted on the walls, throwing flares of light, and swing music came from a hidden source. Frederick Ayer himself was carving a huge steamship of beef, dressed in his tight black vest, frock coat and cravat. The old gentleman had an awl thrust deep into the roast, and Walter trembled as Ayer's face went dark and the bloody meat fell from the bone.

There were several tables laden with delicacies that were common to Lawrence: tubes of pasta with garlic sauce, pork pies stacked up like ammunition, chick peas and Greek olives and tiny onions that gleamed like pearls. Farther down were skewers of lamb, raw kibbee, chubby smelts lined up with their eyes staring at the ceiling—and huge rinds of cheese, radishes, cabbages, artichokes, coins of squash, and peeled carrots floating in a tub of ice water. Although the food was steaming, it gave off a faint chemical odor.

At the end of the last table, stretching into the shadows beyond the torchlight, Walter saw burnt, nasty-looking meats—grilled mice and small, fricasseed rats with whip-like tails, their feet turned up. A few moldy potatoes and buckets of water completed this aspect of the feast. Ragged figures grabbed at the food, and arguments occurred. Some of the guests leaped at each other, wrestling on the floor over the splashings from a bucket. Again, Walter started toward what seemed to be a welcome sight, and then the scene mutated and he turned away.

His father was in the center of the room, surrounded by applauding mill workers. Franklin Beaumont was delivering a speech. Transported closer, Walter noticed Jay Bower standing with his dead grandfather Ray, who wore a baker's apron and hat.

"This fellow is my client," said young Bower, gesturing at Franklin Beaumont. "His image is in the toilet around here."

"That's my father," said Walter, but no sound came out.

Franklin Beaumont stood on a barrel in a plaid tuxedo and homburg hat. The cuffs of his shirt were unbuttoned, hanging from the tuxedo jacket. Walter noticed that the mill workers were silent, looking upon his father with eyeless sockets and skeletal hands that beat together like sheaves.

"MY SON WOULD LIKE YOUR ATTENTION," said Franklin Beaumont. He made several lewd thrusts at his audience. "Get up here, Wally," he said. "Tell some jokes."

Walter looked down at his pajamas. Upon arriving at the party, he had thought himself young again and well-dressed, but now he saw that the oxygen tank dragged behind him and his feet were old and shriveled. "I don't have anything to say, father."

"GIVE HIM A ROUND OF APPLAUSE," Franklin said. " LET MY IDIOT SON KNOW THAT YOU WANT TO HEAR WHAT HE HAS TO TELL YOU."

Several of the mill workers turned to Walter Beaumont, clapping their bony hands in silence and measuring him with their eyeless gaze. Others were motionless, dressed in old-fashioned work clothes, with exhausted faces, like they couldn't stay upright another minute. They stood packed together, with their filthy caps in hand.

"Why don't they just leave me alone?" asked Walter.

The crowd parted as Walter approached his father. "All I know is, the mill was still there when *I* left," Franklin said.

"The Ayer was sold in '59," Walter said. "I told the board to buy municipal bonds with the proceeds, and the directors made a killing." But the music drowned Walter out.

Franklin Beaumont was waving his hands. "MY SON WILL EXPLAIN EVERYTHING." Several of the eyeless mill workers carried him away, and he said, "HE'S THE ONE WHO FUCKED THINGS UP." Then more softly, Franklin Beaumont's voice came floating out of the smoky air: "Where's my cuff links? I gave you my cuff links and you're not even wearing them."

"I'm in my pajamas," Walter said.

"My legacy, pissed right down the fucking toilet," said his father. "It's the little things, you know. The details."

Only a few women dotted the crowd, with thick red arms and faces like fists. Then a light-haired girl in a pleated dress came toward the center of the room. Walter reached out, but the strength of many hands lifted him in the air and deposited him on the barrel top.

"Pier," he said, as the woman glanced up. She was smiling, and the pale orbs of her bosom spilled from her dress.

But soon she was beyond him, pursuing Franklin into the shadows. Bits of conversation were heard, then an organ introduced the strains of a dirge. From the outer reaches, a procession of men came toward Walter Beaumont. Led by torchbearers, the attendants were dressed in black and six pallbearers followed them, carrying a glass coffin on their shoulders. There was the stench of flowers, and Walter could see an old man in a plaid tuxedo stretched inside the coffin.

"Father," said Walter.

Behind the coffin was a woman dressed in black. It was Pier Eriksen— not Walter's mother—who was grieving. The pallbearers stamped to a halt and the mill workers gathered around. From inside the coffin, Franklin Beaumont was staring at his son. His shirt cuffs hung loose and his hands twisted at the hem of his jacket. Still clutching the bloody awl, Frederick Ayer passed through the mill workers like smoke and came to the head of the procession. He took the hand of a small boy with a terrible gash on his head and gave a brief oration that was drowned out by the music.

Perched on the shoulders of his pallbearers, Franklin Beaumont kept his gaze fixed on his son as old man Ayer led the procession away. Only a few eyeless workmen remained clustered around the barrel. The last person to fade into the shadows was Pier Eriksen.

"Your father needs his rest," she said.

Speaking from his heart, the enfeebled Beaumont yearned to know of the past and what his dead father had meant to the young woman. Something was troubling him and he struggled to articulate it.

"Goodbye, Walter," said Pier, from an unreachable distance. In an instant, she had become naked to the waist, her breasts full of milk and standing outright from her chest.

"Are you all right?" Jay Bower asked her.

"It was a shock to see him like that," Eriksen said.

The mill was empty. Walter Beaumont climbed down from the barrel and followed after the procession, but it seemed to glide into a cavern so vast there was no hope of catching up. Then the music died out altogether.

Dragging the oxygen tank behind him, Beaumont sank to his knees and then curled up on the floor. While he was lying there, two men in ghostly vestments came across the room and stood before him. One man rubbed oil on his forehead and wrists that made him feel better for a moment, and another spoke in a low voice, strange words he wasn't familiar with. Walter had the sense that a third man had arrived, and there were echoes of a small, whispered argument. Hands were passing all over him, and Beaumont felt one of the hands remove something from his pocket. Then the men went away.

Next, Walter heard the scurrying of a million claws. The sound of their scratching grew into a din. As the last torch went out, he distinguished a horde sweeping toward him. It was rats. Beaumont clutched at the planks, searching in vain for a weapon.

10

Lawrence, Massachusetts

September 19, 1848

By eight o'clock the sun was riding over Methuen, and Freemasons dressed in their sashes, tanners in leather aprons, and men in silk hats crowded the thoroughfare amid horses, carts, post-chaises and lorries, and the noise of a thousand voices crying out with force. In the Coburn House, Abbott Lawrence encountered the proprietor of the hotel, who had trundled in a load of birch logs and was piling them by the main fireplace. Lawrence instructed the innkeeper to hold his bags until four o'clock, when they were to be loaded into the omnibus and sent to the gatehouse. There an empty strongbox would be added to the cargo, along with the exhausted patron of the New City, both cargo and patron to be delivered to North Andover for the six o'clock train.

"At your service," Coburn said, holding a chunk of birch in his hand.

It was a three-minute walk from the hotel to the gatehouse. Along the way Lawrence saw that a detachment of militia had arrived from Danvers. Their mission was to keep traffic flowing over the Andover Bridge until nine AM, when they would seal it off for the dam dedication, and to safeguard the payroll once the men lined up and began handing in their chits. Among Lawrence's papers was a memorandum from Captain Bigelow, explaining that the militiamen would form a gauntlet leading to Mr. Coolidge's payroll table. The sight of all those muskets would calm the agitation of any employee who had a gram of sense, Bigelow had written.

Rushing past a team of mules, Lawrence noted that several vendors had erected stalls along the Turnpike for the purpose of selling victuals. One man roasted Indian corn on a brazier, behind a sign that listed his price at a copper apiece. Farther along, another peddler sold honey in quart jars that were stoppered with wax. The jars were displayed on a plank slung between two sawhorses, and in front of each was a placard detailing what the bees had fed on: apple blossom, buckwheat, clover, goldenrod, lavender, pumpkin, red sumac, and wildflower. Arranged nearby were the various implements of the beekeeping trade, including the helmet with its gauzy mask, quilted leather gloves of extraordinary length, and a body suit of canvas and leather with intricate straps to join it together, like the padding worn by medieval knights beneath their armor.

Sunlight shone upon the jars of honey, beginning with daffodil hues and progressing through sunflower, maple, and an amber variety that threw narrow rainbows onto the plank. The final row was black and this trait arrested Lawrence's progress, as it was the only brand of honey without a placard.

"It appears you have raised beekeeping from art to science," said Lawrence. He referred to the name that was imprinted in each of the wax stoppers. "I presume you are Mr. Maddox."

Brought to attention by his customer's manner of speaking, Thom Maddox doted on Abbott Lawrence. "I have studied these creatures since I was a wee'un and have determined the three things necessary to making a fine honey: heat, moisture and abundant bees," said the man. Generation after generation of bee stings had raised themselves on his neck, and then dried and whitened into circles. "To an extent, I have learned to industrialize their efforts, creating nectars of discernible taste, texture and appearance. All these characteristics are dependent on the particular flowers the bees visit."

Maddox held one of the nameless black jars to the light, tipping it to make use of the space beneath the wax: its slow, viscous movement was like lamp oil. "But there was a renegade tribe of bees who inhabited a particular hive in my colony," he said. "My efforts to shepherd them toward certain vegetation, either cultivated or native, fell short, as did my attempts to track their nectar gathering. Where they traveled and what they visited I know not, but the honey they have made is dark and secret and rich, with the consistency of molasses and an inordinate sweetness that I have not attempted to categorize." He replaced the jar and pulled at the ends of his hair. "My black honey, although of agreeable taste, is useful to healing burns and softening skin. Married couples hereabouts also report that it has had a marked positive effect on their connubial relations."

"How much compensation do you require for such a mystery?" asked Lawrence.

"One dollar per jar," Maddox said.

Lawrence fished for his purse. "I will take twelve jars, packed six to a box," he said, drawing out a ten-dollar gold piece. "Will this suffice for payment?"

Maddox watched the sun glinting on the coin. "Where can I send your order?"

"Tamp the crates with straw and mark one for Mrs. Katherine Lawrence, care of Back Bay, Boston Massachusetts, and send it to Mr. Coolidge at company headquarters. He will see to the shipment. As to the other, send six of your finest black honey to the gatehouse. I wish to make presents to our shareholders."

Lawrence tipped his hat and went on. The Turnpike was fast becoming more crowded, and from an intricate mental catalogue that included dozens of familiar faces the millionaire sorted out three he recognized from previous visits to the New City. In rapid succession Lawrence nodded to Artemus Stearns who owned the dry goods store, hailed the druggist Nathaniel Wilson, and spoke for a moment to William Sargent who had opened a haberdashery on Essex Street. Each of these men carried a walking stick and was dressed in his finery, especially Sargent, who wore a long brocaded jacket from France that resembled a coffin liner.

Attracted by the scent, Lawrence bought a packet of chestnuts from a man whose roaster was an amalgam of the fantastic and the practical. It consisted of a small pot-bellied stove with a coal fire burning in the lower shelf and a retractable tray for the chestnuts that emerged from the upper half of the device. Rolling his cart by means of two miniature wheels and an iron handle, the dealer was able to take his product to the crowd instead of waiting for the demand to find him.

"Whereabouts did you discover such a conveyance?" asked the millionaire, holding the warm chestnuts in his hands. He cracked one between his fingers and ate the darkened meat.

"I fashioned it out of an old handbarrow and the stove I salvaged from a fish camp upriver," the man said. "I have always loved chestnuts, but could never convince anyone to visit my trees in order to purchase them." He took the penny from the millionaire's hand and deposited it in a pouch slung about his waist. "So one day it came to me: if I rolled my chestnuts down the Turnpike, their aroma might serve as advertisement and I could pursue my customers on foot."

"A wise fellow," Lawrence said. All around them, traffic had thickened and oxen teams and lorries traveled along at paces slower than a man could walk. "But not even a genius can sell enough chestnuts to make his daily bread."

Part of a finger was missing from the dealer's left hand and he stuck the abbreviated digit into the recess of his ear. "My occupation is mason," he said. "I laid many a brick for the Upper Pacific Mill and will soon begin on the Atlantic. Since each day I need walk four miles to the New City, why not push my chestnuts before me and so pay for the shoe-tread?"

Joining in the man's chuckle, Abbott Lawrence thrust out his hand and introduced himself. The mason's grip, roughened by bricks and lacking an element in its lower half, felt strange in the millionaire's palm. "A delight to make your acquaintance," said Lawrence.

"The name is Driscoll," the mason said. "It's a pleasure to know such a fellow as you are."

"The pleasure is all mine," said Lawrence. "Tell me, Mr. Driscoll, what is your prediction for our New City?"

The mason surveyed the crowd of men and beasts massing on the Turnpike and then shifted his gaze to include the mill island and river. "I have to say it passes any muster I would contrive, it does. I see the city standing for many a long year."

Cheered by this, Lawrence again shook hands with the mason and continued on, picking at the chestnuts. Near the Andover Bridge he met the first of his shareholders, lately arrived on the train from Boston and forced by the crowds to make his way on foot. Nathan Appleton was a broad-shouldered man with furry sideburns and a hound dog's face, his complexion reddened by many years in the sun and his sparse hair combed across his forehead. As gentlemen farmers, mercantile experts, and investors in manufacturing, Mssrs. Lawrence and Appleton had the most in common of the Boston Associates. The two men liked each other, and held one another's opinions in high regard.

"Hello, Abbott," said Appleton, striking the ground with a hickory cane as he walked along.

Two militiamen in long blue jackets, cartridge belts, and white leather spats, crossed their muskets at the edge of the gatehouse lot, barring Mr. Appleton's entrance. Amused by this development, Lawrence backtracked towards the militiamen and held out the little envelope he carried. "Care for a chestnut, Nathan?" he asked, thrusting his arm between the muskets.

"No, thank you, Abbott. Following the agitation of my train ride, I'm afraid that even such delectables as those would spit right through me." Appleton placed his hands on his hips and smiled through the crossed bayonets.

"Let him pass, gentlemen," Lawrence said to the militia. "For Mr. Appleton is as much a mainstay of this settlement as yonder factories, and the Great Stone Dam that holds back the river." The militiamen shifted to parade rest and allowed Appleton through. He and Lawrence embraced, held one another at arm's length, then embraced once more.

"What a fine morning," said Appleton. "Surely God has conceived it." He referred to the bedizened hat riding upon Lawrence's head. "Am I to assume that tartans are the latest fashion to reach us from New York?"

Lawrence snatched the hat from his head, examined it, and then replaced it on his noggin. "The device is part of a story there's no need to tell," he said.

Halfway up the drive, the two men gazed upon the dam and its bulwark of stone. In the river below, eight barges had been strung together to make a sort of floating bridge, and already it had filled up with hundreds of men waving their caps amid a general ruckus. Scaffolding rose to the height of the dam, where men were busy fitting the last granite tablet with a harness made from canvas straps. The stone was marked with a large X in red paint, and while the crew prepared it for hoisting another fellow scrubbed at the X with a steel brush and kerosene.

Seeing one of his constables nearby, Lawrence crooked his hand, gesturing the man over. "Can you find a plank of sufficient length to allow our dedication party to creep out from this spot?" the financier asked.

"Aye, sir," said the constable, and ran off.

The two burghers made for the gatehouse. "Why such a shaky bridge?"

Jay Atkinson

asked Mr. Appleton.

"I'm afraid that Mr. Storrow has suffered a misfortune and will be unable to climb the scaffold," said Lawrence.

"Is he in a bad way?"

"I have been told he will recover," Lawrence said. "But let us put our hands in his wounds and see for ourselves."

The undertaker, who had also just arrived, met them near the gatehouse steps. Waiting beside the Turnpike was the hearse, a flatbed pulled by the strangest animal Lawrence had yet seen in the New City. It was something between a mule and a broad-chested horse, and made even more ridiculous by the black feathered plume riding above its forelock. The undertaker's name was Dewhirst and his yellow hair was piled atop his forehead like the cockade of a rooster. Although dressed in mourning clothes and carrying a stovepipe hat under his arm, Dewhirst possessed a jovial nature that was incongruent with his station in life. Apparently one of the militiamen had uttered a humorous remark, and the undertaker's laughter rang out along the drive.

Lawrence had noted among his acquaintances in Washington that so-called "modern" undertakers considered themselves businessmen and aspired to the merchant class. When the financier had attended a party at the residence of Millard Fillmore, he had been taken aback by one such gentleman. The fellow said that his profession entailed the rendering of a service, and once that duty had been carried out, he was subject to the same desires as any man: fine food, enlightening company, and the general pleasures of society. Still, Lawrence had been troubled by the encounter.

The two burghers and the undertaker made each other's acquaintance and then stamped up the stairs and into the penstock room. "Are you here about Mr. Storrow?" Lawrence asked the undertaker.

"Is he the fellow that's died?"

"No one has died. You need only apply some of your greasepaint to Mr. Storrow's face, which has been bruised."

The sound of running water filled the room, and the men zigzagged among a confusion of levers. "I beg pardon, Mr. Lawrence," said Dewhirst, "but not five minutes ago, a boy reached me at Osgood's place and said there was a corpse inside the gatehouse and I was to remove it at once."

His eyes wide with fear, Lawrence stumbled past the undertaker and beat upon the door to the office and it opened up. Inside, the drafting table had been pushed against the wall and there was a powerful odor of horses and saddle leather and tobacco. An unexpected quantity of men filled the close little room and by their arrangement, Lawrence could see that an object lay in their midst. At once he recognized Boston Associates Ignatius Sargent and William Sturgis and the Reverend John A. Lowell, who leaned against a window-jamb smoking their pipes. Also pressed inside were several constables dressed in tunics and carrying their pikes, a number of Essex Street merchants, and Mr. Coolidge, who was bent over the table writing on a parchment.

The assembly melted away and Abbott Lawrence confronted a shape lying on the floor. The dead man was covered in a rough woolen blanket; only his boots were visible, encircled by a puddle of water. An odd, silent figure with an enormous head was seated in the corner. Wrapped in a muddy cloak and with a hat tilted over his eyes, he appeared to be dozing.

Lawrence glanced around the room, shook his head like he was resisting an idea and whispered, "Is it…?"

Just then the door swung open and Captain Bigelow appeared, his blue military cape thrown over one shoulder with the silk lining displayed. The engineer had a roll of documents closed in his fist, and his jodhpurs were covered with mud. Looking toward one of his men, Bigelow said, "I came the moment I was summoned."

"Aye," said the constable. "We knew you would, sir."

"I would ask that everyone beyond members of the corporation and the undertaker, please step outside," said Bigelow.

Nine men gathered their equipage and filed out of the room. The Captain nodded to Mssrs. Sturgis and Sargent and Rev. Lowell, and with difficulty lowered himself to one knee and drew back the edge of the blanket. Abbott Lawrence kneeled on the other side.

Lieutenant Treachey's corpse had stiffened, and his eyelids and lips were the color of slate. His uniform blouse was sopping wet and riverweeds and flecks of algae tarnished his brass buttons and clung to his neck. The hair on his head was white with rime and stood up like a horse's mane.

"They found him lodged against the weir," said Mr. Sturgis, his head wreathed in pipe smoke. "We're told the force of the water broke his back."

Lawrence's stomach heaved up and the taste of bile and chestnuts filled his sinuses. Bigelow returned the blanket and stood erect, the pain of this maneuver crossing his face. Still kneeling, Lawrence waited for Captain Bigelow to offer his prayer but it was the man with the outsize head who spoke first. "This old world is pretty wise and sizes us up pretty well," he said. "If we are useful, she wants us; if we are not, she doesn't."

Although the man's voice was garbled by his deformation Lawrence recognized its cadence and studied him again. Lumps of swollen flesh rose above his ears and flab that was like pastry dough hung from his lower jaw. Battered though he was, the man's gaze convinced Lawrence he was looking on none other than Charles Storrow.

Lawrence went over and clutched the engineer's hands in his own. "My dear Charles," he said. "I was told that your injuries were none too serious. But I see now that we must cancel our business here and get you to a physician."

"What will become of our ceremony, Abbott?" asked Nathan Appleton.

"Blast the ceremony," said Lawrence. He sagged into a chair, lowering himself with one hand while he clutched his midsection with the other. "Mr. Storrow has been pulped like a stepchild, our accounts are several thousand dollars short, and two men in our employ have died."

Mssrs. Sargent and Sturgis halted their conversation and looked for Reverend Lowell to intercede. The minister came forward, avoiding the dead man, and together with Mr. Appleton stooped over Abbott Lawrence. "My dear friend, these two men have departed and I think we can entrust their souls to God, as well as our balance sheet to Mr. Coolidge," Rev. Lowell said, gesturing at the company clerk. "For the sake of the corporation, surely you can be convinced to make an appearance."

"I have no stomach for it," Lawrence said.

Outside, the lot contained a throng of farmers, constables, muleteers and various laborers and peddlers. Rumors were spreading fast and the heads of several death-mongers crowded upon the little window, including a pointy-faced man wrapped in a shawl. Grumbling to himself, Captain Bigelow pulled down the shade. Then he turned back and said, "Gentlemen. Just as a boiling kettle will explode if the steam goes unvented, the top may blow off our enterprises if we neglect to move swiftly."

"I, for one, welcome any suggestions that will allow our company to preserve itself," said Appleton, his hand on Mr. Lawrence's shoulder. Against the wall Mssrs. Sargent and Sturgis nodded their agreement, and Reverend Lowell gazed at Bigelow over his spectacles.

"As Mr. Lawrence has suggested, I'd ask you, sir"—Bigelow motioned Mr. Dewhirst forward—"to apply your powers of concealment to Mr. Storrow's injuries whilst my constables remove Lieutenant Treachey, for the purposes of his interment in Bellevue Cemetery." Immediately Dewhirst began his ministrations, and Bigelow continued: "To avoid attention on this maneuver, I recommend that the procession exit over the weir, followed by Mr. Coolidge and the strongbox. If anything can divert these men from gossip, the appearance of their wages will do it."

The undertaker removed a long flat tin from his coat pocket. Monogrammed with an ornate "D," the case held four small brushes and cylinders of flesh-toned paint. There was the sound of boots upon the weir and before the knock came, Bigelow opened the door an inch. "What is it?"

"Flanagan and Higgins, sir," came the reply. "Body detail."

"Just a minute," said Bigelow.

He latched the door, put his bulk against it and faced the assembly. Coolidge was busy writing again and kneeling beside Mr. Storrow's chair, the undertaker painted over his injuries with a horsehair brush. Nathan Appleton assisted Mr. Lawrence to his feet and the other Boston Associates extinguished their pipes and buttoned up their vests and greatcoats.

"Are we all in agreement?" Bigelow asked.

"I think it's fine, save one detail," said Reverend Lowell. He was an Anglican and wore his burnsides nearly to the point of his chin, where they were separated by a cleft. "The three acres atop Bellevue hill are a Christian cemetery. I know you feel an allegiance to your subordinates,

Captain Bigelow, but perhaps some other arrangement could be made. Surely there is a potter's field nearby."

Bigelow glowered at Reverend Lowell and came to stand beside the wet, stiffened corpse. "I am a thorough man, and the conclusion to which I am led is that Erasmus Percival Treachey drowned upon the weir," he said. Although his tone was low and quiet, it blossomed outward to the eaves. "He served his country for thirteen years and as so, is deserving of a Christian burial. Does anyone care to dispute that with me?" The only hint of his emotion was the quivering of Bigelow's upper lip. "For if he does, it may be best that the discussion take place out of doors."

Reverend Lowell turned the shade of the plaster he stood against and Mssrs. Sturgis and Sargent grasped his elbows in support, otherwise the minister would have tumbled to the floor. Mr. Appleton walked past, touched Reverend Lowell on the shoulder, and then stood beside Captain Bigelow. "No one disputes that this man was a good Christian," said Appleton, removing his hat and canting it under one arm. The fire in the stove had long gone out and all the men wore their overcoats against the morning chill. "Let's get on with it."

Finished with Mr. Storrow, the undertaker rose to his feet. "I provide a full Christian service and have already sent a man up to Bellevue to alert the gravedigger," he said. "I am very experienced in these matters. Leave everything to me, gentlemen."

Solemn nods were issued all around, and Bigelow stepped backward to open the door. He motioned for Higgins and Flanagan to come inside. The constables entered, doffed their caps, and stood gazing at the dead man. "There he is," Flanagan said.

"Aye," said Higgins.

"Remove Lieutenant Treachey's body to the penstock room, wind it in a tarpaulin, and assemble a stretcher. Mr. Dewhirst will assist you," said Captain Bigelow. "Wait for my signal—this is a complicated matter and above all else, I wish to treat Lieutenant Treachey with due respect. Do you understand me?"

"Aye, sir," said the constables.

Bigelow gestured toward the corpse and with one man grasping the boots, they lifted the body. Water streamed from the corpse and from the hanging point of the blanket. Captain Bigelow opened the door and Higgins and Flanagan carried the body into the penstock room.

Feeling a rush through his guts, Lawrence vomited into an empty coal bucket. "Go ahead, Abbott," said Nathan Appleton, slinging his arm across the other man's back. "Purge yourself."

Mr. Appleton gave the financier a handkerchief and he wiped his mouth and chin with it. "Gentlemen: please excuse me," said Lawrence. "I am vexed by bilious fever and a poor digestion."

The stench of the vomitus overpowered the room, driving its occupants onto the weir. No windows illuminated this corridor but a few spears of light entered through the chinks in the planking and the men could hear the roar of voices from outside. At one end, the constables had wound Lieutenant Treachey into a shroud and were busy fixing him to the stretcher poles. Mr. Coolidge emerged last from the office, pushing the strongbox ahead of him on a dolly.

While Mssrs. Sturgis and Sargent attended to Mr. Storrow, Reverend Lowell searched his Bible for an appropriate passage and Captain Bigelow picked his way among the levers, huddling to one side with Abbott Lawrence and Mr. Coolidge. With the trio squeezed into a narrow space, the millionaire stood with his employees facing him on either side.

"I believe we have mitigated at least one of the pressures afflicting our establishment," said Bigelow. He unrolled the document he held in his hand, displayed it for Mr. Lawrence's perusal and then handed it over to Coolidge. "J. F. C. Hayes has agreed to our proposal."

"I would guess that he leaped at such an arrangement," Coolidge said.

Captain Bigelow shook his head. "When I first explained the terms to him, Hayes said that he thought the negotiations were off to a promising start but after further consideration, he had decided upon some additional codicils."

Mr. Lawrence could not contain his exasperation. "Bestowed with a king's ransom and he wishes to negotiate?" asked the millionaire. His voice was heard over the rushing water and at the far end of the gallery, members of the burial detail lifted their heads. Captain Bigelow stared back in that direction, and one by one the constables dropped their gaze.

"Not to worry, Mr. Lawrence," Bigelow said. "I convinced Mr. Hayes that our proposal was a solid one—and final—and he soon agreed to my reasoning."

"Did you present him with a hundred-dollar note?" asked Lawrence.

"That, and some terse private advice is what convinced him."

Abbott Lawrence glanced at Mr. Coolidge. "Do you have a nib?"

The clerk produced this writing utensil and Lawrence placed the contract against the wall and signed it, the ink running from the paper. Then the financier signed two additional sheets that contained Hayes' signature and were otherwise blank. "Make two copies," Lawrence said to Coolidge. "One for Hayes, one for Mr. Storrow's file, and the original to be transported back to Boston in the strongbox. And not a word to my associates about this."

The men said "Aye" in a low voice, and then Bigelow signaled to his constables that they were ready. "Mr. Flanagan: four constables and at least two militia with bayonets will be required to accompany the strongbox," said the captain.

"The militia are waiting for your orders, sir," Flanagan said.

The door opened and a pair of hands deposited a small crate on the tread board and then withdrew. Inside were the six quarts of black honey Mr. Lawrence had ordered from Thom Maddox. All of the men were hungry, particularly those who had arrived on horseback, and since the calamitous events of the past few hours had prevented Mr. Coolidge from setting out breakfast, mouths began watering and stomachs rumbling upon sight of the honey.

Abbott Lawrence bent over the crate to remove one of the jars. Using his penknife, he loosened the wax seal and brought the syrup to his chin. It possessed a dank, earthy odor tinged with sweetness, and the surface of the honey was decorated with a tiny rainbow. "I have requisitioned a jar of this wonderful local product for each of you," said Lawrence. "And would share a taste this instant, only I lack the means."

William Sturgis produced a bundle of cinnamon sticks bound with twine. "My dear wife asked me to purchase these but on an occasion such as this, I think she will understand," he said, dividing the sticks among his fellows. They were as long a man's finger and one-quarter the circumference, hard and hollow like a reed, with a pleasant woody aroma and spiced flavor.

Flourishing the jar, Lawrence invited the men to dunk their sticks into the honey and they each did in turn. "Allow me to propose a toast," said the millionaire, as his colleagues surrounded him, the honey dripping over their fingers. "Just as the bees have produced their fruit for our consumption, so shall the men who fill our enterprise produce nectar for the world."

"Well spoken, Abbott," said Nathan Appleton. "For we should admire the selectivity of bees as much as their industry, for they always know which flowers to dip into."

For a long moment, the burghers and capitalists and financiers sucked at the cinnamon roots, their eyes glazed by reveries of childhood. Finally Mr. Sturgis pulled a gold watch from his pocket and opened its face. "Almost nine o'clock," he said. "We have a dam to cap, gentlemen."

The procession formed near the door with Reverend Lowell carrying his Bible, followed by Mr. Lawrence on the arm of Nathan Appleton, Charles Storrow supported by Mssrs. Sturgis and Sargent, Captain Bigelow, Mr. Coolidge and the strongbox, and bringing up the rear, two constables armed with pistols. Weakened by his upturned stomach and the events of the last twenty-four hours, Lawrence surveyed this assembly and leaned on his companion. "Here we are, then," said the millionaire. "The cream of Boston's elite."

Reverend Lowell drew a ribbon from the Bible, opening the great tome upon the hinge of his elbow. " 'I will seek that which was lost, and bring again that which was driven away, and will bind up that which was broken, and will strengthen that which was sick: but I will destroy the fat and the strong; I will feed them with judgment', " he said.

When all were ready, Reverend Lowell heaved upon the door, and the men were struck by the great clamor of the yard and the light that rushed in. Mr. Storrow descended the gatehouse stairs just as he put the dollop of honey into his mouth. Beside him, he noticed that Bigelow had thrown away the cinnamon stick.

"It tastes like shite," Storrow said.

"Nonsense," said Ignatius Sargent. He frowned at the engineer. "Keep a stiff back now, Charles. The eyes of the New City are upon us."

Mr. Sargent was right. The gatehouse lot was filled with men of every description: masons in their denim shirts, leather-chapped teamsters

Jay Atkinson

and farmers and merchants, calling out in a huge roar. In the excitement, they threatened to overwhelm the procession of burghers until the militia swung their rifles to form a gauntlet. Still, hands were thrust at the Boston Associates and Mr. Storrow stumbled along with his head clutched in his hands.

It was a peculiar affair, Storrow decided. One moment he knew these men and their histories, and gazing at the panoramic distance, he understood the intricacies of their labor and his own calculations that made it possible. The very next instant he had difficulty grasping his own name; the surrounding faces chattered in an obscure dialect and the backdrop of dam and mills and city was as alien to Mr. Storrow as the vista in a storybook.

Just ahead, a man wearing a small, ink-stained hat with a rounded brim intercepted Abbott Lawrence. The tumult carried their voices away, but it was plain that Lawrence and the interloper were acquainted with one another. The man was dressed in a Scottish kilt, bright red with vertical black bars and three horizontal blue lines, and carried a satchel of papers. Reaching for his hat, Mr. Lawrence removed the circular patch of cloth and pressed it into the Scotsman's hand. Then Storrow heard the kilted man say, "You've made a fair bargain."

"Bah," said Lawrence.

As Mr. Storrow approached, the Scotsman displayed the bewildered engineer's tooth, which he had attached to a chain. "A natural charm, if ever there was one," the Scotsman said.

There was a great surge of humanity as several laborers caught sight of Mr. Coolidge and the strongbox heading in the other direction. The gauntlet collapsed on the little procession and only through the effort of several constables was Mssrs. Lawrence and Storrow and the other Boston Associates kept from being trampled upon. From atop the gatehouse a rifleman surveyed the crowd and another man bellowed, "Line up by name. We must keep order here."

"*Carpe diem*, gentlemen," said Lawrence, raising his hand. "A path awaits us."

With one hand on his sword, Captain Bigelow led the Boston Associates across the yard. Scurrying into their path was the newsboy, who would have escaped if Mr. Lawrence had not grabbed him by the collar. The lad's mouth dropped open, his eyes were horror struck, and his feet bicycled through the air like someone in a dream.

"Just give us a paper," said the millionaire. "For a keepsake."

The newsboy flicked one of the papers from his bag. Setting him down, Lawrence handed over a gold coin and the boy stared like it was the treasure of Siam. "Save it, don't spend it," said the millionaire.

Thrilled by his fortune, the lad ran past two soldiers who had been ordered to keep the bridge clear. One of the men, engaged in conversation with a teamster, whirled around with his musket as the boy tried to skip past. At the same instant, a horse attached to the wagon flew out with his hoof and the newsboy darted away, thrusting himself onto the militiaman's bayonet. It passed through the boy's slender frame and protruded out his back.

The militiaman let go of his weapon and met the boy's gaze with a look of abject sorrow. The boy staggered along, freeing himself from the bayonet. Then his knees collapsed beneath him and the young lad plummeted from the bridge. Assuming it was a prank, the boatmen in the water below applauded as he fell. The coin, which the newsboy held so tightly, slipped from his grasp. Body and coin fell at the same rate of descent, the boy spread-eagled and the coin glittering in the sunlight. Amid the uproar, no one noticed and they disappeared into the roiling water.

The plank that connected the berm to the platform was only wide enough for one man to pass at a time. And after Reverend Lowell had skittered across, it was Storrow's turn. His head reeled with the events of the preceding day, and the voices of a thousand men echoed through him. He looked upriver at the sheen of the Merrimack and wondered what had brought him to this place. Building such a settlement seemed the worst sort of vanity, another Babylon.

Beckoning to Mr. Storrow, Reverend Lowell and Captain Bigelow and Mssrs. Sargent and Appleton waited on the other side. As Storrow moved out, the narrow plank quivered beneath his weight and he felt someone guiding him and then Mr. Sturgis's hand fell away. The plank thinned itself in his field of vision, becoming a taut, gossamer thread, and ahead on the platform, the silhouettes of his colleagues were bundled together against the flaring light.

Only Abbott Lawrence stood apart, holding a ribbon that was strung there. Hailing the multitude, in a great voice he said, "Here we are, gentlemen, latitude forty-two degrees, forty-two minutes, thirteen seconds, and in longitude seventy-one degrees, ten minutes, thirteen seconds west from Greenwich, England, on these four thousand, five hundred and seventy-seven acres of the New City. On this site we have been granted the privilege of constructing a dam, canal, locks and other appurtenances, and of holding the adjacent land—as we are charged with providing bridges, maintaining fishways, and establishing the security of the public way. In the course of these endeavors we have striven to treat you all fairly and honestly, as we believe the wealth of the country is founded upon its labor. So, on behalf of the Essex Company, greetings and felicitations to all those who constructed the Great Stone Dam."

Appearing out of the crowd, Mssrs. Carpenter and Gilmore stood nearby, waiting to be invited onto the platform. But Captain Bigelow ordered a man to remove the plank and the two contractors were marooned on the berm, the plump, red-faced Mr. Gilmore shaking his fist and saying, "It isn't a town or a city we've built, it's another trough for the 'Boston Associates' to grow fat upon." His associate tugged at him, but Gilmore expressed his indignation by spitting into the Merrimack River. Finally Mr. Carpenter, his nose turning crimson, encircled his partner in a wrestler's hold and dragged him away.

A few men hooted at this interruption but the majority ignored it, and Mr. Lawrence continued: "The individual most responsible for the recent very great improvements in the leveling down, smoothing off and buckwheatizing of the parallelogrammatical territory lying west of the destitute and dreary depths of the river is a man known to all of you. The man I speak of is the father of the whole enterprise, as he was the sole individual mandated to build the dam, canal and machine shop, purchase and sell the land, and make all the contracts and payments. And now as the final stone is laid three years after the bed stone, on the same day of the month and hour of the day, let us consider the material this fellow was created out of. For just as the Great Stone Dam was bonded with *civita vecchia pozzelano*, or hydraulic cement, this man was fashioned from a sturdy mix of wisdom, technical knowledge and fortitude. In fact, he comes nearer to the ideal of the perfect gentleman than anyone I have ever known.

"This morning it is my great honor to present to you the director, treasurer, agent and chief engineer of the Essex Company, Mr. Charles Storer Storrow!"

There was a great clamor of applause and the beating of paddles against wood. All eyes shifted to Charles Storrow and Mr. Lawrence began clapping and the rest of the Boston Associates joined in. "Huzzah for Mr. Storrow," shouted one of the constables and the throng on the Andover Bridge cheered and waved their caps.

Just below the dignitaries' platform was a scaffold. Here two men cranked the windlass that hoisted the last granite tablet into the air. Gabriel Glass' replacement, William Bower, a huge fellow with unruly hair, shouldered the tablet into its slot and looked at Storrow. What the giant said was unintelligible. But he handed up a small pasteboard card and Mr. Storrow read the words printed there, as men whistled and cheered upon the bridge: *What shall it profit a man, if he gains the whole world and loses his own soul?*

His face stiff beneath the undertaker's makeup, Charles Storrow parted the ribbon with his hand and then gazed at the confused scene. Beneath all the jubilation he heard grumbling about the events in Dublin and more than a few oaths directed his way. Upon the Andover Bridge, Storrow noticed some members of a traveling circus mingling with honest workmen, carrying sandwich boards and walking on stilts. He witnessed the vulgarity of an itinerant clown and decided it was a fitting postscript to the conclusion of the Great Stone Dam. After the consuming labor of masons, millwrights, teamsters and boatman, comes the rush of people without capital or character—gamblers, horse-jockeys and drunkards.

Looking to the horizon, Charles Storrow considered his work. The appeal of the long vista down the canal was enhanced by elm trees, by the handsome fronts of the boarding houses, and by the neat, handcrafted footbridges. But on the island, a fire had been struck in one of the mill sheds. Soon the flames spread to a nearby privy, sending up a loud, crackling noise. Plumes of smoke rose into the air, and the stench of burning offal reached the Turnpike. Covering their faces, the men nearby made a retreat, as Bigelow shouted for the firemen and constables ran toward the blaze with their muskets.

In a letter to a colleague, Mr. Storrow had asked, "Where else can you find as here the elements of society ready to be moulded into a good or evil shape, nothing to pull down, all to build up; a whole town composed of young people to influence and train as you would a school?" Now he understood that, having created the waterpower for the mills and given value to the surrounding land, the sole business of the Essex Company was to hire them out. For the operation of such a company, where the works are completed, is nothing but a process of selling off and winding up.

Beside Mr. Storrow on the platform, Captain Bigelow was calm, almost resigned. He withdrew the chunk of amber from his pocket and studied the well-preserved dragonfly trapped inside.

11

The Present Day

With so much time on his hands, Father Tom found himself prowling around the church, emptying buckets that caught water from the leaky roof, sweeping out the choir loft, and polishing the chalices and the gold doors of the tabernacle where they were kept. The tabernacle was an ornate metal box behind the altar that contained the host. This was the place where Christ was said to reside, that indeed made the cold damp church the house of God.

Lining the walls of the church were statuettes depicting the agonies of Christ, known as the Stations of the Cross. Beginning with His arrest in front of the Pharisees, and progressing through the restoration of a severed ear, His mockery by the Jews and a hearing before Pontius Pilate, Christ was also shown being whipped by olive branches, parading naked in a crown of thorns, and dragging His cross to Golgotha, the place of skulls. En route he was aided by Simon of Cerene, and then put to death and cried over by young John the apostle, His mother Mary, and the former prostitute Mary Magdalene.

The procession around the church ended at the altar. Tom Dailey had always clung to the hope that Christ had endured His betrayal, torture and murder, and then resurrected Himself to burn as a flame of truth inside the tabernacle. The flame trembling inside Father Tom's own heart seemed to be flickering out, as he busied himself at the tabernacle with a flask of metal cleaner. Below the polished metal was a bank of candles, each housed in a sconce made of thick red glass and throwing its light over the carpet. As Tom Dailey scoured the intaglio of Christ—who stood with His arms embracing the congregation—the priest felt his soul joined by the candles, burning with the sacred heart of Christ's presence.

He was disturbed by voices inside the sacristy, an anteroom that the celebrants waited in before Mass. Father Tom blessed himself before crossing the altar to investigate. As he approached, the door of the sacristy opened and a boy went up the aisle, past the candle-lit statues tucked into the alcoves.

Father Tom recognized Ismail Citron, one of the parish altar boys and a resident of the Broadway housing projects. Occasionally, he had driven the young fellow home in his taxi after Masses, and watched Ismail mount the stairs to the apartment where he lived with his mother, Carmelita Diaz, and four brothers and sisters. Father Tom was about to speak to Ismail when he heard a key turning in a lock; then the steps descending onto the aisle groaned with a heavy weight. Ismail Citron glanced back with a frightened look while Monsignor Borinquen glided down the runway toward him, his cassock brushing against the damp stone wall of the church.

Father Tom started to raise his voice but the boy scampered off, throwing light into Holy Rosary as the door opened on the sunlit day. Monsignor Borinquen was caught in the flash, appearing like a robber dressed in black. The light came again when the Monsignor reached the exit and then gloom descended once more, leaving Father Tom in the weak red glow of the candles.

He had given up driving the taxi at Borinquen's request. Although the parish needed money, it was decided that too much contact with the lay population was weakening Father Tom's vows. The time was better spent, the Monsignor believed, in meditation and prayer. Tasks like cleaning, which Father Tom did not object to, washing the pews with oil soap and scrubbing the tiles the way the old women of Common Street scrubbed their floors, would bring God in through his labors like the monks of old.

Monsignor Borinquen often expressed admiration for the hard-working existence of the Franciscans and Benedictines. Yet, he continued to make his trips to the local bakery, and kept his appointments for gin rummy and gossip with Father Daignault in Lowell. Father Tom was beginning to think his superior was a hypocrite—talking about sacrifice and duty and then hiding in the dark with Ismail Citron. This was a strange time for an altar boy to be in church. There was no Mass scheduled until the next morning, and the doors of Holy Rosary had been locked when Father Tom had let himself in with one of the two keys that existed.

Father Tom went back to work troubled by new doubts. While in his taxi, he had overheard the local clergy fighting over the estate of a dying man like the Roman soldiers who had thrown dice for Christ's garments. He had also witnessed pastoral guidance being replaced by bookkeeping, and the relics of the church supplanted by cellular telephones and promotional videos. In addition, young boys were being attacked in church basements all over the world. In the seminary, it had been pointed out that these were aberrations, isolated cases made sensational by an atheistic press corps. But Father Tom agreed that certain men were attracted to the priesthood for the wrong reasons. In the parishes where these monsters lurked, young boys were as common as dinner rolls at a banquet. And some priests believed celibacy only meant refraining from heterosexual activity.

Mistakes were covered by transferring these priests. Then the church would maintain a silence akin to that intact over Rome when innocent Jews were being slaughtered in Europe, or the killing fields of Cambodia ran black with Catholic blood. One thing that Vatican functionaries had learned in two thousand years—of intrigue, ethnic purgation, and bloody deeds that sometimes led to the canonization of the victim—was to keep their mouths shut.

Tom Dailey had joined this exclusive club, in large measure, because of his Irish heritage. Quitting now would mean turning it over to the evil that had infested it, and watching his birthright descend into the murk of cults and commercialism. Irish priests had proven themselves to be sinners, but the devotion of the "sod pastors" was legendary. They wrestled with drink, with their doubts and their consciences, then tried to inch over the crest of mid-life passions into the safety of old age. Back home in the Mount Greenwood section of Chicago, which was now a checkerboard of many different races but had once been the city's Irish enclave, Tom Dailey's mentor had been Father Liam Foley, a reedy little man who smelled of candle wax and Jameson's whiskey.

Growing up, Tom Dailey served as an altar boy at Saint Mary's church, working at Masses and the occasional wedding. When he reached the age of twelve, Tom was assigned to his first funeral. Waiting in the sacristy, as "Forty Minute" Foley drew a white surplice over his cassock and buffed the tips of his shiny black shoes, Tom peeked out at the coffin flanked by silver candles. The priest straightened up while the mourners settled in their pews and the sound of weeping came from the nave of the church.

"Steady, lad," said Father Foley, gripping the boy above his elbow. "We are soldiers in the army of Christ." In that instant Tom Dailey decided to become a priest, and had never wavered until recent events put his decision in question.

*

One day shortly after Ismail Citron's flight from Holy Rosary, when Monsignor Borinquen was in Lowell visiting his friend, Father Daignault, someone rapped at the rectory door. It was Francesca Nesheim, dressed in black tights and a fleece sweatshirt, and without her young son.

"I'm glad you answered," she said. "I felt stupid about missing Gabriel's christening and wanted to make another date."

The priest showed her inside. "Tea?" he asked. When Francesca nodded, he turned a dial on the stove and a whispering flame popped up beneath the kettle. He took cups down from the cabinet, and tea bags with their strings and paper medallions. Father Tom glanced at the fortune printed on his medallion: *Romance is in your future.*

"Does it cost anything to have a baby christened?" asked Francesca.

"Traditionally, the church would expect an envelope with fifty dollars in it," Father Tom said. "But the most important thing is to safeguard the child's soul, not collect a fee." He set out a bowl filled with sugar cubes. "At least, *I* think so."

Father Tom couldn't hide the bitterness in his voice. Then the sound of the whistling tea kettle drew his attention, and he soon delivered two brimming cups of hot water. Francesca dropped a lump of sugar into hers. "Do you officiate the christenings?" she asked.

"Not right now. I've been suspended for three weeks."

Francesca stopped the cup at her lower lip. "You must be very upset about it."

"It's good to weigh my doubts, although I admit it makes me feel like a pretty weak example of a Christian."

"Why wouldn't a priest have doubts, like anyone else?" asked Francesca. She crossed her legs, and the muscularity of her thighs showed through the tights.

Father Tom sat upright in his chair. "What can I do for you?" he asked.

"Joe—that's Gabriel's father—tore up his knee playing hockey, and he hasn't been able to make his support payments," she said. "With another baby on the way, I don't know how we're gonna survive. As soon as they find out I'm pregnant, they'll fire me at the rink."

"Couldn't you just find a job doing something else?" asked Father Tom.

"Not with a baby to take care of," Francesca said. She stirred the tea, raising her eyes to the priest. "I'm thinking about ending the pregnancy."

Father Tom's mind was crowded with church teachings about abortion. But there was the need to let parishioners express their thoughts before breaking in with advice. "Go on," he said.

"I don't have enough money coming in for Gabriel, forget about two babies. And I see what happens to children who don't have fathers. By the time they're twelve or thirteen, these kids are carrying guns, selling drugs, all kinds of bad stuff. Gabriel's father loves him, but he has so many schemes for making money instead of just getting a job." Her face fell into her hands, the silky black hair streaming between her fingers. "I came here, Father Tom, because I trust you. But it's my life and my body—you can't possibly know what it means to consider doing what I'm talking about doing."

Tom Dailey took the young woman by the hands. "Just let remind you that the future for that child—for any of us—is not certain either way, until you end his or her life. You are an intelligent woman, and I'm sure it would be best to have the father of your children involved in their upbringing. This one fellow—Joe—at least, seems willing to do that. Even so, I think you're capable of making a good life for your children. Maybe even relocating out of the city, starting somewhere new."

The two young people sat for a few moments without a word passing between them. Then, her eyes wet with tears, Francesca squeezed the priest's hands. "I've been trying to outrun poverty my whole life. Now I'll be carrying two other people," she said.

"Think about it, and pray about it," Father Tom found himself saying, "and I know you'll do a great deal about it."

Jay Atkinson

The door to the rectory swung open. Monsignor Borinquen stood looking at the couple with their fingers tangled upon the table.

"Monsignor, you're back," Father Tom said. "I didn't hear the car."

"Ye-e-ss," said Borinquen, coming into the kitchen. "I had a flat tire and had to walk here from the bakery." He set a waxed paper bag on the table. Sweat rolled down the sides of his face and he worked his lips together, appearing a bit unsteady on his feet.

"I better go change that tire," said Father Tom. "If we leave the car on Common Street for very long, I'm afraid someone will steal it."

Borinquen shook his head. "I called Triple A," he said. "They'll send someone."

Francesca stood up from the table. "I was just leaving, Monsignor."

"I trust there's been a good result to your visit," said Borinquen, coming between her and the young priest. Exertion had caused the pulse to beat in the Monsignor's neck, and sweat dripped down the pasty flab of his face. "I was sorry we had to scratch you from our christening list. Perhaps you and your son can come in a week from Saturday, and we can try again."

"I've been having some family problems," Francesca said, glancing at Father Tom. "They'll be settled by then, and Gabriel and his father and I will be there."

"Excellent," said Monsignor Borinquen. "God bless you." He walked the young woman to the door. "I'll see you the Saturday after next at nine o'clock, sharp."

When Francesca's heels had echoed away, Borinquen turned to his charge, who was still seated at the table. "I don't think I need to remind you, Father Dailey, that your suspension includes pastoral counseling," he said. "My schedule is posted in the library. If someone comes to the door, make an appointment and then I'll see to it." His eyes shone in his pale sweating face. "Am I clear?"

Father Tom rose from his chair until Borinquen's forehead was level with his own. "I understand your words, Monsignor, but not all of your actions," said the young priest. "Therefore, I resort to thinking on my feet, as I was trained to do."

"Uh-huh," said Borinquen. A wisp of his bad breath could be detected in the air. "Then let me remind you—since our Savior alone sees into the heart of men—that often what is viewed with the eyes and heard by the ears is false testimony."

"Including what you are saying now," Father Tom said.

"I'm no logician, that's true. But I see a path for you, Father Dailey, and it's a hard and narrow one, indeed."

*

A week and a half later, Francesca and her nineteen-month-old son Gabriel and the boy's father, Joe Glass, appeared for the christening. It was the last day of Father Tom's suspension, and he was wearing his cassock and collar when he entered the church. Two infants had already been baptized, and now it was Gabriel's turn. Monsignor Borinquen held the child over the basin of holy water, praying *sotto voce* in Latin.

"Do you reject Satan and all his works?" the Monsignor asked. Just then a loud gasp escaped him, his face twisted itself into a hideous crimson mask, and Francesca reached just in time to snatch away her child. Monsignor Borinquen's knees buckled and he fell to the floor, twitching beneath his vestments, his tongue gone purple and lolling in his mouth.

"Heart attack," said one of the parishioners, bent over the priest. "Call an ambulance."

Someone ran for the phone. Gabriel faced outward from his mother's grasp and for a split second, Father Tom looked into the well of the boy's gaze. Crossing the vestibule, he took the child from his mother's arms and cradled him above the holy water. "Do you reject Satan and all his works?"

"I do," said the mother.

"And all his false promises?"

"I do."

Father Tom poured water over the boy's forehead, and Gabriel wrinkled his brow and became one of Christ's troopers. A moment later, the wail of a siren penetrated the church. Father Tom shooed the families outside and administered extreme unction to his superior. "If there's anything you'd like to reconcile, about Ismail Citron or anything else, I'm ready to absolve you, Monsignor," said Father Tom.

Borinquen made no sign that he cared to respond or even understood what he had been asked, and Father Tom continued with the prayers of absolution. When he was through, the young priest waited beside the Monsignor until the first paramedic came through the doors with her medical kit.

"Over here," Father Tom called to the young woman. Passing in front of the altar, the woman genuflected and made the sign of the cross. While Father Tom leaned over them, the paramedic took Monsignor Borinquen's pulse and looked into his eyes with a tiny flashlight.

"Stroke," the woman said, and began talking into a radio attached to her collar. Loud static followed by a man's voice giving instructions broke over the stillness of the church. Then another paramedic entered with a collapsible stretcher, and the two of them strapped Borinquen down.

The Monsignor began coughing as the paramedics steered him along the aisle. Father Tom gripped his superior's hand, but there was no strength in Borinquen's fingers or his gaze. The young priest prayed over him in Latin.

"Amen," said the woman, when Father Tom had finished. Again she made the sign of the cross.

Darting ahead of the stretcher, Father Tom pushed open the heavy wooden doors and Monsignor Borinquen went headfirst into the sunshine.

Joe Glass and Francesca Nesheim and their child waited on the steps. The sun glittered on the snow, and scrims of ice dotted Common Street. After the stretcher was carried to the curb, Father Tom led the

Jay Atkinson

makeshift family across the street so the paramedics could administer to Borinquen. An oxygen mask was placed over the Monsignor's nose and mouth, and one of the paramedics injected him with something while the other consulted over the radio. In his white surplice and purple vestments, dazzling in the sunlight, Monsignor Borinquen looked like a trussed-up madman. Traffic on Common Street slowed as motorists stared out their windows at the spectacle.

"People would gawk at their own mother if she was dead in the street," Francesca said.

"*Concupiscentia oculorum*—gluttony of the eyes," said Father Tom, shaking his head. "The flesh is weak."

Joe Glass nodded. "You got that right, Father."

Gabriel soon became bored, fussing in his mother's arms until he was allowed to gain his feet and explore the neighborhood. Limping after Gabriel, Joe Glass went down Jackson Street toward the canal. Moments later, the ambulance roared off with Monsignor Borinquen in the back.

"I'm keeping the baby," Francesca said, when she and Father Tom were alone for a moment. "When the baby is born they can do a blood scan, and we'll have paternity tests issued." She glanced at the priest. "Then I'll get child support, no matter what."

"That's a good place to start," said Father Tom, "because it means giving life to a child. How can that be a negative proposition? I don't think it can."

They trailed after Joe and Gabriel toward Canal Street, until Francesca remembered that she had left her purse inside the church and ran back to get it. Traffic over the river was light and the party crossed over the Duck Bridge and began following the south canal. Eventually Father Tom caught up with Joe Glass and his son, joining them near a footbridge. In his white turtleneck jersey and black pants, Gabriel marched alongside the frozen canal, humming to himself.

Standing beside the canal on his bad leg, Joe Glass admitted that he recognized the young priest. He pulled back his hair to display a scar beside his eye. One morning in late December Joe had woken up in the gutter, and Father Tom had helped him to his feet. "It was a pretty tough Christmas," he said.

"But you survived," said Father Tom.

Dressed in his leather jacket, a white shirt with blue piping and black pants, Joe Glass glanced at the priest and laughed. "If you're not a survivor in this town, you're a ghost," he said.

In the instant that Joe was occupied with Father Tom, Gabriel crossed the furrowed ice of the canal. Here and there, the toddler stopped to splash in the puddles. The canal was loosening in the warm temperatures, coming unsprung like fleece until the surface had softened into woolly lumps.

Joe put one foot on the ice and it gave way, soaking him to the ankle. "Keep going, Gabe," he said. "All the way to the other side, buddy."

Joe was running as he said it, toward the closest footbridge spanning the canal, the priest open-mouthed behind him. Less than fifty yards away, the bulrushes moved and a skinny black woman in a short skirt hurried along the canal, her image stretching and then rebounding back to itself in the windows of the Ayer Mill.

Joe Glass barely noticed as he limped along the canal, edging closer to Gabriel on the ice, which bowed beneath his weight. "Hey, little bear," he said. "Come see Daddy."

Another figure rose from the bulrushes. It was Boris Johnson, in nothing but his kamikaze headband, a pair of fluorescent orange shorts, and running shoes.

Joe tried to hunker down, but his bandaged knee caught inside his trousers and he couldn't stoop low enough. With his eyes fixed on the child, Joe gestured toward Johnson. "That's my kid," he said. "I need some help here."

Boris crashed out of the bulrushes to the embankment. Gabriel had wandered in that direction, his attention caught by a huge turbine located where the canal sunk underground. The entrance was a drainpipe filled with ice. Above was an iron ladder joined to a catwalk that surrounded the mill.

The child stood inside the rusted arch of the turbine. He laughed at his discovery, and the sweet timbre of his voice echoed underground. Hobbling along the muddy shore, Joe Glass tried to get closer without frightening his son. "For God's sake, grab him," he said to Johnson.

Father Tom was only thirty feet from the child over the ice but more than a quarter mile around by the bridge. Boris Johnson stared at the priest. He made a gesture toward the bulrushes where he had lain with the black woman, and then pointed at Father Tom. "Don't judge me, holy man," he said.

"All we're asking for is a little help," said Father Tom.

Francesca Nesheim screamed, her cry warbling between the Ayer and Wood Mills. Dropping Gabriel's jacket in the street, she sprinted for the canal.

The priest turned in Francesca's direction. "Wait," he said.

"Just grab my kid, for crissakes," Joe said to Boris Johnson.

Johnson walked along the ice. Then he leaned inside the drainpipe to get Gabriel's attention. "Come on, sonny," he said. "I smell some bad karma."

The child looked at Johnson. "You smell it too, don't ya?" the man asked. He beckoned to the child with his meaty hand. "Come here."

Gabriel swayed in that direction and then Boris Johnson grabbed him, lifting the boy clear of the turbine. "Alley-oop," said Johnson. The child rose in the air, smiling at the funny man dressed in shorts.

Sliding down the embankment, Joe felt the stitches on his knee tear open as he scrambled to his feet. Boris Johnson handed the child to him and bounded away without another word. He ran the length of the mill, his reflection making a series of collapsing X's in the windows. Across the canal Francesca Nesheim wailed, kicking her feet, trying to get across the ice while Father Tom held her back.

"I got him," said Joe, holding Gabriel above his head.

Jay Atkinson

Father Tom let go of Francesca, and they dashed over the footbridge. "My baby," said Francesca, clutching at Gabriel. "Oh my God, I thought something terrible was going to happen."

Peering into the turbine, Joe Glass ran a hand through his long hair. He let out a short involuntary laugh. "I can't believe Boris Johnson saved my kid," he said.

"I can't believe you let him out on that ice," said Francesca.

"It was my fault," said Father Tom. He put his hand on Joe's shoulder. "I was yakking away and distracted him. It all happened in a split-second."

With Gabriel in his mother's arms, the three adults walked back to the church. "We're having a little party at the King of Clubs, if you'd like to come," Joe said to the priest.

"Thanks, but I've got to get to the hospital," Father Tom said. He lifted his cassock and ran up the stairs to lock the church. From there he looked down at Francesca, who stood with Gabriel's arms around her neck. "Good luck to you all," said the priest.

*

A telephone call woke Rick Maxwell just after three AM in his room at the Holiday Inn. Groping for the phone, he croaked into the receiver and the voice of Tug McNamara came through the line. "We had another tip on a body up at Bellevue," the Police Chief said. "Another kid."

Maxwell was already pulling on his black ATF windsuit. "I'll be right there. Bring the tip tape."

Coming into town via South Broadway, Agent Maxwell gazed at the deserted streets and buildings. Lawrence was only seven square miles and seventy thousand people, with a simple downtown layout and a well-defined arson problem. Agency background said that the local police department was corrupt in a small town way, and had incompetent shift commanders and the usual nepotism and Fort Apache attitude. The only bright spot, according to the report, was Chief Thomas "Tug" McNamara, an ass kicker of the first magnitude who had grown up in Queens, New York and served fourteen years as Deputy Police Chief in Boston. He was decorated for bravery in Vietnam, and had once killed a drug dealer during a shootout.

Going up the hill into Bellevue, Rick Maxwell uncovered the Velcro strip that concealed his badge and then checked the safety on his gun. An orange-vested cop with a flashlight waved the unmarked car to the side of the road.

Maxwell rolled down his window. "ATF," he said, and the cop nodded.

Beyond the patrol cars and their rotating turrets, a klieg light sent its arc over patches of trampled snow and a few lonely headstones. Chief McNamara was waiting just outside this arc, wearing a Police Athletic League sweatshirt and department baseball cap. In the flashes of light, his bony face and lean, starched-looking appearance stood out among the surrounding officers in their dark blue uniforms. Eight or nine patrolmen occupied the crime scene; under the Chief's gaze, they hovered between their cars and the arc light trying to look busy.

The Chief had once told Maxwell that he was sleeping only a couple of hours a night attempting to enforce discipline. He made surprise visits to the police station, rode patrols through the Arlington District, and inspected the parking lots and alleys of South Lawrence; maintaining a command presence, he called it. His father had been a New York cop for thirty-seven years, and his grandfather had worn a police uniform in County Armagh, Northern Ireland. He would rather spend time with career criminals than with lousy police officers, McNamara said.

The Chief placed a hand on Rick Maxwell's shoulder when he stepped out of the car. "Over here," he said, guiding the agent forward.

The dead youngster was lying in the remains of a snowbank: another dark-skinned Hispanic boy with curly brown hair. He was younger than the first one. In the glare of the portable klieg light, there were no marks on his body, which was clad only in a pair of briefs.

"Holy Christ," said Maxwell. "He can't be more than five years old."

The other cops stood at a respectful distance, murmuring to each other and drinking from Styrofoam cups. Occasionally the squawk of a radio broke the silence. A state trooper brought Maxwell some coffee, and he held the cup in his hand but did not drink from it.

A patrolman came up and stood beside Maxwell and the Chief. "There's a guy here from the *Tribune-Standard* named Reynoso," the cop said. "He heard us over the scanner."

Squatting by the makeshift grave, Agent Maxwell didn't respond. Over and over, he ran his hand over his forehead.

The Chief's face appeared in the strobe of a turret light. "Escort Mr. Reynoso to the limits of the crime scene—which is Gill Avenue," McNamara said. "Tell him yes, there's an investigation, but right now I've got no information for him."

Maxwell rose to his feet. "Come on, Chief. Let's hear the tape."

McNamara had a portable cassette player in his car. Agent Maxwell leaned in the passenger-side door and McNamara pressed a button, whirring the tape backwards. "Somebody's been messing around with this thing, so it's not cued up," the Chief said.

A lot of the calls were from cranks. One contained a chorus of drunks singing "Ring of Fire." Another caller, mistaking the hotline for some kind of Letters-to-the-Editor, went off on a harangue about the fires being caused by politicians trying to attract more grant money to the city. This was followed by some dead air, then a voice saying, "It's the little things...the details."

McNamara stopped the tape. "Here it is," he said, plunging the start button again.

A hysterical woman began speaking in Spanish and then switched to a sobbing, accented English: "My boyfriend die Ismail in fire. Next he poison Hernan. He say Hernan should be with Ismail." Here the woman broke down, and the tape was filled with sounds of grief mingled with guilt. Agent Maxwell and the Police Chief sat motionless, listening to the woman call on Jesus to strike her dead. Then a thump came out of the speaker.

"Here's the tip," McNamara said.

After a short silence, the woman returned to the telephone—this time speaking in a low tone of voice, like she was very tired. "To use children in fire wrong. Tito wrong. Jesus forgive me my boys." Then the line went dead.

Chief McNamara shut off the tape player. "We're looking for this Tito. As soon as the call came in saying there was another boy up here, I sent a car over to the Broadway projects," he said. "I've got a man waiting there for Social Services to come pick up Carmelita Diaz's kids. My detectives are out looking for her."

"She's gotta be a candidate for suicide," Maxwell said.

Tug McNamara beckoned a patrolman over to the car. "Take a drive over to the Broadway projects and check out the canal," he said.

"What am I looking for?" the cop asked.

"A dead woman."

Agent Maxwell sipped his coffee. "Our man Tito was using his girlfriend's son to start fires. Something went wrong, the kid died, and his mother and Tito dumped him up here. Then for some reason, Tito decides to poison the younger kid and they dump his body in the same place, and a day or so later remorse kicks in for the mother."

"That's how I read it," said Chief McNamara, behind the wheel of the patrol car.

"Let's go to the apartment," Maxwell said.

After giving instructions to a lieutenant, McNamara waved his hand in the direction of the corpse. "Cover the kid up," he said. "Use a piece of plastic—nothing with fibers."

"Do you want him moved?" asked one of the patrolmen.

"No, I don't want you to move the body from the site of a murder investigation," McNamara snapped. "I want that medical examiner up here. Do your job, for crissakes."

The officer hung his head and withdrew. "Let's take my car," Maxwell said.

McNamara spoke when they were on Gill Avenue, speeding toward downtown. "So what's motivating this Tito?" he asked.

"He's some kind of contractor maybe, being paid to burn down buildings," said Maxwell. "And he might have gotten lazy, and started subbing the jobs out."

"So Tito's working for a landlord?" asked McNamara.

Agent Maxwell clicked his teeth together. "Maybe he's a drug dealer trying to scare off the competition. Or he could be just advertising, 'torch for hire,' that kind of thing."

"I don't understand poisoning the other kid, if that's what it was," McNamara said. "And how in God's name could the mother be involved with something like that? It's mind-boggling."

A large white van from the newspaper cruised between the dispensers along Broadway. The driver was putting out the early edition and collecting quarters. Rick Maxwell stopped the car, and the Chief climbed out and bought a newspaper. BODY OF SECOND CHILD FOUND IN BELLEVUE was the headline of a story written by Roger Reynoso.

*

The Broadway projects were originally the Ayer Mill dormitories, set close to the curb, outfitted with aluminum doors and windows. Rick Maxwell shined his spotlight over the facades and then parked in front of building #3. Immediately another car pulled in behind him. A rumpled man carrying a notebook hustled onto the sidewalk. He had a camera hanging by a strap around his neck.

Striding toward the building, McNamara waved off the reporter. "I'm conducting an investigation, Roger, so I've got no comment right now," he said.

"Is it a murder investigation? And is it connected to the death of Ismail Citron?" asked Reynoso. "I'm getting a lot of this over the scanner, so you might as well be straight with me." He followed the two men up the stairs. "My sources say that the body was produced by a tip on the hotline," the reporter said to Maxwell. "Can you corroborate that?"

"No comment," said Agent Maxwell. He pointed back down the stairs. "Please excuse us."

The second floor apartment was tiny and cramped, smelling of urine. Inside, a patrolman watched over four children ranging from a toddler to a young girl about seven or eight years old. Chief McNamara called the patrolman into the hall and elicited a report just by raising his eyebrows.

"No sign of the mother. DSS hasn't shown up yet," the patrolman said. A bar pinned to his shirt identified him as Herlihy.

"All these kids belong to Carmelita Diaz?" Maxwell asked.

Herlihy expelled air from his nostrils. "She's down to four."

"Just answer the questions, patrolman," said the Chief.

Roger Reynoso popped up behind them. "You're confirming that the second body is a child belonging to Carmelita Diaz?" he asked, unfolding a computer printout. "I have their names and ages right here. Just point to the right one."

"All right, Roger," the Chief said, shepherding the reporter farther down the hall. "Why don't you show us what else you got?"

The reporter, who was plump and disheveled and wearing rubber-soled shoes, balanced a pair of reading glasses on his nose. "Carmelita Diaz, twenty-six years old," said Reynoso, scanning his list. "Four sons: the late Ismail Citron, age eleven; Miguel Ramirez, seven; Hernan Diaz, four; Rafael Dominquez, eighteen months. Two daughters: Idalia Citron, eight. Marguerite Puello, five."

The reporter glanced up for a clue to the identity of the dead child. But Chief McNamara and the ATF agent remained stone-faced. "What you might not know is that DSS has a pretty thick file on Carmelita Diaz, going back to when she was living in East Boston," Reynoso said. "She moved here about a year ago, without notifying DSS. Her boyfriend, Tito Jackson, is thirty-three years old, a convicted felon. He's been pinched for assault, and for battering on some other girlfriend—did three months on that—and two counts of accomplice to arson. Both of those charges were filed in Chelsea District Court and later dismissed."

Maxwell and Chief McNamara glanced at each other.

Reynoso continued. "I'm working on a story that says DSS was negligent in managing the Diaz case. They haven't done a monthly interview with her in over a year, as required by law after initial investigations of child abuse," he said. "I'm also ready to include a paragraph that says her boyfriend, Tito Jackson, has been accused of arson in another community, is at large, and may have something to do with the death of Ismail Citron, who was found with burns on his right leg and both hands. Gentlemen, do you have anything to add to that?"

Agent Maxwell nodded at McNamara just as one of the detectives mounted the stairs. "I got it, Chief. See your man," he said, turning again to Reynoso. "Thanks for the abuse tip. Those files are supposed to be sealed, so it's hard even for a federal agency to get that kind of information. I can access it, but it's a lot of paperwork."

"So what are you gonna do for me?" asked the reporter.

"Like I said, we appreciate it."

Reynoso smirked. "Show your appreciation a little more deeply. I got to make a living, too," he said. "Besides, I just might come across other information you'll want to hear about."

"Okay," said Maxwell, gazing into the other man's face. "But I insist on being unidentified."

Reynoso produced a tape recorder. "I refuse to be taped," said Maxwell. Shoving the recorder back in his pocket, the reporter opened a notebook. "Okay, shoot," he said.

"Our preliminary finding is that the body is Hernan Diaz, four years old. There are no burns or visible bruises. The mother is wanted for questioning." Maxwell put up his large hands. "That's it."

"I got that much from your guys up at Bellevue and I can't print the kid's name, anyway," said Reynoso. "What about Tito Jackson? Is he a suspect?"

"No one else has been implicated thus far. The investigation is continuing."

Reynoso hitched up his drooping pants. "That ain't enough to feed the bulldog," he said.

"That's what I'm ready to give you," said Maxwell. He smiled at the reporter. "But let's keep it friendly. I just might come across other information you'll want to know about."

McNamara called to Agent Maxwell, and together with the detective they went inside the apartment and shut the door. The detective's name was Rudy Pattavina, a large, beetle-browed man with thick wrists and a fleshy, boiled-looking face.

"I talked to several other tenants. None of them saw anybody go in or out of the apartment all night, but most of these people wouldn't admit seeing Santa Claus on Christmas Eve," said Pattavina, lighting a cigarette in the pantry. "From what I heard, Diaz just takes off and leaves the kids here. Sometimes she hangs around at the Disco Very but that closed an hour ago. Murdoch is checking the twenty-four hour stores and a couple of private dance clubs, but nothing so far."

"Anything on a guy named Tito Jackson?" the Chief asked.

"Nope."

"You talk to the kids?"

"A little. They didn't say much. 'No ingles, no ingles,' and a lot of crying."

The door to the apartment opened and one of the DSS caseworkers entered, a matron dressed in a raincoat and brown shoes. Officer Herlihy checked her identification and Chief McNamara waved his detective in closer, gagging on the cigarette smoke. "Put that damn thing out," he said.

Pattavina ran water in the sink, extinguishing the cigarette. He washed the ashes down the drain and stuck the nub in his pocket. "Sorry, Chief," he said.

"We just found out that Carmelita Diaz may have a rap sheet," Maxwell said. "That means these kids should have been taken away after the first body turned up."

Pattavina looked stricken. "I ran a check on her at the local office and they had nothing," he said.

"According to the newspaper, DSS had an open file on Diaz when she lived in East Boston, but they lost track of her when she moved to Lawrence," said Maxwell. "Apparently there's an arson conviction on Tito Jackson that we didn't know about, either."

"I'm gonna take full responsibility on that," said Chief McNamara, extending his pinkie toward the detective. "But now I want you to find the mother, and I want this Tito Jackson."

In the living area, the matron from DSS was tugging the children into their filthy parkas. With a hateful look on her face, she stripped the soggy, ammonia-smelling clothes from Rafael, and changed his diaper. Then with the baby in her arms, the caseworker lined the children up at the door.

Chief McNamara introduced himself to the woman. "I need to see your file on Carmelita Diaz, first thing in the morning," he said.

"We don't have a file on her," the DSS caseworker said, tying the hoods on the children. The cord bit into the flesh beneath Marguerite's chin and she began crying.

"Try Boston," the Chief said. "And have your boss call me as soon as he comes in the door."

"*Her* name is Mary Taff-Schoendist," the caseworker said.

"Then please have Ms. Taff-Schoendist call me right away," said McNamara.

The caseworker accepted McNamara's business card like it was a leaf of poison ivy. Just then the oldest child, Idalia, blurted out something in Spanish.

"What'd she say?" McNamara asked the caseworker.

The woman shrugged. "I don't know."

The Chief glanced around the room but no one spoke Spanish. "I'm calling that community college in the morning and taking a goddamn Spanish course. Get on the horn," he told Herlihy. "And get someone up here who can understand what this kid is saying."

The patrolman made the call on his radio and seconds later the *Tribune-Standard* reporter was at the door. "You're on the scanner," Roger Reynoso said. "Let me in—I speak Spanish."

"Be my guest," said McNamara.

Reynoso spoke to the child, who answered with a long breathless sentence. The reporter glanced over his shoulder at the Chief. "She says her mother's in the cupboard."

"What cupboard?"

The reporter asked Idalia to be specific; the child continued for a moment and then Reynoso pointed toward the kitchen. "That one right there," he said.

Tug McNamara glared at Herlihy, who shrugged. "The other guys told me they searched," the patrolman said.

Rick Maxwell glanced at the Chief with a disgusted expression on his face and then opened the largest of the cabinets. Sure enough, Carmelita Diaz was crouched inside, squatting among the stewed tomatoes.

"I want a law-yer," she said.

"I bet you do," said the Chief.

Agent Maxwell reached in and took her by the hand. As Diaz emerged from her hiding place, Roger Reynoso ran over and snapped a picture.

12

Andover, Massachusetts
October 4, 1910

With the façade of his mansion looming behind him, William Madison Wood felt unsteady for a moment, though the driveway was solid beneath his feet. The vast lawns of the estate were dressed in shadow, and the leaves on the elm trees hung black like shrouds. Off to the west, beside the old skating pond, was a large building the children called "the Casino." Through the front windows, the rear windows of the playhouse were visible, and in the sky beyond the night's clouds floated along like specters.

With dawn approaching, a breeze crept over the ground, rolling the leaves along until they scrambled down the slope. Wood reached up and buttoned his overcoat. He was thick in the shoulders, with wavy brown hair turning gray at the temples, brown mustaches flecked with gray, and small, blunt-fingered hands. He wore a tailored suit made of his own blue serge, a stiff collar, and a necktie with a Windsor knot. Wood checked the time on a pocket watch attached to a gold chain and a fob that resembled a human tooth. Behind the shutters of the great house, which he called Arden, his wife and three of his children were asleep. It was shortly after four AM.

Headlamps came toward him, illuminating an iron fence. A perimeter road circled the estate, leading out from the car barns in both directions and bisecting the driveway near the gates. The long black shape of an automobile, driven by Dick Morgan, traveled over this road. The car was a Rolls Royce Silver Ghost. William Wood kept one of the limousines at his home in Palm Beach, Florida; another in the garage beneath American Woolen Company headquarters at Fourth Avenue and 18th Street in New York City; and the third here at Arden.

The passenger cabin of each automobile was equipped with a writing desk; a quadruple telegraph machine, which allowed four simultaneous messages to be transmitted; and the latest addition to what William Wood called his "rolling office," a telephone that his drivers connected to overhead lines by pulling off the road and ascending the nearest utility pole. Dick Morgan was the most adept at this—he could make the "car telephone" operational in less than five minutes—and so was headquartered at Arden and drove Mr. Wood to his mills in Lawrence, where he spent most of his time.

The American Woolen Company was comprised of 59 mills in Massachusetts, Maine, New Hampshire, Vermont, Connecticut, Rhode Island, New York and Kentucky. In these factories, William Wood employed 35,000 operatives, upheld an annual payroll of $25,000,000 and produced 70,000,000 yards of fabric per year. In Lawrence, Wood owned the Washington Mills, Prospect Mills, Wood Worsted Mill, and the nascent Ayer Mill, which was devoted to men's wear worsteds. Located beside the Wood Mill, the Ayer was equipped with 50 worsted cards, 400 broad looms, a total of 44,732 spindles, and nine giant steam boilers rated at 600 horsepower each. These boilers, looms, and spindles were driven by the Merrimack River through its canals, and staffed by workers of Italian, Polish, Lithuanian, Syrian, Irish, English, German, French Canadian and Portuguese origin.

This evening, local dignitaries would gather for the dedication of the Ayer Mill and its forty-foot tower, which housed the largest striking clock in the world. Wood's father-in-law, 88-year-old Frederick Ayer, who had provided William Wood with his first business opportunity many years earlier, would christen the enterprise that had been named in his honor. It was a red-letter day.

The limousine stopped near the front gate and the driver climbed out. Silent Dick Morgan had been a bare-knuckle boxing champion; he was six feet three inches tall and now, at forty-five, as broad as a draft horse. Beneath the shiny black cap his head was bald and heavy slabs of muscle filled the overcoat that fell to his boot tops.

"Good morning," said Wood, as the manservant opened the door of the car.

Morgan tipped his cap and said nothing. He had won sixty-two bouts and was the champion of New York City until he fought a man named Sullivan and was knocked unconscious in the nineteenth round on April 3, 1887. John L. Sullivan split Morgan's upper lip to the bone and the old boxer wore a large mustache to cover that region of his face.

Inside, the limousine smelled of cigars and boiled coffee. There was a vacuum bottle on the desk, alongside late editions of the Boston newspapers and a china cup that was embossed with WMW in gold letters. Leaning into the car, Wood unscrewed the bottle of coffee and poured himself a cup, then walked around the limousine to stand beside Morgan. The two men leaned back on their heels, gazing at the stars that were disappearing from the sky as morning came on. The barking of a dog echoed across the grounds—the mechanic's collie, roused by a skunk—and his alarm rang over the pond and then faded into the trees.

William Wood looked at his watch. Behind him, the idling motor distinguished itself and puffs of exhaust mingled with the rising fog. Yet man and driver remained there, as if waiting for something.

After some time, there was the sound of a car approaching on the Turnpike. The engine clicked upward through various registers as it barreled along, its appearance imminent, but still the visitor failed to arrive.

Suddenly the racing motor permeated the landscape. Next was a screech of brakes; laughter; a bottle falling to the pavement; and loud voices: "A grand goodnight"; "One more for the maestro"; the door closing and the tires squealing and the rising crescendo of the motor. Then it was quiet once more.

Where the car had been, a man stood in a swallow-tailed coat and touring cap. This figure halted in the porte-cochere that surrounded the gates. The flame of a match lit his face for a moment—lean in profile, golden-haired, very young—and then the brick chamber fell into darkness and a voice could be heard, singing:

> A curse on ye, ye millionaires
> Who sit at home in your easy chairs
> And crack your nuts and sip your wine
> While I wail over this son of mine!

There were footfalls and the man emerged, smoking his cigarette. He was singing to himself, and halted when he saw the two men standing beside the road.

"Good evening, father," said the young man. The ember of the cigarette lit his face and his yellow eyebrows stood like tildes. "I'm certain you would like to enumerate your many triumphs, but I'm afraid I have a previous engagement—with a feather pillow." The young man laughed at his own witticism and proceeded up the drive, his head cocked, the cigarette held out like a tribesman's dart.

"Will!" said William Wood. "Do you have the slightest notion what time it is?"

"Indeed I do, father," the youth said. "Time for bed."

William Madison Wood, Jr. was eighteen years old, having just graduated from Phillips Andover Academy. He was a graceful tennis player, a musician and jokester, and also the handsome favorite of many Andover girls.

"Come here," said Wood. "I want to smell your breath. And that cigarette won't help you."

The youth laughed, tossing the cigarette away. "Certainly, father," he said. "Smell the breath of the grave." Will strode over the pavement and surprised his father by kissing him on the cheek.

Wood laughed despite himself. "Ugh. You smell like a toilet," said the mill owner. "That Alex Gardner will be the death of you."

"And I the death of him," said Will, gazing at his father with affection. "Actually, *mon pere*, if I looked as tired as you, I'd report to a sanitarium immediately."

"What you see," Mr. Wood said, "is the result of my seventeen-hour

Jay Atkinson

days."

"When will you earn your free papers?" asked the youth.

All this time, William Wood had been clutching the embossed cup and now he decanted his hand and flung its contents away. "A smart mouth is not as useful as a hard mind, William," said the mill owner. "When you lie on your feather pillow, thank God for being born into such a respected, prosperous family. One of the first rank, like your friend the banjo player."

"Oh, we might play tennis with them, dine with them, and summer alongside them, but the sons of a Portuguese fishwife will never be the Gardners, no matter how many hours you work, *mi padre*."

This was said in a lighthearted tone but it served to agitate Wood nevertheless. He handed the china cup to Dick Morgan and paced to and fro, swinging his arms and muttering to himself. The mill owner snapped open his watch, fretted with the tooth-shaped fob and then tucked the watch into his vest pocket and drummed his fingers there. "Remember, you are descended from the Woods *and* the Ayers, and your grandfather—who expects to see you at the dedication today—is one of the finest old Yankees ever to make his fortune in these parts," Mr. Wood said.

The youth executed a formal bow. "With one foot on the Mayflower and the other mired in a Portuguese fishing barge, I will navigate my way to bed," said the youth.

William Wood pointed toward Arden, where the upper windows grew rosy in the dawn. "Go on," he said. "And be punctual. The dedication is at eight o'clock sharp."

As young Will sauntered up the drive, Dick Morgan reached into the limousine to ignite the headlamps and opened the door for his employer. Inside the car, William Wood unscrewed the top of the vacuum bottle and poured himself another cup of coffee and took up the *Boston Daily Advertiser*. Two small lamps illuminated the interior, and Wood began reading his newspaper as the hatted driver eased the car through the gates.

William Wood's property spread for a mile along the Turnpike, bordered by an iron fence to the limits of Arden and a fieldstone wall thereafter. There was an old settler at the intersection of the Turnpike and Lowell Street that he hadn't bought out, but surrounding the gent's home and extending on all sides was land that Wood had acquired over the past several years. It was more than nine hundred acres, the site of the old Frye Village. Here the mill owner wished to establish a private community: on the south side of the Turnpike, large brick homes for his overseers; to the north, white clapboard structures for the many shop foremen and department heads and their families. Included in his plans, which had been laid out by engineers but scrutinized to the finest detail by Mr. Wood himself, were company meeting halls, civic buildings, playing fields, and houses of worship. Those men staffing the upper levels of the American Woolen Company would enjoy full use of this Arcadia, where they could, after a hard week's labor, borrow a book, sail on the man-made lake, and watch the Wood Mill base-ball team play against the Ayer Nine.

Not every company stockholder in Boston and New York shared Wood's enthusiasm for what he called "Shawsheen Village." Although he had purchased the land with his own money and floated a bond for the plans that had been drawn up, his directors had balked at underwriting what they considered, at best, a peripheral duty of the corporation: i. e., caring for their managers the way one cared for children. Even though the American Woolen Company would amortize the village in their position as landlords and mortgagors, it would take twenty years for the settlement to break even. If their prospects faltered during that time— and it was a huge span over which to speculate—the tenants would leave and they'd be proprietors of a ghost town. This was not good business.

William Wood chafed at the shortsightedness of his directors. By holding paper on American Woolen Company managers and keeping them close to the mills where they worked, he would tether these men for the next twenty years. Had he himself not risen from a bookkeeper's assistant, with a salary of just $4 weekly, to president of the American Woolen Company in this exact amount of time? Did he not, at age 52, earn an annual salary of $1 million plus stock dividends, ranking him among the Rockefellers, Astors, and Carnegies? He had made every one of his directors a wealthy man. And as he gazed upon the land bordering the Turnpike, surveyed and graded at his own expense, Wood imagined the families strolling through phantom streets and the tolling of church bells, and decided to see the project through. He vowed to show them all what he could accomplish, once he set his mind to it.

There in the *Daily Advertiser* was an article containing President William Howard Taft's decision to change Army uniforms from Civil War blue to olive drab—a notion proposed by Teddy Roosevelt two years earlier. Interested manufacturing concerns were invited to submit their bids to Jacob M. Dickinson, Secretary of War.

Immediately Wood thrust the newspaper aside, upsetting his coffee, and mobilized the telegraph key by attaching two copper wires. Reaching to pull the siphon cord free of its holder, Wood blew into the mouthpiece and spoke to his driver, fifteen feet distant at the controls of the limousine.

"As soon as we reach the Bell line, I must make a telephone call," Mr. Wood said.

The limousine rose on its chassis and flew along the Turnpike at double its previous speed. By manipulating the telegraph key with his right hand, Wood clacked out a message regarding Taft's decision that would reach Artemus Twombley at the company headquarters in New York, at his chief wool merchant's office in Boston, and at the dyeing facility in Manchester, New Hampshire. His principle chemist, Mr. Ruffen, had to be reached by telephone at his residence in Connecticut.

As they neared the river, the first row houses appeared and then the dense, reeking tenements: narrow buildings of three and four stories, packed so closely that landlords could stand in one apartment and

Jay Atkinson

collect the rents from across the way. The dye house men and weavers and battery boys that toiled in the Wood Worsted Mill and the Ayer resided here, six or seven families to a tenement and nine or ten to a family. One third of the city's population lived in one-thirteenth of its space, meaning that an average of six hundred men, women and children roosted on a single acre.

The telephone lines, strung on poles of stripped white oak, ran up from Boston and through Andover and crossed South Union Street at a point halfway between Arden and the Merrimack River. Dick Morgan parked the limousine beneath this thick black cable and hauled himself out. Nodding to Mr. Wood, the old boxer passed to the rear of the car, lifted a stepladder from the trunk and unwound a length of electrical cord that was spooled there. He unhinged the ladder with one hand and carried it to rest against the telephone pole, hauling the cable over his shoulder as he went.

Although the landscape was saturated in grainy light, distinguishing the trolley tracks and outlining the houses and sheds, the Turnpike was deserted, except for a dairy wagon making its rounds between the tenements. And while Scannell the milkman hurried into an alley, the old draft horse pulled the wagon some fifty yards and sniffed at Morgan as he wired two clamps to the overhead line and grounded the device to the pole. A bolt of electricity shot down the stepladder and threw sparks over the pavement, startling the horse, which bucked in his traces and stamped his hooves. Dick Morgan was nearly upended, and as he hastened down the stepladder, he saw Scannell running toward him in the street, his hat flying off and the empty wire carrier banging against his leg.

Inside the car, William Wood picked up the telephone and heard the voice of an operator in Boston, inquiring what number he wished to reach. While the milkman calmed his horse and led him off, Mr. Wood listened to the telephone ringing in Connecticut and then Darius Ruffen picked it up.

"Hello?"

"President Taft is ordering uniforms in olive drab. I want our chemists on that immediately."

"What time is it?" asked the bewildered man on the other end of the line.

"Time to be working." Wood grabbed his newspaper and perused some calculations he had been making with a grease pen. "That's roughly one million pieces per year at ten dollars per piece. We need that color, Mr. Ruffen, and we need it fast and cheap."

"Where are you, sir?"

Wood clenched the receiver in his fist. "I could be in Timbuktu, for all it matters to this conversation. Now get busy on that quote."

William Wood took pride in submitting low bids, which always included a fair margin of profit. Although he had little schooling, Wood had spent thirty years acquiring information on textile manufacturing and was a veritable walking encyclopedia in that regard. Recently he had developed a machine for assessing the moisture in raw wool. His buyers could determine shrinkage and therefore calculate which lots provided the most wool for the price offered. Although it might only save a few cents per pound, cast over a million items this was the sort of thing that had put the American Woolen Company on top.

Ruffen coughed into the telephone. "As soon as I get to the office, I'll—"

"Go right now," said Wood. "I'll allow you six hours to get the formula right, then send the details to Twombley in Boston and he'll project the cost. I'll submit our bid by telegraph."

While his driver waited beside the pole, the mill owner tried another call, this time to his head of engineering in Peekskill, New York. The line rang but no one picked up. Wood made a note to have the man fired. What a shock, to arrive at the office with the *Wall Street Journal* under his arm and a smile upon his face, only to learn that he'd been sacked. But the globe spun at a relentless clip and William Wood had no patience for those who failed to keep up.

He tilted the window open. The morning was cool and damp, and Morgan had turned his collar up and stood with his hands in the pockets of his greatcoat. "Take me to the Old Battery," said Wood, shutting the window against the chill.

While Morgan unhooked the clamps, spooled the cable, and returned the cable and stepladder to the trunk, Mr. Wood poured himself more coffee and scoured the news in the *Daily Advertiser* and the *Boston Post*. Outfitting an army was a neat proposition. For the world was a dangerous place and after recent military successes in Cuba and the Philippines, America was growing in power throughout that world. Particularly in Europe, where assassinations and insurgencies had become common and where trade partners like Great Britain and France looked to the United States for support, the prospects for war were gaining steam. Based on the latest information, William Wood decided to buy huge amounts of Scottish and Irish wool. A European conflict would create a double advantage for the company: soon there would be a shortage of foreign wool and an increasing need for olive drab uniforms.

Outside the limousine, a klaxon sounded that shook the tenements to their foundations. Five o'clock; the first bell; meant to wake thousands of workers and send them toward the mills before the second bell, thirty minutes hence. While the horn faded, Dick Morgan closed himself in the car, shifted into gear and pressed the accelerator. A quarter mile down the road, he overtook Scannell's milk wagon and sped past, disturbing the buckets that hung from its tailgate.

Ahead was the Ayer Mill, and the dim faces of the clock that rose above it. At the triangular park between South Union and Winthrop Avenue, the limousine veered onto the right fork, and the first mill operatives to appear waved their caps and cried hooray for Billy Wood.

William Madison Wood was a popular figure in Lawrence. Labor organizers, trying to establish a foothold in the city, called him a robber baron who held down wages and allowed unsafe conditions in his factories. But Wood, who employed thousands of immigrants and had first gone to work at age 12, built a replica of George Washington's Valley Forge headquarters on the grounds of Arden and invited his workers to visit it. The previous spring, when he had raised wages to an all-time high and area grocers inflated their prices, he dispatched a group of agents who persuaded the merchants to bring their prices back down.

That Sunday on the Common, workers had marched behind a hundred-foot banner that read "A Man Without A Stain Upon His Honor." The assembly swelled to ten thousand and filled the Turnpike for a mile, arriving outside the gates of Arden at one o'clock in the afternoon. They clamored for Mr. Wood to appear, singing hymns and offering huzzahs, until the mill owner and his sons, William Jr. and Cornelius, accepted a wreath of daffodils and thanked the workers. In the next quarter, sales dropped off and Wood reduced the prevailing wage by twenty cents an hour, but most workers understood he had their best interests at heart.

At the corner of Haverhill and White streets was the narrow structure of the Old Battery, the first fire house ever constructed in Lawrence. The Essex Company authorized the building in 1856 and within a few years, Major Bonney was appointed commander, naming his regiment the Bonney Light Battery and thus the name "Battery Building" came into existence. William Wood, as afraid as he was of fire and what it could do to the American Woolen Company, revered the art of fire fighting and was somewhat of an authority on its history in Lawrence. A man named Charles Foster, boilerman on the Combination 7 at the Old Battery, assisted him in these pursuits.

Foster was a thin, reedy fellow of 74, who wore his gray hair parted in the middle and could be found, when he wasn't fighting fires, just inside the Battery doors, attended by Jim Syphon, the mascot of the house. An Irish Terrier with a singed tail, Jim Syphon used to run with the Syphon Company but switched his allegiance after meeting Charles Foster in '02. Man and dog had been together since.

The neighborhood around the Old Battery had grown up with tenements and oil houses and garages, now principally occupied by Syrians and a few others from that corner of the world, and teeming with vermin, filthy sumps, and a host of voracious and evil smells. By comparison, the old firehouse was spotless, hung with red, white, and blue bunting and adorned with geranium boxes. The limousine arrived at the corner, hailed by a group of men trudging to work, and Dick Morgan steered the car into the alley beside the firehouse. Leaving just enough of the car exposed to open the doors, the old prizefighter hoped to conceal their arrival. Gangs of urchins, alerted to Mr. Wood's presence, would often press themselves on him, requesting favors and expecting silver coins and other dispensations. But the mill owner's schedule was busy from morning until night and it was Morgan's job to see that he kept it.

Charles Foster occupied his usual position beside Combination 7, smoking his pipe, his feet on the rim of the boiler. Jim Syphon was dozing nearby and Foster beckoned to Mr. Wood and tiptoed past to avoid waking the dog. Guiding Wood by the arm he crossed behind the engine, its boiler emanating waves of heat, and led his patron into the alarm room.

It was a cramped, windowless space, not so much a room as an alcove, with light bulbs covering one wall and marked with little brass plates naming each of the call boxes, as well as three telephones and a dais lined with switches. A man was slumped over this console, his arms flung out and hair glistening with the dust that had sifted down throughout the night.

"I'd rather wake a man than a dog, I would," said Foster, closing the door behind them. "On most occasions, a man can be reasoned with."

Charles Foster had served fifty-nine years as a fireman in Lawrence. His left hand, both forearms, and half his neck were covered with wavy pink scarring. His right eyebrow was missing and when he exerted himself, the breath came rattling from his lungs like an old diesel. He wore dungarees held up with red suspenders and a leather belt, rubber thigh-high boots turned down at the knees, and a double-breasted jacket.

Foster grinned at his visitor. "What brings you here at such an hour, Mr. Wood?" he asked, showing tobacco-stained teeth.

"Every business owner should pay a call to the fire house," said Wood.

William Wood was short, heavy-set, and because he had been reading the newspapers, wore a pince-nez on the bridge of his nose. He was dressed in spats and carried his ivory-tipped cane. Glancing around, Wood felt out of place, not because he smoked Havanas and commanded all that he gazed upon, but because he envied men who slept in their boots and jumped at the sound of an alarm, rushing out to face hell for eight dollars a week. For Billy Wood had labored among the lower strata himself and understood that fire fighters were the undisputed champions of that world.

"It's been quiet," said Foster. "Thank heavens."

Over the years, Charles Foster had ridden to a thousand fires and stoked ten thousand boilers. Caught babies thrown from windows and carried grown men on his back and seen women burned alive and heard their screams. His friendship with Billy Wood was the source of comment in the Old Battery and at the Relief's Inn and across the backs of wagons throughout the neighborhood. But Charles Foster coveted the life and goods of no man.

"Have you completed a tour of the Ayer?" Wood asked. "I'm eager to safeguard myself in every way possible."

"Take all precautions but when it comes to avoiding fire, luck is what you need," Foster said.

Charles Foster had been in his ninth year as a fire fighter when Lawrence was struck by its most infamous tragedy. At 4:45 PM on the afternoon of January 10, 1860, the 670 operatives of the Pemberton Mill, a broad, five-story building on the north canal, were busy spinning, weaving and dying cotton fabrics. In the nearby Duck Mill, men situated near the windows were first attracted by an eerie silence, as all the Jacquard looms of the Pemberton, which were driven by a central gear, halted at once. After a moment, there was a sudden loud rattle, and then a groaning sound as first one, then many more support pillars gave way. As the building swayed, hanging in the balance, horrified onlookers watched as a number of women jumped from the upper-story windows only to be dashed on the paving stones below.

The walls bulged outward and then the floors of the Pemberton, with nothing holding them up, fell to the ground with an enormous concussion, dragging machinery and the screaming workers along with them. In just a few seconds, the Pemberton Mill was reduced to a heap of broken timbers and pulverized brick. Men and women staggered out with their faces gashed open, limbs twisted into grotesque shapes and their clothing in shreds. Immediately a wail rose up from the victims, survivors, onlookers and passersby, and a huge cloud of dust and smoke obscured the wreckage.

Combination 7 arrived within the half-hour. Charles Foster soon learned that every piece of fire apparatus located within ten miles was either on the scene or en route. He stoked his boiler, hearing the cry of those still trapped in the rubble, and the oaths of men who drove teams of horses, heaved at pry bars, and argued and shoved each other in the early minutes of the rescue. The warning had already gone out to beware the dried cotton, oil, and other combustibles that saturated the wreckage. Men with torches and kerosene lanterns, trying to free those caught in the debris, were ordered to take extra heed.

Although a number of workers died in the collapse, many others walked away and hope arose that a large number of souls would be saved. Foster manned his station and watched the other members of his brigade throwing water on the mill, both to keep the dust low and to soak the timbers and planking so they wouldn't burn easily. In the illumination of a bonfire, he noticed a man wandering among the shattered bricks, muttering to himself and picking at his beard. People ran in all directions, jostling the man, but he seemed lost in rumination.

As a public employee, Mr. Foster was acquainted with many of Lawrence's most prominent citizens, including Captain Charles Bigelow, whom he had met at the United States Hotel fire on Essex Street the year before. That night, Captain Bigelow had taken command of the scene, diverting pumps to the canal, organizing bucket brigades and opening a relief center inside the post office. And although flames destroyed the hotel, Bigelow's effort prevented the fire from spreading to other structures on the block and he was named a hero. But the captain deflected all attempts to reward his efforts. It was small compensation for an event that had occurred years before, he said, when a man had plucked him from the Merrimack River and saved his life.

In the torchlight surrounding the Pemberton, Captain Bigelow avoided the officers of the watch, holding up a small object to various bonfires, whereupon he sighted through its translucent surface and then pocketed it again. Leaving his boiler, Foster whispered to the horses and then fetched a cup of broth from a woman nearby, part of a group that was tending to the injured. Foster carried the steaming broth to Captain Bigelow, who stood atop a pile of timbers. Not far from that location, down a shaft that had formed in the rubble, a party of mill girls, trapped so deep they had not yet been reached, sang hymns to keep up their spirits. With an ear turned to this pathetic music, Bigelow was encircled by smoke rising from the fires.

Foster doffed his cap. "Something for you, Captain," he said, handing over the broth.

The retired military man took the cup but didn't drink from it. For some time Bigelow gazed into a long black puddle that had formed at the foot of the mount upon which he stood. The run-off from the bucket brigades and pumps had collected there and, in the strange light of the bonfires, a reflecting pool had emerged: capturing the men who hurried past its edge, the horse's elongated figures, even the constellations hanging in the sky. Bigelow favored his good leg, his left hand pressed against his ribs where he'd been injured when the cofferdam had collapsed.

"All for forty cents," he said, with the object held against his eye. It was an old chunk of amber.

Only later, in the days following the event did Foster guess at Captain Bigelow's meaning. With Charles Storrow residing in Boston and Abbott Lawrence dead, Bigelow was the principal engineer for the Essex Company and its ranking official in Lawrence. During the construction of the Pemberton, he had advised the clerk of the works, a man named J. Pickering Putnam, to purchase wooden pillars and clasps. After deliberating for weeks, Putnam chose iron pillars, along with caps and pintles to bind them to the floors above and below. As signatory, Bigelow made a final argument for the wooden pillars and then withdrew, as he was busy supervising the construction of the Pacific Mill. Mr. Putnam's decision saved a mere forty cents per pillar.

In the aftermath, Putnam and the Boston iron makers foisted all responsibility for the Pemberton's collapse on Charles Bigelow. No matter that during construction one of the defective pillars had rolled off a flatbed and split in half—right before the eyes of J. Pickering Putnam. In fact, a cartoon appeared in a Boston newspaper entitled "The Building of the Pemberton Mill," which depicted skeletons erecting the faulty pillars while Bigelow counted a sack of gold coins. Ministers railed from their pulpits that an "inordinate love of money" was the cause of the tragedy and public scorn was heaped on the figure of Captain Charles Henry Bigelow.

Bigelow had his supporters, although he never uttered a word to rally them. Writing in the *Weekly Tribune*, a fellow named J. F. C. Hayes opined, "But what caused the fall (of the Pemberton) is as much a mystery today as it was on the day the jury conducted its laborious, long continued and utterly fruitless investigation.... After twelve days labor, it aided materially in adding one more, if not the noblest of them all, to the already frightful catalogue of victims of the terrible disaster. For Captain Bigelow preferred to bear upon his own devoted head the full measure of censure rather than even *seem* to cast that censure on others, though to others it might legitimately belong…. The fault, in our view, in this whole matter, falls upon the iron founder."

But standing amidst the wreckage of the Pemberton, Bigelow fingered his chunk of amber while hymns filled the air and the sky above Lawrence blazed with stars. Turning to Mr. Foster, he threw back his overcoat, exposing his breast to the January chill. His black beard and long black hair, streaked now with gray, ruffled in the wind and his eyes were black and cold, sunken into his head.

"What is it, Captain?" Foster asked.

"Render unto Caesar those things which are Caesar's," said Bigelow.

With that, Charles Bigelow descended the little hill and disappeared into the crowd, among boys rushing past with their buckets and the smoke of fires. In less than a year, he would be dead.

The snow that surrounded the mill like fringe on a hat was churned into mud by so many hooves and wheels and boots, and sloughs of water arranged here and there reflected wicks of flame from the bonfires. If not for the general lament that permeated the air, the event possessed all the characteristics of a pagan celebration. By nine o'clock, all but one hundred of those trapped in the debris had been rescued or removed, including twenty-two killed in the initial collapse.

With the water exhausted aboard Combination 7 and the pressure in the lines down to zero, Mr. Foster joined one of the three-man crews probing the wreckage for survivors. He made the acquaintance of Richard Plummer and John Maguire, who were digging at a compacted section of flooring about one hundred feet from the southern corner of the mill. Both were middle-aged storekeepers and had no experience in such matters; called straight from his haberdashery, Mr. Maguire wore a top hat and dress boots, and Mr. Plummer, a grocer, had filled his pockets with maple sugar candy for any youngster who might be in distress.

Charles Foster shook hands with the two men and, poised over a hole the rescuers had made, heard a cry from beneath their feet. Lowering themselves, they descended like miners into the shaft, which smelled of the overturned privies and oil and spent air. When they had traveled downward perhaps ten yards and the last flicker from the bonfires had gone out, Mr. Foster, who was leading the way, called for a lantern. He found himself standing in a cocoon of fabric, a glazed material that was known as cambric and formed the majority of the Pemberton's output. He and his fellow adventurers had entered into a crushed storeroom of some kind, and groping in the darkness, Foster ran his hands over the twilled, figured, striped and carded textiles that surrounded him.

His ears straining for the noise they had heard, Mr. Foster touched something cold and rigid. Then he recoiled in disgust, gripped by the understanding that he had found a corpse.

Digging through his pockets Foster retrieved a match, scratched the tip with a thumbnail, and when it flared up, inspected his discovery. The corpse belonged to a young Irish girl, perhaps 14 or 15 years old, dressed in the flimsy shift necessitated by the heat of the mill. Her bare feet suspended above the wreckage, she hung in the shredded cotton like a fairy, her hands dangling in the threads and her gray eyes fixed in their sockets. In his professional career, Foster had seen a number of burnt and mangled bodies, but this poor girl was notable because of the absence of marks or burns and the delicate surface of her face. Apparently she had been working in the storeroom when the mill collapsed, and had fallen among the reams of fabric, cushioned by the giant wads and spools until it all came to jarring halt. Caught among a thousands strings, her neck had been broken.

Finally, the glow from a lantern extended to Foster, spreading its light into the diaphanous reaches of the cocoon, and he was able to crawl away from the girl—killed for fifty-two cents a week.

The others followed behind. Still groping with his hands, Foster reached a place where some machinery was jammed together and an iron bar was handed down and he tried to pry the twisted metal apart with little success. There was room for Mr. Plummer to join him, a sort of platform made from jagged flooring, and the two men chopped at the wreckage with axes and bars. A voice could be heard now, below and to the left of the ruined loom that faced them.

"My leg's broken," a man said. "I'm caught."

Charles Foster put up his hand. "We'll get you out," he said.

Excited by finding a survivor so deep in the rubble, the men called for more light. A human chain formed overhead, and as the unlucky Irish girl was carried in one direction a number of items traveled toward them, including a small kerosene lantern that would fit through the crawlspace. While they waited for the light to arrive, the trapped man identified himself as Maurice Palmer, an overseer from the Pemberton's spinning room.

Richard Plummer knew this gentleman, an experienced hand from Manchester, England, who traded at his store. A transplanted Lancastrian himself, Mr. Plummer often chatted with his fellow expatriate, in his shop and whenever they encountered one another on Essex Street.

Crawling forward, Plummer reached an aperture they had forced into the rubble and extended his arm through and shook Mr. Palmer's hand. "We'll have you out presently," said the grocer. "And tomorrow you'll be choosing apples and haggling over their price."

"Tomorrow I'll pay my balance," said Palmer, heartened by the appearance of his friend. "And, mind my wife, I'll bring a dram along and we'll toast our acquaintance."

With two men heaving on the bar, the rescuers were able to shove part of the broken loom aside and enter Mr. Palmer's chamber. The victim was bent backward over a pile of rubble and his left leg was lying beneath a timber. A little space had opened among the bricks, preventing the full weight of the timber from resting on his thigh, but the concussion had snapped the leg, just above the knee. Little spindles of bone showed through the fabric of Mr. Palmer's trousers and his eyes wore a heavy, fixed expression. An overturned bowler lay nearby in the dust.

Mr. Plummer cradled his friend's head and fed him a piece of candy.

Voices echoed in the tunnel behind them, as news of Palmer's identity traveled upward. He was dressed in an undershirt and tweed vest, and John Maguire shed his coat and tucked it around the injured man's shoulders. While Mr. Palmer was distracted, Charles Foster slipped the bar under the timber and tested its weight.

Palmer screamed. "No, man, you can't—" he said, writhing over the bricks. "It won't move."

Heads appeared in the porthole they had made and another lantern was brought forward. But despite all the hands touching it, the lantern was dropped, and when the flame struck the wadded cotton, fire at once sprang up. Men beat at the flames but the drafts whistling through such a labyrinth increased the fire, driving everyone located behind the rescue party straight up the tunnel.

Encouraged by the air supply and wads of oil-soaked cotton, the fire spread in every direction. "My God, we shall be burned alive," said Mr. Palmer, beating his head against the rubble.

Screams were heard from all corners of the wreckage. Although the flames obliterated their previous route, Mr. Maguire explored in the other direction while Foster and Plummer attempted to raise the fallen timber. An instant later Maguire returned: he had found a passage.

"Save yourselves," said Mr. Palmer, clutching his injured leg.

"We'll lift that timber and carry you out," Plummer said.

The sound of an inferno howled through the wreckage. Wild-eyed, his body running with tremors that verged on convulsion, Palmer said, "I won't burn." Before anyone could act, he reached into his vest and took out a short, sharp knife meant for cutting fabric from the looms. "I won't stay here," he said, the blade glittering in the firelight.

Flames swept all around, hanging like curtains as they digested the reams of cambric. They reached Palmer's boots, curling the loose threads that hung from his pantlegs. Twice Palmer slashed at his own neck, inflicting a grievous wound with the second blow. He moaned and fell back as thick jets of blood squirted over his chest.

"Dear God, not this," Mr. Plummer said, falling to his knees. He drew out a handkerchief and pressed it against his friend's throat while Mr. Maguire beat back the flames.

Just as the fire threatened to engulf them all, Foster and Maguire heaved together on the bar, the timber rolled away, and Mr. Plummer was able to snatch the injured man from beneath its weight.

Charles Foster tore the sleeve from his coat and wrapped it around the bleeding man's neck. Stumbling forward, they dragged the victim through a narrow passage and into a kind of anteroom, where other rescuers waved them on and pulled Mr. Palmer up a rough-hewn shaft into the starlight.

Flames were consuming the entire mass of the Pemberton and the lament of the previous hours had been replaced by a steady mortal keening from those still trapped in the debris. Laying the injured man down, the rescuers knelt by his side as Mr. Palmer struggled for breath and gagged on the blood pouring down his throat. The fire raised itself before them, devouring materials and choking off the loudest cries, and Palmer struggled to his elbows for a last glimpse of the carnage.

"Tell my children I didn't burn," he said. With that, he fell back and died.

Struggling to his feet, Mr. Maguire rushed to join a nearby bucket brigade. Foster's lieutenant waved to him; Combination 7 was on the move, heading for the canal.

The air was so cold that steam from the boiler turned into snowflakes, angling in a little man-made blizzard. As Mr. Foster slid over the debris, something glinted in the firelight and he bent to pick it up. It was Captain Bigelow's keepsake, and while he rushed to join the brigade, Foster held it up to the light. There was a large winged insect trapped in the amber and he pushed it deep into his pocket, to make sure it wouldn't burn.

Jay Atkinson

13

The Present Day

His stomach tight with veal parmigiana, Kap Kutter was paying for lunch at the Cedar Chest when he noticed the *Tribune-Standard*: BODY OF SECOND CHILD FOUND IN CEMETERY. Kutter's mark, a fellow that wanted to trade hot tubs for some commercials, gestured from the door of the restaurant. He was dressed in a cashmere overcoat and red Hawaiian shirt, chewing on an unlit cigar.

"I wanna meet those Lucky Lager girls," the man said. "Get me laid and I'll throw in a Naugahyde cover."

Ignoring him, Kutter put two quarters in the coin box and took a newspaper from its spring-loaded jaw. The *Tribune-Standard* was reporting that another body had been found in a shallow grave up at Bellevue. Hernan Diaz, age four, and Ismail Citron, the eleven-year-old discovered earlier, were half brothers, and the boys' mother, Carmelita Diaz, had been arrested in connection with their deaths. Diaz's boyfriend, Tito Jackson, was being sought for questioning. Sources identified Jackson as a convicted felon, suggesting that a murder indictment would be handed down when he was captured, and that it was likely the fugitive had something to do with the recent arson wave.

In a sidebar, Police Chief Thomas McNamara was quoted as saying, "Although I'm repulsed by some of the developments in this case, they represent a break in our investigation." And there were small photographs of both victims: a gap-toothed Hernan Diaz and Ismail Citron wearing an altar boy's outfit. Beneath the photo of Citron was the caption, "Lawrence boy loved basketball, church."

Kap rolled up the newspaper and shoved it into his overcoat pocket. He walked by the hot tub man without acknowledging him, and threw open the doors of the Cedar Chest. It was a chilly March afternoon. Sunlight filtered between the buildings, creating a hodgepodge of shadows that gathered on the sidewalk and floated across the hulls of passing cars. Kutter staggered along for a block and then reversed direction, befuddled by the three gin and tonics he had consumed with his cutlet.

Lights that spelled out LAS VEGAS and a pair of mechanical dice were displayed inside a travel agency across the street. A woman pushing a junk-filled shopping cart stopped to watch the dice, bobbing in the same rhythm. Moments later she fell down on the sidewalk, clawing at her face and shrieking. Kap Kutter lurched down Broadway past the Disco Very onto Park Street. He approached a group of teenage boys who began shouting at him in Spanish. One of the teenagers gestured at Kutter's Rolex, and then at his own cheap wristwatch.

"Time is runnin' out," he said, and his crew laughed.

Kutter bulled past them, glancing at the ruined hulks that lined Park Street. Every other house was boarded up or scorched at the windows and doors, the melted shingles covered with soot. Slogans like *Job Action Now, Latin Kings Ruel 2-Nite* and *Fire Bomb Freddy* were scrawled over the deserted buildings. Some of the roofs had been burned through, leaving holes that sent up ashes and other debris whenever a spray of wind dropped down from the sky.

Traveling inches above the pavement, cars equipped with klaxons and strings of Christmas lights drove along Park Street. Their stereos boomed against the abandoned buildings, rattling Kap Kutter's lungs. He turned the corner, arriving at the house where authorities believed Ismail Citron had died. Yellow police tape was threaded along a chain link fence, snapping in the wind. Only the ruins of a chimney and the blackened frame of a tricycle were left in the rubble.

Kutter stood with his fingers in the gate, surveying the wreckage. Riding toward him in a car, the gangsters from Broadway called out again: "Yo, Grand-fucker Time. Got a secon'?"

Another low-rider followed the first one to the curb. Inside were four men in long black parkas, new sneakers, and black and silver baseball caps. Emboldened by these reinforcements, the teenagers and a few girls wearing miniskirts and bright red lipstick surrounded Kutter on the sidewalk.

"You Five-0?" asked the kid with the plastic wrist watch. He wore a gold ring in his nose and another one through his lower lip.

The wind riffled Kutter's hair as he looked into the faces surrounding him. Reaching into his pocket, he took out a cellular phone and snapped it open. Kutter pressed a button that rang through to WKUT, frowning at the teens before he glanced at the clouds overhead. "Yeah, headquarters," he said. "This is Kutter. Send in the team, please."

From the other end of the line, Elise Dominaux asked, "Is that you, Kap?"

"Roger," said Kutter. He held the phone up to catch the music and then drew it back to his ear. "I have an urgent two-fifteen over on Park Street. Over."

Elise spoke to someone else. "He must be drunk as a lord," she said.

Billy Bruce took the headset. "Kap, what the hell are you doing?" he asked.

Jay Atkinson

"I'm on Park Street," Kutter said. "There's trouble down here."

"There's been trouble on Park Street for about fifty years. Look—I'm gonna call Agent Maxwell right now. Stay where you are. I'll get them to send a car for you."

Black-trousered sentries had been posted at either end of the block, and the kid with the ring in his nose again approached Kutter. "Gimme the watch," he said. "This ain' no tee vee show."

Father Tom walked toward them in his priest's collar and denim jacket. He stopped a car by raising his hand and crossed without even glancing at the driver. "What's the problem?" asked the priest.

"Just in time," Kutter said. "I was gonna have to start cracking some heads."

"Not a good idea," said Father Tom, holding Kap by the elbows.

He released the sweaty, liquor-smelling man and fixed his gaze on the oldest boy, addressing him in Spanish. The gang became sullen in Father Tom's presence, but respectful. With eyes cast down to the pavement, they chewed toothpicks and nodded their heads to the music.

A police cruiser appeared and the teenagers evaporated, leaving Kap Kutter and Father Tom in front of the incinerated building.

"This isn't the Easter parade route," the patrolman said. "Better get in."

Kap Kutter and the priest hustled into the back seat of the cruiser. "What are you trying to do?" Father Tom asked Kutter.

"I was here the night of the fire," Kutter said, jerking his thumb toward the blackened lot. "And later on, I saw the dead boy." He gazed out the window. "But I never reported it."

The cop turned on his siren, accelerating past another cluster of teenagers. Over the radio, he identified himself as Herlihy and informed the dispatcher he had a possible witness to the arson on Park Street. The dispatcher spoke back to him and the roar of static filled the cruiser.

Except for his visits to Monsignor Borinquen in the hospital, Father Tom had been submerged in the rectory for more than two weeks. "What fire?" he asked. "What boy?"

Officer Herlihy glanced back for a moment. "Ismail Citron," he said.

Something struck Father Tom's heart. "Are you sure?" he asked.

"He was an eleven-year-old from the Broadway projects," the cop said. "He was beaten to death and burned."

"When did he die?" Father Tom asked.

The cop stuck out his lower lip. "Ahh, let's see—twelve days ago? They found him on February twenty-second."

Father Tom remembered the expression on Ismail Citron's face the last time they had seen each other; the boy looked like he was afraid of something and yet somehow resigned to it. At the time, it seemed to be connected to Monsignor Borinquen and what happened in the church sacristy. But there were other reasons for a priest to meet a parishioner in secret besides those of bondage and abuse. And without a voice to explain what had occurred, Borinquen would be unable to shed any light on the case. Only one thing was certain: the Monsignor had suffered his stroke several days before Ismail Citron disappeared.

Kutter turned to Father Tom. "I was up there," he said. "I saw the body." His head dropped and his fleshy hand waved at the air.

"Just tell the police what you know," Father Tom said.

Kutter took a handkerchief from his pocket and held it over his nose and mouth. "Yesterday they found that kid's little brother in the same place. I should have said something a lot sooner."

While Kutter seemed willing to defer to Father Tom's moral authority, the priest felt that authority ebbing away. His guilt over Monsignor Borinquen was like a stone inside his chest. A discussion with Borinquen probably would not have saved Ismail Citron, but keeping his eyes fixed on the parish might have prevented the death of a second child. Now he was busy praying, as they rode to the police station in silence.

Agent Maxwell, dressed in a gray suit and royal blue necktie, met them in the parking lot at the station. "Thank you, officer," he said, transferring the witnesses to his own car. "I'll take it from here."

"Where's the Chief?" asked Herlihy.

"Chief McNamara's at the arson center. That's where I'm headed," said Maxwell. "You go ahead and log them in. Mr. Kap Kutter of WKUT radio"—he pointed to the gray-haired man and then his finger wavered in the direction of the priest— "I'm sorry, I don't believe we've met."

"Father Tom Dailey of Holy Rosary church."

"Father Dailey—thanks for coming," said Maxwell, shaking the priest's hand. "I was planning to see you today, about Ismail Citron."

Soon the three men were speeding off again: Maxwell at the wheel, Father Tom in the front seat, and Kutter in the back. "I was at Bellevue the night of the fire," said Kutter. "We were chasing some guy dressed in shorts."

"Boris Johnson," the ATF agent said. "Go on."

"Up at the cemetery, I saw two other people carrying something," Kutter said.

"Can you identify them?" Maxwell asked.

"They were too far away. Then I followed their footprints into this real shabby part. It was a little hill, sort of. The guy in the running shorts was looking at something in the snow," said Kutter. "It was a body."

"Which turned out to be Ismail Citron?" Maxwell asked.

Kap Kutter couldn't bring himself to say the name. "Yeah. It was the kid." He fumbled in his coat for a pack of cigarettes. Before it was in sight, Maxwell asked, "Do you smoke Kools?"

"Yeah," said Kutter, removing the striped green package.

But Maxwell pre-empted him. "Not in my car, you don't." He made a U-turn toward Bellevue, which could be seen in the distance, against a lowering gray sky.

"Where we going?" Kutter asked.

"I want you to show me where you spotted these two people, where Boris Johnson was in proximity to them, and in what direction they were headed. I want a walk-through of all your movements, and the precise location of the body. Then I want to hear what was said, and who said

Jay Atkinson

it."

From their vantage point, the cemetery appeared like a sepulchral dome under its pall of snow. Maxwell gunned around a rotary that was decorated with a large stone cross, and then zoomed up Gill Avenue toward the cemetery. Over the radio, he called for a patrol car to meet them there.

Kutter told Maxwell to stop at the entrance to Bellevue. The three men disembarked, leaving the doors open behind them. Kap Kutter lit a cigarette and began puffing on it. The road was dry, and he walked downward into the bowl of the cemetery. "I was right about here," he said, "when I saw two people. The bigger one was carrying something that looked like a rolled up rug."

The cemetery was a checkerboard of mud and snow to the horizon. Honeycombs of ice were lying in patches over the terrain, leaching into the grass as they melted.

"Where were they headed?" asked Maxwell.

"Over there," said Kutter, pointing with his chin. "I started to follow them"—he paused at the edge of the lawn— "and then I saw Johnson again." Kutter squatted down, indicating the path just ahead. "He was going along that road."

Rick Maxwell set off across the marshy turf, beckoning after Father Tom and Kutter. "Okay, then what happened?" he asked.

"The snow was deep," Kutter said. "I got in the limo, and we drove over to the woods." He remained on the pavement, gesturing back toward the car. "The easiest way is to drive," he said.

Rick Maxwell shook his head. "You and Boris Johnson were the first to see the kid after he died. And when I visited you the next day, not a word was said. That means you withheld information related to a capital crime." Maxwell began slogging across the turf. "So you're gonna have to get your shoes a little dirty as we work through this thing, since otherwise you'll be subpoenaed and find yourself in front of a grand jury."

It was almost a mile to the crime scene, and the three men trudged in that direction with hands in their pockets. Upon gaining the road, the only sound was the scrape of shoes on the asphalt. "Where were these people the next time you saw them?" Maxwell asked.

Kutter pointed a little farther ahead. "Over there. By the time we drove up, they were gone."

"Let's cut across," said Maxwell, walking between headstones. "Did anyone else in the limo see anything?"

"No. I guess the driver, Joe somebody-or-other, was busy watching the road. The limo barely fit down here."

Shadows fell over the gravestones, and the scream of a crow preceded the long black shape that glided overhead. "You can stay here if you like, Father," Maxwell said. "There's no reason for you to wade through all this muck."

"Please—I'll go along," said Father Tom. "I knew Ismail Citron."

Pockets of cold air lurked among the trees. The three visitors traveled in and out of them like they were passing through a series of refrigerated envelopes. At times the mushy snow grew deep, higher than their knees, and they moved in a slow, high-stepping motion to keep their pantlegs dry. In the thickest undergrowth some of the vines and low lying vegetation were adorned with tiny buds, one of the few signs that winter was ending. Occasionally warm air hovering over the snow created a strange tropical sensation, but no one spoke of it.

Led by Kap Kutter, the visitors walked past some strips of yellow police tape that were strewn over the ground. All around them hundreds of footprints dimpled the earth. On the spot where Ismail Citron was discovered, the snow had melted until just a box-shaped outline remained on the ground.

Kutter halted. "That's where I saw Johnson standing over the body," he said.

Father Tom came to Ismail Citron's resting place. He removed a purple scarf from his pocket and looped it around his neck. Then the priest knelt at each corner of the snow outline and pressed the cloth to the ground, murmuring in Latin. With his hand cleaving the air, Father Tom stood where the boy had been and made the sign of the cross.

Rick Maxwell waited until the priest was through before asking Kutter some questions. "Did Johnson say anything? Was there any sound from Johnson or the boy before you came into the clearing?"

"He told me that he saw a man and a woman burying something," Kutter said. "We followed the footprints and Johnson dug up the snow and we found the kid. Then Johnson ran away."

"What'd you do?" asked Maxwell.

Kap Kutter glanced at Father Tom. "I left."

Maxwell stretched his lips into a grimace. "First you smoked two cigarettes," he said. "I have 'em sitting on my desk in a plastic bag."

"Yeah, well, I screwed up," said Kutter. "I never should've come up here."

Father Tom was pacing around Ismail Citron's temporary grave. "But this young boy was murdered and you didn't do a thing about it," he said. The priest raised his eyes to Kap Kutter. "And now another child is dead. Sometimes you have to put your own fears aside—can't you understand that?"

Kutter swung his head toward Maxwell. "I had nothing to do with any of it."

"You, Mr. Kutter, are a material witness to a murder who withheld information from the police," Maxwell said. "Your cooperation from this moment on will help decide whether you are charged with that crime or not."

Maxwell turned to Father Tom. "Let's go see the Monsignor," he said.

They rode across town to Lawrence General. Inside the lobby was a vacuum cleaner, standing near the gift shop. It had been left running, and the smell of a burned-out motor filled the air. Rick Maxwell used his foot to knock the plug out of the wall. "That's a fire hazard," he said.

On the dingy carpet they ran into Father O'Connell from Manchester

Jay Atkinson

College. "We're on our way up to see Monsignor Borinquen right now," said Father Tom.

Father O'Connell arched his eyebrows. "Monsignor Borinquen is ill?"

"Oh, I'm sorry. I just assumed—" said Father Tom. "The Monsignor is in the cardiac unit."

"Actually, I'm here to see about a patron of the college who died this morning. I wanted to be sure his needs were being met."

At that moment the electric doors were flung open and the Cardinal Archbishop marched into the lobby wearing an expensive raincoat and his red satin skullcap. "Eamonn," he said, crossing the room to greet Father O'Connell. "I came as soon as I heard."

There was the smell of burnt offerings where the heavyweights of the Catholic church embraced. With Kap Kutter and Agent Maxwell standing beside him, Father Tom was at a loss. He couldn't understand why O'Connell and the Cardinal Archbishop would visit a dead man when the hospital chaplain was capable of performing the last rites and contacting the family. Then it dawned on him: they were busying themselves with the poor fellow Reverend Cruikshank had mentioned in the taxi. Someone named Beaumont had died and they were sniffing around for his money.

Father Tom felt sick. Such high-level urgency, bustling in with their cellular phones and calculators, as if Walter Beaumont's death was a piece of official business. If it had been within their powers, the Cardinal Archbishop and Father O'Connell would have resurrected Beaumont and made him sign documents. On the other hand, Joseph Borinquen and his thirty years of service to the church were not even a concern—and the Monsignor still clung to life. His heart was beating in a room on the third floor.

To Father Tom, the thought of "death" came freighted with the associated meanings of teeth and tear and deed and dearth and dear and heath and head and hearth, jammed together with earth and ear and eat and dread, then tea, heart, art and health. But life, life meant only the sacred heart of Jesus Christ, wherever He could be found.

The three priests, the federal agent and the radio station manager regarded each other like so many foreign diplomats. Then Reverend Cruikshank came in, slipping along the wall toward the elevator, and Eamonn Carr O'Connell stared thunderbolts at him. "Good afternoon, gentlemen," said Cruikshank. The elevator doors opened and closed again and he descended toward the morgue.

The Cardinal Archbishop's face indicated a question. "Episcopal," said Father O'Connell, and the two clerics frowned at each other.

As everyone hesitated with one foot in the air, unsure of what to say and where to go next, Philbin Bates strode through the electric doors. With a briefcase tucked under his arm, the attorney zoomed past the congregation in a blur.

Eamonn Carr O'Connell patted Father Tom on the sleeve. "You go ahead up to the Monsignor," he said, flagging down Bates. "I have some business to take care of."

Baffled now, the Cardinal Archbishop swiveled toward Father Tom. "What's this?" he asked.

"Monsignor Borinquen has suffered a stroke, your Excellency. He's here in the cardiac unit."

"My, my," the Cardinal Archbishop said. "How bad is it?"

"It's very serious, I'm afraid."

His Excellency made a clucking sound. "Ugh. That's tragic. Why wasn't I informed?"

"I called your office three weeks ago," Father Tom said.

"I don't recall receiving that message," said the Cardinal Archbishop, stammering a little. He surveyed the lobby. "Well, I'll certainly mention him during my appeal for the sick. And if I have a moment, I'll stop in."

Rick Maxwell took a call on his phone just as the Cardinal Archbishop received one on his. Their elbows touching. Father Tom and Kap Kutter edged toward the gift shop. Not to be outdone, Kutter unfolded his own telephone and called the radio station. "Elise? I'm at the hospital. No, someone else is going under," he said. "Is my hot tub guy still around?"

Near the elevator, Eamonn Carr O'Connell intercepted Attorney Bates. "Is everything in order?" Father O'Connell asked.

"The funeral arrangements are being taken care of, if that's what you mean," said Bates.

"What about Walter's other wishes—were they transacted?" O'Connell wanted to know, his eyes steady beneath snowy brows.

The lawyer's face stiffened. "Probate issues are always very sensitive," he said. "But rest assured that as executor, I'll be sending out prompt notices to any person or entity with an interest in Mr. Beaumont's estate." Bates paused for a moment, his displeasure apparent in the weight that seemed to be pressing his jaw downward. "I thought I'd hold off until the man was given a decent burial."

"Of course," said Father O'Connell. "We at Manchester College are concerned about the life and legacy of Walter Beaumont, in every respect. If there is anything we can do, please let me know."

The two men shook hands. "You could pray for him," said Bates, maintaining his grip.

"Don't worry about that," said O'Connell. "Walter Beaumont is on everyone's mind at Manchester College."

"I'm sure he is," said Bates.

The Cardinal Archbishop waved Father O'Connell to the door. "What's going on?" he asked.

"That's Walter Beaumont's attorney," said O'Connell.

"It's all in the hands of lawyers now, anyway," the Cardinal Archbishop said. "Eamonn—I have to get going. Why don't you ride with me?"

The two clergymen went through the doors into the parking lot. Then the elevator returned to the lobby and Agent Maxwell, Kap Kutter, Father Tom, and Attorney Bates, who had ducked into the hospital office for a moment, crowded on board. The men gazed up at the ceiling where "heaven" was scrawled in blue ink. Kap Kutter glanced down and noticed "hell" written at his feet.

Agent Maxwell and his companions stopped at the third floor. The wards were filled with the odor of urine smothered with disinfectant. A gurney carrying an enfeebled old woman rattled past into the elevator, and they hesitated when the woman began staring at them and reached out her hand. Father Tom took it for a moment and blessed her. "Christ be with you," he said.

Maxwell held the elevator door for Attorney Bates and the lawyer shook his head and smiled for a moment. "I'm going down," he said. "But it's nice to see you again."

Father Tom led the way to the cardiac unit. Pausing to take another telephone call, Maxwell signaled for the priest to wait a moment. Ahead of them in the corridor, a pretty young nurse streaked from one doorway to the other, and Father Tom glanced at the woman's backside.

"Ha," Kap Kutter said. "I saw that."

"I don't know what you're talking about," said Father Tom, turning red.

Kutter smirked at him. "Don't kid a kidder," he said.

Agent Maxwell finished his call and then pocketed the telephone, waving them forward.

"Hell, I thought priests were gay," said Kutter. When Father Tom scowled at him, Kutter added, "What do I know, I was raised by a bunch of atheists."

Monsignor Borinquen's face was ashen and his eyes were closed when Rick Maxwell entered the room. The priest's arms hung from the hospital gown, exposing his tattoos. Beside the bed several machines recorded Borinquen's heartbeat, which rose as high as one hundred-eighty and then dropped into the forties. A nurse poked her head in the door and frowned at the visitors, but kept silent upon recognizing Father Tom. She checked Monsignor Borinquen's vital signs, scribbled something on a chart and then padded away.

The Monsignor was asleep. Maxwell and Father Tom waited for several minutes while Kap Kutter lingered in the hall with an unlit cigarette hanging from his lips. Finally, Borinquen opened his eyes and they could see that the left side of his face was immobile.

"I'm sorry to bother you, Monsignor," said Father Tom. "This is Agent Rick Maxwell from the bureau of Alcohol, Tobacco and Firearms. He's investigating the death of Ismail Citron."

The side of Borinquen's face twitched and his gray eyes stared at the ceiling. "Monsignor, a few days after you became ill, Ismail Citron was found dead of asphyxiation with burns on his legs." said Maxwell. "His four-year-old half brother is also dead and we have the mother, Carmelita Diaz, in custody."

"I know this is taxing, Monsignor; we won't stay very long," said Father Tom.

"When Ismail Citron came to see you, did he mention the name Tito Jackson?" asked Maxwell. "He's the mother's boyfriend and he's been implicated in the death of the two children."

Monsignor Borinquen made a tiny sound deep in his throat. Amounting to less than a syllable, its meaning was inscrutable. With his palm held out, Father Tom indicated that the visit would not grow more productive, and he and Agent Maxwell retreated to the corridor.

"How long has he been like this?" Maxwell asked.

"Three weeks."

"Before Monsignor Borinquen had his stroke, did he say anything about Ismail Citron coming to see him."

Father Tom shook his head. "I didn't bring it up," he said.

Maxwell sighed. "I'm going to give Mr. Kutter a ride back to the radio station. Can I drop you somewhere, Father?"

"No, thanks. I'll stay with the Monsignor."

Kutter and Maxwell disappeared into the elevator. At the bedside, Father Tom dropped to his knees and petitioned for Ismail Citron, Hernan Diaz, Monsignor Borinquen, Rick Maxwell and Kap Kutter, Francesca Nesheim and Gabriel and Joe Glass, and for Eamonn Carr O'Connell and the Cardinal Archbishop and the soul of Walter Beaumont. Shifting into Latin, he glanced up and was surprised to see Monsignor Borinquen's lips moving over the prayers.

*

It was impossible for Rudy Pattavina to blend in with the crowd at the Disco Very, so he didn't even try. The police detective was off-duty, his badge and gun stuck in the pocket of the raincoat that was thrown over the stool beside him. The nightclub, about thirty feet wide and seventy feet long, was upholstered in some sort of dusty black mohair. Latin music that sounded like engine noise blasted from dozens of speakers, setting Pattavina on edge, and making it difficult to hear anything below a scream.

Rudy held a drink in his right hand and surveyed the chubby women wearing silver lamé gyrating on the dance floor, the men draped with gold chains eyeing him from along the wall, and the middle-aged couples who sat beneath a haze of cigarette smoke. For three straight nights, Rudy Pattavina had come to the Disco Very and emptied a quart of Scotch. This kind of detective work was like bottom fishing, waiting for something to drift to him on the currents.

No one spoke to Rudy but the hired help. Even at that, the bartender, who wore his hair in a glistening black pompadour, seemed upset whenever Pattavina said yes to another drink. But the detective continued his assault on their supply of Dewars, until the barman shook the last few drops from the bottle and smiled, revealing his gold tooth. Then Rudy would pay his tab and go home.

Each time he came into the nightclub, Pattavina sensed that the bartender and the chunky dancers flashing over the mohair floor and the men slinking along the walls knew why he was there, and who he was looking for. But the detective never asked for information regarding the whereabouts of Tito Jackson. Staking out a spot along the wall, Rudy just smoked cigarettes and held his ground.

On the fourth night, the bartender tried a new tack. "No more Scotch," he said, leaning over the bartop. "You drin' *todos.*"

Pattavina could smell the mixture of garlic and peppermint mouthwash on the man's breath. "Got any rum?" he asked.

An entire shelf was taken up with Ecuadorian rums, squat brown bottles of *Ron Rico de Cuba*, and rums from the Dominican Republic, Barbados and Puerto Rico. "*Si.*"

"Rum it is, then," said the detective.

When his glass was delivered, Rudy sensed someone looming behind him. "*Vamonos, cochino,*" said a voice. "Drink up."

Pattavina turned to face a barrel-chested man wearing leather pants and a sports coat that was too small for him, with dozens of metal buttons decorating the lapels. The man also wore a denim cap covered with buttons. Some of them advertised cigarettes and alcohol and were printed in Spanish, but one hanging from the brim of the cap was in English. Stamped on the button in tiny letters was *nosy little fucker, aren't you?*

"I'm not bothering anyone," said Pattavina, hoisting his glass.

"You botherin' me. I don' like pigs."

Pattavina looked in the man's gold-colored eyes. "I don't see any pigs," he said. "Just you."

Rudy drank undisturbed for another hour, working through the first bottle of rum and his package of cigarettes. It became obvious that the *hombre* in the denim jacket was some sort of enforcer. Loud discussions became quiet ones whenever he looked in that direction and several patrons left the bar when the man jerked his chin toward the exit. In addition, each guest paid homage to him, at least a nod of the head or a sign made with the first two fingers of the right hand. But the barrel-chested man ignored these tributes.

VIPs approached the man for a double handshake or an embrace, which he received stiffly. A few of the women danced faster when he was in their vicinity, but most shied together like ponies, averting their eyes. Suspended between these mysterious duties and an awkward form of socializing, the barrel-chested man wasn't a bouncer in the traditional sense. He stayed away from the hatch-like door of the club, preferring to navigate around the room in disinterested fashion. Every twenty minutes of so, he tapped his glass against the Formica and the man with the pompadour refreshed it with a syrupy concoction.

After midnight, when a good portion of the crowd had been siphoned off to the Boca Mal disco, the enforcer came back to the bar. Rudy Pattavina was rum-drunk in a way that Scotch never affected him. The walls of the club palpitated with his heartbeat, and he kept misplacing his cigarettes that burned across three different ashtrays. Rudy wished to go home, but his head was swimming and his various joints had ossified against the bar stool. The thump of the music was so constant that only sudden bright passages flared up in his consciousness. Flashes of silver lamé on the dance floor joined with the music and then flickered out, like fish disappearing into murky water.

"*Otra vase,*" said the enforcer. The bartender slid to the wall and removed a top-shelf bottle of rum. He filled a tumbler to the brim, placing it in front of Rudy.

"For you," the barrel-chested man said.

The detective waved at the rum. "No more," he said.

"Then get out," the enforcer said.

Pattavina rose to his feet. He wriggled into his coat, the reassuring weight of his gun swinging in the pocket. "I wanna talk to Tito Jackson," he said. His jaw felt like it had been shot with Novocaine.

The barman smiled. "Not tonight," he said, shaking his brilliantined head.

"*Que?*" the enforcer asked, blinking at Rudy. When his eyes opened again, the gold irises were runny with light. "Wha' you wan'?"

In his drunken exhaustion, Rudy shouted, "I want Tito," and several patrons jerked their heads around and began staring at him.

The man in the denim sports jacket shoved off from the bar, parting the crowd like a tugboat, and Rudy hitched up his trousers and followed him. The music throbbed in his groin, and Pattavina felt like he was squeezing through the bowels of an animal. In the corner there was a door, unrecognizable from even a few feet away. The barrel-chested man opened it and Pattavina descended a set of mohair stairs into a room paneled with driftwood.

A Latino man dressed in black velvet trousers, a tight black jersey, and black shoes was inside, dancing with two young women. Against the wall was a bar, its surface cluttered with glasses and bottles and a filmy mirror. The enforcer closed the door behind them, sealing off the racket from the discotheque. Immediately the room filled with marijuana smoke, along with several varieties of perfume and cologne.

"Wha's this *cabron* doin' here?" asked the young Latino. Around his neck was a gold chain thick enough to tow a car. He wore two gold rings, one on each hand that spelled out *New* and *York*. On his right wrist was a bracelet identifying him as *Kuko,* and he had a crown tattooed on his neck.

"He wanna know somethin'," the barrel-chested man said.

"He don' know nuthin' with that bug ass raincoat and them wash 'n' wear pants," said Kuko.

This bit of theater set the young woman on his arm braying like a mule. She was taller than Kuko and had long black hair and an enormous, bubble-shaped rear end. Her dress, which stretched over an ample frame, was made from a bright red material that whistled when she moved. Kuko rubbed her hindquarters and the woman slinked against him like a cat.

"I wanna talk to Tito Jackson," said Rudy. "You know where he is?"

The two women made a ululating sound, like Rudy had breached etiquette and was about to face the consequences. Kuko leaned toward Pattavina until their noses were touching. "Maybe I could stuff Tito up your ass," he said.

"I'm looking for a guy that killed two kids," said the detective. "You can help me out, or I can shut this place down for fire code violations, serving alcohol to minors, the presence of drugs and drug paraphernalia, and maintaining an after hours club without a license."

Rudy Pattavina saw Kuko's punch coming and braced himself; it felt like a bee sting. He turned to face the enforcer and kicked him in the groin when he came forward. The man fell to the ground and the two women bent over him, throwing their rear ends toward the ceiling.

"Okay," said Pattavina. "Let's talk about Tito Jackson."

Kuko shrugged his shoulders. "He's free-lance," said the gang leader. From his pocket he took a fob attached to a gold chain. "An old *cabron* paid for some job, and Tito fucked it up."

"Who was he working for?"

"Some old *jefe*. He's dead now," said Kuko. He turned over a glass and poured himself something from one of the decanters on the bar.

Rudy took a cigarette from a package on the bar and lit it. Looking at Kuko's fob he realized it was a gold-plated tooth. "So where's Tito?" the detective asked.

"I don' let him in my place. Maybe he's at the Boca Mal."

The detective scanned the walls. Hanging over the bar was an old sepia photograph of a man with gray hair inside the Ayer Mill tower. He stood beside another fellow, who had a long white beard. Attached to the gray-haired man's watch chain was a human tooth.

"I'll see you," said Pattavina, heading toward the door.

"Yo," Kuko called after him. "Latin Kings rule."

Rudy Pattavina checked his footing on the mohair steps. "Better work on that punch," he said.

*

Broadway was deserted, and the night sky was mild and starless. Rudy swayed on a patch of sidewalk, lighting a cigarette. Out of nowhere, a hearse drove by headed for Lawrence General, and then the thoroughfare was silent. Rudy took a drag on his cigarette, looking up and down the street, but couldn't remember where his car was parked. Lost in the old neighborhood, he was thirsty for another drink. He wanted Scotch—all that rum weighed on him like a giant ball of sugar.

The detective got his bearings and headed downtown, his footfalls loud on the pavement. He stopped once and listened to them echo in the doorways across the street, continuing for a distance beyond where he stood and then fading out. Rudy could feel the pressure of the old buildings looming above him, moving like glaciers along Broadway. As he staggered toward the Boca Mal disco, swaying in and out of the garbage piles lining the sidewalk, an old tune formed in his head and he began singing:

> *There's no business like show business*
> *Like no business I know*

His voice was reedy and thin, floating among the vacant grocery stores and shoe shops. Rudy Pattavina had grown up on Broadway, roaming with his pals Wimpy Latulippe and Spitty Hayes and a funny little guy named Chicken Riendeau. Back in the 50s, Lawrence was teeming with fruit stands and bakeries and appliance repair shops. The gang hustled from noon until midnight, selling newspapers, shining shoes and running errands for the shopkeepers when they weren't stealing from their stores.

When Frank Sinatra or Vic Damone came out with a new song, the gang would sit on Rudy's fire escape listening to WKUT. Later Spitty would gather them in the alley between the Palace and Apollo Theatres, where they would harmonize on original numbers like "Sugar Boy" and "Homesick on Haberdash Street." All that brick made for great acoustics, and their snapping fingers sounded like gunshots. Once in a while, the head usher Tommy Maloof would come out for a smoke in his embroidered red suit and bellman's cap. After a rousing serenade, Maloof would let them in the back door for a free matinee: Ward Bond and Lillian Russell in the latest B western, or something with Robert Montgomery and dark-eyed Myrna Loy. There was no story to most of these pictures, just women in cocktail dresses and tall, narrow-waisted men, gliding around in rooms filled with smoke.

The Capri Cafe on Essex Street was the most popular club, attracting GI's in their uniforms, the late moviegoers from the theaters along Broadway, and the politicians like Wilson X. Wilson and Paul Quebec, Sr. In those days, Bronco Castricone worked the door at the Capri. He was forty-five years old, a former boxer and professional wrestler who could crack walnuts between his fingers. If an under-age person showed up, blustering like a swell and waving cash around, it was impossible to fool Castricone. The barflies used to say that he was Lawrence's only heavyweight truant officer.

But one night Chicken Riendeau put lifts in his shoes, padded the shoulders in his father's jacket, and sneaked past Castricone in a snap-brim hat. Rudy and Wimpy Latulippe and Spitty Hayes watched from Joe Binette's diner as Chicken, unsteady in his elevator shoes, wobbled up to the bar and ordered a drink. For a ten minutes he played the part, sipping a Manhattan and trying to disguise his adolescent neck inside a collar that was three sizes too big. Then Bronco recognized him and heaved Riendeau through the door.

Chicken Riendeau sprinted down Essex Street, losing his hat into the canal while Rudy and the boys killed themselves laughing. When they caught up with Riendeau alongside Holy Rosary church, they convinced him to piece the disguise back together and purchase a bottle of whiskey at Halloran's Package Store. When this gambit proved successful, they retired to the canal and passed the bottle around. Drunk for the first time, they went arm in arm down Broadway singing "A Fellow Needs a Girl" at the top of their lungs. For hours, the gang marauded up and down the strip; if a cop came along, they just darted into one of the alleys. Rudy felt like the lord of the city, his head full of wild plans for making money and living the high life.

It had been forty years since Rudy Pattavina had been drunk and singing on Broadway. In place of the Palace and the Broadway and the Modern and the Strand movie theaters were vacant lots filled with trash, and the dingy facades of Jiminez Travel and the Windsor Hotel. The Capri had long since burned down. Tommy Maloof and Bronco Castricone and all the old matinee idols were dead. Spitty Hayes had been run over by a streetcar when he was nineteen. In 1953, Chicken Riendeau joined the Marine Corps and shipped out to Korea; three months later he disappeared in a plane crash. Of the old gang, only Rudy and Wimpy Latulippe were still alive. Wimpy lived up in Salisbury, and the two childhood pals had not seen each other in decades.

As he stumbled past his old haunts, Rudy's off-key rendition of "Summertime" wafted along the storefronts. In recent weeks, WKUT had been playing the songs from Rudy's salad days and he listened at home, in his car, and at the station house; he even had a transistor radio hanging in his bathroom and that morning had blasted "Take the A Train" when he was in the shower. The big band sound had always been there, dancing in Rudy's bones, and the recent flood of Duke Ellington and Sinatra and Bing Crosby had prompted him to stake out the Disco Very during his free time. He needed to thank Billy Bruce, the disc jockey—the man was a programming genius.

Right now he needed a piss. He hurried past the used clothing stores and *bodegas* with what felt like a bag of mush growing in his abdomen. Rudy tried the doorknobs of a few abandoned buildings and turned the corner onto Annis Street, but one alleyway after another was sealed with concertina wire or boarded shut.

The detective arrived at a flimsy wooden gate. He looked up and down the sidewalk, his bladder grown rigid. Pattavina leaned over, but couldn't reach the lock on the other side. Rearing back, he kicked the gate off its hinges, and the wood made a splintering sound as he trampled over it and moved into the alley. Painted over the bricks was an advertisement for Knickerbocker Beer; a man in a cocked hat drinking from a great frothing mug. It was on this spot in 1952 that Rudy Pattavina had seen his first naked woman. Mary Lou Tardiff had been with Wimpy Latulippe in the balcony of the Palace Theater and then, after a showing of *The Best Days of Our Lives*, she became separated from Latulippe and ended up here, with Rudy.

The strip was crowded that night as three movies let out at once, and the streetcars jangled up and down Broadway. A quick glance at each other, and Rudy and Mary Lou dashed away holding hands. Over the rooftops, they could hear Wimpy calling for them. Rudy felt like Arthur Kennedy in the movie he had just seen, mysterious and wavy-haired and full of unexpressed passion. While the other kids streamed past the alley, Rudy pressed against Mary Lou and ran his hands over her soft breasts. Eyes closed, the little brunette stood against the wall with her arms down at her sides. In a moment, Rudy was groping at the clasp on her brassiere. When she didn't offer any resistance, he took down Mary Lou's plaid skirt and underpants.

Tommy Maloof had made her in the balcony at the Palace and had seen her there the next week with a sailor from Lowell. Now Rudy himself was confronted with Mary Lou Tardiff's hairy plum, and didn't know where to begin. He put a finger in there and it came out smelling like burlap. A moment later, the cop on the beat hallooed into the alley and Rudy abandoned his conquest. Going faster and faster, over brick walls and through yards hung with flapping laundry, he ran for his life.

*

Feeling better after a torrential piss, the detective found his way back to Broadway. A breeze swept along the sidewalk, circulating within his trousers. Rudy's zipper was caught on his shirt and he tugged at the loose end, jiggling the tiny lever. Just then a sedan rolled to the curb and someone called his name. With his pants undone Rudy looked around at all the cement and brick, and a nameless terror flashed through his chest; the Latin Kings could have had an arsenal trained on him, and there was no time to react and nowhere to go. His raincoat was twisted around his legs and he couldn't find the butt of the gun. Then the driver of the car leaned out and Rudy saw that it was Chief McNamara.

The Chief waved. "Get in."

Rudy climbed into the passenger seat. His shirt tail was hanging from his zipper and the wings of his raincoat were tangled between his legs. "Hiya, Chief," said Pattavina. The music from the nightclub still rang in his ears. "I'm a little drunk."

Tug McNamara exhaled through his nostrils. "I guess you are."

"I been in that Spanish joint," Pattavina said. "Tryin' to find Tito Jackson."

"And trying to drink the bar dry, by the looks of it," the Chief said. He scratched at his crewcut, amused at Pattavina's condition. "Did you see anything?" he asked.

"Yessir," said Rudy, patting the bulge in his raincoat. "I'm getting an eyeful."

McNamara noticed the welt on Rudy's face. "What happened?" the Chief asked.

"Kuko Carrero says an old guy hired Tito Jackson for some torch work, and Tito screwed it up. I heard he might be in the Boca Mal."

Chief McNamara wrote something on a little notebook attached to the dashboard. "Why don't I drive you home?" he asked. "I'll go down to the Boca Mal myself." The Chief was dressed in coaching shoes, a pair of dark blue slacks and a Police Athletic League sweatshirt.

"Not in that get-up, you won't," said Pattavina.

McNamara laughed. "I guess you're right," he said. "I'll swing around and park out back. Are you carrying your weapon?"

"Affirmative," said Pattavina. He screwed up his face.

"Give it to me," McNamara said.

Pattavina untangled the ends of his raincoat and removed his gun, a nine millimeter Beretta. "I can't shoot straight, anyway," he said.

"At least zip up your fly, detective," McNamara said.

Once on the sidewalk, Pattavina got his zipper and the wings of his raincoat in order, and then sauntered toward the Boca Mal disco. The nightclub was covered in stonework lined with fluorescent pink grout.

Rudy walked beneath a cowl-shaped awning that was straining in the wind and heaved on the doorknob. A great puff of smoke escaped from inside.

Idling at the curb, Chief McNamara watched his detective enter the Boca Mal. A minute later, the cell phone buzzed on his hip; it was Rick Maxwell.

"What's happening?" the ATF agent asked.

A louvered purple Mustang with tinted windows pulled up in front of the nightclub. "I'm outside the Boca Mal," the Chief said. "I see a guy wearing a dungaree sports coat, and another guy with enough gold around his neck to fill a thousand teeth. Kuko Carrero and his bodyguard."

"I'll be right over," said Maxwell.

*

The Boca Mal was hot and smoky, with music that sounded like angry chimpanzees banging on sheet metal. Pattavina spotted one of the witnesses from the Ismail Citron case: Joe Glass, the limousine driver. He was with Brenda Steffanelli and they had their arms around each other, whispering and giggling. Brenda was waving a cigarette around and the limo driver was trying to knock it out of her hand.

More than two hundred people were contained within the pink interior of the Boca Mal, when half as many would have been a crowd. Rudy ordered a Scotch. The bartender nodded his shaven head, took Rudy's ten dollars, and produced five cans of beer. "*Cervesas,*" he said.

"I asked for Scotch," said Pattavina.

"*Si*. But you get *cervesas,*" the barman said.

Rudy lumbered onto the dance floor, elbowing his way along until he found Joe Glass and his date. Brenda's hair was sprayed into a lion's mane, and she wore heavy purple mascara.

"Have a *cervesa,*" Rudy shouted at them.

Glass took one of the sweating cans. "Cheers," he said.

The music went around like something unspooling from a reel. "Seen Kap Kutter lately?" Rudy asked.

"The last time I saw him he was puking in a wastebasket," said Glass.

One thing Joe Glass and Detective Pattavina had agreed upon during their interview was that neither of them liked Kap Kutter very much. But Glass had signed a statement indicating he was with Kutter that night in the cemetery, except for five minutes when the radio station manager had disappeared into the woods. So Kutter couldn't have had anything to do with Ismail Citron's death.

Pattavina ripped open a can of beer. "What are you doing here?" he asked.

"There aren't many places you can go at two o'clock in the morning," Brenda said.

Rudy herded the young lovers behind one of the speakers. The effect was like stepping behind a rock during a hurricane. "I'm looking for a guy named Tito Jackson," Pattavina said.

Brenda looked gimlet-eyed. "There's a Tito who comes around," she said.

"Ever heard of Kuko Carrero?" asked the detective.

Just then Kuko entered the nightclub with his bodyguard following him. "Yeah. He's right there," said Joe. People on the dance floor avoided eye contact and got out of Kuko's way.

"If he comes near me I'll blast him with my stun gun," Brenda said.

The detective turned. "Got it with you?" he asked.

"I'm packing a stun gun, mace, and an air horn," said Brenda, patting the bulge in her purse. "Fear no evil."

Rudy led the way across the beer-slicked floor. The music beat down from everywhere, including speakers attached to the ceiling, and the dancers were halved and quartered and then made whole again by the rotating lights. A marshy smell filled the room, punctuated by patches of jasmine and rosewater. The hair of the women flew in all directions, making a spray in the air while the music pulsed louder and faster.

Brenda Steffanelli grabbed Rudy's elbow. With her other hand, she directed his chin toward the far wall. Sunk down in a chair was a man wearing a black leather hat, yellow dungarees, and a pair of sandals. Everyone was bopping to the music except for him.

"Tito," Brenda said in Pattavina's ear.

The detective slipped his hand inside the purse, fumbling for a weapon. His fingers closed on a stubby pistol grip. It had a stock and trigger mechanism, but no barrel.

"He's gonna run on you," Brenda said.

Kuko was talking to the barman, while the man in the denim sports jacket scanned the club from behind a pair of sunglasses. Then he nudged Kuko, and the gang leader turned from the bar and stared at the man in the easy chair.

Rudy lunged forward, scrambling between a huge woman in a bright orange dress and two men in straw hats who were dancing with her. Before he could reach Tito's chair, the woman in the orange dress grabbed Rudy by the collar. She had a grip like a wrestler, and turned Pattavina half-around until her face was only inches from his.

"Don' cut in on Mama Lopez if you ain' gonna dance," she said, laughing at him. Her face was like a melon, with spots of color in both cheeks. Opposite her, the two men in straw hats danced on, their white socks flashing.

The straw hats looked worried. Although rivals for Mama Lopez's affection, they presented Rudy with a unified front. "Go away," one of them said.

Kuko Carrero reached Tito first and kicked at his sandal. In the flash of a strobe light, Rudy got a look at Tito Jackson. The brim of the hat came up, revealing bloodshot eyes, jaundiced skin, and a cruel-looking mustache and goatee.

"Get up," Kuko said.

"Leave me alone," said Tito. "I'm sick."

Kuko kicked him again. "Up," he said.

In an instant, Tito was running for the exit. The man in the denim

Jay Atkinson

sports coat tried to tackle him, but he missed and rolled onto the dance floor, knocking down Mama Lopez and her admirers.

Rudy Pattavina cleared a space in the crowd, aiming what he thought was the stun gun. "Police! Get out of the way," he said, and pulled the trigger. There was the terrific blast of a siren.

"That's the air horn," Brenda said.

"No shit," said Rudy.

Tito sprinted for the door. Someone tried to talk to him, but he pushed the man away and jumped the stairs. Joe Glass clutched Brenda to his side, as Kuko and his bodyguard and Rudy Pattavina converged on the exit.

"Adios," Joe said.

When he hit the sidewalk, Tito Jackson ran down the alley and out through the parking lot. The enforcer chased after him, but Kuko stayed with the Mustang, leaning against its glossy purple flank, his eyes shining in the streetlights. Rudy Pattavina took one look at the distance between where he was standing and the murder suspect, and went over beside Kuko.

"Off," said the gang leader when Rudy touched his car. "I polish that shit all day long."

"You're sitting on it," Rudy said.

Kuko picked at the seat of his pants. "My ass is buffin' the thing."

Rudy's hand left an impression in the wax. "Pretty soon your ass is gonna be buffing a jail cell," he said. "Then you'll see *me* tooling around in this rig."

"That ain't tonight," Kuko said, laughing.

Two patrol cars flashed by on Broadway, their blue lights rotating against the storefronts. "Tito sure is a dumb fucker," said Rudy.

"One monkey don't stop the circus show," the gang leader said.

Cop and crook stared up at the mild blank sky. The Ayer Mill clock glowed beside the risen moon, its face turned toward the light. "Beautiful city, man," Kuko said.

Detective Pattavina reached into the Mustang, helping himself to a pack of Kools on the dash. "What're you, the Chamber of Commerce?" he asked, lighting a cigarette.

"You got it, bro," the gang leader said. "Account representative."

Pattavina drew on the cigarette. "The wages of sin is death," he said.

"Word up," said Kuko. The gang leader mused on the great clock face. "Fish gonna eat the little fish, and then get eaten by the big fish. Everybody need a competition."

The detective pointed his cigarette at Kuko Carrero. "Think of me as the great white whale," said Rudy.

"It's a good thing you got away from Mama Lopez," Kuko said. "She stuff you with rice and beans, and suck your cock inside out. Get yourself a straw hat and move to French Street."

*

Attached to the Boca Mal was a joint called the Lucky Dragon, and then a gravel lot that led to Daisy Street and the Spicket River. Rick

Maxwell was in the parking lot talking to McNamara when a man in a leather hat ran past, leaped a fence with his heels sailing past his ears and disappeared into the alley. Moments later, a barrel-chested man charged through the parking lot, struggling over the same low spot in the fence.

"Get some back up," said Maxwell, running off.

The fence was still quivering from the last vaulter and went into spasms when the ATF agent mounted the rail. He felt the chain link spring back under his weight and catapult him into the alley.

Bullet holes through the window of a tailor shop made starbursts in the glass and empty shell casings littered the pavement. Maxwell unholstered his Beretta and took a flashlight from his pocket. Gliding over the asphalt, he shined the beam into one narrow space after another. The rest of the neighborhood was comprised of vacant lots and an appliance store that looked as impregnable as a bunker. A car that had been stripped to its chassis was the only vehicle on the street.

Behind another fence was the Spicket River, with patches of foam speckling the surface. Shattered bricks tumbled down both riverbanks, and half-sunken appliances jutted above the water. The river followed Daisy Street for a block and then veered off through a cluster of tenements standing black against the sky. Maxwell examined the fence for man-sized holes, but there were none. He sent the beam from his flashlight scaling over the water, and stopped on a washing machine resting in the shallows. Wisps of plastic clung to the fence and the branches of the trees, swaying in the wind. Over the first bridge, Maxwell found some old rusted gearing and a stack of wooden pallets but no Tito.

Footfalls came over the houses from the next street. Maxwell took a diagonal line across several vacant lots, heading for the noise. Then he jumped two more fences and sprinted for seventy or eighty yards. At the conclusion of an empty block, the man in the denim sports jacket stood in the roadway. He looked at Maxwell, and raised his hands and shrugged. A patrol car turned in behind Maxwell and the man ran off.

Agent Maxwell signaled the patrol car to wait, lodging itself in a bottleneck that divided Annis Street from the rest of the neighborhood. Beyond where Maxwell stood was a well-lit section of Broadway, with billboards advertising the Marine Corps and Naval Reserve. Along an arc, the Spicket ran for half a mile until it again bisected Annis Street. Getting over an eight-foot fence and into that nasty water seemed unlikely for a part-time arsonist and junkie. That meant the crescent where Tito Jackson was hiding contained no more than two dozen buildings, most of which featured bars on the lower windows, steel-reinforced doors, and padlocks.

A clang of the Ayer Mill bell marked the time as 2:30. Maxwell came to an alley that was crowded with garbage cans and he went along peering into each one. Then he took out his phone and made a brief report to Chief McNamara. Maxwell asked that the neighboring streets be blocked with cruisers and two other ATF agents summoned. The Chief said that several men were already on the ground, and Maxwell rogered that and hung up.

Jay Atkinson

Agent Maxwell checked the safety on his Beretta, and shined his flashlight into every nook and cranny along Spruce Street. A warehouse was flying a banner that read *Bargain! Building for sale Cheap!* Beside the warehouse was a dirt road that didn't appear on any city map. The ATF agent started down the road and a wind came up, throwing grit against his jacket. Shining his light ahead, Maxwell discovered a lot filled with salt and sand.

The wind ran over the dunes, until the sand undulated in every direction. The ATF agent pocketed his flashlight, and set off with his gun pointed ahead of him. As he climbed the first hill, he heard the sound of running water. It reminded him of the underground river at Bellevue, and he had the eerie feeling that he was mired in the silt of bones—granulated dead that had washed up in a final arid place.

Maxwell realized he was wandering through the municipal salt and sand supply, left over from a winter that had been cold and wet but not as bad as the meteorologists had predicted. He was more than halfway across, slogging in the deep sand, when he spotted a set of footprints in the lee of a hill. He descended the slope into a large white valley that carved aside the remaining elevation. Far off, Rick Maxwell heard the rumbling of trucks along Route 495 and much closer, the sound of denim gliding over the sand.

Quickly he withdrew his flashlight and held the gun and flashlight together, his arms raised to chest level. Maxwell dropped to one knee. Ahead of him, dimples spread out over the landscape for a hundred yards or so. They formed little foxholes where a man could crouch undetected. Again there was the sound of denim and then the ground shook when something thudded against it.

Duckwalking forward, Maxwell dropped into a foxhole, crawled out, and slid into the next one. Backed against the sand, he glanced at the sky and then his watch. It was a minute or so before three AM. Several yards away he heard a rustle of fabric and then the landscape around him grew quiet again. Maxwell waited for the mill clock to begin tolling and then leaped up, sprinting toward the suspect. At the last instant he stopped short, flinging himself into another depression. At the bottom of the hole his foot touched something; it was the suspect's leather hat; *Tito* was written in large black letters inside the brim. The ATF agent stuffed the hat into his pocket.

When the final clanging of the bell had trembled over the landscape, Maxwell heard something off to his right. On hands and knees, he gained the edge of a foxhole and peeked inside. Curled up in the fetal position was a man in yellow dungarees, pretending to be asleep.

Agent Maxwell shined the flashlight at him. "Get up, Tito," he said.

The man opened his eyes. "I no Tito," he said, raising his hands.

Maxwell yanked the suspect's arms down and applied a pair of handcuffs. Then he removed the leather hat from his pocket and turned it inside out so the man could read what was inscribed there. "Gimme a break," he said.

The ATF agent directed the suspect out of the hole. They crossed several dunes and came upon a U-shaped iron pipe thrusting out of the sand.

"Stop," Maxwell said. He unfastened one side of the cuffs and chained Tito to the pipe. A quick search of the suspect turned up neither weapons nor contraband.

"I di'n't do nothin'," said Tito.

"You used Ismail Citron to set fires," said Maxwell. "Then, when the kid got scared, you suffocated him with some rags. Ismail's four-year-old brother said he knew about the fires and you killed him, too—with rat poison."

Tito Jackson sat cross-legged. "You didn' read my rights, man," he said.

"All you jailbirds are experts," said Maxwell.

He squatted down; the sweat was pouring out of Tito's face and he looked yellow in the beam of the flashlight. "This is bullshit," Tito said.

"You killed two kids," said Maxwell. He pushed the barrel of his gun beneath Tito's chin. "*That's* bullshit."

Agent Maxwell lowered his gun and put his flashlight away and stood up. He contemplated the desert that surrounded them, cursing before he took out his phone.

The Chief answered right away. "Where are you?" he asked.

"Some big sand pile off Spruce Street. I got him."

"Fuck you, man," Tito said. The whites of his eyes were jaundiced, their dark centers floating in puddles of yellow. "Latin Kings rule."

Maxwell spotted Chief McNamara struggling toward them over the sand. He knelt to unlock the handcuffs, using a judo sweep to knock Tito down when he tried to run. Yanking Jackson up by his wrists, the ATF agent re-fastened the handcuffs.

McNamara wore his gold shield around his neck. "Any problems?" he asked.

Maxwell shook his head. He switched on his flashlight and, together with Tug McNamara's, the two beams of light converged on Tito Jackson's face.

"Was he carrying a weapon?" the Chief asked.

Maxwell shook his head, and the Chief grasped one of Tito's hands and examined it with his flashlight. There were brown spots on some of the fingers and several roughened areas dotted the suspect's left palm. "These burns are pretty old and he's tried to file them off with an emery board or something but he's a torch, all right," said McNamara.

"I want to take him to the outstation before we book him," Maxwell said.

"Okay, but we're on foot," said McNamara. "I don't have a unit."

Tito Jackson was roused to his feet, and Chief McNamara led them past several piles of rock salt onto Daisy Street. As they went along, Tito Jackson began crying. The two cops ignored him: a lot of people shed tears when they were arrested and remorse had little to do with it. Usually the perpetrator, who had eked out a living by stealing, selling dope, or in Tito's case, setting fires, was about to trade familiar surroundings for a world populated with second-rate lawyers, distracted judges and nasty, ill-tempered guards. It was a source of amusement in police stations all over the country that degenerates like Tito Jackson murdered children without thinking twice, and then got choked up over their own lost freedom.

The Chief looked at Maxwell and with a jerk of his chin, urged the ATF agent forward. "Tell me what's wrong, Jackson," McNamara said, when they were out of earshot. "Get it off your mind."

Jackson raised his face as they passed beneath an old crown-and-bulb streetlight. "Those fuckin' kids don' ever shut up," he said. "The oldest is saying Jesus is gonna save me and all this bullshit. One night I was sick and couldn't do the job."

"Who hired you?" McNamara asked.

"Some ol' white dude," Tito said. He wet his lips with his small purple tongue. "The dude say if he can see the fires, I get my money. The fuckin' kid, he's hanging around; he wan's a dollar, so I say sure, I'll give you ten fuckin' dollars, *pollo*. Just take this can over to Park Street, hide it there, and come back and tell me you done it. But he comes back and it ain' done. The kid say he went to church and tol' the fuckin' *padre*."

"What'd you do to the kid?" the Chief asked.

Jackson made fists inside the handcuffs. "I went into the room and grabbed the little square-headed one—"

"Hernan Diaz," McNamara said. His face was taut, and he leaned toward the suspect when Jackson's voice dropped to a mumble. "Then what happened?"

"I ran hot water in the sink and grabbed the little shit..." Tito buried his chin in his chest. Increasing the pace, he went along the sidewalk in silence.

The skin on Tito Jackson's face settled around his cheekbones like cement. "I put the kid near the water and he started screamin'. Then I tol' his brother to get the can, and he'll get his fuckin' money."

They arrived at a storefront on Bradford Street where the arson command post was located. Maxwell unlocked the door and went inside.

"Ismail Citron set the fire and then he came back to the apartment," McNamara prompted Tito.

"He didn' come back. So I wen' down there and some guy started chasin' me," said Tito. "But I got away and foun' the kid. He was gonna go back to the *padre*."

"So you did Ismail with the rags. And dumped him up at Bellevue."

Tito looked away. "Don' mess with me—I tell 'em that all the time." He shrugged. "But they don' listen."

"Who paid for the jobs?" asked the Chief. He stood with his arms folded over the Police Athletic League sweatshirt, his face rigid along the jawbone.

"Some dude on a oxygen machine."

Rick Maxwell came back out, accompanied by a man with curly black hair who wore a leather vest over his Temple University T-shirt.

The Chief nodded. "Hi, José," he said.

"That's the guy I was chasing," said the curly-haired agent. "Has he been Mirandized?"

McNamara glanced at Rick Maxwell, who shook his head.

"I'll take care of it right now," said Jose, leading Tito Jackson inside.

"Did he cop to it?" Maxwell asked the Chief.

McNamara shrugged. "None of it's worth anything."

"Why not?"

The Chief spat into the street. "I guess I'm just a 'due process' kind of guy," he said. "But we'll have enough to sink his ass. And the sponsor, too."

"Who is it?" asked Maxwell.

"An old white guy, he says."

There had been one hundred ninety-two fires of suspicious origin in Lawrence over an eighteen month period, and the cops knew that no single person could be responsible for so much damage. The Latin Kings had their hands in it, and some of the action came from free-lances and start-up gangs. For instance, the South Side Sultans were branching out from car theft to the more lucrative practice of selling crack cocaine, and burning down Ferry Street was their way of advertising a new service.

These were tactics used by any business that was struggling to survive. However, Rick Maxwell had been working on a new hypothesis. The ATF agent had learned that Lawrence Savings & Trust held paper on a number of abandoned properties, insuring them against fire. He was studying records at City Hall and the county probate court, in an effort to trace lien holders on each of the incinerated buildings. City tax records always listed the mortgagor, but many of the owners had defaulted and titles had to be searched to find out who had taken possession. Nothing in Lawrence was computerized: copies of tax bills were heaped in file cabinets and stored in boxes, along with dusty old parking tickets and fishing license applications. And the records at the probate court were even worse. Rick Maxwell's hunch was turning into a long, dirty bookkeeping exercise, but that was often the nature of police work.

"As soon as we get a list of Tito's jobs, we should be able to figure out who was bankrolling 'em," the ATF agent said.

Chief McNamara spat into the gutter. "I guess I should call the mayor," he said. "She'll want to organize a press conference, so she can tell everyone the case is solved."

"You've got a mayor who moonlights as a waitress," said Maxwell. "No wonder the city's going to hell."

14

Lawrence, Massachusetts
October 4, 1910

By the time Charles Foster wound up his tale of the Pemberton disaster, sleepy-eyed men were entering the firehouse and the night shift was going out, hauling their lunch pails and bidding one another good day. William Wood and Mr. Foster adjourned to the great wooden doors and stood for a moment beneath the arch.

"Come to the Ayer tonight and I'll stand you to a good meal," said Wood. "It isn't every day a fellow like me watches his dream rise up in brick and stone."

Three urchins were loitering beside the car when Wood strode into the alley. The tallest boy, about eleven years old, wore a moth-eaten jacket, knickers, and a scrap of wool around his neck, and his two confederates were dressed in little more than rags. They waited behind the limousine, out of the driver's sight. No doubt Mr. Morgan had already chased them away.

"Hey Mac, can you give us a dime?" the boy asked.

Wood hadn't noticed the trio and now he swung around to look at them. "A dime is a lot of money," he said. "What's your name, son?"

"Glass."

"What about your fellows—what's their part in this?"

"What I get, I share. But they don't speak English." The oldest boy pointed to the youngest, who had a head of fine black hair. "This one, he's Syrian. And Giuseppe"—he indicated the other lad, who wore a garment made from a tablecloth and a pair of old fashioned ladies' boots with the heels knocked off—"just come on the boat from Italy. He don't have nothin', so he don't say nothin'. "

"A successful man is always in a hurry, remember that," said Mr. Wood. "But if you come by the Ayer Mill, I might have something for you."

The oldest boy raised himself on tiptoe. "A dime?" he asked.

"You just ask for Mr. Beaumont," said Mr. Wood, opening the door to the limousine.

At that instant, the second bell rang, marking the time as 5:45 AM. Entire families poured from the tenements, joining the dormitory girls who linked arms and strolled toward the mills, four and five abreast. "What's this fellow going to give us?" the boy asked.

Wood paused with one leg inside the car. "What every boy needs," he said. "A job."

Soon William Wood was traveling along Haverhill Street and onto Jackson, his newspapers scattered over the floor and the mill workers peering in from either side. "There goes Billy Wood," said a fellow on the side of the road. "The best man what's ever lived in Lawrence, by God."

Wood rolled down his window for a blast of morning air. As the limousine rumbled over the Duck Bridge, the Ayer Mill grew in perspective, looming above the river. Its windows were shining with the dawn, their regularity broken only by the steel fans, spinning out the hot, damp air from the looms. High above, the clocks had their hands fixed at eight o'clock. During the ceremony this evening, they would be set in motion—the largest striking clock in the world.

Dick Morgan steered the car beyond the bridge, lingered as a wagon rattled past, and then turned onto Merrimack Street beside the Ayer Mill. Halfway along he stopped the car, and William Wood reached for the siphon tube. "Richard," he said. "I'll ask you to fetch Mr. Mills."

For fifty years, Hiram F. Mills had conducted experiments at a laboratory on the banks of the Merrimack, and with his hand-picked chemists, engineers, and biologists, had learned to accurately measure and control water pressure, leading to his benchmark treatise, *Flow of Water in Pipes*. Because of this work, the south canal on the Merrimack, recently extended to reach the Ayer Mill, operated with more efficiency than any other turbine system in existence.

Mills' crowning achievement, however, was a lengthy investigation into water purification spurred by the Lawrence typhoid epidemic of 1891. By examining the residue that Lawrence factories dumped into the river, and experimenting with various sorts of filters, Hiram Mills determined that typhoid fever was carried by polluted water. After constructing a 2 1/2-acre sand filter, Mills had caused the death rate to fall sixty percent and earned the title "the Father of American Sanitary Engineering."

Mr. Wood disembarked and went through the archway, beneath the word "office" carved in granite letters, and into 200 Merrimack Street. Beneath the clock tower, stairs led into a central pavilion that contained the timekeeper's room, mill agent's headquarters, countinghouse, and William Wood's executive office. In this region of the facility, little expense had been spared: tongue and groove joints created seamless mahogany paneling, and the walnut doorways and joists were decorated with handcarved Shawsheen Indian heads and American eagles, two of Wood's favorite motifs.

Passing through, Wood acknowledged the only employee occupying the countinghouse at such an early hour. His assistant treasurer *pro*

Jay Atkinson

tempore, Moses J. Stevens, sat huddled over the Ayer Mill ledger, writing out his accounts in a tight blue script. His efforts were fueled by a glass inkstand and scratched over the wide-lapped pages with a nib.

"Are we still in business, Mr. Stevens?" asked Wood.

"Robustly so, Mr. Wood," said Stevens.

Mr. Wood circled the desk, leaning over the treasurer to peruse his work. After a stint as a bell time worker in New Bedford, Massachusetts, Wood had started his career in bookkeeping and knew how to flush out the snipes hidden in a column of figures. For an entire minute, Mr. Wood scrutinized the accounts while beads of perspiration appeared on Stevens' bald head.

"One number disturbs me," said Wood.

His pen drying at the bottom of the page, Moses Stevens wet the nib once more and twisted halfway around to meet his employer's gaze. "Which number is that, sir?"

"Puzzle it out," said Wood, agitation creeping into his voice. The mill owner ran his finger along the left-hand column. "The cost of our new turbines here"—he stopped at an entry for six hydroelectric turbines listed at $9,000 apiece, and then moved across the page—"and the profit from those looms where their power is manifested over here."

In the past month the Ayer had begun changing over to Victor-Standard turbines, modern high-speed devices that helped convert waterpower to electricity, but the switch had brought along a marked fluctuation in profits.

"It's a plain reckoning," said Stevens. "Although the output of the new turbines is half again that of the old, the amount of time the turbines were inoperable has doubled—a total of seventy-four hours in the month of September." The assistant treasurer *pro tem* reached for a scrap of paper and executed a rapid algebraic formula. "We've lost approximately three percent of our gross production over the last thirty days."

"Three point two percent," said Wood. "But you've had your 'eureka' moment, Mr. Stevens. And from it certain recommendations are forthcoming, are they not?"

Stevens multiplied another column of figures by 'x' and then found for x. "Projecting our usage at full capacity, the new turbines will increase our output by eleven percent," said the clerk. Again he met Mr. Wood's gaze. "Surely that is desirable."

"When I purchased the new equipment, my calculation was twelve percent increased output," said Wood. "But that means running the Victor-Standard turbines at capacity for the entire month. Adjust for breakage, obstruction, acts of God, I'll come down to eight percent. But minus three point two? That's unacceptable."

William Wood's voice had risen over the past few moments, until Mr. Stevens snapped off his nib against the desk. He cowered as the mill owner upended a wastebasket and kicked it across the room. "Tell the foremen to keep those turbines running or look for new employment," said Wood.

"Am I really to tell them that, sir?" asked Mr. Stevens. "After all, I'm only temporary here."

"Be precise in that regard, Mr. Stevens, or your tenure will end sooner rather than later."

William Wood thumped his cane against the countinghouse floor and stalked off, muttering to himself. A moment later, he slammed through the door of his private office, startling the two women inside. One of the secretaries was sharpening a jar of pencils and she dropped it, shattering the glass and throwing its contents to the floor.

"Good morning, Mr. Wood," the woman said, kneeling to gather her pencils.

The mill owner grunted his reply and passed through a second door into his chamber. This office reflected none of the trappings of its occupant's wealth or status: a plain oak desk and chairs, a sideboard that contained five telephones, and hanging on the wall, photographs of his father-in-law Frederick J. Ayer and various business associates.

The secretary who had dropped the pencils appeared in the doorway. Miss Halliman was a prim young Englishwoman wearing a tweed skirt and jacket, her chestnut hair already threaded with silver and swept up in a bun. "Do you need me, sir?" she asked.

"Take a dictation, please," Wood said. "Memorandum to all overseers, foremen, inspectors, and second hands of the Ayer Mill, regarding the Victor-Standard turbines and their operation."

Miss Halliman produced a notepad from her skirt. "I'm ready, sir," she said, examining the tip of her pencil. "Memorandum eight-nineteen."

"'Gentlemen: our gross profitability was down three point two percent in September, on account of idleness in the turbine pit. It is imperative that our new turbines remain in operation at all times.' Emphasize last three words. 'Any loom remaining inactive more than one hour in a single week will result in three hours' dockage for all workers and terminations from pit to pulley to line shaft. Signed WMW.'"

Miss Halliman folded the top sheet over the back of the notepad, removed the carbon paper, and detached the memorandum. "Very good, sir," she said.

The other secretary, Mrs. Litwack, a short, heavy woman with black hair, entered the room carrying a pot of coffee and a salver that contained three raisin turnovers. William Wood poured himself a cup of coffee and ignored the sweets. "A second memorandum," he said. "To the overseer and foremen of the dyehouse."

Again Miss Halliman moistened her pencil, while Mrs. Litwack took the first memorandum and its carbon copy and left the room. "Memorandum eight-twenty," said the Englishwoman.

"'Gentlemen: we will soon be entering a bid for an important new item. It is imperative that the workers in your department commit to an additional hour in the morning and two hours in the evening, at the standard rate of pay, commencing immediately. Boys under fourteen exempt from the morning hour. Signed WMW.'" The mill owner fussed with the tooth on his watch chain. "Please hold this last memo until I give you the word."

Wood picked up the telephone to dial the operator. "That's all for now, Miss Halliman," he said, the receiver pinched against his shoulder.

"Very good, sir," the secretary said, detaching the carbon on her way out.

The telephone buzzed and then the operator broke in. Wood recited the number for Hiram Mills' residence and a few moments later, the gruff old engineer came on the line. "Mills," he said.

"Hiram, William here. I need you to have a look at my turbines."

"I'm afraid I'm very busy," said Mills.

"A professional courtesy," Wood said.

Mr. Mills hemmed into the line. "All right," he said.

Mills hung up and the in-house telephone rang. It was Frank Beaumont, the overseer's second hand. Young Beaumont was an up-and-comer, with the brisk, practical manner of his birthplace in Yorkshire, England.

"Good morning, sir. I'd like your permission to take a photograph at the clock dedication," said Beaumont. "A burnished plate featuring you and Mr. Ayer would be a nice keepsake."

"Will this interfere with your other duties?" Wood asked.

"I can take a photographic impression in less than a minute with my new equipment."

Wood gestured when Miss Halliman re-entered the office, motioning for her to unlock the door to the room where the safe was located. "If it won't cause an interruption, I see no reason to prevent a photograph from being taken," said Wood. "Anything else, Beaumont?"

"Yes, sir. There's an Italian weaver in Room Five, a man named Gallitelli, who meets with the other Italians in the worker's hall."

"So—he eats with other Italians. To each his own."

Beaumont cleared his throat. "Yesterday Gallitelli was overheard saying that once again his meal consisted of spaghetti drenched in olive oil, and skilled workers such as he and his countrymen should be able to afford a tomato on occasion," said the second hand. "I don't speak Italian, but one of the battery boys laughed and afterward I asked the lad what Gallitelli had said."

"Some nights I tell my wife how much I detest this place," said the mill owner. "Would you have me turned out of my office?"

The second hand continued in the same steady tone. "Gallitelli organized a weaver's guild in Milan and was one of its chieftains," he said. "He might be one of these labor agitators, sir."

"Why didn't you say so?" asked Wood. He stood clenching the receiver in his fist, using the other hand to wave his secretary about. "I'll have no *foreigner* organizing a union while resting at my table. These damned socialists should be thrown out of the country."

"Gallitelli's the most skilled weaver I have, taking charge of eight looms while the next best worker in the line handles three," Beaumont said. "If we need to maintain Room Five at capacity—and I know that we do—right now I can't manage it without Gallitelli. He's a talented fellow, sir."

"These damned Italians and their scheming," said Wood. "I don't treat my workers good enough, they want unions? We should put them all on a barge and send it over the Great Stone Dam."

The mill owner made Frank Beaumont wait as he chewed his lower lip. "Here's what you do, Beaumont," he said. "Take the best smash piecer you've got, the sharpest in the bunch, and apprentice him to your agitator for a week. When he's grasped the basic operation of the looms, assign two of them to your second best man and have the new fellow take two and you take four, until you can apprentice another fellow to the second best man. Then send that worthless guinea bastard through the door. Is that clear?"

"Yes, it is," said Beaumont.

Wood was as rigid as a beam, his knuckles white against the receiver. Out the windows, he could see the embankment of the river, dotted with the saplings he'd planted last spring. Directly across the Merrimack was his competitor in worsted woolens, the Kunhardt Mill. A segment of the bridge was also visible, crossed by horse-drawn wagons, pedestrians, and the occasional automobile.

"Is that all, Beaumont?" Wood asked.

"Three boys said you'd promised them jobs. They were a ragged bunch and I sent them away."

"I did speak to some boys this morning," said Wood. "You might use the oldest one to replace that smash piecer. The other two are useless: a couple of foreigners."

"Perhaps they'll come around again, sir."

"If not, someone will," William Wood said. "Your commission, Mr. Beaumont, is to keep those looms running. And don't you forget it."

"I won't, sir."

*

After discharging his passenger, Dick Morgan steered the Rolls Royce along Merrimack Street, and then turned between two stone pillars and through the main gates. Morgan angled the car beneath a drawbridge and into the courtyard located within the interior of the building. He drove to a sign that read "William Madison Wood," yanked on the handbrake, and climbed out of the limousine.

Gathered around the dock were the loom fixers, sweepers, scrubbers, change-over men and bobbin boys of Loom Rooms Four and Five, smoking their hand-rolled cigarettes and waiting for the third bell to ring them inside. The courtyard itself was flocked with pigeons and curlicues of excrement were scattered over the ground. An enclosed walkway connecting the buildings ran overhead, and occasionally the boards creaked when someone used this passage to save a trip around the complex.

"Hey, Dick," called a smash piecer named Gus Hearin. He was a tall, stringy man, thirty-one years old, with short blond hair that was like yarn. "Have you been riding on your ass all morning while having it ridden by Billy Wood?"

Dick Morgan's reputation preceded him into every nook and cranny of the American Woolen Company, and he felt no need to answer any such challenge. He was paid ten dollars a week to drive one of America's most powerful businessmen to his appointments and hear some of his most intimate conversations. Battery boys ran to hang up Dick Morgan's coat when he entered the mill and ran to open the door when he departed.

"If I worked as much as Morgan speaks, I'd be in the poorhouse," said Hearin.

Several Italian weavers leaned against the wall, conversing in their native tongue and smoking cigarettes. They were wearing alpaca coats and black sheepskin hats that came down to their eyebrows. One of the men, Enrico Marrone, winked at his companions and said, "If you keep at Dick Morgan, your teeth will be on the ground."

"Maybe I'll take a knock at you first," said Hearin, laughing back at him. He threw several punches at the air and then stopped. "But wait, you don't have any teeth."

In the midst of the weavers, a short, gray-haired fellow named Gallitelli spoke to his countryman in Italian and Marrone answered back with a few soft words and nodded his head. Looking satisfied, Gallitelli continued a monologue that had begun a few minutes earlier. He spoke with great passion about something while gesturing with his hands, and Dick Morgan found himself leaning that way, captivated by this dissertation though not understanding a word of it.

Across the courtyard, something disturbed a large gathering of pigeons and they soared in all directions, their wings beating the air. Two boys were running up from the canal, scattering the pigeons and then a bevy of drop wire girls, who gathered their skirts in a haste to clear the way. The boys were shouting and their warnings competed with one another and echoed off the bricks. They were saying that the river was filled with softwood and some of these timbers were being drawn into the canal.

The Ayer Mill and its neighbors relied on waterpower. The Merrimack came over the dam, was diverted into the canals, and then drawn under the mills through various penstocks. This energy was harvested by a 13-foot drop in the flow, through pipes and into the turbines, causing them to rotate. Through a system of gears, belts, and pulleys, the rotation was transferred to the power looms, which produced the cloth. Although there were grates protecting the sluiceway, any debris that fell against the turbines would cause damage and potentially halt operations. Therefore, the Essex Company had long ago purchased timber rights from adjoining landowners and barred all corporations from using the Merrimack for conveying lumber.

The crowd of workers in the Ayer courtyard surged toward the river. With the two battery boys racing ahead, even Dick Morgan felt himself being pulled along, his long legs devouring the pavement. Spanning the mill was a catwalk that provided an unobstructed view of the dam, the river, and four large pipes where the water returned to the canal after its power was extracted. Coming through the archway, the boys reached this catwalk first and the iron girders rang beneath their feet as they went.

The Merrimack was teeming with softwood. A variety of timbers, some over fifteen feet long and some as small as hurley sticks, ran in the current. Men from the Kunhardt Mill had also been drawn to the embankment and from across the river they shouted at their fellows, queuing upon the catwalk.

"It's half the trees in New Hampshire," Gus Hearin said. "They'll be turning us into a paper mill."

Dozens of workers thronged over the catwalk. Forty feet below, timbers were being driven against the grate that covered one of the penstocks. "If those turbines seize up, they'll be turning us out of our jobs," said Finbar Maloney, who had a three-tined metal claw where his right hand once was.

Since there was nothing to see but logs floating downriver, the workers from Loom Rooms Four and Five passed beneath the archway and once again congregated near the loading dock. Dick Morgan ambled back with them, smoking the nub of a Havana he had retrieved from the limousine's ashtray. Puffs of smoke garlanded his head, and boys jumped in his wake and put their hands through the rings.

There were four docks within the courtyard, and a few minutes before their shift, workers from the various departments began to gather in front of each one. The weavers from Rooms Four and Five hadn't budged. They were still leaning against the soot-covered wall, arguing in Italian. A teamster led a pair of giant Clydesdale horses down the slope, beneath the drawbridge, and into the courtyard. Their hooves made a smart noise against the cobblestones and men hurried to either side, wary of being kicked. The weavers were especially shy of the horses and flattened themselves against the wall.

Just then Frank Beaumont came to stand on the dock. He was dressed in a bowler hat, vest, and linen shirt with gaitered sleeves. Mr. Beaumont was neither a large nor a small man, with an open, fleshy face and brown hair. It was well known that his ambition soared beyond his current job, and the air of competence and dispatch that attended him ran all the way to Billy Wood.

Beaumont's tie was askew and he carried a wrench in one hand and a pocket watch in the other. Immediately groups of men extinguished their cigarettes and began walking toward the iron gate beside the dock. Gus Hearin and Finbar Maloney and two of the change-over men fell in behind them. That began a general migration toward Loom Rooms Four and Five, even though most workers estimated several minutes to the third bell, which signaled the beginning of their shift.

Only the group of Italian weavers remained in place when Mr. Beaumont appeared; finally Carmen Gallitelli took out his watch and surveyed the time. Beaumont glanced at his own watch and then his eyes met those of the Italian. After a few seconds, Marrone said something in a low voice and Gallitelli shook his head; there was more than a minute remaining until the third bell.

Frank Beaumont handed his wrench to a passing loom fixer and stood upon the concrete dock until the bell did ring. Promptly the weavers

Jay Atkinson

broke up their gathering and mounted the steps. *Rooms Four and Five* was painted overhead in large white letters and Mr. Beaumont waited here for the Italians. "I like people who want to work," he said.

Enrico Marrone snorted at him. "We work hard. But extra time, we don't give."

The weavers climbed the stairs to the second floor, passing through the 12-foot doors. Marrone and Gallitelli went into Room Five on the left and the other three weavers said "arrivederci" and entered the door across the hall. Mr. Beaumont paused to note the time on a clipboard and then followed Carmen Gallitelli into Room Five. The weavers removed their overcoats and sheepskin hats and hung them on pegs fastened to the wall.

Arranged in long rows, 50 Compton & Knowles looms filled the room, joined by overhead belting and separated from one another by a mere twenty-inch workspace. Weavers stood in this narrow lane armed with a steel pointer that was heavy enough to depress levers and still used to separate individual strands of yarn.

Young women and boys scurried about, threading the drop wires, replacing empty bobbins, and generally preparing the looms while the weavers jotted notes in the manifest that Frank Beaumont carried to them. A buzzer announced the power surge, and one by one the looms started up. Immediately the noise in Room Five was constant and deafening. There was the hum of the belts overhead, the clack of harnesses bobbing up and down, and the ping of the shuttles traveling back and forth at 56 miles per hour. The shuttles made a racket as they pounded over the grooved raceways, caught by the picker sticks on either side and thrust back.

To prevent the yarn from breaking, the loom rooms were hot and humid and the air was filled with tiny fibers, dust, and dried sputum. The work was tedious, interrupted only by equipment breakdowns or other emergencies, and due to poor overhead lighting, the belting and machinery were treacherous. Although men and women worked in close proximity, there was very little socializing and laughter was a rare occurrence.

Mr. Beaumont received the manifest from the one of the weavers, uttered a voiceless "thank you" among the clamor, and made his way toward Carmen Gallitelli. As he edged between the looms, holding the heavy black book against his chest, Beaumont signaled with his eyes for one of the smash piecers to come along. Gus Hearin tucked his steel pick into the apron draped about his waist and followed Mr. Beaumont toward the final eight looms in the row.

Gallitelli was a wiry man in a striped blue shirt and blue workpants, sorting and assembling individual yarn fibers on a wheel adjacent to his looms. Like only the most skillful weavers, Gallitelli had the knack of isolating a single loom and replacing any broken parts without shutting down the row; or using the steel rod to perform functions on several machines at once, keeping each problem separate in his mind like a great military strategist.

So Beaumont found him, using his left hand to remove an empty warp beam while the steel rod in his other hand stayed the picker arm on a second loom. Two of the change-over men and an inspector leaned over the next row, watching this display of mechanical virtuosity. One man looked at the other and shook his head. The expression on his face was no different than if a pigeon on the windowsill had recited lines from Chaucer.

"Gallitelli," Beaumont said over the tumult. "Sign the manifest."

The Italian braced the steel rod against his knee and flipped open the book and affixed his signature on the appropriate line, never once glancing at Beaumont or the smash piecer. There was a single bulb hanging above the aisle and it cast light on the wires of the loom and the three men, crowded together in such a small space.

"I'm putting Hearin on this line," Beaumont said. "I want you to train him."

The weaver shifted his gaze toward Gus Hearin for an instant and then back to his superior. "No room," said Gallitelli. He indicated the first row, where the space between the looms grew to thirty-six inches on account of the hat rack. "Try Romano's line."

"I'm putting him here," said Beaumont. "And you're going to train him."

Gallitelli reached for the steel rod, lifted it free of the belting, and cruised its tip within inches of Beaumont's head. "I didn't come to America to train anyone," said the Italian. "I came to work."

"You do what I say or find another job," Beaumont said.

Gus Hearin was immobilized by this discussion. He dwarfed the other two men, and stood so high above the looms that the top of his head nearly touched the shafting. Static electricity from the belts caused his hair to stand on end, and the combination of his height and the waving fronds of his hair drew attention from around the shop. Hearin had worked in Lawrence since the age of nineteen; before that he farmed in Peterborough, New Hampshire, until a wet summer drove him south toward the mills. But for all his time in the loom room, Hearin's skill was limited. As a smash piecer, he was called when a significant number of threads broke during the weaving. Using his pick and handknotter, he tied the threads together and allowed the weaver to continue. That was the extent of his ability.

The workings of the loom were as mysterious to Gus Hearin as the beating of his own heart. All around him, the harnesses raised themselves up and down, the shuttles went rocketing to and fro, and the drop wires vibrated like the strings on a banjo. Although Gallitelli's response to Mr. Beaumont was lost in all the noise, Hearin saw the reproach in his eyes and felt uneasy. He was trapped among three fears: Gallitelli's scorn, Mr. Beaumont's authority, and his ignorance of the loom. Gus Hearin closed his eyes for an instant, hoping it would all go away. His head was jerked sideways, the clamor of Room Five echoed in the distance and he began screaming. Only then did Gus Hearin realize that he had been lifted off the floor.

Jay Atkinson

His hair was caught in the belt from the loom behind him and he was picked up by the ear and transported several feet.

Carmen Gallitelli was the first to notice, even before Hearin cried out, and jabbed at two levers with his steel pointer and shut down the line. When the shaft stopped rotating, Hearin's weight dropped him to the ground, but not before his right ear and a large hank of hair were torn from his head. Although the looms were suspended the belting still ran and the workers in that vicinity watched Gus Hearin's ear and the bloody mass of hair travel across the room. They caught against the pulley at the end of the line and were ground to bits.

Wedged between the looms, Gus Hearin bled in a great pulse. Beaumont used his knife to cut a swath of fabric and wrapped it about the injured man's head.

Two of the battery boys raised Hearin to his feet and helped the bloody smash piecer toward the exit. He looked like the victim of a cannon blast, his head elongated by the makeshift turban, the blood already soaking through. Mr. Beaumont told another boy to clean up the floor and then restarted all eight looms under Gallitelli's supervision.

The noise resumed. "When Hearin comes back, train him," said Beaumont to the Italian.

*

Inside Billy Wood's office, a small brick room with steel doors occupied one corner. Within this fortress was a Corliss Cannon Ball safe, delivered to the building by steam-driven cranes and lowered into the pavilion before its roof had been constructed. The mill owner waited until he was alone and then drew back the outer door. Miss Halliman was busy delivering the work orders to various departments, and his other secretary, Mrs. Litwack, was out of the building entirely. For many years, Lawrence's post office and jail had occupied the same building at the corner of Essex Street and the old Turnpike. Of the secretaries, only Mrs. Litwack cared to make this trip when the stamps ran out, as her son Norman was incarcerated there and she could pay him a visit.

In the afternoon silence, William Wood twisted the dial on the safe until all the tumblers clicked and then heaved open the door. Since the payroll was kept at Lawrence Savings & Trust, the safe contained only a few hundred dollars in petty cash. More importantly, all the company ledgers were stored here, along with background records on every single employee. Standing in the open well of the safe, Wood fetched the small leather-bound journal that contained his dye formulas, placed it on a side table, and then sorted through the personnel books until he found Volume G-H.

He located the entry for Carmen A. Gallitelli, master weaver, Room Five, written in Mr. Beaumont's neat hand. Gallitelli was forty-seven years old, a native of Monterosso in the Cinqueterre region of Italy, the father of six, and Roman Catholic. His wife, Antonia, was a loom scrubber in the Wood Mill. Two of the Gallitelli children, ages 11 and 9, worked in the Pacific Mill. The final bit of information was the most telling: Gallitelli held office in the Knights of Columbus.

William Wood, on the other hand, worshipped at Christ Church in Andover and was a Republican. Fingering the tooth on his watch chain, he reminded himself that Papist Knights were unwelcome in his company. He had little use for their high-mindedness, their secrecy, and their penchant for organizing. Carmen Gallitelli and his brood would have to seek employment elsewhere.

Wood's .38-caliber revolver was also contained within the safe. It possessed a long barrel, hand-carved ivory stock, and his initials stamped in gold upon the handle. Feeling its weight in his hand, the mill owner withdrew the gun from the recesses of the vault. Wood raised the gun to eye level and spun on his heel, leveling the barrel. His mind was filled with the dreams of youth.

There was a boy standing in the doorway. Somehow he had passed through the outer rooms and entered Wood's office. "What in blazes are you doing here?" asked the mill owner, lowering his gun.

The lad snatched the cap from his head, moving his lips without making any sound.

"I could have shot you dead and been well within my rights," Billy Wood said.

Still, Wood was embarrassed by the gun and replaced it and closed the safe. "I remember you," he said, looking at the boy. "From the fire house. What was the name?"

"Glass, sir," the boy said. He stepped backward into the office, allowing the man to emerge from his storeroom. "There wasn't no job."

"That was a misunderstanding." Mr. Wood regarded the boy, dressed in patched, threadbare clothing. A hundred more important thoughts raced through his mind. "Come with me," the mill owner said. "And be quick about it. I haven't all day for the likes of you."

Wood noticed that the boy coveted the pastries on his desk. "Go ahead," he said. "Take them."

The boy scooped up the turnovers. He stuck two of them in his coat pocket and began eating the third. "It's good," he said, chewing as he went.

"Will you eat all three, then?" asked the mill owner.

The boy shook his head. "Two is for my friends," he said.

Again William Wood regarded the boy. "Mind you, don't breathe a word about this," he said. "Or I'll have you put in the post office."

At the far end of the room was a hidden door and Wood pressed a lever on the molding and a portion of the wall sprang open. Stepping through this porthole, Mr. Wood and the boy were halfway along a corridor that separated the main pavilion from a gangplank that led into the turbine pits. A rope blocked the way hung with a sign reading "Authorized Personnel Only."

As they walked, the boy devoured the pastry. "Have you eaten today?" asked Wood.

"No, sir."

"I imagine you could make short work of those other two pastries, then," said Wood.

Jay Atkinson

The boy's hair was matted and dirty, soot permeated his clothes, and there was a vast longing in his gaze that no number of raisin turnovers could satisfy. It was a look of perpetual want; of simultaneous expectation and the thwarting of it. This was the reason Billy Wood rolled up his car windows and sped through the streets. As a child, he had worn that very same look and detested the memory of it.

Near the door to Loom Room One, which shook with the racket inside, Finbar Maloney overtook Mr. Wood and the boy. The pit boss wore rubber waders and a greasy shirt, canvas gloves protruding from his belt. The echo of his footsteps caught up and Wood realized the man had been running; he slowed and doffed his cap when he spotted Mr. Wood and now his breath came shallow and he began to sweat.

Billy Wood had a thousand things to do before the arrival of his father-in-law for the clock dedication, and wished to rid himself of the boy. "You there," he said to Maloney. "I have an errand for you."

"At your service, Mr. Wood," said the pit boss.

"Take this lad"—he swung around to the boy—"what's your name again?"

"Glass, sir."

Wood thrust the boy forward. "Take him down to Beaumont and put him to work."

Maloney grabbed the boy by the collar. "I'll see to it, Mr. Wood."

The mill owner turned and made for his office while Maloney jerked the boy in the opposite direction, toward Rooms Four and Five. "I'm going for Beaumont all right, and it's lucky as a coin in a cupboard full of buttons that Mr. Wood's going the other way," said the Irishman. "Because he'd bring down the thunder if he a-heard what I'm going to report."

Beyond the door to Room One, they veered to the right, traveled along another empty corridor, turned left, and found themselves at the bottom of a stairwell. A tall man with a bandage wrapped around his head was mounting the stairs and Maloney called to him. "Hallo, Gus," he said. "Where's Mr. Beaumont?"

"He's on the dock. The new bales are coming in, and the fellows are saying we're going to make Army uniforms."

"I'd rather make 'em than wear 'em," Maloney said. He indicated Gus Hearin's bandage. "What's happened to you, now?"

"I sent my ear out to be cleaned," said Hearin.

Finbar Maloney stood dumbfounded while the injured man laughed and resumed climbing the stairs. Then he hauled on the boy's collar, passed through the iron gate and went outside.

The courtyard was bustling with horse-drawn wagons and trucks. They were delivering a month's supply of wool, and two men on the drawbridge waved them toward a third fellow who marked a chalk X where each wagon should set its brake. With a cigar fixed in his mouth, Frank Beaumont tallied the shipments as they arrived, writing down the number scribbled on each one.

"Mr. Beaumont," said Maloney, approaching with the boy.

"You'll have to wait," Beaumont said. "I'm not halfway through these accounts."

Maloney removed his cap and stood twisting it in his hands. "The turbines are seizing up and all the looms in Four, Five and Six are stopped," he said.

Mr. Beaumont flung his clipboard and pencil against the wall, spinning around to face the pit boss. "God's curse upon this place," he said. "If the looms are down an hour we'll be docked. Any more than that, and we'll be sacked. Didn't you see Mr. Wood's memorandum?"

"I don't read, Mr. Beaumont."

"Apparently you don't think, either," said the second man. "What's causing the stoppage?"

"It's the softwood, Mr. Beaumont. All manner of sticks are clearing the grate and lodging against the first turbine. It can't turn."

Beaumont struck out for the catwalk with Maloney and the boy following. They dodged men with hand trucks who were unloading the wool, and trotted among lumps of fresh manure and cast off wire and other debris that littered the pavement. Just then, Mr. Wood's limousine rolled into the courtyard. Noting the passenger, Beaumont called for Dick Morgan to stop the car.

Hiram Mills occupied the rear seat and Mr. Beaumont stooped to meet his gaze and beckoned to him. Tugging at his vest, the engineer disembarked from the limousine and surveyed the chaos of the Ayer Mill. Hiram F. Mills was an imposing figure: thick white hair, heavy browed, with a footballer's jaw covered by white whiskers and draped over with regimental mustaches.

"Welcome to the Ayer, Mr. Mills," said Beaumont. "We've got softwood clogging our turbines and I was wondering if you'd have a look."

The engineer stared. "Is Wood here?"

"In his office. But this won't take long, if you'll come this way, sir."

Horses were shitting on the pavement and men calling out orders and a fellow in a stovepipe hat was doing sums on the concrete with a piece of chalk. "Just as well," said Hiram Mills.

Leading the way, Beaumont gestured for the engineer to follow him and the one-armed pit boss and young Glass came after. Operatives tipped their caps at this procession and men pushing trolleys and hand trucks darted out of the way. They passed beneath the arch and found the catwalk, tramping in unison along its length, with the mill to their immediate left and the Merrimack on the right.

Logs rolled and bumped each other in the current, leaving a greasy iridescence on the water's surface. Grumbling to himself, Mills shook his head and spat. For while the managers of the Ayer were concerned with production, his foremost goal was the salvation of the river: as conveyance, life source, and habitat. What these loggers were creating was a genuine hazard—a negation of all that Hiram Mills had accomplished. "What a disgrace," he said.

Mr. Beaumont peered over the railing at the sticks and branches jammed against one of the grates. "It's a crime against every working man in Lawrence," said the second hand. "They might as well fill the river with corpses."

Joining the party on the catwalk were the two ragged boys traveling with Master Glass. They stood to one side as Frank Beaumont and Mr. Mills went past, all but invisible in their wake. But the older boy greeted his comrades with a smile, digging in his pocket for the raisin turnovers he had saved. The urchins greeted this event with wolfish delight, especially the Italian, who gamboled over the iron rungs with his skirts lifted, the turnover protruding from his mouth.

The party halted at the terminus of the catwalk, above a ladder that descended to the main intake pipe. Bending over the rail, Hiram Mills inspected the detritus that had lodged against the grate and then straightened up, gazing toward the Stone Dam.

"God save us from ourselves," said the engineer.

"Shall we take a closer look?" asked Beaumont, pointing downward.

The engineer nodded and first Beaumont, then Mr. Mills and Finbar Maloney descended the ladder, his claw ringing against the iron. Twenty feet below was a concrete landing, which sat a few inches above the canal. From this vantage point, the men had a view of the intake pipe, the grate, and the first turbine.

Mr. Mills instructed Maloney to unhinge an I-beam that was connected to the mill, lowering it flush with the canal. This prevented further debris from clogging the turbine and the engineer indicated his surprise that it hadn't been done already. Then Maloney stuck his claw and his free hand in the apertures of the grate, using his considerable strength to haul it open despite the force of the canal. For a few moments Hiram Mills stared into the drainpipe, turned to express his opinion on something, and he and Mr. Beaumont shook hands. Then Mr. Mills excused himself, his shoes clattering against the ladder as he ascended to the catwalk. While he smoked a cigarette, Beaumont made a remark that was lost in the wind, then swung around and gazed at the boys waiting above. He beckoned them down the ladder.

Glass came first, followed by the dark-haired Syrian boy. The Italian was reluctant, but his comrades jeered him, whistling in a sustained, high-pitched tone. Finally the boy gave in. He lowered himself one rung at a time, eyes pinched shut, his checkered skirt writhing in the breeze. At the bottom of the ladder, Glass chucked the Italian on the shoulder and all three boys yelped in triumph. What a lark! They were poised just inches above the canal, the river churned past with its cargo of softwood, and the intake pipe offered a strange view of the mill's interior. Its water source diverted, the huge blade of the turbine lay exposed in the passageway, jammed with debris.

Frank Beaumont made sure of something with Mr. Maloney and then approached the boys, who congregated by the tunnel. He flung his cigarette into the river, glanced up at the mill, which was huge from this perspective, and cleared his throat. "So you want work, boys," he said in a strange, thick voice.

He looked into their eager faces. "How many children at home?" he asked the oldest boy.

"I'm the only one," said Glass.

"And how many are you?" Beaumont asked the young Syrian.

"He's got three sisters. His father died on the boat," Glass said.

Crouching down, Mr. Beaumont placed his hand on Giuseppe's shoulder. "What about you?" he asked. The second hand reached in his pocket and took out a silver dollar, which he held in front of the boy. "You look like a strong lad."

"He don't speak English," said Glass.

"Does he have a family?"

The oldest boy shook his head. "None."

"Here," said Beaumont, handing Giuseppe the coin. "This is for you."

The other boys whooped with glee. "And we ain't even worked yet," said the oldest, who was dancing with the Syrian.

Mr. Beaumont looked at them. The only sound was the purling of the canal through the sluice gate. "Maloney. Take these other two boys to Mr. Gorham. There's plenty of work in Room Five right now."

"Yes, sir," said Maloney, who had turned pale. The pit boss spread the tines of his claw and pointed toward the catwalk. "Up you go, lads," he said.

Anxious to have a dollar themselves, the boys scrambled up the ladder. Giuseppe raised his head and watched them go, the sky dark behind him and the wind roiling his tunic. "*Buona fortuna*," he said, and the other boys paused, staring at him. The Italian put his mournful gaze on his friends and waved them upward, then turned to Mr. Beaumont.

When the others had gone away, Beaumont escorted the Italian boy to the edge of the tunnel. There was a dank, swampy odor and they could hear the clatter of machinery from somewhere deep inside the mill. Beaumont squatted on his haunches, but Giuseppe walked straight into the pipe, his legs trembling. Halfway along the boy turned and expressed his bewilderment. Using pantomime, Beaumont instructed him to remove the sticks and other debris that jammed the turbine.

While Giuseppe picked at this flotsam, Beaumont raised the I-beam and the canal began seeping into the pipe again. Soon the boy was knee deep inside the tunnel, his skirt rising with the water. The turbine, which stood six feet tall and loomed above the boy, groaned with pent-up torque. Bent at the waist and digging with his hands, Giuseppe managed to pry several chunks of softwood from among the blades of the turbine and it moved a few inches.

Suddenly the turbine made a complete revolution and then stalled for a moment, which set off a grinding noise that echoed throughout the tunnel. The boy turned toward the opening, his eyes white against the startled expression of his face. He cried out, but Beaumont had already begun climbing the ladder.

Giuseppe's feet were mired in water and his arms slapped against the current, which drew him backward toward the turbine. There was a gulping sound and the canal became red with backwash and then the stain was drawn through and the gears smoothed themselves, water

Jay Atkinson

filled the pipe, and the turbine began spinning again.

The boy was gone.

*

Frederick Ayer's chauffeur-driven Bebe Peugeot arrived outside the mill at six-thirty. A man dressed in livery stepped out of the car, polished the rear window with his handkerchief and opened the leather-hinged door. Immediately someone burst from the entrance of 200 Merrimack Street and greeted Mr. Ayer as he emerged. "Hello, Father," said Billy Wood. "So good of you to come."

"I'm pleased with your success, William," Mr. Ayer said.

"What's mine belongs to you, sir."

Frederick Ayer smiled with his ancient teeth. "I'm happy to stay out of it, now."

The old man wore a frock coat, bell-bottomed trousers, and a low-crowned hat, all in black; a white collarless shirt, doeskin gloves, and he carried an umbrella on account of the season. Ayer's most prominent feature was a long white beard, which fell in a ruff from his ears and chin, tapering to a point just above his belt buckle. He allowed his son-in-law to take his arm, though he was capable of walking unassisted, and together they mounted the stairs.

Vases of pink and red azaleas lined the outer office, countinghouse, and mill agent's headquarters. In each of these rooms, gentlemen congregated around a linen-covered table, drinking punch and eating calves' liver. These men applauded the dignitaries as they passed, while Billy Wood, who clutched his father-in-law's arm, shooed his employees back to their luncheon.

Frederick Ayer possessed the indifference of someone who had made money at every turn; who, at 88, maintained the hard, healthy vigor of a person half his age; and who had mingled with the prior century's most influential figures. The pomp of this evening's ceremony affected him as little as the dust upon the windowsills: if he noticed either, he did not remark upon it.

In his younger days, Ayer had been partial to the use of 'West India goods,' which is to say rum and tobacco. In 1855 he joined his brother Dr. J. C. Ayer in the manufacture of Ayer's Cherry Pectoral, sarsaparilla, ague cure, hair restorer and other patent medicines, enjoying success for a good many years. Later Frederick Ayer diversified into railroads, lumber, and textile manufacturing, making the acquaintance of an eager young man named Billy Wood, who began selling cotton goods for $2,500 per year. Mr. Wood succeeded, and eventually Ayer called him back to Lawrence and paid him $20,000 to manage his factory.

William Wood married Ellen Wheaton Ayer on November 21, 1888, when he was 30 and his wife was 29. Most of the Ayers drew a straight line back to the Mayflower and had attended Harvard University; Wood's family had emigrated from Portugal and none had ever finished high school. But the business partnership and the marriage prospered, and it was Billy Wood who escorted his father-in-law toward the reception area he had created beneath the clock tower.

When they reached Wood's office, Frederick Ayer paused to retrieve a box from his pocket. In a quavering voice, the old man said, "Ellie had these made at Shreve, Crump & Low."

Inside the box was a pair of cuff links shaped like the Ayer Mill clock. A diamond chip represented each of the hours, and the hands, inlaid with pearl, were fixed at eight o'clock. "Your generosity is overwhelming," said Wood. Indeed, his face took on a purple blush, and the hair at his temples seemed very white by comparison. "I'm speechless."

"Bosh," the old man said. "They're a trifle."

Billy Wood removed one of the gold cuff links and saw that '1910' was inscribed on the top and bottom edge. The workmanship was very fine and the item weighed more than twice what its size indicated. "I neglected to purchase a gift for you, Father Ayer," said Wood. "But I promise to find something appropriate to commemorate the occasion."

Ayer regarded his son-in-law with puzzlement. "You named the building after me."

"But that's…generally known," Wood said. Try as he might, the mill owner could not reduce the flush that had overtaken him. "This evening, I've done nothing to surprise you."

The old man laughed. "I don't like surprises," he said, in his tuneful voice. "Not at my age."

"Still, I am touched," said Wood. He removed the cuff links he was wearing, tacked the new pair on, and deposited the box and his old cuff links in a desk drawer. "I shall treasure them."

Ayer looked at his watch. "We should be getting on," he said.

Just then the mill whistle sounded, dismissing all hands, and the ceiling shook beneath their footfalls. Billy Wood extended his arm, showing his father-in-law the way, and the two men passed through the exit hidden in the wall. At the base of the tower, Wood had prepared a device that would start the Ayer Mill clock and save the guest of honor from climbing the stairs.

As soon as Mssrs. Wood and Ayer came through the door, the Columbian orchestra burst into "Yankee Doodle Dandy." The honored guests, including ex-Congressman James T. McLeary of Minnesota; Hat manufacturer Charles H. Tenney of New York; Attorneys Ignatius J. Bates of Lawrence and Vaughn Jealous of Andover; Hiram F. Mills and several others, left off sampling the victuals and sang along with the orchestra.

Old George Kunhardt, owner of the mill that bore his name, drew laughter when he began conducting the music with a large smelt from the buffet, and William Wood Jr. and Alex Gardner, dressed in tennis clothes, unfurled a scroll of red fabric, creating a path to the center of the room.

While the music was still playing, Kunhardt flung away his baton and sidled up to Billy Wood. The German wore an old campaign coat and spats that bulged about his ankles, his stubby legs clad in riding trousers. Pinches of snuff glistened in his beard and his sideburns stuck out like a pair of brushes. "I hear you want to make uniforms," said Kunhardt.

"Nice thick wool for the Army."

"The Army *has* uniforms," said Billy Wood.

Opening his snuff container, the German laughed. "You should leave military outfitting to the military men."

"Like who?"

"Like Colonel G. E. Kunhardt," said the German, with a bow. "Of the Prussian cavalry."

Wood kicked at the smelt lying on the floor. "Why would the United States do business with a Hun?" asked the mill owner. "If they need something, they'd do better to contract with the *American* Woolen Company."

"You are Portuguese," said Kunhardt, throwing out his paunch.

"I am part of the most venerated Yankee family in America," said Mr. Wood. He indicated Dick Morgan, who stood nearby wearing his chauffeur's cap. "If you insist otherwise, I'll have you escorted out—by the ear."

His clothing spattered with mud and his hair in disarray, Colin Isherwood hurried into the reception just as the orchestra began playing "My Faith Looks Up To Thee." Isherwood owned the *Weekly Tribune*; a tall, slender young man whose background was quite different from the other "newsies" surrounding the beverage cart. He had served in the Army during the Spanish-American war and graduated from a business college in New York.

"Here's Ishy," said Jack Wermers, who ran *The Telegram*. Mr. Wermers was a nervous fellow who's black beard shone like a pelt. "Where've you been, buggering Greek misses as they step off the train?"

Bart Quimby laughed. Red-faced and corpulent, he was the oldest and most successful of the local journalists; his paper, *The Lawrence Daily American*, had been published for eleven years under his stewardship. He leaned over the trolley upon which rested a silver coffee urn, pitchers of milk and cream, and two dozen mugs. "Mrs. Isherwood would have none of that," Quimby said, uncorking a hip flask and adding a dollop of whiskey to his coffee. "Isn't that right, Colin?"

The new arrival held out a mug for some whiskey. After taking a drink, Colin Isherwood smacked his lips and eyed the other men crowding around the urn. "There's no reason to shag an immigrant when Mrs. Isherwood is in the prime of life," he said, dropping his voice. "A man wouldn't bother taking coals to Newcastle, would he?"

The men gathered around the trolley laughed at Isherwood's comment and before their mirth had evaporated, the young newspaperman smoothed his hair into place and scratched at the mud affixed to his coat. "Jack, you may aim at throttling a Greek girl, but some of us are concerned with the news," said Isherwood. He nudged Mr. Quimby. "What do you say, Bart?"

"Depends on the girl," Quimby said, and the men laughed once more. He winked at his colleagues. "If one of those Greeks were to bend over while fastening her shoe, an immigrant would become an emigrant in very short order."

Mrs. Litwack entered long enough to distribute two boxes from Haynes Cigar & Tobacco and then retired. Soon the guests lingered among dirigibles of cigar smoke, talking politics while dining on asparagus and pork pies and herring. The three newsmen watched from a distance, sipping their coffee.

"Where'd you get all that mud, Colin?" asked Jack Wermers.

"Since you'll read it in the *Weekly Tribune*, I won't spoil it for you," said Isherwood.

They were joined by 74-year-old fire fighter Charles Foster. "Evenin', gents," he said.

Foster took one of the mugs and Mr. Quimby added a generous amount of whiskey. "I see you got mud on your pants, Charlie," he said. "How'd you come by it?"

"Pulling a body from the canal," said Mr. Foster. "It was just a kid and he was all broken up. Ask Colin. He was there."

Isherwood uttered an oath and, reaching inside Bart Quimby's jacket for the flask, topped off his coffee. "There's no hope of making a living when your tongue is loose," he told the fire fighter.

"It's no secret," said Foster. "There were fifteen or twenty men by those locks."

"But none of these," Isherwood said, indicating the present company.

Taking up his notebook and a pencil, Mr. Wermers kicked Charlie Foster in the shin. "Who's the kid?" he asked.

"Nobody knew him. The mortician said he was about nine years old."

"Dewhirst?" asked Wermers, scribbling notes. "Is that who's got him?"

"The devil's got him now," Foster said. "For doing whatever he was doing, right where he shouldn't have done it."

Wermers wrote to the bottom of a page, and then scratched at his beard with the pencil. "Stick to the facts, Charlie," he said.

"Dewhirst said that every bone in the kid's body was pulverized," said Isherwood. "He surmised that the boy had passed down the canal, and through the turbines of the mill."

"Ground up like a sausage," said Wermers. "How'd he get in there? Somebody push him?"

"There were two kids standing by the locks, but when I tried to talk to them they ran away," Isherwood said.

Mr. Wermers filled several pages with his scrawl. After a few moments, he glanced up at Bart Quimby. "Ain't you gonna put this down?"

The old journalist pointed to his temple. "It's all right here," he said, and drank from the flask.

While a man with a cornet played "Home Sweet Home," several members of the orchestra crowded around the buffet. A fat saxophonist, his maroon tunic unbuttoned and the epaulets darkened with perspiration, gathered six large smelts and a jar of horseradish and stole away. Once he had hidden his spoils beneath a chair, the musician returned for two bottles of ginger beer and a liverwurst sandwich. Then he retired to the corner for his feast.

Jay Atkinson

On the other side of the room, Hiram Mills was busy explaining the declivity of the south canal to the gentleman from Minnesota. It was the only time all evening that Mr. Mills had shown the least bit of animation; his hand planed downward while he gave the former Congressman a lesson in the natural sciences. "The water passes through the gratings, then through six feet of vertical pipe to a sixty-by-sixty-inch tee, where it is deflected horizontally into the main line whence it is conducted to the locks," said the engineer.

"I'm nothing but a Minnesota farm boy," James McLeary said.

"It's a forty-eight-inch tar-coated cast iron pipe. The velocity of flow is—"

Billy Wood hailed Mr. Mills, directing him over to a space by the windows. Outside, the river glinted in the moonlight and the bumping and complaining of timbers could be heard. When Mills excused himself, Mr. Wood shook the engineer's hand. "I'm told that you inspected the turbines and gave advice for restarting them," Billy Wood said. "It worked to a T."

"I inspected the first turbine," Hiram Mills said. "But all I did was second the notion that timbers were clogging your sluiceway. Any fool could see that."

Those same timbers gleamed in the moonlight, floating downstream in great bunches. Billy Wood glanced out the window at them, and then turned back to Mr. Mills. "I understood you gave directions to clear the turbine," said Wood.

"I told—what's his name? Beaumont? —there was no way to do it without shutting down the works, and disassembling the turbine. If Beaumont got things moving again, he must've devised a solution on his own. Because there was only one thing I could think of."

"What was that?" Wood asked Mills.

"For someone to climb in there and chock out the debris. But it wouldn't work."

Mr. Wood stared at Hiram Mills. "Why not?"

"If the turbine began rotating with a man standing close like that, he'd be drawn right through and under the mill."

Just then the orchestra struck up with "Wait Till the Sun Shines, Nellie" and Frank Beaumont came through the door with his camera and tripod. "Here's the man you want to talk to," said Mills, without a trace of good will.

Mr. Wood approached Beaumont in the midst of setting up his camera. The second hand spread the legs of the tripod until the leather straps grew taut; he unfurled the shroud attached to the camera and unsnapped the front housing, slid in the appropriate lens, and clipped the housing into place again. Lifting the canvas shroud, he bent his eye to the viewfinder and sighted his object: the table where the clock switch was mounted.

"Congratulations are in order, Beaumont," said Wood. "Mr. Mills tells me you devised a solution to the canal problem."

"I suppose I did, sir," said Beaumont, coming out from beneath the shroud.

"We were the only mill in Lawrence that made our goal today," said Mr. Wood.

Beaumont was saved from replying when Frederick Ayer approached with his pocket watch displayed. "Time to get on with it," said the old man.

Immediately Mr. Wood silenced the orchestra. He took his father-in-law by the arm while Beaumont ducked beneath the short hanging cape and then Billy Wood gathered the assembly together by clasping his hands and raising them over his head. "Attention, everybody," he called out, and then in a much lower voice, he spoke to Mr. Ayer: "All this, thanks to you."

"It's the little things, William," said the old man. "The details."

Across the room, the orchestra stood poised with their instruments. "Thank you all for coming," said Billy Wood. "We're about to start the clock."

Before the assembly was a switch that connected with the clock mechanism up in the tower. "My dear gentlemen, with Mr. Wood's kind permission, I will now show you how easy it is to start the largest striking clock in America," said Frederick Ayer.

Stooping over the table, Mr. Ayer snapped the switch into place. Immediately the gears were heard, the hands on the clock face notched into position, and the great bell started chiming eight o'clock.

"Gentleman, three cheers for Frederick C. Ayer," said Mr. Wood, over the applause.

Mr. Ayer returned the compliment, and then Wood directed attention to the men gathered around the beverage trolley and called three cheers for the Lawrence press: "Hip, hip, hooray!"

Since the newspapers in town used drawings instead of photographs to illustrate their stories, the journalists crowded around Mr. Beaumont as he made ready for the portrait. The camera was a brand new Eastman Kodak, and the newsies watched as Beaumont stripped the backing from a roll of film, spread the thin, gelatinous emulsion over the flexible strip and then loaded the roll into the camera.

"I'm ready, Mr. Wood," said Beaumont, and the mill owner and Mr. Ayer broke off their conversation. At that moment, the orchestra played "Auld Lang Syne."

The photographer ducked beneath the truncated cape, peered through the viewfinder, and drew his subjects together by raising his arms and compacting the air. "A bit closer, gentlemen," said Beaumont.

In 1840, Frederick Ayer had had his portrait taken at the family's summer home. He was asked by the technician to stand before a window overlooking the lake. A sheet of silver was attached to a copper plate, and sensitized by being placed over a box of iodine crystals. During sixty minutes of exposure the iodine reacted with the silver, preserving the light and dark segments that appeared in the viewfinder. The silver sheet was removed from the camera, transferred to another box with a dish of heated mercury and the vapors formed an amalgam with the silver.

What resulted was called a "sun drawn miniature:" a slender young man, dressed all in black, and gazing out the window.

Here the old man felt Billy Wood's hand on his shoulder and then the fellow behind the camera said, "Steady, gentlemen," and there was a brilliant flash of light.

15

The Present Day

The stained glass across the front of the Beaumont home rattled when Philbin Bates came up the stairs, his mind crawling with details of Walter's estate and the other filings he needed to make at the probate court. With no light behind it, the glass rendering of the Merrimack River and mill buildings and canal was nothing but dark gloomy shapes flowing along the porch. The putty in the joints had fallen away in several places, leaving abscesses where there should have been blue sky and the sun-reddened bulk of the mills.

It was a breezy morning in May. The lawyer stopped on the welcome mat and felt its thickness, like an animal's hide, beneath his shoes. He remembered when a visit to the Beaumont's meant some important business was about to be transacted, a decision that would affect hundreds and perhaps even thousands of people. Inserting a key in the lock, Bates yanked downward on the brass door handle and entered the house.

It reeked of sickness and death. The parlor contained an unmade bed, the pillow dented with the shape of a skull and the covers thrust downward like the sleeper had been called away. An oxygen mask with a flimsy elastic strap hung over the bedpost and yards of plastic hose led to an oxygen tank with a gauge that registered zero pressure. The lawyer glanced up at the chandelier, appraising it. In the dining room, he could see a cherry-cabineted ship's clock, as well as the old grandfather clock lurking beneath the stairs, but neither one was ticking. For more than a month, Walter hadn't been there to wind them. An opulent hush reigned over the premises.

Bates took another step, and his foot brushed against weeks' worth of unclaimed mail scattered over the hallway. The lawyer stooped to examine the envelopes, sending them across the floor with a dash of his finger. He picked one up that contained a dividend check from the bank; then he made sure the door was locked behind him and went on down

Jay Atkinson

the hall. Bates tiptoed but there wasn't anything to disturb; he could have gone marauding through the rooms and no one would have heard him.

The more familiar smell of Walter Beaumont—damp wool and a pinch of ammonia—greeted Bates in the study. Leaving the shades drawn, he clicked on a brass lamp that flooded the desk with light. At the edge of the blotter was a photograph of Beaumont *père*, the Ayer Mill overseer. Bates studied the haughty look on the old man's face and then drew back. There he was—the wily businessman who had always remained two steps ahead of everyone in Lawrence. The positioning of the photograph left the impression that Franklin Beaumont still ruled here. But he had died of a cranial embolism, back before Philbin Bates had even made partner in his father's law firm.

Bates inhaled the odor of creosote from the fireplace and stared into old Beaumont's eyes. His earliest memory of the overseer was mingled with that of his own father, the late Ignatius J. Bates, who had served for more than thirty years as a Massachusetts Superior Court judge. During his lifetime, Judge Bates had contributed to local charities, as had Franklin Beaumont. Churches and hospital wings sprouted up and each man competed to have his name engraved above the other on their cornerstones. To this day, Philbin Bates could hardly enter a public building in Lawrence without seeing the judge's oil portrait, the white eyebrows, sharp chin and two prominent front teeth—unremarkable in his looks but a smart jurist, industrious community leader, and faithful husband.

Walter Beaumont had often fidgeted through speeches that lionized his own father and praised the innate Beaumont savvy and goodwill. At a dinner dance commemorating the hundredth anniversary of Lawrence General Hospital, Bates and Beaumont *fils* received plaques engraved with the likenesses of their fathers. Cloistering himself in a private reception area, Walter hammered away at an expensive bottle of bourbon. "Believe me Phil, it wasn't all daisies and daffodils at 621 Haverhill Street," he said, struggling to hold up the bronze tablet.

Franklin Beaumont's enigma consisted of a meddling man who could somehow remain aloof, a formidable but distant force in his son's life. The mill overseer believed in independence, rewarding his son with the customary signs of approbation: unerring stock tips, scads of money, and access to prized information about company business. But he was stingy in his affections and hoarded his free time. As a result, Walter remarked that his father was better known on Essex Street than he was in his own home.

In fact, Beaumont and Bates were familiar names throughout the Merrimack Valley, endowed with an indefinable quality that boosted them a few inches above the ground everyone else walked on. To the short order cooks and secretaries and mill workers they came in contact with, Judge Bates and Franklin Beaumont and Colin Isherwood I, the publisher of the *Tribune-Standard*, never left so much as a drop of sweat on the landscape. Yet an air of dominance over the century attended them. Everything that occurred in Lawrence—legal decisions, the furious construction of new buildings, even the thick black headlines that announced bank mergers and election results—was the conjuring of their minds. Such men didn't build the city—they willed it into existence.

In conversation, Judge Bates had expressed admiration for Franklin Beaumont and the way he did business, but only once did Philbin remember the mill overseer visiting the Bates home. One Saturday evening, father and son were playing a game of billiards when Franklin appeared, disheveled and without his eyeglasses. "Sorry, Ignatius," said the mill overseer. "Katherine let me in."

Judge Bates poured his visitor a glass of Armagnac. Since he had not invited Franklin Beaumont for a chat he felt no urgency to dismiss his son, who he had treated as an equal since his eighteenth birthday. Young Philbin was conscious of his father's pride and basked in importance, wearing his Penn track letter. Holding their snifters of cognac, the two older men watched the lad attempt a bank shot.

"What can we do for you?" the judge asked Beaumont, when the ball had fallen into its pocket.

The mill overseer glanced at Philbin and asked, "Is there a way I can divorce Maeve and still keep the house and bank accounts?"

"What would possess you to do that?" asked Judge Bates.

"I'm in love with another woman," said Beaumont. "But I'm not willing to give up everything I've worked so hard for."

Judge Bates replaced the decanter of Armagnac inside his liquor cabinet. "Forget about this other woman," he said. "If you were in love with her, one way or another, you'd have done it—consequences be damned."

"An affair will ruin me," Beaumont said. He sat down, covering his face with his hands. "And it would jeopardize Walter's future at the bank."

"Then end it right now," the judge said. "Everything that has been said here will be kept in the strictest confidence. You have my word on that."

Franklin Beaumont soon vanished into whatever turmoil had delivered him to the Bates' doorstep that night. The judge never mentioned the episode again and Philbin Bates also lived up to the pledge. If Walter hadn't learned of his father's infidelity in some other way, it was not Philbin's duty to inform him. That much Bates had learned from studying the law: take action in sight of an attainable result and then apply pressure until the goal is reached. Otherwise, pass on to other matters.

Bates opened the top drawer of Walter's desk. Among the items there was an old scorecard from the Andover Country Club. Walter, a sixteen handicapper, had won the round with a seventy, the best day of his golfing life. On the back of the card was a quotation from Heraclitus: "You can't step in the same river twice." The lawyer smiled at that. Apparently a hot pitching wedge had brought out the philosopher in his old friend.

Philbin Bates' name also appeared on the scorecard. He was a first year law student, out for an afternoon of duffing with Beaumont, Colin Isherwood II, and Wilson X. Wilson. The middle-aged State Senator dribbled one tee shot after another, an uncoordinated man who blamed his ineffectiveness on the Republicans. Paired with Bates, thirty-two year old Walter sailed from hole to hole, bending his fairway shots around trees and lakes and tossing in putts like he was dropping coins in a fountain. They approached the eighteenth green with Beaumont leading by more than a dozen strokes. Isherwood, their usual champion, threw away his club when he failed to come near the pin with his fifth shot.

"Colin's about to pop," Bates said to Walter.

"He's had a thousand good days. This is mine," Beaumont said. He unleashed a sweet swing with his wedge and threw the ball high in the air, a black dot against the sky until it dropped and came to rest a foot from the cup. "I'm in love," said the banker, the club at a rakish angle over his shoulder.

They strode over the green and Walter tapped in the putt. "But I'm not sure how my father is going to react," he said.

The two men watched as Isherwood mounted the green, and then putted to a triple bogey. The smell of roast beef wafted down from the clubhouse, and they could hear a jazz band on the patio.

"I've sought my father's opinion on every decision I've ever made," Walter said. "A marriage is a partnership. Every aspect should be examined, every fact thoroughly vetted."

A tall, well-dressed man with a high forehead, Walter Beaumont was vice president at Lawrence Savings & Trust, executing the sort of deals that his young companion had only read about in books. But Phil Bates was already developing a Socratic mind and he felt the questions lining up. "Is there something in this woman's background to make you think she's not suitable for marriage?" he asked. "Has your father conducted interviews with her or hired an investigator? Has this woman been married before?"

"She's an exotic," Walter said. On the huge sprawl of grass, Senator Wilson picked up his golf ball and chucked it toward the flag. "She comes from Norway originally, and for several years lived in the Far East, where she studied herbal medicine and Zoroastrianism."

As preparation for the law, Bates had studied philosophy at the University of Pennsylvania and was familiar with Eastern thought and mysticism. "Does this woman believe in the occult?" he asked. "Has she practiced free love? And have you pressed forward with your own inquiry?" The young lawyer stood his bag on end, placing numbered socks over each club. "Because you should."

"Lawrence has never seen anything like this woman before," Walter said, "In the East, she visited plantations where wool and flax were being harvested into great bundles and sent to an ancient port by train. She endeared herself to the engineer and rode with him to the sea. She booked passage on the steamer that contained the bales—first to Tangiers, then to London and on to Boston." Bates whistled through his teeth, and Walter put up his hand. "She acquired several bolts of cloth from the Ayer and is dying the fabric by hand. As we speak, she's in the midst of designs for a line of clothing."

Walter gazed at the huge green valley of the country club and shook his head. "This isn't double-breasted suits and Navy print dresses we're talking about. They look like tunics and Arabian outfits, things like that."

"It doesn't sound very practical," said Bates, glancing down at his madras shirt, pink chinos, and white golf shoes with black tassels.

" 'A glorious raiment,' she calls it. The clothes that children and poets would wear if they had the temerity to have grown the fibers themselves, and then colored them with roots and berries."

On the eighteenth green, Wilson X. Wilson was sprawled beside the hole with a golf ball clenched in his hand. He wore cleats meant for aerating his lawn and his scrawny ankles were exposed beneath the cuffs of his trousers. After lying motionless, he bent his arm across his forehead and dropped the ball into the cup.

"She didn't know the wool was coming here until she had reached Gibralter," said Beaumont. "A seaman told her that Lawrence was a planned community—a city of immigrants filled with giant mills and commerce."

Dusk was settling over the golf course. An invisible hand turned on the sprinklers and arches of water fluttered back and forth. Feeling the spray, Senator Wilson picked himself up and wandered off toward the smell of roasting meat. Colin Isherwood had long since disappeared. In a pique, he had tossed his monogrammed golf bag into the weeds and gone home.

"Does your father know all this?" asked Bates.

"He advises caution," Walter said.

This revelation, coupled with Franklin Beaumont's unexpected visit to the Bates' home, had plunged young Philbin into gloomy circumspection. In his mind, he made the obvious leap to where the evidence was leading him. But Philbin Bates' advocacy didn't extend to matters of the heart, and so he decided to keep his own counsel.

*

As he had done for some forty years. Bates slipped the scorecard into his pocket, a keepsake of their golf outing. The rest of the drawer held souvenirs, including an insect trapped in amber, along with Lawrence Savings & Trust paperweights and other dross from Walter Beaumont's long career. There was an ancient package of Chesterfield cigarettes.

Bates also discovered a small notebook that had been recently filled out and contained a list of addresses, all of them in Lawrence. Beside each address was an account number in Walter's shaky handwriting, then a figure that sometimes rose as high as $90,000. Scattered over the pages was an occasional fourth entry that was usually $100 and, on just two occasions, $250.

Bates was puzzled by the ledger. Since Walter's retirement at the age of sixty-five, his financial portfolio had been managed by a brokerage firm, with incidentals like his pension and annuity drafts funneling through the Bates' law office. And these pencil scratchings were insignificant if one knew that the retired banker's wealth grew by as much as $10,000 a month, regardless of what additional investments he made. Also, Philbin Bates had presumed that Walter's illness barred him from conducting business, but the notations were accompanied by recent dates.

The remaining pages of the ledger were blank. Flipping through, Bates came across an old photograph lodged in the binding. It was Beaumont *père*, sitting in an empty room with white-columned mansions and weeping willows printed on the wallpaper. Depicted in the photograph from the waist up, the mill overseer was wearing his hat and nothing else. For several moments, Bates considered this portrait of a naked, middle-aged man. He had been dead for thirty-seven years but in some quarters, the photograph would have still constituted a scandal. Apparently, Franklin Beaumont had hidden aspects of himself from an entire city, but evidence of his peccadilloes had not eluded his son.

Bates stuck the pasteboard photograph back inside the ledger and pocketed the book. He glanced at his watch; there was just enough time to take a look around the property. Soon all Walter's possessions, including his municipal bonds and stocks, his car, and every stick of furniture in the house, would be liquidated to pay estate taxes, legal fees, and the distributions itemized in his will. Philbin Bates, as executor, had a maximum of one year to catalogue Walter's assets, coax them to the highest possible level, and then dissolve the estate.

Extinguishing the lamp, the lawyer placed the chair in its slot and came around the desk. Something gleamed, and he bent to pick up an object from the floor. It looked like a bullet, so small he had nearly missed it. Carrying the object in his hand, Bates re-entered the hallway and glanced at the cylinder in the light. He tugged and it came apart: a woman's lipstick.

The rest of the house was immaculate, except for a patina of dust that had begun to settle over the furniture. Bates went up to the second floor, glanced around the rooms, and then returned to the main level and entered the kitchen. On the counter was a bone-handled knife and the severed heads of half a dozen strawberries. Their bloody scalps left stains on a paper towel, and Bates could see from two red fingerprints on the table that Walter Beaumont's last meal had been the strawberries and a cup of black coffee, which was skinned over with mold. He dumped the coffee into the sink and ran the water after it. Screwing the tap shut, he heard the water gurgle in the pipes, then a last little echo that sounded like a person laughing far beneath the house.

Walking down the hallway something compelled Philbin Bates to open the door to the cellar. From somewhere beyond the crooked steps came the smell of turpentine and spilled heating oil. Because of Walter's condition, it had probably been quite a long time since he had ventured downstairs to adjust his furnace or tinker with the hot water heater. For a period of years, his life had been confined to the first two floors. Then, as the emphysema progressed, the bathroom, study and kitchen had formed Walter's universe, until he lay in bed with just a piss bottle and his medic-alert button. Under such an exile, parts of Walter Beaumont's own house had become as remote as the moon.

Bates remembered the coal chute in the Beaumont cellar. When he was a boy, the coal wagon came around early in the morning. The driver would unhinge a door in the foundation and then lower a metal trough from the wagon. By lifting a spring-loaded blade, he sent his delivery rumbling into the coal bin accompanied by a large cloud of dust.

After the old furnace was removed, Franklin Beaumont had walled up his coal bin to make a darkroom. For many years, amateur photography had been the only diversion from his seventy-hour work weeks. The old man became quite a fanatic, ordering chemicals and glass lenses and special acid-free paper through his buyers at the mill. He started with portraiture and gradually moved into esoteric images like the giant fans that cooled the dye house, and shots of an egg-and-dart molding above the Ayer Mill entrance that he fussed with for months. One project involved spigots of water that ran under the baling machines before dumping into the canal. Beaumont would stand in the August heat of a Sunday, waiting for the light to drop over the mill and strike the flowing water. Then he would shoot plate after plate of what looked like nothing, just a shining bar of effluvium truncated by an ocher paper.

Franklin Beaumont spent every free minute in the darkness of his cellar, introducing an agent that solidified these columns of water and made stone ripple like grasses in the wind. After his infamous visit to the Bates home, Franklin entered the abstract phase of his hobby; depicting the velvety inside of a tea rose and gnarled old sticks lying in the gutter. Perhaps there were antique cameras and other paraphernalia still down there, but Philbin Bates did not investigate. He preferred to make his appearance in court that morning without any coal dust smeared over his neat blue suit.

He lingered for a moment at the head of the stairs. Philbin Bates was only twenty-seven years old when his own father had passed away. A call came into the law office about some sort of attack and before he could reach the hospital, Judge Bates was dead. Philbin made the funeral arrangements and greeted visitors while mired in a slow gray funk, like he was swimming in syrup. His hand ached from the hundreds of men who grasped and shook it, nodding their heads in mute befuddlement. The one image he retained was Colin Isherwood I, in front of the Bates mausoleum. Isherwood tried to hold back his tears and then the good-humored newspaperman sat on a marble bench and wept, his long fingers splayed over his forehead. He admitted later that it was the only time he had ever cried in public but that it felt good, because Ignatius Bates was as fine a person as he'd ever known.

Cool air emanated from the darkness, bringing an odor of moss and tubers up from beneath the faint chemical smells. In the shadowy gray vault of the cellar, Bates imagined a netherworld where Franklin and Walter Beaumont and all the rest of their clan had gathered. Over long stretches of time the house had emptied itself of the mill overseer, his wife and his son, and what was once solid about them had become

Jay Atkinson

insubstantial, fading into the recesses of memory. It was the same with the entire city. Lawrence had prospered and then failed, and men like the Beaumonts and Colin Isherwood and Judge Bates had all rumbled down the slope into dust.

Bates reached down to adjust the slim gold buckle on his belt. He was sixty-nine years old. Although his blood pressure was normal and his most recent examination in the office of Montgomery Tattersall had turned out quite well, sooner rather than later he would join the thronging shadows at the bottom of the stairs. He remembered some lines from Thomas Hardy about the running of Time's far glass. But in his case, that distance had been foreshortened. Everything about the future was close at hand, refracted in such proportion that it loomed grainy and indistinct, almost unrecognizable. Bates thought of his granddaughters Nina and Rose, shining like pennies, their heedless laughter and coarse red hair. He had seen them growing up in the photographs he received at Christmas, from mismatched toddlers in short pants to young ladies arrayed in pinafores and school uniforms. Just when his little granddaughters' flames were beginning to sparkle, his own taper was running out. His last will and testament was specific in providing for the girls' education, yet he wanted something more for them—although he wasn't quite certain what it was. Swallowing drily, Bates closed the door to the cellar.

With the ledger flapping against his hip, Attorney Bates proceeded to check the lock on the rear exit and all the windows on the first floor. He made a note to have the bed in the parlor removed, along with the oxygen tank and the other appurtenances of Walter's illness. Out on the porch, he drew in great lungfuls of fresh air and regarded the sun climbing over the hemlocks. Mayflies twirled about him in the rays of light, and he felt the infinitesimal weight of their bodies as he dispersed them with his hand. Unseen ground insects, buzzing and making sounds like those of tiny sirens, joined a sweet warbling from the trees. Bates broke off one of the green shoots from a shrub that overhung the porch and broke it apart in his fingers, inhaling the fresh wet scent of evergreen.

He passed alongside the glass mural and clattered down the stairs. In the garage was Walter's dark blue Oldsmobile. Bates found the key on his chain and slid into the front seat. The car was two years old, but still smelled of the showroom and had only two hundred and fifty-three miles on the odometer. After his retirement from the bank, Walter had kept up his practice of buying a new car every spring, even though he hardly drove them and took a financial beating when he traded them in. It was the one luxury he could never give up, a symbol of his independence. This show of wealth was in marked contrast with Franklin Beaumont, who had driven the same '37 Pierce Arrow for years. The lawyer wondered what had become of the old touring car. For a generation, the Pierce Arrow was a fixture at noontime in front of Murphy's Cafe on Essex Street. Bates was surprised that the car wasn't occupying the other stall in the garage, but that side was empty.

He thought of his friend dressed in cardigan and touring cap, clutching his oxygen caddy as his breath came in gasps and he measured the distance from the porch to his car. How many times had he marshaled his strength, forced himself outside and then given up, retreating to his day bed? Bates opened the glove compartment and removed the registration slip. On the passenger seat was a small glass tube bent upward with a metal fitting at one end. Assuming it was part of Walter's oxygen set-up, Bates put the pipe in his shirt pocket and locked up the car.

A sedan turned onto the property as Attorney Bates emerged from the garage. Slowly the car rolled toward him, crunching over the gravel. Agent Maxwell got out and stood on the whitewashed stones of the driveway. "Is this the Beaumont residence?" he asked.

"It was," said the lawyer. "Walter Beaumont died a week ago."

"That's too bad," Maxwell said.

"I'm representing the estate," the lawyer said. "Is there anything I can do for you?"

Maxwell unbuttoned his jacket and spread it wide, hands resting on his hips. "Don't know," he said. "I'm working through a line of reasoning on some of the arsons and talking to local bankers about insurance indemnity and a few other things."

"Walter had been retired for years," said Bates. "Have you spoken to Chuck Prescott at Lawrence Savings & Trust? He's the president down there now."

"I talked to him yesterday. Mr. Prescott told me that the bank had written a lot of mortgages and taken out fire insurance on some of these properties back when Mr. Beaumont was overseeing things. He also said that until this past year Mr. Beaumont had been one of the bank's directors and had given him some advice on acquisitions and so forth."

Bates was conscious of the ledger in his pocket. "If you don't mind me asking, how many fires have occurred in properties owned by Lawrence Savings & Trust?" he asked.

"Seven out of the last thirty," said Maxwell.

The twittering of birds filled the silence. Frowning, Bates glanced at his watch. "I have to get to court," he said. The lawyer started for his car and then turned back. "Could Walter have benefited personally from those fires?" he asked.

"Not directly, according to Prescott. You could say that, since the insured value was greater than the market value of the properties, and since none of them were selling anyway, that the bank profited from cashing in the fire policies. As a shareholder of the bank, Mr. Beaumont also profited." Maxwell's shrug was an admission that his logic stretched awkwardly over the facts. "But the margins were small, and divided among all the shareholders they'd be considered almost negligible."

Bates scratched his ear and nodded. "Another point is that Walter's condition had deteriorated so rapidly these past few months that, in addition to it being impossible for him to have been involved in any wrongdoing, it's arguable that his quality of life prevented him from enjoying or making use of any profit he might have received," the lawyer said. "I'm not violating my client's trust in saying that he was a wealthy

Jay Atkinson

man and a clever investor. I've helped keep track of those investments for forty-something years, and what you're talking about is very pale in comparison."

"All I'm doing is serving the taxpayers by running out every lead we get," said the ATF agent. "Are you compiling an account of the estate?"

"Someone in my office will be starting that process very soon. I just came by to make sure everything was all right. Walter was a friend of mine."

"Would you mind if I had a look around?" asked Maxwell. "I mean, we're not ready to get a warrant or anything, but just to satisfy my curiosity."

Attorney Bates looked at his watch again. "I'm going to be late," he said. "In Walter's interest, I'd like to accompany you inside. Can we make an appointment to do it later?"

"How about tomorrow? Nine AM?"

The lawyer agreed and walked off toward his car. Rick Maxwell, with one foot on the berm that separated the driveway from the lawn, stared up at the massive old house.

Philbin Bates drifted through traffic and parked in a lot near his office. Behind locked doors, he spread open Walter Beaumont's ledger and did several calculations on his adding machine. The numbers dismayed him. For five minutes, he stared out his window. The lawyer turned back to the adding machine and finished his computations. By dividing the percentage of Walter's shares in the bank by the amount of the insurance policies itemized in the ledger, he ended up with a close approximation of what Walter's profit would have been on each transaction.

Adding the seven numbers in the ledger, the lawyer discovered that their total was the same as Beaumont's estimated profit from the fires as a shareholder in the bank—$1,000. Bates fished a copy of the *Tribune-Standard* from his wastebasket. One of the addresses in Walter's handwriting corresponded to the site of a recent fire on Annis Street, a warehouse that the lawyer recalled had once been a storage facility for the Ayer Mill. Equally distressing was the fact that, after writing down the address, Walter had died three days before the fire had occurred. It was a short march from this to the incredible notion that the dead banker had something to do with arson in Lawrence. Bates reasoned that Walter Beaumont had been unable to visit any of the sites personally, although the extra line of figures, which were negligible amounts, might have represented payments to an accomplice.

On the surface, Bates' whole theory seemed ridiculous. More than once, Walter had expressed his anguish over the blight that had afflicted the city. His generosity and advice had kept many of Lawrence's institutions functioning beyond their natural lifespans. But the dogged line of Bates' intelligence could not be turned aside: Walter was in it up to his neck. Scratching at this intuition had led to the first piece of hard evidence. The lawyer didn't want to see any more.

He opened the window, letting in the cool morning air. Philbin Bates stood on top of his desk and unscrewed the smoke detector. Then he dragged the wastebasket over near the window. Balling up pages of the newspaper, he lit a match and got a blaze going inside the metal drum. One by one, he added pages of the ledger to the fire. A tornado of smoke came from the wastebasket and, before it became too hot, he lifted the drum onto the windowsill.

The lawyer removed the old photograph of Franklin Beaumont from the ledger. The mill overseer's face looked rubbery, the lower half twisted around sideways. He appeared to have been drugged. For a few seconds, the lawyer contemplated the puffy slope of Beaumont's torso, exposed like the larva of an insect. Then Bates scaled the card into the flames, throwing fresh smoke from the window—a signal that something had been decided.

16

Lawrence, Massachusetts
November 2, 1932

The corridor outside of the Ayer Mill office was still as Gus Hearin slowed to open the door, the echo of his footsteps coming up behind. Except for Miss Halliman, who was typing, the outer office was deserted, and the secretary hardly looked up when she gestured toward one of the chairs against the wall. After the pungency of the dye house it took a few moments, but Gus detected an unpleasant smell lingering in the room. Then an electric box on the desk made a noise and Miss Halliman answered it by pushing a button. The voice that came from the intercom was garbled but the secretary said, "Yes, sir" and directed her gaze at Mr. Hearin.

"He'll be with you shortly," she said, and resumed tapping the keys.

Originally the office had contained two desks and now there was only a light spot on the carpet where Mrs. Litwack's had been removed after she'd died. Three chairs separated by an old spittoon and a dustbin comprised the rest of the furniture. At age 47, Miss Halliman's small, dry face had taken on the look of parchment. She used to walk home from the market with a single pork chop and the men on Essex Street laughed and called her "Miss Doesn't Have-a-man."

The mill offices were quiet on Saturdays because Shipping & Receiving was closed, although the manufacturing plant was busy from six AM until noon. Gus Hearin, foreman of the dye house, had been talking with the chemist when a boy ran up and said he was wanted in the office right away. Twice the chemist asked if he should drain the tanks, it being nearly 11 AM, but Hearin was fondling the nub of his ear and staring in the direction the runner had gone.

Now Gus sat drumming his fingers on the arm of the chair. He had been toiling in the Ayer Mill for twenty-six years and never once been summoned to the office. Since making foreman Gus reported to the superintendent, Mr. Gorham, a fat, bitter man who had predicted he would be passed over in the search for a general overseer and whose prediction had proven correct. After Billy Wood's death in '26, the American Woolen Company's board of directors, acting from their headquarters in New York, had appointed a temporary committee to run the Ayer Mill. As the recession deepened, the company had been so occupied with consolidating its business, that it had taken six years to install an overseer. Finally they had done it.

In the dustbin was a two-week old copy of the *Lawrence Tribune-Standard*. Casting a glance at Miss Halliman, Gus withdrew the newspaper and spread it over his knee. On the front page was a photograph of a man wearing rimless spectacles.

> *Franklin Beaumont, age 43, a prominent executive in the local textile industry, has assumed new duties as general overseer of the Ayer Mill. He was a member of the interim committee running the mill since the death of its founder and president William Madison Wood.*
>
> *Mr. Beaumont has been connected with the Ayer Mill for many years. He is a member of the American Association of Textile Executives and formerly served as chairman of the northern New England division of that organization.*
>
> *Married, Mr. Beaumont makes his home with his family at 621 Haverhill Street in Lawrence. A son, Walter, age 22, is soon to be discharged from the Army.*

The noon whistle sounded throughout the building and at that instant, the mechanical hum that gripped the Ayer Mill ceased to be heard. Again Miss Halliman's intercom squawked and she beckoned to Gus Hearin.

"Mr. Beaumont will see you now," she said.

Before Hearin gained his feet, the door to the next room opened and he and Miss Halliman were confronted with the specter of Dick Morgan. A terrible odor filled the room and although it was impossible for such a large fellow to make himself inconspicuous, Morgan was hunched over at the waist and his legs rustled when he moved. The coat that he wore, if it could be called that, was fashioned from a number of smaller overcoats and formed a great, parti-colored mass that hung to the ground. His boots were stuffed with newsprint and there did not appear to be a viable tooth in his head.

Morgan crossed the room, staring toward the door with baleful eyes. As he passed near Miss Halliman's desk, the secretary took a bank note from the drawer. "Mr. Morgan," she said, holding out the note. "Mr. Beaumont wished you to have this."

The former strongman took the five dollar bill without making a reply. He rubbed the dirty green paper between his fingers and stuck the bill in his pocket. Turning for the exit, he saw Gus Hearin, his old coatroom nemesis, standing on the light spot in the carpet where Mrs. Litwack's desk had been. The men regarded each other, and without a sign of recognition Dick Morgan looked away.

Jay Atkinson

Gus Hearin, too, had aged. His hair was sparse and gray and stood up on his head like wires. Although tall, he had grown fat around the middle, and his mangled right ear and a portion of his scalp were gray with scarring. But Morgan had fared worse in the years since they had last seen each other. Another man's tragedy had separated him from his occupation, his health, and his dignity.

On August 15, 1922, Billy Wood had received a telephone call informing him that 30-year old Will, Jr. had been in an automobile accident, along with his friend Alex Gardner. The caller said that Major Gardner was driving his Rolls Royce at high speed and had struck a telephone pole. Hastening from his office, Mr. Wood had ordered Dick Morgan to bring the limousine around and then followed his chauffeur through the mill, intent on gaining the accident scene as rapidly as possible.

On a wooded section of the North Reading-Andover road nine miles from the Ayer Mill, they came across a policeman in his double-breasted tunic and jodhpurs. A short distance away, two horses with shiny leather tack were hitched to a mile marker. The policeman had erected a barricade from several large tree limbs and there he stood, signaling for the limousine to approach with caution, to slow down, and finally, to stop.

"Sweet, merciful God," said William Wood as he bolted from the car.

Beyond the policeman was an empty stretch of roadway, marked with two long streaks of rubber. Just off the shoulder was a cream-colored Rolls Royce, lying on its side with the roof smashed flat. Parked farther along the road was an ambulance with two Red Cross men in their white uniforms and visored caps.

The millionaire waddled along as fast as he could. "Will," he said. "No, no, no."

Dick Morgan overtook him just as the policeman moved aside the barricade, allowing another vehicle to pass. Gliding toward them was a hearse, polished to a black so deep and perfect it collected iridescent highlights from the air, curved human figures in its gleaming chrome, and the reflection of inverted fir trees. Wood caught sight of the hearse, the wreck, and the policeman's face all in the same instant and let out a shriek. The two corpses were lying on matted grass, their feet extending beyond the single horse blanket that covered them. William Wood, Jr., the taller of the two, wore a pair of white bucks and Major Gardner had on military boots and puttees.

Billy Wood grasped at Morgan's lapels, his face drained of blood and a dark flush along his scalp. "What is it?" he asked. His voice became strangled in his throat; he coughed in a deep, raspy tone, and the muscles along his forehead and jaw contorted like a man suffering an attack of palsy.

The mill owner collapsed on the pavement as the white-jacketed attendants grabbed their valises and ran toward him. Then an even stranger thing happened. William Wood began to curse his son in the foulest, most profane terms imaginable. While Dick Morgan staved off the ambulance attendants with a glare, this malefaction of his own spawn continued until Mr. Wood allowed himself to be hauled up and set on the pavement.

Two men in black suits retrieved the corpses from the roadside and loaded them into the hearse. Then the undertakers climbed into the front seat and the long black car swung in an arc and passed through the barricade, embossed with fir trees.

"That's what lawn tennis will do for you," Billy Wood told his chauffeur.

In the months that followed, Wood's health continued to fail and the scope of Dick Morgan's duties grew smaller. Some time later Dr. Griffin surmised that Wood had suffered a stroke that day on the North Reading-Andover road, the first in a series of these attacks over the next two years. Even when the mill owner was strong enough to work, his temper became uncontrollable and he paced the halls of the Ayer Mill swearing under his breath. His interest in Shawsheen Village faded, to the point where he didn't bother to attend the ribbon cutting. With the American Woolen Company's stock plummeting, the board of directors forced Billy Wood out and a short time later, the Man Without A Stain Upon His Honor was dead.

Dick Morgan had been wandering the country since Wood's death, living in hobo encampments, working as a strikebreaker in Chicago, and panhandling in Omaha. He had seen a fellow killed in Tennessee by a mob that wanted the man's shoes and he had squatted in firelight eating "Hoover ham" while teen-age boys fought over the scraps. Morgan had never singled out Lawrence as a destination; rather, his peregrinations just led him back there, as the rest of the country had been trammeled and exhausted. But there was no work in the mills or anyplace else and soon the old prizefighter would be hiding in a copse of trees with other bankrupt men, waiting for the next train out.

The fright of seeing him that way, ill-smelling and toothless, had distracted Gus Hearin from his own troubles. But as Morgan crossed the rug and the door flapped shut behind him, Hearin marched toward Beaumont's office with a sense of dread. He had no reason to worry: the dye house had made all its goals since he had been named foreman and he had worked like the devil to please his bosses, often staying until nine o'clock at night. Perhaps this meeting was a formality and Hearin would soon be laughing about it with the fellows. But his heart thundered in his chest and his legs were numb.

Reaching for the doorknob, Gus looked back and Miss Halliman began typing again and he moistened his lips and went in. Beaumont was seated at the desk, studying an oversize ledger and making notations with a pencil. He waved Hearin toward a chair and they sat that way for an entire minute, the general overseer jotting notes and the dye house foreman clasping his hands and perspiring. An old photograph of William Wood and Frederick Ayer hung on the wall, inscribed: *October 4, 1910. Dedication of the Ayer Mill clock.*

Finally Beaumont settled his gaze on the dye house foreman. The

Jay Atkinson

general overseer's face was pink with burst capillaries and his hair was turning white. "I'm letting you go," he said. "See Mr. Stevens for your pay and get out."

Gus Hearin felt a lump growing in his throat and before he could choke it away, Mr. Beaumont was dialing the telephone. He pointed to the door.

It had been unpleasant for the general overseer, but business was business. The Great War had been over for thirteen years and the Ayer Mill's largest profits had gone with it. In retrospect, Billy Wood's finest moment was the creation of an inexpensive olive drab dye. Throughout the war and for almost a decade afterwards, they sold woolen blankets and uniforms to the Russians and French, as well as the Americans. All three armies were stockpiled now; it would take another war to dent their reserves and that didn't seem likely at present.

Franklin Beaumont knew he must lower wages and tighten operations or the Ayer would fail. He had begun by promoting Moses Stevens to treasurer and summoning this Hearin from the dye house, but he had been sidetracked by the appearance of Dick Morgan. It was a sad case, all around. Beaumont gazed at the picture of Billy Wood and remembered the years they had spent together, particularly during the war. He was not a sentimental man but Mr. Wood had been a fine example to him, the paradigm of a textile executive. In his opinion, Billy Wood's firing and his exodus from Lawrence had heaped shame upon the corporation.

*

Gus Hearin received a tiny paper chit from Miss Halliman and passed through the exit, walked along the main corridor, and knocked on the door to the countinghouse.

"Come in," said a voice.

The sole occupant of the room, Moses Stevens, was perched on a stool behind one of the highboy desks, with a cashbox at his elbow, several timecards stacked together and a gold-nibbed fountain pen. Stevens wore abbreviated spectacles attached to a length of black ribbon and his feet dangled off the ground. "I'll take that," he said, gesturing toward the chit.

Hearin gave him the paper and the treasurer of the Ayer Mill scrutinized Mr. Beaumont's signature and then opened the box on his desk and counted out several banknotes. Then he shuffled the bills into an envelope and handed it over the desk.

"You shorted me," said Hearin.

The treasurer shook his head. "I most certainly did not," he said, studying the chit and Hearin's timecard, which was on top of the stack. "You've been paid for fifty-nine hours."

"It's a sixty hour week."

"According to Mr. Beaumont, you were in his office for an hour this morning and we're not obligated to pay for that," said Stevens.

Hearin's jaw dropped. "I went to the office because Mr. Beaumont told me to go, and I waited because he made me wait," he said.

In a gesture of finality, the treasurer stretched a rubber band around the timecards and stowed them and the cashbox in the desk. He wiped the tip of his pen with a chamois cloth, unscrewed the gold nib, and placed the nib and stock in the little wooden reservoir beside the ink well. Then Stevens removed his spectacles, allowing them to hang about his neck by the ribbon.

"This office is closed," he said.

Gus went into the main pavilion and onto the street with the last of his wages in his pocket. Without thinking, he crossed the road and headed over the Duck Bridge, his shoes chiming against the metal and the river fast and black through the apertures. A truck passed and the driver blew his horn and shouted at Hearin to make way. He was going to get himself killed, the truck driver said.

At the next intersection several men were climbing the battlements of Holy Rosary church, installing a green slate roof. They scrambled over the ridgepole without harnesses or straps, calling to one another in Italian. Hearin rounded the corner and piles of slate blocked the way, forcing him into the gutter. The electric car slowed and he had time to get aboard but suddenly a nickel was dear and he let the car pass. It sang against the wires overhead and the wheels made a rhythmic noise on the tracks.

The sky was overcast and Essex Street was dressed in various shades of gray. Bundles of *The Lawrence Tribune-Standard* were piled against the curbing; on the cover of each paper was the headline ROOSEVELT TOUTS 'NEW DEAL'. Soon men would be fighting over the bundles when in years past it was only boys that hawked newspapers. In front of Lawrence Savings & Trust, other men stood before pyramids of shiny red apples, two for a dime. Just yesterday, Hearin had lingered there with a fellow named Glass, sharing a bottle the apple vendor carried in his pocket. It was a cold, clear evening and to the delight of the apple sellers, Gus belted out "There's No Endurance Like the Man Who Sells Insurance," to shouts and applause. But now he trudged along with his hands in his pockets, his collar up, without saying a word to anybody.

Gus Hearin shuffled along Broadway, ignoring the panhandlers and hawkers and shoeshine men that crowded the sidewalks. He turned down Spruce Street and entered the three-decker where he and his family rented by the week. He had no idea how he was going to tell Elena he had been sacked or what they would do next. Last June he had received a letter from his younger brother stating that the family farm was affected by blight and he'd rented the barn and smokehouse to other families. Gus had left that barren patch of ground in '06 and wouldn't be going back.

The smell of lye overpowered the fish heads in the sump. On his way upstairs, Hearin paused for Mrs. Driscoll, who was scrubbing the treads with a bar of OK Soap. Since her husband had lost his arm in the war, she did odd jobs around the neighborhood. Mrs. Driscoll looked up as Gus passed by her, making wet footprints on the stairs.

When he reached the landing, Elena opened the door to greet him. Gus could smell the burnt orange peels on top of the stove and reached into his pocket for the envelope and handed it to his wife. Behind her on the table was a cake with eighteen candles. His grown son, John, who had been struck by an automobile when he was twelve and was an idiot, sat wearing a tiny paper hat. He swung his gaze toward his father and pointed his finger and started laughing: Gus had forgotten his son's birthday.

17

The Present Day

The sun drew a scalloped line of shade along the pavement. Rising over the downtown buildings, it glinted on cars and shimmered across the roof of WKUT, before ducking behind a cloud. In the strange eclipse that followed, Francesca Nesheim heard a sizzle from the WKUT antenna. For an instant the vibration electrified the sweet June air, and then passed straight through her. A moment later, she felt the sun again, warming her skin. The young ice skater hesitated on the sidewalk, and then someone inside the radio station pressed the security buzzer and she entered the lobby.

Behind the reception desk was a woman with gold-blonde hair. "Can I help you?" she asked.

"I want to see Kap Kutter," said Francesca. "It's urgent."

"Do you have an appointment?"

On the wall was a moose head with widespread antlers, along with several photographs of Charlie Kutter, the famous announcer. The central portrait was of the square-jawed Kutter in middle age, posing in his yellow network blazer. The rest of the pictures had been taken when the sportscaster was out hunting or fishing. Kap appeared in three of them—as a seven-year-old, a teenager in a New York Yankees cap, and then a handsome young man with none of the gray hair or paunch that he had now. His celebrity father never seemed to change as Kap went through this remarkable transformation, each time holding up a smaller fish or pheasant than the one that dominated the photograph.

Francesca introduced herself to the receptionist. "I doubt Kap would have given me an appointment," she said. "I'm pregnant."

Elise Dominaux ducked around the moose antlers and grasped Francesca's hand. "You poor thing," she said. "Did Kap dump you? He's such a bastard."

"He doesn't even know about it yet."

Filling a paper cup with water, Elise put her hand on Francesca's lower

Jay Atkinson

back and attempted to steer her into a chair. "Here," she said. "You must be exhausted."

"I feel great," said Francesca. She placed the tiny cup on the desk. "Is Kap here?"

The receptionist fluttered her lips. "His father's in town, so he's on his best behavior," said Elise.

"Where are they?" Francesca asked.

"Over at Bachop's, having lunch," said Elise. "The old man drinks like there's no tomorrow."

The women turned to behold the portrait of Charlie Kutter, beside which the regal head of the moose was somehow diminished. Upon his face was a satiated look, like a man who celebrated Christmas every day. Charlie Kutter held the two women in his powerful blue-eyed gaze.

Francesca gulped. "I'm going over there," she said.

"I'll come with you," said Elise. Reaching over the desk, she picked up the telephone and dialed a single number. "Sheryl—cover the phones, will you? I'm going to lunch." She grabbed her handbag, and she and Francesca went out.

Francesca marched over the radio station lawn toward Bachop's. She was now three months pregnant—illustrated by a slight tilt in her abdomen. Elise double-timed it alongside, chopping at the pavement in her high heels. Although cinched in a brassiere, her chest bounced in several directions as she walked.

A man in a delivery van shouted, "Hey, nice tits," and Elise gave him the finger.

"It's been a tough year," Francesca said. "Now with another baby coming..." She sighed, looking down at her sneakers. "Things will be even worse."

"Especially if it's Kap Kutter's baby," Elise said. High above Common Street, a woodpecker knocked at a utility pole and the sound echoed over the rooftops. "What did you ever see in that jerk?" she asked.

"One night we took a drive in this car he had, a Jaguar or something." Francesca shrugged, and a diamond of muscle formed between her shoulders. "The next thing I know, we're parked in the cemetery and he's telling me how beautiful I am."

In front of them was a municipal parking lot and Elise and Francesca zigzagged through the cars, toward the spot where Bachop's shimmered like an oasis. A fellow in a plaid tuxedo greeted them at the top of the stairs. "Good afternoon, ladies," said Aram Bachop, a squat, balding man with tight gray curls above each ear. "Will there be just the two of you?"

Francesca shook her head. "We're just looking for someone."

"Very good," Aram said. He swung the glass door open to accommodate the two young women, the smile dropping from his face as they passed.

Inside Bachop's, two stone jars flanked the entranceway and a carpet figured with golden camels and palm trees lay over the terra cotta floor. The atmosphere was cool, the lights were dimmed, and a redolence of braised lamb shanks, garlic on the skewer with fresh vegetables, and marinated feta cheese wafted from the dining room.

Amir, nearly identical to his brother and also dressed in a tuxedo, beckoned Francesca and Elise forward. He was standing behind a counter filled with various brands of cigars and netted bottles of Bachop's famous marinade. "Two?" he asked.

"We're looking for Kap Kutter," said Francesca. "Can we go in?"

The restaurateur glanced at her shorts and sneakers, then moved his hand. "Go ahead," he said.

Glass tables ran down the center of the main dining room and booths upholstered in pale blue Leatherette lined the walls. The Bachop coat of arms—a camel standing under a palm tree—was embossed on each of the tables. Faint paths in the carpet were visible from the lobby to the kitchen.

Tambourine music was playing over the public address system and the buzz of conversation filled the room. The waiters carried trays filled with dinner salads in little cut glass bowls, and trenchers of baba ghanough and hummus sprinkled with paprika, accompanied by sliced red onion. Moving among the tables, these tired-looking men handed out baskets of pita bread and smiled at the customers with their dentures.

Francesca spotted Kap Kutter and his father and strode toward them over the thick blue carpet. Charlie Kutter was waving his glass in the air. "Garçon, another bourbon," he called to the waiter.

The retired announcer wore loose-fitting khakis and a polo shirt with *Pebble Beach Classic* stitched on the left breast. He was thin, with a droopy neck and shimmying wet eyeballs. Charlie and his son were accompanied by a third man, fleshy and red-faced, who had adorned his massive head with an admiral's cap that read:

> *Pick Byer's Professional Bass Fishing*
> *Ocala, Florida.*

Francesca came to the booth and stood for a moment looking down at one of the Leatherette menus, with camels and sheiks emblazoned on its cover.

Pick Byers spoke first. "What can I do for you?" he asked, studying Francesca like she was a glossy-hulled bass boat. "Because I would gladly do it, yessir."

"I need to speak to Kap," said Francesca.

Byers winked at his companions. "Who would want to talk to a worn-out old bass fisherman?" he asked. "My wife won't even tell me what time she's serving dinner."

Kap Kutter didn't recognize Francesca right away. But he noticed Elise Dominaux marooned in one of the shipping channels to the kitchen, staring at him. Kap squirmed into the far corner of the booth and gulped his drink.

Pick Byers ogled Francesca, a stuffed grapeleaf pinched between his fingers like a cigar. "If I could be a young man again for about an hour," he said.

Charlie Kutter put his rheumy eyes on her. "Are you a waitress in this

Jay Atkinson

dump?" he asked. "Because if you are, how long does it take to pour a shot of Jack Daniels?"

"I don't work here," said Francesca.

A waiter passed by and Charlie Kutter raised his arm with the glass tumbler at the end of it. "Damnit, where's that drink?" He glanced at the young ice skater, annoyed by her presence.

"I need to speak to Kap," Francesca said. "It's personal."

Pick Byers put his large red hands on the table. "It's not polite to keep a lady waitin'," he said to Kap, inching sideways to allow him out of the booth.

"Come see me in my office," said Kap. "We're discussing business right now."

Charlie Kutter motioned for Kap to stay quiet. "Say what you got to say," he told Francesca.

"I'm pregnant," Francesca said. She glared at Kap Kutter, who refused to look at her. "When my baby's born, you're gonna have to take a paternity test."

Charlie Kutter shook his head in disbelief and then pointed at his son. "Jesus Goldstein," he said. "Don't you have any sense? What about my granddaughter?"

"It's bullshit," Kap said.

"Is this some stupid attempt to squeeze money out of me?" asked the retired announcer. "Because it's not gonna happen."

Elise Dominaux came over to the booth. "I don't know anything about Francesca's baby, Mr. Kutter," she said. "But I can tell you that your son harasses women, cheats on his wife, and spends about as much time at the radio station as you do."

"You're on my payroll and you're making accusations like this?" asked Charlie Kutter.

"I'm just getting warmed up," Elise said.

Heads turned, and whispering began among the tables. Charlie Kutter scowled into his empty glass.

"If this son of yours can't keep his plug out of the lily pads, Charlie, you best take him off the water," said Pick Byers. "Radio is dead. Get out while you still have your pants on, and we can make this bass business fly."

Aram Bachop approached, smiling at them. "What seems to be the trouble?" he asked.

"Him," said Elise, pointing at Kap Kutter. "He's an alcoholic, womanizing bum who's guilty of sexual harassment and embezzlement, and may have gotten this poor woman pregnant."

With the grin of a corpse, Aram bent forward, his eyes darting from Elise Dominaux to Kap Kutter. "Would you like the check?" he asked.

"I can't make it through an afternoon on these turds," said Pick Byers. He tossed the grapeleaf onto the tablecloth. "Bring me that prime rib I ordered. And Charlie needs another drink."

The women stepped back as the food arrived: a skinned fish with white sauce, lamb kabobs, and a bruised and bloody prime rib. As quickly as he could, the waiter unloaded the main dishes and platters of French fried potatoes, adding another basket of bread. Then he placed fresh glasses of whiskey in front of the men, and beat it back to the kitchen.

Kap looked at Elise with bloodshot eyes. "She's just some double-talking bimbo," he said.

"You're just a drunken slob whose father used to be famous," said Elise.

Pick Byers stood up, his chest shifting downward until it bulged at the spot where a belt cinched his trousers. "No need for everybody's underwear to get all wadded up," he said. "This-here kind of thing should be discussed behind closed doors."

"Bullshit," said Francesca. "Kap Kutter—you might be the father of my baby and if you are, you're gonna take legal responsibility for this child."

Shuffling his feet, Pick Byers studied one of the golden camels figured on the carpet and made a sound against his teeth. "I'm going to the head," he said, barging off through the tables.

"What are you—some kind of imbecile?" said Charlie Kutter to his son. "Forty-two years old, and not enough sense to keep your pecker dry." The retired announcer waved his hand at the ceiling. "Pick and I have been discussing a venture down in Florida. But I needed to put up some capital and until today, I didn't have it. Now, I most certainly will." He drained his bourbon and slammed the glass down on the table. "Better start reading the want ads, because the station is for sale."

The loose flesh beneath Kap's cheekbones was yanked into a grimace. "But Dad—"

"But Dad nothing," said Charlie Kutter. "To think at your age, Ted Williams clubbed a five-hundred foot home run and here it is you can't even pee straight." He poured Pick Byers' drink into his. "Why is it other men have sons that accomplish great things and look what I get: a nincompoop."

"Mr. Kutter, I—" Francesca began, but the retired announcer refused to look up.

"He'll take the goddamn paternity test," he said, waving her off. "Now get outta here."

Francesca hurried out of the dining room, nearly bowling over Aram Bachop in the process. For another moment, Elise stared at the Kutters, and then turned and stalked across the carpet. In the coolness of the lobby, she met Pick Byers coming back from the men's room.

"I admire your gumption, Miss," said the bass fisherman. They stood watching Francesca zigzag between the cars in the parking lot.

"You sure helped me convince Charlie that Lawrence is dead," said Byers. He chewed a toothpick, squinting at the gray noontime sun. "Any fool can see that."

*

After her obstetric exam, Francesca Nesheim took the elevator to the basement of Lawrence General Hospital. She found herself in a corridor that housed several laboratories, a storage area, and departments like

Jay Atkinson

CT Scanning and Medical Records. The passageway bent to the right and was crossed by another corridor with an arrow pointing toward the "Counseling Center." Francesca squeezed past dozens of folding chairs stacked against the wall and entered an ancient section of the hospital, where the paint was chipped and beads of moisture clung to the ceiling. At the end of the hallway, she knocked at the door to the counseling office and a woman told her to come in.

The room's sole occupant was an elderly woman with her white hair gathered upward to form a tulip shape. Eyes that were a brilliant shade of blue shone out of the woman's face, which swayed on its framework of bone when she turned her head. Gazing over the nameplate on her desk, Pier Eriksen had an elegant bearing and skin the color of marzipan. Her face was smooth and radiated health, considering she was at least eighty years old.

Mrs. Eriksen was engaged on the telephone, indicating that Francesca should remain in the office until the conversation was completed. Dressed in a pink smock with a tag that read *Volunteer,* the old woman lifted one arm like a symphony conductor and began nodding her head over some point that was being made. "Yes, of course I will," she said.

Hanging up the telephone, the old woman rose to greet her visitor. "Hello, my dear," she said. "You look wonderful." Herbal fragrances circulated around her, and the glow of her white hair filled the dank little room. "Is everything all right?"

"I went to see Larry Harrah and Kap," Francesca told her. "They know about the baby and they'll both take the paternity test, but they're not very happy about it."

"Sit down, dear," said Mrs. Eriksen. She lifted a chair, settling it in front of the desk, and the two women sat knee to knee. "I spoke to Legal Aid, and they said they'd help you get a court order for all three blood tests," Mrs. Eriksen said.

"I only need two. Joe volunteered to take the test."

Several fine white hairs had loosened themselves from the arrangement on Mrs. Eriksen's head. "Men can very easily change their minds about responsibility," she said, without any trace of malice. "They've had centuries honing that particular skill, from the men who took to the sea in boats, to the ones who went wandering over the plains and climbing mountains. Fathering children was something like a biological accident to them." Mrs. Eriksen's eyes became blue slits. "You must meet strength with strength. It's the only thing men understand."

"Have you ever had any children?" Francesca asked.

The old woman's eyes were opened to their limit again and Francesca saw herself reflected in their jet-black centers. "No, I haven't," said Mrs. Eriksen. "It was almost fifty years ago that I came to Lawrence. I had experienced places and things that were unheard of. The pyramids by moonlight. *Tsars* and *tsarinas.* I rode a bicycle around Lawrence and they were all afraid of me because I was so foreign. The city in those days was little more than a struggle between management and labor, and I had no interest in either one. But one fellow didn't let that deter him; we were in love. Then his family objected, and there was quite a mess."

The old woman threw her yellow-toothed smile at the ceiling. "I counsel young women because I understand men," said Mrs. Eriksen. "And the first thing is, they are indispensable."

Francesca giggled. "Oh, yeah."

"Having a man with you is like keeping an animal. The hairiness of their bodies. The way they sleep, turning in the sheets. But never quite tamed. Never quite yours." The old woman stood tall and smiling and white-haired. "Really, it's having an ambition that truly defines a woman. Put that aside to support a man, take on the role of a bit player, and you're throwing away half your life."

Mrs. Eriksen removed a hot plate from the filing cabinet and plugged it in, then filled her teapot with water. After awhile Mrs. Eriksen took a little satchel from her handbag and poured hot water into a pair of mugs. She pinched grit into the mugs and then stirred her concoction with a sterilized tongue depressor. "Have you been eating those seeds I gave you?" she asked, handing one of the mugs to Francesca.

"Every day."

"And how have you been feeling?" asked the old woman, sipping her tea.

The ice skater crossed her legs. "I'm still skating every day. I feel strong."

Mrs. Eriksen picked up a glass paperweight from her desk and pressed it to her forehead. "Reaching old age with your mind intact is like looking through a fisheye," she said. "The shapes of the past are stretched along the perimeter, and the present is large and clear." Her eye was pink-veined and huge, the center as blue as a gemstone. "You see in three dimensions—everything except the future. Of course, all that is for nothing. The future cannot be plumbed."

"Don't you ever worry about it?" Francesca asked.

Mrs. Eriksen lowered the glass disc and her eye shrank to its normal size. "I remain fixed on the present. That's what I see the most clearly. That's where I am." She held her arms out and flexed her hands, and her jaw fell and hollowed her cheeks. "The world is where we live, and through the senses is how we live there," she said. "There's no need to go beyond that, when sensation is the pinnacle."

"What do you mean?"

The old woman returned both hands to her lap. "That telephone call was from a lawyer, telling me I'm listed in the will of an old acquaintance who died a month or so ago. There was a sum of money in question, and I said I'd give the money away. The lawyer was put off by this. For old time's sake, didn't I want to visit my friend's house before it was sold? No, I said. I never was asked to visit while he was alive, and see no reason to visit there now. As far as this acquaintance was concerned, I had disappeared. But I was always right here where you see me, in the midst of my own life."

"I should get going," Francesca said to Mrs. Eriksen, rising from her chair. "By now, Gabriel is probably wondering where his mother is."

Mrs. Eriksen collected the mugs and placed them on the desk. "You're my last appointment this morning," said the old woman. "I have my car outside. Let me give you a ride."

Together the two women navigated the bowels of the hospital. Behind the building was an old touring car with chrome fenders and plump whitewall tires. Inside, Mrs. Eriksen donned a beret with two pheasant quills through the brim. The feathers were smooth and almost black, bordered with several lighter shades of tan and brown. Mingled with strands of Mrs. Eriksen's long white hair, the quills drooped over her shoulder like plumage.

"My crash helmet," she said.

The elderly woman reached into the glove compartment for a slender glass tube with a flexible bulb on the end. Glancing upward, she squeezed a drop of fluid into each eye. "I take crushed holly berries and mix them with oil of vitriol, in a pure mineral solution. It helps me to see better," she said. The drops glistened there like jewels, and Mrs. Eriksen's eyes ran with tears for a moment. "I hardly need a car, to be honest. It was a gift from a man I used to know."

"He must have been a great friend to give you a car like this."

A security guard opened the gate with his lever, and the old woman steered the car between the metal posts. "He was very generous. But he was a self-conscious man and a little weak, I'm afraid," said Mrs. Eriksen, her eyes darkening. "That was a long, long time ago."

A man in front of Tivoli bakery stared at the old car, clutching loaves of Italian bread like a quiver of arrows. "I like to walk, usually," said Mrs. Eriksen. She glanced over at Francesca. "I plan to give the car to you and Joe. You can take Gabriel on rides in the country."

"I bet it's worth a fortune. You could sell it and give the money to charity."

"Charities are top-heavy franchises operated by hypocrites for their own enrichment," Mrs. Eriksen said. "If I'm in a position to feed the hungry or comfort the sick, then I best deliver the food and make bedside rounds myself."

Soft breezes followed the Merrimack, riffling its surface. Mrs. Eriksen turned at the light and crossed over, her tires singing on the metal bridge. "Where can I drop you?" asked the old woman. "Is Gabriel at the baby sitter's?"

"His father took him to a carnival," Francesca said. "He's gonna ride on a Ferris wheel."

"Before I was born, the American engineer George Ferris came to our summer home in Antibes," said the old woman. "He'd invented the wheel for the Chicago World's Fair and told my father it was inspired by the Roman coliseums. It wasn't until years later I had my first ride on a Ferris wheel, at the Centennial Exposition in Paris. All the lights glittering in Montparnasse and along the quay. I was with my husband and he had smuggled a bottle of champagne and some petit fours under his coat, and when we rode to the top we munched on biscuits and toasted our youth and freedom. Paris at night was like caves filled with gold. It was breathtaking."

"Whatever happened to your husband?" asked Francesca.

"It was 1937 and they were playing all these American songs on the radio. 'Who Stole My Heart Away?' was my favorite." Mrs. Eriksen hummed part of the air. "My husband and I became separated shortly afterwards. It was inevitable, I suppose. He was a Frenchman with socialist tendencies and I was an anarchist. Later he was killed in the war."

Francesca dipped her head. "I'm sorry."

"We all knew the war was coming—even in '37. Michael was a sportsman, several years older than I was, but vigorous and athletic. He had beautiful yellow hair. I remember that night on the Ferris wheel, a flock of birds came up from the Seine, flying over us, and Michael threw a biscuit high in the air. It hung there for an instant and then began to drop like a stone. One of the birds plunged into a dive. Several feet from our chair the bird threw his wings back, stopping himself in mid-flight. He looked at us with strange golden eyes; the biscuit tumbled past and he snatched it in his beak. 'Bravo!' my husband said, waving the bottle of Mumms. He rocked the chair so wildly we almost capsized and his hair stood straight out from his skull. 'Bravo, black bird!'

"Michael became an aviator after that. He was shot down over Auvergne. I found out later that he jumped in a parachute—fell from the sky like a biscuit. The Germans machine-gunned him."

On South Broadway, they encountered a string of antique fire apparatus: old pumper trucks, horse-drawn wagons topped with smoking boilers, and men riding spindle-wheeled bicycles and carrying yoked buckets across their shoulders. Vendors hurried along the sidewalks, pushing carts filled with noisemakers and pinwheels and foam rubber hats. Craning their necks in every direction, Mrs. Eriksen and Francesca laughed at the spectacle and looked for clues to its meaning. Just ahead of them, a ladder truck zigzagged back and forth. A flag fluttering from the crazy seat proclaimed "Fireman's Muster Today. Veteran's Stadium."

"I remember when those trucks were new," said Mrs. Eriksen. She flattened a pile of horse manure and the pungent smell wafted into the car. "And I remember horseshit, too."

They became trapped between the ladder truck and a hand-drawn pumper manned by cheering boy scouts. Each of the side streets was cordoned off, and traffic flowed in only one direction. Reaching a checkpoint at the intersection of Boxford Street, the occupants of the old touring car were waved through by an auxiliary policeman wearing white gloves.

"I guess we're going to the show," Francesca said.

Mrs. Eriksen waved to the onlookers congregating in front of O'Neill's Market. "I think we're in it," the elderly woman said.

The notes of a fife came piping along the storefronts, and then the thump of kettledrums. More spectators began to accumulate on the sidewalk. Francesca dangled an arm out the window and was surprised when a clown riding a tiny motorized scooter put a lollipop in her hand.

Jay Atkinson

His eyes were made up with blue stars and he winked at her, doffing his hat to reveal a peeping chick nesting in his hair.

"A 1937 Pierce Arrow coupe. Awwright," yelled a man in front of the vacuum cleaner shop. Ensconced in a rickety lawn chair, his stomach ran in folds to his knees and he put aside a wand of cotton candy in order to applaud. "They don't make 'em like that no more."

"They surely don't," Mrs. Eriksen hollered back.

Blasts from air horns mingled with the steam whistles, and the piping and pounding from the unseen marching bands. The din was punctuated by sirens, the hawking of street vendors and the occasional firecracker. Inside the touring car, Francesca touched the old woman on the arm. "I have to get home," she said, pointing. "Would you like to rest? We could get lemonade or something."

Mrs. Eriksen pulled up the handbrake. "I'll just drop you here, if you don't mind, and proceed on to the stadium."

Francesca emerged from the car to a ripple of applause. She reached the sidewalk, glanced about at the crowd and then darted behind one of the metal barriers. Leaning from the window, Mrs. Eriksen gave a final wave and quickly the touring car was lost in the procession of bright moving shapes.

Francesca watched the spectacle for a few moments and then made her way toward one of the side streets. As a shortcut, she chose an alley between South Broadway and a row of three-deckers. The alley was covered with pieces of shingle and tin cans and the broken necks of bottles. Weeds sprouted from the foundations and cardboard had been torn up to make pallets that bore the impression of human shapes. A drum major cried out from over the housetops and the Lawrence High School marching band launched into their fight song. For a moment, Francesca thought she detected another set of footfalls behind her.

Glancing over her shoulder, Francesca started to run but the man lunged forward. He rode his weight upon her back, until she stumbled and fell among the cinders and broken glass. The man scrambled onto her, using the ball of his knee as a pivot. Then shoved her head down with his forearm, and she heard him scraping at the waistband of his shorts. Francesca's elbows were pinned at awkward angles, and the man's torso was crushed against her hips. She felt a scream go out of her lungs, but it was overwhelmed by the fireman's muster.

She felt a short hard prodding at the top of her buttocks, still on the outside of her shorts. "I'll pay you," the man said.

He stood, allowing a gap to form between his crotch and the ground. In that split-second, Francesca spun around and released a mighty kick at the man's testicles. They were raw and red like meatballs, hanging below his penis. "You little bitch," the man said, lunging at her again. Rolling back on her shoulders, Francesca drove her feet into the man's midsection, knocking him down.

Francesca's recoil sent her into a backward somersault. She sprang to her feet and ran off down the alley, the man charging behind her. "I'll fuck you up," he said.

Garner Street was deserted, and a ladder with balloons attached sailed above South Broadway. Francesca sprinted in that direction, hands slicing the air, her feet padding on the sidewalk. The man closed within a few feet of her and Francesca heard the snarl of his breath. She created a small gap and her attacker veered off, like he was in pursuit of something else.

Francesca ran until she reached an auxiliary policeman—a slender, hollow-chested fellow with a whistle around his neck. "Help me," she said.

The policeman turned from the splendor of the fire trucks. His cap was pushed back and he wore an uncomprehending look on his face. The young woman knelt before him.

"Help," she said. Drops of blood came from her, freckling the pavement.

18

Lawrence, Massachusetts

November 2, 1932

The first thing Walter Beaumont did when he arrived in Lawrence was buy a copy of the *Tribune-Standard* from one of the vendors on Essex Street and a Macintosh apple from another. He was tall and slender and wore khaki pants, a khaki blouse, and his web belt and barracks cap with shiny shoes. He had his Army pay and tossed a coin to each of the apple sellers in front of the Lawrence Savings & Trust. For some reason Eddie Heath was not manning the little newsstand on the corner and Beaumont wondered about him. He bit through the skin of the apple and tasted the hard, sweet flesh as he walked along. There had been no such apples in Kentucky.

This was Beaumont's first trip home in almost two years. It had been his father's idea to join the Army, since it provided regular employment despite the recession and had supplied a certain limited education on how the world worked. Walter underwent basic and advanced training in 1928, and then spent three years as a payroll clerk attached to battalion headquarters at Fort Campbell, Kentucky. He got himself physically fit and learned how to shoot a rifle and mastered the basic principles of accounting. He was discharged as a corporal.

Although the sky was cloudy, dimming the landscape, the streetcars and sidewalks were busy with people, many of the shop windows were lit up, and the smell of bread from Tivoli's filled the air. A man named Driscoll was selling chestnuts outside Rokel's Tea Room, his left arm missing and his coat sleeve pinned up. He was a war veteran and raised his good arm and saluted Walter Beaumont when he saw the uniform. The ex-corporal went over and handed the man a dollar and spoke in his ear: "For the Ardennes."

The fellow smiled at him, revealing a mouthful of broken teeth. He wore the Croix de Guerre on his lapel. "For Black Jack Pershing," he said.

The sky tilted back and façades loomed over the street in the early winter sundown. At the corner of Essex and Newbury Street, Beaumont smoked a cigarette and flipped through the newspaper while several automobiles bumped along and an electric car discharged its passengers. Inside the paper was an item mentioning that Eddie Heath had fallen on bad times. Sightless since birth, Heath had maintained a vigorous trade selling newspapers, coffee, chewing gum and other sundries, until the depression had forced him out. In the article, friends and patrons noted his "laudable spirit of independence" and said that Eddie had been too embarrassed to seek charity.

Beside this article was a paid notice for Joe Annaloro and his Sophisticated Swingers, appearing all weekend at the Capri Café, "New England's most conservative nightclub." Tonight Walter's parents were having a party for him at their new address on Haverhill Street, but first he was going to stand Monty Tattersall to a drink. He had wired his friend from the Philadelphia bus station, arranging a rendezvous at this precise hour. It was something out of the pulp novels they had read as children and Walter Beaumont was sure that Monty would be there.

The passengers from the streetcar walked toward him and down the street and off the other way, scattering in all directions. Walter spotted a fellow with one ear, a good portion of his scalp flapped over and sewn to his head in a jagged line. Then the man passed by and there was a woman in a fur stole, two policemen swinging their nightsticks, another soldier, an enormous fat man carrying a tiny dog, and finally, Montgomery Tattersall, in a woolen suit and polka dot tie, motionless against the hurly-burly of the street corner. "You made it," he said, his arms flung out and his face pale and scholarly beneath its crown of thick black hair.

Walter tossed away his cigarette. "It's a pleasure to see you, Dr. Montgomery," he said, embracing his friend.

"I'm not a doctor yet," said Tattersall.

"What do I know? I'm just a corporal," Beaumont said. "Can we get a drink?"

Monty Tattersall clapped an arm over his friend's shoulder and they headed in the opposite direction. "I know a place where a man may purchase a constitutional," he said.

Tattersall steered them into an alley, where they climbed an iron ladder, tip-toed along the edge of a roof, descended another fire escape and emerged on Trimble Street. There was a streetlight burning over the last little building, with a sign hanging from two leather thongs that said "Jerry's."

"The candy store?" asked Beaumont.

They glanced at each other and laughed and then ran to the door. Wearing his paper hat, old man Jurek was busy dipping cherries into a kettle of molten chocolate. There was a display case filled with penuche, mallow caps, taffy in waxed paper and other candies, and the smell of burnt sugar permeated the room. Nodding to the proprietor, Monty Tattersall led Walter through the shop and down a flight of stairs into the cellar. The walls were brick, except for one place where cement formed a

　　　　　　　　　　　Jay Atkinson

kind of vault. An old Victrola occupied a fringed table against the wall, surrounded by thick wax records.

Jurek's twelve-year-old son presided over the bar, which was fashioned from a battered walnut door and two sawhorses. His stock included several liters of Canadian whiskey and a large metal tub filled with shattered ice and bottles of beer. Near the kid's elbow was a milk bottle filled with cigars and a placard that read *5 cents each*. One other fellow was standing at the rail. Young Jerry poured whiskey into a glass; the man put up a half-dollar, swallowed the whiskey and then asked for another. He wore an old jersey and a porkpie hat.

The boy looked at them. "What'll you have?" he asked. Undersized for twelve, he had sandy hair and a long, thin nose and wore a spattered candy apron over his dungarees.

"Two whiskies and two beers," said Beaumont.

"Dollar-fifty." The boy poured the liquor into two glasses.

"To the hope of new friends and the memory of old ones," said Beaumont, raising his glass. "To youth and beauty and all good things,"

The whiskey burned their throats and the man in the porkpie hat said *"Salud"* and drank his own down. Beaumont gestured to the boy for three more. "Have a drink," he said to the other man.

"Grazie," the fellow said. *"Cent anno."*

His trousers were powdered with slate dust and his hands were raw and chapped where they fell from the sleeves of his jersey. He drank the whiskey, his third in the space of a minute.

"You working?" asked Tattersall.

"No," the Italian said. He gestured at his dirty trousers. "Work for church. Free."

Monty turned his back. "Pretty tough around here," he said.

"In Kentucky I saw farmers eating their horses," said Walter.

"What are you going to do now?" Tattersall asked. He opened the bottles of beer and handed one to Beaumont.

The ex-corporal drank his beer. "My father said he'd help me out. He's doing well."

The Italian lifted his hat in their direction and staggered toward the exit while Enrico Caruso swooned from the Victrola. On his way the man stopped by the vault, knelt down and prayed for a moment, then continued toward the stairs. After the boards creaked overhead and the Italian went into the street, the boy walked over and lifted the arm of the Victrola, silencing the music, and for a moment the little hovel beneath the candy store seemed dark and poor and sad. But the young bartender replaced Caruso with Al Jolson and the beer tasted good and the occupants were happy again.

Tattersall gestured toward the spot where the Italian had knelt. "What was that all about?"

"There's supposed to be a body in there, so we get a lot of wop business."

"Who is it?" asked Beaumont.

"I dunno. A kid. They say he died in the canal, a long time ago," Jerry said.

Taking his beer, Monty Tattersall went over to inspect the bulge in the wall. He struck a match and sheltered the flame for a moment. Someone had written *Giuseppe Oct. 1910* in the wet cement and it had dried that way.

"What is it?" Beaumont asked.

Tattersall shrugged. "It doesn't look like anything to me," he said.

Walter motioned toward their glasses again and they took up fresh shots of whiskey. "How's medical school?" he asked.

"There's nothing I want more than to be a doctor."

Young Jerry pointed to Beaumont. "I'd rather be a soldier," he said. "They get to have uniforms and go to war, like Sergeant York."

"This is the last time you'll ever see me wearing one," Walter said. He laughed and drank from his beer. "I'm going to college and learn something."

"Like what?" the boy asked.

Walter paused in his drinking. "I'm not sure," he said. "Maybe architecture. Or engineering."

"Okay, one more for the architectural engineer and then I have to go," said Monty Tattersall, slapping Walter on the back. "There's a cadaver at the lab with my name on it."

They drank another whiskey, shook hands, and after Monty promised to stop by later that evening, he excused himself and Walter was alone with the young bartender. For a short while, he listened to the Jolson record and drank his beer.

On the floor above, the bell jangled and two voices were muffled by the ceiling, then there was a heavy tread upon the stairs. Into the cellar came a fellow hauling a basket supported by thin iron rods. He limped toward them, set the basket on the floor and gasped for breath, his face reddened by the exertion and his apron marked with gravy stains. Inside the basket were dozens of small meat pies.

"Where do you want 'em?" the man asked.

Young Jerry motioned toward the counter and the fellow squatted behind his basket, grabbed the wire framework and hoisted his pork pies onto the bar. The smell of the pies filled the room and Walter's mouth began to water. "Aren't you Mr. Bower?" he asked.

The man took a pencil from behind his ear and produced a thick pad of paper. "That's my name," he said. Walter remembered Ray Bower when he had a storefront on Broadway and a dog named Lisa that sometimes rode the trolley by herself. Every morning Walter passed by the shop on his way to school and the butcher-baker would give him a twist of dough sprinkled with cinnamon or a misshapen pork pie.

Calculating a sum, the butcher-baker tore the page out and rested it on top of the basket.

"How much do we owe?" asked the lad.

"Nine dollars," Bower said. "They're a dollar-fifty per dozen."

The boy was confused. "We sell 'em for a quarter," he said.

Mr. Bower glanced at Walter and smiled with his blue eyes. "Better

Jay Atkinson

ask your father," he said.

The boy banged on a pipe that ran vertically and there was the sound of wood sliding back and old man Jurek stuck his head through a hole in the ceiling. "What?" he asked.

"How much for a dozen pies?" asked Jerry. It was strange to see the old man staring down at them. His paper cap fell off and wafted to the floor.

Jurek looked at Mr. Bower. "What do I owe you?"

"Nine dollars."

The old man's disembodied head shifted its emphasis. "Give him nine dollars," Jurek said. "And stop trying to be so smart."

Walter put a half-dollar on the bar. "I'll take a couple," he said.

Jerry deposited two of the pies in front of Beaumont and swept up the coin. "I'm not trying to be smart," he said.

"You're just trying to help your father, is all," said Bower.

Walter ate one of the pies. It was salty and marbled with fat and he could taste the white pepper and the smoothness of the lard in the crust.

Mr. Bower turned for the stairs but Walter reached over and touched him on the elbow. "I'm not sure if you remember me," he said. "But I used to visit your shop when I was a kid."

The butcher-baker squinted for a moment and the light of recognition appeared in his pale blue eyes. "How long ago was that, now?" asked Bower.

"I went to the Amesbury Street School during the war."

The butcher-baker smiled, his eyes crinkling at the edges. "It looks like you've done well for yourself," he said. "Good for you."

Apparently Mr. Bower had spoken to the candymaker, because when Walter departed a short while later old man Jurek insisted he take a box of chocolate-covered cherries despite the fact they didn't know each other. Walter thanked him and the bell rang over the lintel and he passed onto the street. Darkness had arrived and he hurried to the trolley with the small white box under his arm, the city grown quiet at the supper hour and his shoes loud against the pavement.

Halfway home, Walter realized he had forgotten his duffel bag at Jurek's. Getting it back would mean a trip out to the car barns and all the way around and he decided to retrieve the bag later. Walter rode the trolley from Common Street to the base of Tower Hill and he climbed alongside the houses with their pebbled finishes and large gloomy windows and turrets. At the crest of the hill, he spotted Judge Bates' old Ford and peered between the hedges at number 621. Workmen tramped over the porch, installing a huge stained glass mural and Beaumont lingered for a moment, inspecting the gravel drive and outbuildings and craning his neck to survey the apex of the roof.

It was strange to think that the mother who had nursed and raised him and sung hymns by his cradle and the father who disciplined him and lectured about alcohol and women and other vices from his chair beside the kitchen stove, first in their apartment on Jackson Street and later in the white frame house in Shawsheen Village, had a life separate from his own. They had new occupations and preoccupations Walter was unfamiliar with, and in the months since he had been home last his mother and father had eaten hundreds of meals and taken part in thousands of conversations that would forever be lost to him. A tremor ran through his limbs when he considered the fact that *anyone* could be forgotten, no matter how charming or special or dear.

Mounting the stairs, Walter saw that the stained glass windows depicted the Lawrence cityscape with its factories and river, crowded by rowhouses more stylized and sanitized than they were in fact. Two men wearing gloves eased a large panel into the space that remained while a fellow on either side of the window stretched the rubber gasket over the edge and puttied the sections together. Someone turned on a light inside the house and as Walter passed by, the river seemed to flow along the porch and the dial of the Ayer Mill clock was situated in the exact center of the mural.

Walter reached for the doorknob and suddenly the door didn't exist and his father was there, wearing a herringbone suit and paisley tie. Franklin Beaumont kept his eyes on the tall, uniformed man in the doorway and spoke into the silence that encompassed the house: "Maeve. Your son is home."

His mother rushed from somewhere inside, darted past her husband and flew into Walter's arms. "My baby," she said, weeping against his shirtfront. "The good Lord has delivered you to me."

"I think it was the Boston & Maine," said Franklin.

Walter's father was turning gray and his mother looked older, too. Ensconced inside a cloud of Park & Tilford perfume, Mrs. Beaumont wore a sleeveless dress patterned with flowers and her hair was bobbed in a style that had been fashionable ten years earlier. Fat dimpled her elbows and her left eye twitched whenever she turned her head.

A workman in overalls passed by, his hands full of limp rubber gaskets, and Mrs. Beaumont led her son deeper into the house. "Where's your bag?" she asked. "You smell like a sewer. Those trains must be awful."

"I left my bag downtown," said Walter. "I'll get it later."

Although the hour of Walter's homecoming had never been fixed, several guests congregated in the parlor. Judge Bates leaned against the mantle, examining a cherry-cabineted ship's clock and smoking his pipe. His son, Philbin, a lad of fourteen, was beside him clutching a glass of lemonade. They were conversing with Mayor Quebec, a dumpling-shaped fellow who held a pickle in one hand and a hunk of soda bread in the other. And Colin Isherwood, whose son was at Dartmouth, stood by the windows, a tall, lightly built man in a gabardine suit and bow tie.

The newspaperman smiled as Walter entered the room. "Hail the conquering hero," he said, holding a copy of the *Tribune-Standard*. "May we have a quote for the late edition?"

Walter Beaumont was surprised at the prestige of his welcoming committee. His father had been friendly with Ignatius J. Bates since 1918, when they had served together on the War Relief Board. But as far as he knew, Mr. Isherwood and Mayor Quebec had never visited the Beaumont home prior to Walter's military service. With friends of such caliber, Franklin Beaumont was making a name for himself in Lawrence.

"I'm happy to be home," Walter said.

The newspaperman frowned in mock disappointment. "You're not exactly W. C. Fields with a quip," he said, and the others laughed. Isherwood folded his newspaper and tossed it onto the mantle.

Conviviality reigned, as each guest shook Walter's hand and pounded him on the back, while young Philbin stared at the uniform in awe. The house was redolent of braised mutton and here and there little crystal bowls were filled with mints or shelled peanuts. Walter handed his mother the box of chocolate cherries and she cried when she opened them, dabbing her eyes with a napkin.

"What a thoughtful boy," she said. Then Mrs. Beaumont ran to fetch more lemonade and Judge Bates insisted that Walter have his chair by the fire.

"No, thank you, sir," Walter said. "I've been sitting on a bus for two days."

"Leave the boy alone, 'Natius," said Mayor Quebec, the flesh along his throat quivering like a wattle. "He's not one of your law clerks, to be ordered about."

Colin Isherwood gave Walter a sly look. "By all means, Mr. Mayor, defend our guest of honor's freedom to stand as he pleases." The newspaperman pretended to dust off the chair. "Creating space where one might exercise one's own right to sit down."

"Thank you, Mr. Isherwood," said the Mayor, seating himself in the chair as the other guests laughed. "In this great country of ours, all men are free to do as they wish."

"Except work," said Judge Bates.

Franklin Beaumont lingered near the entrance, watching his son and measuring the reception he was being given. "The men who are best suited to work *are* working," said Mr. Beaumont. "Any fellow may clear a path for himself if he has the will and the energy for it."

"Like Eddie Heath?" asked Judge Bates, flourishing the newspaper. "There's a man who's been clearing a path for sixteen years, against obstacles none of us can imagine. Now look at him, poor fellow."

Franklin Beaumont rubbed his chin. "It's a harsh thing to admit, but life has a way of thinning out the competition," he said. "Eddie Heath's failure opens up a chance for another man to succeed. That's the way our system works and I think we should celebrate it. Otherwise we're no better than the Bolsheviks, who would tear down our mills and put the corn fields back in."

"In my opinion, some men deserve special consideration for their circumstances, even under the doctrine of free enterprise," said Judge Bates, displaying his prominent front teeth. "The able-bodied fellow will make his way, I agree. But others need a little help, and it's a duty of we who are in positions of influence to supply that impetus."

The judge's pipe had gone out and he sucked on the stem while gazing at Mr. Beaumont. "Some may 'celebrate' the failure of Eddie Heath, but pardon me if I defer," he said.

As gloom descended over her son's homecoming, Maeve Beaumont announced that the dining room had been laid out and the cassoulet was ready. She asked Philbin Bates, who was a responsible lad, if he would call the other guests from the hall telephone and invited the men to seat themselves while she managed things in the kitchen.

Rumbling along the hallway, Mayor Quebec leavened the proceedings by grabbing Walter's barracks cap, placing it sideways on his own head and leading the party into the dining room. The table was covered in white linen and decorated with a bouquet of irises, snapdragons and gladiolus. A tureen of mashed potatoes smoked like a volcano and the gravy boats on either side bubbled like lava. Dishes of peas, carrots, artichokes, yams and Brussels sprouts ran down the center of the table and each place was set with silver and bone china. Tall white tapers were spaced throughout and the smell of candlesmoke mingled with other pleasant aromas.

"Are you expecting President Hoover?" asked Mr. Isherwood, placing his chair back from the table to accommodate his long legs.

Judge Bates harrumphed. "Soon to be ex-President Hoover," he said. "If he had insured the banks in '28, we wouldn't be in this mess."

"Gentlemen, please," said the Mayor. "No more politics. It gives me indigestion."

Isherwood poured himself a glass of wine from the decanter. "We'll stop, then," he said. "You mustn't attempt to run the city with a bellyache."

Although he didn't say another word, Ignatius Bates pulled out his empty trouser pockets in a gesture known as Hoover flags and the men laughed. Then their hostess carried in the leg of mutton on a platter garnished with tiny onions, and young Phil entered the room just as the doorbell chimed.

"Answer that will you, dear?" Maeve asked, and her husband got up from the table.

Judge Bates swatted at Franklin as he went past and said, "No rest for the wicked."

A short while later, more guests filed beneath the chandelier and greetings were exchanged all over again. Mayor Quebec and Judge Bates rose to kiss their wives and settled the plump, well-coifed ladies into their assigned places. Reverend Metzemaekers from United Church of Christ arrived with his wife, Vivian, and a female cousin who was visiting from Baltimore, and after they sat down there was no room for young Phil. Amidst much discussion, an extra chair was carried in and the youth had the butler's sideboard to himself.

"If Mrs. Quebec continues with her amorous proposals, I'll trade with you, Phil, while supplying a job at the City Dump," the Mayor said.

Mrs. Quebec punched her husband on the arm while the others laughed, and Philbin Bates said, "If you'll get me a job in the District

Jay Atkinson

Court, I'll think about it."

"Smart lad," said Mr. Isherwood.

Reverend Metzemaekers pronounced the blessing, and then Mr. Beaumont rapped on his wineglass and stood up. "On behalf of Maeve and I, welcome to our new home," said the general overseer. "Today we celebrate our son's return to Lawrence and we want you all to know how proud we are of him and how excited about his future."

There was more chiming of glasses while the recipient of this attention smiled and looked at the floor. Franklin quieted them by pressing his hands downward on the air and then continued. "I'm also happy to announce that my son and I will be working together." The host raised his wineglass and instructed the others to do the same. "So allow me to propose a toast: to Walter Beaumont, soon to become dye house foreman at the Ayer Mill."

The diners cheered and then set themselves to the groaning board: white bean stew flavored with garlic, the mutton, potatoes, gravy, vegetables, three large decanters of wine, followed by consommé, sherbet to clear the palate, and the apple-and-cherry tart that was Mrs. Beaumont's specialty. After this feast, the women retired to the kitchen, Reverend Metzemaekers and Phil Bates went out to explore Haverhill Street, and the others filed into the parlor for cognac and cigars. Their talk revolved around government dry agents, who after several years of focusing on the lower class establishments, had begun raiding speakeasies favored by the gentry, including Nick's Supper Club and the Tip-Top.

"I have it on good authority that we won't be troubled this evening," said Mayor Quebec, "so long as I am winning at canasta."

While Judge Bates told a story about an arsonist that had set twenty-eight fires in a single building, Walter tried to catch his father's eye. He wished to discuss something but knew he must wait an appropriate length of time before they would be able to hold a private conversation. So he listened to the judge's tale of a man who, returning to Lawrence after many years, had used kerosene to incinerate the boarding house where he had been raised.

Finally, an opportunity arose when Mayor Quebec complained of intestinal disturbances and Judge Bates was summoned to the telephone. Walter signaled to his father and asked, "Can I have a word with you, please?"

They went down the hall and into the study, another unfamiliar room since there hadn't been time yet for a proper tour of the house. Franklin seated himself behind the wide oak wale of the desk and his son took one of the chairs positioned in front. A blaze occupied the fireplace and they could hear it drawing up the chimney. On the desk were some sort of amber paperweight and a box of cigars, which Franklin offered to his son.

"No, thanks," said Walter, taking out a small, foil-lined package. "I'll have one of these."

"Since when do you smoke cigarettes?" Franklin asked.

"When you're on guard duty at three in the morning, there's nothing to do but smoke."

Franklin held out his hand for the cigarettes. "A gentleman may enjoy an occasional cigar and not look foolish. But cigarettes are an unattractive and idle habit."

He put the cigarettes in a drawer and gazed at his son. Nobody referred to Walter Beaumont as handsome, but he had a narrow, well-proportioned face, thin-lipped, with high cheekbones and impassive brown eyes. He wore his hair in the short brush cut preferred at posts like Fort Campbell; his brass insignia shone in the firelight and his collar was stiff with starch.

"Father, I plan on going to college," Walter said. "Not working in the mill."

The general overseer lit one of the cigars, flapping his arm to put out the match. "Men go to college so they can study for a career," he said. "You're going to earn sixty dollars a week and you'll *have* a career. Besides, it took a lot of trouble to create that position and you have to take it now, not four years from now."

"There's more to education than just studying for a career," said Walter.

"Not when thirteen million Americans are out of work," his father said.

On the bus trip to Philadelphia, with second and third legs to new York and Boston, the train trip to Lawrence and a stint on the electric car, and later, his walk through the dim and darkening streets of his hometown, Walter Beaumont had seen evidence of the privation that his father was alluding to. Near Roanoke, Virginia, he watched a family dine on corn husks and rainwater, the husks cut up and browned over a fire and the water served in a china cups taken from the family's trunk of belongings. Driving through the Alleghenies, he saw two men hanging from a linden tree and the bus driver remarked that they were suicides. The coal region from West Virginia to Pennsylvania had been crippled by the Depression and more than half the mines were shut. This was his regular route and the bus driver witnessed men hanging from trees Monday through Friday, he said.

"How much money have you saved?" Franklin asked.

"Nearly six hundred dollars."

The general overseer dispatched cigar smoke toward the ceiling while his son examined the paperweight on the desk. There was a large insect trapped inside the amber. "I couldn't lend you money right now, anyway," said Franklin. "This house cost us a pretty penny."

Walter took a handful of shelled peanuts from a bowl upon the desk. Aiming for another bowl on the side table, he began pinging them off the glass.

"Stop that," said Franklin. "I don't want to spend my Sunday picking up peanuts." He rested the cigar on the edge of the desk. In the electric lamplight, his face was gray and his clothing looked shopworn. "You're welcome to stay here, so you can save some more money," he said.

"I'll take a room at the Y," said Walter.

His father began nodding, and said, "That's what I did when I was your age. Of course, if you wish to entertain a young woman you may do so in the parlor whenever you like."

"I appreciate it."

"Perhaps in a year or two, you'll find a nice girl and settle down and have a family. At least, your mother and I hope so. But college is out of the question."

Rising with his cigar, Franklin Beaumont pointed their way toward the door and the company of the other guests. "You'll have to work hard," he said. "The dye house is no place for shirkers."

"I'm not afraid of hard work," said Walter.

His father smiled. "That's why I hired you."

The gentlemen were seated around the canasta table when Franklin and Walter emerged from the study. Maeve had covered another table with linen and brought out a steaming silver urn and two trays filled with pastry. A fire rampaged in the hearth and the aroma of coffee permeated the room.

"Here comes my partner now," said the Mayor, who had recovered from his attack and was enjoying a cream puff. "Have a seat."

"Are you claiming the father or the son?" asked Judge Bates.

Mayor Quebec laughed. "Rummy is a game of stamina. Why on earth would I want a broken-down old carthorse when I can transport myself on a steed?"

"I hope you're not going to sit on the boy," said Mr. Isherwood. "You'll kill him."

Just then, Reverend Metzemaekers and Phil Bates returned from their jaunt, accompanied by a neighbor paying a call on the Beaumonts. His name was Egonne Shiebel and he lived in the massive Victorian across the street. "We found Mr. Shiebel on the walkway," said Reverend Metzemaekers. "And thought he might help us dispose of these pastries."

"By all means," said Franklin. "I'm pleased to make your acquaintance, Mr. Shiebel."

Introductions followed, and the newcomer shook hands with each of the guests in turn. He delivered the traditional housewarming gifts of bread and salt to Mrs. Beaumont and laughed and shook his head when asked if he wanted to play cards. Egonne Shiebel was a small, dark-haired man with a compressed forehead and thick black eyebrows. His suit was baggy at the shoulders and knees in the Old World style, and his shoes were made of patent leather.

Behind his back, Mayor Quebec looked over at Mr. Isherwood and mouthed the word "Jew."

Mr. Shiebel accepted a cup of coffee and stood beside the card table in silence. Judge Bates asked how long he had lived on Haverhill Street. In a faint European accent, Shiebel replied that his family had occupied their home for two years but that his duties for Hasselblad Fotografiska kept him away for long periods of time. Franklin Beaumont lit up at the mention of Hasselblad. A long-time photography enthusiast, he had read of the Swedish company in trade journals. When he mentioned his passion to Mr. Shiebel, the company's American representative was only too happy to fetch his samples. Was it too much trouble, he was asked.

"Never refuse an opportunity to talk business," said Mr. Shiebel.

He bowed to the ladies and went out. While the card players awaited his return, Walter kissed his mother on the cheek and excused himself. Franklin trailed him onto the porch where Walter reminded his father that he'd left his bag downtown and needed his clothes and shaving things.

"Of course," said Franklin. He stood for a moment against the rail, breathing in the night air and staring off toward downtown. "It's good to have you home."

"I'm happy to be here," said Walter.

He went down the stairs and along the gravel driveway and turned onto the sidewalk, just as Egonne Shiebel hurried across the street with a large case under his arm. Walter looked back as his father allowed the stranger to pass inside with his valise. Then the door closed and the neighborhood was still and Walter descended on foot toward Broadway.

It was after nine o'clock and the streetcars were no longer running. There was a klieg light mounted above the Palace Theater but the rest of the boulevard was dark. Walter passed beneath the sign for Murphy's Café, which was decorated with a giant Pepsi-Cola cap. Just ahead, a man was coming along the pavement, sweeping the way in front of him with a cane. As this metronomic sound grew nearer, Walter made out the figure of Eddie Heath, a big chap, thirty-six years old, with a cannonball for a head. He wore an old tweed overcoat and a knitted cap.

While he was in high school, Walter discovered Heath's newsstand during one of his forays through the city. Most afternoons, he'd stop by for a package of Beeman's chewing gum, or Black Jack if they were out of Beeman's. Eddie Heath would start grinning as soon as his friend approached, detecting Walter's presence by the shaving lotion he always wore and gazing with those sightless eyes, which never remained fixed in any direction for long.

Eddie's voice began deep in his chest. "Ain't it Walter?" he'd ask, persecuted by lousy grammar as well as his blindness, although cheerful to a fault and delighted by the young man's friendship. They would discuss the weather, a phenomenon that Eddie Heath insisted he could predict with his liver, which would swell in anticipation of rain and shrink before dry spells. Or they would talk about the Lawrence Independents, a local baseball team that played its games on Water Street. When Walter was a teenager, he would climb the fence at O'Sullivan Park to watch the Indies. And there was Eddie sitting behind home plate, eating a bag of popcorn and listening to the snap of leather and crack of the baseball on wooden bats.

Just then, Eddie Heath came in range of the streetlight. His eyes were pinched shut and he moved at a considerable pace. As Eddie passed by,

Jay Atkinson

Walter felt his tongue mired in his throat and said nothing. Stitched across the blind man's overcoat was a notice that read "Shop at Heath's Newsstand."

19

The Present Day

Outside the stadium, Joe Glass shouldered his son between the antique fire engines, and on past men in red suspenders and a pyramid of wooden barrels marked "Sasparilla." There was a rattle of drumsticks as one of the marching bands finished and broke ranks, dispersing across the parking lot. They teased each other, playing little solo pieces and scaling their stiff hats into the air. Chubby teenagers strapped to bass drums and clarinet players and oboists wandered toward the lemonade stand beneath the stadium, or else stood on patches of tarmac and jeered as the next band arrived.

When a truck backfired nearby, Gabriel wound both his arms around his father's neck and gave a little shriek. "It's okay," said Joe. "Daddy's right here."

Gaudy clowns and cops and horses were mixed together in a great riot. Underneath an oak tree, a group of firemen in white shirts and visored caps stood drinking cans of beer. The departmental chaplain, in his priest's collar and blue greatcoat with silver buttons, refused when one was offered to him. A moment later, glancing up at the small white sun, he reversed himself. The priest leaned into a group of firemen to secure one of the dripping cans and the men cheered him. A smile spread over the chaplain's face and he popped open the can, dousing his jacket with foam.

One fire truck after another drove into the parking lot, and a man with a walkie-talkie sent them rumbling toward the football field. Crew members leaped to the ground, walking ahead to guide their trucks through the gate. A boy in a Cub Scout uniform stood open-mouthed, watching them pass.

Joe ducked beneath one of the stone arches and through a turnstile onto the grass. He let Gabriel down so the boy could walk, but he began to cry and Joe picked him up again. After another look around the field Gabriel made a noise that indicated he wanted to get down, and father

Jay Atkinson

and son strolled hand in hand along a grassy corridor that was roped off for spectators. The trucks parked themselves in front of numbered stakes and the crews shouted good-natured challenges to one another, or else prepared for the judging with rags and brass polish; the fittings on all the equipment gleamed like gold.

Some of those on foot migrated toward the elms on the visitors' side of the stadium. Brightly-colored mummers in spangled pants and fringed cowhide boots trooped over the grass, unhinging their feathered arms. Going past a Shriner who was inspecting his tiny motorcycle, Joe and Gabriel headed for the huge continent of shade. Behind them, the Shriner adjusted the tassel on his fez and zoomed off aboard a motorbike, his knees jutting up almost to his ears.

Out on the football field, steam engines and hand-pumping teams competed to see who could propel water the farthest. Joe and Gabriel paused in front of a shiny copper boiler that was throwing smoke, interrupted by ear-splitting bursts of steam. Men in long yellow ulsters and rubber boots leaned on their prods, discussing the optimum temperature of the boiler. It occurred to Joe that most of the equipment before the modern era was pretty useless. The utilitymen in dusty yellow coats, their prodding sticks buried in the turf, were trying to recreate the good old days of firefighting. That wasn't very difficult, Joe figured, since mostly they just watched things burn.

Above the whining boiler the facade of Veteran's stadium rose five stories high. The empty tunnels were spaced evenly across, letting in glimpses of the sky. When the boiler reached its highest pitch, two of the men picked up the fire hose and upon a signal from their chief, sent a spume of water into the upper reaches of the stadium. The point of its arch caught the sunlight above the concrete bulwark, and the stream shattered into millions of diamonds that rattled down onto the seats of the stadium. The crew raised their prodding sticks in the air and gave the effort three cheers.

Gabriel pushed at the back of Joe's knee. "Dad-dee," he said. They continued between the trucks and around teams of horses who stamped against the turf, flicking their tails. At midfield was a canvas pool where the children could splash each other and play with toy boats.

Bent over the pool with his arms immersed, Gabriel cocked his head and grinned at his father, showing two rows of small white teeth. "Uh-oh," he said, lifting his arms up so the water streamed down the neck of his sunsuit.

Two of the older children began splashing each other, and Joe plucked Gabriel from between them and carried the boy away, until he squealed in protest and Joe set him back down. Beyond the fence was a carnival: some bumper cars arranged on a temporary metal floor, a set of flying swings, and a Ferris wheel that as yet had no passengers. Gabriel ran down the center of the football field toward these attractions. With nothing in the way Joe let him run, the boy marveling at his freedom as he chopped through the grass and his small bare arms jittered in every direction.

Iridescent soap bubbles shot from a calliope on the other side of the fence and Gabriel went into convulsions of mirth as the bubbles, hundreds of them in various sizes, descended toward the earth. Unable to choose, the boy swatted in all directions, tangling his legs, and then fell down weeping with laughter. Sprawled on the grass, Gabriel was instantly fatigued, his smooth round face turned up at the sky. A pulse beat in his neck, and his rib cage was delineated and trembling with each breath. His eyelids at half-mast, Gabriel lay in a satisfied torpor while the calliope maintained its bombardment.

"All gone," said Joe, lifting Gabriel in the air. He deposited the boy on his shoulders. "Let's ride the Ferris wheel."

After the military opulence of the fire trucks, the carnival felt small and seedy. It consisted of three decrepit rides and a midway, with games of chance arranged on both sides. Only one was being attended: a boy about nine years old fished in a pool stocked with miniature cement whales. Nearby, the boy's father stood drinking beer from a paper bag, as bluebottle flies zigzagged through the air.

Joe Glass tipped Gabriel over his shoulder and bought tickets from a woman with bloody skulls tattooed on her arm. Then he gave the small orange papers to a man standing beside her, in order to ride the Ferris wheel. Joe used two more tickets for a bag of animal crackers with elephants printed on it.

The attendant stopped the Ferris wheel, and they went aboard and Joe closed the safety bar. Creaking at each turn, the wheel rolled onward until the other man and his son approached the ticket booth. Then the attendant lowered Joe and Gabriel to the starting position.

"That's it," he said, raising the bar.

"Not for six bucks, it ain't," Joe said, pulling the gate down again.

The attendant folded his arms. "If you wanna 'nother ride, that's four more tickets," he said.

The other customer and his son wandered off to try the air rifles. "I never heard of a Ferris wheel where you didn't stop at the top," said Joe, throwing more tickets on the ground. "Keep it going."

The rows of fire trucks tilted toward them as they ascended, and crisscrossing plumes of water formed helixes above the muster. Joe tore open the animal crackers and some pigeons flew over and began orbiting them.

At the top of the arc, Joe and Gabriel were nearly thrown from their seats when the attendant pressed a button and the wheel lurched to a stop. Gabriel pointed toward the fireman's muster, and talked in an excited patois of words and syllabizing.

"Daddy! Hi! Car! Mama!" the boy said.

Joe hailed the attendant. "Hey! Get us down."

Gabriel tried to lift the safety bar and squirm out, crying when his father pushed him back into the seat. "Easy, magoo," Joe said. "Just a second."

Joe whistled between his teeth for the attendant. "Bring us down RIGHT NOW, or I'll have so many city inspectors looking at this piece of shit you'll be *rolling* it back to whatever hole you crawled out of."

The man pressed a green button without looking up, and Joe and Gabriel rode backward to the starting position and disembarked. Gabriel was crying.

"Didn't the little fella like it?" asked the attendant.

Joe looked into the other man's eyes and smelled the alcohol saturating his flesh. "Another time, sport," he said. "I'll shove this Ferris wheel right up your ass."

"Whoa, a tough guy," said the attendant.

As Joe and Gabriel walked back to the stadium, firemen in blue uniforms were lining up on the football field. A silver bell had been hauled onto the grass, and then a color guard made up of decorated fire fighters marched out. Fire Chief Driscoll was making a speech, most of which was carried away by the great open spaces above the stadium: "...together this sacrifice we...never to answer the alarm...the good people."

With Gabriel in his arms, Joe wandered among the crowd until he found Billy Murphy standing there. Murphy was dressed in cut off dungarees with red suspenders, and an old blue T-shirt stretched over his enormous torso like a sausage casing. A fireman's cap with a crinkled brim rode the back of his head, marked by a badge for the Sanbornton Volunteer Fire Department.

"What's going on?" Joe asked, shifting Gabriel to his shoulder.

"Sshh," said Murphy.

Upon command, seven policemen drew their weapons and pointed toward the sky. At the first discharge, Gabriel's body twitched and he clung to Joe's neck. Several more volleys pierced the quiet. They sailed out in concentric rings until they broke against the stadium, reverberating in loud dry echoes. There was the smell of gunpowder and when the last pop had died away, another fireman began striking the bell with a silver hammer. The bell rang out nine times, the hammer flashing in the sunlight. Then the fireman turned to Chief Driscoll and the two men saluted each other.

The high school band struck up "God Bless America," and Murphy leaned toward Joe Glass. "One each for the firemen who died in the Vendome Hotel fire in 1972," he said. "It was the worst loss of life in Massachusetts firefighting history."

Chief Driscoll dismissed the ranks, and the firemen picked up their children and strolled back over the football field toward the muster.

"If I could pass the physical, I'd sign up for the Civil Service," said Murphy. He pointed to a card table against the stadium. Behind it was a man wearing a short-sleeved shirt. He sat alone beneath the lower stand, his fist resting on a stack of papers to keep them from blowing away.

From across the gridiron, Billy Murphy was being called to rejoin his pumper team. "You're in good shape," he said to Joe. Again he indicated the man sitting there with his application forms. "The fire department is hard work, but it's fun." The saloonkeeper started for the muster in his slow, pigeon-toed walk. "Whaddaya got to lose?"

Joe Glass picked up Gabriel and went over to the table. Above it was a sign that said "Civil Service Exam." The man in charge wore glasses and had a waxed crew cut that stood up all around. He sawed at his scalp with a pencil and before Joe could speak, fired off several questions. "Are you a United States citizen? Lawrence resident? Under thirty-six years of age? Do you have a Massachusetts driver's license? Any felony or misdemeanor convictions? Any warrants? Physical disabilities? History of heart trouble or mental illness?"

Joe answered the questions, lying about his bad knee, and the man shoved one of the papers across the table and a pen that was stamped *Commonwealth of Massachusetts*. Joe set Gabriel on the grass and the man frowned, collecting his loose pens. With his arms resting on the card table, the boy stared at the Civil Service man while Joe filled out the application.

"If you pass, you'll get a letter directing you to psychological and strength testing," the man said. "If a spot opens up, the highest grade usually gets endorsed by the Chief and his recommendation goes to the City Council for a vote."

"What's a top grade?"

"Somewhere around ninety-eight or ninety-nine," said the man, handing over an instruction booklet with the seal of Massachusetts on the cover. "The fee is twenty dollars."

"Huh?"

"It costs twenty bucks to take the test. Usually you send in a check, but since you're turning the application in here, you have to pay now. That's the rule."

Joe Glass chewed his lower lip. On the stadium grass, pumper teams were sending arches of water into the air and the copper boilers threw steam and blew their whistles. Joe dug into his pocket and removed a small wad of money. He had twenty-six dollars. "I guess I can do it," he said.

Joe straightened out a few bills and put them into the man's palm. "I'm in," he said.

"You'll be permitted to take the test," said the man, writing out a receipt. "Whether you're 'in' or not remains to be seen."

Gabriel hadn't taken a nap because of all the commotion and now he was exhausted. The boy hung over his father's back as they passed between the antique fire trucks and out beneath the stadium. The streets were littered with snapped balloons and paper cups and lumps of manure, which sent up a musky odor. On the way home they stopped at Lawton's Frankfurters, a narrow red and white structure beside the canal. A team of Little Leaguers crowded the tiny restaurant, and Joe and Gabriel queued up behind them. When the counterman was ready, Joe ordered one plain, and two with the works, and they stood by while the frankfurters were grilled in Lawton's special oil.

When the hot dogs were rolled in wax paper, Joe and Gabriel sat on a bench outside and threw bits of bread into the canal. Joe had fished there as a boy and knew that eels and gigantic carp swam in the deep troughs between the mills. Once he had caught a slimy black fish and brought it home to show his father and been whipped for it. He was made to dump the fish into a sewer and when he forced it through the grate the fish swam in circles for a while before disappearing. Joe cried and his father told him to shut up; the fish would end up back in the canal and he could catch it again tomorrow.

It seemed impossible to Joe that only a few weeks earlier Gabriel had wandered onto the frozen canal. Now the sun lit the fronds that grew along shore, and breezes ruffled the water and made a hot dog carton skate past them on the sidewalk. Gabriel had no memory of his ordeal as he gnawed at the frankfurter, kicking his legs against the bench. Each passing minute was a different world for him; right now it was hot dogs. The meat had a metallic taste, sharpened by the onions and sweet pebbly relish.

From a parked car, Joe could hear the Red Sox game over the radio. The pitcher was working with men on base, and the sound of the hawkers and the low hum of the crowd became audible. There was another splash, and the Little Leaguers cried out when their ball was lost in the canal. Shouting and waving their caps, they passed along the sidewalk in a rout.

At the appointed hour, Joe hustled Gabriel up the stairs to Francesca's apartment. He knocked, but no one answered. Joe took the key from above the sill and unlocked the door. The boy's eyes grew wide and he ran from room to room with his arms in the air. "Ma-maa!" he said.

Francesca wasn't home. There was no note and nothing on the answering machine and Joe began roaming the apartment with Gabriel at his heels. It was a brief inspection. The three rooms were piled in heaps of sweatshirts and skating costumes and other gear. The apartment was like a warehouse of clothing, some of the items in doubles and triples. Joe had no idea what Francesca did with all her outfits. Most were still wrapped in plastic and had never been worn.

While the boy played on the living room floor with his stuffed animals and cars, Joe turned on the television, picking through the channels with a remote control. Gabriel pushed the cars along on their routes and made a guttural noise to complement the activity. After a while, the child left off playing and spoke to the mouse that was lying beside him on the rug. Joe doused the television. "You wanna go night-nights?" he asked.

The boy rolled toward his father. "Yes," he said.

Joe carried him into the bedroom. Inside the crib was a star-shaped toy that played "Twinkle, Twinkle, Little Star" when the top half was pressed. After changing Gabriel's diaper, Joe lowered him into the crib. "Goodnight, son," he said, kissing the boy's forehead.

Gabriel cried, believing that his father was about to desert him, and he only stopped when Joe handed him the star-shaped toy and promised to remain in the room. He lay down on Francesca's canopied bed, and watched the shadowplay on Gabriel's face as he sat playing with the chime box. The tune repeated itself until the child was asleep and Joe stared up at the canopy, which reminded him of a funeral awning. He wondered how hard the Civil Service test would be.

Once when he was a kid, Grampa Gus took him to the fire station on Park Street. His grandfather spoke to a man out front, tilted against the bricks in his wooden chair. Behind him the fire engines were dark and metallic, like holstered guns. Up a staircase was the dormitory, several tiny rooms each containing two cots and a dresser. Grampa Gus went into the first room and spoke to another man lying on one of the beds. They shook hands, and his grandfather put something the man had given him into his pocket. Then Joe was allowed to jump through a hole in the floor, sliding down on a brass pole. He remembered hoping for a fire but it was a quiet summer afternoon, the men chatting out front and the great smooth trucks waiting in the darkness.

Jay Atkinson

20

Lawrence, Massachusetts
October 16, 1941

Emerging from the Ayer Mill, Franklin Beaumont folded up the speech he was about to deliver to the Chamber of Commerce and stowed it in the pocket of his best serge suit, hurrying along the sidewalk. The last golden light was fading from the sky and looking up, he saw that the hands of the clock above the mill were no longer rotating. His watch said quarter to seven but the great clock was stopped at five-thirty. There was no money to fix it and if things kept up the way they were going, Lawrence would be under blackout soon and the clock would remain unlit.

His car was the last one in the lot, and he paused as two buses approached: green and yellow monoliths with high flat fronts and silver wheels. The rotating sign on the first bus was emblazoned with "Canobie Lake Park." and the second one read "Essex Street." As they whizzed past, singing over the corrugation of the Duck Bridge, Franklin wondered why he had paid almost three thousand dollars for his Pierce Arrow when he could ride the bus for a dime.

As he unlocked the door to his car and eased himself into the leather-driving seat, Beaumont decided to give the four-year-old Pierce Arrow to his son. Riding the bus was good enough for an old mill hand like him, a fellow who never traveled beyond the Mayfair Café on a Saturday night. If Walter was going to start at the bank he should cut a certain figure around town. Besides, the walking would do Franklin good. He hadn't worn this particular suit of clothing since he and Maeve's thirty-fifth wedding anniversary and it felt tight across the middle. He had left two buttons of the vest undone.

The car engine started up and he rolled onto South Union Street and over the bridge. It had been an eventful day, filled with good news for the Ayer Mill and ominous tidings for the world in general. Beaumont had just learned that he was going to produce 500,000 yards of fabric for the British Navy. And while several other mills were engaged in competition for lesser amounts, the U. S. Department of Defense had ordered one million yards of olive drab wool because of the Ayer Mill's superior performance during the Great War.

Beaumont drove as far as Holy Rosary church and turned onto Essex Street. Here he joined a throng of automobiles and buses and delivery trucks, inching along the broadest commercial thoroughfare in the Merrimack Valley. Calling to one another, men and women in overcoats and soft hats rushed along the sidewalk, their arms filled with packages. Vertical signs hung from the buildings on either side, advertising Kane's and Brockelman's and Gale the Jeweler. Covered in oversize light bulbs, the marquee above the Warner Theater announced *The Maltese Falcon*, starring Humphrey Bogart, Mary Astor, and Sydney Greenstreet.

It was five minutes till seven. Franklin steered onto Lawrence Street and began hunting for a parking space as he neared the YMCA. To his right was the great oblong of the Common, shaded by elm and oak trees and crisscrossed with gravel paths. Beaumont spotted room for his car but someone backed into the space before he could claim it and there was Judge Bates, climbing from the sedan and giving him a raspberry as he drove past. They were both late for the same meeting.

Beaumont circled the park before he found a space near City Hall. The streets were filled with moviegoers and late shoppers and teenagers in "straw hats and spats." They congregated on the shaded walkways of the Common and in front of Ritzy's Diner and the Puritan Tea Room. Franklin dodged in and out of their loud, laughing hordes as they pounded toward Essex Street. The path was covered in leaves brought down by the night rain, some blazing reds and a particular repeated gold, and stamped underfoot they sent up a thick, marshy odor.

Judge Bates met him beneath the red neon arrow that spelled out YMCA. "Well, if it isn't the barefoot boy from Wall Street," said Franklin.

They laughed and shook hands. "Did you hear about the sinking of the *Kearney*?" the judge asked Beaumont.

The other man nodded. "We're getting into this fight," Franklin said. "And soon."

As the Chamber's incoming president Mr. Beaumont had decided, with the country on the brink of war, that 1941-42 would be dedicated to the young people of the city. His inaugural speech was entitled "Youth, Democracy and Defense," and the night before he'd stayed up late committing it to memory.

They climbed a stairwell to the auditorium and were greeted by two sturdy young men who pinned white carnations to their lapels. The room was deep and wide, lit by electric sconces along the wall and crowded with tables. The basketball hoops and their metal staging were folded against the ceiling and the room smelled of solvents and floor wax.

Men in business suits were drinking coffee from porcelain cups and chattering in a huge, indecipherable mass. At the far end of the room was the head table, garlanded with ferns and a sign that read "Flowers courtesy of Venti the Florist." A young man named Charlie Kutter was installing a radio microphone in front of Mr. Beaumont's place and another fellow sat wearing headphones and plugging wires into a console.

"We were afraid that you'd ended up like McKinley," said Mayor Quebec, gesturing toward Beaumont.

The Mayor was not well. He had lost a great deal of weight, so that his skin hung from him in folds, and his complexion had long since taken on a waxy tint. He stood in the space between tables with Franklin Beaumont and Judge Bates while dozens of conversations raged about them.

"I would never resort to assassination," said Judge Bates. "But I'm not above slander: please take note that Mr. Beaumont's car is illegally parked."

Franklin registered a mock protest. "I left it in the space marked 'Reserved for Mayor' knowing that its signatory has no automobile."

"I've been on foot since they took out the gaslights," said Mayor Quebec, picking at the billow of his shirtfront. "I've walked myself half to death."

Just as Mr. Kutter began waving them toward the head table, Franklin Beaumont spotted his son Walter holding a cup and saucer and looking uncomfortable in a suit purchased off the rack at Bon Marche. Walter was standing near one of the potted palms supplied by Venti's for the occasion, and the general overseer moved a chair aside and squeezed through duos and trios of congratulatory merchants in an attempt to greet his son before the program began.

"Welcome to the Chamber of Commerce," said Franklin, taking his son's hand.

Walter Beaumont was thirty-one years old, a lanky, trim-waisted fellow, his hair longer in front than in back while slicked with pomade and combed toward the rear. He was clean-shaven and wore his father's old paisley tie with a close-collared shirt and suspenders. Tacked to his wrists were diamond-studded cuff links depicting the Ayer Mill clock.

"I wanted to hear your speech," said Walter. "They were talking about it on the radio when I was getting dressed to come over."

Franklin dropped his son's hand. "I've seated you between Judge Bates and Mr. Prescott from the bank," he said. "Just be yourself. Be polite. Be firm. A good impression will go a long way."

"I'm not sure I want to work at the bank," said Walter, who was scheduled to interview with Charles Prescott the following Tuesday.

After serving as foreman of the dye house, the younger Beaumont had been promoted to supervisor upon the retirement of Mr. Gorham. Over the course of his employment, Walter had impressed all hands with his ability to take orders from above and translate them for the operatives at the machinery. "Besides, you need me," he said. "We're going to get busy."

"You're a very useful employee," Franklin said. "But banking is a respectable career, with great promise of advancement and prestige in the community."

That very afternoon Franklin Beaumont had ordered five wool suits with matching homburgs from McCartney's on Essex Street. He earned an annual salary of $100,000 with stock options and had autonomous control of the Ayer Mill and a voting interest at the Wood Mill. Even without the new orders, Mr. Beaumont had turned a profit for eleven consecutive quarters, the first time that had occurred since 1922-24.

"When they open up in North Carolina you can help me get the overseer's job," said Walter.

Franklin shook his head. "The war may provide a quick fix, but the American Woolen Company is stuck in the nineteenth century," he said. "That's why I persuaded you to take that night course. Look around." He indicated the men in various grades and shades of wool, browns, tans, checks and charcoals, in tight collars, their hats on the chairs. Some wore hounds tooth vests and draped slacks, the more prominent fellows dressed in handtailored American suits, but all were bedecked in the local product of local toil; even Judge Bates, who was natty in his tweed jacket and bow tie.

"All I see is wool," said the younger Beaumont.

"For now," his father said. "But they're always going to have money, and that comes from banks."

Mayor Quebec was beckoning them to the head table. The uproar increased as the members devolved into their chairs, a chaotic undertaking as none of the places in the auditorium had been assigned and there were just as many table settings as guests.

Franklin withdrew a set of keys from his pocket and slipped one off the ring. "Here," he said, handing over his automobile key.

"The Pierce Arrow? Father, you must be kidding."

"I'll have Miss Halliman switch the title out of my name and you can pay for the new one. A banker needs a reliable automobile."

"I don't know what to say."

Franklin clapped his son on the back. "The most important thing is what you say to Prescott," he said.

Huge crescents of red, white and blue bunting adorned the head table and covered the dingy windows and brickwork of the auditorium. Tiny white cards announced the seating plan: State Senator Wilson X. Wilson; Reverend Metzemaekers; Mayor Paul Quebec, Sr.; Colin Isherwood I, who had not yet appeared; Franklin Beaumont, his place marked by the tall silver radio microphone and a bateau of orchids; then yellow-haired Mr. Jordan from the YMCA; Lawrence Savings & Trust president Charles Prescott; Walter Beaumont; and at the far end, smiling with his bucked teeth and winking at one of the lawyers in the gallery, Superior Court Justice Ignatius Bates, LL.B., JD.

Mayor Quebec recognized those seated at the head table, apologizing to Reverend Metzemaekers before stating that the younger Beaumont was the only innocent among them and sure to be spared if lightning were to strike the YMCA. All the men laughed, including Metzemaekers, who stood and pronounced the blessing: "May the Lord our God share his bounty with the Chamber of Commerce in the year 1941-42 and

Jay Atkinson

allow its membership to prosper in His service, amen."

Charlie Kutter came forward with a miniature glockenspiel and struck the three ascending notes that comprised WLAW's signature and then Franklin Beaumont rose to the microphone. "I am honored by your invitation to address this annual meeting of the Lawrence Chamber of Commerce, which has met to consider the all-important problems of youth," said the president-elect. "I have no hesitation in saying that the success of Nazism in Germany and Fascism in Italy is due to inculcating into the minds of youth the feeling that the old social order had failed and that a new order based on totalitarian principles would restore the glory of the fatherland, and assure their people of employment and prosperity. If the schemes of Europe are based upon the training of youth, how important is it that we who believe in democracy should train the youth of America so that they will have an abiding belief in democratic principles and be willing to defend them at all costs."

In the applause that followed, Mayor Quebec said to Wilson X. Wilson: "Speaking of orders, if Mussolini wanted five hundred thousand yards of black wool, the Ayer Mill would be first in line."

Forty-two year old Wilson giggled like a schoolboy and added, "Imagine, telling us to base our youth programs on the Nazis. What an unmitigated disaster that would be."

Reverend Metzemaekers glared at them while Beaumont continued with his address: "—Youth, as I define it, covers that critical period after the primary education has been finished when boys are inducted into their life work and become self-supporting citizens of the state. In this period from age sixteen to twenty-four, there must, of course, be definite training for life—"

On the other side of the dais, Walter caught the eye of Judge Bates. "I guess I missed the boat," said the younger Beaumont.

In a manner he had perfected in court, while talking to a bailiff or stenographer without disturbing the testimony, Bates spoke between his teeth. "I'd gather he's talking *about* you, rather than to you," he said.

It was true that Walter, at his father's urging and with his father supplying the tuition, had completed a three-week course in finance at the Macintosh School of Business, a private college located on the eighth floor of the Bay State Building, half a block from where they were sitting. Four nights a week, Walter sat listening to an elderly man in a cravat mumbling about federal bonds and the Dow Jones average. Along with what he had learned in the Army, Walter supposed that the course provided a rudimentary benefit and that without it, he wouldn't even bother to interview with Mr. Prescott. But while he was studying at the "University of Franklin Street," Colin Isherwood II was finishing up at Choate and Phil Bates was starring on the Penn track team.

"—Finally I believe that the trend of our civilization, with its technological advance and specialization of industry, is toward the ever shortening of work hours. Already the five-day week is becoming universal throughout the manufacturing industry. That means more than two-sevenths of the year must be filled with recreation or by other activities that have no connection with earning a living. So what must our young people do with their free time? They must strive, in every way, to better themselves through education. They must aspire to mount the next rung on the ladder of success and they must make the world they inhabit a richer, bolder and more democratic place."

Immediately following Mr. Beaumont's address there was sustained applause. The dapper young radio producer came forward and again struck three tones on his glockenspiel, whereupon the broadcast shifted elsewhere to list the evening's sponsors, including Kelvinator and the Beach Soap Company, located at Maple and Lawrence Streets. During this interval, Mayor Quebec announced that Colin Isherwood had been elected second vice president *in absentia*, and that the newest member of the Lawrence Chamber of Commerce was seated to his left on the dais.

"Gentlemen, I give you Walter Beaumont," said the Mayor.

"Speech, speech," called out a wag.

The Mayor laughed. "Please," he said. "One Beaumont per evening is enough."

"Fewer than one is enough," said Wilson X. Wilson, sotto voce.

Winking at the younger Beaumont, Mayor Quebec noted that Walter had joined the Chamber of Commerce as "unaffiliated" rather than under the aegis of his current employer. "Stay tuned for developments in Mr. Beaumont's career," said the Mayor.

While those near the console heard an announcer enumerating the benefits of Father John's Medicine, Mr. Jordan scrambled from his place and arranged the YMCA choir in a semi-circle behind the microphone. When the commercial ended, the producer signaled to Mr. Jordan, whose hands were poised in the air, and with a flourish the eleven-member chorale launched into a medley of "Visions," by Sjoberg-Balough; "Song of the Jolly Roger," Chudleigh-Candish; "An Evening Pastorale," Shaw; and "Laudamus," by Protheroe.

The younger Beaumont had been studying the weave of the tablecloth since his unfortunate introduction by the Mayor, and while the choir reached for the tremolo of Sullivan's "Lost Chord," he heard Mr. Prescott from the bank shift in his chair. Charles M. Prescott was a prim-looking man of fifty-four, dressed in an Edwardian suit of light gray wool, a blue and gray striped tie, and a folded silk handkerchief in place of the boutonnière worn by most Chamber members. His sparse hair was stretched across his pate and he wore a pair of wire-rimmed specs. When Mr. Prescott leaned toward him like he was about to speak, Walter's face reddened and his collar grew hot.

Walter mastered himself, raising his eyes to Mr. Prescott and seeing only the glittering orbs of his spectacles. He wondered if he would be able to match the bank president's wit and whether a piece of Yankee wisdom was about to come his way.

A phalanx of waiters had begun moving out of the kitchen, rolling their carts in single file along the wall. "I hope it isn't chicken," said Mr. Prescott. "I detest chicken."

*

Walter Beaumont descended the stairs of the YMCA, his cleats popping on the metal treads. He hesitated between the chopped-down wisteria, made pink by the neon above; a slender, roseate figure with the landscape of the Common gaping before him. By leaving the banquet early Walter had claimed the better part of the evening for himself, but the young executive had forgotten to ask where his father's car was parked. He swung his gaze up and down Lawrence Street, scrutinizing the various automobiles hunched along the border of the park. The senior Beaumont had arrived late and there was little chance he had found such a prime spot as these. So Walter headed for Broadway, knowing he could find a good cigar there, if not his father's automobile.

It was a short walk. After the quiet neighborhood he passed through, the boulevard was lit up like the Great White Way. Four consecutive theaters lined the street: the Palace, the Broadway, the Modern, and the Strand, each glowing with a thousand light bulbs and attended by a man in a braided overcoat and visored cap. The Palace featured *Rangers of Fortune* with Gilbert Roland; *Citizen Kane* starring Orson Welles was playing at the Broadway; the Modern was home to Alfred Hitchcock's *Suspicion*; and the Marx Brothers were at the Strand. Although cars were lined up on both sides, Walter didn't see the Pierce Arrow.

Just before nine o'clock, the main features were in progress and the sidewalks were empty but for an occasional stroller, hands clasped behind his back, perusing the coming attractions. At the corner of Broadway and Essex Street, a policeman occupied the traffic pedestal in front of Liggett's Drug Store, whistling cars through the intersection.

Not far from the Victoria Theater, which stood across Broadway from the others, Walter encountered the wooden Indian that marked the entrance to Haynes Cigar & Tobacco, est. 1909. Inside the narrow, tar-smelling shop, eighty-one year old David Haynes, wearing an upright collar and black tie, presided over the boxes, netted bales, painted tin drums and glass tubes of his establishment. A buzzer announced Walter's arrival and he moved into the tiny shop, which could only host a single customer at a time.

"What'll it be?" asked Haynes, sitting on a barrel in the corner. He was wreathed in shadow; only the tip of his nose and his hands, clutching the head of an ivory-tipped cane, were visible.

"'Evening, Mr. Haynes. It's me, Walter."

The old man emitted a cackle. "I didn't recognize you in that monkey suit," he said. "Thought you were a goddamn banker or something."

David Haynes, like Ray Bower and a scarce number of other old-timers, had maintained his Broadway establishment since the days of Walter's youth. Although he kept a small supply of expensive cigars, the majority of his clientele were working fellows from the Washington and Upper Pacific and Ayer Mills, who queued on the sidewalk just after six PM and filed in for their nickel cigars or a plug of Bowie chewing tobacco. Feeling the sting of the old man's wit was part of the bargain, and when a patron came back out, he often repeated what Haynes had said to the line of other customers, waiting for their barrage of laughter and smoking his cheroot.

Walter chose two cigars and handed the old man a banknote.

"One for before you make an ass out of yourself and one for after," said Haynes.

Beaumont smiled at the old man. "I was thinking of them as victory cigars," he said. "One for each of my achievements."

"And what might those be?"

"A new car, and maybe a new job," the young man said.

Haynes snorted. "Your feet are propulsion enough, if you ain't got a horse," said the tobacconist. "And a fellow who covets another man's job sees a fool when he looks in the mirror."

Another customer was peering through the glass as Walter turned to leave. "Have a good night, Mr. Haynes," he said, chuckling at the old man's proverb.

"Every night is saved from what's left," said the octogenarian.

Walter passed along the broad panes of the sidewalk with the two maduros in his pocket. At the corner he waited for the traffic cop to spot him, standing beneath one of the gaslights that had been wired for electricity forty years earlier. Buildings loomed all around and a clock outside Morton's Shoes indicated that it was five minutes after nine. Essex Street was teeming with cars and trucks and men in brimmed hats; Walter had never seen such a collection of souls. People rushed along, preoccupied with thoughts of war but certain that America could whip the Nazis. The street was humming with talk of it.

Just then the policeman raised his big Irish mitt, halting a panel truck from Maroun Bros. and the line of cars beyond. Whistling through his teeth, the cop pointed the index finger of his right hand at Walter Beaumont, swung his forearm across his torso and indicated the far side of Essex Street. Walter tipped his hat as he went past.

Not far from the *Tribune-Standard* building, Walter spotted Colin Isherwood through the windows of Pinky's Café. The newspaperman shoved his drink aside and reached into his pocket for a crumpled bill and tossed it on the bar. With his hat pushed back on his head, he circled the pool table and came outside.

"We missed you at the Chamber," Walter said.

"Working late," said the publisher. "You hear about the *Kearney*?" Walter nodded, and Isherwood continued: "We just got another bulletin."

Walter raised his chin, encouraging Mr. Isherwood to go on. "You know Mrs. Campagnone?" the publisher asked. His hair was gray and there were deep pouches beneath his eyes.

"She lives across from the Common," said Walter.

"Her son was on the *Kearney*," Isherwood said. He looked in the direction of his errand. "Albert Campagnone is Lawrence's first casualty of the war."

Colin Isherwood shoved his hands into his pockets and walked away, in and out of the light cast by the windows along Essex Street. Half a minute later, Walter ran into Mr. Shiebel in front of the Sutherland's

Jay Atkinson

building, its metal wings folded shut over the doors and secured with padlocks. Dressed in a shapeless wool coat, Egonne Shiebel was carrying a package from Brockelman's and examining through the grate some item lodged in Sutherland's front window.

"Mr. Shiebel," Walter said. "Are you going home?"

The man squinted through his eyeglasses and, recognizing Walter, smiled and extended his hand. "I'm just wandering," he said. "And you?"

"I'm coming from my father's speech at the YMCA. We hoped to see you there."

"I'm neither young nor a Christian," Mr. Shiebel said.

"The Chamber is open to everyone."

"Of course it is," said Mr. Shiebel. "Did you enjoy your father's talk?"

"I thought he made several good points."

"So did I." While the younger man looked puzzled, Mr. Shiebel leaned over and rested his package on the sidewalk. "Not only did I hear it on the radio, but your father read it to me over the telephone last night. Twice."

Walter laughed. "He does things to death."

"Your father is a thorough man." From beneath his heavy brow, Mr. Shiebel's eyes were steady on Walter. "And from what he tells me, you'd be wise to accept that job at the bank."

"It hasn't been offered yet."

Mr. Shiebel looked off down Essex Street, which was crowded with automobiles and buses, then returned his gaze to the man who stood before him. "Your father will see to that," he said. "And please don't begrudge his influence. As one grows older the thing one misses most is the advice and guidance of one's father." Mr. Shiebel could see his own *pater*, sitting by a rude fire, his eyes glistening as he told little Egonne to make way for America. That in America, if he saved and prayed and worked hard, he would find what he was looking for. What all the Shiebels were looking for.

This was more than Egonne Shiebel had said to Walter Beaumont in all the years of their acquaintance and they stood before the Sutherland building gazing at automobiles and then at the night sky. Somewhere above the clouds droned an airplane.

"There's a war coming," Shiebel said. "And every man must take stock of himself."

Walter bent down and then handed Mr. Shiebel his package. "Have a pleasant evening, sir."

"And you."

Farther along the sidewalk, Walter heard music coming from the Capri Café. Lumps of manure were littering the roadway and Bronco Castricone, the large, hairy-handed doorman, was inspecting the manure and shaking his head. "Here it is 1941 and I'm cleaning up horse shit," he said.

"How's the action tonight?" asked Walter.

The former athlete was several years older than Beaumont and inflated with muscles. "Slow," he said.

A quarter mile down the boulevard was the Connolly Coal wagon, one of the last horse-drawn vehicles in the city. While Bronco cleaned up the manure with sheets of cardboard, he spotted Jim Connolly emerging from Summerfield's with a large coal scuttle in each hand.

"Son of a bitch," said Castricone. He disposed of the manure in a neighboring alley and began lumbering down the sidewalk.

Beaumont watched with his arms akimbo. "What are you going to do?" he asked.

"Boot Jimmy in the ass," said the doorman.

Since Monty Tattersall had gotten married a year earlier, Walter hadn't been to the Capri or any of their other downtown haunts. Nowadays he spent most nights at home, listening to "One Man's Family" and "Duffy's Tavern" on the radio. Lately Edward R. Murrow had been broadcasting from overseas and Walter, like millions of other Americans, heard bombs falling on the city as the great man intoned "This…is London."

Inside the Capri, Joe Annaloro and his Sophisticated Swingers played a fast number while cigarette smoke drifted above the tables. On a platform behind the bar was a stuffed deer with a large rack of antlers, its glassy eyes aimed toward the bandstand. The buck had been salvaged from the Park Hotel when that place burned down, carried from the scene by revelers who occupied the bar when the fire broke out.

Standing at the tall, cadmium-plated bar was a young Negro, Chet Collins, who played drums in the Troy Brown orchestra and was there, he told Walter, to hear a saxophone player named Carl Thomas. Dressed in flannel trousers, white dinner jacket, and a neat bow tie, Collins explained that he was on a break from his gig at the Manhattan Lounge.

Beaumont knew Collins and had stayed late at the Tip-Top and Nick's Supper Club for his jam sessions. As he drank his beer, the drummer said that he'd enlisted in the Army and was heading out the next morning for training in Georgia.

"Why'd you do that, Chester?" asked Beaumont. "You must be thirty years old."

"Thirty-five," said Collins, who wore a goatee and a little mustache that crawled across his upper lip. "Anyhow, we're all gonna go eventually."

Beaumont shook his head. "I got four years prior service and the draft board says I have 'sub-standard respiratory function.'"

"You did your time, I'll do mine," said the drummer. "Just happens to be war time. My pappy fought in France, my granpappy in Mexico. We're a fightin' bunch, the Collinses."

Walter motioned to the barman. "Two cognacs, please."

The drinks were poured and Chet Collins raised his snifter toward the ceiling. "I get to France, I'll drink cognac straight out of Hitler's hat," he said.

While they were talking, three swells in mohair jackets got up from one of the tables and danced with their dates. The girls wore ankle-length wool skirts and short beaded jackets with fur collars. When the

Jay Atkinson

song finished they sat back down and the swells, perspiring from the effort and their faces glowing with alcohol, came over to the bar.

"Three Rupperts," said the tallest one, who wore a straw boater. They crowded to the rail and the barman opened the tap and poured the beer into three mugs. The men were very close to Walter and one of them jostled his elbow. "Good evening, friend," said Beaumont.

"Evenin', " said the man in the boater. "Got your shadow with you?"

"Pardon me?"

The man jerked his thumb toward Chet Collins and looked back at his friends, who were laughing into their beers. "I didn't know shadows drank whiskey," he said.

"It's cognac," said Collins.

One of the men, a short, bearded fellow, pushed against Walter Beaumont. "Your shadow is talking, mister," he said. "Tell it to pipe down."

"Listen here," said the barman. "You fellows go back to your seats. Leave them alone."

The man wearing the straw hat knocked his mug over, spreading its contents over the bar like quicksilver. "I don't like drinking with niggers," he said.

Walter Beaumont and Chet Collins removed their jackets and handed them to the barman. At the same time, Carl Thomas jumped down from the bandstand and rushed over, carrying his saxophone. He was an anemic-looking fellow with brown hair and watery blue eyes.

"We don't want no trouble in here," said the barman. "This is a respectable club."

The bearded gent laughed and spit into his hands before raising them as fists. "If it was respectable you wouldn't have niggers at the bar," he said.

Just then Bronco Castricone returned from his errand. Sprinkled with coal dust, the old wrestler stood on the planks of the Capri, arms folded, surveying the faces of Beaumont and Collins and the bartender. The club's patrons, about thirty in all, were staring toward the bar and Joe Annaloro, distinguished by his pink boutonniere, was clutching a fire extinguisher.

"There ain't gonna be no fighting, is there?" asked Castricone, towering over the three swells.

Castricone's arms were as thick as pillars and his neck was like a tree trunk. The men put their jackets back on and left the bar while Carl Thomas returned to his place and Joe Annaloro set down the fire extinguisher and took up his baton. He tapped the lectern four times and the orchestra began playing "In the Still of the Night."

That's the moment that Walter Beaumont spotted Pier Eriksen. She had entered the Capri unnoticed and stood combing out her hair. It was plentiful and golden with a long white feather caught in the tresses and she wore a man's short traveling jacket over a diaphanous gown of some sort. Beside her was a small case of lacquered straw, from which she removed a notebook, jotted something down, and replaced the notebook in the bag.

She was tall, with very long legs and slim hips and a full, pleasing bosom. Her hair was shiny under the gaslights and the contour of her face, lacking any trace of makeup, radiated health and wellbeing. She had brilliant white teeth, skin like satin, and eyes the color and depth of the ocean. No one in the room had ever laid eyes on such a woman before.

Tossing her jacket over the lacquered case, she walked toward the bar. Beyond, Joe Annaloro and his orchestra drummed and tootled and strummed, filling the room with music. "It's been a long trip," said the woman. "And now I'd like to dance—" she looked at Chet Collins—"with you."

The others watched as she led the drummer onto the dance floor. Then Chet Collins and the mystery woman waltzed over the polished wood, cheek-to-cheek, her fairy-like complexion floating above his while they swayed to Cole Porter.

Collins and the woman returned to the bar. "Thank you, miss," said the drummer. "Now, if you'll excuse me, I'll be going back to work."

"It was my pleasure, Mister…?"

"Chester Collins."

The dancers shook hands. "Pier Eriksen," the woman said. "I wish you luck."

"Thanks again, miss. Good night."

The drummer went out through the kitchen. Bronco Castricone helped the barman sop up the beer with some towels and then returned to his post, leaving Beaumont and the woman alone.

"Do you come here for the dancing?" Pier asked.

Walter laughed. "I don't dance," he said. "And I don't fight, either."

"There are two forces in the world," said Miss Eriksen. "Spenta Mainyu, the beneficent spirit, and Angra Mainyu, the hostile spirit. Who and what you are depends on your choice between good thoughts, good words and good deeds, and evil thoughts and evil deeds."

"Is it some kind of religion?" asked Walter.

On stage, Carl Thomas stood up behind the riser and played an extensive solo. His eyes closed, fingers skittering over the keys, his song went low, mellow and deep. "These words were spoken by Zarathustra," Eriksen said, "more than three thousand years ago."

"I'm an Episcopal," said Walter.

Pier Eriksen stared into Walter's eyes, thrilling him to the bone. "These men who despise Mr. Collins are evil because of their bad thoughts," she said. "You chose 'asha,' the side of the truth. The man who possesses 'ashavan' will attain enlightenment. He is the one blessed after death."

The barman returned with a towel draped over his shoulder. "Can I get you folks something?"

Walter ordered a beer and Pier Eriksen requested a glass of tomato juice. When it arrived, she removed a tiny cloth bag from the waistband of her skirt, took pinches of grit from the bag and added them to the juice and drank it down.

Jay Atkinson

"Its called haoma," Pier said. "If I add Ephedra, I can produce haoma from any natural drink."

Walter set down his beer. "What does it do?"

"Haoma is given to the dying," said Eriksen. "It acts as a kind of viaticum that permits them to obtain immortality and be resurrected."

On the bandstand, Carl Thomas completed his solo and the orchestra returned to playing in harmony. For several minutes Walter and Pier stood against the bar, listening to the music. Finally Pier said that she had just arrived that evening and would like to tour the city. "I want to see everything," she said.

They left her bag with the doorman and went onto Essex Street, horns honking, globes of light thrust against the facades of downtown and the motorized buses passing like ships. Pier Eriksen had a light, graceful step and when Beaumont asked where she had come from, the woman laughed and said she'd been just about everywhere but had been born in Norway. And Walter understood that he would gladly live there with her, on a hillside dotted with milk cows and sheep, up early to do his chores, drinking great mugs of buttermilk with platters of ham and fresh eggs, a whole life left behind him, if only for the chance to lie down at night in the great feather bed of the cottage loft.

Walter had known women before—in the backseat of a roadster parked behind Lawrence High, on blankets spread over the grasses of Kentucky, and in rooms at the Ambassador Hotel. But strolling along with Pier Eriksen, he had the sensation of climbing a vast obstacle and for the first time, glimpsing the territory on the other side. Her presence opened up a strange new land and across this vista were fresh sights and sounds even as they walked among the familiar landmarks of Essex Street.

Miss Eriksen had delivered this vista at great peril. After her husband's death at the start of the war, she had been in North Africa, upon Gibraltar, and then in London, squatting each night in the underground while bombs fell on the city. Finally she had inveigled a place aboard one of the merchant ships bound for New York; the *Asilah Star*, a Moroccan freighter in a convoy of seventeen other vessels, including a military escort comprised of two British frigates, a Canadian destroyer and a French man 'o war. Crossing the Atlantic was a dangerous business, as German submarines hunted in packs astride the shipping lanes, and every night Pier Eriksen and her fellow travelers saw hulks burning on the water. Great tonnages were going to the bottom.

On the fifth night of the voyage, alarms rang throughout the ship and Pier was hustled to the deck by wild-eyed Moroccan seamen. Arcs of light dashed over the water as the frigates searched for the nub of a U-boat, their semaphore blinking on and off like eyeballs. Pier huddled against the rail, studying the sea and tasting the oily spray. Around her, seamen prostrated themselves and prayed to Allah, or else clung to the railing and cursed the darkness. Suddenly a whistling sound pierced the air and half a mile away the sea erupted in a geyser, followed by the bellow of an explosion. The escort ships had zeroed in on a target and begun shelling, walking their cannons up and down the stretch of ocean where they believed the enemy was lying in wait. The sky was illuminated with great flashes of light, which the Moroccans insisted were the protests of Allah.

Pier gave herself to the splendor as the nearby deck gun went *crump crump crump* and shells burst over the water in such rapid order there seemed no space between them, just one sea-rending eruption. A phosphorescent wake spread out from the *Asilah Star* and Pier was gazing into this soft glowing foam when the U-boat popped to the surface less than one hundred yards astern. Its rusted hull was streaming with water and she could read the Nazi insignia and see the nets flung over the conning tower. She attempted to cry out, but her voice caught in her throat. It was like seeing Death itself.

There was the hollow sound of an implosion as the submarine loosened its torpedo, and then the klieg lights found the silhouette and hell was unleashed upon the Germans. The U-boat dived; Pier had a feeling of dread for the men entrapped there. Then she saw the torpedo riding the surf like a porpoise, heading straight for the oil tanker that followed the Moroccans in the convoy. There was half a second of calm as the torpedo sank into the metal, then the freighter rose higher and higher, like a skyscraper emerging from the sea. Steel plates were rent with a groaning sound, then the vessel exploded in orange, red, and blue flame, disintegrating the heavy black ship upon the waves.

No sound came from the crew and the ship bubbled into the depths. The next freighter gave the wreckage a wide berth and the convoy sailed on, flinging depth charges in its wake.

With her *visa de sortie* Pier could have sought refuge in a neutral country, but as a "textile artist" she had accompanied a load of Egyptian cotton and wool and flax from the Nile to its ultimate destination, which turned out to be Lawrence. In front of the W. T. Grant & Co. building, Walter asked Pier what she intended to do now that she had arrived.

"Coming to this city is 'ayathrima,' the homecoming spoken about in the *Gathas*," said Eriksen. "I feel content here."

She and Walter strolled along the huge darkened windows, which trembled in the wake of passing trucks while leaves danced about their ankles. A squirrel zigzagged ahead of them and Beaumont asked what Miss Eriksen had written in her notebook upon entering the Capri.

Pier took out the notebook and Walter leaned under a streetlight to read the inscription: *Why do we kill the things we love?*

21

The Present Day

Rick Maxwell lingered between the metal wings of the old Sutherland's building, which were fastened to the brick with massive steel bolts. He was hidden in a well of shade, watching Elise Dominaux stroll past the boarded-up storefronts. Elise came toward him in the windows along Essex Street, first as a montage of elegant parts—the whirl of an arm, slim bare legs, the rounded buttocks—and then made whole again, her figure reassembled into sharp, sculpted outline.

"Over here," Maxwell said. In tan slacks and an oxford shirt, the ATF agent twirled his sunglasses like a propeller. He and Elise had decided on a last night out. "How's it going?" he asked.

"I'm starving," Elise said.

It was six o'clock on a mild sunny evening. Elise and Maxwell went along the sidewalk, gazing at the soaped windows and old dented signs. "Where is everybody?" Elise asked.

"At the stadium," said Maxwell. "There's a big fireman's muster today."

"I can imagine what all the firebugs are doing," Elise said.

They stopped in front of the defunct headquarters of Lawrence Savings & Trust. It was a stone building with massive columns out front and a polished granite slab that led into the foyer. Maxwell rubbed some of the grime from the window and they peered inside. Light was refracted through the rotunda, splintering into four separate beams. Dust rose toward the ceiling, ascending the shafts of light, and bits of mica glowed in the marble floor. The teller windows and ink stands and desks had all been romoved, and the one remaining counter, about ten feet long and made of rose-colored marble, looked like a sarcophagus.

"It's sad," said Elise, standing on tiptoe.

"They buried their retired president about a month ago," said Maxwell. "The last of the Brahmins."

"I know," Elise said, as they passed along the sidewalk.

In the alley a figure emerged from beneath a jumble of cardboard, leaving a terrible odor in his wake. The besotted man glanced at Rick and Elise and worked his toothless jaw, his gaze cutting up and over their heads. Behind him the cardboard was on fire, and Maxwell strode into the alley and stamped it out. Soon he emerged, brushing off cinders that had attached themselves to his trousers.

Elise took his hand. "We're going to miss you around here," she said.

They walked past a vacant lot strewn with tufts of upholstery. "I'm on my way to Utah next," Maxwell said. "They've got some guys out there who refuse to pay taxes and are stockpiling weapons."

"I'm going to San Diego," said Elise. "If I'm gonna struggle, it's gonna be someplace with grass and trees."

"Let's get something to eat," Rick said. "How about Bachop's?"

"Anyplace that serves food."

A mass of clouds eased over the horizon. The sun sank beneath this thunderhead, illuminating its ribs and bathing the Ayer Mill in unearthly light. Not far along they approached WKUT, a turret-shaped building with a fence around it. There was a "For Sale" sign staked on the lawn.

"Kap ran this place into the ground," Elise said.

The windows glowed in the light and the door, papered with Dominican campaign posters, was fastened with a padlock. "When did they close?" Rick asked.

"About three weeks ago," said Elise. "You should see the crowds at the Unemployment Office. It's like waiting for a lifeboat on the Titanic."

They turned onto Common Street and Maxwell ran his fingers along the chain link. "You know, I was a little disappointed when we got Tito Jackson's confession," he said. "I had a feeling Kutter was part of it, somehow. Those footprints in the cemetery..." Maxwell trailed off, staring through the fence. "I mean, how could a guy be such an asshole and still be innocent?"

The security gate was locked and Kap Kutter's Porsche was the only car in the lot. "They're not broadcasting, are they?" asked Rick.

"They leased the tower, so Kap has to go in once a day," Elise said. She glanced at the shining black hull of the the Porsche. "Billy Bruce works his tail off for thirty years and all he gets is a piece of fax paper with 'Thank you' printed on it."

"What's he going to do now?"

"One of the advertisers offered him a job selling cars, but Billy and his wife took a drive up to the White Mountains. They haven't had a vacation in years."

"I hope things work out for him," Maxwell said.

"The day I left, Billy was on the air. He started playing 'Rhapsody in Blue,' and ran out to the lobby to say goodbye. Before the tears could start, he took me by the elbow and said, 'May I have this dance?' and waltzed me out the door. When I started down the walk, he bowed and his toupee fell off. He caught it, and then laughed and said, 'For you, my dear, the real me.' "

"What a classy fella."

Jay Atkinson

Elise Dominaux forced a smile. "They should put up a statue to the guy," she said.

A sign in the window announced that Bachop's was closed due to a kitchen fire. Aram and Amir Bachop thanked their loyal clientele and mentioned plans to re-open within a few days. "Another fire," said Maxwell. "What a surprise."

Elise pointed the way toward Jackson Street. "There's a ton of Dominican and Puerto Rican restaurants up this way," she said.

Passing the Greek Orthodox Church, they emerged beside the YMCA and cut a tangent along the Common. Inside a little storefront called *El Casa de Lopez*, they stood at a makeshift bar and Rick Maxwell ordered a couple of beers from the large Hispanic woman behind the counter. Two bottles of *Carte Blanco* were brought up dripping from the cooler, and the proprietress flipped the tops onto the floor. Three admirers of the woman huddled by the window, watching her movements like starveling dogs. Empty bottles littered their table and cigarettes burned in the ashtray, sending up ribbons of smoke. Whenever the proprietress glanced at them, the men gulped the cold, sweet beer and waved their hands for more.

Elise pumped two quarters into the jukebox and played a handful of salsa tunes. She did a little dance step over the floor, stamping to a halt in front of Rick Maxwell and giggling into her beer.

The other customers never took their eyes off the proprietress, her huge breasts swinging beneath the fabric of her moo-moo. They made Elise Dominaux's implants look like cantaloupes beside two championship watermelons. Another man entered the *bodega*, dark-skinned and feral with a metallic sticker of a Corvette on his black T-shirt. He purchased a beer and stood against the wall, joining the intense study of the barmaid.

In the midst of another salsa tune, Rick and Elise finished their drinks and asked for the bill. "One dollar, fifty cent," said Mama Lopez.

A few drops of rain splashed the pavement and a yellow dog no bigger than a cat leaped in front of the window, yipping at the change in the weather. Maxwell gave Mama Lopez three dollars, gesturing that she should keep the change. "At these prices, I don't know how you do it," he said.

Mama Lopez winked at him. "Smile a lot, sell a lot," she said.

Heavy black clouds sailed above the mills, casting a gloom over downtown. Rick Maxwell took Elise by the hand and they hurried down Jackson Street, breaking into a run as the rain pattered on the eaves overhead.

Soon it fell faster, coming in large drops that crashed against their foreheads. They crossed the empty squares of Campagnone Common, ravaged by the sudden thunderstorm. An oak tree was creaking in the wind and the bronze statue of the doughboy slanted toward Essex Street, rain clattering from his helmet. Elise paused beneath the statue to remove her sandals, and they started running again.

Rick thrust out his arm like a halfback breaching the line. "Where to?" he asked.

"This way," Elise said, running past him. "It's not far."

No space existed between the raindrops; they fell everywhere, warm and dense. Elise veered through the parking lot of Tivoli Bakery, heading for a restaurant on Newbury Street.

"Is this place any good?" asked Rick.

"It has a roof."

Yellow cabs were parked on both sides of the street. Squeezed in between Rivera Dry Cleaning and Merrimack Taxi, *La Bahia* restaurant advertised itself as *Comidas y Bebidas por Muchachos y Muchachas*. Rick and Elise were drenched. They hesitated beneath the awning, staring into each other's eyes. The breasts of the young woman were held upright by a sheer, flesh-colored bra and several times Rick Maxwell's gaze slipped down to examine them.

"They're fake," Elise said. "Implants."

"Science is amazing," Maxwell said, and they kissed. He felt Elise's technology, like two firm balloons, crushed against his chest.

A waitress thrust open the door and they were welcomed into the pungent, air-conditioned restaurant. The bedraggled couple stood leaning together, water pooling on the rubber mat beneath their feet. Elise put her sandals back on and pinched at the front of her blouse, but it was soaked through and clung to her breasts no matter what she did. "It's embarrassing," she said in Rick's ear.

No one seemed to notice. The waitress wore a T-shirt tied off above her bulging midriff. She was braless, jiggling as she wiped off a table, her black hair pinned up by a spray of plastic flowers. *"Aqui,"* the waitress said, directing Rick and Elise to a table.

In a minute she brought over their drinks, rum mixed with fruit juice. Outside the storm had already lessened. Rain dotted the windows, but columns of sunlight appeared here and there on Newbury Street, steaming now from the abrupt temperature change. "Utah," said Elise. "That sounds pretty remote."

"If you have more than five teeth you're the governor," said Maxwell.

The door opened and Kuko Carrero entered *La Bahia*, accompanied by two young women wearing spandex, their hair swept back in shiny black torrents. Immediately a pitcher of rum punch was brought to their table.

"Hola," Kuko said to Maxwell. "Funny freakin' weather."

Suddenly this new party was the center of attention: Kuko in repose, his arms folded over his chest. He ordered cold shrimp and pineapple and the two young *Latinas* sat to either side, picking at the shrimp with their fingernails and gazing at the ceiling. Even the cook ventured out to shake Kuko's hand and two men from the taxi stand came to the window and were acknowledged. Just as Maxwell considered going elsewhere, the waitress took his order.

Across the room, the *Latinas* dipped shrimp into the rum before shoving them in their mouths. Their make-up was garish; ruby lipstick that hadn't washed off in the rain, and purple eyeshadow and half moons of blush painted along their cheekbones.

For Kuko, who slept all day, this was breakfast. Soon he would shed the Tutamara sisters and meet his bodyguard, and they would drive over the river between South Lawrence and downtown. In these hours, Kuko collected money from the street dealers and laid some wood on the other "biznessmen" and freelances that were cutting into Latin King profits. A little rum, some toots of cocaine, and his night would be eaten up by threatening, hassling, and driving by crack houses with guns displayed out the window.

Since he had arrived in Lawrence, Kuko had only zapped one guy; a heroin dealer from East Boston, some Portuguese dude who was hardly worth shooting. Kuko had one of the Tutamaras lure this *cabron* to a house where they speedballed until the guy was nearly comatose, and then Kuko popped him. They left him there for several hours, flies buzzing around two holes in the guy's forehead. Then a couple of Latin King wannabes loaded the body down with scrap iron and dumped it in the river.

Offing one little *cabron* was easy. And since the guy was from out of town, there was no heat. Not so much as a dirty look. Kuko was like a lumberjack in a town with one tree.

Kuko's phone buzzed in his pocket and he noticed the *cabron* eyeballing him from across the restaurant. The gang leader smiled at him and clicked on his phone. "Yo," he said.

Little Eddie told Kuko the deal was on. After making final arrangements, they'd leave for New York in a few hours.

Kuko hung up. The idea of going home made him happy, and he saluted the black dude and his squeeze with the beautiful tits. In Spanish, he told the waitress to send them a round of drinks. The black dude was tall and well muscled with a good haircut. Kuko didn't recognize him.

The drinks arrived. "*Salud*," Kuko said, raising his glass. "To your health, my fren.'"

Rick Maxwell knew Kuko's rap sheet backwards and forwards, and worried that he'd been identified as Five-0. Since his arrest, Tito Jackson had been locked up at the state police barracks in Andover. He made four calls to the public defender's office and received no visitors. So there was no way Kuko could've been tipped off about Maxwell's identity. Still, the ATF agent was curious over the attention he was getting, and wondered if he and Elise had been followed into *La Bahia*.

"What's happenin'?" asked Kuko, his eyes trained on Elise's breasts.

"*Nada*," said Maxwell.

The gang leader's phone buzzed again. Listening into the receiver, Kuko grunted a couple of times, then folded the plastic device and returned it to his pocket.

"Bizness," said Kuko. "You can't get away from it."

Maxwell's beeper went off, and he glanced down at Chief McNamara's cell phone number on the tiny screen. "You got that right," he said, switching off the noise. His gaze darted around, looking for a pay phone, but there wasn't one.

"You need to make a call, my fren'?" asked Kuko, extending his phone. "Be my gues'."

Taking Elise by the elbow and bringing along their drinks, Rick Maxwell joined Kuko and the Tutamara sisters. The shrimp gave off a briny odor, and there were the additional smells of sweat and cigarettes and cologne. Rick took the cell phone and punched in McNamara's number.

"What is it?" asked Maxwell, when the line was picked up. Beside him, Elise was fidgeting under Kuko's scrutiny, and the Tutamara sisters crossed their hairy forearms and glared at her. Chief McNamara wanted to know where Rick was calling from. "Cell phone," he said.

"Call me later," McNamara said. "I think you'll want to hear what's going on."

Rick Maxwell hung up, using the keypad to erase the chief's number. Kuko smiled as he took the telephone back.

"What are you doin' here?" asked Kuko, drinking his rum.

"My friend and I"—Maxwell circled an arm around Elise— "are leaving town, so we're out celebrating."

Kuko grasped Elise's wrist with his damp, fish-smelling hand. "This is my las' night, too," said the gang leader. "I'm history aroun' here, man."

"Where you going?" Maxwell asked.

Kuko laughed, showing his gold teeth. "Anywhere," he said. "This inchworm don' crawl fast enough for me."

Elise tried to free herself, but Kuko maintained a grip on her wrist. His clammy fingers moved up her arm. Yet he smiled like it was nothing.

Unable to speak or understand much English, the Tutamara sisters were ready to scratch the eyes out of this yellow-haired bitch with the *tetas grande*. As soon as Kuko was through pawing her, they hoped to entice him out to the car to smoke a few rocks. Once high, they didn't care what Kuko did or where he went. The sisters would spend the night watching television and scrounging pebbles of cocaine from the living room floor.

But the gang leader showed no signs of quitting the restaurant. With a glance at her sister, Gloribel slipped her hand beneath the edge of the table and began massaging Kuko's balls. The gang leader flashed a look at her, and she let his cock go and it flopped against his leg. "Gimme *Nueva York* any day, man," Kuko said to Maxwell.

"What do you do for work?" asked Maxwell.

Kuko looked down at the shrimp casings on his plate, which were fringed with little pink legs. "Marketing and sales," he said. "How 'bout you?"

"Same thing," Maxwell said.

Kuko's eyes were like two dirty coins. His teeth flashed as he drank, and then his fleshy lips covered them again. "It ain' easy when everybody's got a bug up his ass," he said.

The waitress came out of the kitchen with a tray balanced on her shoulder. The food was steaming, piled high on green ceramic plates. "Ready to eat?" Elise asked Maxwell.

Jay Atkinson

"I sure am," Rick said. He shook hands with Kuko, crushing the man's slimy knuckles. "Thanks for the phone call."

"Listen, you around late, stop by the Disco Very. That's my crib."

"I will," Maxwell said.

Dropping a fifty-dollar bill beside his plate, Kuko stood up, addressing the Tutamara sisters in Spanish. "You wanna get high—okay. But first you're gonna suck Kuko inside out. Maybe we'll stop downtown and I'll buy you some blonde wig and a furry sweater."

From the sidewalk, Kuko looked through the rain-spattered window at the blonde. "Gimme five minutes," he said. "I'll break her to the pipe and fuck her silly."

"I don' think her boyfren's likin' that," said Gloribel.

Kuko laughed. "I'd put a cap right between that *cabron's* eyes and he wouldn't care no more."

*

Inside *La Bahia* the smell of barbecued pork overpowered the odor of sweat and cologne. "Do you know that guy?" Elise asked Maxwell.

"He's no 'fren' of mine."

Elise dabbed a napkin in her water glass and wiped her hands with it. "He acts like he's King Shit," she said.

"Another guy'll come along who's smarter and then boom, he's history. Kuko's what—twenty-eight, twenty-nine?" asked Maxwell. "In that business, he's pushing it."

After dinner, Maxwell found a pay phone outside and called McNamara. "What's up?"

"I have some pretty good news," said the chief.

"Tito Jackson has cancer."

"It's not that good," McNamara said. "Rudy Pattavina called to tell me something's happening tonight, and the Latin Kings are in on it. We're not sure what."

Rick Maxwell glanced at Elise, who stood looking at her reflection in a puddle. Her skirt was clinging to her ass, and the curve of her breasts was visible on either side. "I was just talking to Kuko when you called," Maxwell said. "He told me to stop by the Disco Very."

"Call back in an hour on the land line," said McNamara.

"Roger that," said the ATF agent, and hung up.

Arm-in-arm, Rick and Elise walked down Common Street. All the rum and pork sandwiches had a mellowing effect on them, and the sun cast a glow over the dooryards and vacant lots. At the corner, Elise skipped into Halloran's liquor store and came out with two bottles of *Malta Vitarroz*, with tropical sunsets painted on the label.

"How about dessert?" asked Maxwell.

Two blocks down, Jerry's Variety was dimly lit and packed with candy of every size and description. There were segmented bars and ducklings and one-sided rabbits made from chocolate, and other confections like jellied fruit and horehound lozenges and gumdrops arranged in glass jars: blue raspberry, lemon, pineapple, cherry and many more. The smell of burnt sugar filled the room.

Beside a display case filled with gleaming slabs of fudge and rows of peanut butter cups and almond bark was the only customer, a tall elderly woman with beautiful skin and a mantle of white hair. In the woman's right hand was a paper bag twisted at the neck, and she held a baton of chocolate in the other. "Nothing will trigger a memory like the taste of something," the old woman was saying.

Even though a bell tinkled above the door when Rick and Elise entered, the proprietor didn't notice them at first. In his apron and weightless paper hat, he danced across the candy store with arms spread wide to illustrate how much popcorn he could make from fifty pounds of seed.

Many items in the shop were on the grand scale: twenty-pound chocolate rabbits, six-foot sheets of fudge and cashew turtles the size of real ones. On the stove behind the counter a batch of peanut brittle was simmering, and the proprietor stirred the molten candy with a paddle.

"How long has *Jerry's* been here?" asked the woman.

"Eighty years," the shop owner said. "My grandfather's name was Ash Jurek. He was from Hungary, and none of the Eye-talians in the neighborhood could pronounce Jurek so they called him Jerry. Years ago back, we even had a speakeasy in the basement. In them days you did what you had to do to get by."

"I used to come here with my sweetheart and your father would give us what he called cordial cherries," said the old woman, smiling with long yellow teeth.

The candyman reached into the display case, taking out a stemmed cherry as large as a small plum that had been glazed with cream fondant and dipped in chocolate. "This is what you're talking about," he said. "The only hand-dipped, stemmed cherry left in the country, I figure."

Holding the confection by its bright red stem, the elderly woman took a bite and then closed her eyes. "My sweetheart and I would have cordial cherries and lemonade for supper."

Finally Mr. Jurek hailed Rick and Elise, shifting toward them on his rubbery legs. "Can I get you folks something?"

"Do you have any fudge?" Elise asked.

"I'm just whipping up some penuche," said the candymaker. He began tossing supplies onto the metal bench. "It's fun to watch, but making candy is hard work," Jurek said.

To make penuche, Jurek weighed the empty kettle to make sure there was no sugar residue from the last time it was used—even a small amount could change the taste of the fudge, he said. The copper kettles, water-cooled metal table, the saltwater "kisser" machine, and the gelato maker that his grandfather had once owned were still in use. New technology hadn't had much of an effect on making candy by hand, said Jurek. "A piece of equipment that's fifty or sixty years old is the same as what you can buy today," he said.

"Usually what you buy today is thrown out tomorrow," Elise said.

"And believe me, the world suffers for it," the elderly woman said. She introduced herself. " 'Newer' doesn't always mean better, just like 'older' isn't necessarily a synonym for wiser."

Standing beside the old woman, Elise could have passed for her daughter: the same erect carriage, the hair abundant and waxy in the dim light, and the long, elegant hands. Their body English was also identical, and the two women had large eyes spaced well apart beneath prominent foreheads. Elise watched the penuche being made with her elbows bent upon the display case. A couple of feet to her left, gravity pulled the old woman's face down around her jaw and deflated her breasts.

While the candymaker bustled around the shop, Rick Maxwell picked up one of the metal molds that was lying on the counter, for a three-inch Morgan horse. It came in two halves and was dated 1865.

"My God," said the ATF agent. "This was made during the Civil War."

Mr. Jurek said his grandfather had bought one of the copper kettles and the various nickel molds around 1900, from a Greek candymaker in Lowell. The kettle was scarred from the Greek's system of tapping on the rim with a spatula. "One tap meant a pound of butter, two meant a cup of sugar. If the guy fetching the supplies was too slow the Greek kept smacking the kettle, and that meant your ass was in hot water," said Jurek, glancing over his shoulder. "Sometimes we forget, but years ago back the people were just like us."

Over the next few minutes the water was boiled off, until a dollop of the candy dropped into cool water turned into a hard, crackly ball. Then Jurek paddled in the evaporated milk, cream, and several one-pound blocks of butter.

"It's very rich," said Elise.

The old woman dug into a satchel worn around her neck and took out a single dried leaf. "Have this afterwards," she said. "It will eradicate most of the fat and leave a pleasant sensation in your throat. Chinese soldiers used this herb during the Twelfth and Thirteenth centuries, when all they had to eat on the march were balls of rice candy."

The last step entailed cutting pieces with a spatula and paddling them back together with the soft salted mixture, which was still hot. Then the combined mass was poured into a wooden tray lined with waxed paper, and California walnuts were steered into it. The result was twenty pounds of handmade penuche that old man Jurek would have been proud to call his own.

"Thirty or forty years ago, there were a dozen candymakers in Lawrence," said Jurek, cutting off pieces of fudge with his spatula. "Now there's only me."

Rick Maxwell and Elise and the white-haired woman tried slivers of the penuche. The taste was smooth and heavy and sweet, textured by the walnuts.

A car arrived out front. Then the door burst open and Gloribel Tutamara came in waving a fistful of money. Her eyes darted around the shop and she walked straight toward the corn syrup, the hair hanging in strands from her forehead when she leaned over the pail.

"*Me deseo comprar eso,*" she said.

"I don't have the slightest idea what you're saying, young lady," Jurek said.

"She wants to buy what's in the pail," said Mrs. Eriksen.

"Necesitamo ese ahora," said Gloribel, throwing a fifty dollar bill on the counter. Her bra had been unsprung beneath the tube top she was wearing, and her breasts tumbled this way and that when she moved.

The *Latina* reached for the pail, but Jurek yanked the handle from her grasp. "You can have the corn syrup, but not the pail," he said. Reaching in, he patted the syrup into a round transparent globe as large as a basketball and set it on the metal bench. "Go ahead," he told her.

Digging her fingers into the quivering mass of syrup, the teen-age girl lifted it from the counter, balancing it as best she could. As she passed by Maxwell, her eyes blazed and she made a half-turn in his direction, wiggling her backside. *"Come eso, cabron,"* she said, laughing at him.

Smeared with lipstick, her breasts hanging in their tunnel of fabric, Gloribel Tutamara was wild-haired and smelled of cigarette smoke, body odor and liquor. Inside the globe of syrup her red fingernails were sharp and jumpy, magnified several times. Freeing one hand, she opened the door to the shop and crossed the threshold onto the sidewalk. The car door opened and despite the smoke filling the interior, Maxwell glimpsed Kuko in the passenger seat. The gang leader's shirt was unbuttoned to the waist and his eyes were fixed on the ball of corn syrup with a heavy-lidded, bloodshot stare. Beside him on the driver's side was a large, middle-aged man wearing a denim jacket.

"I'll fuck it," said Kuko. He grasped the ball of syrup and with a deft maneuver, flopped out his erect penis and shoved it deep inside the globe. *"Ah, cabron,"* he said, the syrup resting on his lap. Kuko flexed his hips and began thrusting up and down, his magnified penis looming in the syrup.

Squeals came from the back seat as Gloribel deposited the syrup on the stick shift, and grabbed two fistfuls and smeared them on her breasts. While the driver plunged his arm into the remaining syrup to shift gears, Gloribel clambered onto Kuko's lap facing the backseat and the car zoomed off.

"I've never seen that before," said Jurek. "Not in forty-three years of candy making."

Rick Maxwell hurried outside to record the license plate. Gnawing on her chocolate baton, Pier Eriksen glided across the shop and craned her neck to see out the window. "How remarkable," she said.

"We just had dinner with them at *La Bahia*," said Elise. "Chewing with their mouths open. Talking on the telephone, and bumping around under the table. It was very scary."

"The most interesting things in life are often frightening," Mrs. Eriksen said.

Maxwell entered the shop. "Can I use the phone?" he asked. The candymaker pointed out back.

Behind a curtain was an office that contained Jurek's desk and a clunky black telephone. The ATF agent dialed McNamara's number. "Chief,

I'm down at Jerry's Variety," he said. Against the wall, several chocolate rabbits stood in a row. Their ears had been shorn off and still they were nearly three feet tall, with clenched teeth and slick, coppery limbs. In the dark they looked like an army of club-footed pygmies. "Kuko just stopped here and bought fifty dollars worth of corn syrup."

"What the hell for?" asked McNamara.

"You don't want to know. But the reason I'm calling is the car he's in. A brand-new Toyota. And he's got two women and Little Eddie with him."

"The infamous Little Eddie," the Chief said.

There was a basket of shattered white rabbits on a shelf and Maxwell removed one of the ears. It was smooth to the touch, with a buttery flavor. "The car's a dark green Toyota with Mass. plates: 111 ELM," Maxwell said.

"Let me run that," said McNamara.

While Rick was on the telephone, Elise and Pier Eriksen stood in the doorway watching the sun drop behind the tenements. The final rays were angled over the rooftops, glowing with iridescent dust and other pollutants. "It's not unusual for a girl to please her lover," Mrs. Eriksen was saying. "When I was your age, I was in love with a very special man and we would try all kinds of love-making."

Mrs. Eriksen played with a strand of her long white hair. "We fingerpainted each other's bodies, indulged in ritual eating, we even tried tetherings and lashings," she said. "And that was the 1940s. When you realize your life is curving toward oblivion, especially if that realization comes in the flower of youth, you take license." A bird streaked across the sky and the old woman fluttered her hands. "Marvelous things can occur when you let go of other people's expectations."

"Whatever happened to your madman lover?" asked Elise.

"In my life I've had several affairs, but none so fulfilling. Ending it was difficult," said Pier. She placed one of her hands on her abdomen. "It left an ache right here. But finally I was able to see what I had gained from it."

Elise made sure Rick was still on the phone. "Once I made love inside the Ayer Mill clock," she said. "My boyfriend was a big mucky-muck, and he had the keys to get up there." She went on in a rush. "There I was, feeling like a woman down to my bones."

"The top of the Ayer clock will do that," said Mrs. Eriksen. She clasped Elise's hand and smiled at her with glittering blue eyes. "Believe me, you weren't the first one to scream up there."

*

Chief McNamara came back on the telephone. "The Toyota was stolen an hour ago," he said.

"If you want, I'll come down," said Maxwell.

"We'll try to pick them up," the Chief said. "Make it easy for you."

The bell rang above the door and a new customer entered. Mrs. Eriksen and Elise Dominaux made way for him: a hairy fellow wearing only a bathing suit and running shoes. "Ladies," he said.

Mr. Jurek intercepted the man. "This is a candy store, not a sweat shop," the candymaker said.

"I want something for my girls," said Boris Johnson, indicating the chocolate rabbits on display. He moved his arm, and perspiration flew everywhere. "One of those big ones."

Mr. Jurek stabbed at the air, trying to block all the droplets like an ice hockey goalie. Then he leaned against Johnson's slick frame. "Get out," said the candyman. "You're ruining my chocolate."

"I want one of those bunnies," said Johnson.

"Send a car to Jerry's Variety," Maxwell said to the Chief, and hung up. Coming around the display case, he pulled one of the rabbits up by its cellophane cap and handed it to Boris Johnson. "Let's go," he said. Maxwell indicated to Elise that she should wait with the proprietor.

The two men went out front. "I'm a federal agent," said Maxwell. "We've been watching you."

Boris Johnson tightened up his pectoral muscles, which rose beneath the hair like two iron plates. "I've been watching you, too," he said.

A cruiser pulled up, and Maxwell handcuffed the prisoner and opened the rear door. "They wanna ask you a few questions," he said. The hairy man went into the back seat, resting the rabbit on his knees to avoid knocking its ears off.

"What kind of questions?" asked Johnson.

"About Hernan Diaz," Maxwell said. "He was one of the kids we found up at Bellevue."

"I've seen him. He died in the fires."

Maxwell was leaning toward the prisoner. "Hernan Diaz was poisoned," he said.

"He died in the fires," said Johnson. "You'll see." The prisoner hammered at the Plexi-glass with his head. "Let's go. My bunny is melting," he said. Maxwell shut the door, and the police car swooped away from the curb.

Jay Atkinson

22

Lawrence, Massachusetts
December 7, 1941

Established by Charles Storrow and Nathan Appleton in 1863, Lawrence Savings & Trust was a three-and-a-half story building located at the corner of Lawrence and Essex Streets. The bank featured a protruding clock encased in a bronze sleeve and the entrance, which was made of polished granite and etched with the bank's motto—*Labor Omnia Vincit*—was catty corner to the intersection. A frieze of marching figures appeared over the cornice: early Lawrence workers proceeding toward the Great Stone Dam. After serving as assistant branch manager for five weeks, Walter Beaumont joked that his place of business was the finest mausoleum in the city.

On a cold, gray afternoon he returned to the bank from his lunch hour with snow lining the curbstones and sliced into furrows by passing automobiles. Someone had already shoveled the entryway as the snow, which was still falling at noon, had been turned back and the sidewalk bared once again. Walter stamped his galoshes on the pavement and entered the building. As he squeaked across the floor, Blind Eddie Heath, who was allowed to operate his sundry business inside the vestibule, rose to his feet. "Good afternoon, Mr. Beaumont," he said.

Walter approached the table where each morning Eddie Heath spread out his packages of chewing gum, cigarettes, cigars, newspapers and cellophane-wrapped pastries. "Give me a package of doughnuts, please, Eddie," said Beaumont.

"Playing a little hooky, Mr. Beaumont?" asked Eddie.

Walter pressed a finger to his lips. "Ssshh," he said. "You don't want to get me sacked, do you Eddie?"

Although this was a running joke between them, Eddie Heath turned the cannonball of his head in all directions, trying to sense any eavesdroppers who may have entered the vestibule. "If you were ever fired, Mr. Beaumont, I don't know what I'd do," said Heath, twisting the end of his necktie. "I would…challenge Mr. Prescott to a duel."

"You've been listening to the radio too much," Walter said.

Heath wore an ancient paisley tie and a dilapidated suitcoat that was too small for his ample frame, but he was neat and clean-shaven and the gay little packages that comprised his business were smartly arranged. With help from Judge Bates, Walter and his father had located Eddie Heath at the Peabody School for the Blind and engineered his return to Lawrence. Walter had then convinced Mr. Prescott that Eddie's stand would be unobtrusive, and perhaps even a boon to their customers.

"Here you are, Mr. Beaumont," said Heath, passing over six tiny doughnuts dusted with confectioner's sugar and wrapped in cellophane.

Walter thrust out a banknote but Eddie put his hands in his pockets.

"Not a chance," said the blind man.

"All right," Beaumont said. He reached over and feathered the dollar bill into Heath's cash box. As he turned to leave, Eddie was smiling, his eyes turned up and aimed at the ceiling.

"Thank you, Mr. Beaumont," he said.

Walter heaved on the inner door. "Don't mention it," he said.

Although Walter was active inside the bank, greeting depositors and perusing mortgage applications, he had been spending his free time at the Lawrence Public Library, engrossed in books. Day by day he was absorbing volumes on Zoroastrianism, Eastern philosophy and the occult, both as a primer for lenghty conversations with Pier Eriksen and as supplement to his meager education. For every fact that Walter Beaumont discovered led to hundreds of other facts that teased him onward and often reduced his lunch hour to a mere ten minutes.

Entering the bank's rotunda, with its Ionic columns and polished marble floor, Walter sensed a figure that rose up from the shadows and followed him, casting a stench in the air. The teller's cage, with its ornate iron bars, appeared vacant and the door to Mr. Prescott's office was closed, as was Mr. Eaton's, the vice president. Mrs. Peachtree's reception desk was also empty. Opposite, the branch manager's and assistant manager's carrels, divided from the main floor by a balustrade, were unoccupied and none of the office boys were loitering in the wings. Walter could see into the empty coffee cup on his desk.

The intruder was a wild-looking fellow dressed in soiled clothing, his skin almost black, tinged underneath with the redness of drink. His eyes bulged and his hair was twisted with grime and standing upright on his skull. Where his left ear should have been was a stump of cartilage that resembled a seashell. "My job wasn't enough," the man said. He pointed a skeletal finger at Beaumont. "You had to turn somebody else out, you bastard."

The figure looming before him was more pitiful than frightening, but Walter was transfixed by the man's eyes, which pierced him to the quick. He did not recognize his accuser nor have the slightest idea what he was talking about.

A plaintive note entered the man's speech and he asked, "Why would you want to ruin my family? We've done nothing to you."

Jay Atkinson

Just then Evelyn Peachtree came stalking across the bank's rotunda, her heels popping on the marble floor. She wore an astrakhan coat with a mink collar, her shoulders capped with fresh snow and tiny icicles affixed to her hat. Shaking out her coat, Mrs. Peachtree was presented with two figures obstructing her path and reached for the spectacles looped about her neck.

She sighted along her nose at the pungent, filthy man. "Shoo," said the receptionist, waving her hand. "Get out."

The vagrant took a last baleful look at Walter Beaumont and scuttled across the marble floor and out through the vestibule. Like actors in a play that had all been cued at once, several bank employees appeared at the instant Mr. Beaumont's antagonist made his exit. A teller emerged from behind the door of the vault, which had been left ajar; two office boys crossed the rotunda from opposite directions; and Mr. Prescott came out of Fred Eaton's office, walked along the runner, and shut the door to his own office with a clattering of frosted glass.

The receptionist proceeded to her desk, stowed her outer garments in the drawer and looked up to find Mr. Beaumont standing there. "Yes?" she asked.

"Was all that necessary, Mrs. Peachtree?" Walter asked. "Perhaps he just meant to get out of the weather."

"He can find a church basement, then," the receptionist said. "I am not running a charity."

Walter beckoned to one of the office boys and handed him a ten-dollar bill. "Give this to the fellow who just went out," he said.

While Mr. Beaumont circled to his desk, Mrs. Peachtree motioned the boy over and held out her hand. "Here," she said, replacing the note with a one-dollar bill.

"What about Mr. Beaumont's sawbuck?" asked the boy.

"He'll get it back and won't even realize it," said Mrs. Peachtree.

During the afternoon Mr. Prescott's daughter Kitty arrived and was talking to Mrs. Peachtree in the rotunda. While most girls her age wore tartan skirts and Peter Pan collars and ganged onto the downtown buses in a vast noisy troop, Kitty Prescott favored gabardine jackets and décolletage, traveling back and forth to Manchester College by jitney. She had a habit of standing in the first ballet position and was that way now, heels together and toes pointed outward with her arms hanging down from her shoulders.

The dark-haired beauty struck another pose as she explained some hilarity to Mrs. Peachtree and the older woman smiled, gazing upward through the ellipses of her spectacles. Walter had business at the teller's cage and as he rose from his desk, unlatched the gate hidden in the balustrade and clicked over the marble floor, the receptionist called out to him. "Walter, you must come and say hello to Kitty," said Mrs. Peachtree.

"How do you do, Miss Prescott?" Walter asked. The air surrounding the girl reeked of violets.

"I'm just peachy, Mr. Beaumont," said Kitty, mocking his seriousness.

"How's every little thing at Daddy's bank?"

"No one has learned the rudiments of high finance in a shorter amount of time," said Mrs. Peachtree, touching Walter's hand.

The young woman laughed. "Would you go to a doctor who had two months of schooling?" she asked. "I prefer acquiring my skills by going to college."

Just then the door to the president's office swung open and Charles Prescott marched across the lobby. "Mr. Prescott will certainly settle *this* dispute," said Mrs. Peachtree, winking at Mr. Beaumont.

"Katharine," said Mr. Prescott. "Why aren't you in class?" He smiled at the two older adults. "I'm not paying all that tuition so you can gab with Mrs. Peachtree and flirt with Mr. Beaumont."

Father and daughter embraced with Kitty's arm slanted across her bosom in the third position. "Quiet, Daddy," she said. "Mr. Beaumont was just about to detail his career in banking."

"What a saucy tongue you have, and you smell like cigarettes. You'll turn that wonderful skin of yours to leather, if you don't watch out," said Mr. Prescott. "Now scoot back. I expect high marks this term. Otherwise, how can you expect to become president of the bank?"

Prescott withdrew several bills from his money clip and stuffed them into Kitty's purse. "Get on back and *study*. Mr. Beaumont, will you please show my daughter out?"

"Yes, sir," Walter said. He turned to the young woman. "Miss Prescott?"

"Hold your horses," Kitty said. She kissed her father's cheek. "Try to brighten this place up, Daddy—it's like a cemetery in here."

She turned around. "Come on, *Walter.*"

On their way out they passed Eddie Heath and the blind man sniffed the air. "You sure smell nice, Miss Prescott," he said.

She ignored his remark, stalking over the runner in high heels, Walter darting ahead to open the door. Snow was falling over Essex Street, capping the turrets of Brockelman's and adhering to the automobiles and delivery trucks as they waddled along. A good-size drift blocked the entrance to the bank. "I don't want to get my ankles wet," Kitty said.

Beaumont kicked the drift aside and proceeded to the gutter, where he raised two fingers and whistled for a taxi. He waved and the driver cut across traffic and veered to the curb. "Here you go, Miss," said Walter.

"What's the matter, don't you like me?" asked Kitty.

"I like you well enough, Miss Prescott."

"If you were smart, you'd like me a whole lot more."

Walter looked at her. "I guess I'm not very bright," he said.

Kitty Prescott stepped into the taxi, sweeping her coattails after her. "Run along, then," she said, revealing her spectacular cleavage. "Help Daddy count all our money."

For quite some time, Walter busied himself with telephone calls, sorting through pleas for the bank's charity (saying no was a duty of the assistant branch manager), and going over the huge, leather bound 'Summary of Daily Accounts' that was kept on the marble catafalque opposite the vault. Here was the record of every single transaction that occurred at Lawrence Savings & Trust in the course of a day, week, month, quarter and year, and by studying it Walter was supposed to predict the future of the bank like a shaman sorting through his bones. He marveled at the punctiliousness of the tellers' recordkeeping and examined the tiny universe of each and every decimal point as the hours raced by.

At the midpoint of afternoon Walter switched to other labors. Centered on his blotter was a mortgage application filled out by Mr. Gianni Quirinale who lived in an apartment above Finno's Pool Room and wished to borrow $20,000 to purchase a home in Methuen. Written in a neat hand across the top were the words *completed by Father Lorenzo Andolfi* and in place of Mr. Quirinale's signature was an 'X' countersigned by the priest, who had acted as his translator.

Mr. Quirinale could neither read nor write and the press had listed his references as "Ha Ha Reitano" and "Louie 8-ball." He had worked at Tivoli's bakery for many years but at age fifty-six, he was rather old to take on a twenty-five year obligation. And though he paid his rent without fail, the amount was less than half of what he would owe to the bank each month.

When asked why he felt the bank should lend him money, Mr. Quirinale listened to the question in Italian and then replied to the priest. "He wants to own a few grapevines," said Father Andolfi.

After Quirinale left the bank, Walter carried the application to Mr. Prescott's office. The bank president was sitting in his brass-riveted chair, wearing an old fashioned wing collar and pencil-striped trousers, a fountain pen in his hand. When he heard the details of Quirinale's application, Mr. Prescott motioned his protege over to the window. "The automobile demonstrates the man," said Prescott.

From their vantage point the bankers could see Prescott's dark blue Studebaker, the Pierce Arrow, Mr. Eaton's Ford with the oak sides, and a smattering of old Dorts and Saxons owned by the bank's customers. Mr. Prescott explained that when he had begun at Lawrence Savings & Trust as an office boy, Mr. Appleton would rush to the window to examine a particular horse tied to the hitching rail. "If the horse had good teeth and a sturdy carriage, the bank did business," said Prescott. "If it was swaybacked, no loan."

While Prescott and Beaumont peeked through the blinds, Father Andolfi and the baker stood talking in Italian and gesturing with their hands. Finally, Quirinale bowed his head and Father Andolfi pronounced his blessing and made the sign of the cross. Then the two men shook hands and exited the parking lot on foot.

"I'm afraid you'll have to resort to more scientific methods," said Mr. Prescott.

As Beaumont pored over the application, he spotted Father Andolfi in the teller's line and waved to the priest. He wore the floor-length alb and chasuble with a square-shaped biretta riding the crown of his head. Lorenzo Andolfi was a bemused, even-tempered fellow, with the habit of snuffling through his nose before he spoke. Next to Holy Rosary Church was the White Way Service Station and one day while a boy filled Walter Beaumont's car with gasoline, he watched Father Andolfi climb a ladder to paint the church. The priest hadn't applied a brush full and Italian men, on their way to work, ran over to help. Since there was only one bucket of paint, Father Andolfi clung to the window frame as three men crowded the ladder and several more pushed each other back and forth while arguing in Italian. Finally, the priest convinced his parishioners that it wasn't a good day to paint the rectory after all. He hid in the tool shed until after the second bell at the mill and then emerged, whistling and swinging his bucket of paint. Walter imagined that the balding, middle-aged vicar enjoyed the physical exertion.

"How is Mr. Quirinale's application coming along?" asked Father Andolfi. He snuffled through his nose. "I promised him that I would inquire."

Walter closed the file on his desk. "I'm just not sure Mr. Quirinale can afford this loan. He and his family will be living on very thin margins."

"Whatever your decision, I will pray for you and trust in the Lord," said Father Andolfi. He raised his arm to free himself from the cassock and described a small cross with the first two digits of his right hand. "In Nomine Patri, et Fillii, et Spiritus Sancti, Amen."

"You're not trying to bribe me, are you Father?" asked Walter, smiling at the priest.

"If that was the case, I'd give you two free tickets to the Ham and Bean supper."

Mr. Beaumont stood up and came around the desk and put his hand on the priest's shoulder. Leaning over, he sprung open the walnut door and guided Father Andolfi back to the teller's cage, where he was handed a passbook with his deposit and interest stamped into it. "I'll do my best, Father," said Walter.

"Think about it, pray about it, and I'm sure you'll do a great deal about it," said Father Andolfi.

Shadows lengthened along the marble floor. Near four o'clock the door swung open and a fellow dressed in work clothes entered the bank. Mr. Beaumont watched the filthy young man as he went to the teller's cage, passed words with Mr. Burroughs, retreated to Mrs. Peachtree and was handed a loan application and stared after disapprovingly; then completed a triangle by marching straight to Mr. Prescott's door. The fellow was admitted and seconds later discharged, whereupon he proceeded to Beaumont's desk and hovered there, attached by a distinct and penetrating odor: fried fish mingled with camphor. "I want to borrow some money," the man said.

Walter indicated the chair opposite his desk. "Please fill out the application," he said.

The applicant looked at the paper in his hand like he was seeing it for the first time. He was of medium height, with short dark hair and brown eyes. Beneath the detritus of old chicken guts and fish scales, his outfit crackled when he sat down. There was a long raised scar on his forehead, just below the hairline. "When will I get the money?" he asked.

"Complete your application and I'll have an answer for you tomorrow."

The speed of the bank's decision, which avoided the laborious vetting by committee and triplicate copying out required by other institutions, was not sufficient to please the man. He plopped into the chair, scrambled among Mr. Beaumont's pen enclosure for a ballpoint, and jotted down his facts and figures in a messy script. Accustomed to reading upside down, the banker learned that the applicant's name was Joseph G. Glass, that he was thirty-three years old, and had a wife and child. An itinerant, Mr. Glass worked as a short order cook Tuesdays, Wednesdays and Fridays at the Tiger Club, Thursdays at Cestrone Poultry, and Mondays and Saturdays at Gangi's Fish Market. He wished to borrow three thousand dollars with a term of five years and left the reason for the loan blank.

"Here," said Glass, shoving the paper toward Mr. Beaumont.

Walter clicked on a ballpoint, poised over the space on the application that read *For Bank Use Only*. He stared into the man's eyes and cleared his throat. "What is your reason for borrowing the money?" he asked.

"Do I have to tell you that?"

"Since the amount is relatively small, we figure the ratio of your income to your expenses and base the decision on that. But it helps if we know the reason for the loan."

"If it ain't none of your business, then it ain't," Glass said.

Walter made a tiny hieroglyph in the space provided. "Do you have any other debts?"

"What do you mean?"

"Exactly what I'm saying, Mr. Glass. Do you owe anyone money?"

"I never borrowed from no bank in my life."

"That's not what I asked you."

"That's what I'm telling you."

The man's impertinence fascinated Walter Beaumont. Most people would crawl across the floor to secure a loan; or at least dress up their application with official sounding narrative and wear their Sunday best when presenting it to the bank. Joseph Glass was a hardworking fellow and the income from his patchwork of jobs minus his rent and sixty five percent of the remaining figure for expenses left enough to make sixty payments of $52.50, which covered the principal plus five percent interest. But Walter was compelled to ask a few more questions.

"Do you always work three jobs?"

"Sometimes more, sometimes less," the applicant said. "Everybody got to work."

Beaumont raised the paper from the desk, nodding his head while scrutinizing it. "How long have you held these jobs?" he asked.

"I've been working as long as I can remember," said Joseph Glass.

"How long at these particular jobs?"

The applicant shrugged. "I've been working at the Tiger Club since August."

"That's not very long," Beaumont said.

"I haven't had a day off besides Sunday in ten years."

"But you don't have a full-time job, or a particularly well-paying or steady one," said Mr. Beaumont. "Is there a reason for that?"

Glass picked up a chunk of amber from Beaumont's desk and examined the insect trapped inside. "Am I applying for a loan or being arrested?" he asked.

Mr. Beaumont extended his hand and took back the entombed dragonfly. "We'll have an answer for you by tomorrow afternoon," he said.

"I ain't holdin' my breath," said Glass, and he went out. The two men did not shake hands.

By five o'clock the skylights were dark and Mrs. Peachtree crossed the rotunda and drew the iron grate across the entranceway and fixed it with a padlock. Eddie Heath had long since pushed his table against the wall, covered it with an old baize tablecloth and departed in the company of the office boys. While Burroughs and Willoughby finished tallying their accounts, Mr. Eaton and Mrs. Peachtree replaced the cash drawers inside the vault, Mr. Beaumont carried the leather bound summary in, and then all five employees stood watching as Mr. Prescott swung the door of the vault into position and turned the knobs that secured it.

Mr. Eaton said goodnight and went home and Mr. Prescott returned to his office. Willoughby and Burroughs fled across the darkened lobby and, after tarrying for a moment by her desk, Mrs. Peachtree climbed into her alpaca coat and called to Mr. Beaumont who followed her to the exit. Unlocking the grate, Walter stepped aside and peered through the frosted glass at Essex Street. "Are you sure I can't walk you to the bus stop?" he asked.

In a voice that echoed throughout the vestibule, Mrs. Peachtree said, "I've been walking home since Christ was a corporal." She touched him and her hand was cool and dry as parchment. "Now, stay at your desk until Mr. Prescott calls it a day. That's how you'll get ahead."

"I will," said Beaumont. "Goodnight, Mrs. Peachtree."

He drew the grate together and locked it, returning to his desk. Behind Mr. Prescott's door a light was glowing and the president could be heard talking on the telephone. Walter glanced at his wristwatch; he was supposed to meet Pier Eriksen at six o'clock and hoped that Mr. Prescott was wanting his supper. To pass the time, Beaumont retrieved the folders containing the two loan applications. Using the shiny new adding machine he had been given, he demonstrated that Mr. Glass had enough of an income to repay his note and the Milanese baker probably did not. Mr. Quirinale's margin for error was so slight that any other expense—a child's illness, several days out of work—would jeopardize his ability to perform on the loan.

A beaded chain hung down from the lamp on Mr. Beaumont's desk and he gave it a tug, illuminating the applications. The grumbling in his stomach reminded Walter of the doughnuts in his pocket and he took them out and opened the package. Confectioner's sugar fell onto the blotter, obscuring parts of Mr. Quirinale's application. After three of the pastries Walter threw the rest away and clapped his hands against

Jay Atkinson

his pant legs. Rummaging in a drawer, he withdrew a pair of inkpads and spun the little hanging rack at his elbow until he produced the stamps that he required. Reading over the applications one last time, Mr. Beaumont flipped open the inkpads and wiped the bottom of the two stamps with his handkerchief. The light went out in Mr. Prescott's office and he heard footfalls; the catch of a doorknob hastened his decision.

Walter knew the figures by heart. Then he remembered something his father had taught him and consulted his gut. Inking the *Approved* stamp in black, he marked the appropriate box on Mr. Quirinale's application. For a long moment, he hovered over the two inkpads before taking up the other wooden knob, applying red ink and stamping Mr. Glass's application *Denied*.

"Are you through, Walter?" asked Mr. Prescott, who was holding two overcoats in his hand.

"Yes, sir." He clicked off his desk lamp and stood up. "All done."

"Lights out, then." Half a second later, the bank was plunged into darkness.

*

A few minutes later Walter followed Mr. Prescott out of the bank, said farewell beneath the streetlight and walked along Essex Street, late for his rendezvous with Miss Eriksen. He passed Liggett's Drug Store and there in the window was Philbin Bates, his arm around a pretty girl. Across the table was a dark-haired youth cuddling with a brunette in a tight sweater. Beaumont recognized him as Jack Dulouz, the hero of the 1938 Lawrence v. Lowell Thanksgiving Day football game. The two friends were both Ivy Leaguers, Bates at Penn and Dulouz on the freshman team at Columbia; and while the Lowell kid laughed at something his girl was saying, Mr. Beaumont glanced into his eyes and Dulouz winked at him.

Walter envied the youths and the intimacy they shared despite the clamor of Liggett's. As a teenager he had enjoyed a love affair with a raven-haired Italian girl and had his heart shattered when she left him for another boy. At age 31, he seemed past that epoch in his life, where he might eat a banana split and laugh with a girl and not have a concern in the world. All around him, Walter felt circumstances bearing down the pressure of a new job, his father's expectations, the threat of bombs that could start falling any moment. The sky was overcast and black and he could make out a single star in all that darkness and was reminded of Pier Eriksen. No other woman had ever meant as much to him no one appealed to him in so many dimensions. Of course, Walter felt a tingling in his groin when he encountered Kitty Prescott. He knew that Kitty had designs on him; that by choosing an "older man," she was rebelling against her father. But despite her charms, Kitty's banter masked an insecurity that was transparent and tedious. He wanted to shout in her face.

Walter entered the SAC club, where he was supposed to meet Pier for a drink. Beside the cash register, Farris Marhd, a swarthy fellow in a dazzling white shirt, waited on two men who were drinking champagne. Beaumont signaled to him, and the Syrian returned the champagne to the ice chest and walked along behind the bar. "She just left," said Marhd, handing over a page torn from Miss Eriksen's notebook: *I'll see you on Essex Street. The snow!*

"Can I get you something?" asked Marhd.

"I'm going," Walter said. He placed a dollar on the bar. "If she comes back, hold onto her for me," he said.

"I'll do that for nothing," said the bartender.

On his way out, Beaumont held the door for a man in a raccoon coat and then turned back toward Essex Street. Passing Vermont Tea & Butter he heard the door open and there was his father, carrying a box that said 'Extra-Fine Frankfurts.'

Franklin rested the parcel on the ground and shook his son's hand. "What are you doing out?" he asked. "Come home and have dinner with us."

"I can't," said Walter. "How's mother?"

"Not so good, you know. Her sugar," said Franklin. "How are things at the bank?"

The younger man couldn't conceal his pride. "I'm writing loans now," he said.

"American Woolen Company is selling their lot on Merrimack Street and you're going to get the escrow and deposit. At least two hundred thousand."

"Why sell? You might need it."

The elder Beaumont shook his head. "I'm taking this deal straight to you," he said. "I already cleared it with your directors, thanks to Judge Bates."

Walter reached for the parcel and handed it to his father. "I'll do my best," he said.

"Don't forget dinner on Sunday."

"I won't be able to make it this week," said Walter.

"Is it that woman again?"

Walter nodded. "She's wonderful."

"Please don't make any rash decisions," said Franklin. "Be certain of your intentions and the young lady's."

"Has your new camera arrived?"

Franklin brightened at the mention of his hobby. "Mr. Shiebel went through a great deal of trouble to acquire one," he said. "I threw my Kodak straight in the bin."

"I look forward to seeing it."

"After I finish my darkroom, I'll invite you over," said Franklin. "You and your lady friend. Perhaps she can be convinced to have her photograph taken."

Walter laughed. "Your camera will love her," he said.

They parted ways at the intersection, Franklin tramping uphill toward the bus stop and his son along Essex Street, gazing into the nooks and crannies for Miss Eriksen. Here he might find her conversing in any of the dozen languages she spoke. More than once he had discovered her on Common Street enjoying "souppa"—hard bread and coffee—with the old Italian men of the neighborhood.

He found her at the entrance to Bachop's Restaurant. It was a humble place: nothing more than the kitchen of a tiny house. A counter barred the way and Pier Eriksen stood there talking to an old woman with stout legs and a nest of black hair. Near the doorway were barrels of olives and soft flaky disks of lamujoun and baked kibbee piled up like bricks. Mrs. Bachop retrieved a tray from her oven and slid the hot, smoking pastries onto the counter. They were packed with spinach and onion and garlic, and Mrs. Bachop carved a fresh lemon in half and squeezed it onto the pies, handing one to Miss Eriksen and another to Mr. Beaumont, who had joined her at the rail.

"Hello, love," said Miss Eriksen.

She wore a snug black coat with a mandarin collar and a black beret with a feather through it, her hair golden in the lamplight. She bit into the pie and doubled over, then placed her free hand over her mouth and bulged out her eyes. "That's hot."

Mrs. Bachop added a bowl of hummus tahini to the fare arranged on the plank. Behind her in the kitchen two curly-haired boys wrestled on the tiles. Mrs. Bachop spoke to them in Lebanese and they quit grappling and returned to the sink where one boy washed and the other dried the pastry pans.

"How'd she do that?" asked Walter.

Pier was standing close, the warmth of her hip pressed against Walter's side. "She said she'd put them back on the ship," said Miss Eriksen. "And if the German submarines didn't get them, they could live in the desert with their father."

Mrs. Bachop wrapped three more pies and a handful of black olives into a length of oiled paper and Walter handed her a few dollars and took the parcel from the old woman's hand. Usually Walter preferred steak or chops for dinner but he enjoyed Miss Eriksen's forays into the unknown quarters of the city. Taking her by the arm, he ate the pie that was cooling on the mailbox and Mrs. Bachop said something in Lebanese as they strolled away and Pier looked back and waved her hand. The spinach was hot and sweet with the tartness of the lemon saturating the dough.

As they walked along, dipping their pies into the container of hummus and watching the snow fall past Brockelman's, Walter felt the young woman swaying against him. "Where're we going?" he asked.

Pier indicated the Ayer Mill, which lay across the river. "Over there," she said.

"I suppose you can fix clocks, too," Walter said, laughing.

They turned south on Broadway and passed over the little bridge above the canal, beyond the old gatehouse and along a walkway that ran parallel to the bridge and then to the railroad trestle beneath. Lights threw their image against the Great Stone Dam, making a silhouette forty feet high: the gentleman leading his lady, their *pas de deux* visible to the automobiles that whisked overhead. Here they picked their way across, just a few yards above the ice-choked river.

A number of wooden ties began to go missing and they heard a train in the distance but Pier continued ahead in her light dancer's gait. Dropping her hand, Walter crossed from tie to rail with a stork-like hesitancy. "I can't see," he said, his voice echoing against the vault overhead.

Pier glanced over her shoulder. "Trust yourself," she said.

They could hear bells chiming as the train crossed Broadway and drew toward them. "I have to go back," said Walter. He was two-thirds of the way along the trestle.

"Remember the *Gathas*," said Pier, as the train drew nearer. "Every soul crosses the Chinvat Bridge but only a few succeed, for the width narrows to a razor's edge." Her voice was calm, filling the vault overhead. "The souls of the evil will fall into the abyss," she said.

A steam whistle rent the air. Walter saw the onrushing shape of a train and leaped once, twice, three times like a stag and Miss Eriksen grabbed his arm and yanked him aside as the engine rocketed past. They tumbled down the embankment, landing in a thick clump of brush by the river's edge.

"That wasn't very dignified," said Walter, brushing himself off. They laughed and he pulled Miss Eriksen to her feet. "Come on," he said.

They climbed the embankment and walked along Merrimack Street. Just ahead the Ayer Mill was arranged in a vast L-shape, the clock faces looming above. On a metal ring in his pocket, Walter still carried the key to the shipping door located at the base of the tower. Leading Pier by the hand, he stepped over the entrance chain, descended the ramp that sloped beneath the drawbridge, and examined his keys by moonlight. The courtyard was empty and most of the windows were dark; the only active shift at this hour was located in the dye house, at the far end of the complex.

Walter unlocked the steel door and they passed into the dense, oil-smelling gloom of the tower. He squeezed Pier's hand and they began mounting the stairs. The tower contained an accumulation of heat from the machinery and furnaces and as they squeaked over the treads, Pier loosened her coat and stuffed her beret into the right-hand pocket. Whirring above their heads startled the trespassers, but as pigeons dashed against the bricks, Walter pulled Miss Eriksen closer. "We're alone," he said.

At the bell landing, they encountered a wooden ladder and the gentleman went first, brushing aside the cobwebs. The trap had been flung open and he gained the platform and hauled Miss Eriksen to her feet. With the lights doused, the tower afforded a panorama of the city and the roof held in the warmth and made the space comfortable. Walter removed his overcoat, folded it in half and placed it on the floor beside the dusty workings of the clock.

"Watch out for the pigeon shit," he said, indicating the seat that he had fashioned.

Pier sat down and they felt the exertion and heat of the climb. Soon Walter was in his shirtsleeves and the young woman wore only a camisole of white silk, her long legs slanting upward at the hips and down from the knees as she hugged her shins and gazed at the city.

Jay Atkinson

There was a subdued glow from Essex Street, half of whose merchants had blacked out their lights in anticipation of war. But the marquees were illuminated along Theater Row and they could see the electric newsboy perched above the *Tribune-Standard* building. Walter leaned toward Miss Eriksen and they shared a kiss. "Now," she said.

"Here?" he asked.

"Yes." They spread their coats over the floor, exposing the satin linings. Pinned to Miss Eriksen's blouse were the gold cuff links he had given her. "They're so beautiful," she said.

"Everything I have is yours," said Walter.

She undid the blouse, handing the cuff links to Walter, who deposited them inside his hat. Pier bared her shoulders and allowed the camisole to slide to the floor. The line of her neck fell to her bosom, large high orbs tipped with rose and poised above the flat diagonals of her torso. Her hips were small and round, and the silky blonde hair formed a triangle above legs that ran straight as a colt's. Reaching behind to undo the pins, her hair cascaded in a shining gold ream.

Walter took off his shoes and then his wristwatch and placed it in the overturned hat. Stripping off his tie, he unbuttoned his shirt and lowered his trousers. She laughed as he hopped on each foot to remove his socks. Then he peeled off his boxer shorts.

Pier reached into her things and removed a tiny flat silver box and dipped her fingers in its contents. Taking Walter's penis in her hands, she rubbed a salve over the tip and along the shaft. Immediately his member grew numb and radiated a steady pulsating heat. "I knew a Fijian poet who said we must burn with the fire of love," said Pier.

She drew her fingertips along his arm and he watched the tiny hairs stand up. "I'll burn every building in the city," Walter said.

They began in tenderness but soon Walter cupped the tightness of her breasts as he smothered himself there. His mouth wandered, giving her pleasure, and she yanked at the roots of his hair and flexed her hips. Shifting and coupling, they lay entangled for a long while, grunting like beasts.

Afterward, they reclined on the overcoats and he sifted her hair between his fingers. "Let nothing come between us," said Pier.

The dust caught in Walter's throat and he began coughing. "Never," he said.

Through a porthole they watched the revolving light of a fire truck speeding along Essex Street. One of the buildings near Lawrence Savings & Trust was ablaze. Several more emergency vehicles came from the opposite direction and a crowd gathered as large sheets of flame erupted from the roof.

"Upon the last judgment, good men will be separated from evil by a river of molten metal," said Miss Eriksen. She looked into Walter's eyes. "An ordeal by fire."

It was nearing time for the watchman to come around and the lovers stood and dressed themselves. Walter donned his hat and fastened on his wristwatch and as they descended the ladder, a passage from Luke entered his mind. *From he who has been given much, much will be required; and from the one who has been entrusted with more, much more will be demanded.*

The night was cold and starless and they strolled along Essex Street, past Sutherlands and Bon Marche, trailing those who gravitated toward the fire. People were saying "Brockelman's" and great flames rose up and sparks drifted on the air like fireflies. In front of Silver Sweet Candies a policeman opened a box that was mounted on a telephone pole. He picked up the receiver, turned the crank three times and spoke to an operator at the firehouse.

"Send everything you got," the traffic cop was saying.

Walter stopped him. "Is it bad?" he asked.

"The worst fire in sixty years," said the cop.

Pier squeezed Walter's arm and they hurried on. At the *Tribune-Standard* building, a message was rotating across the bulletin board. Because of the fire no one paid any heed but Walter began to follow the news as they rushed along. JAPS BOMB PEARL HARBOR…19 SHIPS LOST…2,400 DEAD…ROOSEVELT DECLARES WAR.

Pier clung to Walter as the message repeated itself and people began to take notice. "Those dirty Japs," said a man with boils on his neck.

Jay Atkinson

23

The Present Day

The muscles in Little Eddie's jaw were tightened into strips. Although he loomed over the man beside him, he didn't move. The fidgety courier handed a paper bag over to Kuko, motioning for the gang leader to look inside. Kuko stuck the bag under his arm while Little Eddie took off his denim cap and laid it on the roof of the Toyota, his gaze steady on Kuko.

The courier glanced at Kuko and then at the bodyguard, trying to gauge if danger lie in one or the other. Nothing about Little Eddie's exterior suggested he was upset, or ready to harm anyone. As always, the bodyguard's face resembled a silent, pockmarked eggplant. The courier decided to focus on Kuko and in so doing, turned his back on Little Eddie.

May Street was deserted. Looking up and down the block, Little Eddie squared himself to the curbstone. He was wearing black chino trousers with deep pockets and he reached inside with his left hand while Kuko searched the courier. The man put his hands in the air and Kuko patted him down.

"You hot?" Kuko asked the man. He frisked the courier around the hips and ran down his trouser legs. "Nobody comes without carrying no knife or no gun." Kuko found only a plastic comb with some teeth missing, and he tossed it aside and smiled. "Nobody except this idiot," he said.

"I got nothin' to hide," said the courier, whose name was Lopez.

His hands were still raised, and Kuko smacked him just below the wrist, knocking his arms down. Tommy Lopez was a nervous man of about fifty, wearing a black T-shirt with a shiny Corvette emblazoned on it, his feet shod in green plastic sandals that looked like fruit containers.

It had become full dark. On the corner, Haffner's gas station was decorated with a glowing red horse that kicked its hind legs as the neon shifted back and forth. The changing light stretched halfway down the street.

They were standing in front of the water station. The spring came up from underground, housed in a concrete bunker with slit windows and covered over by loops of concertina wire. Inside, four spigots were running with cold, clean water, as they did twenty-four hours a day. The bunker was lit by a single bulb contained in a rusty fixture and the water drained into steel gutters, making a din that sounded like toilets. Bordered on one side by tenements, May Street also faced the lower reaches of Bellevue cemetery. It was dotted with tombstones and plenty of weeds. Across from the men was a vacant lot, glinting with broken glass.

"I'm jus' tryin' to keep everybody happy," said Lopez.

"If this guy don' shut up, you're gonna give him a headache," Kuko told Little Eddie.

The bodyguard nodded. Glancing over his shoulder, Lopez hung his head and shifted his feet against the pavement. "I'll shut up," he said. "I'll shut up."

The object in Little Eddie's pocket was a steel ingot nearly a foot long and an inch and a half in diameter, padded with electrical tape. He slipped the bar outside his pocket, keeping it concealed in his shirtsleeve. Parked at the curb with its engine running was the dark green Toyota.

Lopez pointed to the bag under Kuko's arm. "You do the job, and you'll get the other half."

"Tell me what to do one more time and I'll fuckin' smoke you."

In just a few hours, Kuko and Little Eddie would ghost for New York. The Tutamara sisters were gone, dispatched with one of his lieutenants and a vial of cocaine to an out-of-town nightclub. Never again would he have to listen to their endless bitching. Or find tweezers in the sink, or their dirty rags in the wastebasket. All day when Kuko was trying to sleep they roamed the apartment, creaking over the floorboards, with nothing to do until he got up and shared his stash. Or else they watched TV in their underwear, eating potato chips and farting like cowboys.

Kuko took off his shirt and threw it down. He asked Little Eddie for a blunt and lit it up; the smell of marijuana filled the air. Kuko's torso was covered with gang insignia, and crosses encircled with barbed wire were tattooed on his chest.

"Do it here?" Kuko asked. Little Eddie shrugged his shoulders.

The only witness was a dog about fifty yards away. The sound of the pit bull's chain could be heard slithering along the pavement; then the dog leaped against the fence and howled in the direction of Bellevue. High above the cemetery, the brick water tower was spectrally lit.

Tommy Lopez insisted that he had fulfilled his part of the bargain, and asked for permission to be on his way.

"I wanna know who I'm doin' bizness with," Kuko said.

When he arrived in Lawrence, Kuko's task was to make sure that every player was identified and put on the payroll, intimidated into making themselves scarce, or eliminated altogether. He was a businessman, and the Latin Kings were all about expanding in a businesslike manner. One fucking thing he didn't need was a silent partner that handed out bags of money without revealing himself.

"I called the number that Tito gave me, and then a note came to Mama's telling me to go downtown for the bag," Tommy Lopez said.

"You related to Mama Lopez?" asked Kuko.

The courier stared at the ground. "She my ex," he said.

"But haven't I seen you with the other *cabrons*, buying her drinks, following her aroun' with your potato hanging out?"

Tommy Lopez shook his head. "I don' think so," he said.

"What a *cabron*. Sittin' there while everybody fucks your ex-wife."

"I love her," said Lopez.

"You love somebody who shits on you? That's not too smart," Kuko said. He shifted his eyes to Little Eddie. "All right."

The two men led Tommy Lopez into the vacant lot, as the man's sandals dragged on the ground and he began weeping. "You should thank me," Kuko said. "Now you don' have to watch everybody stickin' his dick in your fat old whore of a wife."

Lopez faced his oppressors, shivering even though the night was warm. Streaks of perspiration appeared as dark spots on his T-shirt. "What are you doing?" he asked, trembling in his limbs. "This is bad for business."

"I got my 'fuck you' money," Kuko said.

Little Eddie raised his arm and thrust the ingot deep into Tommy Lopez's skull. The sound was like a hammer striking a coconut; the *cabron's* teeth snapped together and his knees gave out.

Kuko stood over the lifeless body of Tommy Lopez, watching the blood leak from his head. "Stupid *cabron*," he said, drawing on the blunt. "Stupid for having a wife who is a whore, stupid for meeting me without any back-up, and stupid for being dead."

Little Eddie wiped the ingot with a rag and then replaced the weapon in his pocket. He motioned toward Lopez using the toe of his boot. "Leave 'im there," Kuko said. He stubbed out the blunt. "It sends a message."

Squatting down, Little Eddie rifled the dead man's pockets to make sure he wasn't carrying any identification. Then he removed the corpse's shirt and sandals and the gold chain around his neck, stuffing these items in a plastic bag that had wound itself against the fence.

Kuko looked into the bag filled with money, and then rolled up the edge and shoved it into his pants. "The man wan's a fire, I'll fire up this whole fuckin' city."

The neon clicked back and forth above Haffner's, throwing a fan of light onto the pavement. Little Eddie was bareheaded, just a few hairs stretched across his scalp. Down the block came the sound of a chain rattling; the pit bull had disappeared into his ramshackle doghouse.

Kuko crossed the street, his metal heels popping on the asphalt. "Every town got its whores and its heroes," he said, tugging on the door to the Toyota. He paused with one foot in the driver's seat, and Little Eddie stared at him over the hood. "But this fuckin' place, man. I don' know."

24

Lawrence, Massachusetts

April 26, 1942

Franklin Beaumont's hand shook as he raised the knot of his tie and fixed it in place. All he could think about was Pier Eriksen. While bits of Chopin emanated from the radio, Franklin dressed himself with a quickening pulse and the feeling that a long lost moment in his life was about to be reclaimed.

From down the hall came the entreaties of his wife, Maeve, who was bedridden. They had occupied separate rooms since the illness had progressed, weakening her kidneys and dimming her eyesight. Because of his position on the hospital's board, Franklin had arranged medical care and companionship for his wife that freed him from providing it himself. He looked at his wristwatch; the nurse who drove over from Lawrence General was expected any minute.

He glanced through the window just as the small white emergency car arrived out front. The nurse set the parking brake and climbed out and passed along the hedge in her winged bonnet. Crocuses were pushing through the duff beside the fence and the hemlocks he'd planted years ago were thick with new growth. Franklin heard the nurse use her key to enter the house and then he crossed the runner at the foot of the bed and shut the door, muffling his wife's complaint.

This was originally the guestroom. The only item on the dresser was a newspaper clipping. It was a month old and Franklin surmised that Walter had forgotten it during a recent stay while his apartment was being painted.

> *U. S. Army Corporal Chester C. Collins, 36, a popular jazz drummer who played in several Lawrence orchestras, was killed during a commando raid in France. Originally from Pointe Coupee, Louisiana, Collins resided at 42 Quarry Road in Pelham.*
> *A talented musician who once played in Tommy Dorsey's band, Collins moved to Lawrence in 1937. While appearing in several*

Jay Atkinson

orchestras, Collins was a fixture on Essex Street and a soloist in WLAW's Christmas concert of '39. He finished his local career with the Troy Brown Orchestra and enlisted in the Army last October.

    Collins is survived by his wife, Belle, and a brother, Lester Collins, of Pointe Coupee, Louisiana. For his exceptional bravery under fire, Corporal Collins has been nominated for the Congressional Medal of Honor, posthumous. Burial was in France.

The photograph accompanying the obituary depicted a smiling Negro in his khaki shirt and insignia. Beaumont was not aware that his son associated with jazz musicians, but he expected there was a lot about Walter and his activities that had been kept from him. This was due to Franklin's initial encounter with Pier Eriksen, which had been one of the most remarkable meetings in his life. Originally planned as a get-acquainted luncheon for the three of them, Walter was called away on business and Franklin proceeded to the Cedar Chest restaurant and waited in one of the scented booths for Miss Eriksen.

His guest arrived in silhouette, taking on a pleasant shape as she drew closer to him. Pier Eriksen was a tall young woman, rather well built, with high cheekbones, a profusion of golden hair, and an irrefutable sense of authority despite her feminine appearance. Immediately on his feet, it occurred to Beaumont that he had risen on a command that was neither seen nor heard and which had little to do with chivalry.

They shook hands and sat down. Afterward Beaumont did not have the slightest recollection of his consommé, the salad nicoise with Roquefort dressing, the roasted chicken and French-fried potatoes, or the three neat whiskies and black coffee. In truth, when he reflected on the hour spent with Miss Eriksen he remembered only the frankness of her gaze and how exposed she made him feel. That all his talk of the weather, the war and his business was nothing but drivel and that together they would be privy to some titanic secret whose meaning he could only guess at.

He heard the nurse on the stairs and turned off the radio, waiting for her to gain the hallway and enter his wife's room. Only then did Franklin make his exit, descending the stairs with a light step, his coat thrust over his shoulder. In the first floor bathroom he sprinkled powder on his toothbrush and popped the soft gold bridge from his mouth. Running water into the sink, he dampened the brush and scoured the eyeteeth attached to his bridge and then cleaned what was left of the natural ones.

With his thumb against the roof of his mouth, he replaced the bridge and smiled into the mirror like a chimpanzee, inspecting his hygiene. He ran a comb under the water and parted his fine white hair and then splashed his cheeks, which were crimson after years of little exercise and so rich a diet. It occurred to Franklin Beaumont that he had nothing to show for his pains but the money in his bank account.

What was it that he wanted? Certainly not to climb mountains or fly an airplane or go to war. In fact, what the world considered masculine adventures were trifles to him. But as the woolen industry began to founder, Beaumont had the concomitant feeling that thirty-five years of his life had been given to an activity that was essentially meaningless. How many nights had he remained in his office calculating the amount of shrinkage in lots of wool, or puzzling over the accounts payable until his head pounded with the effort. And for what?

When Mayor Quebec was diagnosed with cancer he traveled to the Ayer Mill and sat there with the doctor's report while Miss Halliman diverted Beaumont's other appointments. "There's a mystery solved," said Quebec, letting the report drift to the floor. "Next up, the mystery of oblivion."

Franklin was shaken by the experience. For Paul Quebec was a man who reveled in the give-and-take of politics, enjoyed the local acclaim and indulged his appetites to the *nth* degree. And now faced with eternity he was as cowed as anyone else. Franklin recalled Billy Wood saying, "Any man who gets paid for telling me I'm going to die is a charlatan. Of course I'm going to die, and if I have anything to say about it, it'll be right here at my desk."

On January 5, 1926, Dick Morgan had brought the car around for the last time and Mr. Wood limped down the stairs of the Ayer Mill and was spirited away. His family steamed ahead on the train, and after a perfunctory stop at company headquarters in New York and a farewell luncheon among his old buyers in the nation's capital, Wood was driven to his winter home in Florida, down the lonely turnpike in the post-holiday quiet. An unexpected snowstorm fell across Virginia and they made slow progress, but the embankments along Route 1 melted away and at the Georgia state line Dick Morgan tilted open the windshield and let the coastal breezes in. Occasionally he caught sight of Mr. Wood huddled in the back, still wearing his overcoat.

When they arrived in Florida, Wood decided it was too much trouble to open the house and settled instead at the Hotel Ormond in Daytona. Along with Mrs. Wood, who had been an invalid for many years, Wood's party included his physician Dr. Griffin, a nurse, two maids, and Dick Morgan. For several days, Wood remained in his suite, never venturing so far as the lobby. Then on the morning of February 3rd, he summoned his chauffeur and asked to be driven through the orange groves. Dick Morgan had spent his time polishing the long black body of the limousine and buffing its chrome; when he drove it around the hotel cul-de-sac and stopped beside the fountain, passersby gathered to see what captain of industry they were sharing an address with. But as Billy Wood came laboring through the door, a cane in each hand, most turned away; the old man and his infirmities embarrassed them.

It had rained the night before and the groves were vast and dripping, threaded with roads made from beach sand and rife with the sweetness of oranges that were lying on the ground. At a nameless intersection some fifteen miles west of the hotel, Mr. Wood asked Dick Morgan to stop. The millionaire was dressed in a blue serge suit with watch chain and fob, his spats, and a pair of Italian shoes. Wood emerged without his canes and told the chauffeur to stay with the car. Then he walked back the way he'd been driven, around the curve and out of sight.

Trade winds cascaded through the groves and the sky was vast and blue and dotted with shapeless white clouds. There was a loud report.

Dick Morgan sprang up, running toward the sound in his loose-legged gait. He found Billy Wood a short distance from the road, with dozens of oranges lying all around. The side of his face was blackened by gunpowder and large amounts of blood poured from the wound. The gun was still smoking when Morgan picked it up. It was an ivory-handled revolver with WMW stamped on the butt, and after the headlines, the inquest, an autopsy and a funeral, Wood was buried next to his oldest son at Arden. The gun was shipped back to the Ayer Mill and Franklin Beaumont locked it in the safe.

*

Beaumont replaced his toothbrush in the rack, fastened his collar buttons and retrieved his new homborg from the closet. His appointment with Pier Eriksen was for three o'clock at her home, where he planned to make a photograph of her. During their luncheon, Miss Eriksen was eager to hear of his passion for photography and treated the subject with more deference than she had any chatter about his business. And thus it had been decided that Franklin would demonstrate his Hasselblad camera while visiting the house that Miss Eriksen had recently purchased on Bailey Street. No mention was made of Walter or his intentions, nor did Franklin discuss his wife's illness or invite Pier to visit their home. He left the Cedar Chest filled with new inspiration and unburdened of his concerns, with a hint of spring in the air and all the bustle of downtown as new and wondrous to him as the streets of paradise.

Now he made his way to the kitchen and descended the cellar stairs. Where the handrail ended, he swung an arm up and groped in the darkness for the light cord. Batting the nib to and fro, he caught the thread between his fingers and tugged on it, illuminating the dank mossy cavern beneath the house. At the south end where the coal storage had been, Franklin had built a darkroom using two by fours and tarpaper he found in the garage. Light bulbs and timers and camera parts were strewn across an old table outside the room and he gathered two of the lenses and opened the door. In the dim, velvety darkness, strips of film and various prints gleamed on wires he'd strung overhead and the enclosure smelled of developing fluid and other chemicals. On the counter that acted as his workspace, Franklin moved aside a ceramic tub and several little brown bottles and gathered the elements of his camera.

Into one of the developing trays Franklin poured a measure of distilled water, and then added a gelatin strip and solutions of potassium iodide and potassium bromide along with the silver salts. Choosing a piece of paper, Franklin immersed the sheet and an image began to appear as he gripped the sheet with a pair of tongs and washed it back and forth in the emulsion. It was an attractive young blonde woman, emerging from the Lawrence Savings & Trust. Her hair fell below her shoulders and, because of the f-stop he had chosen, one foot blurred as she stepped

City in Amber

onto the pavement.

He hung the print on a wire and looped the camera over his shoulder and exited the darkroom. Pausing at the foot of the stairs, he heard the nurse enter the kitchen, the floorboards creaking beneath her weight. Water ran in the sink and he heard it rush by in a succession of pipes. Then it was quiet again.

Franklin mounted the stairs. The hallway was empty and he proceeded again to the wardrobe and put on his hat and overcoat. Then he groped in the closet and located a flat walnut box and took out a key and unlocked it. Inside was a .38 caliber revolver with an ivory stock and WMW stamped on the butt. During a recent inspection at the Ayer Mill, the fire marshal had discovered the weapon in the vault and asked Beaumont to remove it. To avoid troubling his wife, the general overseer kept the firearm a secret, taking it once to the Methuen Rod & Gun club where he familiarized himself with its operation. Otherwise it had remained in the closet.

Beaumont opened the cylinder to make sure the gun was loaded and then stowed it in his pocket. Earlier that day, as he counted down to his rendezvous with Miss Eriksen, Franklin had occupied the steam room at the YMCA alongside his oldest friends. Judge Bates sat nearby with his graven face and long legs, a patch of hair sprouting on his back. Beside him was Mayor Quebec, displaying the jagged scar on his abdomen where the surgeons had removed his cancer. On the other bench was Colin Isherwood I.

Lounging amid billows of steam, the Mayor and Judge Bates droned on about their secure marriages and predictable complaints. Opposite them, Franklin's heart was rattling like the steam pipes that throbbed and pulsed against the wall. His appointment with Miss Eriksen stirred him in a manner that his colleagues had not entertained for many years. He was going to see a young woman, and let the chips fall where they may.

He felt Colin Isherwood's gaze despite the steam that obscured him. Perhaps the newspaperman sensed Franklin's excitement, although he had been careful to provide no outward signs. Or maybe he took the extended silence as a portent that something was amiss. When Judge Bates and the Mayor filed through the door, Colin stood up, his penis dangling like a rope. He stretched his arms overhead, palming the ceiling, and fixed Beaumont with his watery blue eyes.

"How's Walter?" he asked. "I hear he has a ladyfriend."

Franklin cinched the towel about his waist and followed Isherwood toward the showers. "He seems to be doing well."

Isherwood stopped at the sink and ran some cold water. "Are you all right, Frank?" he asked.

"Right as rain."

Now Beaumont felt the weight of the gun in his pocket as he traversed the hall. Just last week a German spy posing as a Belgian had been arrested in Hartford, Connecticut and the newspapers were filled with rumors of the Nazis targeting American manufacturers. Miss Eriksen was no spy; she was not dangerous in any conventional sense. There was nothing conventional about her and that very idea gave Franklin Beaumont cause to worry.

Easing through the front door, he left the house and passed along the stained glass window. Canted toward each other on the wide expanse of the porch were two sturdy Adirondack chairs that Walter had given them for Christmas. Painted forest green, they matched the railing and flower boxes and provided a quaint setting for visitors. Franklin and his wife were meant to retire into those chairs. But with the house looming in the background, he felt the arch of Haverhill Street tilting him toward downtown and his meeting with Pier Eriksen.

25

The Present Day

Joe Glass dozed for a while in Francesca's bed. When he woke up Gabriel was asleep, his soft exhales rising from the crib. An odor of vanilla permeated the room and for a while Joe lay among the rumpled sheets, breathing in Francesca's scent.

He went into the kitchen, squinting at the light. Outside he could hear sirens; just a few in those early moments, the wails increasing as they came from several directions at once. It was eleven o'clock and still no Francesca. Joe turned on the television and all three Boston channels were leading off their newscasts with stories about a tremendous fire in Lawrence.

It was the Ayer Mill. Live video showed horns of fire curving upward from the lower windows. At first there was no commentary, only depictions of the blaze from several vantage points accompanied by a loud crackling sound. After a while the cameras panned the crowd sitting in lawn chairs or pushing babies in strollers. A great deal of fire apparatus lined the canal, throwing streams of water into the blaze. A reporter called the fire "an epic disaster," which appeared ready to "eradicate one of America's most significant industrial landmarks."

Joe rushed to the window, but all he could see was a slight glow on the houses opposite. From the bedroom he heard Gabriel's voice. He walked in and the baby was gripping the bars and smiling.

"Do you wanna go look for Mommy?" asked Joe, scrambling for Gabriel's clothes.

"Yes," the boy said.

Joe dressed his son and they hurried down the stairs. Just as they reached the sidewalk, a large mote of ash drifted from the sky, alighting on the curb. It was black and smoking, honeycombed with tiny holes. Gabriel reached for it and Joe pulled him away. "No, little bear," he said.

Hundreds of ashes were falling. Along South Broadway they came to rest on the sidewalk and parked cars, chopped into dust as Joe trod

Jay Atkinson

them underfoot. Gabriel twisted this way and that holding out his hands, while the ashes brushed against his skin. In the distance, sirens thronged together in a chorus.

With Gabriel clutching his neck, Joe Glass approached the O'Leary Bridge and saw flames thirty feet high and dozens of figures reddened in the glow. There were fire trucks lined up for blocks, antique pumpers and horse-drawn carts and ladder trucks with more than six lines running out toward the blaze. Except for the peak of the tower and the clock faces, the Ayer Mill was engulfed in flames. Here and there firemen and rescue workers stood in silhouette, arrested in various poses like a dumb show. Arches of water flew in every direction, but no one spoke and the inferno enveloped the sky, throwing hot cinders into the canal.

Although the fire stood a quarter mile off, Gabriel was uneasy. "Daddy," he said, attempting to crawl on top of Joe's head.

"It's okay, bear. We're gonna look for Momma."

Nearby a television reporter was interviewing Boris Johnson. He was clad only in a pair of iridescent briefs, his running shoes and a metal fireman's hat. Soot covered his chest and his eyes were blackened like a raccoon's. "Don't know why I did it…fire everywhere…sheets of flame to the ceiling," Johnson was saying. He took gulps of fresh air and his body shook with adrenaline.

One of the technicians called Johnson aside and the reporter stood alone in the light from the camera. "There he is, ladies and gentlemen, Boris Johnson, who just moments ago broke through a door that you see in flames behind me, and carried a night watchman to safety. That man is now at Lawrence General Hospital being treated for smoke inhalation."

Joe Glass walked by with his son and Johnson hailed them with his eyes and they went over. The soles of his running shoes were melted from the heat and his eyebrows were singed and bits of ash shone like mica across his chest.

"Sounds like you're a hero," Joe said.

Boris spit into the canal. "Kamberelis owes me six hundred bucks," he said. "I wasn't gonna let him die in there."

Joe Glass crossed the bridge toward the mill and walked along the railroad tracks, his son mute in his arms. The fire was less than a hundred yards away: pouring through the windows, timbers crackling, the vast tulip of flame drawn upward and encompassing the tower. Joe noticed Father Tom among the volunteers drinking coffee from Styrofoam cups. Just then a fireman ran up, his face blackened with soot and his clothing scorched at the elbows and knees. "Father, come quick," he said. "One of the guys from Ladder Seven didn't get out."

The priest threw down his cup and together they ran toward the entrance of the mill, doubled over like they were being shot at. Twenty yards from the engulfed doorway, three more colleagues of the ladderman were wringing their hands and cursing. Father Tom was given a helmet with a plastic visor and uttered some words of comfort to the distraught firemen and then advanced a few yards beyond them, his figure outlined in red.

City in Amber

The archway of the mill was whirling in fire. At that moment the windows on the far side of the Ayer must have blown out, for the draft suddenly increased and bits of refuse and coffee cups and shredded paper were drawn over the ground. The debris went past Father Tom in mid-air and disappeared into the flaming doorway.

Father Tom was joined by one of the firemen, gesturing with his ax. But the priest laid his hand on the man's shoulder and turned him back toward his company. The aggrieved fireman was helped to a safe position and Father Tom continued ahead, until the fire roared outward and he was forced to draw up. He stood in his leather boots and jeans and his priest's collar beneath the whorl of flame. Raising a hand above his head, Father Tom described a cross in the air.

In a loud voice, he cried, "Eternal Father, I offer Thee the most Precious Blood of the Thy Divine Son Jesus, in union with the Masses said throughout the world today, for all the holy souls in Purgatory, Amen. Eternal rest grant unto them oh Lord and let Perpetual Light shine upon them and their souls and all the souls of the faithful departed through the Mercy of God, rest in peace. *In Nomine Patri, et Fillii, et Spiritus Sancti.*"

And kneeling among the gravel and debris the firemen joined in saying "Amen."

Someone called to Joe and Gabriel from the other side of the canal. There in the crowd was Francesca Nesheim, standing with an attractive blonde and a tall black man in sport clothes. Francesca called again and waved her arm and Joe stumbled over a firehose, catching himself, and with the heat of the blaze pressing him onward, he clutched Gabriel to his chest and doubled back, along the weedy canal and over the footbridge.

"What are you doing here?" asked Francesca, running to meet them. "My baby." She took Gabriel in her arms.

"Mama," said the boy, smiling at her.

"When you didn't come home, we were worried," Joe said.

Francesca drew him aside. "Joe, I was attacked," she said. "In an alley during the parade."

"*Je-sus.* Are you all right? What the hell happened?" he asked. Joe walked in a tight circle, pounding himself on the side of the head. "I'll kill that motherfucker."

"Joseph Anthony Glass. Don't you ever talk that way in front of my son."

Joe swallowed with a crunching sound and tears ran down his face. "Look, Frannie. I'm sorry," he said. "I don't know what to say."

"The main thing is, the baby's okay," said Francesca.

"Gabriel's fine. He was with me."

Coming nearer, Francesca looked Joe in the eye. "I'm pregnant. I didn't want to tell you until I knew what I was going to do. I'm keeping it."

"Oh, brother," said Joe, rubbing his eyes. "Am I the father?"

"I'm not sure."

More sirens keened in the distance and half a dozen state troopers came over the bridge in their flat-brimmed hats. As the fire grew more

Jay Atkinson

intense, the troopers were determined to move the crowd back. A new perimeter was being arranged along Broadway and on South Union Street.

"Why don't you just stab me in the heart?" asked Joe.

Gabriel began crying and Elise Dominaux approached, offering to take the child while the adults hashed things over. "You're the one that didn't want to get married," said Francesca to Joe, as the mill grew skeletal in the flames.

"I can't even find a job," Joe said. "What kind of life can I make for anyone? I'm just one step out of the gutter."

They embraced. Burying his face in Francesca's hair, Joe said, "Maybe I should get out of this shithole once and for all."

Francesca gripped the sleeves of his leather jacket. "You're a good father," she said. "Gabriel loves you very much. If you move away, you'll hurt him." She held Joe at arm's length. "You'll hurt us all."

Gabriel squirmed loose and came running over, with Elise following right behind. The child leaped into his parents' arms and the three of them swayed there for a moment, against the great aurora of the flames. Then Francesca introduced Elise and her friend Rick, and Joe disengaged himself and shook the man's hand.

They turned and stared at the Ayer Mill. Somehow the great clock had remained in operation as the hands neared the stroke of midnight. Flames reached the height of the tower and the crowd, which had grown into the thousands, watched the clock faces burn up like giant paper disks.

On the ground, three men from Ladder Seven raced toward a burning doorway in their helmets and padded suits. Carrying a hose, their faces grimed with sweat and dirt, the trio were thrown sideways when pressure came through the door. Waves of soot, ash, sparks and intense heat emanated from the burning wreckage and moments later, only two of the firemen came back out. Father Tom was summoned again and one of the men broke down and the priest cradled the fellow in his arms like a child.

"I can't believe they're allowing teams in there," said Rick Maxwell.

"What sort of work do you do?" asked Joe, wiping his face on the cuff of his jacket.

"I'm a federal agent," Rick said.

"What are you doing here?"

Just then a telephone rang and the ATF agent drew a small black object from his pocket. "Hello? Okay. I'm going." He replaced the telephone in his pocket and directed his attention back to Joe. "We've been working on the arson problem," said Rick.

In the distance, tiny figures threw streams of water onto the Ayer Mill. "Oh," Joe said.

*

After saying goodbye to Joe and Francesca, Rick Maxwell whispered to Elise that he would return as soon as possible and kissed her on the cheek. "Be careful," she said. Taking out his phone, Maxwell switched it over to walkie-talkie and Tug McNamara came on the line.

"Where are you?" asked the chief.

"A quarter mile south of the dam. I'm on foot."

Two lanes were backed up in either direction, the cars at a standstill with their occupants leaning out to gawk at the fire and salsa music booming from everywhere at once. Pedestrians wove in and out of the stalled traffic and a number of motorists had abandoned their vehicles and congregated in the roadway, talking and gesturing at those few that beeped and shouted and wanted to move on. Maxwell angled to the sidewalk and down an embankment and made his way along an overgrown path toward the river.

"There's a dark green Toyota in the southbound lane on the bridge, Mass. license plate 111 ELM," Chief McNamara said. "We think its Kuko and Little Eddie."

Near the railroad tracks, Maxwell encountered a youth about sixteen years old and his girlfriend, writhing in an embrace. He shined a flashlight on them and the girl bolted upright, hands covering her breasts, and the teenagers grabbed their discarded clothing and ran off.

"Are we going to pop Kuko on the stolen car?" asked Maxwell. He shined the light near his feet and saw the girl's bra lying on the railroad tracks.

"A few minutes ago, Rudy Pattavina got a tip about an incident on May Street," said the chief. "We found the body of one Tommy Lopez, his head just about bashed in."

"Any relation to Mama Lopez?"

"Ex-husband. He's got a rap sheet. Small-timer."

"Who clipped him?" asked Maxwell. He followed the weedy track to the old paper mill where it ascended a rise and joined the sidewalk at the foot of the bridge. People had spilled from their cars and formed a gigantic block party that stretched back to Essex Street.

"We weren't aware of an association between Lopez and Kuko Carrero, but Rudy found a piece of evidence on the scene," McNamara said. "A big piece."

Maxwell slipped the telephone into his pocket for a moment and with both hands free, raised himself onto the concrete abutment of the bridge and stood up. He took out his phone while scanning the bridge. "Late model Toyota, dark green, about forty yards away," he said.

"I'm going to open up the channel," the chief said. "You there, José?"

The line crackled with static and the voice of the young ATF agent broke in. "I see you, Rick," said José Padilla.

"Where you at?" Maxwell asked.

"Over near the gatehouse. Right next to a monument for...Arthur Flynn, 'the Toy Bulldog.' "

With the Ayer Mill behind him, Maxwell scanned along the Great Stone Dam until reaching the gatehouse and then a figure waved its arms. "I got you," said Maxwell.

The chief said, "Rudy's there, too, somewhere. Right now I'm holding back the uniforms. I don't want Kuko to panic and try and shoot his way out."

Jay Atkinson

"I got the car about thirty yards away," said Padilla.

"Do it fast," the chief said. "Before they spot you."

Maxwell jumped down from the abutment and walked toward the Toyota, looking over the hoods of cars. "With me, José?" asked Rick.

Agent Padilla began advancing down the other sidewalk. "Making a beeline," said Padilla.

Maxwell left the sidewalk and zigzagged among the bystanders and their cars, ignoring the bottles of malt liquor and the sweet, pungent smell of marijuana. He came at an angle for the Toyota, the phone in his pocket now. José Padilla closed on the suspects from the opposite direction.

Although the preoccupation of every bystander was the fire, Maxwell noticed a commotion in the middle of the bridge. Coming toward him was a tall, white-haired woman, wearing an operatic cape and matching tunic that was drawing remarks and stares from other pedestrians. Rick Maxwell recognized the woman—it was Mrs. Eriksen, whom he had spoken to earlier that night at Jerry's Variety. She had changed her clothes and as Maxwell drew nearer, the fabric of the old woman's cape acquired more detail, and took on the meaning that attracted so much commentary as she walked along.

Her outfit was arrayed in various hues of black and gray and blue, and rather than the geometric sameness that appeared from a distance, the regular and irregular check in the pattern turned out to be hundreds and perhaps even thousands of individual faces. The faces were idiosyncratic and distinguished by each and several of the characteristics that marked real people everywhere: wrinkles and freckles and bisected eyebrows and broken noses. As Rick Maxwell came within a few feet of Mrs. Eriksen, he could see that the garments were hand-woven and hand-dyed and that the myriad faces represented the heretofore nameless and unrecognizable mill workers of Lawrence.

It was plain that the faces had been studied and assembled and compiled into such a unique garment only through a commitment of years and under a single-minded directive that Maxwell could not begin to fathom. Just ahead was the moribund green Toyota, its windows dark and implacable and Mrs. Eriksen brushed past the fender and continued along, heedless of the remarks being made and ignoring the stares.

José Padilla arrived at the Toyota first. He reached around to the back of his jeans and produced his service revolver. Duckwalking forward, he approached the passenger side while Agent Maxwell, gun drawn, hovered about twenty feet from the driver's door. Rudy Pattavina was nowhere in sight.

With only the top of his head visible, José inched to the rear bumper. The Toyota was idling, all its tinted windows rolled up and the fixtures shaking from the concussion of the radio playing inside. With both hands on his weapon, Padilla raised it to his ear. He gave a signal and Maxwell rushed forward, his gun trained on the windshield of the Toyota. "ATF," he shouted. "Get out of the car."

Onlookers ran away in all directions and a woman screamed. In a swift, practiced movement, Padilla yanked open the door and aimed his weapon into the front seat, the back seat and the front again. At the same moment, Agent Maxwell smashed the driver's side window with his foot and shoved his gun into the gaping hole. The car was empty.

"Hey," said Padilla, pointing over Rick's shoulder. Maxwell spun around just as Little Eddie threw himself over the abutment, disappearing toward the river.

"Find Kuko," said Maxwell.

Women shrieked as Rick Maxwell dashed through the cars with his gun raised. He ducked behind the concrete bulwark, about five yards from the spot where Little Eddie had gone over. Slowly he raised his head and peeked over the edge. A truncated iron ladder hung from the abutment, extending three quarters of the way to an old railroad bridge underneath. Maxwell shined his flashlight for a moment, inspecting the span, then turned it off.

There was a ten-foot drop from the ladder to the trestle. Maxwell shoved his gun into the waistband of his trousers and heaved himself over the bulwark and scrambled down the ladder. The river was fast and black, crashing over the jagged rocks below. When he had cleared the abutment, Maxwell stared through the rungs at the Great Stone Dam. The two bridges formed a cowl and the reflection of flames from the burning mill gamboled over the dam. At the terminus of the ladder, Maxwell grasped the final rung and extended his legs, hanging straight down. He prayed the railroad bridge was intact and released his grip, falling through space.

His foot struck one of the iron rails and he sprawled forward, one hand breaking his fall as the other swam in the gap between two ties. He gashed his chin on a protruding spike and as he fumbled for his weapon, Maxwell was struck behind the right ear by something heavy and solid. He blacked out.

When Maxwell awoke Little Eddie had taken his gun and telephone, straddling the ties with a long steel ingot in his hand. Rick felt the bridge spinning out of control and fought to keep his eyes open. His tongue was inert and he discovered that his arms and legs would not respond to the ideas he had about getting up.

Little Eddie opened the stock of Maxwell's weapon, checked the ammunition, and chambered a round. Glancing toward the fire, he seemed to consider the wisdom of shooting a federal agent, right there on the bridge above the Merrimack. Then he eased the hammer down and shoved the gun in the pocket of his denim jacket.

Rick Maxwell couldn't form any cogent thoughts. He felt nothing like pain; just a constant vibrating sensation that wracked his entire body and an internalized hum that obscured all sounds coming from the world around him. Hovering overhead, Little Eddie divided into two's and three's until he resembled the faces on Mrs. Eriksen's cloak, his voice thin and hollow like the cry of birds.

"Get up," said Little Eddie. When Maxwell failed to respond, the gang member wedged the toe of his boot under the man before him and

Jay Atkinson

heaved upward. Rolling sideways, Maxwell felt his leg fall between the ties, dangling now beside his right arm.

Little Eddie was seized by an idea. Stepping over the prone figure, he examined the next tie and saw that it was rotted halfway through. Keeping most of his weight on the rail, he inched his left foot onto the rotten tie and pressed down with force. There was a cracking sound and he drew back. Harder this time, he shoved the tie downward with his foot and it broke away and dropped thirty feet to the river, where it flipped over and was carried away on the current.

Swinging back around, Little Eddie squatted beside Maxwell and grabbed hold of his belt and shirt collar. Maxwell was a good-sized man and the gang member found it difficult to budge him. Finally he rotated the ATF agent onto his side. One good shove and he would plunge from the bridge into the river.

Little Eddie wanted to make sure their combined weight did not snap the other tie and kill them both. He stepped back, lowered himself onto the secure base of the rail, and positioned his feet against the ATF agent's back. "Can you swim?" asked Little Eddie.

There was a click and Rudy Pattavina rested the muzzle of his revolver against Little Eddie's skull. "Can you?" the detective asked.

Little Eddie stood up and raised his hands. "I was helping the guy. He fell."

Pattavina snapped the open end of his handcuffs onto Little Eddie's wrist, yanked it backward, then knocked the other arm down and joined his hands with the tight metal rings. "You're creative, I'll give you that," said Pattavina.

Maxwell was lying on his back. He indicated the suspect by moving his eyes.

Rudy patted Little Eddie down and relieved him of the telephone, Maxwell's gun, and the steel ingot. "Just helping the guy, right?" asked Pattavina. "Because he fell."

Rudy found the open channel on Maxwell's phone and hailed Jose Padilla. "I got Little Eddie and Maxwell is hurt," said Pattavina. "We're on the railroad bridge. Call an ambulance."

"Roger that," José said.

Maxwell worked his lips together and managed to utter the word "Kuko."

"You got anything on Carrero?" Rudy asked Padilla.

"Nothing," said José. "He's gone."

Rudy pocketed the telephone, shoving Little Eddie toward the start of the bridge. "I'm arresting you for the murder of Tommy Lopez," he said.

"I got fifty people who'll say I was at the Boca Mal," said Little Eddie.

Pattavina produced an object and held it out, catching the light from the Ayer Mill. It was a denim cap, glinting with dozens of metal buttons including one that read *nosy little fucker, aren't you?* "I guess you dropped your hat and Lopez tripped over it and stove his own head in," Rudy said.

Epilogue

At the appointed hour, Joe Glass reached the zenith of High Street in the old roadster and fixed the parking brake and sat with his lights off. Along the curb were some triple-deckers raised up with a view of the park and an old Victorian home protected by shade trees. To Joe's left, spread over a rundown glade, were a few moonlit benches cemented into the ground and plastic barrels stamped with "L. P. W." Beyond them was a lot strewn with broken glass and an overgrown basketball court with empty poles and a tennis court with no net. Among the trees that began in the glade and ran down the hill on the other side was an electrical transformer locked inside a chain link fence.

All Joe knew about his errand was what Mrs. Eriksen had told him. He would meet a man in Storrow Park at 1 AM and give him the paper bag that was rolled up and wadded in his pocket. He didn't know who the man was or what was in the bag and he didn't care. Joe needed the fifty bucks he was being paid for his end and could keep his mouth shut. The Ayer Mill was still burning and Joe could see pillars of flame rising from the site, which was hidden in the trees.

The tenements were dark and silent with a glow from the fire reflected in the upper windows. An old washing machine and two rubber tires littered the curb, otherwise the street was deserted. To keep the way clear for fire trucks, the mayor had established a midnight curfew. It was 1:15 and Joe fretted that a police cruiser might appear any second.

He released the parking brake and drove alongside the park without using his headlights. After the basketball court Joe turned left onto a short vacant street that cut diagonally along the shank of the hill, ending at a concrete barrier marked with fluorescent paint. He got out of the car and zipped up his leather jacket. Past the barrier was a walkway that descended the hill, flanked by undergrowth and a sloped iron railing. Soon he reached an open area where several trees had been cut down to clear the view. From here, a vista stretched over Lawrence General Hospital to include the gasworks and the Wood Mill and several other buildings, including, half a mile distant, the wreckage of the Ayer Mill.

Jay Atkinson

Emergency vehicles surrounded the fire, throwing swaths of red over the canal, and occasionally one of the revolving lights broke away, made a zigzagging path across the darkened, silent town and turned into the hospital driveway.

Halfway down the ramp, a staircase covered in graffiti dropped to the four lanes of Prospect Street. As Joe watched, a shirtless figure emerged from the darkness beyond the hospital and crossed the intersection. His cleats made noise on the pavement as he started up the long steep flight of stairs. Dressed in leather trousers and heaps of gold jewelry, Kuko Carrero made a sign with the first two fingers of his right hand.

Joe waited for him to reach the landing and then produced the wadded up paper bag. "You looking for this?" he asked.

"I'm lookin' for lots of things," said Kuko, glancing around. He indicated a spot halfway up the stairs where they couldn't be seen from the street. "I know you?" asked the gang leader.

"I been around," Joe said.

"Gimme the bag."

Joe handed over the parcel and Kuko shoved it into his pants without looking inside. The gang leader had not bathed in several days and the funk that permeated him was an admixture of perspiration, boiled sugar and ammonia. The graffito beneath his heel read *Latin Kings Rule* but another writer had crossed out the last word and substituted *Die*.

"Hey—are we done?" asked Joe.

Under the streetlight Kuko's torso was glazed with some sort of dried paste and his hair was sticky with it. "Who's the *jefe*?" he asked.

"Whaddaya mean?"

"Don't shit on me, *cabron*," said Kuko. "Who's feeding the money?"

Joe stared back at him. "Fucked if I know," he said.

A patrol car drove along Marston Street, scaling a light into Storrow Park. Hidden among the trees, Joe and Kuko froze in place as the spotlight ran up the walk and into the trash-strewn undergrowth. The car stopped in the middle of the intersection and they could hear voices over the police radio, then easing back into gear, the cop negotiated the curve and went out of sight.

In the distance, the flame-wracked tower of the Ayer Mill broke with a loud cracking sound and tumbled into the river. There was a cry from the firemen and rescue workers that could be heard in Storrow Park and Joe and Kuko watched as the mill buckled like papier-mâché and firemen abandoned their hoses and equipment, running in all directions.

"Holy shit," said Joe, as the mill crumpled into itself and disappeared.

The gang leader spat into the weeds. "History is bullshit," he said.

They climbed the walkway, Joe going ahead and Kuko a few paces behind. When they neared the cement barrier Kuko spotted the roadster and whistled through his teeth. "Hold it, *cabron*."

Joe took a deep breath. "What?"

Kuko's jewelry shone like ambergris in the moonlight. He wore a gold tooth on a chain around his neck and attached to the cartilage of his right ear were the Ayer Mill cuff links. "Gimme the keys," said Kuko.

Joe handed him the keys to the Pierce Arrow. He stood with his hands in the pockets of his leather jacket and Kuko motioned for him to take them out. "Whatever you say," Joe told him.

Kuko gazed toward the Ayer Mill, which was obscured by the trees. Finally he spat into the tall grass and took out a fistful of hundred dollar bills. He unrolled two of the notes and displayed them. "You like money?" he asked.

"Usually," said Joe.

Kuko reached over and stuck two hundred dollars in Joe's pocket. "So you just made some. And you didn't half to do nothin'."

Joe eyed Kuko from the midst of an enormous calm, ready for anything the gang leader might do. But the boss of the Latin Kings surprised him.

Kuko took a cellphone out of his pocket and gave it to Joe. "I call you up, tell you to go somewhere, do something." He took another bill from his wad and stuffed it in Joe's pocket.

"I'm listening," Joe said.

Kuko jangled the keys and brought himself nose to nose with Joe Glass. "Listen good, *cabron*," he said. "Because if you don', something bad's gonna happen."

Hopping over the barrier, Kuko unlocked the door to the Pierce Arrow and reached over and stuck the key in the ignition. "You're gonna torch whoever gave you the money. Tha's free enterprise."

Kuko watched Joe's face until he was satisfied that the message had been received and then he slammed himself inside the Pierce Arrow and started it up and drove away. For a moment Joe Glass remained at the top of the walkway clutching the phone and gazing after the departed car. Then he descended toward Prospect Street and the river and the smoldering hulk of the Ayer Mill.

In Joe's pocket were Kuko's phone and his stub for the Civil Service exam. Halfway along the walkway, he reared back and threw the cellphone as far as he could, hearing the whir of plastic through the air as it clipped the tall branches of the trees.

THE END

Jay Atkinson

When *Ice Time* was published in 2001, *Publisher's Weekly* called it "a bonafide masterstroke" and named Atkinson's memoir a Notable Book of the Year. In it, Atkinson returns to his old high school hockey team as a volunteer assistant coach 25 years after he played for the Methuen High varsity. Jay Atkinson is the author of the bestselling narrative nonfiction books, *Legends of Winter Hill* and *Ice Time*. He teaches writing at Salem State College.